# JACKSON

BOOK ONE: THE LOSS OF CERTAINTY SERIES

# JACKSON

T. P. JONES

Synergy Books

Jackson
Book One: the Loss of Certainty Series
Published by Synergy Books
P.O. Box 80107
Austin, Texas 78758

For more information about our books, please write to us, call 512.478.2028, or
visit our website at www.synergybooks.net.

Publisher's Cataloging-in-Publication
(*Provided by Quality Books, Inc.*)

Jones, T. P., 1941-
        Jackson / T.P. Jones.
        p. cm. -- (The loss of certainty series)
        LCCN: 2008911769
        ISBN-13: 978-0-9821601-8-3
        ISBN-10: 0-9821601-8-6

        1. Meat industry and trade--Iowa--Fiction.  2. Plant
shutdowns--Iowa--Fiction.  3. City and town life--Iowa--
Fiction.  4. Local government--Iowa--Fiction.  5. Iowa--
Fiction.   I. Title.  II. Series: Loss of certainty series.

PS3610.O6298J33 2009              813'.6
                        QBI08-700257

This is a work of fiction. Many of the scenes in this as well as the later volumes
are written from the points of view of people who are technically trained. The
author has attempted to be as accurate as possible in his portrayal of these professions, but if any errors have managed to slip through, they are the author's
responsibility entirely. Furthermore, the characters themselves are fictitious. Any
resemblance to actual people is purely coincidental.

10  9  8  7  6  5  4  3  2  1

For Elisabeth, the person who,
beyond all others, has made this possible.

# Author's Note

~

In the mid-1980s, I had the idea of writing a novel, set in a Midwestern river city, that would represent my interpretation of political life in "the heart of the heart" of the country. First I would dramatize the day-to-day administration of local government affairs, and then, having established the dynamics of my characters' interrelationships, I would show how those dynamics changed when a massive calamity threatened. That was the idea.

So late one spring, my wife Elisabeth and I drove around the Upper Midwest and I spoke to government officials in nearly a dozen midsize cities. The community that appealed to me the most turned out to be Dubuque, Iowa, on the Mississippi River, and after discussions and a presentation to the city council, I was able to spend two years there as a participate-observer in a number of city departments. *The Loss of Certainty* trilogy is based on that research.

What started as a straightforward four-year project became an anything-but-straightforward eighteen-year struggle to turn the mundane cycles of city business into the stuff of compelling fiction. The linear plot that I had originally envisioned elaborated itself into a network of the interwoven and complex lives that people actually lead in places such as Dubuque. And the political novel became as well a novel of business and race and religion, the story of a strife-filled year in the history of an American city.

# PROLOGUE

~

Skip Peterson didn't mind taking his time. Except for the city's dredge, he had the river to himself. Later, pleasure boaters would be out trying to shed the overcoat of September heat, but no one yet. The western bluffs behind downtown Jackson were now reduced to mere suggestions by the smog, while in the east the gray haze soiled the disk of the morning sun.

Skip aligned the bow of the johnboat on a daymark upstream, beyond the Wisconsin bridge. Decades ago, as a kid, he remembered a summer like this one. His grandfather would dig red worms out of the piles of horse manure packed around the railroad water tower on the far shore, and the two of them would fish for bluegills and crappies in the sloughs. The manure was long gone and the water tower, too. He couldn't even remember exactly where they had stood.

In slow motion, the dredge swept back and forth, vacuuming sand off the bottom and up onto Apple Island. The river had fallen in the droughty weather, exposing sandy flats where the dredge's floating line lay stranded. On the island behind it, nothing stirred. The drowsy Sunday morning seemed held in the thrall of the long, rainless summer.

And yet, as Skip followed the sinuous course of the dredge's pipeline disappearing into the distance, something disturbed the stillness, a slight movement caught in the corner of the eye. He turned to look.

Upstream, beyond the abutment of the bridge, a heron-like figure disappeared. Odd. He couldn't recall ever seeing great blues around there. And so, interested, he kept his eye on the spot as the johnboat continued to beat its way along, passing into the shadow cast by the roadway overhead. A short distance farther up the shoreline stood an abandoned cottage, engulfed in shrubbery gone wild, and he felt the movement around it without quite seeing his quarry.

Finally, as the boat slid free of the bridge's shadow, a figure emerged from behind the disintegrating building, not a heron at all but a man, high-stepping through the undergrowth.

Skip got out his field glasses and trained them on the fellow. "I'll be damned." Walter Plowman. He hadn't seen Walter in ages. Except on TV, of course.

Skip swung the johnboat around and headed in. When he felt the river bottom rising beneath him, he killed the motor, tipped it up, and let the boat drift steadily forward until it grounded with a hiss on the flats. In the sudden quiet, he paused and listened to the tires of cars crossing the bridge behind him and, farther away, the rumbling of the dredge. The heat embraced him, sweat beginning to prickle his forehead. Tossing the anchor out, just to be on the safe side, he climbed overboard.

Plowman, large and untidy, was down on all fours, peering under the porch.

"Looking for something, Walter?"

"Mud daubers." Plowman trained his flashlight up along the stringer of the front steps. "Take a look."

As Skip came around to kneel down beside him, he tried to remember something about Walter and mud daubers. Probably some bit of local lore. He talked about so many folk beliefs on his weathercasts, it was hard to keep track.

The house had been constructed on stilts to lift it above the spring rises. At the joint where the steps were nailed to the building, supported by a header, he could make out the remnants of a wasp nest.

"Found her last year," Walter said. He got back to his feet, knocked the dust off his knees, and shook Skip's hand. "Long time since I've seen you out on the river."

"Busy."

"I bet. How's it going?"

Such a question invariably referred to his company more than himself, so Skip gave his answer. "Good. Holding our own. And you? How you doing?"

"No complaints."

"Mud daubers?"

"That's right," the weatherman said, and without explanation, he started circling the building again, probing the dark corners with his light. Skip followed, curious.

"You're not exactly dressed for this kind of work," he observed.

"Came from church."

Walter's linen suit, old and bagged out, showed signs of many impromptu field trips.

"Saw you out on the river, thought you were a fisherman," he said.

"Got my gear, at least. Heading up to Cappy's Slough." Skip intended to go through the motions. Mostly he wanted to get away and forget about the rest of his life for a few hours.

"Didn't know you had a johnboat."

"Borrowed. I know a guy."

"Ah."

Walter nodded slowly. He had stopped to rest, taking out his handkerchief and wiping the sweat from his forehead and cheeks and chin. Skip was always struck by the man's youthfulness. He had to be well into his fifties, hair gone mostly to gray. But not his skin. His skin remained as fair as a schoolgirl's. Even the weight Walter had put on over the years resembled adolescent pudginess more than a middle-age spread, and his awkwardness more like the eager variety of a child growing into his coordination.

And there was something youthful in his way of paying attention, too. Lacking the typical adult's ability to dissemble, Walter expressed both interest and disinterest without reservation. Others were undoubtedly put off. If they couldn't say something engaging about the river or the climate or the sins of TV station managers, Walter's indifference was immediate and complete.

Now he was inspecting the riverscape. In the distance, through the smoky air, tiers of fleeted barges lay at anchor, their mooring lines sagging. A Burlington Northern freight moved slowly along the far shore. Skip heard droning overhead and looked up to where, from the haze into the bull's-eye of blue directly overhead, a plane emerged and then banked sharply toward the south. That would be the little feeder airline serving Jackson, completing its morning run from O'Hare. Suddenly, Skip saw something else.

"There!"

A wasp had looped past them, only a couple of feet away. They pivoted to watch its flight. Walter stampeded in pursuit, around the corner of the building.

"Aha!" he said as Skip caught up and looked where he was pointing, toward a small porthole-like window at the very top of the gable.

Walter climbed the front stairs two at a time. Skip followed, more gingerly, up through the missing screen door and across the porch. The boards meant to seal the front door peeled away easily.

"Probably not a good idea to go inside," Skip said, just for the record.

The door sagged on a single hinge. Sunlight, shining through rents in the building, left streaks and splotches on the walls. The floor flexed ominously beneath them.

Walter craned backward and flashed the beam of his light into the rafters.

The nest, large and irregular, a patchy gray color, had been constructed in the exposed framing and anchored to one of the studs immediately beneath the small round window.

"That's a beauty," Skip said. He squinted through the sunglow, trying to make out the female wasps, with their delicate abdomens, hovering like miniature hummingbirds as they added bits of mud to the elaborate structure.

Walter was elated.

"And just what was it you said you wanted this for?" Skip asked.

Walter held a finger up for patience. From one of the pockets of his Sunday best, he extracted a steel tape measure and set about calculating the distance up to the nest.

"I got the city survey crew to shoot me an elevation a few years ago," he explained as he went, jockeying around the rickety building and adding one vertical calculation to another. A metal stake had been driven at a corner outside.

Suddenly, Skip remembered what it was about Plowman and mud daubers. "Ah, yes, that's it. You think the wasps can predict how high the river's going to go next spring." A hoary bit of local wisdom.

Walter smiled. "Listen to this," he said, "almost exactly twenty-seven feet." He looked wide-eyed at Skip and nodded and repeated the number, waiting for a reaction. Skip understood. If the figure happened to be right, that would mean a record spring rise in a few months, a doozy of a flood. Skip, however, thought it was all hooey.

So he simply smiled. "Tell me, Walter, have you been drummed out of the—what is it?—the American Meteorological Society?"

Walter ignored this. "Twenty-seven feet," he repeated yet one more time, with a sage nod.

"And what did they say last year, these mud daubers of yours?" Skip asked.

"Seventeen five."

"And how high did it go?"

"Not quite fourteen."

"So, there you are."

Plowman remained unfazed. "Been doing this for years, Skip. The daubers are statistically significant."

Skip had to laugh. "Oh, they are, are they?" Leave it to Walter to come up with something like that. "With all due respect, Walter, the world is filled with all sorts of wacko correlations. Just because—oh, I don't know—the price of hogs is correlated with… let's say, a rise in the murder rate, that doesn't mean people are killing each other in fatal porker disputes."

"Go ahead, make fun," Walter retorted loftily.

"Anyway, even if it's true, I guess Jackson isn't going to get washed down the river. Floodwall's thirty-three-foot, if memory serves."

"Protects against a thirty-foot flood. The rest is freeboard." In some matters, Walter was apparently a stickler for precision. "Anyway," he now said, "that's not the point."

"I'm afraid to ask."

"It would mean a wet spring after a droughty summer, just like in '37 and '38, just like '64 and '65."

"Is that right?" Skip hadn't heard that one before, and as far as he was concerned it didn't make much more sense than the mud daubers' reputed prowess. Although it was true, there had been some talk recently of weather extremes. "Is it supposed to have something to do with global warming?" he asked.

"Could," Walter said. "The mechanisms are not well understood."

Was that really possible? Catastrophic flip-flops? Skip didn't know, but with not much more than a decade until 2000 and all the apocalyptic pronouncements sure to be bruited about, he had his doubts.

"What do we really know about the weather?" Walter continued. "I'll tell you—diddly, that's what. Maybe ten percent. Maybe less."

"Of course you're correct." Skip was always happy to grant human ignorance. "Don't expect," he said, "that those mud daubers of yours are such mental giants, either."

Walter seemed to have stopped listening. He was staring intently over Skip's shoulder, out toward the river.

Skip turned.

A cabin cruiser had appeared. He couldn't tell whether the boat was bound upstream or down, for the person at the helm had lost control and the craft swung broadside to the current.

"Looks like he's hung up on something," Walter said.

"That far out?"

They walked toward the shore.

Skip shook his head. "Boy, the river *is* down, isn't she?"

The little cruiser had wandered away from the channel in midstream, perhaps with the intention of saving some ground by cutting across the inside of the river bend.

As Skip and Walter watched the guy trying to extricate himself, they chatted about the drought and Skip mused over Walter's prediction. He didn't believe it for a moment, but he decided that he'd make an effort to remember the mud daubers and their nest. Come next spring when the Noachian flood didn't materialize, he could give Walter a hard time.

The pleasure boater remained hung up, listing to one side, his efforts to free himself only making matters worse.

"Suppose I'd better go out and give that fellow at hand."

"Want some help?" Walter asked.

Glancing down at Walter's dress shoes, well-scuffed but dress shoes nonetheless, Skip said, "Expect I can manage."

He threw the anchor back in, pushed the johnboat out into the shallows, and climbed aboard. As he poled toward deeper water, he looked back on shore in time to watch Walter disappearing behind the broken-down cottage, high-stepping through the undergrowth, indeed, thought the CEO of the Jackson Packing Company, just like a great blue heron.

# PART I

# CHAPTER I

~

The small commuter plane balanced in midair, the engine noise and the floor vibrating beneath Rachel Brandeis's feet the only evidence it moved at all.

She peered out the window again, to see if the view had changed. It hadn't. They inched along above the forbidding landscape, where the morning sunlight mixed with the smog, creating a featureless, ocher sea, less like the earth, she thought, than some alien, gaseous planet.

Going into internal exile, her favorite uncle Myron had called it when he heard about her sudden offer of a full-time reporting job in Jackson, Iowa.

She leaned back and closed her eyes. The mystery novel she'd been attempting to read lay on her thigh, her index finger the bookmark. She talked silently to herself, forming a callus of words around her anxiety. The plane began its descent, the male flight attendant picking up cups and peanut wrappers. There already? Events tumbled one after another.

Less than a month ago, Jackson, Iowa, had meant nothing to her, just another name she'd heard from time to time, another Midwestern burg, less a place than a symbol of a place, America reduced to the lowest common denominator. No matter, she'd sent off her résumé to the *Jackson Tribune* upon learning of the opening, and a sampling of her work, too. For years, she'd been firing off her résumés and clips in all directions. Who wanted to be an AP stringer in Albany forever? This time—suddenly, inexplicably—an offer had come.

The plane banked and she turned back to the window, looking straight down, the ocher sea parting beneath her to reveal a city.

She picked out what little she could, a golden glint that would be a courthouse or some other government building, a grid of streets, and a river, the famous Mississippi. Like a braid unraveling, it wound southward, losing itself in the mist. Tear-shaped islands resembled boats in the stream, seeming almost to move with the current. Along the city's waterfront, the harbors and shoreline had been machined to straightedges. She was too high to make out the topographical relief, but she could see where, like waves, the pattern of downtown streets broke upon bluffs behind the city center.

The plane righted itself, the scene disappeared, and her internal organs shifted, a reminder of her anxiety. She leaned back, closed her eyes, and waited.

~

The cab ride from the airport both alleviated her anxiety and left her vaguely dissatisfied. She had expected Iowa to be a tableland of sod houses and women in poke bonnets and cornfields stretching off into eternity. Okay, maybe not literally, but some vision of the heart of the heart of the country, at least, some evidence of her internal exile. What she found instead were long loping hills, small farmsteads, woodlands and rock outcrops, then motels and auto supply stores and the other detritus of modern urban approaches. She could have been entering Albany.

She didn't talk to the cabbie. Words would have gotten in the way of seeing. They descended between rock cuts, down toward the floodplain where downtown Jackson stepped off beneath the line of bluffs, losing itself in the soiled air. The bluffs themselves, perhaps two hundred feet high, resembled a junior version of the Hudson River Palisades.

As they drove through the streets, the place became more and more familiar, just another Rust-Belt city, but too small to be Albany, really, more like Troy, she decided. In one way, however, it differed from both.

Rachel had been curious about national press coverage of Jackson, and so she had looked up recent stories, or tried to at least. Not much ever happened in Jackson, according to the rest of the world. She found one piece of some interest: Several months earlier a busload of black tourists on their way from somewhere to somewhere else had stopped there briefly, but not briefly enough for a gang of local toughs. The ensuing fight—or scuffle, the reporter covering the incident couldn't seem to decide which—ended with one injury and two arrests, and the resulting wire service story merited a few inches at the bottom of the national page of the *Albany Times Union*; Rachel could find no follow-up.

But now, as she entered Jackson for the first time, she had her follow-up. Jackson, Iowa, a city of sixty thousand, contained no blacks. If they did exist, they were at the moment otherwise engaged, for every motorist and every pedestrian she passed was unequivocally white. No Asians, either, or Indians—American or otherwise—or anybody else of color. She had come, she thought ironically, to the real America.

She took a room at a downtown hotel, deposited her luggage, freshened up, put on an outfit a little more formal than her traveling clothes, and then, filled with nervous energy, went directly to the paper.

～

Leonard Sawyer, the *Tribune*'s owner and publisher, was eighty-two. As happened to some, he had been reduced in old age, too much of him already gone for Rachel to get much of a reading. Even his voice had a threadbare quality, tinny, without resonance. He wore clothing with many pockets and drove a red Jeep, the vehicle as worn and minimal as its owner.

Sawyer had, immediately upon Rachel's arrival in his office, announced that he would show her the city, and so for an hour they drove around, although it turned out that as a tour guide he left a good deal to be desired. He seemed only interested in the waterfront, and even there he pointed out each landmark with a backward flip of the hand, as if simultaneously dismissing it.

They passed along the city's floodwall and levees, the straight-edges she had seen from the plane. To the landward side stood commercial establishments: a tank farm, a grain terminal, a lumberyard, and others. On a Sunday afternoon, not many people were about, but those few she did see, as before, were all as white as white could be.

"Are there no blacks in Jackson?"

"Got a few. About three hundred."

Rachel did the calculation. Less than one percent of the city's population, then—in fact, way less. "Why not more?"

Sawyer laughed, a single bark. "Simple. Civil rights movement never got here. Everybody knows who Martin Luther King is, but you ask them about, say, Rosa Parks, you're pretty much beyond their depth." He nodded in agreement with himself.

By that standard, Rachel thought, there were lots of towns in America still waiting for the civil rights movement. She didn't know what she felt about being in such a place. Not unhappy, she supposed. A place with stories waiting to be written.

"What has the paper done?" she asked.

"About the blacks? Something happens, we run a piece."

"Still—" she started to say, but the publisher cut her off, impatiently whisking the word away with another flip of his hand.

"Forget about that. I got something else for you to do."

"What?"

"We'll get to it. Keep your britches on."

They passed a brewery. They passed a power-generating plant, alongside which piles of coal smoked in the heat.

At the north side of town, they crossed a small bridge onto an island in the river. The road led along a causeway to a second, larger bridge, which the signs overhead informed her would take them across to Wisconsin. But Sawyer wasn't going to Wisconsin. He turned off the causeway, down a steep ramp onto the south side of the island, and drove along a gravel road until they reached the far shore and a vessel that Rachel recognized at once as a dredge, a tiny version of the similar craft she had seen at work along the waterfront in Albany.

He parked.

"Got to see a fellow," he told her. When she started to get out, he stopped her. "Best you wait here. Pretty dirty out there." Rachel said she didn't mind, but he merely repeated, "Best you wait." An order, then.

She watched him pick his way along the catwalk laid on top of the discharge pipe. Something of danger was suggested by his age and the narrowness of the gangway, although he moved nimbly enough.

After he had disappeared, she climbed out of the Jeep and walked along the road, away from the racket. For the first time, she could inspect the Mississippi up close.

It lay shriveled by the drought, hardly broader than the Hudson and totally lacking the presence required of such a legendary waterway. Like tiny ice floes, scuffed-up patches of light crept along in the current. Hundreds of miles to the south, the Missouri would enter and even farther along, the Ohio. Then the legend began, she supposed.

She broke off a tall stem and, as she walked along, idly switched the wild grasses growing beside the road. Slowly, tentatively, the rushing sensation of the last few days began to ease. She was there. She had begun.

After a while, she turned and started back. The causeway formed a massive dam-like structure across the island. Along the top of it a few cars were passing, going to and from the bridge to Wisconsin.

As she slowly returned, she glanced from time to time toward the deckhouse on the dredge and wondered about events unseen. The craft turned one way, then the other, sweeping out a slow, smooth arc as it worked. Despite this graceful movement, however, the thing itself was a contraption, holes rusted through its super-structure and arthritic machine noises accompanied by a variety of eerie screeching sounds. At the stern, a necklace of water sprayed from an elbow in the discharge line. The line passed over several rickety-looking pontoons and up onto the shore, finally disappearing behind the causeway.

She had returned about halfway when Sawyer showed himself again, whatever business he'd had concluded, and began the trip back down the catwalk. Rachel quickened her step toward the Jeep.

"What was that all about?" she asked as they started up again.

"Not important," he told her.

*Okay*, she thought.

The causeway loomed above them and then disappeared as they passed under it, emerging on the northern side of the island, where the vista opened once more, a landscape of sand dunes and plateaus. They turned and drove beside the discharge pipe. In the distance, she could see lappets of fluid spilling from its end and a bulldozer mounting up the sand hills as it pushed the slurry-like dredge material before it, water streaming from its treads.

"What's all this?" she asked.

Sawyer had parked again, pulling next to a couple of cars in a turnout.

"Used to be the city dump, good while ago." The dust kicked up by the Jeep drifted slowly back over them. "Now they're raising the site, got to make it match the floodwall. Going to build a dog track."

"They?"

"The city."

As the dust settled around them, she could see two men standing on one of the platforms of sand.

Sawyer got out again, and because he didn't stop her this time, Rachel followed.

They climbed toward the two men, the sand giving way beneath Rachel's shoes. From the brilliant surface, heat ballooned up, and pinpricks of light flashed all around her.

"Come for the ceremony, have you, Len?" one of the men asked as they neared, a natty, official-looking fellow who seemed surprised at the publisher's sudden appearance.

"Nope. Checking my operation," Sawyer told him.

"Ah." The fellow nodded, as a man might who, after a moment of doubt, had had his low opinion of the world reaffirmed. "Still a lot of downtime."

"You'll get your sand."

Rachel, naturally, didn't understand exactly what this was all about, except that it obviously had something to do with Sawyer's visit to the dredge. Apparently the newspaper publisher dabbled in dredging on the side. Of course, newspaper work and dredging went together like hand and glove.

"I hope you've got somebody coming out to take a picture at least," the talking man said.

"I expect," Sawyer replied.

The talker wore crisp trousers the color of wheat and a dress shirt with barely visible vertical stripes. A camera hung around his neck, a Pentax single reflex. He was an old man, and as often happened to redheads, his hair had faded to an apricot color. His full features seemed to have been worn to pleasantness, as if by a lifetime of smoothing things over.

As the exchange progressed, he had been regarding Rachel from the corner of his eye and finally, since Sawyer showed no sign of making an introduction, took matters into his own hands. "And who might this be?" he asked.

He nodded as Rachel introduced herself, his focus on her both mild and precise.

"And you are?" she asked.

"Mark O'Banion, work for the city." He came over to shake her hand, a generous gesture, she thought, nothing that he had to do.

"Miss Brandeis is my new investigative reporter," Sawyer informed O'Banion in a kind of bragging voice.

At these unexpected words, Rachel started, her hand tensing slightly as she withdrew it from O'Banion's gentle grasp.

Investigative reporter? In her résumé, she'd listed investigative work among her various aspirations—she had no shortage of aspirations—but that would be later, another town, another paper. On the *Jackson Tribune*, she'd start out on general assignment stuff or, if she got really lucky, be given a beat. So she'd assumed.

To cover her momentary confusion, she made an effort to sound offhand as she said, "I understand you're going to build a dog track, Mr. O'Banion."

He at once held up his hands in a deprecating fashion. "I just pay the bills. Here's the fellow doing the hard part." He indicated his companion, who had removed himself from the conversation but now, apparently taking his cue from O'Banion, came forward, a pained expression on his face, and repeated the ritual of introduction.

"Jack Kelley."

"Jack's the construction manager for the project," O'Banion explained.

Kelley gripped Rachel's hand firmly, briefly, then retreated and resumed his pose of patient noninvolvement.

A brief silence descended on the little group, until Rachel asked, "Isn't this a rather odd time to be starting, this late in the year?"

"So it's been said," O'Banion admitted casually. "I'm not especially worried. Mr. Kelley here is famous for bringing in jobs on time, isn't that right, Jack?"

The praise might or might not have been ironic, but Kelley didn't react to it either way.

"What's the deadline?" Rachel asked.

"June fifteenth…" O'Banion stopped and stared at her intently. "New York City? Is that it? Is that what I'm hearing?" It took her a few moments to realize he referred to her accent.

"I grew up in Westchester, north of the city," she told him.

He nodded. "Ah, yes…I thought I heard New York." Then, with a sly smile, he added, "Maybe a little north of the city, now that you mention it."

Sawyer, who had not been taking part in this phase of the conversation, said abruptly, "Got to be going," and started off without another word.

"We'll have to talk one day," Mark O'Banion suggested to Rachel. He nodded, half to her, half in the direction of the retreating figure, as if to acknowledge the difficulty of having such a boss as Leonard Sawyer. Rachel said good-bye quickly and hurried after the publisher.

"Investigative reporter, Mr. Sawyer? Is that why you hired me?" she asked as soon as they were back in the Jeep.

"Yup."

"Investigating what?"

"You'll see."

A minute later, they were driving back along the road, retracing their route.

She tried another tack, asking the follow-up question that she hadn't had time to put to O'Banion.

"Building a dog track in the middle of winter? Why?"

"State passed a pari-mutuel law a while back. City's trying to build first, beat everybody else."

Rachel wet her lips with her tongue, then rooted around in her shoulder bag for a ChapStick. She could feel the moisture on her face cooling in the breeze. She touched her cheek, gritty with sand.

Her sense of headlong rush had returned. They weren't going very fast, twenty-five or thirty, but the road was rough and Sawyer drove intensely, almost ferociously. His clipped responses and willful, self-absorbed manner had really begun to annoy Rachel.

"So," she said, "you're providing the sand for the project? Pardon me, but isn't that a little unusual for a newspaper publisher?"

"I'm chairman of the dock board."

"Dock board?"

"Been chairman thirty-five years. We run things down here on the waterfront." He jerked his chin up, a single sharp pointing movement. "There!"

She turned and peered through the haze. They were crossing back over the small bridge connecting the island and mainland. In the distance, the smoky blue bluffs formed a rampart hemming in the bay of land on which the city had been built. "There!" Sawyer repeated, now pointing with his hand. She shifted her gaze.

For a moment, rather than seeing, she was aware of a slight uneasiness. Then her eyes adjusted, and she made out the great welter of buildings lying before her. In the haze, no details were visible, just a central massif and profusion of outbuildings like faulted geological strata. In front of the Jeep, a truck had slowed and begun to turn into one of the gates of the huge facility.

"What is it?"

"The Jackson Packing Company."

"A slaughterhouse?"

"Hogs. Used to do cattle. Sheep, too. In fact, just about anything you could kill and cut up and sell. One time the largest single operation of its kind in the world, bigger than anything in Chicago, bigger than anyplace."

As they passed the truck, Rachel could make out the pinkish flanks of animals pressed against slots in its side, and beyond the truck a long driveway lined by rows of single-story structures.

Sawyer slowed but did not stop.

"That, miss," he said, as they glided by the plant, "is why I hired you." Unable to fix her eye on anything for more than a few moments, Rachel was left with only the impression of enormous size and complexity.

"You want me to do a piece?" she asked uneasily.

"Said you were interested in business." True, she had, indeed, put that on her résumé, along with her desire to do investigative work. The business of America being business, she dreamed of specializing in such journalism, but like the other, it was something for one day, not today. She'd included such wish-list stuff merely to show that she was a serious person.

"What do you have in mind?" she asked, chary but imagining Sawyer must be thinking about some fairly routine feature-type articles.

"Don't know," he said. "That's for you to find out."

"You must have some idea."

"Something's going on at the Pack, don't know what. Company's in trouble, been in trouble for a long time. Just keeps getting worse. Now something's going on. I want to know what it is."

"Why me? You must have other reporters."

"Had people on it. Getting nowhere fast. Decided we needed somebody doing it full-time."

"Full-time?"

"Yup." He turned and glared at her, hunched and gnome-like behind the steering wheel.

"But why me?" she asked again.

"Liked your clips. Liked your ambition. Anyway, I figure a woman's got to be better than a man if she thinks she can make it in this racket."

"Pfft," Rachel said before she could catch herself. This ringing endorsement for women everywhere was not what she wanted to hear just at that moment. "Frankly, Mr. Sawyer, this sounds like the kind of thing that would require a team of reporters." A team of reporters with a helluva lot more experience than she had.

"Don't have a team. Got you. Don't have to take the job if you don't want to."

That was right, she didn't, but when a genie pops up and offers you your heart's desire...

Rachel reminded herself that she didn't believe in genies.

"I figured," Sawyer added, "being as how your father is Morris Brandeis...I got that right, don't I? You are his daughter?"

"That's right." This wasn't something she wanted to hear, either.

"Saw the name on your application. Did a little research. That's how I found out. Figured any kid of Morris Brandeis wouldn't mind a little rough going."

This was just wonderful. She was hired because she was a woman and Morris Brandeis's daughter. Affirmative action at work.

"I'm not anything like my father, Mr. Sawyer." The old man continued to look straight ahead, but she could see the smile of disbelief. "I'm not," she repeated, but all he did was dip his head to one side. We'll see, the gesture said.

"So what's it to be?" he asked.

She probably should reject the offer. It had no basis in reality. She wasn't her father's daughter, whatever Sawyer might imagine, and she lacked the requisite experience. "I still don't get it. What's so important about the company that you'd hire someone just to work on that one story?"

"Two thousand jobs, that's what. This ain't your New York City. Two thousand jobs mean something here."

In other circumstances, such an answer might have been convincing, but not here. It wasn't even close.

"Privately owned. Family named Peterson," Sawyer went on. "Never tell anybody anything. But I can feel it. Something's going on. I want you to find out what."

"I see," she said.

They had been zigzagging through the city streets, Rachel in her excitement and irritation paying no attention, but now she recognized the newspaper building. Her sense of hurtling pell-mell into the unknown had not abated one iota, but the possibilities here—admittedly from any reasonable perspective totally *meshugge*—were beginning to get the upper hand.

"You say the firm is closely held, Mr. Sawyer?"

"That's right."

"They're hard places to research." Closely held companies weren't required to do filings with the SEC. They had lids notoriously difficult to pry off. Or impossible.

"Need somebody good," Sawyer said. "Are you that person, miss?"

She had a vision of herself as this tiny figure in the corner of a huge Chinese painting, the rest of the canvas filled with the oriental complexity of the Jackson Packing Company. It didn't make sense. If Sawyer was so hot to unmask the place, then why not hire an experienced reporter? One answer suggested itself at once: money. A real reporter would cost real money. She stared carefully at the outline of the old man, trying to decipher something, anything, from its sparseness. If only he didn't seem the spitting image of some buccaneering newspaperman straight out of the nineteenth century—aggressive, partisan, unprincipled, barely literate. A little bit like her father, in fact, except for the barely literate part. The pockets festooning his clothing were like so many small caches where he could hide away little bits of this or that. She thought about the dredge. A contraption. She glanced at the ancient Jeep. Another contraption. Probably the *Jackson Tribune* was a contraption, too.

But finally, she realized, it made no difference. This gift horse might have a mouth full of bad teeth, but so what?

Another thought occurred to her. She wasn't exactly crazy about the idea of hog slaughtering. She thought about all the horror stories she'd heard about packinghouses. She thought about *The Jungle*. She even thought about her kosher grandmothers and what they'd say if they ever found out. But once again, so what?

"Well, Mr. Sawyer," she told the tense, staring specter beside her, "whatever you think, there's very little of my father in me. But if, beyond that, it's a woman you're after, it might as well be me."

And in this way, with this nervous and doubtful affirmation, her new life began.

# CHAPTER 2

~

Mark O'Banion had only a short time to finish his conversation with Jack Kelley before the ceremony began.

As they had watched Len Sawyer and the young woman moving away, Mark mused, "I wonder what he's up to. Not the Len Sawyer I know, squiring around one of his recruits like that."

"She certainly didn't waste any time before she started in with her reporter's questions," Jack responded.

Mark had always gotten along with reporters, but he'd noted their strange semi-blindness, as if they could only see light of certain wavelengths.

"I suppose," he half agreed. "You best get used to it." The dog track project was going to attract a lot of attention, and not just because of the winter construction schedule.

They continued talking, mostly Jack going over technical matters concerned with the project's start-up, while Mark, who enjoyed people, even fancied himself something of an ethologist in the human zoo, let his thoughts return to the young reporter. Given her name, a Jew no doubt. She had a different look about her from the recent run of *Tribune* reporters. A jump-right-in look. Not particularly pretty. Handsome, perhaps. Or striking. He sought the right word. She possessed interesting features, a thick, ebony mane flowing straight back from her low forehead, a purposeful mouth and dark expressive eyes, eyes not recessed in shadow but right on the surface of her full face, with which she took him in boldly.

In the distance, from behind the causeway, vehicles began to materialize, the ceremonial participants finally arriving.

Yes, Mark thought, *that* was the word—expressive. Miss Brandeis surely wasn't pretty or particularly handsome but most definitely expressive. Full of words. A woman, perhaps, with whom to have a care.

Jack had stopped speaking and looked toward the approaching cars. In profile, his features betrayed a certain sadness, a trace at the corners of eye and mouth, but as he turned back to continue talking, the sadness disappeared.

Rachel Brandeis had asked the obvious question. Building a track in the middle of winter? What *were* they thinking?

Too late now. Mark had noted the collective mind-set, which had taken possession of the others involved in the project, confidence the order of the day. As for himself, well, he was prepared to be confident, too, although he wasn't a man to kid himself in the privacy of his own thoughts. And what about Jack? He was the man responsible for pulling this thing off. What did he think, in the privacy of *his* own thoughts?

And so, Mark said casually, "I'd still feel a lot more comfortable if we'd found a private developer."

"Jackson's not big enough."

"Yup. Be a terrific stretch for any of the locals."

Jack squatted down and picked up a handful of sand, letting it run through his fingers, leaving behind a shell fragment, which he inspected and then tossed away. He waited several more beats before canting his head back to look up at Mark, squinting against the glare. "You'll have your track."

The silence before he spoke seemed to contain his reservations.

Jack Kelley was a decent fellow. Another man would have introduced all the mitigating circumstances into evidence—an accelerated job, the kind of facility none of them had ever built before, winter coming—but once the decision had been made, Jack had never mentioned these complications again. He didn't now, either.

Nevertheless, the sense of the man's sadness remained, so perhaps his private reservations were even stronger than his silence seemed to suggest. Anyway, the difficulty had been broached, and some sort of understanding established, or reestablished—a moment of shared reflection before it all began.

Red ribbons tied to the tops of the surveyor's stakes hung limply in the humid air. Tomorrow, gravel access roads would be laid across the sand, a construction trailer hauled onto the site, temporary utility connections made.

Mark felt the heat of the sand rising through the soles of his loafers, which reminded him of himself, his own needs. His own sadness, for that matter. Sixty-three wasn't supposed to be such an advanced age anymore, but it felt old enough to him. Had he been king, he would have had a statue of himself erected down in Washington Square—something nice, tasteful—and then abdicated.

He'd have to settle for this more prosaic monument, a dog track—a gaming facility, although he didn't gamble himself, in fact, didn't even approve of gambling.

He watched the other ceremonial participants approaching and thought that probably he did want to be king, all right, but less for the power of the position than the sense of entitlement he supposed kings possessed as part of their birthright. How delightful it would have been to live for a day, even just a day, freed from all the double and triple meanings in things, the elaborate summations of the bad and the good into something that was neither.

The ceremonial gold shovels had arrived. The mayor, too, looking fairly presentable for a change. The *Tribune* photographer Len Sawyer had promised came forward laden with his equipment.

Seeing this person, with his burden in the heat, Mark suddenly realized that nobody there represented the dogsbodies charged with actually building the track, and so he reserved a small place in his consciousness for the poor drudges who would earn their bread on this particular job, less by the sweat of their brows than the frostbite of their fingertips.

The officers of the racing association formed a phalanx as they advanced toward Mark. He noted that they just naturally assumed that where he stood had been designated as the official groundbreaking spot. He also noted the sense of satisfaction he felt that this should be so. Pride.

Yes, it would have been so much nicer to be king.

"Well," he said finally to Jack, who had remained silent, "shall we get this over with?"

# CHAPTER 3

~

Thinking his second thoughts, as if there really was a right thought and he really might think it, Jack Kelley resisted going to the meeting with Father Mike. He decided several times that he'd call and cancel. But five o'clock came, and he found himself walking up the steps of Saint Columbkille's rectory.

In the cramped triangular entrance hall, Father Mike had placed two lecterns. On one was displayed a Bible that had belonged to Bishop Reinert, the first Catholic prelate in Jackson. On the other sat a copy of Fowler's famous treatise on the virtues of octagonal buildings.

The sister who had let Jack in told him that father expected him, and soon Mike appeared, wearing civvies. Chatting of inconsequential matters, he led the way to his private study, another triangle on the opposite side of the building.

"Can we have sister get us something, Jack? Coffee? A nip?"

Jack shook his head.

Rooms inside octagon houses didn't possess the virtues of the octagons themselves. The study hadn't been large enough for built-in bookcases, but Father Mike would have them anyway, so when Jack had renovated the building, he accommodated him. But now the priest had to shift the chairs around in the odd, whittled-down space until he was satisfied they could make themselves at least half-comfortable. He patted the seat he wanted Jack to sit in, then settled himself in the straight-backed desk chair opposite, their knees in intimate proximity.

Jack liked Mike Daugherty. He liked his energy. He liked his imperfections, too: the obvious pleasure he took in gossiping with someone he could trust, the need for approval, the sense, as well, of some unnamed difficulty. Jack could hardly have unburdened himself to a man who didn't need a little renovation work done on himself, as well. That much, at least, offered some hope.

Mike propped a hand on each thigh. "Good! You know, a little while ago, as I was waiting for you, I was thinking, 'Trusty old Jack. What a blessing it is to have such a man in St. C's.'"

Since this speech had obviously been prepared with some purpose in mind, Jack replied, "Beware the priest bearing compliments."

Mike grinned. "Well, yes, perhaps my motives at the moment aren't the purest, but the sentiment is genuine." His awkwardness lasted only briefly, for where awkwardness was concerned, Mike had amazing recuperative powers. "I'll tell you one thing, Jack. Around you, I can relax. I never feel I'm on duty."

"But we always are."

"Alas." Mike waved his hand in a gesture that might have been irritation or submission. "Well, who shall we do first, you or me?"

"You."

"Sure?"

"Yup."

Mike paused, composing his expression. In slacks and polo shirt, he hardly looked like a priest, more like some working-class Irish kid who had made it in business and then taken up golf.

"You've always been a rock in the parish, Jack," he began. "I mean that. I'm dead serious now. You've been involved, you've led by example, you've increased your giving year by year."

"But I don't tithe."

"Ah, yes, well, who does anymore? We've got as many envelope holders as we ever had, but the giving's just not there. As you well know."

Jack didn't want to get on parish finances again, an old, old subject. That wasn't the reason he'd come. He'd spent too much of his energy over the years on such matters. It ought to be possible to do both, he knew—to have a rich spiritual life and deal with the everyday stuff, too—but somewhere along the way, he'd lost the knack.

"I don't blame people," Mike went on, "what with the emphasis on material things, on television, on sports, on all the rest."

"Perhaps you should," Jack suggested. Perhaps you should blame me, too, he thought. Television and sports weren't the only problems.

The priest shook his head sadly. "Yes, yes. But blame, you know…it's so easy. We beat each other over the head all the time.

I'll tell you what I think. I think, more often than not, it's just a way to avoid the real business at hand."

Jack nodded. Of course, the man was right: put the past behind us, move on. But Jack had done that all his life; he was an expert at it, always pursuing the next project, as if...he didn't know, as if it might possess some magical power to atone for all the rest.

At the moment, however, he'd lost the strength needed for such self-delusions. He remembered the elliptical conversation he'd had barely an hour earlier with Mark O'Banion over the difficulty of the dog track project. Before big jobs, it was always the same. Jack passed through cycles of confidence and despair. He dismissed them, of course, both the euphoria and the gloom. For all their apparent intensity, what were they but the rather commonplace emotions attached to such work, perhaps even necessary to it. If so, he wondered, where was the even greater intensity that should be part of his faith life?

He had ceased hearing what Mike Daugherty was saying until the words "dog track" penetrated his reverie, and for a moment he had the eerie sensation that perhaps he'd been talking out loud without realizing it.

"I'm sorry, Mike, what was that?"

"The track, Jack, I was asking about the track."

Jack paused.

"What about it?"

"I've been thinking about the electrical contract."

Jack nodded slowly, surprised and yet unsurprised. He settled back, on his guard. "An odd thing, I must say, Mike, for a priest to be thinking about."

"Oh, I don't know, in my line of work there's hardly a subject doesn't come up from time to time. I suppose there'll be a good-sized electrical contract...at the track, that is."

"Correct." In the time it had taken for this brief further exchange, Jack had figured out what was going on. "This is about Tony Vasconcellos, isn't it?"

Mike conceded that it was. What he said was, "Not so much about Tony. More about his family."

"I see. Well, Mike, it's a public project. Anybody can bid. That includes Vasconcellos."

"Yes, I know. The problem is, he's not going to."

"He told you."

"Angela did."

"Ah. Well, then." It pissed Jack off that Mike would take advantage of their friendship like this.

"These are good people, Jack. This is a good family."

Jack stared at the priest's earnest expression. "For you, Mike, that might be enough."

"Apparently Tony believes this other outfit—I can't remember the name—will underbid the job just so nobody else gets it. A cheap contract is good for you, I suppose, but if nobody makes a profit, is that right?"

"Is that what Vasconcellos says?"

"That's what Angela told me."

"An interesting criticism, coming from Vasconcellos."

"What's the problem, here, Jack? Can't Tony do the work?"

"He understands the technology, if that's what you mean. It doesn't take a genius to pull wire and make connections. When contractors fail, Mike, that's not the reason. This is a cyclical business. Successful contractors know how to ride the cycles."

"But if Tony understands the technology, like you say, then he could do the dog track job, isn't that right?"

Jack didn't answer. Probably he'd lose the argument. Mike usually got his way. But Jack would make his points, at least.

"Between you and me, Vasconcellos is a shitty businessman."

Mike nodded slowly. "Is that right? He's always seemed to have plenty of work."

"The problem wasn't that. If anything, it's the opposite."

The priest shook his head, perplexed. Jack hesitated. He saw where this was going. Mike's fascination with the particulars of the situation, however, wouldn't alter his request, just make it harder to resist.

"I can't tell you what's happened," Jack told the priest, "not exactly. Frankly, about some things, I'd just as soon not know. But if you bid the jobs wrong, you can have all the work in the world and still go belly up."

"So, on the other hand, if he bid the jobs right…"

Jack frowned, unable to keep his unhappiness at this suggestion to himself. Of course, Mike picked up the gesture at once and turned it to his own purposes. "It would be better, I know, Jack, if you could just concentrate your energy on completing the project. 'Spare me all these complications.' Right?"

"That's right, Mike, spare me. Come the middle of January and it's twenty below on the job site, I don't need the Marx Brothers out there."

"But Tony can perform. You said he's competent, he knows the technical stuff."

"So go tell him to bid."

"But he won't. I can't tell him."

"Don't look at me."

Father Mike held his tongue for a time. They seemed to have reached a stalemate, but Jack didn't kid himself that it would last for long.

"I'm not asking you to do anything illegal, Jack, heaven forbid."

"I know what you're asking."

"It is possible, isn't it, to do something? A man with your ability."

"This is not the moment to try flattery on me, Father."

The priest smiled. "Ah, yes, I see, I've done it this time. You're really mad."

"You blame me?"

"Nope. Not at all." Among Father Mike's variety of smiles was a kind one, and he now bestowed that on Jack. "You know, I often tell myself, wouldn't it be nice, wouldn't it be wonderful if I could just tend to the spiritual needs of the parishioners? It would be; it'd be damn nice. But I couldn't do it, and I'll tell you why. I'd lose the respect of people like you." Mike had often expressed regret at the practical necessities of his vocation, but this codicil was new.

"No, you wouldn't," Jack said.

"Oh, yes, I would. But no matter. I know I shouldn't envy the Trappists, tucked away out there in New Melleray, but I fear that sometimes in my weakness I do. I think of the monks enjoying their lives apart. They're a gift to us all, of course. But me, what am I? Nothing more than a simple parish priest."

"Not so damn simple."

"But I'm out in the world, Jack, and the world's a messy place."

"Yeah."

"And so sometimes I have to do things like this. Impose upon my friends. I don't like it any more than you do."

"Then you don't like it much."

"No, I don't. But from them who give, more is asked..." The kind smile again. "And you can help Tony Vasconcellos, right? You can sit down with him?"

What was the use? Jack thought. "Yeah, I can sit down with him."

"And there's a way."

"Sure," Jack conceded, "you can get the man you want on the job."

"I knew you could."

"I've negotiated with contractors before. I've even done it on public jobs." Jack, recognizing the brag, listened with disgust as these words came out of his mouth.

"Good," Father Mike said, duly modest in his triumph.

Jack tried to backtrack. "But there's still no guarantee, Mike. I can only do so much."

"Of course."

"And the man's got to perform. You better make him understand that."

"I'll make Angela understand it. That's even better."

"Okay, whatever, but I'm not kidding. If Vasconcellos doesn't perform, I'll get rid of him. Electrical contractors are not so hard to replace. You tell Angela that, too."

The priest smiled, a different smile now, with a touch of relief in it.

"I understand, Jack, I really do. You've got a job to do." Despite the affirmation, Jack heard the faint, probably unintended, dismissal in the priest's tone.

Mike was pressing his lips together and shaking his head, the picture of sympathy. He understood Jack's predicament. He understood the unfairness of what he was asking. He understood it all, but he was asking, anyway. And how, in the face of all this sympathy, could Jack possibly refuse? Well, obviously he couldn't.

Mike sat back and composed himself. Jack had a sudden urge to ask for the drink he'd turned down earlier.

"I don't propose you should be the only one helping out here, Jack. We'll be working together on this. They're a good family. Devout. They say the rosary together before dinner. How often do we see that nowadays?"

"Not enough, I'm sure," Jack conceded, a little sourly.

"This is a good thing we're doing, Jack," the priest assured him.

"Perhaps." The moment to be gracious had arrived, but Jack couldn't quite manage it. He'd do this thing, but there was no way he could pretend to like it.

The Tony Vasconcellos matter disposed of to the priest's satisfaction, he settled himself benignly in his chair and said, "Okay, good. Now, Jack, what about you? We've put you off too long. So out with it, what can I do for you?"

Jack had all but forgotten. His own problem, so fresh in his mind when he'd come through the door, now seemed remote. Under the best of conditions, he didn't know how he'd manage to talk about it, and here, on top of everything else, he and Mike would go and get themselves into a conversation like the one they'd just finished.

Perhaps, he thought, trying but failing to summon back the earlier feeling, Mike was the last person in the world he should confide in. Perhaps he should go out to New Melleray and talk to the monks. Perhaps on a retreat, if only he could find the time.

Anyway, at the moment, he had Mike's question to answer. The priest, having gotten what he wanted, was ready to reciprocate.

"That's okay, Mike," Jack told him. "It can wait. Another time."

"Really?"

"Yes."

"Are you sure?" Jack saw the pain in Mike's expression and understood at once the unfairness in not allowing him to extend a helping hand now, after the Vasconcellos business. Jack understood, but he could do nothing but nod and repeat, "Another time."

He couldn't possibly imagine when that other time might be.

# CHAPTER 4

～

At seven a.m. on Wednesday morning, three days after arriving in the city, Rachel Brandeis stood outside the Jackson Packing Company. The facade of the slaughterhouse's main building ranged before her, a vast, featureless brick wall—an industrial version, she supposed, of the plain brown wrapper.

Inside, narrow stairs led up to a reception area, little more than an alcove punched out of the hallway, an afterthought. Clearly, here was a place with scant interest in visitors. While she waited, she seemed to have trouble breathing, as if the air had been evacuated from the tiny space. Clutching her notepad, she listened to muffled sounds from deep within the building and imagined the worst.

The youthfulness of Skip Peterson startled her. He shook her hand firmly and immediately suggested a tour of the plant, and before she knew what had happened, she found herself following him at a brisk clip through an office area, past a huge ceramic or plastic pig that in her impressionable state she momentarily thought real. A faint animal odor scented the place.

Peterson's young appearance wasn't the only thing that surprised. Given the general disdain private companies showed to the press, she'd been surprised to get any access at all, and when she did, she had expected to be dealing with some PR flunky, not the man himself.

"You'll need a frock," he said, pausing at a closet. "These come in two sizes, too small and too large."

After she had donned one of the white coats, Peterson appraised her. "Hmm. Looks like you're auditioning for the Ku Klux Klan." She smiled and held her arms out, conscious of a little-girl quality in the gesture. The coat cascaded down from her shoulders and arms.

"Here, try this one." The second choice was smaller but still a couple of sizes too big. "Perfect," he said, handing her a hardhat to complete her ensemble. Then, without another word, he was off again, double-time, as she struggled to adjust the band on the inside of the hat.

They passed through a door, and the temperature suddenly dropped fifteen or twenty degrees. The odor was stronger, a kind of tainted bacon smell. They walked along dim brick passageways filled with machine noises. They clattered down iron stairways, moving so quickly that Rachel's fear was barely able to keep up. She could feel the cool air on the backs of her hands, at her temples, in her mouth.

Peterson talked in machine gun bursts. "In meatpacking, we work on narrow margins. Razor thin. Less than one percent. And that, Miss Brandeis, is during the best of times. Which, as you know, this ain't." She was conscious that he hadn't automatically used her given name. She liked that.

He greeted workers without stopping, turning around and walking backward for a few steps to conclude some snippet of conversation as they passed and were gone.

"Number one problem: the plant—old, multistory, inefficient." They went down another steep, narrow stairwell. Descending, descending...Rachel took rapid, shallow gulps of air as they sped along.

And then, all at once, Peterson pushed through a door and into a huge, open area. The noise was deafening. Men in white frocks and variously colored hardhats were everywhere. A line of pigs hung spread-eagled from an overhead conveyer moving toward them along the right-hand wall. Peterson pointed the other way, at the blank wall on the left, and leaned toward her so that he could be heard above the din. "Used to have a beef kill! No longer—uneconomical! Now it's just waste space!"

She wasn't, however, much interested at the moment in what used to be. She was staring at the carcasses, pink and glistening and hairless. She pointed. "How do you kill them?"

"Follow me!"

They were almost jogging now, through the machine noise, in the direction from which the animals were coming. The smell was very strong, but she found it not entirely unpleasant. Like the odor of shrimp boiled in their shells. Shrimp were *trayf* too, of course.

Ahead, indistinctly, the scene unfolded. She could hear squealing, and then finally she saw them, the row of animals still alive. She stopped and stood riveted. They were being herded into a chute, which narrowed until it was wide enough for only one at a time. At the end, a worker stood with a U-shaped device, which he placed against the head of each animal as it arrived. A brief click and sizzling sound followed, and the pig dropped off the end of the chute and slammed onto the brick floor several feet below. Another worker caught one of the legs of the fallen animal in a noose and it was pulled upward and along, dangling upside down from the conveyor.

Rachel gestured toward the animals that had just been hoisted aloft. "Dead?" Through its bristly white hair—like an old man's, she thought—its skin appeared delicate and vulnerable.

"No! Just stunned!" Peterson pointed at the U-shaped instrument. "That knocks 'em out! Five hundred volts! If we didn't bleed 'em, they'd all wake up with whopping big headaches!" He led the way along the platform to a point where they could look down on the next step in the operation. She watched the worker there make a short, quick cut in the throat of the animal she had asked about.

"Some of the blood is used by pharmaceutical houses!" Peterson yelled. "Most of it ends up as protein supplement in animal feeds!"

Rachel had expected to be nauseated but at that moment felt almost nothing except curiosity. She studied the man below as he bled another animal. He paid no attention to her or to Peterson. It was as if they weren't there. His indifference seemed to her like a kind of anger. After each animal, he dipped his knife into a vat of steaming water. Occasionally he drew the blade back and forth across a sharpener, which hung down from his waist. He moved slowly, gracefully, in time with some inner rhythm as if conserving energy, speeding up only to make each cut, a quick slashing motion, the blood gushing out of an animal, pulsing briefly and then draining evermore slowly away. Life ebbing.

"The work must get to you!" Rachel shouted.

"I think the basic problem is it's boring!"

As they were walking back in the direction from which they had come, Peterson said, "That's the thing! Most of the people here are too smart for the jobs they've got! Now, you take a company like Modern Meat! They bring in a lot of Asian and Mexican immigrants! Pay them next to nothing! You know about Modern Meat?"

"Oh, yes!" Over the last three days Rachel had been doing furious background reading on the industry. Each story, it seemed, contained an obligatory reference to the infamous Modern Meat. Without unions, using the most modern equipment, subdividing jobs until they required almost no training, Modern Meat gave no quarter in their competition with older firms, like Peterson's. And they were about to open a plant in Maquoketa, a town a couple dozen miles to the south, right in his backyard. The two companies would be buying animals from the same farmers.

"You'll be going head-to-head with them! How can you do that with an old plant like this and narrow margins?"

"It's very common for buying areas to overlap! Got to work smarter is all!"

This answer seemed rather too facile. "But still! The shakeout in the industry! A company like Modern Meat! Aren't you living on borrowed time?"

Peterson stood stock-still and regarded her cannily for a few moments, and then, stabbing his finger toward the floor, some of the friendliness gone, said, "Good people! Creative people! We'll be okay!" before wheeling and starting off again at a full clip.

Some of the workers, like the one she'd seen bleeding the hogs, seemed sullen and looked at their capo de capos without expression. Others were friendlier. Peterson seemed to know most of them by name. A few were effusive, sycophants. Many eyes she felt on her, appraising. She glanced down at her shapeless white coat and self-consciously fingered its nap, rough from many washings.

Peterson pointed again toward the abandoned area where he'd once had a beef kill. "Used to have rabbis come all the way from Cincinnati to perform the ritual slaughter! They did it for the Arabs, too! We supplied kosher beef for the entire Midwest!"

Rachel listened to this and remembered something her father had once told her. It didn't matter whether she dismissed the fact she was a Jew; other people wouldn't, Jews or Gentiles. The comment, anyway, reminded her of another one of the questions she'd intended to ask.

"If your margin's so narrow, how can you afford to have this much unused space?"

"Mostly there's a big psychological issue about empty space! Drives people crazy! The real problems are process, labor costs, and the cost of animals!"

"Lots of problems!"

"Got to work smarter!"

*Mnyeh*, Rachel thought sarcastically, the man's found the solution to all the world's ills. But she'd learned enough to know that Peterson's outmoded plant was the anchor hung around his neck, and the few people she'd talked to so far had told her it would drag him to the bottom. "But dead space is dead space!" she prodded. "It still costs money!"

"We've got loyal customers, Miss Brandeis! We put out superior products! You can't measure everything in dollars and cents!"

About this last, Rachel had her doubts, at least in the niche that the Jackson Packing Company and Modern Meat were fighting over. Peterson's responses, meant to deflect, merely heightened her curiosity. Her new boss, Len Sawyer, about whom she wasn't crazy but whose lead she was destined to follow, insisted something out of the ordinary was going on at the company, something beyond the mere struggle to survive, which was old news. So what was it? Encouraged by Peterson's breezy style, she wondered if the company might not be less anal-retentive than everybody seemed to think. Perhaps she could establish a relationship.

When Peterson stopped to talk with an official-looking fellow in a green hardhat, she had the opportunity to pause and study the CEO a little more closely for a minute. At the paper, she'd gone through the morgue and learned a fair amount about the man. In person, he looked younger than in the file photos. Attractive. Chestnut brown hair combed back in two waves, the style a little old-fashioned. Impossibly thin, the sort of person who would never have to worry about his weight, unlike Rachel, who had a lifetime of fad diets in her future. A third-generation Peterson. Somehow he looked third-generation. *Skip*, she understood, was a boyhood nickname he had never quite managed to shuck. She stared at him, seeking that which was implied in his gestures as he bent close to talk to his subordinate. His pose had a certain tension in it, like flight arrested.

They continued the tour. The conveyor doubled back upon itself as it crisscrossed the floor, the room filled with the bodies of slaughtered hogs, slowly being dismembered, like an assembly line in reverse.

Peterson, ever in a hurry, stopped only occasionally to say a few words to her. The problem with overhead. The by-product markets had gone to hell over the last few decades. Money cost more. The environment. She understood that he was arguing management's point of view, defending himself against his competitors, against his unions, against his bankers, against the city, against fate. Nonetheless, she found his sincerity and intensity attractive.

She watched the chest cavity of an animal being split open. "The lungs are inedible!" he yelled, leaning close. She could feel his breath on her cheek. "They're used in animal feeds!" A worker cut down vertically with his knife across the belly of a carcass and the viscera were exposed. Rachel stopped and stared at it. The small intestine, brown, packed in tight coils, glistened from the moisture on it. "The men who work these stations are highly skilled! If they nick the intestine, the edible meat is contaminated and has to be thrown out!" She casually wondered if contaminated meat really was discarded. But she also thought that Peterson seemed genuinely loyal to his employees. Nice.

Staring at the intestine, hardly different than looking at an anatomical diagram, she remembered her earlier expectation of being revulsed. Hadn't happened, not at all, not the least little bit, and she felt a small joy.

"Not a pretty sight, I know!" Peterson said, misinterpreting. One of the workers dipped his knife in his vat of hot water and glanced down at her. She looked into his eyes and smiled, and he smiled and nodded. He was a young man, and in his smile was something sly. Another misinterpretation, she thought, but it pleased her.

"Reminds me of biology class!" she said. "Bigger frogs is all!" She felt good. Yes, she thought, this is okay. I'm glad I came. To the Midwest. To Jackson. Now to the packing company, to the kill floor itself that only an hour before had seemed a place of such primal horrors. But no more. She could do this.

"I'm fine!" She reached out and put her hand familiarly on Peterson's sleeve. "What's next?"

# CHAPTER 5

～

As he approached the dog track construction site, Mark O'Banion, the city's public works director, drove slowly by the dredge's discharge pipe, the end man nowhere to be seen, the dozer idle, no slurry fanning out from the spreader mounted on the end of the pipe. Every time he discovered that the dredge had gone down again, a small bleakness would set in.

It was early yet, he told himself, happy, for the moment, to rationalize. Perhaps they just hadn't begun.

As he was about to drive on, he spotted two men nearby, Jack Kelley and somebody he didn't know, standing at the foot of a swale in the sand. He pulled off the access road, got out into the heat, and went down, half sliding, through the trash that had worked its way to the surface from the ancient city dump beneath. In the distance, at the far northern edge of the site, he could hear the slow but steady report of a pile driver, muted by the heavy air.

Jack squatted next to a small pool of water. He looked up as Mark neared.

"Morning."

"Jack. What's up?"

"Just showing my man here the bubbles."

A tiny clay catchment, half-filled with dredge sand, cupped the water. From blisters in the yellowish, unhealthy-looking clay, several stringers of gas bubbles rose: methane.

Jack gestured up at the third man and made the introductions. Don Adagian, the field manager, second day on the job. So, Mark thought, Jack had finally managed to round somebody up. Adagian possessed the florid complexion of a drinker.

"I was just telling Jack here," Adagian started off as soon as he was introduced, "about a project I was involved in up in Madison. Subdivision. Maybe you heard about it. Landfill was across the street. Nobody thought nothing about it. But what with methane being odorless and colorless, a regular stealth gas, you might say," he chuckled. "It just crept across the road there, seeped into one of the houses, spark touched it off, and boom, that's all she wrote—"

He kept on talking until Jack cut him off and drily remarked, "So Don here understands our problem."

Jack and Mark would have left a small space in the conversation for contemplation at this point, but apparently this Adagian person abhorred a vacuum, for he rushed back in with more chatter until Jack cut him off again and turned to Mark.

"We're through here. I'll meet you up above."

Wondering about the new man, Mark watched them climbing toward the top of the plateau, then turned to climb back up himself. The brief ascent winded him, and he stopped to take a blow and empty the sand out of his loafers. He really should exercise, he told himself for the hundredth time or the thousandth. Since the end of the dredge pipe lay close at hand, he walked over to it and ran his fingers across the metal spreader, although he could see perfectly well that it was bone-dry. He looked at his watch: 7:35. Not that early. They should be pumping.

He stared disconsolately at the spreader—nothing more than a roughly fashioned piece of sheet metal used to broadcast the slurry—thought about the fateful decision to let Leonard Sawyer do this work with his little dredge, and said softly, "Oh, Leonard, Leonard, Leonard, why did I let you talk me into this?" Sadly, he climbed back into his car. He knew why, of course. Politics.

In the distance, the rigging of the pile driver rose above the construction site. Mark's old Caddy rocked in the potholes of the road. The morning sunshine, smudgy and glaring, seemed less like something new than some unhappy past taken up again. Almost October and still the drought hung on.

Jack had already returned to the construction trailer and come back out, alone now, carrying a hard hat. Mark got out, and Jack handed him the hat.

"Thanks for coming."

"Not a problem. What can I do for you?"

"Let's take a walk."

They moved toward the pile driver, into the steady, metallic concussions of the machine.

"Is the dredge down again?" Mark asked, hoping against hope.

"Sometime late yesterday."

"Um." Not so long. Could be worse.

"At the moment, the dredge is the least of my worries," Jack said. "You saw." He obviously meant Don Adagian.

"Your new friend's quite the talker."

"Yes, he is."

"Expect he's been known to take a drink on occasion."

"Expect he has."

"Where did you find him?"

"Contact in Madison. Friend of a friend."

Mark clucked sympathetically. "Too bad your original guy bailed."

"Adagian's supposed to be a good field man…that is, if he lays off the bottle and doesn't get too cozy with the help."

They had neared the pile driver, becoming engulfed in the intense shroud of sound. The machine, suspended from a crane and cradled in the harness used to align the piles, was powerful and compact, perhaps fifteen feet high, narrow, its intricate guts exposed, black and gleaming with oil.

"Are they getting count?" Mark asked, raising his voice just loud enough to be heard.

"No."

A brief discussion followed about the schedule and how much pipe they were using and just how serious this problem of driving it to refusal might be. Puffs of black smoke punctuated the relentless echoing of the hammer blows, the blows themselves only visible as a vibration of the device. They next talked about the methane seeping up from the old dump beneath the site, an enormous potential liability. At least, Mark comforted himself, it was a liability they knew about.

One of the pile driver's crewmen was taking a leak, shielded partly between the treads at the rear of the crane. Then he zipped up and strutted back, taking his time.

Beneath Mark's feet, the sand vibrated. He liked the slow rhythm of the work. He liked the ironworkers, too, with their earmuffs, with their faces and clothes spotted with oil from the hammer, with their confident manners.

"Anything else?" he asked.

Jack squinted off into the early morning glare. "I suppose not."

Mark looked at him speculatively. If they continued having trouble driving the piles to refusal, that might necessitate a change order. More important, it would suggest that McDermott, the engineering firm that did the soils tests, had screwed up: the same firm, as luck would have it, that was designing the methane barrier. Something to think about. But these matters, as important as they were, could have been handled with a phone call. So why, Mark wondered, had Jack wanted him to come down to the site? Guessing, he said, "You're worried about the new man, this Adagian fellow."

"We're gonna be joined at the hip the next eight months." Jack stared off into the glare, shaking his head. Then he shrugged. "Anyway, construction workers drink. So what else is new?"

They stood silently contemplating this reality.

Mark had been in AA for nearly thirty years. Jack knew that. Everybody in the city knew it.

"Still," Mark said after a time, "there are drinkers and there are drinkers."

Jack nodded. "I've already told him how important this project is to the city, for whatever good it'll do."

"Yes. We can hope that will help." Mark had dealt with many drunks over the years. He wished he could do something to help Jack out, something preemptive. Maybe one day, depending on how things turned out. But not now. With people like Don Adagian, more often than not, it made no difference how important the work was; it was never important enough.

~

As he drove back past the end of the discharge pipe, on his way uptown, Mark saw that the dredge still wasn't running. At the moment, feeling sufficiently burdened, he had no interest in tangling with old Joe Turcotte. This was the dock board's problem, he rationalized, and succeeded in driving another quarter mile before this small rebellion had been put down and, with a sigh, he'd turned the Caddy around and headed back.

The dredge lay near the shore, the pair of tall spuds on which it pivoted rising high into the air from the stern, while at the bow, the cutterhead jutted forward like the proboscis of a giant mechanical mosquito.

Mark felt slightly off balance as he walked along the duckboards laid on top of the floating line. Far forward, he could see the dredge master standing in a workboat and swinging a small sledgehammer against the shaft of the hydraulic motor, which drove the cutterhead. The workboat recoiled slightly with each swing, the sounds reaching Mark a split second after he saw each blow fall, a trivial, futile sound after the massive noise of the pile driver.

Sidling past the deckhouse, stepping over lines and come-alongs and other gear strewn carelessly about, he made his way to the bow, where Petey Grace, who normally operated the dozer at the discharge, now merely stood and watched his boss work. Petey nodded but made a point of not seeming too interested in Mark's arrival. Turcotte had stopped hammering, but he didn't bother to look up at Mark. The man possessed a full measure of the river rat's disdain. By stopping, he acknowledged Mark's presence. More he wouldn't do.

"Problem?" Mark called down to him.

Turcotte worked the wad of tobacco in his cheek and then spit. "Shear pins."

Mark thought about climbing out on the framework to take a look for himself, then decided he'd better not. No point, really. He shifted his position and leaned out over the bow. Forward of the motor, the shaft was flexed and partially twisted. What would have happened, he could surmise. The shear pins, which held the flanges of the drive shaft, had failed to break off cleanly when the cutterhead lodged against something on the river bottom. Turcotte had been trying to free the pins with his small sledge.

"There's a hydraulic ram at the city garage. Why don't you borrow that?" Mark suggested.

Turcotte turned his head just enough so that he could look up with one eye. He was a thin man, a handful of years older than Mark, wearing olive-colored work pants and a dirty, shapeless T-shirt. His thin arms had the long, stringy muscles of a lifetime of manual labor. "I'll take care of her," he said. Mark could barely hear him.

Mark gave him a look that was meant to indicate a certain impatience and said, "You'd better use the ram."

Turcotte didn't bother to answer.

Mark nodded at Petey Grace as he left, and Grace nodded back, and that was that.

Relieved to be in the Caddy again, his fruitless task performed, Mark drove slowly uptown meditating upon the latest set of problems to land in his lap. Turcotte, of course, was not a new one, but a golden oldie.

As he pulled into the city hall lot, he wondered what had ever happened to his legendary ability to keep problems from eating him up. He parked and went inside, making his way along the downstairs corridor, greeting its denizens. Upstairs he looked in on the city engineer.

Chuck Fellows was sitting at his desk, his thick arms crossed, his flagon of black coffee in front of him, ready to spend another day not suffering fools gladly. Mark closed the door and sat down.

The office was strictly utilitarian, no pictures of the little lady and the kids, nothing on the walls except USGS seven-and-a-half-minute maps of the Jackson area. When Fellows left the room, nothing of himself remained behind.

The two of them nodded but did not speak. Mark crossed his arms so that he was almost a mirror image of his subordinate, whom he liked enormously, a barbarian with an education. He had his PE, of course, and an MBA as well. He played rugby. He read Dickens. He liked up-front, in-your-face situations. He was like a mythical beast made up of diverse parts. And he had a knack for alienating people, a knack Mark rather envied.

"You look like shit," Fellows said finally.

"Didn't get much sleep last night." They lapsed into silence again until Mark said, "I once met a lady at a party who told me what a lucky guy I was to have so many opportunities to fix problems."

"What did you tell her?"

"That disasters were not as much fun as they were cracked up to be."

Fellows grinned. "That's because you give a shit."

"Yes, I suppose I do. A failing, I know."

"What is it this time?"

From his collection of problems, Mark selected the one he'd talk to Fellows about.

"Dredge. Down again."

"When?"

Mark told him what he knew.

"Shear pins are no big deal," Chuck said.

"Right. Unless the motor's been damaged."

Chuck frowned.

"Any suggestions?" Mark asked.

"Me? Sure. Start over. I'd've never used the city's dredge in the first place. It's undersized. I'd run Turcotte off the job and get somebody out there who's got the proper equipment. That's what I'd do."

"Not very helpful, I'm afraid," Mark said, but he was smiling. He knew what Chuck would say.

"You asked. Maybe you've got a better idea."

Mark shook his head. "Wouldn't it be nice to just start over?"

"Shit, I'd do it. Screw the cost. Get the job done right."

"Right, screw the cost." But it wasn't just the cost. It was the history, the inconvenient fact that the lifetime chairman of the dock board and the publisher of the local daily newspaper happened to be one and the same. Old Len Sawyer thought river rats like Joe Turcotte were the salt of the earth. Not, of course, that Chuck Fellows gave a fig about such complications.

Mark looked at Chuck, thinking what a marvelous luxury the man's frankness was. The city engineer hadn't moved. He sat with his arms folded across his chest, a man without doubts. He had a civil engineer's mentality. Mark, on the other hand, from his many years in the private sector before joining the city, had the mind of a general contractor. For Fellows, everyone was either right or wrong, part of the solution or part of the problem. For Mark, everyone was a subcontractor.

But still, what a temptation. Just give the problem to Fellows and stand aside. Sometimes Mark even fantasized about what Chuck would be like as the public works director. He smiled. It wouldn't be pretty.

"So tell me," Chuck now asked, "what *are* you going to do?" He spoke with the little swagger and snicker of a bully who's backed off for a moment and dared his victim to stand up again.

Mark shook his head.

"Have another chat with Len, I suppose."

Chuck snorted. "Waste of time."

"You're probably right."

Chuck just smiled and nodded, satisfied, no doubt, that he hadn't heard anything in the last five minutes to threaten his low opinion of his fellow mortals.

And Mark was satisfied, too. He'd had his cold shower. He felt refreshed, a little. He could get on with his day.

# Chapter 6

⁓

*As of January 1, Albert T. Swenson Inc. will no longer market products of the Jackson Packing Company. For the past five years, Swenson, which has corporate offices in Minneapolis, Minn., has been marketing Jack 'n' Jill brand products under an agreement with Jackson Packing. "We are presently establishing new marketing arrangements to replace those expected to be lost," Jackson Packing Company President William F. Peterson stated today. "Given the high quality of our products and the long-standing loyalty of our many customers, we are confident in the future of the company."*

Just after lunch, Rachel Brandeis had returned to the *Tribune* to discover this news release from the packing company on her desk. She had read it standing, then sat down and read it again, as if such a blunt announcement could possibly be open to interpretation. She knew about the agreement. It was a big deal. Since it was set to end, that would be another big deal, a major blow to the company, as if Peterson didn't have enough problems already. He was going to have to work even smarter.

In quick succession, she felt mystified, then angry, and finally deflated. She'd spent more than an hour with the man that morning. In her mind's eye, she watched him charging across the kill floor at the packing company, firing volleys of facts back at her as he went. But nothing, not a word about the garroted marketing deal.

Her immediate superior, the assistant local news editor, was nowhere to be found, so she went in search of Neil Houselog, the news editor, and held the offending news release out toward him.

"Came in while you were gone," he told her. "We've already assigned people to it."

"I don't understand." Hearing the sense of violation in her voice, she paused a moment. When she continued, she had filtered out the pain, leaving only the irritation. "I just toured the company with Skip Peterson. He didn't say a word about it."

Houselog considered that. "About par for the course, I'd say."

"Par for the course? Why even talk to me then? Why the tour of the place? Why not just stiff me like I expected?"

The editor didn't answer right away. In their few brief dealings since her arrival, Rachel had detected something not quite definable in Houselog's demeanor toward her. She had met him the previous Sunday. He possessed a pleasant expression, which hid the kind of watchfulness that Rachel associated with cops. He had worn a tie clasp in the form of a musical notation, a G clef, and managed, in the short time they were together, to tell her three times that the *Tribune* was the paper of record in Jackson, a fact he needn't have mentioned at all, since the paper was the only daily in the city.

Now he had on a tie with a violin motif. His cop-like detachment remained.

"Probably," he suggested, "it was more about Skip Peterson seeing you than the other way around."

"But he could have told me about Swenson, anyway," she complained. "What difference would it have made? It wasn't like we were going to scoop anyone."

"I suppose." He seemed completely undisturbed by this.

Halfway through this conversation, the editor had leaned back in his chair and planted his feet on his desk. Now he was stroking the corners of his walrus mustache with thumb and forefinger.

"So what should I do, then?" she asked him.

"About the story?"

"Yes. I thought JackPack stuff was mine." Once again she heard the note of poor-little-me creep into her voice.

"Have you looked at your messages yet?" he asked. "No? I suggest you do."

Dispirited, Rachel returned to her desk, her head filled with images of Peterson and the tour of the packinghouse. What a schmuck she'd been to fall for his breezy, buddy-buddy style. Suddenly, her thoughts lit on one particular moment. They were standing near the man who slit the throats of the stunned hogs. Peterson had just mentioned working smarter. She'd continued to harp on the company's decrepit condition and the shakeout in the industry, and all at once Peterson had stopped, just for an instant, frozen in place, as still as judgment, peering at her. She had seen the slight constriction of his hazel eyes, the slight adjustment of his mouth, and made a mental note but then in the rush of events forgotten it, until that moment. Maybe, after all, she could have left the plant with the press release in her hand. Shit!

Still standing, propped on one hand, she called up her messages. Message. A single one popped onto the screen. In the instant before she began to peruse it, she felt the poverty of having only one message. And this barely a line long: Rachel. My office. 3 p.m. Sawyer.

She groaned and threw herself down in her chair, where she slouched and thought her paranoid thoughts. *Kvetching* voices inside her were in full cry, and she had to wait for them to quiet down so that she might try to think clearly about her situation.

Since other reporters had been assigned to the story, that left her with nothing to do. She could take Neil Houselog at his word—that he'd assigned the stories to others simply because she wasn't available—but then what was the rush? They weren't on deadline.

Another explanation lay close to hand. Sawyer was having second thoughts about hiring someone so inexperienced. That would explain Houselog's move. And why Sawyer wanted to see her up in his office. What good was she? She'd been warming up her engines while the rest of the world zoomed by. Of course. It all made sense. In fact, nothing else made sense.

It wasn't fair. She'd only been in Jackson for four days; what did they expect? But then she remembered her own surprise, shock really, when Sawyer had offered her such a plummy job to begin with, investigative business reporting. Now second thoughts must have set in; he'd decided she wasn't the hotshot overachieving woman he'd fantasized hiring, and so she was to be given the old heave-ho.

Oddly, as she laid these facts out neatly for herself, one after the other, this sense that reality had reasserted itself almost pleased her. She'd go back East, take up her old work as an AP stringer, and put this whole sorry episode behind her. Good.

She looked at her watch. Barely after two. She had nearly an hour to kill before she went upstairs.

Satisfaction over getting fired being what it was, she had soon taken herself off to the cafeteria where she sat in the far corner with her Coke and candy bar and thoughts of revenge. What she wanted most of all was to call up Skip Peterson and give the jerk a piece of her mind. If he'd told her about Swenson, she would have come back to the paper knowing something, at least, perhaps too late for today's editions but before anybody else had it. Then she wouldn't have looked like a complete idiot.

As she contemplated the pros and cons of a second candy bar, she visualized the tour of the kill floor again, and her pride that she hadn't fainted dead away at the sight of all those slaughtered animals. She had been like a little schoolgirl, tagging along after Peterson and letting him charm the pants off her.

She decided against the second candy bar and reminded herself that she was still a reporter for the *Jackson Tribune*, if only—she looked at her watch—for forty minutes more. Time for a call or two, at least. But to whom, about what?

"Okay, okay, Rach, think. Forget about yourself. Think about Swenson. What exactly does this all mean?"

Since JackPack traditionally shunned publicity, why announce the failure of the marketing agreement at all? Probably because Swenson was going to do it even if JackPack didn't.

She listed all the problems Peterson faced: purchasing, production, and marketing, all in deep trouble. Cutthroat competition. An ancient, decrepit facility. How could they survive? Probably they couldn't. Probably they were going down.

On her feet at once, she hurried from the cafeteria, telling herself she couldn't actually yell at Peterson. Fair enough. But she would call him on all this "gotta work smarter" crapola. She would make him explain just how he proposed to continue fighting when he was out cold on his feet.

Back at her desk, she immediately dialed the number she had for JackPack, identified herself, and asked for Peterson. The woman who answered told her to wait and after a minute returned and informed her that "Mr. Peterson is not available. But I'll transfer you to Mr. Bates, the director of human resources, if you want."

Itching to have another go at Peterson, Rachel's first impulse was to ignore this lesser mortal. But then what?

"Okay," she heard herself say. She waited to be transferred, thinking, the director of human resources? A fancy-shmancy term for the personnel manager. What did he have to do with marketing?

"Bates here," a new voice said.

When she identified herself again, he said, "I just talked to somebody from the *Trib*. Don't you people coordinate?"

Off to a good start. Rachel covered as best she could. "This is a big story, Mr. Bates. Several reporters are working on it."

With this new person to talk to, the urge to complain returned. Bates, however, didn't wait. "I hope you aren't going to overplay this. It's a concern, but we're prepared to deal with it."

"A concern? Sounds like more than that to me, Mr. Bates. If my company suddenly lost the bulk of its markets, I'd be pretty nervous."

"See, there you go," Bates shot back at her. "We didn't lose the bulk of our markets. Nobody said that. We have institutional customers. We process meat for other firms. We have our own retail and wholesale ties. You better get your facts straight, Miss... Brandeis, is it?"

"Yes. What percentage of your marketing have you lost, then? How much did Swenson sell for you?"

"I'm not prepared to discuss the details of our business."

"In that case, how are we supposed to know how serious the problem is?"

"Read the handout."

Okay, she thought, so she was talking to the wall here, but she wouldn't let this guy go without extracting a little something. She listed for Bates's edification all the obvious problems JackPack faced. "And I've only been in Jackson four days, Mr. Bates. If I'm here a couple more weeks, what else will I discover?"

"Look, these are all problems, okay? But you take any one of them, it's not such a big deal. A few years ago, as it so happens, we *were* in serious trouble, I won't deny it, but since then we've made considerable strides. We're just not as vulnerable anymore."

"It would be nice, then, if you could convince me of this. I've got plenty of time."

"Is that right?" Bates said drily.

"From where I'm standing, Mr. Bates, it appears that your company is in very, very serious trouble. If it's true, the public has a right to know." This was all bluff, since Rachel only had...twenty-three minutes left to work for the paper. "Frankly," she forged onward, "if you're not about to go bankrupt, I'd imagine you'd want the information out there in a convincing fashion. Otherwise, people are going to think the worst. Do you really want that?"

"They won't think the worst if you people don't print the worst—all these wild speculations of yours. Print the press release. I gave some quotes to your man a few minutes ago. Print those. The rest is just irresponsible gossip."

"At this point," she extemporized, "we don't know how we'll handle the story."

"Right."

She noted the sarcasm. "You don't give us much to go on, Mr. Bates, not with this just-print-the-handout approach to press relations."

"But it's all there. That's the trouble with you people. You're not happy unless you're covering the run-up to Armageddon."

The conversation lasted another minute or two, adding nothing to the nothing Rachel had already accumulated. After she had hung up, feeling energized and utterly defeated at the same time, she looked at her watch again. A quarter to three. Just enough time to call somebody else and make an ass of herself one last time.

"Pfft," she said.

~

At three o'clock, she went up to the penthouse.

The receptionist took one look at her, said, "Go right in," and Rachel gave a small, involuntary shudder.

The previous Sunday, Sawyer had met her in the outer office, and now she entered his private sanctum for the first time, a loft-like space whittled down by a series of upright panels, less a wall than an indication of where the wall would have gone had there been one. On all of the panels hung pictures, a frieze running entirely around the room depicting the waterfront.

Through the gaps between the panels the rest of the huge room could be glimpsed, what an archaeologist would call a midden, perhaps, since in the poor light she made out ancient machines and tools of the journalistic trade: a graceful curve that must have been the silhouette of a rolltop desk, the corner of some large machine (maybe a Teletype), stacked font trays, and much else unidentifiable in the dimness.

Sawyer's desk and computer workstation sat catty-corner to the left, raised on a platform. He had doffed the safari gear of the previous Sunday and now wore a conventional business suit, too big for him, as if since purchasing it he had continued to steadily waste away. He sat regarding her, something greedy in his old eyes, she thought. He didn't ask her to sit down.

"So…" he said.

She waited for the end.

"So," he repeated in his threadbare voice. He rubbed one skinny hand over the other, back and forth, back and forth, as a child rolls a ball of clay into a rope.

Apparently he intended to drag the thing out.

"Tell me what you've got." His hands ceased their rubbing. He sat perfectly still, staring at her as if he knew damn well what she had but was giving her a chance to introduce evidence in her own defense. She had none. No way did he want to hear about her delvings into the history of JackPack and the meatpacking industry. Yet, she had to say something.

"I think the company's on the verge of bankruptcy."

"Do you know it?"

She gave him the reasons she believed so.

"But do you know it? Do you have any hard information?"

She shook her head.

His leaned on his elbows. "I don't need you to tell me what anybody with eyes can see, miss."

She apologized. He stared at her, unsympathetic, and she thought, here it comes.

"Tell me what you've done," he demanded again. "Everything." Once more, the invitation to submit mitigating evidence.

So she gave him her small potatoes.

As soon as she finished, he snapped, "Forget the past. Forget Peterson, too, and forget his flunkies. I didn't hire you to waste your time on them."

"Yes, I see…although I don't know how I'm going to dig anything up if I don't do the background work and talk to company officials."

"Talk to anybody you want to. Just don't expect to get anything out of 'em. You're gonna help me out here, you gotta be more imaginative than that." The tics in his expression served to add intensity, and Rachel had to struggle to hold his gaze.

Evidently, she wasn't about to be fired. The relief she felt resembled more a letting go than anything like joy, as if something had floated free inside her and sunk down and made it more difficult to move.

The publisher's expression had changed. A certain calculation remained but joined now by interest and even a hint of perplexity.

"You know, I'd expect any daughter of Morris Brandeis to be a pretty resourceful young woman."

That again, the real reason she'd been hired. Well, it would have been so very easy for Rachel to trade on her father's reputation, but then people would have expected her to be like him.

"He's a labor lawyer, not a journalist."

"But a man of determination."

That Sawyer had gone to the trouble to find out who her father was ticked Rachel off. "He's an advocate, Mr. Sawyer. I didn't go into journalism to be an advocate."

Sawyer's forearm was propped upright on the edge of his desk, his thumbnail scratching along his chin thoughtfully as he took in this disavowal.

"Didn't hire you to be my lawyer, miss, if that's what you mean."

All of Rachel's apprehension had disappeared, replaced by irritation. So what if her last name was Brandeis? So what? She was related to Justice Brandeis, too, three generations back, but what did that mean? Nothing, that's what. "I want to do investigative work, Mr. Sawyer, and I'm not anything like my father. I don't already know who the heroes and villains are. How close I can get to the truth, that's what I'm interested in."

Sawyer nodded slowly, his fingernail still working. "Fair enough," he said. "So I ask you—is the Pack going to close? That's the question. Is it? The people of Jackson—our readers—want to know. You find that out, Rachel, you'll have done all I ask. Understand?"

Rachel, still possessed by the need to exorcize the spirit of her father from the conversation, wasn't ready to reach an accommodation, but she saw it was pointless to pile any more disclaimers on top of the ones she had already made.

"Yes," she said, "I understand."

"You need anything, you tell me."

"I will."

"Then we understand each other. Good. That will be all."

~

Back downstairs, Rachel slouched at her desk, her mind caroming from subject to subject.

She loved her father, but she wasn't one of those nice Jewish girls who set their fathers on pedestals and went running to them for approval every two minutes. Her father's fame had been nothing but trouble, as far as she was concerned, its imagined advantages swamped by all the assumptions people made about her. As soon as his name came into the conversation, Rachel all but disappeared. She could see it in Sawyer's gaze, too, staring not at her but at his fantasized picture of what Mo Brandeis's daughter must be like.

The nattering in her mind gradually subsided. What came in its place, however, hardly offered comfort. If it was true that Sawyer had hired her because he imagined she was her father's daughter, a grim specter arose. She might not be good enough. She might fail. Forget about all the left-wing stuff—her father got results. People loved him, people despised him, it made no difference; he got results.

And her? Results? She'd been given a reprieve by Sawyer. Big deal. She had no idea how she'd manage to unmask Skip Peterson, not an inkling. All her wise words about the anal-retentiveness of closely held companies had merely served to hide her own naive assumption that somehow she'd waltz right into JackPack and the truth would be made manifest. Good grief.

She felt a tingling in her scalp, followed by a sensation like cold water purling down her spine. She looked at her watch and took herself back to the caf—for tea this time—where she continued to contemplate the ruins of the last hour and a half and finally set about laying out a strategy for herself that might generate enough of a breeze to lift the veil from the Jackson Packing Company.

# CHAPTER 7

~

At 5:30, Jack Kelley entered the business establishment of Anthony Vasconcellos, electrical contractor, serving the tri-state area since 1967 (as the sign outside informed him). The office staff had gone for the day, leaving the small reception area deserted and in twilight.

Originally the building had been a gas station. A stab had been made at remodeling, but gas stations were too specialized ever to look like much of anything else. Vasconcellos was a hermit crab living in someone else's shell. Jack walked slowly back through the old lube area, taking everything in, imagining he could still smell the oil.

He knew more about Tony Vasconcellos than he had let on to Mike Daugherty the other day. Jack had been with Vasconcellos on a couple of jobs, including a big one during the electrician's salad days. The man wasn't truly rotten, just slightly on the other side of marginal. Decent electrician, lousy manager. Never quite learned how to run a job right. Of late, Jack knew, he'd been having a lot of trouble with his suppliers, a bad sign. Jack could have told Father Mike all these things, of course, but it wouldn't have changed anything.

Computers, of various brands and vintages, were scattered about. That was something else that Jack knew about. Vasconcellos had been having a deuce of a time switching over from his old manual bookkeeping system. In a nutshell, he was the kind of guy Jack could do without.

He found Vasconcellos in his office in the back, which was the old parts supply room.

"Tony."

The electrical contractor nodded slowly. He sat stoically behind his desk. "Jack."

"How you?"

Vasconcellos paused several more beats. "Been better."

"So I understand." Jack's intent was to strike just the right note of sympathy here, not too little, not too much. "Tough times," he said.

"Yeah, well, what can you do."

Vasconcellos didn't seem any more enthusiastic about this business than Jack. They weren't the principals here. Father Mike and Angela were. The contractor's wife and kids overlooked the scene from the top of a nearby file cabinet. Except for her willingness to form unholy alliances with Father Mike, Jack knew nothing about Angela Vasconcellos.

He walked over for a closer look, conscious of being watched. The photographer's art had eradicated any trace of the wife's personality, leaving behind a pleasant, round-faced woman, plump in the Jacksonian manner, the perfect image of a benevolent household deity.

"Nice-looking family."

"I think so."

They say the Rosary together, Father Mike had made a point of stressing. A good family, he had said. Mike laying the holy lumber to Jack.

"All your kids are still at home, then?" Jack asked, just to say something, in no rush to get to the subject at hand.

"That was taken some time ago. Lonny's the oldest—he's on the far left there—working with me now. Next to him is…" Jack half listened, letting his eye trail from child to child as Vasconcellos told each brief story.

Jack wondered if maybe the two of them might strike a bargain to forget this business about the electrical contract. A tempting idea, except that one way or another, given the sliding scale of loyalties here, it would get back to Mike Daugherty.

The chance to talk about his kids seemed to loosen Vasconcellos up a bit, and he was almost friendly as he waved Jack to a seat. They chatted for a few minutes about this and that, and Jack tried to take the current measure of the man. They hadn't had much contact of late, not having been on a job site together in several years. As for the parish, Jack belonged to the 9:30 congregation and Vasconcellos went some other time.

He looked a little like his wife, although without the benefit of the photographer's art. Despite his powerful physique, some vital force seemed to have been drained out of him, like a wild animal that, in being tamed, loses the very qualities for which the taming was necessary in the first place. He resembled a man of few skills, deeply ingrained. A gas station attendant.

"I notice, Tony, you haven't gone down to City Hall and picked up a set of plans yet."

Taken aback by this sudden jibing in the conversation, Vasconcellos shifted in his chair and looked briefly away. "Been thinking maybe I won't bid the job."

"I see. Why?"

"Don't know. Never much liked public projects, I guess. Everybody and his brother bids them. No profit margin."

Maybe you leave too much on the table, Jack started to say but then changed his mind.

Vasconcellos had gone on. "Anyhow, I figure one of the non-union outfits will buy the job." He shrugged.

"They can try." Contractors like Vasconcellos, who ran union shops, could get a little paranoid where non-union operations were concerned. "We're running a two-gate system," Jack told him, "one for union, one non. I expect to have both on-site."

Vasconcellos didn't seem to hear. "You try to be decent," he said, "and what does it get you? It gets you screwed, that's what."

Boy, Jack thought, the starch really has gone out of this joker. Jack wondered what minimal effort would suffice to discharge his promise to Father Mike.

"You've got to bid the job right, Tony."

Vasconcellos just shook his head.

"Anyway," Jack told him, "you'll never know if you don't look at the plans." With each statement, each grudging encouragement, Jack asked himself, Is this enough? Except for the unfortunate fact that whatever happened there would find its way back to Father Mike, Jack would gladly have abandoned the effort. But it *would* get back to Mike, and so something more *was* required. "I'll tell you what, Tony, if it was me, I wouldn't have any trouble making some money here."

Vasconcellos rubbed his fingertips back and forth across his forehead as he regarded Jack coolly.

"Perhaps you're just smarter than me." The words had an edge. Jack's flat contradiction had stung him.

Jack said, "Perhaps I am, on this job."

Vasconcellos didn't react to this provocation. He continued looking at Jack. Then his fingertips lifted off his forehead in a small dismissive gesture, and he subsided.

Enough? Jack wondered again. A little more. He'd give the man a little more. "This is an accelerated job. Only 40 percent of the electrical work is in the base bid."

Vasconcellos merely shook his head at this revelation, as if he saw only the problems in it and remained blind to the possibilities. Perhaps it didn't matter what he said, Jack thought. Perhaps he could lay the whole thing out for Vasconcellos and it wouldn't make one damn bit of difference.

"On the base bid, Tony, the successful bidder won't get more than a 7, maybe 8, percent markup. But on change orders, well, any contractor worth his salt could make 25 or 30 percent on them. You don't lowball, you just bid the documents."

Again Vasconcellos seemed impervious to this new bait and again Jack asked himself what was enough. But now, as he began to retail this information for Vasconcellos's benefit, he found himself drawn into his own recitation. He went on, letting out more and more line, waiting for Vasconcellos to bite.

"You understand," he repeated, almost angry now, "this isn't an invitation to lowball the project, Tony. You bid strictly on the basis of the documents."

Vasconcellos nodded slowly. It was impossible to tell just what impact all this was having on him, for he had continued to interject down-in-the-mouth comments. Nevertheless Jack imagined he felt a nibble.

He could have stopped there. He'd discharged his duty to Mike Daugherty and then some. But he'd gone this far, so what that hell.

"Do I dare ask what your relationship is like with your suppliers?"

Vasconcellos shrugged, the gesture confirming in all the detail necessary what Jack already understood—trouble paying bills, creditors pulling the plug. But, as Jack had bragged to Father Mike, there was always an angle. There was always somebody willing to supply you. So he said, "I know a guy down in the Quad Cities is looking to get a toehold up here. He'll give you very nice terms." Even as Jack heard the words coming out of his mouth, he wondered, was he crazy? He was just asking for trouble.

Finally, preparing to leave, he remembered what he'd seen earlier as he came through the old lube area. "Oh, and one more thing, Tony. If you *do* get the job, you'd better run it manually. Forget about using your computers for anything but backup."

Jack's irritation continued to prickle him enough so that he turned back at the door. "You could at least thank me."

Vasconcellos, who looked decidedly more comfortable now, drummed the desk with his fingers.

"Sure, thanks. You doing this for me, Jack?"

"No, that's right, I'm not doing it for you."

"Well, good, then, why don't we leave it at that?"

"Fine."

And Jack left, neither Father Mike nor Angela having been mentioned. Outside, he got into his car and drove slowly away, thinking he'd helped Vasconcellos out. He'd done enough; he'd done more than enough. Given that last exchange between them, probably something would get back to Father Mike about his lack of enthusiasm. That was okay. Jack hoped it did.

But that still left the question of whether he could stomach having Vasconcellos on the job site. Tony would probably figure that Jack owed him, not the other way around. He'd expect Jack to make sure the change orders were as plentiful and lucrative as promised.

And as if having to baby Vasconcellos along wouldn't be bad enough, there was also the matter of Don Adagian, Jack's last-minute hire as his field manager. About Adagian, Jack had an awful foreboding. Add Vasconcellos to the mix and Jack had this vision of himself taking on one cripple after another, as if the damn project was being run by Catholic Charities.

"Shit!" He pounded the steering wheel. He wouldn't do it, Father Mike or no Father Mike. No way he wanted Vasconcellos on the job. Maybe the SOB wouldn't bid, after all. But if he did…if he did, Jack would take steps. He knew just what to do. It meant becoming a double agent. He thought about that. Damn, he'd do it.

Submarining Vasconcellos was unworthy of Jack, of course. He'd feel bad about it, too. But he'd done such things in the past for the sake of a job. What would this be but another item for the debit side of his life? Could he live with himself? Well, he'd been living with himself for fifty-two years. He supposed he could do it for a few more. Father Mike or no Father Mike.

# CHAPTER 8

∼

With the plans and specs under his arm, Don Adagian walked through the wide gate in the floodwall and down to the marina, a large rectangular harbor surrounded by a dentition of boat slips, some covered by corrugated metal roofs, others without protection, open to the sky, like the one where the Do-Si-Do lay solitary and faded in the afternoon heat.

On board, he found a message taped to the hatchway—an invitation to come for a drink from someone named Kate Sullivan, complete with directions: "See the houseboat across the harbor. Looks like a shoebox. That's us."

Kate Sullivan. He liked the sound of the name. The "us" he was less enthusiastic about.

Below deck, in the steamy mildew odor of the stateroom, he threw the plans onto the counter and opened a can of beer. The beer was barely cold, the first slug from it bitter. That was the trouble with old boats like the Do-Si-Do that only pulled thirty amps of power. Couldn't hardly keep anything cold. Rubbing the can across his forehead, he thought vaguely about going up to the marina's bar. Or over to the houseboat. He wondered what Kate Sullivan looked like.

Trouble was, first thing in the morning he had to be back on the job site. Damn. He unrolled the plans, pinned them open with spare marine hardware, and began halfheartedly leafing through the drawings. As Kelley had said, almost no detailing.

He propped himself on his arms as he stared down at the plot plan. Sweat dripped onto it, the cabin of the Do-Si-Do a heat sink. He swore but then decided he might as well enjoy it while it lasted. Come January he'd be down on the job site freezing his keister off. He turned to the next sheet, the layout of the grandstand crawl space. Did Kelley believe everything he said? he wondered. Finish by June 15? No way, not if they had to work off shitty drawings like these all the time. There was enough detailing for the piling contractor. The form work could get started, too. But that was about it.

Not that Don gave a rat's ass. Three days ago he'd been on his last job, he still had a shitload of closeout work to do, and here he was, on another frigging project. He thought about that for a while, then shook his head and said, "Fuck." He got himself another beer and went topside, where he sat in the bass fishing chair and put his feet up on the rear deck.

At the far corner of the harbor lay Kate Sullivan's "shoebox," broad and low, with beige clapboards and dark brown shutters and fascia. It squatted on a nearly rakeless barge-like bottom and was hedged in by wooden pontoon walkways. Nearby somebody was playing Frank Sinatra. Shit, Don thought, Sinatra. The son of a bitch still topped the pop charts in marinas everywhere.

"What the hell."

Below, Don brushed his teeth, combed his hair, and slipped into a pullover that pretty well hid the beginnings of a beer gut. He studied his face in the tiny mirror in the head and decided that he still looked pretty good. A little jowly. He practiced smiling, the upside-down smile that spread to a crinkling at the corners of his eyes. The age lines, he imagined, added an aura of maturity. Even the hint of dissolution could be charming, from the right point of view. A man who knew how to have a good time.

Back on deck, he unlashed the dinghy from the swim platform in the stern and got out the trolling motor. It was well after five o'clock, but a midday heat still lay on the breathless water. The egg-beater sound of the tiny kicker echoed off the surrounding boats and embankments as he cut catty-corner across the harbor.

He'd deal with the plans later.

~

Kate Sullivan held the screen door wide open for him. "So you're the one came in on the Connie last night," she said.

Around her neck, on a delicate chain, hung a gold cross. Her hair was a wispy, pastel orange, her face round and smooth, her skin transparent where sunburned patches had peeled away. No great beauty but 100 percent colleen was Katie Sullivan, right down to the trace of a lilt in her voice, although her words were as strictly practical as the boat she lived on.

"You managed your hook-ups okay?" she asked.

"Yeah."

"Need to use the pumpout?"

"I'm fine."

She looked suspiciously at him and said, "I hope you're not one of those people who dump their shit into the harbor." Don inadvertently shifted slightly away from this bluntness.

"No," he lied.

"Good."

As his eyes adjusted to the dimness inside, he realized they were not alone. A man worked standing at a drawing board on the other side of the large, low room. The other half of "us," no doubt.

"That's my husband, Reiny Kopp," Kate Sullivan confirmed breezily. "Say hello, Reiny." The fellow raised one hand briefly but did not speak or turn to look at Don. "He's having a bad day," his wife explained. "Beer, Don?" she offered.

He smiled. "You're singing my song."

"Got whiskey if you'd prefer."

"Beer's fine, Kate." He liked the sound of her name on his tongue. "I'm laying off the hard stuff. Got a job to do."

Except for the low overhead, the large room, a combination lounge and galley, pretty much resembled a place you might find ashore.

"Job?" Kate said as she opened the refrigerator in the galley and twisted a can off a six-pack.

"Out at the dog track they're building. I'm the field manager."

A massive aquarium took up one wall, but the fish in it weren't the standard tropical varieties. Don stooped and stared through the murky water. He recognized a bullhead cat, buffalo, several panfish, even a carp.

Kate had come over and handed him the beer and gestured back toward the sofa and easy chairs arranged in one corner for sociability.

"Field manager? Sounds important."

Don shrugged. "Honest buck."

"I bet."

Her husband apparently had nothing to say for himself. Reiny Kopp, strange damn name. Don was glad Kate had kept her family name. It made her seem less married.

"So what's he do, your husband?" Don asked.

"He's the director of the historical museum." She raised her voice. "We're talking about you, honey." She smiled at Don, then shook her head and changed the subject.

"So, you got a place to stay yet?"

"My boat."

"Really? What about this winter?"

"Until the job's done. Why not?"

"Well," she said slowly, "for one thing, it's illegal."

"That so?"

"City code. No live-aboards during the winter."

"I see. So where do you and your husband there spend the winter?"

Don had every intention of living on the Do-Si-Do. No way was he going to fork over good money to rent some dump.

Kate took a sip of her drink. A gin-and-tonic, maybe. Don wasn't sure.

"You might ask the dock board," she suggested, "see if they'll make an exception for you. But I don't know, an old wooden boat like that." She shivered.

"So that the way you did it? The dock board?"

She smiled and said, "It's a long story."

He took a pull on his beer. Kate Sullivan was okay to look at. Nice smile. Nice set of knockers.

"Living on a Connie in the middle of winter," she mused. "I'll tell you, Don, I wouldn't do it."

Nearby, a big woodstove sat amidships. In one of the windows, an air conditioner rattled away.

"We got to build the damn track in the middle of winter," he told her. "I'm gonna be freezing my butt off out there. A little more won't make no difference."

She shook her head over and over. "A fun time."

"Yeah," he chuckled, "dumb. Living on the boat's dumb, building the track's dumb, but there you go."

"Ha!" Reiny Kopp barked from the drawing board. One word, that was all.

"Reinert has some pretty strong views on the track project," Kate explained.

"Does he now?"

Kate nodded but showed no interest in elaborating. Instead she inspected Don over the rim of her glass as she took a sip. Don performed the little trick he had with his expression—his upside-down smile, the crinkly eyes.

"Expect something can be done," Kopp said into the silence. He hadn't moved from the drawing board. He had a surprising bass voice.

"Done?"

Kopp turned, abandoning his work for the moment. "About living on your boat. Ask the guy you work for. Somebody at City Hall will be able to pull the necessary strings."

Now he advanced casually across the room, his eyes fixed on Don.

"You're gonna be their fair-haired boy since you're working on the track." His low, low voice echoed in the room.

"Thanks, I'll do it," Don said. "So...you don't think much of the project, do you?"

Kopp gripped the backrest of a chair with long, bony fingers. "The city decided they were gonna build this thing come hell or high water. Promoted it, got the bond issue passed, the whole nine yards. Then they started going around to construction outfits who, being sensible fellows, kept on telling them, no way, building in winter like that, and what the hell did they know about dog tracks? Nobody around here had ever built one. The idea was deranged. But the city wouldn't give up. They kept on asking, and finally, lo and behold, they got the answer they were looking for."

"I believe it," Don said.

Now Don could get a good look at Kopp. He didn't much like what he saw. He was tall and skinny. His Adam's apple bobbed as he hammered home his points in that bass drum of a voice. He resembled nothing so much as a cross between an English rock star and some kind of bird of prey.

"I'll tell you why people voted for the project, too," Kopp said. Once you got this guy started, Don noted, he wasn't so damn quiet. "They thought it'd knock a few bucks off their taxes, that's why. That noblest of all human motivations."

"Not because they wanted to patronize the track themselves?"

"A few, maybe. That wasn't why it passed."

Don didn't mind making a wager now and again. But poker was his game. Couldn't see himself betting on the doggies. Too unpredictable. "Anyway, gambling's big now," he said to Kopp. "Expect it will, like you say, knock something off the local taxes. I mean, you'll be getting all the niggers from Chicago coming out here to blow their welfare checks."

Kopp's head jerked around. "I don't know how you talk around your friends," he snapped, "but you better watch your mouth around us."

"For your information, Don," Kate informed him, "my husband is currently working on an African-American exhibit at the museum."

"Shit. Sorry."

Kopp said nothing.

"Hey, look," Don told him, "I don't have anything against the blacks. Hell, they use the word as much as we do. I didn't mean nothing. Live and let live, that's my motto."

Maybe Kate had fallen for the rock star, but it was the bird of prey who was at that moment sizing Don up. "Just watch your mouth," Kopp said finally.

"Hey, I said I was sorry."

Kopp shook his head, then turned around and retreated to his work.

Shit, Don thought, another hard-ass. As bad as frigging Jack Kelley.

"You do need to watch it," Kate admonished him, more softly than her husband.

Don's impulse was to get up and leave. He didn't need the grief. Jack Kelley was bad enough, nothing he could do about him, but these uptight liberals or whatever the hell they were he didn't have to put up with.

Still, Kate Sullivan had become more pleasant to look at by the minute. And what did he have waiting for him back on the Do-Si-Do? Warm beer and the damn track plans. Fuck.

So he set about trying to repair the damage.

The rest of the evening, however, wasn't much of an improvement on this rocky beginning. Kopp was some sort of leftover hippie or something. He inserted comments into the conversation from time to time. Why somebody as foxy as Kate would have married such a blowhard was just another one of life's mysteries. What a frigging waste.

Finally, as he prepared to cast off, Kate stood on the deck and looked down on him and asked if he was really serious about living on his boat all winter.

"Yup."

"But those old Chris Crafts have wooden hulls. What are you going to do about the ice?"

"Bubblers."

In the dim light, almost nighttime now, he could see her shaking her head.

"I wouldn't do it, if I were you."

"I've got everything figured out," he lied.

Kate was just a silhouette. Around her head stars were appearing in the deep violet sky.

As he steered back across the harbor, trying to pick the Do-Si-Do out of the dark line of hulls, Don remembered the lies that he'd told. Finally, as he pulled the dink up onto the platform and lashed it down, he decided that he'd worry about one thing at a time. Concrete stuff, that's what he'd worry about. Tomorrow he'd start seriously considering how he was going to winterize the boat. And he'd climb down into the bilges and flip the switch at the Y of the discharge pipe so that his shit started going into the holding tank rather than the river. Then after a while he could use the pumpout. He'd do it for Kate. Kate was okay. As for Kopp, fuck him. Fuck him and all the hard-asses.

~

When Kate went back inside, her husband paused long enough to say, "I hope you're not going to make him into one of your projects, cupcake."

Kate stared off into space and considered the matter, tempted. They would have some contact with the man. Why not put it to good use?

"Lounge lizard like that," Reiny added, completing his argument, "he'll just be trying to get into your drawers."

"Yes," she said wistfully, "I suppose you're right."

And so she put the idea aside.

~

# PART II

~

# CHAPTER 9

~

With her latest collection of JackPack quotes, Rachel stood outside the converted store front used by the local meatpacking union, at the end of a block filled with the small stuff of city commerce. Everybody she had talked to so far had a different opinion. Her piece, if written with what she'd gleaned so far, would be a typical bit of rabbinic scholarship. Rebbe A says this, Rebbe B says that, Rebbe C disagrees with both of them. According to this babble of wise men, JackPack was on the point of signing a marketing agreement with another packer or being sold outright or going into Chapter 11 (or perhaps Chapter 7) or trying to scare the *kishkas* out of its union, with which negotiations had been stalled for months, or planning to shut down the Jackson plant and set up operations in K.C. or Omaha or Kathmandu. With this information, she could maybe write a novel, but a decent investigative piece, fugedaboudit.

Her trolling on the phone hadn't turned up much, either. She'd talked to scores of people, even her father, although that had been inadvertent and probably shouldn't be counted. He was almost never at home now, being in the middle of a big court case—the rights of immigrants to speak their native tongues in the workplace, the kind of nasty battle that was right up his alley and might end up in another opportunity for him to strut his stuff in front of the Supreme Court—but a few nights earlier, when she'd called, he'd been the one to pick up the phone.

"Pussycat, pussycat, we miss you," he cried. "When you coming back to your poppa?"

"Not just yet, Daddy," she said drily, although she loved the sound of his voice. If only he didn't fill up a room quite so completely. "How are you doing? How's the case coming?"

"Ah, don't mention it." The preamble to many of her father's harangues. "Listen! Can you believe these weasels? They think the First Amendment has a sign on it—English only. You speak Spanish or Vietnamese, the Bill of Rights doesn't apply." And off he went, merrily excoriating his opponents for the immoral bounders they were.

When he was through, he immediately repeated, "We miss you, pussycat. When you gonna have enough clippings to find a job someplace with indoor plumbing? Your mother tells me you've got only one assignment, could that be right? A packing company? Is that true?"

He next put on his cross-examination hat and made her repeat everything she'd already told her mother.

"This is a private company, yes?"

"Yes."

"You got the D&Bs yet?"

"Give me a break, Daddy. Don't you think I know anything?"

"What does the trend look like?"

"Not good, but everybody knows that. The company's been limping along for years."

"So they're getting ready to say *kaddish* and sit shivah, that's what you're supposed to prove?"

"If it's true. Maybe it isn't. The company's totally in denial."

"Look," he told her in the consider-this-an-assignment way he had, "here's what you gotta do. Find the local watering hole where the middle managers go, where they hoist a few on Friday night after a hard week in denial." And so off he went again, giving his standard spook's approach to investigative work.

She resisted. She liked doing research, but the kind of derring-do her father got off on had little appeal to her, even something as simple as wheedling her way into a drunken conversation and playing head games with her marks. Although, who knows, maybe with the Pack that was the only way.

Pursued by these dispiriting thoughts, she set off on foot back toward the *Tribune* building, only a few blocks down the street from the union hall. Locust Street. Locust trees had been planted along it, although they were still quite small, probably replacements for the original trees, maybe—who knows—the third or fourth generation of such signature specimens. In the early afternoon sunlight, their finely divided leaves threw dusty shadows on the pavement.

Her failure to penetrate the packing company's shroud intensified her sense of estrangement from her surroundings. She walked on, past apartment houses occupied by people she didn't know, past cars driven by more strangers, through a landscape whose history she couldn't read; for every one thing known, ten thousand unknown. Probably such was always the case, but she felt the loneliness more keenly in this Midwestern burg.

The situation at the newspaper wasn't much of an improvement. Arriving back there, she took the elevator up to the newsroom on the third floor. At this time of the day, almost everyone was out on assignment. She passed through the hum made by the cooling fans of the computer terminals until she arrived at her desk and her own small hum, where she slipped off her shoulder bag and fetched her notebook, flipping it open to the interview just completed. Then for the next five minutes she did nothing, merely sat idly, her mind adrift.

Next to the notebook sat the three-day-old *Trib* edition containing her story about mysterious groups recently spotted touring JackPack, the one piece she'd written so far, the gift mostly of the contacts she'd made within the JackPack union. So the company had turned out to be not quite a black box, more like one of those stretch limos with tinted glass where, if the light were just right, dim figures might be glimpsed. She knew now, or almost knew, that other companies had been sending teams to look at the plant, what official spokesman Ted Bates insisted were nothing more than consultants.

But the union provided no help in bagging her real quarry—was JackPack on the point of going bankrupt? If Skip Peterson was trying to shop the company, that might mean anything. Maybe he was simply tired of working and wanted to buy a yacht and make an around-the-world cruise. Who knows? People had money, they traveled.

Everybody at the paper had been treating her with scrupulous courtesy. The other newsies were friendly enough, but always the friendliness had an asterisk, and a footnote she couldn't read, exactly as it had been with Neil Houselog, the news editor. Maybe it was nothing. Maybe she was just being paranoid as usual.

She wanted to take someone into her confidence, to make a friend, but who? Not Houselog, with his musical clothes and cop's reserve. And certainly not her nominal boss, Margaret Foss, the assistant local news editor, a woman with whom Rachel shared her gender and apparently nothing else. And what a title, she thought, assistant local news editor, each word failing to undo the damage done by the last.

Along with these two went the rest of the newspaper's hierarchy—the local news editor, the managing editor, the executive editor (a post currently vacant but soon to be filled again, no doubt) and probably a few more that Rachel hadn't run into yet, a regular Soviet-style bureaucracy, the place filled with the bustle of apparatchiks, although it all for some reason seemed to have nothing to do with her. Instead she got summonses to ascend into the clouds for an audience with the godhead himself. Go figure.

Finally, no new insight coming, she shook herself free of these reveries and went back to work, first by adding notes to the bottom of the interview just concluded with the president of the JackPack union, a fellow who had seemed too nice to be a union head and called Homer Budge. What a name! She next tried again to reach Peterson's ex-wife and got her answering machine and didn't bother to leave a message this time.

She hadn't spent all her time sitting on her tush. She'd gone down to the county courthouse and looked for any proceedings that might have been brought against Peterson or other top company officials. She'd also been scouring court records looking for suits against the company by consumers, former employers, contractors, anybody with a beef, but JackPack had the disconcerting habit of reaching settlements out of court. She had managed, however, to cadge the names of a couple of disgruntled ex-employees and the lawyer who had handled a class action suit against the company. After failing to reach Peterson's ex, she tried these three, only managing to speak to the lawyer, who, of course, told her that he was bound by confidentiality because of attorney-client privilege and because the case had been settled before coming to trial and for any number of other lawyerly reasons.

She flipped to the back of her notebook, the to-do list.

She hadn't talked to the mayor of Jackson yet, a fellow named Fritz Goetzinger, who conveniently worked for JackPack, although in some lowly position. As mayor he must be plugged into all kinds of networks, he must know something, although a couple of days before, when she'd gone over to Neil's desk and asked him about Goetzinger, he'd just shaken his head. "Go ahead, talk to him if you want, but he's out of the loop. He likes to fancy himself a man of the people..." at which point the news editor had paused for effect, "...and I'd say he pretty much knows what the people know."

Even so, she would talk to the fellow, Rachel decided. Just in case.

Back at her desk, she made a couple more calls, one to *The Provisioner*, the meat industry's weekly news mag, the other to a contact name she'd been given at Oscar Mayer. Two more dry holes.

Finally, she gave up for the moment and went down to the caf for her Coke and candy bar, which was fast becoming an afternoon ritual, the small reward she allowed herself as recompense for all this frustration. She'd either get her story or get fat, and the way things looked at the moment, fat it would be.

# CHAPTER 10

~

Mark O'Banion wanted to sit down. He stood with Chuck Fellows, the city engineer, at the drafting board in the public works offices. Laid out before them was one of the working drawings, incomplete, for the dog track.

"You can talk about overlap as much as you want," Chuck was saying, "but as soon as you cut the membrane, it loses its integrity."

"How do you fit it around the pile caps then?"

"I'm sure McDermott will come up with some brilliant solution," Chuck said, by which, Mark understood, he meant precisely the opposite. Chuck had little use for the firm doing the foundation design, less for McDermott himself.

Except for the inconvenient possibility that several thousand people might get blown to smithereens, this problem of venting the methane at the track could have been quite interesting.

"I know what I'd do," Fellows said.

"Which is?"

"Redundancy."

"Yes, of course." In certain situations, engineers were happy to over-design. Mark didn't have the energy at the moment to start second-guessing anybody, however. "Best wait for McDermott's brilliant solution. If we don't like it, we'll make him do it again."

"Make sure the SOB signs off on it, too."

"Of course," Mark agreed.

Mark had had enough of standing. He rolled the swivel chair out from behind the nearby desk and sat down.

He looked at his watch. Almost six p.m. Probably they should just pack it in, he thought. The end of another long, hot week, certainly no time to wake up sleeping dogs, of which Mark had a kennel full. Still...

"Let's take a gander at the Turner drawings again."

Saying nothing, Chuck replaced the track plans with a second set. Mark held his hand out and Chuck gave him several of the large sheets, which Mark unrolled on his lap and slowly leafed through, letting each one in turn drop to the floor. Sketches of engineering mechanisms, details of machine parts, assemblies, plans, sections, electrical schematics. They looked exactly like what they were, exercises from a drafting class. Not bad. Mark hardly needed to look. He'd seen them enough already. Chuck, for his part, ignored the few still lying on the drawing board.

"Yet," Mark said, picking up a conversation where they had left it two days earlier, "he might be brought along."

"You're just like my wife," Chuck said, "you think you can wear me down."

"That would be nice." Certainly Mark didn't want to force the issue. "Look at it this way. You acquire merit by doing this."

"Bull. Nobody ever acquired merit by rolling over and spreading his legs."

"Such a mouth."

"I need somebody can pull his weight right away."

"He isn't bad." Mark inspected a diagram of loads on a truss bridge, noted the evidence of corrections, then dropped it on the floor.

"He isn't good either," Chuck said. "Look, Mark, I need someone with experience. I've got a shitload of work."

"No job, no experience. No experience, no job."

Chuck was quiet for a few moments, about the length of time a fighter would spend feinting before launching a blow from another direction.

"There are other ways to get experience than on the job. Did you look at the dates on those drawings?"

Mark's thoughts had gone to images of Sam Turner going from engineering firm to engineering firm in the city, a black man with only entry-level skills. It didn't take a genius to figure out what would have happened in shops like John McDermott's. No indeed.

Reluctantly, he put these thoughts aside and looked at the dates on the drawings, three years old. Of course, he'd looked at the dates before. He knew what the dates were.

"He should've been busting his hump on his own," Chuck said, "trying to get better."

"Perhaps. But people get discouraged. And as for a black man, in a town like this…"

"Then maybe he should go somewhere else."

Mark jerked his head up. "Oh, is that right?"

"I don't care where he goes. He can stay here, he can go to the moon, for all I care." Impatiently he added, "Look, Mark, if Turner could cut it, I'd hire him in a heartbeat. Okay?" Challenged, Chuck became even more aggressive than usual. "Anyway, you just wanna look like some kind of saint to that damn committee of yours." He meant the Integration Task Force. "Tell me you don't have a conflict of interest here."

"Yes, I suppose I do, and I suppose it's important to keep that in mind." For Chuck, undoubtedly, such a fact filled his radar screen, but for Mark, the situation was rather more nuanced, so he said, "However, I like to think of it as an opportunity. God, in His infinite wisdom, has seen fit to give us this small test of our character." Certainly, it was quite a coincidence that one of the handful of black city employees should just then have decided to bid on a job for which he was only marginally qualified, just when Mark and the other members of the ad hoc committee were struggling with the issue of racism in the city. Or, then again, maybe it wasn't a coincidence, maybe someone had put Sam Turner up to it. Not that that made any difference. Life was not meant to be easy.

"Test of character, my ass," Chuck was saying. "Look, Mark, my people are swamped. We got projects up the ying-yang. I need a real draftsman, somebody who can turn out finished work from day one, I don't need this." And he gestured with scorn toward the drawings scattered on the floor.

Mark tried another tack.

"Have you ever noticed," he said, "how we like to tackle problems that are tough but not too tough? We don't seem to have the stomach for the truly difficult. Ever noticed?"

Chuck grinned. "You old fox, don't think you can con me with that shit."

"It's true, you know." Mark discarded the next drawing without looking at it. "We all manage to wriggle out of good stiff challenges, the ones with long odds." He wasn't thinking of Fellows now. He was thinking of himself.

He parceled his attention out across the complex landscape of his life and absolutely depended on a certain level of competence and motivation in others. Perhaps Sam Turner would work out just fine. But what if he didn't, and Mark was off doing something else, and Chuck, well, Chuck was his usual benevolent self, what then? The prospect saddened Mark. Like a good physician, his first commandment was to do as little harm as possible.

Could he, he asked himself, take the young man under his own wing? He remembered Len Sawyer's unusual interest in his cub reporter. No, not just unusual, but improper, that was the way Mark had seen it at the time. And so how would it look if he dedicated himself to Turner's survival as a draftsman? Well, he knew how. The question was—did he have the guts to do it anyway?

Mark couldn't share all this with Chuck Fellows, as much as he might have liked to. Such sharing was beyond the pale of their friendship.

So all he could finally say was "Don't be surprised if I promote the fellow after all."

Mark held up an isometric drawing that he rather liked. Fellows showed no interest. Mark paused and then let the sheet slip from his fingers.

The two of them said nothing for a time.

Fellows would not back down, of course. As for Mark, well, he could wait only so long. As a matter of professional courtesy, he wanted to thrash the thing out with Chuck before going to the city manager, but it had already been a week since Turner had showed up on their doorstep.

He looked at his watch again, a reflex gesture, then struggled up out of his chair.

"How's Diane?" he asked, as they walked down to their cars through the deserted building.

"She's got me taking the kids camping."

"I thought you liked camping." They descended the City Hall steps into the lingering late-afternoon heat. "In fact, I thought you loved it."

"Not buckskinning, I don't. There's a damn rendezvous coming up this weekend."

"Buckskinning?" Yes, Mark understood that that was a different breed of cat for some reason. "Still, isn't that getting back to nature, where men are men and all that?" They had never talked about

Chuck's experience in Vietnam, but Mark had always assumed his love of the outdoors had something to do with that. This buckskinning business was new.

"Like hell," Chuck said now. "I go into the woods to get away from people. Buckskinners go there to get together." Then he added glumly, "Diane's the one who insists on turning everything into a social event."

"I couldn't approve more."

"Yeah, right."

"I realize that your idea of a social occasion is a scum in a rugby match."

Chuck smiled despite himself. "You mean scrum."

"Whatever."

Chuck shook his head. "Shit..." He stared down at the fender of Mark's Caddy, and for a long moment neither of them spoke, and his tone had changed when he said, "I don't know, Mark...I'll tell you, if I stick around here much longer, you won't be able to tell me and Diane apart."

Mark laughed. "I frankly doubt that."

"But it's true." Chuck looked up. "I mean it, Mark. It's got so that sometimes I have to make an effort to be unpleasant." He said this quite seriously.

Mark didn't believe it for a moment, but what a delightful idea. "You could do worse than ending up like Diane."

Chuck didn't respond to this. He was gazing off into the distance. "You talk about rugby. Know how long since I played? Two years. My damn knees are gone. I'm fat. If I could get up an old boys' side, then maybe...who knows? But Jackson ain't exactly the rugby capital of the world." He looked at Mark. "I know this doesn't mean anything to you, but it does to me." He paused, and Mark was stunned by the genuine pain that he saw in his friend's eyes. "Everything's got too damn easy, Mark. Too friggin' comfortable. Something's gone out of me. I don't know...I'm different, and I'll tell you what, I don't fucking like it."

Mark was touched and a little embarrassed by the frankness. So he said, "Well, perhaps you can have my job one day. That'll provide some discomfort, if that's what you want."

Chuck frowned, his look changing. Again he didn't respond immediately, appearing to seriously consider the matter. When he did speak, it was clear he had just been choosing the worst among his various dislikes. "I couldn't abide those assholes on the council."

Mark recoiled slightly. Certain statements still had the power to shock, like the crack earlier about spreading his legs. They reminded Mark of all the irreconcilables of the world.

"Pretty strong talk."

"Well, that's the way it is."

"Not quite," Mark said.

They continued to chat, but the bond of sympathy had been broken for the moment, and so finally they went their separate ways.

# Chapter 11

~

The farm, on the western side of the city, stood at the top of a long winding road that rose gradually from the river's floodplain to the brow of the bluffs and then wound through country that reminded Rachel Brandeis a little of Westchester County.

From the road, she drove up a narrow, weedy driveway. When she had asked Neil Houselog to describe the place, all he would volunteer was, "When you get there, you'll think you're in the wrong place." Patchy field grass skirted the long-unpainted house and petered out in anemic-looking rows of corn. One end of the barn had collapsed. The other outbuildings appeared deserted. Her editor had been right.

As she rounded the back corner of the house and parked in a place that seemed as good as any other, she spotted a man sitting on a bench next to the back door and smoking a pipe. She had not met him yet, but she'd seen pictures in the newspaper's files—the mayor of Jackson, Fritz Goetzinger. Even at a distance, the strong asymmetry of his features was evident.

Getting out of the car, she heard the squealing and snorting of pigs somewhere behind her. She could smell them, too, an odor riper than in the packinghouse.

As she approached, her eye was drawn to the boots he wore, of thin-looking black rubber, like cheap rain boots. Next to him on the ground stood a second pair, identical to his, almost, she thought—remembering suddenly her own childhood—as if he had an invisible friend.

"Got something to do," he said without preamble. "We can talk as we go along. Here." He pointed at the extra pair of boots.

She thanked him for the thoughtfulness.

"No need. Don't want you tracking foreign organisms into the confinement buildings is all."

He banged the bowl of the pipe against a bench slat, knocking out a half-burned plug. "Wife don't like me to smoke in the house."

In order to stand, he leaned forward and pushed down hard on his thighs, rising slowly, and Rachel could see the exhaustion she'd missed at first.

As they walked, he took out a tobacco pouch. He had strong hands and he kept them in view as he fiddled with his pipe.

"Ever been on a hog farm before?" he asked.

"First time."

He nodded to indicate that he'd figured as much.

He wasn't a tall man. He wore jeans and a blue work shirt faded almost to white. He carried himself erect, as small men often do. When he gave her a quick look now and again as they walked, the deep jagged furrow that descended from the middle of his forehead to the bridge of his nose became visible. His black hair, clipped short, had begun to go white, but in no particular pattern, a half-moon over one ear, a small patch above the opposite eye. One side of his mouth scowled while the other merely disapproved.

"Them's the farrowing houses," he said, waving toward a warren of low buildings at the center of which what had once been a mobile home was now studded with vents and dirt. "That's my wife's domain. In that part of the operation, what she says, goes."

Rachel thought about that, and it irritated her enough to say, "Women, of course, take care of the young."

"That's right."

"However, when men start insisting on the fact, Mr. Goetzinger, I begin to get suspicious."

"Might as well call me Fritz. Everybody else does." He stuck the pipe, unlit, into his shirt pocket.

"I'm Rachel."

After a few paces, Fritz said, "I'm a breeder. I sell to commercial farmers. Some of the men who come here won't buy a boar from my wife. I'm not of that view. I say if there's work to be done, it don't make any difference who does it.

"This here is where I mix and store feed, Rachel." They were passing a tall circular bin. "I like to feed my animals corn I grow myself. The commercial stuff is full of fines and dirt and who knows what all."

It was difficult to envision this man as the mayor of a city of sixty thousand. But, of course, pols of his type were common enough at certain levels of American political life, blue collar stiffs who make a religion out of the practical and take special pride in their limitations. "This has been a real bad summer," Goetzinger was saying. "Real bad. Most of the corn in my upland fields has burned up in the drought."

They were approaching a pair of barns with a fenced-in area between them. As they neared, she could make out the pigs, some all white and others mostly black, with white feet. They weren't particularly large, a couple of feet at the shoulder, she guessed, about the same size as the pigs she had seen being butchered.

"These here are the gestation and breeding buildings," Goetzinger explained. He opened the gate so they could slip through and in amongst the pigs, some of which shied away while others hustled over to inspect Rachel, sniffing at her with their dirty and sensitive noses. Their eyes were quite small but very much like human eyes, with delicate eyelashes. Fritz found the animal he was looking for, one of the black ones, and nudged it around with the side of his leg so that Rachel could see the raised area beneath its tail.

"This here's a gilt, a young female. When the vulva's pink and puffy like this"—he poked it with a finger—"she's ready to accept a boar."

Feh! Rachel thought. She'd hardly met the man, and already he was showing her vulvas?

He herded the pig toward one of the barns, where, he informed Rachel, the boars were isolated in pens. He kept up a steady stream of chatter. "Had an old sow bite the vulva right off a gilt the other day. The gilt was blocking the sow's way to the feed trough. Nice little pig, that gilt, a good prospect. Liked her blood lines. Course, until she drops a litter you can't really tell. But I liked her as well as this gal." He tapped the young female he was herding on the rump, and she skittered into a small enclosure.

Rachel's discomfort grew by the moment. Maybe this was just a farmer thing, she tried to tell herself.

Inside the barn hung a strong libidinous odor of animal heat and feed grain and excrement.

"Look at him," Goetzinger said, pointing at one of the boars, another black pig, about the same size as the female. "Look at how long he is." He reached over and ran his hand over the back of the animal. "Good underline, too."

"What kind of a pig is it?"

"Berkshire. An old breed, making a comeback. It's hardy, can withstand the pressures of confinement operations, which is what a lot of the commercial farmers are running now."

The male pig had poked his snout between the slats of his pen, and his broad, pink nose twitched as he sniffed at Rachel. She asked, "So you don't sell animals to slaughterhouses?" Her voice was not as steady as she would have liked.

"I sell some animals to the Pack. As I like to say, 'If the help don't get along with me, they get shipped.' I raise Berks and Chester Whites. Them gals you saw outside are Chesters. Basically, what I do is sell seed stock to commercial operators who crossbreed 'em. Hybrid vigor and feed efficiency and all that."

He swung the gate open, and the male started to wander away. "Still too young to know quite what's up yet. I tried to put a sow under him a bit ago, but she was just too big."

Rachel was busy trying to decide whether she was ready for this.

Goetzinger steered the young boar into the pen with the gilt, and the boar immediately climbed up on her back, slipped off, climbed back up again. The gilt, skittish, sidled up against the boards of the stall. "Amateurs," Goetzinger said with mock disgust. Rachel could see the boar's long thin penis bobbing as he poked it ineffectually against the gilt's rump. Her own breathing had become more shallow and rapid.

"Your tool's not doing you any damn good waving in the breeze," Goetzinger said to the boar. He reached down, grabbed the animal's penis and guided it into the vagina of the young female. While he did this, he glanced up, as if to make sure that Rachel was still watching. She started to look away, but then stopped herself. Goetzinger's eyes were small and intelligent, like those of his animals. She held his gaze. She felt exposed and angry.

A few pokes and it was over. A typical male.

The mating complete, Fritz checked the small gelatinous mass that had formed at the entrance to the vagina. "Jelly plug," he said, satisfied.

As they walked back toward the house, Rachel's sense of violation and outrage increased. She said nothing.

Goetzinger had gone on talking about the principles of hog breeding, casually, as if nothing had happened. He'd taken out his pipe and lit it, the big stove match flaring in the twilight.

Still unable to find the words to express her true feelings, Rachel blurted out the first thing that came to mind.

"So, tell me, Mayor Goetzinger, if the Jackson Packing Company closes, where will you send the help you can't get along with?"

He stopped and turned, obviously aware that something had happened. Too dark to make out his expression clearly, but she imagined she saw a trace of a smile.

She said, "I suppose you think that that was pretty funny back there."

"What are you talking about?"

"You know what."

He took the pipe out of his mouth and studied her.

Finally, what he said was, "If you read anything into what just happened, you read too much."

They had stopped in the middle of a large dirt patch, at the intersection of the service roads for the various outbuildings. He didn't rush as he re-lit his pipe. "I farm, I work full-time at the Pack, I'm mayor. Something needs to be done, like breeding my animals, I do it. Thought you might be interested. Guess I was wrong." She listened impatiently to the sucking sound of the flame being dragged down into the plug of tobacco. Then, all at once, he took the pipe out of his mouth, turned his head away, and coughed, a violent, rasping cough. He stepped away a couple of paces and continued to cough, bringing a mass of phlegm up which he hawked into the dirt.

"Hog dust," he said as he checked to make sure his pipe was still lit and then calmly took a drag on it.

"Acts have meaning, Mr. Goetzinger." Rachel still felt violated, whatever the hell he thought he was doing. "You can't define them any damn way you please."

Goetzinger took the pipe out of his mouth and spit off to the side as he considered this.

"I suppose. But you're in Iowa now. This ain't New York anymore."

"It isn't the moon, either."

"Nope, that's right."

This last exchange seemed to bring them to a point of stalemate, and they fell silent briefly.

The long dusk of the early fall evening gathered momentum, darkness rising up out of the ground. The heat of the day remained, muted, stale. Inside the farmhouse, a single light had been turned on.

Rachel's anger having begun to trail off into the kind of irritation with which she felt more at home, she remembered that she was a journalist and why she had come.

"So," she said, gathering herself together, "what will you do if JackPack closes?"

"Where will I ship my animals? Modern Meat, most likely, when they start their operation, down there in Maquoketa. You know about that, I suppose."

"Yes, I do. And the company, is it going to close?"

"Don't know."

"Everybody else I've talked to seems to have an opinion, one way or the other."

"That right? Well, a lot of people around here got their little games they like to play. Maybe they'll tell you what they think, maybe they won't. You won't get that from me. I dispense with all the political shenanigans. I'll always tell you exactly what's on my mind. That's why people vote for me."

"Frankly," she said, unimpressed with this snake oil, the standard-issue politician's claim not to be a politician, "my impression is that the situation at the Pack is very bleak."

"That the way you're gonna write it up? Pack's done for. That what Sawyer told you to do?"

This schmuck really could be irritating. "He didn't tell me anything, except to find out what's going on. And it wouldn't make any difference if he had."

Goetzinger nodded. "Hope so. Be interested in what you uncover." He put his dead pipe back into his mouth and scratched under his eyebrow. "Tell you this much, the Pack's been mismanaged for decades. Wouldn't be surprised if it does go down."

"Mismanaged?"

"Too much production concentrated in one place, to begin with. Always a day late and a dollar short when it came to modernizing. Back in the sixties, when land was cheap, they could've built themselves a one-story operation out west of town. Didn't happen...How much time you got? I can go on all night about the sins of the Petersons."

"I've got time."

He pointed the stem of the pipe at her. "Trust. That's the big thing. The Petersons are not to be trusted. They don't operate out in the open." He continued, finding the subject of the Petersons' duplicity convivial, and Rachel added more items to her list of indictable offenses that Skip Peterson had committed. Which, per usual, told her nothing about what he might be planning to do.

~

As she drove away from the farm, Rachel wondered whether the pig mating business had really been nothing more than Goetz-inger claimed, or had he been coming on to her in some weird farmer way. It had always been her fate to have older men more interested in her than men her own age. But perhaps he had told the truth, perhaps he wasn't a lech, just crude and insensitive. Or, who knows, maybe—despite all evidence to the contrary—he had a sense of humor and it had simply been his metaphor for life in Jackson. Supervised fucking.

Anyway, another rebbe heard from. She decided that prob-ably Neil Houselog had been right. Whatever the wit and wisdom of the mayor, he showed all the signs of being someone out of the loop, a man from whom the occasional quote must be extracted to fill out a story but who might otherwise be safely ignored. Based on her first evening with him, she certainly hoped so.

# CHAPTER 12

~

The buckskinners' encampment ranged along the edge of a cornfield. A short distance away, the primitive camp had been set up, a thin brake of cockleburs, velvet leaf, and other weedy species that besiege corn crops now serving as a symbolic barrier separating the purists with their tepees from the pilgrims, with their hodgepodge of camping arrangements. Chuck Fellows and his son Todd, age seven, were putting up the old Army surplus tent Chuck still insisted on using.

Todd, at the moment, was whining because they didn't have a tepee themselves, and in an attempt to take his mind of this imagined injustice, Chuck explained the engineering principles incorporated into the idea of the tent. He showed Todd the fabric in tension, the poles in compression, the whole system in equilibrium. "Here," he said, pulling on one of the guy ropes, "feel the pull." Todd held the rope, the tent fabric sagging, as Chuck drove in one of the pegs and then took the rope back from Todd and snugged it up, feeling the pull inside himself, the sympathetic tug shared by his muscles and the rope.

As he worked, he began to get hot and so stripped down to his T-shirt. He observed how Todd's eyes were immediately drawn to his right elbow, the remnant of his last wound in Vietnam. Chuck had been lucky. The field medic knew what he was doing. But still the reconstruction looked odd, a large ball of flesh missing, the bones articulated strangely, giving his forearm the appearance of a mechanism, a lever. Todd would look at this misshapen appendage with awe. But though his son had recently begun to show a lot of interest in warfare, Chuck hadn't talked to him very much about his wartime experiences. That would come later. If ever.

Todd wore the buckskins that Diane had sewn for him. Chuck and Todd were both dressed as frontiersmen, Diane and Grace as

Indians. A short distance away, Diane had gotten out her sour-dough starter and was preparing to bake bread, and next to her, three-year-old Grace performed some sort of pantomime, perhaps her version of what her mother was doing. Chuck observed, with a secret edge of envy, how easily Diane's homemaking skills had been adapted to this ersatz frontier life.

In her deerskin dress and leggings, hair neatly braided, quilled pouch, Diane was the very image of the woodland Indian, a converted Indian, for dangling down the front of her costume was a necklace with a bead cross. She had sewn more costumes as well and made other items to be bartered. When the skinners laid out their trade blankets she'd take her fresh bread and buckskin clothing and swap for whatever else she imagined they might need to become properly accoutred buckskinners. Chuck, for his part, had brought a copy of a Fenimore Cooper novel to read later; that was his contribution to the authenticity of the occasion.

Despite Diane's enormous effort, Chuck guessed that she wasn't much interested in the frontier life and did it solely for the sake of the kids. Although, with Diane, you could never be entirely sure. She had always been a good sport, and took pleasure in the pleasures of others, and so her own pleasures had remained something of a mystery to him.

At any rate, whatever she liked or didn't, she had apparently convinced herself that Chuck would eventually grow to accept this ludicrous version of early Americana.

With an irritated tug, he cinched down the last of the guy ropes, and stood up to judge his work. The olive drab tent with its drop sides could easily sleep four. He walked slowly around it, making small adjustments until he was satisfied.

"Can we go shoot now?" Todd asked impatiently.

"First we stow the gear."

After that had been done, Todd renewed his question.

"Ask your mother if she has anything else for us to do."

"Aw."

Diane looked up at the two men in her family, standing with their rifles.

"Don't forget to tell everybody about our potluck." She squinted into the midmorning sunlight. Her skin remained perfectly smooth, but with a slightly puffy look because she had never taken off the extra weight she put on during her pregnancies.

"Okay," Chuck said glumly. He liked the physical labor of putting up the tent but had no desire to go over to the primitive camp and invite a bunch of people he didn't know and didn't want to know to share a meal with them. But Diane, who enjoyed experimenting, had decided to cook a turkey in an authentic frontier manner, and she needed some people to help eat it. A raised mound of earth near the campfire provided the only evidence of this experiment.

"Okay, sport," Chuck said to his son, "now we go shoot."

Todd's enthusiasm concentrated in his grasping and fumbling hands. "Let's go learn to use this thing the right way," Chuck admonished him as they set out, but the boy seemed almost blind and deaf in his rush to gather in and use the .40 caliber flinter Chuck had given him.

Among the tepees, Todd stared wide-eyed at all the artifacts the buckskinners had gathered around themselves. Chuck liked the smell of the leather, but all this stuff seemed too new to him, too carefully crafted, the tepees with their wing-shaped smoke flaps too geometrically precise. He moved through the setting, obsessively noticing the details, each one a new irritation.

As he went from tepee to tepee, passing along Diane's invitation, a figure approached from the other direction, sauntering along and passing the time of day with fellow enthusiasts. His outfit dripped with fringes. When he walked, the fringes whipped around him as if he was going up in flames. He wore a bear-claw necklace, a beaded sheath for his bowie knife, a powder horn slung around his shoulder, some kind of French voyageur cap, Chuck guessed, with metal thingamabobs pinned to it, and a shit-eating little grin on his kisser that said, "Ain't I the coolest dude you ever saw?"

"Howdy." He looked at Todd. "Mighty fine set of duds you got on, young fellow."

"My mother made them."

"Did she now?"

"Yes." Todd, encouraged by this attention, said, "She can make anything."

"Is that so? You don't suppose she's got some possibles pouches to trade, do you?"

Todd looked blankly at the buckskinner, then at his father. Chuck didn't know what the hell a possibles pouch might be, either, and he wasn't about to ask.

He waved back toward the pilgrim's camp. "Go ask her."

The buckskinner nodded, bestowing on Chuck the grin of good-fellowship and said, "Reckon I will."

He propped the butt of his fowling piece on the ground and settled in for a little palaver.

Chuck merely passed along Diane's invitation and kept on going, leaving the asshole to palaver with himself.

Finally, the tepees behind them, they marched out toward the shooting range, Chuck carrying his .54 caliber Hawken and Todd his flintlock. The barrel of the flinter dipped toward the ground like a dowsing rod, and Chuck had to keep reminding Todd to carry the gun correctly. "You don't want to act like a damn pork eater, do you?" Pork eater, Chuck had learned from Diane, was the buckskinner's phrase for a boor. It had the desired effect on Todd, but Chuck regretted the words, for they tasted bitter in his mouth, other people's words.

The targets had been set up in an old quarry beyond the end of the cornfield. Some of the skinners were already practicing.

The weapon was too heavy for Todd to fire from a standing position. Even Chuck, who believed in the virtues of a finely honed perversity and was already beginning to instruct his son in some of the basics of in-your-face diplomacy, had his doubts about teaching a seven-year-old to shoot.

"If we're going to do this, we're going to do it right," he repeated, but he had the impression Todd hardly heard him. His son's stubby fingers, in miniature uncannily like his father's, were white with the effort to grasp the rifle.

"Now watch me carefully," Chuck said as he took the flinter and loaded it. "You're going to do this next time yourself."

The hill from which limestone had been quarried stood hollowed into an elaborate tower of ragged stone battlements topped by a fringe of brush and scrub evergreens. Chuck got Todd to lie down and fitted the weapon into his shoulder.

At the foot of the battlements, the targets, a row of bottles and cans, had been ranged along a low stone shelf, but they were too far away for Todd to have a realistic chance of hitting them. His first shot ricocheted off the ground, the recoil making him cry out. Another little boy might have decided then and there that he didn't like shooting very much, but Todd had a stubborn streak that came out at times like this. Chuck helped him reload and try again. This time, with a stone propped under the barrel, he managed to miss the ground, his shot hitting several feet above the targets. Chuck fired off a shot himself, missing high right. On his second try he aimed low left and nailed one of the cans. Todd cheered. Then it was Todd's turn again, and he missed again, a little closer this time.

Chuck encouraged him, but Todd's attention span couldn't be counted on, and soon he became bored and barely took aim before each shot. He began to look around and pick up stones that had interesting shapes and inspect them and stuff those that passed muster into his pockets. Collecting had recently become a passion, and his room at home was filled with an odd assortment of found objects for which Chuck could summon no enthusiasm.

Soon Todd abandoned his rifle altogether, and Chuck felt as if he had been deserted as well. He liked the way that his own attention sometimes would gather about his son. But at other times, like now, the reverse process seemed to occur, an unpacking and scattering of his sense of self.

He stared after Todd, who had wandered away in his search for interesting collectibles, swatting at weeds with his ramrod. Chuck's thoughts were intense and wordless, and after a minute he took up his weapon and began firing again, but without enthusiasm. More of the buckskinners had arrived by now and the firing had become more intense.

Chuck's dissatisfaction became sharper. The image of the buckskinner they had encountered earlier stuck in his craw. He hated this thing Diane had dragged him into even more than he thought he would. Such trivial playacting he experienced as a violation, a violation of the very woodlands themselves, and his anger sat in the center of his chest.

He took his time reloading, keeping an eye on Todd, who had drifted beyond the firing line.

"Keep away from the firing range!" Chuck yelled at him. Todd seemed to ignore him. "You hear me!" Todd nodded, barely, looking intently down at an object Chuck couldn't make out at that distance. Not satisfied with the response, Chuck yelled, "Remember frontier justice!" which was what he called a spanking.

But Todd seemed impervious to his father's threats. He reached down and picked up the object he had been studying and brought it over and held it up for his father's approval.

"Neat, huh?"

The object was S-shaped, and Chuck had to hold it up close to make out the flattened and dried corpse of a small snake. More interesting, he thought, than most of Todd's finds. Chuck turned it over. Light side, dark side.

"A piece of advice," he said. "If you want to take this home, don't show it to your mother."

# CHAPTER 13

~

On his way out of City Hall on Monday morning, Mark O'Banion ran into Chuck Fellows coming in; the city engineer decked out in work boots and a slicker, despite that it hadn't rained in many weeks.

"I suppose you're not wearing that stuff just to be on the safe side."

"Seth found another one of the old stone sewers."

"Where?"

Mark listened to Chuck's tale with only passing interest. The assistant city engineer's enthusiasm for holes in the ground knew no bounds. One day Seth would probably make a decent enough PE, but now he seemed more like an amateur spelunker who had lucked into a dream job.

"Did you tell him not to explore it?"

"I told him if he went near it again, I'd cut off his balls."

"Good."

For once, Chuck's choice of language seemed just about right. Of course, it wouldn't keep Seth out of the next old sewer or lead mine or whatever that he happened to stumble across. The place was honeycombed with them. "It would be nice," Mark noted, "if he paid more attention to his job." Maintaining the existing storm and sanitary systems should have kept him busy enough.

"Seth is a ditz. But you pay chickenshit wages, that's what you get."

"Sigh."

They had stopped near Mark's Caddy, almost exactly where they had last spoken, on Friday afternoon.

"How was the buckskinning?" Mark asked.

"You really want to know?"

"No, I suppose not."

Chuck made a motion as if to leave and then hesitated, as a man will who has something to say but is reluctant. Mark noted the wavering, so very un-Chuck-like, but having something more to say himself, he didn't read into it the meaning he might have.

"We were just talking about what happens if JackPack goes down," Mark said.

"We?"

"Paul Cutler, Harvey Butts, a few others."

Whenever he mentioned the city manager and city attorney, Mark could count on Chuck's little dismissive gesture.

"The subject of retraining came up," Mark told him.

"Of the Pack workers?"

"Yes."

"That's a job for the feds and state, isn't it?"

"Yes...in such circumstances, there's always a routine, of course. But that doesn't mean we couldn't do a little something ourselves."

Chuck thought about this.

"Pretty old workforce."

"Yup."

"So what's the idea, make 'em all welders and computer programmers?"

Mark considered this skeptical question and said, "The idea is to do something."

Chuck, who was not a man given to symbolic gestures, simply shrugged.

"Anyway, it set me to thinking," Mark told him, "about the drafting position."

"About giving it to one of them?"

"No. About an age when people move from job to job and we can't expect all our new hires to be mint perfect." He paused before finishing the thought. "So I'm thinking maybe I will give this fellow Sam Turner a try after all, see what he can do."

Mark said this, mentally bracing himself for Chuck's counterpunch, but the city engineer only shrugged as he had earlier. He didn't offer even so much as a snide comment.

Surprised at this show of indifference, Mark said, "You seemed pretty damn adamant last week."

"I just did it for drill."

"That right?"

"Sure. Shits and giggles. I saw the look in your eye. I know when you get into your do-gooder mode, I can pretty much forget it."

Something rang false in this claim, but Mark was willing to take it at face value, if it got him where he wanted to go.

"Then I can assume you'll do your bit for the cause?"

Yet, even as he said this, even as he entertained hopeful thoughts, Mark understood that this wasn't a simple matter of making a decision and then getting Chuck to sign off on it, as if the world wasn't chock-full of consequences. Certainly he didn't confuse his liking for the man with a conviction that all would, therefore, somehow turn out for the best.

"I plan to be involved myself," he said, the carrot that went with his stick, "but I'm not going to be the only one carrying the load here."

He watched as Chuck made some sort of calculation, his eyes calm, no trace of the keenness and scorn so often present.

"Yeah," was what he finally said, hardly more than an acknowledgment that he understood. Not much, but for the moment it would have to do.

"That's all I had to say," Mark finished and turned toward his car, but Chuck stopped him.

On turning back, he could see that Chuck's look hadn't changed and understood at once that whatever he meant to say now had been part of the earlier calculation.

"Yes?"

"To tell you the truth, Mark, there's a reason I don't give a shit about how you deal with Turner." Chuck's voice had softened in a way that Mark didn't like one bit.

"Which is?"

"I'm starting to look for another job."

"Don't tell me that."

"It's true."

"Because of Turner?"

"No, it's got nothing to do with that." Suddenly, Chuck became animated. "Look, I've been here nearly six years. A friggin' lifetime. If it wasn't for you, I'd've left a long time ago. But now…I mean, shit, Diane's starting to grow roots. I figure I've got one more move in me before the kids get old enough to begin taking her side, and then I'll have them all on my case."

Mark shook his head. "You've picked a wonderful time."

"Don't give me that. Whenever I left, you'd say the same thing. The way you live, you're always up one shit creek or another."

"I suppose."

"I'm sorry, I really am, but I gotta get outta here before I turn into vegetable matter. I mean it. I'm not like you. Hell, you're good at all this crap."

Mark continued to shake his head. What a miserable day. He looked at his watch. Not even nine o'clock yet. "I wish you'd reconsider. Have you actually applied somewhere?"

"There's an opening in Yellowknife."

"Yellowknife?"

"Canada. Northwest Territories. At the end of the Mackenzie Highway."

Mark whistled. "The end of the what?" He smiled in spite of his pain. Leave it to Fellows. "I have no idea where that is, but knowing you, it's gotta be the edge of civilization as we know it."

"I heard about the job a couple weeks ago. It was just this weekend that I decided to apply."

"The buckskinners?"

"That was part of it."

"And what does Diane say?"

"We're discussing the matter."

"I'll bet."

With anybody else, such a proposal would have been hardly more than a negotiating position. But Mark knew Chuck well enough to realize he was in dead earnest.

Mark sagged back against the Caddy, frowning and looking at nothing in particular, while Chuck said, in as kindly a manner as he ever used, "I just wanted to let you know. You've been a good CO. You've kept all the assholes off my back. But every year now, it's just the same damn things over and over and over. There's nothing else for me here."

"I wish you'd stay."

"Yeah."

They stood without talking, and Mark looked up, and the two of them gazed at each other speculatively, as friends might when a decisive move had just been made in the middle of a chess match. Mark hated the idea of losing Chuck. He knew that the only reason the city had been able to get an engineer of his caliber in the first place was because of the reputed defects in his personality. Mark tried to imagine what Yellowknife might be like, a place of grizzly bears and primordial pine forests, or polar bears and permafrost. Probably, it occurred to him, if Chuck was ever really to fit in somewhere, it'd be such a place, the back of beyond.

Clearly, Mark decided, his only hope lay with Diane. In no way could she be enthusiastic about such a move. He said a silent prayer on her behalf. To Fellows himself all he could think of adding was "I wish you luck. I really do. But I hope to hell you don't get the job."

# CHAPTER 14

~

As she walked across the campus of the University of Jackson, Tuesday morning, just over three weeks in the city, Rachel Brandeis noticed several students wearing yarmulkes entering a Hillel chapter house—the first evidence of Jewish life she'd encountered in the city—and she remembered with a slight start that the next day would be Yom Kippur. The previous week a Rosh Hashanah card had come from her parents, who went to temple only on High Holy Days and whose religious practice was mostly a kind of mourning. Since then, the days had been struggling past as she tilted at the meatpacking story, and now she remembered Yom Kippur, the Day of Atonement. Rachel wasn't observant but sometimes she would catch herself, even as once more she violated sacred writ by working on the holiest day of the year, thinking of the final service, just before God is supposed to close the book for the next year, having written her future in indelible ink. Her future. Feh!

Her father had called a few days after the card arrived. He'd undertaken to check up on the Jackson Packing Company on his own, not that Rachel had asked him to, certainly not that she wanted him to, but Mo Brandeis never waited to be asked.

"The place is history, pussycat. They used to do a lot of kosher slaughtering there, did you know that?" He asked the question as if he suspected she probably didn't. He was always the instant expert.

"I know it, Daddy."

"It's really quite interesting. They'd import some *shohet* from Cincinnati, put the guy up in a local hotel, and he'd spend x-number of days or weeks or whatever doing the ritual slaughtering."

Rachel knew about the *shohet*, although not that he'd come from Cincinnati. She said, "He used to do it for the Muslims, too,

*96*

did you know that?" When her father paused just an instant, she thought, Aha, gotcha!

Undeterred, he plunged on, "Makes sense, makes sense, but it's neither here nor there now. Ritual slaughter or not, your company doesn't have a prayer."

"Very funny."

"I mean it. You might as well write an obit and move on to something else."

When she'd asked where this information had come from, he got very cagey. Mo Brandeis didn't reveal his sources, not to anyone, not even his own daughter. Probably he talked to a guy who talked to a guy.

"You see, that's the problem, Daddy, I'm surrounded by prognosticators, but none of them can give me any hard evidence. It's all circumstantial."

"Ah, but, pussycat," her father said, "circumstantial evidence is so wonderful. You can do so much with it." And it was true, he was some attorney, he could make a ball gown out of a *shmatte*, evidence-wise. But that wasn't for Rachel. She wanted to find the gown still in one piece.

Yet her own pile of circumstantial evidence had certainly mounted up. And probably her father had it right, probably the Pack didn't have a prayer. She'd continued going down her lists, talking to the multitudes—rank and file people within the company, farmers, operators of hog buying stations, meatpackers, industry analysts, traders in pork futures, labor organizers, other journalists, more meatpackers, stockyard managers, consultants of various stripes, people of uncertain affiliations, friends of people of uncertain affiliations, and so on and so forth, hundreds of calls through a fine gradation of diminishing returns. And now this, a meeting with the dean of the business school at the University of Jackson, a man who as far as Rachel was concerned was only one step up from interviewing people picked at random from the phone book.

Behind the Hillel building, she found what she was looking for, the business school, housed in a Victorian mansion set somewhat apart from the other, rather nondescript academic buildings. The dean occupied a corner office, where the ancient chandelier that must at one time have hung from the high ceiling framed by the elaborate molding had been replaced by a powerful but ugly modern fixture. Like an overturned ice-cube tray, it eradicated any trace of a shadow, casting a pitiless glow on stacks of spiral-bound volumes, the sorts of documents that committees prepared and no one reads.

The dean, Dr. Douglas Sample by name, invited Rachel to a small, formal sitting area in one corner, where plush, claw-footed chairs and a dark, polished coffee table held out against the encroaching modernity.

"I've been waiting for you to come see me," Sample told her as soon as they were settled.

"Oh?" Rachel answered, her interest piqued.

"Yes," he said and then, for the moment, fell quiet. He might have been fifty. His mouth a little disapproving, his eyes melancholy. In the manner of some balding men, he had combed his hair straight across the top of his head, the part low on the left side, suggesting that he was right-handed.

"We're a very good school," he said when he spoke again. "Have you heard of us?"

"Not before I came to Jackson," Rachel admitted. "I take it you're familiar with the story I'm working on?"

He nodded. "I heard that Len Sawyer had hired someone. I was told the Pack was your only story. Is that right?"

"I've done a couple of other things, but mostly the Pack, that's right."

"I see." Rachel noted the wry smile and shake of the head that went with this comment.

"You're surprised?" she asked.

"Not at all. Old Len and the Peterson family go back a long way."

"And there's some hostility."

"As you must know. Anyway, you didn't come here to talk about that, you came to ask me if the Jackson Packing Company is going out of business."

"And you were expecting me to come. Perhaps you can help then."

"Well, I don't know about that." He looked at her more intently, although the sense of melancholy remained. "But certainly anyone doing what you're doing should have checked in with us. I'm rather surprised you didn't come sooner."

"You've been on my list," she assured him. Apparently she had committed some sort of venial sin by not rushing up here first thing to sit at his feet. "My research to this point has focused directly on the meatpacking industry."

He nodded slowly and stroked his beard, or rather what would have been his beard. Perhaps he had shaved one off recently and still felt its presence, like a phantom limb. "Let me tell you something about ourselves," he said.

"By all means."

Rachel settled back to listen. Being at the end of her rope, she had plenty of time. The school, Sample told her, was among the one hundred top business schools in the country. Many graduates worked for Fortune 500 companies. The dean provided statistics of the world-beaters he had sent forth—grade point averages, starting salaries, numbers of women and minorities enrolled. Once he got going, he had plenty to say, but he spoke like a man who didn't quite believe his own words.

Rachel listened gloomily, thinking her father had been right, not only about the fate of the company but also about the way she should do her research—by hunting down JackPack middle managers in their lairs and plying them with booze and pretending she was Mata Hari.

When Sample had finished his standard spiel, she gave him hers, worn down to the essentials from so much use and every bit as much a set piece as the dean's braggadocio. He nodded slowly as she talked, as if he knew already.

When she had finished, he repositioned himself in his chair, arching his back and grimacing before he settled down again, stroking his imaginary beard. He spoke slowly. "Of course, firms don't like to talk about closing their doors. A self-fulfilling prophecy, you might say." The dean looked up. "Buzzards are circling."

"I'm aware of that. But at some point, the public has a right to know. And the packing company has been anything but forthright in the past."

He nodded, serious, although she had no idea whether he was agreeing with the moral or just the factual content of her statements. She found herself becoming interested, however. Something in his demeanor suggested he might actually have something useful to tell her, if he chose.

She set about trying to help him decide. "The Pack's in trouble, Dr. Sample, that much is clear. Everybody knows it. Certainly, JackPack's creditors and competitors know it. I believe many of them have already written the company off. It's only the people of Jackson who are still in the dark. They don't have access to the kinds of information these others do. Or perhaps that you do. They have nothing but rumors to go by. I've heard all kinds of crazy theories as I've interviewed people."

"Such as?"

She outlined a few. She couldn't read much from his expression as he listened. He seemed rather more formidable than he had at first, and while she talked, his doleful eyes didn't move from her face. Since he thought her remiss for waiting so long to come see him, perhaps he was deciding whether she should be punished for that slight to his dignity.

"It's a judgment call," she ended, "but I believe the situation has gotten bad enough at the Pack so that a little light should be shed on the situation. Companies, even private companies, have some obligation to their communities."

With a forefinger he beat a meditative tattoo against the arm of his chair.

"I can't tell you anything, I'm afraid…"

Shit, Rachel thought.

"I could give you my own theory, I suppose, but you've obviously got enough already. However," he continued, "I wonder, do you happen to know who Kevin Osborn is?"

"Yes. He's the controller at the company."

"That's right. Have you talked to him?"

"He didn't return my call."

Sample nodded. "A few years back, while he was working at the Pack, he came into our MBA program, looking to upgrade his résumé."

"I see." Rachel waited. His forefinger continued to tap thoughtfully.

"The Pack had just signed the marketing agreement with Swenson, the one that's about to be cancelled. After some rough years, it looked like the company might be turning around. Anyway, one of our professors and Osborn cooked up the idea of doing a case study. Did I tell you that we use the Harvard case method here?" He had, but it was certainly something that bore repeating. "Anyway, they decided to look at the shakeout in meatpacking from the local company's point of view. They got about two-thirds of the way through the work—a neat little case, it would've been, too—except suddenly the company called it off. That's always the understanding. If the company doesn't like what we're doing, we tank it."

"Why did they change their mind?"

"You'll have to ask Osborn."

"Do you have a copy of the case?"

"They've been destroyed. Oh, there's probably one around here somewhere, but I couldn't give it to you. You want to talk to Osborn. Did you try to reach him at home? No. You should try there. If he's not in the book…" Sample extracted a slip of paper from the breast pocket of his sports jacket and handed it over—a telephone number.

"Thank you. I'd also like the name of the professor he was doing the case with. I'd like to talk to him."

"Sure." He smiled. "But *she* probably won't be of much help. Osborn's your man."

Annoyed at the assumption she'd made, Rachel wondered what the chances were that a randomly chosen business prof at a dinky, backwater business school like this would be a woman.

"And Osborn was upset when they got cold feet?"

"At the time I believe so. Whether he still is…" He shrugged.

"Talk to Osborn," she said.

"Now you've got it."

~

And so she did.

And suddenly, just like that, she had her story.

It took three phone calls. Osborn refused to meet in person. On the first call, after he answered and didn't hang up at once, she did her little song and dance, and he hemmed and hawed, and that was about it. But he called back after a couple of hours and demanded that whatever information he gave her, it didn't come from him. So they discussed attribution and agreed on the way he might be adequately disguised in any article that was written—a person familiar with the internal workings at the packinghouse, something nice and vague—after which he seemed to lose his nerve and hemmed and hawed some more and the call ended inconclusively. Osborn was young, still in his thirties, although over the phone he sounded even younger. In the file photo Rachel had found of him and which she kept before her as they spoke, he had a sleek look, reminding her for some reason of a goose. Based on his picture and voice and hemming and hawing, she wasn't impressed, but then again she hadn't thought much of the dean, either. You never knew, you just never knew. The third phone call had been the charm. Mr. Kevin Osborn would take his revenge.

It turned out that Skip Peterson had approved the case study, but when the corporate counsel, a man named Mel Coyle, discovered what had happened, he'd put the kibosh on it. Coyle she knew about, the gray eminence in the company, right-hand man to JackPack presidents since time immemorial. Which brought them to the nub of the matter.

"Has there been talk about bankruptcy, Mr. Osborn?"

"The *b*-word. That's what we call it."

"So people have brought it up."

"Oh, yes."

"Has Peterson himself?"

"Yes."

"Mel Coyle?"

"Yes."

"Are these just casual references, or has there been serious discussion?"

"Pretty serious discussion."

"Is it going to happen?"

"We still hope to find a buyer."

"What are the chances that you might do that?"

"Realistically?"

"Yes."

"Slight."

"Slight?"

"Very slight."

"So the odds are that the Jackson Packing Company is going out of business, that's what you're saying."

Osborn hesitated, and she could hear the hesitation lingering in his voice when he did speak, but he'd gone too far to back out now. "Yes, I believe that's true. The odds are very long. Most likely the Jackson Packing Company is going out of business."

Rachel had what she needed.

# CHAPTER 15

~

As Jack Kelley got out of the company car, the air clung around him as still as before a storm, but the sky remained cloudless, just dull and smudgy, like old snow.

In the distance, piles were being driven for the paddock building. Concrete trucks lined up waiting to unload at the southeast corner of the grandstand site. At the opposite corner three men stood talking.

He knew all three and not one of them lifted his spirits. Certainly not Jack's own man Don Adagian, who had demonstrated that he knew the work but also that he had a fondness for the bottle. Or Cletus Dickey, the cagey foreman for the contractor doing the foundation work. Every time Jack came on the site, Don seemed to be hobnobbing with Dickey. Getting too cozy with the help, just as Jack feared.

Adagian and Dickey at least were necessary evils. The same could not be said for the third man, none other than Father Mike Daugherty. He knew why Father Mike had come; there could be only one reason.

The priest stood bareheaded, so Jack went into the trailer to fetch an extra hard hat before walking over.

"You better put this on," he told Mike. "God might protect you from falling objects, but He won't protect us from OSHA."

Mike smiled and took the hat. "We've all been waiting for you," he said.

"I'm sure you have."

Nearby, concrete had been poured for the grandstand grade beam, but the forms were not yet stripped. The first of the materials for the system to vent the methane from the old dump lying beneath the site had finally arrived.

"Donny and me been explaining to the Father here how we're

gonna seal the crawl space." This from Cletus Dickey, Don Adagian's good buddy.

"Is that what you and Donny been doing?"

Dickey had the habit of strutting around with his shoulders thrown back, as if his beer gut was some kind of trophy. He had opinions, too, lots of opinions.

"It's really quite interesting," Father Mike was saying.

"We was telling him about how tricky the installation is," Dickey said.

"Yeah, a regular Swiss watch we're building here, right, Jack?" Don added.

Why they were saying this to an outsider Jack couldn't fathom. Maybe they thought they were in a confessional.

Jack turned to Father Mike.

"You wanted to see me?"

"A few words, if we might."

Before he turned to walk away with the priest, Jack jabbed a finger at Adagian. "In ten minutes, I want to see you back at the trailer." He was going to take care of this "Donny and me" crap once and for all.

When they were by themselves, Jack said, "I'd appreciate it, Mike, if you didn't start noising around this business about the methane."

"Just how serious is it?"

"Not very. We've been aware of it from the beginning, part of the cost of building on a dump site. The last thing we need is a lot of people who don't know what the hell they're talking about trying to make an issue out of it."

"I understand," Mike said. "And I know you, Jack. You'd never put anybody at risk." His tone was like honey spread on the rough toast of his words. Annoying as hell.

They walked around the site, Jack pointing out where various structures would eventually go up—tote board, track oval, paddock, kennels. A couple of dozen men were working the job now. When they really got rolling, there'd be four times as many.

Jack waited for the inevitable. He could have broached the matter himself, but he wouldn't do it. This was Mike's baby. If he wanted to talk about it, then let him. Of course, he did and he would. They were approaching the line of concrete trucks, and the priest had slowed to a meditative pace.

"I stopped by, Jack, because I was wondering how things were coming along with our mutual friend."

"Can't tell you."

"Has he made a bid?"

"Not the last time I looked."

"When do all the bids have to be in?"

"Deadline's next Friday."

"And his bid isn't in yet?" Mike didn't try to hide his concern.

"Not that I know of. Most contractors wait until the last minute, anyway." Tony Vasconcellos undoubtedly was shopping prices and running every cost-cutting trick in the book.

"But you have talked to him?"

Jack said skeptically, "You mean, you haven't been checking up on me, Mike?"

The priest smiled and dipped his head in acknowledgment. "I wouldn't call it 'checking up.' But I've been talking to Angela. I talk to Angela a lot these days. The Vasconcelloses are, you might say, a little project of mine. Anyway, she told me you'd seen Tony once. Have you seen him other times, too?"

"Once," Jack said. "Once should be enough. Did she tell you he was going to bid?"

"Perhaps you should talk to him again."

"I don't know what I'd tell him."

"You don't need to tell him anything. Just encourage him to put in a bid, that's all. I'm sure if you did, it would carry a lot of weight."

Father Mike had probably been informed of Jack's ill-disguised hostility during the exchange with Vasconcellos. Anyway, he didn't respond to Mike's request. Instead he said, "The Vasconcelloses are a project of yours? What does that mean?"

Father Mike clasped his hands behind his back and walked very slowly, with eyes cast down, as he thought.

"Let's just say they've been going through some rough times lately. Between you and me, very rough times."

Jack heard these words, and the prospect of having Tony Vasconcellos on the job site grew more ominous by the moment.

"Did it ever occur to you, Mike, that you've crossed over the line here?"

The priest did not respond at once, and their steps now brought them close to others, at the southeastern corner of what would be the track grandstand, where the grade beam was being poured. They stopped briefly.

A concrete truck had just backed into place, and Jack explained the slump test as it was made—one of the laborers scooping the first concrete down the chute into a truncated cone, turning it upside down onto the ground and measuring the sag.

"If it's more than five, the truck goes out. Too much water in the mix."

Jack smelled the faint but distinctive odor of the wet material and listened as it scraped against the rotating drum of the truck.

They moved along the grade beam a few steps and watched another laborer probing the wet concrete with a vibrator to remove air and properly settle the material, the device making a low moaning sound.

"Are you on schedule?" Father Mike asked.

"We're on schedule," Jack said.

"That's good news, then."

"We should be ahead. Almost anything could put us behind, and you don't pick up at the end of a project what you lose at the beginning." It was a hoary old adage of the construction trade, but true for all that. They moved on.

Mike said, "I know you don't like this business with Tony Vasconcellos, Jack. Do you think I like it? Well, I don't. I try to listen to what the Spirit is telling me, but I won't pretend my hearing is always so good."

Jack, encouraged by this admission, said, "If Vasconcellos can't compete, he shouldn't be out here. This project is important for the city."

When Mike began again, he began slowly. "You asked me before, have I stepped over the line here? I don't know, perhaps I have. On the other hand, what does that mean, to step over the line? Do you suppose that God recognizes lines that He shouldn't step over? Do you suppose that the Church should recognize lines we shouldn't step over? People come to Mass an hour a week and the rest is—what?—the free enterprise system?" Mike, beginning to show signs of annoyance, had the big artillery, and he didn't hesitate to roll it out.

Jack shook his head and swore softly to himself. They had stopped on a small patch of vacant ground.

"You don't know how much this contract might mean, Jack. And we don't need a miracle here, just the kind of mutual caring and support that used to be the hallmark of life in a parish like ours. But, okay, I can see you're not willing to do it." He lifted his hands in a gesture of surrender. "This is possible, but it's obvious that you're dead set against helping. I won't put any more pressure on you."

This last, of course, was the finishing touch, the coup de grace, and when he began to walk away, Jack called him back.

"All right, Mike, you win. I'll talk to Vasconcellos."

His priest turned back gravely. "I don't want to win, Jack. I want to help that family."

"Okay, but you understand, Mike, I'm not promising anything. I'll talk to the man, again, but that's it."

"All we can do is try, Jack. I won't forget this. It's a good deed you're doing. And I'll be working on my end, rest assured. I'll help out as much as I can"—he winked, his normal buoyant mood wondrously restored—"even if I have to step over a line or two."

But Jack wasn't reconciled as he watched Mike walking smartly away, mission accomplished. As far as Jack was concerned, all this business about troubles in the Vasconcellos family just made the situation that much more ominous, for people with lots of personal problems had the nasty habit of dragging them onto the job site. Well, he thought, as for stepping over lines, he could step over one or two himself. There was another way to keep Vasconcellos off the job site.

Father, forgive me, he thought, and mentally he crossed himself before he headed back to the construction trailer to have it out, once and for all, with Don Adagian.

# CHAPTER 16

~

One more time, Rachel read over the lead to the first of the three articles she would write about the crisis at the Pack:

> *Despite the Jackson Packing Company's claim that the recent cancellation of a major marketing agreement will not undermine the long-term viability of the firm, the* Tribune *has managed to piece together from company, industry and other sources the story of a company on the verge of bankruptcy.*

In the second graf, she mentioned the competitive pressures the company faced, particularly the ultra-modern facility soon to be opened in Maquoketa by Modern Meat, the most aggressive company in the industry. Then she revealed that officials inside the Pack itself had begun using "the b-word."

Playing the devil's advocate, she scrolled slowly through the piece. She hadn't shown it to anyone yet. One other thing she hadn't done, either. She hadn't called JackPack for a reaction.

She sat staring at the computer screen. Her few exclusives in the past had been mere nothings compared to this. She felt like a god rearing back, about to fling her thunderbolt at JackPack. Okay, maybe not a god. Certainly not God. Let's not get carried away here. No piece of mere journalism had ever been written in indelible ink.

But her story might force Peterson's hand. Could it precipitate the announcement that the company was, indeed, about to close? What would happen then? Might another packer step in at the last moment and buy the place, the assets at least? She didn't know. The employees were probably screwed either way, for surely whatever the potential impact on the alligators here, it was death to the frogs.

She had to get reactions, she couldn't put if off forever. She decided to go treat herself to a snack first. She'd try to reach Peterson as soon as she got back.

Away from the computer, settled with her Coke and candy bar at a back table in the caf, she could take some enjoyment from the moment. Her exhilaration as she'd written the stories had died down to a steady inner glow.

She inspected the half-finished Coke and balled up candy bar wrapper. Pretty soon, if she didn't watch her step, she'd look like every other *schlump* in this godforsaken burg. Something would have to be done. But not just then. Just then she felt a little bit of all right.

Into the room, empty except for her, came Bruce Moss. He stopped, as if lost, and took his bearings. About her age and a reporter like herself, Moss was nevertheless of an entirely different subspecies of Journalistus printus. He spotted her and detoured over.

"Hi," he said. He lingered, waiting for an invitation to sit down. Among the *Trib* people, Bruce had been as friendly as any. Probably he was interested in a little fling, if he could manage it.

She nodded toward the chair opposite and he slipped into it. He wore his standard uniform—chinos, a patterned shirt, and a solid tie. His ears were a little too big, his nose a little too small. He lacked, she suspected, the heart for a really good fight.

Yet Bruce wasn't a bad sort. Somebody somewhere, maybe a favorite high school teacher, had told him he could write. And he'd done a little reporting, no doubt on his school newspaper—all her images of him seemed to have something to do with secondary school—and he'd found that people generally liked to get interviewed, so that didn't turn out to be a problem. Being a newsie of a certain type required only the most modest of gifts, and she could imagine the relief he'd felt upon discovering that he possessed them.

"What's up?" he asked.

She hesitated. Did she want to tell him? It suddenly occurred to her that she did, in fact, want to tell someone. She planned to call her best friend Sheila back in Albany later. And her parents, of course. Her father would approve, even though she hadn't used his hugger-mugger tactics to make her score. And she'd call Uncle Myron to give him a report from internal exile.

But she had no one in Jackson, no friend with whom to share her triumph. So, she decided, Bruce would have to do.

He listened attentively, but as she spoke, Rachel became aware of a certain oddness in his demeanor, something off-key. He sat with one arm propped on the table, wrist crooked in front of his chin. His soft brown eyes revealed little, just the blank look of a man engaged in some sort of mental triangulation. Rachel began to become anxious. Had she missed something, something so obvious that it was immediately spotted by a person as dim-witted as Bruce Moss?

"Well?" she demanded when he didn't react after she had finished. He picked at the hairs of his mustache.

Finally, speaking very carefully, he said, "The old man will like it."

"They're good stories."

"Yes, they sound very good." His tone had something speculative in it, as if he was listening carefully to what he said.

"What's the matter, Bruce?" He shook his head, but said nothing, so she repeated, "They *are* good stories, you know. And nobody else has them. Nobody else has done the legwork or made the contacts." She was beginning to feel positively defensive.

He nodded and then got up, and she thought he meant to leave, but he went to the counter and started to make himself a cup of coffee, and then stood undecided and finally abandoned the coffee and returned and sat down again.

"Perhaps it doesn't make any difference," he said.

"What doesn't?"

Again he said nothing for a time.

"This is just between you and me, okay?" he said.

"We'll see about that."

"I mean it, Rachel."

What could be so infernally important? With her irritation went a sinking feeling, the awful possibility that all the work she'd done and the exclusive she'd finally managed to write were about to turn into cottage cheese.

"I won't use your name. That's all I'll promise," she told him.

He leaned back and rubbed his eyes, then crossed his arms over his small beginning of a paunch and told his story.

"Have you heard of Ben Morrissey?"

"I've heard the name. He was the executive editor before I came." Morrissey had come up in conversation a couple of times, and she'd been told he had left the paper to take another position.

No big deal. Or at least that was what she'd thought. She remembered the similar question from the dean of the business school—did she know who Kevin Osborn was?—that had led to her big breakthrough. Every place had a history. She steeled herself.

"Do you know why he left the paper?" Moss asked.

Rachel leaned her elbows on the table and looked closely at Moss. "No."

"Because of you."

"You're kidding."

He shook his head glumly. "When the reporter before you left, Ben wanted to go out and hire somebody else for general assignments. He already had a guy picked out. But the old man came up with the idea of hiring an investigative person to concentrate on the Pack. You. The two of them got into it. Ben quit in protest."

This was very interesting. "So it was a turf battle," Rachel said. "What about the rest of the people on the *Trib*? What did they think?"

She watched as Moss chose his words carefully. "Ben was very popular."

"For instance," she said, "you liked him a lot."

"Yes, I did." He hesitated. The look on his face told her there was more.

"And?" she demanded. They were launched. They'd complete this little journey.

"It was true, everybody was on Ben's side. None of the editors, or anybody else for that matter, wanted to hire a reporter just to investigate the Pack, but Sawyer forced the issue. Nobody believed it has anything to do with the union or saving jobs or anything like that."

"They thought it was personal, then, that it had to do with the animosity between Sawyer and the Peterson family." This was not news, but the possibility disturbed Rachel. "My stories are good stories, Bruce, whatever Sawyer's motivation."

He paused a long time now, and she could see he was even more reluctant to say whatever was left to say. But eventually he continued.

"Sawyer and the Petersons go back a long way."

"So?" Rachel's interest was beginning to turn to irritation.

Moss told her, "Back in the thirties—I think that's when it was—Skip Peterson's grandfather and Sawyer owned a boat together. That's what I heard, at least. There was some sort of falling out, I don't know about what. Anyway, that started it."

"Started it? Back in the thirties? Skip Peterson's grandfather?" Spare me, Rachel thought.

"All sorts of stuff has happened since then. During World War II, Sawyer is supposed to have prevented the Pack from getting an Army contract worth beaucoup bucks. I don't know if that's true or not, either. There are lots of stories. One I do know happened was during the flood fight back in fifty-one. Or maybe it was fifty-two. They had a couple of big floods back-to-back. Hard to keep them straight."

"It's not important," Rachel snapped. "What happened?"

"Sawyer was supposed to be in charge of the fight. Back then the dock board was a lot more powerful than it is now. Anyway, the Petersons ran their own flood fight around the packinghouse. One thing led to another, and pretty soon there were two flood fights, the Petersons at the north end of town, Sawyer at the south end. The old man was totally ticked off, what with the Petersons poaching on his territory. Anyway, he waited two years, and then there was a big strike at the Pack. A bitter strike. One man was killed. The paper came out strongly for the union and succeeded in turning public opinion against the company. The strike was finally settled, but it had been so divisive, some people say the company has never really recovered from it."

"I know about the strike," Rachel said. "Why don't I know about any of this other stuff?"

Bruce shrugged. "Who's gonna tell you? No way you'll figure it out by going through the morgue, either. The announcement in the paper when Ben left didn't talk about the real reason he left. As for the fights between Sawyer and the Petersons, most of it happened so long ago that people hardly think about it anymore. The *Trib's* been pro-union for decades now, and generally the people on the paper are in favor of that, although their reasons are different from the old man's. They're not just out for revenge. There's a lot of union support in the community, too. Jackson's always been a strong union town. So people forget. But not everybody."

"Not the people on the paper."

"No."

"And Ben Morrissey was very popular."

"Yes, that's right. The people here liked Ben…a lot."

Rachel didn't want to hear this.

"So that's all, what you've just told me?"

"Yes, pretty much."

"Pretty much?" She wanted every last jot and tittle here.

"It's all I know."

"Why are you telling me this, since obviously nobody else around here has seen fit to?" She remembered his earlier hesitations.

"I like you."

Oh, good grief, Rachel thought, he likes me.

Moss sat hunched, elbows on the table. He had taken his glasses off, as if seeing a little less clearly helped him get the words out. He was rubbing his eyes. He still had something of the schoolboy about him, although he certainly understood now, if he hadn't at the beginning, that this note he was passing in class wasn't likely to advance any amorous designs he might have.

Rachel shook her head. Could you believe this?

"These *are* good stories, Bruce. And the public does have a right to know."

He was playing sadly with the saltshaker, tipping it this way and that, and watching the salt slide from side to side.

"Yes," he said without conviction.

Behind the paling of his mustache, he compressed his lips. His sadness had gathered in his downcast eyes.

"So, okay, what you're telling me is that it doesn't make any difference if we're talking Pulitzer Prize here, everybody just assumes the worst, right? I'm Sawyer's cat's-paw, plain and simple."

"I don't."

"But the rest?"

His gesture started out as an uncertain waggle, then faded away.

She'd known about the dislike between Sawyer and the Petersons. Nobody had spelled it out, but it had come up from time to time, and she'd thought, okay, Jackson might have sixty thousand people in it, but it was still like a small town, and this sort of thing happens. It didn't make her work any less important. That's what she had told herself. Now she understood that she'd been kidding herself; she'd been naive. Even the most legitimate stories can be fatally tainted.

Everything fit—her summonses up to the penthouse, the fact that others at the paper kept their distance. Maybe they thought she was ignorant of all this underlying horseshit or maybe they didn't. Maybe they thought it didn't make any difference one way or the other. She was an ambitious outsider come to Jackson, a New York Jew looking for the main chance. So what if her story was Sawyer's way of telling Peterson to go fuck himself? So what if two thousand jobs hung in the balance? A good story was a good story, right? And all she cared about was her clips, anyway, right?

"Tell me about him."

"Who?"

"This Ben Morrissey person."

And so Rachel settled back to listen, having learned what she had really known all along. The job was, as she had told herself on the day she stepped off the plane in Jackson, just too good to be true.

# CHAPTER 17

~

Nothing in the office had changed. Vasconcellos sat exactly where Jack had left him two and a half weeks earlier. The family portrait still commanded the heights of the file cabinet.

Jack looked at the picture on his way by, taking about the amount of time that a rubbernecking motorist does in passing an auto accident. There was, of course, nothing to see that he hadn't seen the first time, the smiling faces more like masks, perhaps, and perhaps somewhat more interesting, too.

As for Vasconcellos himself, well, he sat comfortably behind his desk and regarded Jack with uplifted chin and lowered eyelids, as the cat feigns a sleepy disregard of the mouse. "I didn't expect to see you back here," he said.

"Father Mike asked me to come." Jack sat down but didn't make himself comfortable.

"Did he?"

"He wants me to try and convince you to put in a bid."

"Is that what you're doing?"

"He asked me to come, and I've come."

Vasconcellos nodded slowly. "Father," he said, "can be a pain in the ass."

Jack weighed his response to this assertion. He could see in Vasconcellos's demeanor that something had changed significantly since the last time. Instead of a man burdened with a sense of defeat and injustice, he now resembled the cocky electrical contractor Jack had once known.

Deciding against any gossiping at Mike's expense, Jack said, "I told him that contractors wait until the last minute."

Vasconcellos leaned far back, the swivel of the chair creaking under his weight.

"But he wanted you to come anyway."

"Yes."

"If you'd had your druthers, though…"

"I told him that contractors wait until the last minute," Jack repeated.

Vasconcellos nodded slowly. He seemed rather amused by this whole business. The change from Jack's last visit was really quite amazing. It pissed Jack off.

Vasconcellos continued when he was ready. "I will, as you said, wait as long as I can, but yes, I do plan to bid. You can tell Father that. It'll make him happy…although I expect it doesn't do much to improve your day."

As pleasant as it would have been to go on in this vein, progressively laying their cards on the table, Jack realized that the situation called for some diplomacy, and so he said, "Look, Tony, we're in the same parish, okay? That means something. But I've got a track to build, that's what I'm worried about. I'm worried about the accelerated schedule. I'm worried about the weather. Winter's coming. It could get mighty nasty. I need people who can perform. Can you do that? Can you? That's all I ask."

Vasconcellos's gaze now changed, becoming cooler, as he said, "I can handle the work."

"I hope so."

"Let me tell you something, Jack. Tony Vasconcellos finishes jobs."

"For your sake, I hope so" was all Jack had to add, and soon, with his small gesture of civility accomplishing nothing, the interview came to an end.

Next, without calling ahead, Jack drove down to One Jackson Plaza, the largest commercial building in the city, where Ralph English had his insurance offices. English handled the bid bonds for all the contractors in town.

Jack walked slowly through the three-story atrium of the building, reluctant to go upstairs. He sat briefly on one of the marble benches bordering a fountain with tropical plantings. The plashing of the water covered the low, almost inaudible hum of the building's HVAC system, and Jack could feel the coolness from the fountain bathing the back of his neck.

He went over the meeting with Vasconcellos, wondering at the change in the man and trying to decide if his newfound arrogance might be translated into job performance. Jack doubted it. And he wasn't prepared to take a chance. A quiet word with Ralph English was in order.

He'd already tried to arrange an accidental meeting with English, but that had proved trickier than Jack had anticipated. If he was determined to submarine Vasconcellos, he'd have to forget about being subtle.

Still, he was having trouble bringing himself to do it.

Around him, several old people sat or walked, alone with their thoughts. In the hot weather, they would come from the retirement high-rise a few doors down the street to take advantage of the air conditioning and atrium of One Jackson Plaza. Although it wasn't so hot today. Autumn had finally begun to set in. Soon it would be cold.

Jack got up and walked across the promenade to a café and ordered a cup of coffee. As in the atrium, the appointments of the café—antique soda fountain decor with richly veined marble counter and tabletops, polished bentwood chairs, quarry tile flooring—were top-of-the-line. It was the same everywhere in the building.

Jack never failed to notice these amenities when business brought him there. Or to remember the history, either—the developer who kept on insisting on one upgrade after another, the ballooning budget and discarded schedule, and finally the bank foreclosure. He remembered it because he'd been the general contractor during the massive retrofit. It had been his finest work and his worst job, his sense of success nested in the greater sense of failure. And that was not all. On that project, Tony Vasconcellos had been the electrical contractor.

Jack had never been comfortable with the man, although he'd found his discomfort hard to put into words. That was the way with people who weren't out-and-out bad but rather failed at the margin. Vasconcellos didn't care how many change orders there were or how long it took to complete a project. Maybe, like he'd bragged, he did manage to finish every job he'd been on. It might take until kingdom come, but the son of a bitch finished.

Yet, Jack thought, that wasn't why he didn't like him. Jack had known contractors who were bumbling idiots, yet whom he'd liked for all that. But Vasconcellos…well, if he'd been the best damn contractor in the world, Jack wouldn't have been able to stomach the man.

As he toyed with his coffee, he thought about all these things. And about Father Mike Daugherty, too. Going behind

Vasconcellos's back hardly bothered Jack at all, but Father Mike was another matter.

He stopped thinking and stared intently at nothing, feeling a deadness lodging just behind his eyes. Sometimes he seemed to know nothing, the million practical things he'd learned over the decades adding up to not much of anything. He would have tried to talk to Mike about this the other Sunday, if they hadn't got onto the Vasconcellos business first.

What difference did it make what he did? So what if he finished some project on time, within the budget, according to the specs, so what? How could that be measured against the noble goals of someone like Father Mike Daugherty?

Yet Jack resisted this idea. He had made his commitments. The dog track might be a trivial thing, but he had made his commitments. He valued his good name, and he wasn't about to put that in jeopardy if he could help it. And whatever penances Mike might be prepared to endure himself, Jack had no interest in wearing a hair shirt like Anthony Vasconcellos. The job was going to be tough enough as it was.

He felt a hand placed lightly upon his shoulder and turned and looked up into a familiar face.

"Ralph!"

"Long time, no see," English said. "Mind if I join you?"

It took Jack some moments to regain his composure after this sudden materialization.

"I must say, you look awfully surprised to see me, Jack," English said. "I work upstairs, you know."

Jack couldn't believe it. Perhaps Ralph English had been sent as a sign, perhaps God did care about finishing projects on schedule. With this pleasing thought in mind, Jack led the way to a table in the farthermost depths of the café.

# CHAPTER 18

~

After Bruce Moss's revelations, Rachel didn't return to her desk. She left the building and walked, going up one street and down another, without plan or destination. Few people were about at that dead time of midafternoon, the streets as quiet as photographs.

Outside the post office, an old woman, wearing a respirator because of the smog, stood vigil, protesting U.S. intervention in Central America. In the park nearby, two retirees sat ignoring her and each other, watching the seasons change.

Rachel tried to envision Ben Morrissey, who had quit the paper rather than acquiesce to her hiring. All she could think of was Jimmy Stewart in Mr. Smith Goes to Washington.

At the last, Bruce, in a kindly gesture, had suggested that Morrissey quit more because he felt his prerogative to hire reporters had been compromised than because of any scruples over the reason she had been hired. As she wandered aimlessly, she tried to tell herself that Bruce was right, that the affairs of others have little emotional power over us compared to our sense of personal violation. Yet she was too honest not to sense the disingenuousness that lay at the core of Bruce's gesture.

She walked and walked, as if in walking itself lay her solution, as if the scenes around her hid some answer for her, like a figure disguised in a drawing.

She noticed especially the street plantings, hedged all around with asphalt and concrete, barely alive after the long drought.

On one of the service roads, which lay in shadow and cut the downtown blocks in half, she passed an old brick apartment building from the roof of which descended a narrow patch of lighter-colored bricks, as if a lightning strike had once opened a fissure, later patched. In a sunlit corner, where a small burned-up garden was tucked into the angle between a wooden garage and the building, she came upon thousands of bugs, drawn to that island of greenhouse heat, black creatures with red piping, the size of throat lozenges, moving restlessly, like strange small wind-tossed flowers.

Entering the orbit of the heat, she stood watching them, putting aside the desire to know what kind of bugs they might be and how they came to be there, and instead simply observing them and imagining after a time that she could detect some pattern in their intricate movements.

When she resumed her wandering, she had begun to perspire, and the shadows had acquired a sharp coolness. She came to a quiet residential street, not a soul about, only the faint restless sounds of the heart of the city behind her. From a tree in a yard someone had hung a wreath, dried to a cinnamon color. She had no idea what its significance might be, perhaps just a Christmas wreath from the previous year, hung there for who knows what reason.

Suddenly, she remembered that Yom Kippur had passed. She'd been so busy that she'd forgotten. She'd missed the Day of Atonement. Yet, miss it or not, ignore it or not, she knew the message of Yom Kippur as well as anyone. It was impossible not to know. Pure acts from pure hearts come. She moved on, sadder than ever.

Not wanting to, but feeling she must, she thought about her dilemma, about Leonard Sawyer. Publishers were the same as other people, weren't they? At one extreme ideologues, at the other pure businessmen, and every kind of creature in between. Still, meddlers like Sawyer must be rare, a throwback to the age when newspapers were the weapons of the men who published them. Feh. Just her luck.

She walked for a whole block with the soothing illusion that she had become a time traveler, that Jackson lived in some sort of weird time warp, and the moral complexities of the late twentieth century simply didn't apply.

But then the reality of her situation returned, slashing through this trivial fancy. Better she was still in Albany, scurrying around looking for her little off-beat human interest stories, living in a mouse hole of an apartment.

She walked a block intent upon not thinking at all. But who could not think? She attempted to imagine a life without Leonard Sawyer, a less rocket-like career in which she earned her reportorial badges through good writing and the occasional modest exclusive. She imagined a blameless life.

Who was she kidding? A blameless life? Didn't all reporters have to cover shit stories sometimes, didn't they have to intrude crassly upon innocent people, didn't they throw away the wheat and make bread from the chaff? Didn't they, finally, have their life's lie just like everybody else?

She could storm up to Sawyer's office and challenge him to an accounting. She could do that. But then what? Such an act seemed senseless unless she was prepared to quit. Was she?

Back on the downtown streets, she moped along a commercial block, past an income tax service, a comic book shop, a store selling grave markers. She passed an auction and realty service, tavern, barbershop, pawn broker—each disappointing in its own way—while above them the sad dripstones of the dingy old Victorian-era buildings frowned down from the upper-story windows.

She approached the city center again. In the distance, near a Catholic retirement home, she could make out a nun in full habit, moving as sedately along as a sailing ship on the horizon. The city was filled with nuns, she knew, but they mostly wore civilian clothes now, and this was the first one she'd seen in a habit. Two blocks farther, she passed a Moonie selling flowers beside a boarded up gas station.

She envied such people their acts of moral clarity—the woman she'd seen earlier standing her vigil, the nun, even the Moonie here. But she felt a certain pride, too, pride in the complexity of her own dilemma, pride in the sense of an outcome not foretold.

She continued to make her ramshackle progress along the street. As she approached a building, a large black man came out, confidently descending the half dozen steps to the sidewalk, head up, looking neither right or left, then setting off down the street in front of her.

She read the plaque on the building as she passed, a simple historical marker:

### KJAX
Founded in 1921, the first radio station in Jackson, Iowa

She followed the black man for a half block. He walked steadily, with an economy of motion, at a rate that suggested he had no interest in catching anyone or being caught himself. Then abruptly he turned into a parking garage and disappeared from sight, leaving Rachel alone with herself once more.

But she found that she had fallen into his rhythm and no longer moved along at a hangdog pace. This seemed to have a tonic effect upon her thoughts because she at once decided she had to make up her mind; she couldn't wander around Jackson all day bewailing her fate at having fallen into the hands of Leonard Sawyer.

And the mere thought that a decision must be made told her that a decision had been made. She simply didn't have the heart to go back and destroy the story and tell Sawyer what he could do with his damn job. With this admission, another possibility occurred to her, that the last hour of struggle had been nothing more than window dressing, her attempt to arrange the mannequins and drapery at the forefront of her thoughts so that she could no longer make out the darker reality behind, where the real business was transacted.

Was that what she was doing? Her honesty reasserted itself, and she had to admit it might be true. She did not know.

She crossed the street with the light, then stopped on the curb, but only for an instant before she turned and recrossed and started back toward the paper.

# CHAPTER 19

~

Near the end of the day, Don Adagian made his last tour of the job site.

He walked past the section of grade beam where the concrete had been poured that afternoon. He walked past the formwork at the far end of the grandstand. He walked through the noise of the pile driver at the paddock-building site. It almost felt like he was going back in time. Where the kennels would be built, nothing had been done yet. In front of him, the platform of sand, with swales and crests like choppy water, still looked exactly like it had on the day he arrived. And in the distance, he could see the river, and he imagined traveling farther back—upstream to La Crosse, past his failing marriage, too, past the day he'd gone into construction because he didn't have anything better to do, past it all.

The bees, which had been skimming the surface of the sand only a few days ago, had now disappeared. The sun had descended beyond the western bluffs, and he could feel a slight chill. Behind him, he listened to the workers knocking off for the day. The pile driver fell silent, then the rotary saw and hammers used for the formwork. Voices dying away. Doors slamming and pickup trucks driving into the distance. And finally nothing. Just the ghost of the noise of the pile driver, which seemed to haunt the site.

And in the quiet, Don remembered Jack Kelley ripping into him after the priest had left.

When he got back to the Do-Si-Do, Don thought a drink or two with Kate Sullivan might pick up his spirits, so he cleaned up and launched the tender from the stern of the Chris Craft and motored over to the houseboat on the other side of the marina.

Nobody home. Shielding his eyes, he peered through a window. The silhouettes of Reiny Kopp's drawing board and the tank filled with native fish appeared abandoned and lonely in the gloom.

Back on his own boat, Don got out the bottle of Black and White and a tumbler and poured himself two fingers of scotch. He stood undecided and then carried the glass and bottle back on deck and sat in the fishing chair and put his feet up on the stern deck. A film of rich amber clung where the liquor had slid around inside of the glass. Don took a sip and held the liquor in his mouth, his eyes closed, his chin tilted up. Then he swallowed.

He never gave a shit when he started a job. Who could look at a job site and give a damn about the tract housing or strip mall or whatever the hell you were about to build? Or dog track? But somewhere along the way, even with the most piddly-assed job in the world, Don would begin to take an interest in what he was doing. When the thing was half-built or two-thirds, he would suddenly realize that with a little attention to the detailing, with half-decent landscaping, with the right owners and tenants, this was something a man might drive by in a few years and take some pride in. So, for a time, he wouldn't mind so much getting up in the morning.

Could he hang on long enough to begin to give a shit about the dog track? When would that be—February, March? But what about December, then? What about January when he was out there freezing his butt off?

He poured himself another drink and rolled the glass between the palms of his hands as he thought.

He remembered something that Clete had said to him, a couple of hours after the scene with Kelley and the priest, after Kelley had reamed him out, and Don had gone out to check on the placement of the clean stone for the methane system. Clete, who was shooting elevations for the formwork, came over as soon as he spotted him.

Don knew that Dickey was sucking up to him, something else to add to his grievances.

"What the hell was wrong with Kelley, Donny? Did he have a hair up his ass or what?"

Don shook his head. He didn't want to talk about Kelley. Or see Kelley. Or think about Kelley.

"And the priest, what was that all about? What's a guy like that want with Jack Kelley?"

Don didn't know. Didn't care much, either. His thoughts went off on a tangent of their own. The priest had interested him. "For a priest, he didn't look like much," Don said.

"What's a priest supposed to look like?"

"I don't know, but different somehow. The way I got it figured, you wanna be religious, Clete, I mean *really* religious, none of this nine-to-five shit, you gotta wear sackcloth, whatever the hell that is, pray twelve hours a day, whip yourself until you're bleeding, sleep on a bed of nails—that sort of crap. That's what I think."

Cletus whistled softly. "Whew. Guess Kelley got just the right guy to run his job for him."

"Yeah, watch out, Dickey," he chuckled.

As Don was about to leave, Dickey asked him did he want to play a little poker. "I know a game I can get you into."

Don, thinking about what it took to be really religious and mindful of the reaming he'd just gotten from Kelley, shook his head and said good-bye and walked off.

"Don't worry, buddy, we're gonna take good care of you," he heard Dickey say to his back.

Now he regretted that he hadn't taken him up on the offer of a game.

Don blew out a puff of cigarette smoke and watched it hover uncertainly in the still air above the rear deck, then slowly break apart.

Clete would try to use him, of course. Jack Kelley was right about that much. A time would come, Clete would need a favor, something not quite on the up-and-up, and he'd come to Don, and how could Don say no? That was the fucking world, you scratch my back, and I'll scratch yours. But for all of that, Clete wasn't such a bad guy. And shit, you gotta take your friends where you find them, right?

~

About halfway through his second drink Don stopped worrying about other people. He touched some wellspring deep inside himself. He became disentangled. Like a boat freeing itself from a snag, he floated clear. Once more, as at such moments in the past, some large possibility lay before him, some vast potential within himself, and the way to tap it almost within his grasp. For one minute, for two, he sat relaxed and stared off into the distance and dreamed of what might be.

After a time, he saw Kate and her husband returning to their boat. They didn't look his way. He thought about going over. Maybe he would have if he'd been drunker, or sober. Something else.

He still felt pretty good. To hell with Kate, he thought suddenly. He was kidding himself if he imagined he could get anything going with her, and what difference did it make, anyway, who cared? And while he was at it, to hell with all the other assholes in this burg.

Don rested the empty glass on his belly. He was feeling pretty good. Yeah, to hell with them all, he thought pleasantly. He might not be much, but shit, at least he hadn't sold his friggin' soul to the Devil like Kelley and the rest of his lot. To hell with Clete Dickey, too. If Dickey thought he could wrap Don around his little finger, he had another think coming. If any of 'em did, they were sorely mistaken.

He considered his options. Unlike all those other jokers, his house wasn't planted in the ground. He could cast off any time he wanted, head on downriver, take his chances somewhere else. And, by god, if they gave him too much shit, he damn well would.

He poured another drink.

# PART III

# CHAPTER 20

~

He showed his ID at the guard gate and went inside. Others arrived alone or in pairs. The hallway, silent and cool, with runs of ductwork overhead, was filled with animal smells left over from the previous day. At the laundry, he turned in his chip and picked up his whites. Upstairs in the men's locker, he changed as others drifted in and out, talking about the series of articles in the *Tribune.*

He put on his whites and over them his yellow rubber apron with the bib turned down. Then he pulled on his calf-length rubber boots. He dressed carefully.

His legs ached. He was losing the feeling in his right hand. To help him stay awake he'd had two cups of coffee even though he couldn't hold it anymore and later would have to ask one of the floaters to spell him on the line so he could take a leak. That meant his name would go into the book again.

Finished dressing, Fritz Goetzinger sat on the bench, perfectly still, breathing slowly and deeply. Someone else came in, wanting to talk about the stories being published in the paper. He shook his head. Not yet. There'd be plenty of time for that later.

Finally he heaved himself up and looked around for the rest of his equipment: hard-hat, mailed glove, and the scabbard with his knives.

Out on the floor, he got a pair of earplugs at the supervisors' office and then walked toward his workstation across the swells and gullies, which turned the brickwork into a shallow, man-made watershed. The room clattered with machine noise, but the line wasn't moving yet. In the distance, he could hear the hiss of the dehairing machines.

A few yards ahead, Billy Noel, who worked opposite him, was fitting in his plugs as he rolled along above his bad leg. Billy had been forced back onto the kill floor, too, either that or get laid off. He had a massive torso balanced above match-stick legs, one slightly shorter than the other. For a man with good pins, the work was bad enough. That rock-hard floor would suck the last ounce of strength out of you. Once, after the end of a shift, Fritz had found Billy in his car in the parking lot, slumped forward, his great round head pressed against the steering wheel, eyes closed, mouth wide open. Fritz thought at first he'd had a seizure, but it turned out that he was just asleep. He'd dozed off the moment he sat down in his car, the car door still open.

Billy smiled when he saw Fritz, and then, as if suddenly realizing joy was inappropriate just now, he grew serious.

"Did you see the last story?" he asked.

"I did."

"Could it be true?"

"Of course it's true." Still, Fritz wasn't prepared to talk about the situation yet, not even with his friend. First, he had a day to get through. "How many we got today, Billy?"

"Heard seven six."

Fritz nodded. Seven thousand, six hundred hogs.

"Seems like every time I'd as soon get home a little early, they find some extra animals somewhere," Fritz said.

The line was moving now. The first carcasses of the day had appeared at the far side of the room, hanging spread-eagled upside down from the chain, hairless, slightly bloated.

Fritz rolled the plugs he'd picked up into thin cylinders and inserted them into his ears. As they expanded, they muted the sounds around him, creating a kind of isolation. Crisscrossing the kill floor, the spastic conga line of pale, hairless carcasses approached, so closely spaced that they bumped into one another as the line jerked along.

Fritz took one of his knives out of the scabbard and began to work it quickly back and forth over his steel. Above him, he was conscious of the metallic rubbing of the chain. Almost immediately his earplugs had begun to itch. He held his right hand up to the vent from the overhead blower. The air was hot. They must've turned off the pumps from the wells, he thought. Damn.

He continued to work the short, scimitar-shaped blade back and forth, trying to feel the rhythmic movement of the knife through the numbness and stinging of his hand. He couldn't hear the blade against the steel or see it either except as a gray blur. For a few moments his eyes began to close. He dreamed of taking a nap...

"Hey, wake up, ol' buddy!" Billy yelled at him. "Time to go to work!"

Fritz shook himself, then rubbed the knife across his steel one last time and finally put on his mailed glove.

The first carcass—one of the large packers, probably a sow past breeding age—approached the steel workbenches where he stood with the thirty other headers. The neck bone had been severed, and the head of the animal, hanging off the rest of the carcass by only a thin strip of flesh, was now cut free and mounted on a spike so that the flesh of the jaws and snouts could be loosened and peeled back from the bone. Then one of the tonguers cut out the tongue, and the skull was clamped to the snout puller where metal hooks on a rotating drum yanked the flesh below the eye sockets free and dropped it at the side of Fritz's cutting board. The remainder of the skull passed along to the chiselers, who further loosened the meat for the skullers behind him. Most of the people Fritz worked with were okay, except for the chiselers, a bunch of wise-ass kids.

Fritz trimmed the snout, removing the nostrils and inspecting them for hair or blood clots. The good meat he piled under water spraying down from the nozzle between him and Billy. The bad went into the black inedibles can. Billy cut off the cheek meat.

Fritz had to work quickly. Every four seconds the snout puller dropped another slab of flesh at his elbow. The trick was to get a rhythm and hold it and stay alert while thinking as little as possible, just enough not to nick the bony gristle-like meat.

Fritz just wanted to find his rhythm and let the time pass as fast as possible, but no sooner had he begun to settle in before a buzzer sounded, filling the room with a sound like sizzling, and the line immediately stopped, the carcasses rocking back and forth briefly, then becoming perfectly still. He looked at the row of lights behind him: red. One of the inspectors had shut down the line to have an animal removed. They'd probably found an abscess. He looked at Billy, who nodded.

Nobody would admit it, but with the scarcity of animals, it was generally believed that the people in the JackPack buying stations weren't looking at hogs so carefully anymore.

As they waited for the line to start up, some of the chiselers started to fool around. If it had been late in the day, they would have been the first to yell, "Get the fuckin' line moving," but this early they didn't give a shit. Fritz and Billy cared, though. They hated dead time. Fritz glared at the young men, but they ignored him. They were, so far as he could tell, kids without a future, like most of the other youngsters who had been hired on after Jack-Pack signed the marketing agreement with Swenson. It had been a long time since people who came to work at JackPack thought they were starting a career for themselves. If the plant were shut down, they'd just drift off, picking up whatever work they could wherever they could.

He'd have to yell to get them to shut up. Which he finally did. "Righto, your honor," one said sarcastically.

The chain started to move again. Fritz turned back to the cutting board, trying once more to find his rhythm, but almost immediately he had to go to the john. The need came on him quickly. Sometimes he had to take a piss two or three times between avalons, and then he was the subject of jibes from the other headers and suspicious looks from the supervisors, and, of course, his name went into the book. He could try to hold on, although then, when he absolutely had to go, he might have to wait to be spelled. He looked at his watch. It wasn't even eight o'clock yet. He hadn't even been working for an hour yet.

And so he waited.

Finally, just barely able to hold it in, he spotted Dickie Streuer, his foreman, and yelled at him. Dickie pretended not to hear. The muscles clamping Fritz's bladder shut were fluttering. He walked over to Dickie.

"I need to be spelled."

Streuer began preparations to say something.

"Can't wait," Fritz told him and handed over his glove and knife. His urinary muscles quivered, and as he rushed toward the john, he could feel warm spurts of urine trickling down one leg.

He rested with his head pressed against the wall above the urinal. A cold thread extended the length of his leg. He was breathing hard, as if from violent exercise. He felt ashamed at his weakness.

Someone came through the door, and he immediately straightened up and zipped his fly and went back to work.

"Thanks," he said to Streuer.

"Yeah."

Dickie had fallen behind, of course. When Fritz began to

work, he realized that Dickie had nicked the blade of the knife, too, for it no longer laid the flesh open with the buttery smoothness necessary for the work. Heaven help the man whose knives all went sour on him. At the end of the day, his arm would weigh a thousand pounds.

Ignoring the snide comments and giggling from the chiselers, he took out his spare blade and worked it quickly back and forth a few times on his steel. If this one got nicked, he'd be out of luck. He took a deep breath, set himself squarely at his cutting board, and went back to work.

By nine thirty, when they got their avalon, he felt a little better. He and Billy went to the john, then down to the cafeteria. They got coffee and wandered over to a group of the dissident union members sitting together in a far corner.

"Wha'd'ya think, Fritzy?" Arthur Vogt said. A copy of the *Tribune* lay before him with Rachel Brandeis's last story beneath a three-column headline. He made a space for Fritz to pull up a seat. Billy grabbed a chair from a nearby table and established a listening post behind the others.

"This new gal reporter the *Tribune* got looks to be a cut above what we been used to, Arthur."

Vogt sniffed. "If bad news makes a good reporter, this lady's a pip."

Since he had lost the union election, Vogt had gone back to shaving only when he felt like it, and his flat, fighter's face was studded with a salt-and-pepper two-day growth. The corners of his eyebrows were turned up, giving him an odd look, either sinister or comical, Fritz had never decided quite which.

"Some of us," Vogt said, "figure it don't mean nothing. It's just old Len Sawyer pullin' Skip's chain."

"I wouldn't count on that, Arthur." Rachel Brandeis had been a little oversensitive when she'd come out to the farm to interview him, but Fritz was inclined to accept her claim to independence.

"Anyway, you ask me," Vogt said, "even if it is true, it still don't mean nothin'. Skip Peterson's a helluva lot more worried about losing his job than any of us at this table are."

Fritz yawned and stretched, "Yeah, so you say." Vogt, like everyone else, had his pet theories.

The old-timers—didn't make any difference if it was the dissidents like Arthur here or the more housebroken members of the union—

they all believed the Pack would never close. Fritz knew different. The Brandeis woman had tapped into a vein.

"Tell you what," he said, "how about I go upstairs come dinnertime. See what Skip's got to say for himself."

"Sounds good," Vogt agreed.

Fritz stretched and yawned again and then shook his head. He'd only taken a couple of sips of his coffee, the aroma less a smell than a clogging of the nostrils, like a local anesthetic. "Seems so it gets tougher and tougher out on that floor, gentlemen."

"Any more it's not fit work for a human being," Bernie Osterkamp observed, sitting, as he always did, at the far edge of the gathering.

"Amen," said Arthur Vogt.

When Fritz got back to the floor, he decided that if he waited until dinnertime, Skip Peterson would probably have gone somewhere. So he hunted down Dickie Streuer and told him to find a floater to spell him.

"Haven't got anybody."

"Don't give me that shit, Dickie. The company's about to come down around our ears. I need to go upstairs."

Now, as always, Streuer stood expressionless, his blue hardhat planted squarely on his head, his white frock neatly laundered. The two of them had a strange relationship. The fact that the foreman had the Mayor of Jackson as a subordinate added a bit of swagger, even haughtiness, to his manner toward Fritz. On the other hand, Streuer was basically a follower, and his natural posture toward those he knew, or suspected, were his superiors was one of subservience. The contradiction was beyond his capacity to resolve.

He shrugged. "I'll try and find someone."

"Don't try. Do it."

Finally, the floater arrived. Streuer must have hunted high and low until he found just the guy he was looking for, the worst of the replacements.

Upstairs, Fritz walked by the life-size porcelain pig in the common area surrounded by the general offices. Skip's secretary said, "He's busy."

"He's busy, is he?" Fritz raised his voice. "You tell him there's a city council meeting tonight. Tonight I'll be busy. You tell him that."

He spoke loudly enough to be heard through the door to Peterson's office and walked away slowly enough to be called back. He wasn't and went downstairs with the familiar mingling of regret and grim satisfaction that had marked so many of his dealings with people like Skip Peterson.

By the time Fritz had detoured over to the smokehouses for a word with Arthur Vogt and at last got back to his workstation, the floater had fallen way behind, a pile of untrimmed snouts next to him.

Damn that Streuer, Fritz thought. "Let a man in there, son," he told the replacement. Suddenly, for no good reason, he was in fine spirits, and as he filled Billy in on his misadventure, he fell at once into the proper rhythm, working swiftly and skillfully, and well before the line halted for dinner, he had caught up.

After dinner, however, after all the speculations in the cafeteria over how events might play out, Fritz still had to face the afternoon shift on the line. The jolt of energy he had finished the morning with did not return, and he felt more tired than ever.

He struggled with his exhaustion. He stopped working and let the snouts pile up, hoping that rushing to catch up again might give him another shot of adrenaline. The drum which tore the faces from the heads deposited another next to his cutting board. He counted the seconds. One thousand one, one thousand two, one thousand three, one thousand…Another snout dropped onto the pile.

He looked at his watch. Still a lot more animals to do. Another snout revolved into view and dropped off the drum. The time stretched out in front of him without end. His muscles felt paralyzed as he watched the slabs of flesh pile up, one after another, in mindless accumulation. As a hand truck hauled away full vats of meat, the brickwork vibrated beneath his boots.

Finally he began working again, but still his muscles were filled with a dreamlike lethargy. He rested, his arms rigid against the cutting board, propping himself up. He put his face up into the warm air from the blower.

"You okay?" Billy asked.

"Tired."

Billy shook his head, a sympathetic gesture. Another snout dropped onto the pile. Out of the corner of his eye, Fritz saw a chiseler looking at him and grinning and working with great energy. Shit, he thought, and he grabbed a snout and began to trim it.

And that was when he nicked the edge on his spare knife.

# CHAPTER 21

~

Rachel Brandeis called up her messages. The other reporters, being on deadline, were bent to their work. Rachel rather envied them their deadlines. They lived like mayflies, a day at a time, their stories completed in a white-hot rush at the last minute and then done with and forgotten. Meanwhile, she was back on the phone, feeling less like a journalist and more like a...she wasn't sure what. She didn't work for the paper, that much was sure. She worked for Leonard Sawyer, who had come to her with a proposition she couldn't refuse.

She had more messages now. She had a couple from previous contacts, several from locals, including one from somebody named Ron, who claimed he worked for the Pack and possessed some interesting information, although he wasn't free to divulge it at the moment. About this wannabe CIA agent she had some doubts, but being able to scroll through a bunch of messages was nice.

The last one in the queue, however, although certainly the most interesting, destroyed this small pleasure. JackPack, it said, had formed a plant-closing team. If true, this would add another fillip to her stories about the company's imminent demise. Unfortunately, the source was the last person in the world Rachel cared to get unsolicited material from at the moment—none other than Leonard Sawyer himself.

She decided to call him to find where he'd gotten his information, then just as quickly decided that she had no interest in talking to the publisher. She hadn't confronted the *alter kocker* yet. She was biding her time. For the moment, she simply stewed, listening to the clacking of computer keys all around her.

Finally, having to do something, she got up and went in search of Neil Houselog. She zigzagged toward the news editor, past the other reporters, whose computer terminals were set at right angles to one another, spaced across the room like houses on suburban lots.

She told Houselog what she had and where she got it. With a silent sweep of his hand, he conducted her into the vacant room where the editors and sub-editors and sub-sub-editors held their daily story meetings. The huge oval conference table filled the space, leaving barely enough room for chairs and a coffee machine.

"Did you know about this?" she asked.

He pinched his lips together and shook his head. "No surprise," he said. "Len has his own sources."

"The union?"

"That would be a good guess. Not the union itself, but someone in the union."

"Someone who's likely to be reliable?"

"Can't tell you."

"Presumably there are people at the company who hate Peterson and would be glad to embarrass him."

Houselog nodded. "Presumably."

This was not the first conversation the two of them had had on the revenge motive, Sawyer's and others', and Rachel could already see that Neil, being powerless to alter the situation, would just as soon ignore it.

"Tell me, Neil, I've been wondering about this: am I the first, or have any other reporters been hired just to do the Pack?"

"You're the first."

Except for his walrus mustache, his face was efficient, parsimonious, but when he smiled—a smile in search of humor—deep fissures appeared, like an eroded landscape a geologist might read with profit. She had noted that with the other newsies, he could be quite funny. But one look at her apparently drove away all humorous thoughts. She was this strange new species at the paper, occupying her own ecological niche, Sawyer's hopeful monster, and Houselog just didn't want to know about it.

"As far as the plant-closing team is concerned, Rachel, you should do the usual stuff. Does the team, in fact, exist? And if so, just what does that mean? Probably in situations like this, it's all SOP."

"And suppose it is? Do we run the story?"

"Can't tell until I see the piece. But as I've said to you before, we won't violate the canons of good journalism. And we're quite aware that because Len's attitude is so well known, we run an extra risk here."

"You know," Rachel couldn't help twitting the guy, "it would have been nice if you'd told me all this on the first day." She'd complained about this before. This time he made a small concession.

"Perhaps we should have."

"And perhaps Hitler wasn't too crazy about the Jews." Could you believe this schmuck?

He studied her, as if trying to decide something. "You're right, yes. And if I could rewrite history, I would. But despite all that, you understand that there are matters of emphasis, there are honest disagreements."

"What's that supposed to mean?"

He opened his hands, palms up, as if he thought it was beginning to rain in the room.

"Anyway," he said finally, "you understand the situation now."

"Ah," she said, "I understand the situation now." She did, most definitely. And now she understood something else as well.

As she returned to her desk, Houselog's last words went with her, and with them a still sharper sense of the hard reality by which she would henceforth live. But for Leonard Sawyer, she wouldn't be there. No doubt, if Sawyer died tomorrow, she would be on the next plane back to Albany.

During the golden age—last week, that is—when she had been semi-ignorant of the old man's bloodlust, she had at least been an almost innocent victim. But now she knew in no uncertain terms. And everyone in that room knew that she knew. Now she had no one to blame but herself. Sawyer's personal motives in the matter of the Pack had become her own personal motives, whatever she might care to imagine to the contrary.

She could still quit, of course. But what would have possessed a righteous spontaneity a few days ago had in the interim become something less, something suspect, an act with its own tinge of guilt...or cowardice.

She would write the story. Probably it would be run. And there would be other stories. And she'd write them, and they'd be run. And so it would go.

Was that it? she wondered desolately. Was there nothing else she could do, some third way? She didn't know. And in this frame of mind, she set out to find if, indeed, a plant-closing team had been created at the Pack.

It had. The story was run.

# CHAPTER 22

~

After the shift, it took Fritz Goetzinger some time to find Buck Tekippe, the best butcher in the plant, who had a steady sideline regrinding blades for people. To him Fritz gave the two knives that had gone sour, and arranged to pick them up before work the next day. Then he and Billy Noel turned in their whites and drove to the Riverview for a cup of coffee.

They sat in a back booth, talking about inconsequential matters. Darlene, the waitress, silently topped off their cups after a while. Fritz yawned and massaged his wrist.

"What a day, Billy. Got to get home, attend to my animals, council meeting tonight. Never seems to end."

The coffee made no impression on his fogged brain. He knew he should be thinking about the situation at the Pack, but each time he tried, he began to fall asleep, a velvet blackness coiling about his half-formed thoughts. Yet he knew that whatever was to be done must be done quickly. If he let tonight's council meeting pass without acting, he would have to wait two weeks for another chance. Could be too late by then. Events had a way of running away with themselves.

A couple of Pack workers who had followed them into the café stopped on their way back out to exchange the latest rumors and speculate about what they might mean. Fritz went to take a leak, and by the time he got back to the table, they had left.

Even the simple act of sitting seemed to drag him toward sleep. Billy, his second cup of coffee barely touched, sat quietly, even quieter than usual. Fritz pushed his own cup aside and leaned forward, feeling the cool metal rim of the tabletop against his forearms. As parts of him seemed already to have dozed, others possessed an unnatural vividness.

"So, Billy, tell me, what do *you* think?" Fritz narrowed his focus, holding in his thoughts the question he had just asked and waiting for whatever Billy might care to say.

Billy would occasionally become talkative, when he felt strongly about something, but mostly he remained silent and watchful. As was the case with essentially good but vacillating people, he lacked the ability to act decisively. Yet others observed his sincerity and the sense of fairness, which lay at the bedrock of his character, and Fritz had noticed how often in groups someone making an argument ended up addressing it to Billy. Fritz, not given to easy relations with others, found Billy more sympathetic than almost anyone he knew, and a kind of bellwether, too, a man whose ideas, arrived at after so much earnest wrestling, had, if not inevitability, then at least the kind of substantiality totally lacking in the drivel that usually passed for wisdom.

"Talk to me, Billy. I've been watching you thinking about the situation all day long."

"I don't know, Fritz." Billy spoke to the table, a shock of his fine, light hair falling forward over his large, round forehead. "It just occurred to me, you know, how we've always said the Pack would never close. Somehow the Petersons would find a way to keep it open."

"That's what those two guys believe." Fritz jerked his thumb at the space left vacant by the departure of their co-workers.

"But it's not true." Billy looked up, his mouth open, as if he was having trouble breathing. "We're gonna close. Ain't we? We're goin' down."

Fritz could see clearly, even through his exhaustion, how much Billy had been shaken by these words, his own words.

And Fritz himself for a moment was shaken, too, freed from his lethargic state. He hadn't known what was coming. He hadn't expected anything so direct and forceful as this out of Billy. And if Billy had come this far in his reasoning, others would have, too.

"That's right," Fritz said softly to his friend, "we're going down."

Billy shook his head. "What will I tell Margaret?" When troubles arose, Fritz knew his friend always thought of his wife first, of the pain he was about to cause her.

"You'll tell her what you just told me. You'll tell her the company's going to close. You'll tell her that, and you'll tell her something else, too."

Billy said nothing, only looked at Fritz, not understanding.

"Ain't it obvious?" Fritz asked, although he knew that to Billy it would be anything but, despite that Billy himself had contributed the critical fact. If he thought the company was going down, many others must as well, Fritz was sure of it. The myths, like Arthur Vogt's, that Skip Peterson was more afraid of losing his own job than the hourly people were of losing theirs, or the widespread belief that there were two sets of books and the company's financial situation was always better than Skip ever admitted, or even the simple faith that the company was just too important to the community and would never be allowed to fail—if these fantasies had finally lost their power to bewitch people, then from this new reality flowed an inevitable conclusion. Anybody ought to see it.

But Billy was made of different stuff. His former belief in the longevity of the Pack had been built on little more than his desire always to go from here to here, and if he had now lost that faith, the other darker side of his view of things would have taken hold of him. Over the many years of their friendship, Fritz had come to understand that Billy clung to the present as an exhausted swimmer might cling to a bit of wreckage. To let go was to drown. So as obvious as the next step might be, he could never propose it. That would be left to Fritz.

"We've got to buy the Pack, Billy."

Billy did not react.

Fritz repeated himself. "The employees have got to buy the place from Peterson." As he spoke, he yawned again, his exhaustion rolling back over him. Even as he was making what might turn out to be the most important proposal of his life, he could barely stay awake. "Other folks have done that, Billy, haven't they? Companies given up for dead, then saved by their own people. Ain't that right? And I'm telling you, we can do it, too."

Billy nodded at these last assertions, but the assent, Fritz understood, didn't amount to much. Other companies had been saved, okay, but JackPack was not other companies.

"I don't think people will go for that," Billy said.

"That's because they believe Skip Peterson will find some way to keep the place going. But you said it yourself, Billy, not this time. Others know it, too, even if they don't want to admit it just yet."

Billy grimaced, trapped in his own reasoning. "I don't know."

Fritz could see his friend was closing down, the idea of buying

JackPack too enormous to talk about at the moment. Billy would have to begin the long and tortuous process of turning it over in his mind and listening to what others had to say and trying to hear what his own heart was telling him. Fritz understood all this. Later Billy would have some further contribution to make. But now, no.

"Okay, Billy," Fritz told him, "don't worry about it. Just remember what you said. The plant's going down. That's God's own truth, Billy. You remember that."

But *something* had to be done. And Fritz would have to do it. There was nobody else.

# CHAPTER 23

~

In the city council chambers, which were dim and cooler than the rest of the building, Rachel Brandeis felt a little odd, as she always did in places reserved to public ritual. The thick wooden columns and high ceiling were out of proportion, giving a sort of comic seriousness to the smallish room, like the kind of distortion you see in political cartoons. Across the back wall, a mural had been painted, a rural-to-urban panorama, badly faded.

Bruce Moss, in his official capacity as the *Trib*'s city hall reporter, sat with others at the press table. As soon as she saw the man sitting next to him, however, Rachel lost all interest in Bruce.

She would have talked to Fritz Goetzinger first, except that the meeting was on the point of being called to order, so she turned her attention back to the press table. Bruce obviously didn't know quite what to make of her sudden appearance, whether she'd come to poach or what.

"The mayor called me," she said.

Then she looked at the large black man next to him, without a doubt the very same man she'd seen walking out of the radio station the other day. At the council table, Goetzinger was already gaveling the meeting to order.

She lowered her voice as she reached out to shake hands. "Rachel Brandeis."

"Ah. The lady with the exclusive." Despite his formidable appearance, the black man barely squeezed her hand as they shook, leaving more a sense of texture than pressure. "Johnny Pond," he said, also sotto voce, "KJAX. Here, sit with us."

All the seats at the table were taken, and so Pond reached back to the first row of spectator chairs and grabbed one. "Scooch over there, Bruce. Let the lady in."

The mayor was already speaking, and so they settled down to attend to the meeting, leaving the getting-acquainted for later.

The proceedings began pretty much as all such gatherings in her experience, an invocation by one of the local ministers followed by proclamations. The five council members, including Mayor Goetzinger, sat in high-backed leather chairs, in which they could lean back and swivel around, masters of their domain, surveying the citizenry through lowered lids as these opening ceremonies were gotten out of the way.

Rachel sat jammed between Pond and Bruce, feeling the large man's heat from one side and nothing from the other.

A report on the progress at the dog track came next. Then—as the items to be set for public hearings were about to be considered—the mayor made his move.

"Before we go any further," he said, "I've got something to say about the situation at the Jackson Packing Company."

The message on her desk late that afternoon from Goetzinger had suggested she might want to come to the meeting, that something interesting might happen. And so she thought, Okay, here we go.

"Point of order, Mr. Mayor," one of the men on the council interrupted Goetzinger. "This matter isn't on the agenda, and with all due respect, you have a clear conflict of interest here since you work at the Pack."

"That's Bob Pfohl," Johnny Pond leaned over and whispered, "the parliamentarian on the council."

"I see," Rachel whispered back. She knew Goetzinger, of course, but the other four council members—two women and two men—were pretty much terra incognita. She had heard of several of them, had read a few stories about them, but she couldn't have put names to faces without the little nameplates in front of each chair. Pfohl, however, was totally unknown to her. At that distance, his face appeared to be hardly more than a quick sketch, all his emotions residing in his dark eyes, his nose and mouth barely visible, suggested by the small shadows they cast. "Does he do this all the time, or is it just that he's no friend of the mayor?" Rachel and Johnny Pond leaned even closer to speak under their breath, too close to look directly at each other, so that the feeling Rachel had was simultaneously of intimacy and distance.

"Nobody's a friend of the mayor," Pond whispered. "They all have their weapons of choice."

The city attorney was reading out the appropriate statutory language from the Iowa Code, which supported Fritz Goetzinger's interpretation of the situation.

Pfohl, however, wasn't quite ready to back down. "That still leaves the fact that this isn't on the agenda. I'm tired of getting blindsided all the time."

Goetzinger, with his piebald hair and complex frown, stared straight ahead, as if his head was held in a vice. He spoke with sharp emphasis and impatience. "With the indulgence of the council, this is a matter of two thousand jobs. Does Councilman Pfohl claim that his point of order is more important than two thousand jobs?"

"You do this to us all the time, Fritz," Pfohl said, addressing Goetzinger directly and with what appeared to be deeply felt sincerity.

"Does Councilman Pfohl claim that his point of order is more important than two thousand jobs?" Goetzinger demanded again, his eyes still fixed rigidly forward.

The councilman formed a single silent word, "Shit," before subsiding into his chair with, "No, of course not. Say what you want to say."

And so, on both issues, Pfohl had been routed, but the exchange had provided Rachel with a little more of the lay of the land, a sense of the almost spooky implacability of the mayor when his ire was raised.

He now looked slowly left and right, taking in the other council members, silently inviting them to object if they wished. None did.

The two cameras of the local-access channel, one on either side of the room, dollied forward and focused in on the mayor as he prepared to speak.

"First off," he said, "I want to acknowledge the presence in the chamber of Miss Rachel Brandeis."

Rachel went rigid.

"I would like Miss Brandeis," the mayor continued matter-of-factly, "to confirm for the benefit of the people in this room and for those watching in their homes that the stories she wrote and which have been published in the *Tribune* over the last several days are correct. Can you do that for us, Miss Brandeis?"

Conscious of the eyes of the other council members on her and that the TV cameras had swung quickly around and now pointed directly at her, Rachel said, "I stand by what I wrote."

The mayor wasn't satisfied. "I'm sorry, Miss Brandeis, could you speak a little louder? I'm not sure everybody heard."

"Yes. I stand by what I wrote," she repeated, speaking more than loud enough this time.

"Thank you."

This affirmation in hand, Goetzinger went on with what he intended to say, leaving Rachel to make what she would out of what had just happened. The other council members were still inspecting her with interest.

Pond leaned over. "Looks like the mayor had his own reasons for inviting you up here."

Rachel realized that, yes, indeed, Goetzinger had done it to her again. First pig fucking, now Rachel Brandeis, Exhibit A. Yet she felt a kind of thrill, too, as if she had suddenly become visible after her ghostly existence at the paper. Goetzinger had pointed out that her story had an author and that she was here, among them.

As she mused over these somewhat contradictory feelings, she only half listened to what he was saying. Most of it, anyway, was just the obvious blah-blah about saving the dear old Pack. Only when he got to the nub of the matter, a proposal that the employees buy the company, did she perk up and begin to take notes. Here was something new.

Finally, she leaned over to Pond. "Could he actually pull that off?"

"Leading a buyout?"

"Yes."

Pond shook his head. "Probably not."

The attention of the other council members had not long remained on her, but from time to time she saw one or the other of them turn back toward her and spend some moments in contemplation.

Woodward and Bernstein had become famous, of course, but they were the exceptions that proved the rule. Reporters were supposed to be the anonymous chroniclers of the times. And Rachel certainly wasn't in Jackson to become a celebrity, just to add to her clips and then get the hell out. Yet, for the moment, she enjoyed being visible, perhaps even a little notorious. Yes, that was a bit of okay.

She remained in the meeting through the public hearings and then the first of the items on the agenda requiring council action. From time to time, Johnny Pond would lean over to impart a nugget of information. He had peppermint on his breath. He leaned lightly against her each time he spoke. She found him rather puzzling. The man who had come out of the radio station the other day had carried a certain hauteur about him, a person who would insist most definitely upon his territorial integrity. Yet the Johnny Pond she was sitting next to appeared quite comfortable in these close quarters, modest, easily familiar, with no more territorial sense than a penguin.

At the break, she sought out the mayor with the idea of giving him a piece of her mind again, but she hesitated when, close at hand, she realized the man was exhausted, practically out on his feet. He drew her aside, over to an unoccupied corner of the room, partially screened by towers of electrical equipment.

"I would appreciate it, Mr. Mayor, if you'd let me know in the future when you plan to drag me in front of everybody."

"Not important," he said and started to continue but she interrupted.

"It's important to me."

"All right, fine," he said brusquely, then at once returned to what he wanted to say. "Tell me again, this story of yours, how confident are you that it's true? This isn't Sawyer, is it?"

"I beg your pardon."

"If this stuff is coming from Leonard Sawyer, I need to be absolutely sure."

"I'm not going to respond to that."

"All right. But you're certain...about this source you found who'd talk to you. This is somebody who knows what he's talking about?"

"Who said it was a he?"

"This person then." He eyed her as if trying to decide whether it might actually be a woman, whether that possibility might make sense. "You're sure? That's all I want to know, Rachel."

"I stand by what I said in the meeting."

"No doubts." He clutched a hand in front of his midsection. "This is important. There's no point in pursuing an employee buyout unless there's no other way."

Did she have any doubts at all? "I'm confident that some form of bankruptcy has been discussed, Fritz. I'm even more confident that all the numbers are running against the Pack. Beyond that, I can't say."

He relaxed.

"That will do. That's enough. I think you've got it right. I think a buyout's the only way."

He was speaking rapidly and briefly, like an exhausted athlete trying to end each point as quickly as he could. "This is the next thing you've gotta do—" he started up again but she interrupted.

"I'll make that choice, if you don't mind." She already worked for one asshole, and one was quite enough. And more important, she knew enough about Goetzinger to understand that the only way to deal with him was by meeting strength with strength.

"No, listen to me," he rushed on, undeterred. "You've got to convince people."

"Of what?"

"You've written these stories. You've piled up all this evidence. Makes no difference. Most everyone believes Peterson's denial. They want to believe him."

"I'm a reporter, Mr. Mayor. What people choose to believe is their own business."

He ignored this. "You got to do more digging."

"Is that right?"

"That's right. You want people to believe you, you got to do even better. All right?" He raised his eyebrows, and for a moment his face became open and questioning. But only for a moment, as a seal on all that he'd just said. "All right," he repeated.

She asked her own questions, but it became clear at once that the buyout idea had just occurred to Goetzinger, and he had nothing to add to what he'd said at the council table.

When the interview ended, she watched the retreating figure, his exhaustion evident even from the back, and her first thought was, no, she didn't care if people believed her stories or not. She put them out there, how people took them or what they did with them, well, that just wasn't her business.

With this conviction in hand, she got ready to leave, having no reason to stay for the rest of the meeting. She walked over and arranged with Bruce to write a companion piece to his general account of the meeting. She said good-bye to Johnny Pond.

Before she left, Pond introduced her to the other reporters, and in this way, she found that she was already quite well-known to the local news establishment, who had been doing their own pieces for the past several days, basically cribbing off her material. For a few minutes before she left, she enjoyed being the center of attention at the press table. Invisible no more.

# CHAPTER 24

~

After the lunch break on Friday, Cletus Dickey came over to the construction trailer just to shoot the breeze. He walked around, peeling back pages of the sheaf of blueprints on the drawing board like somebody looking for dirt under a rug, reading the papers on Don Adagian's desk, inspecting the detailing of the trailer itself. Don was reminded of the lame old dog that accompanied one of the day laborers to the job site. "Is he applying for work?" someone had joked. The dog wandered aimlessly, sniffing here and there, stopping to scratch or attend some other minor personal need, ignoring the workers as if it had spent too much time with humans to have any illusions left. That was Clete, cynical but sniffing, always sniffing.

At the moment, his canine interest had come to a focus on something outside the miniature picture window above Don's desk. "Well, well, well, what have we here?"

Even before he'd spoken, Don had heard the unmistakable sound of car tires skidding on the gravel access road, and by the time he turned to look, car doors had slammed shut and three men were stalking toward the site.

"Shit."

John McDermott led, followed by two of his flunkies, one of them the inspector that the civil engineer had been sending over to keep tabs on the methane system as Cletus's people installed it.

"My boss tells me one thing," Clete said as he hitched up his pants and sauntered toward the door. "Don't let McDermott fuck us over. You coming?"

"I suppose. Got something to do first."

"Suit yourself."

As soon as Clete had left, Don called uptown and told the secretary that Jack Kelley better get himself down to the job site ASAP.

Then he sat down and debated whether he should go talk to McDermott or wait for Kelley. He didn't want to go outside. He hated it when people started climbing all over his shit. On the other hand, maybe McDermott didn't have a hair up his ass. Maybe this had nothing to do with who got the blame when the grandstand blew up. If the visit was friendly, Cletus could handle it, he didn't need any help from Don. Then again, sitting in that perfectly quiet trailer, Don couldn't help but wonder just what the hell was going on.

In this way, he cycled through his small set of pros and cons, and had begun on a second run-through when somebody knocked.

"Yeah?"

One of the laborers working for Clete stuck his head in the door. "Cletus says you should come."

"Yeah, yeah, tell him I'm working on it."

Left alone again, Don decided he might as well. He had no desire in the world to tangle with McDermott, but he might as well go. What the hell. From his desk he took a small bottle of eyedrops, and tipping his head back, squeezed a couple of drops into each eye. Then he downed four aspirin. Then he got up.

He stepped outside and looked back along the access road. No sign of Kelley.

By the time he walked through the gap left in the western end of the grade beam, McDermott was already returning from the area where the methane barrier had been glued. Even at that distance, Don could tell that some of the plastic had been ripped free.

McDermott bore down, still a half dozen paces away but already talking at Don. "I don't know what the hell you people think you're doing here. This is goddamn gas we're dealing with, did anybody tell you that?"

"What's the problem, John?"

McDermott was short, square-shouldered, a slab of a man with a sunken chest, as if his heart had been removed. "What's the problem?" he snapped. "I like that. Installation's gotta be flawless, that's what the fucking problem is. I don't believe this. First you try to hide in the trailer there, and now you pretend you're just totally fucking ignorant of what's going on out here."

Don looked at Cletus, who said, "Mr. McDermott claims that he found a place where the membrane wasn't glued."

"Are you calling me a liar?" McDermott turned on him.

"I'm not calling anybody anything."

"Where wasn't it glued?" Don asked.

"Find it for yourself. What the fuck good are you if you're not out here inspecting the work?" McDermott, even as he continued talking, had ceased paying attention to Cletus and Don and begun to look intently around his feet.

"I'm not an inspector," Don told him, thinking he'd better make a statement for the record. "Our position, John, is that your man Phil here is to inspect and to relay supplemental information from you to Cletus Dickey." Phil stood as far away from his boss as he could without appearing to be disconnected from the group entirely.

"What the hell is this?" McDermott knelt down and scooped up a handful of the aggregate in which the pipes used to vent the methane were to be buried. "This is supposed to be clean fill. Look at this!" He held it out to Don. "Look at all the goddamn fines in it!"

They were standing immediately south of the temporary ramp through the west end of the foundation.

Shit, thought Don. "The excavation contractor has been removing his surplus sand from the southwest corner of the foundation. When that's done, we'll replace this with clean."

McDermott flung the material down.

"It's clear to me," he said, standing up and dusting off his hands, "that you people just don't give a shit."

And with this parting shot, he stalked off, his unhappy subordinates forming a kind of rear guard.

By the time Jack Kelley arrived, McDermott was long gone. Don told him what had happened, watching Jack's expression grow darker, and every time Clete Dickey seconded something, Don winced, waiting for Jack to start laying into both of them for the way they'd handled the situation. But Jack just continued to listen and then said, "Show me," and they walked out to the pile cap with the membrane pulled loose and inspected the seam where it had been installed, looking for the place where McDermott claimed the plastic had been left unglued. When they didn't find anything, Don felt a little better.

"The fucker tried to tell me we should be doing the inspection, Jack. I told him that's not the CM's job."

Kelley nodded.

Next it was Cletus's turn. "We want one of McDermott's people out here, full-time, and my boss says we're not gonna do shit on the basis of verbal orders anymore. We don't proceed until McDermott confirms, in writing, that his design works."

Again Kelley nodded.

They ended up back near the temporary ramp where McDermott had discovered the fines in the washed stone.

"You explained we planned to undercut this area and replace with clean aggregate?" Kelley asked Don.

"Yes."

"Good."

"Tell him what McDermott said when he left, Donny."

Don told him. Kelley nodded. He even managed a smile of sorts. The expected outburst not having come, Don began to feel considerably better.

"Okay," Kelley said to Don, "what I need from you is a memo for the file. Details. Leave nothing out, including McDermott's parting shot."

"You got it."

"And I want it yesterday."

That was all, not a hint of criticism. They talked about other steps to be taken, practical stuff, and then Jack left as abruptly as he had come.

Don returned to the trailer and began working on the memo.

Late in the afternoon, Clete paid another visit, and the two of them discussed what had happened and agreed that, all in all, their asses were pretty well covered for the moment. Don felt good. For once, somebody else was the villain.

"So, wha'd'ya say, Donny," Clete suggested, "how's about a little celebration? There's a game tonight. You say the word, I'll get you into it."

"I don't know, Clete."

Probably, Don thought, he should treat this business as a second chance and become a monk or something.

Yet he felt damn good, too, a kind of grinning inside that, with a little effort, might be turned into laughter. What would it hurt to have a little fun after the misery of the last several weeks? He'd never had a break since the last job. Was one night too much to ask?

"What kind of game?" he asked.

"Dealer's choice. Nothing fancy. Mostly we play seven card stud."

Don liked that. He enjoyed different kinds of poker but hadn't played enough to get good at the Hold'em games that had started to get so popular.

"You gotta have five hundred to sit down," Clete said.

Don only had about three hundred dollars in his bank account at the moment. Perhaps, he thought again, he shouldn't. "No problem," he said anyway, thinking what the hell, he felt good for once. This was starting to look like his lucky day, and he might as well grab for the brass ring while he had the chance.

# CHAPTER 25

～

Jack Kelley sat up straight and listened. The ultramodern public rooms of Steadman and Associates—Jack's firm, the firm with the construction management contract for the track—had been furnished with museum-quality antiques, and on quiet afternoons such as this, the plangent knelling of the grandfather clock in the reception area would carry through the corridors, reaching even Jack's afterthought of an office at the far reaches of the floor. He counted the chimes. Four. Four o'clock. The time for the opening at City Hall of bid pack C for the dog track—plumbing, HVAC, sprinkler…and electrical. His old friend Tony Vasconcellos.

Earlier in the day, he'd checked to see who had submitted bids, a useless exercise since contractors often hand-carried their proposals to the opening itself, and so when he discovered that Vasconcellos hadn't yet submitted anything, that proved nothing, except perhaps the depth of Jack's own anxiety over the matter.

He pushed aside the schedule he'd been fretting over and held himself perfectly still, as if he might hear several blocks away the sound of envelopes being broached by Mark O'Banion and the amounts read off. He knew that that was exactly what was happening, for bids were opened with the promptness of space shots and executions.

Despite his quiet word with the insurance agent, Jack couldn't shake the idea that Vasconcellos might have gotten his bid bond, anyway, and that Jack's attempt to cut his legs out from under him been wasted, perhaps even revealed.

He waited until nearly five before calling public works to ask about the results. The secretary said she'd go get them, but then, without Jack having asked for him, Mark O'Banion came on the line.

"What's up?" he asked.

It wouldn't do to seem too anxious, so Jack started off with, "McDermott showed up at the site today. He threw a fit, claiming the installation wasn't being done properly."

"Is it?"

"According to the specs."

Jack paused to let Mark consider this intelligence.

"I suppose," Mark said, "we ought to get all the principals together and thrash the thing out."

"Suppose."

They chatted about this for a couple of minutes, and then Mark said, "Joyce told me you were interested in the results of the bid opening."

"Yes."

"Any one in particular?"

"No," Jack lied.

Mark rattled off the low bids.

"Electrical," he said when he got to it, "now there's a bit of a surprise. Tony Vasconcellos."

Jack made an effort to sound conversational as he observed, "Wouldn't think he could get bonded for a job this big."

"As a matter of fact, he didn't."

"He came up with the ten percent?" Jack didn't even try to disguise his shock. Vasconcellos had come up with sixty thou in lieu of the bid bond? Impossible.

"Got the check right here in front of me," Mark said.

Where the hell, Jack wondered, could Vasconcellos get that kind of money? It took him only moments to come up with an answer. Mike Daugherty, that's where. Father Mike must have twisted the arm of one of the wealthy parishioners and gotten him to pony up a loan, no doubt at a favorable rate of interest in the spirit of the enterprise. All Jack's subterfuge, all his elaborate efforts to help Vasconcellos and screw him at the same time, had accomplished nothing but put another parishioner in jeopardy. Damn Father Mike!

He finished his conversation with Mark O'Banion as quickly as he could and sat gloomily reviewing the history of this debacle, one moment cursing Mike for his determination, the next himself for his own duplicity in the business. He perceived as well the bitter humor in the situation. And the justice, too.

Along the still corridors of Steadman and Associates, the report of the grandfather clock rolled, five times.

On his way out of the building, Jack encountered Don Adagian, coming in and looking worried.

"Now what's happened?"

"Nothing. I just wanted to see you."

"Yes?"

They were standing in the reception area, surrounded by cream yellow walls and two-hundred-year-old mahogany furniture. Adagian still had on his work clothes, but he had made some effort to tidy himself up, his hair still damp from a combing, his shirt snug from a tucking. No doubt it being Friday night he would go out and drink himself into a stupor. At the moment, however, Jack envied him his simple defects.

He needed money.

"A couple hundred, that's all, Jack, to make up what I'm supposed to send for child support this month."

Jack chewed on the corner of his mouth as he considered the request. He didn't believe Don, and another time, he would have refused the request. At the moment, however, still oppressed by his role in the Vasconcellos bid fiasco, he felt a need to trust in something; if not in Adagian, then in his own capacity for generosity.

Perhaps Don was telling the truth. Perhaps he did need money to help support his kid. Perhaps in this way he sustained whatever tenuous grasp he retained on a responsible life. At least Jack was prepared to entertain such an idea.

"What did you say your daughter's name was again?"

"Donna Maxine Adagian. Her friends call her Max. She was named after me, would you believe it?" Jack found something appealing in the sheepish grin that accompanied this acknowledgment of the improbability of such a state of affairs.

"How are things with your wife at the moment?"

Adagian shrugged. Jack didn't know much about his personal life, or want to know much. Don was separated, which seemed about right, since he didn't impress Jack as a man with the gift of finishing projects decisively, not that Jack as a good Catholic would wish a divorce on anyone.

"Perhaps," he said as he took his wallet out, "you'll be able to patch it up."

"I don't know. Maybe. Hope so."

Jack started to hand the money over, then drew it back.

"If you could settle down and get through this job in good

order, who knows what might happen?" Jack eyed his field manager, who seemed to be making an effort not to look at the money. "I mean it, Don."

"Yeah, I know, Jack. You don't have to worry about me, I'll be okay."

"I hope so."

Finally, he relinquished the bills, and Don in a few moments had thanked him and given him the payment of a couple more assurances of his good behavior in the future and disappeared out the door.

Jack listened to the elevator open and close in the distance, and he regretted the promises he had felt compelled to extract from the fellow. The money, after all, had not been given on condition. It had nothing to do with Don at all, only with Jack's own desire to perform an act of generosity, however slight, an act uncontaminated by other motives. He saw now that he hadn't been able to do even that.

# CHAPTER 26

~

Chuck Fellows sat in his office staring at the grid of USGS maps on the opposite wall. At that distance, he couldn't make out detail, just color and shape. The Mississippi flowed south, leaving one map and entering the next, while along its tributaries and the tributaries of tributaries, the green woodland fringes were as complex as the bronchial trees of lungs. Chuck loved the topo maps— the great blue artery of the river, the dendritic green of the creek bottoms, the fine network of red contour lines invisible at that distance but present nevertheless in his mind's eye. He loved the complexity of the map, the hint in it of military campaigns and so, for him, memories of Vietnam.

Five o'clock had come and gone, but he continued to sit there, doing nothing, thinking about nothing.

Finally, Mark O'Banion looked in and made a great show of checking his watch and then said, "Go home."

Chuck didn't react.

"Go home," Mark repeated. "Talk to your wife about Yellowbelly."

"You mean Yellowknife."

"Isn't that what I said?"

Chuck had no interest in talking to Diane. What he wanted to do was go out and get hammered.

He and Mark walked out to their cars together, taking their time, as men who enjoy each other's company will. Mark brought him up-to-date on the methane controversy, concluding, "The design is questionable, as we knew. McDermott's claiming the problem is shoddy installation."

"Figures." Chuck had had a couple of run-ins with McDermott, a real piece of work. "So what are they going to do?"

"Consult their lawyers."

Chuck snorted.

"Jack Kelly called and pleaded his side of the case," Mark continued. "Do you know Kelley? No. Doesn't matter, not your type. Not into tundra and polar bears and such. I called McDermott up, too, and he's talking about some sort of backup system."

"Like maybe fans?"

"Yeah."

"Redundancy." He and Mark had had this conversation before, so Chuck had the sense of a solution foreordained. But Mark was clearly unhappy. He rubbed his thumb and first two fingers together—money.

"What choice you got?"

"None. But I dream of some elegant solution."

"Elegant? John McDermott? That great exponent of meatball engineering. You gotta be kidding." They stood next to Mark's Caddy. Chuck was concerned about him. Mark had too much of a stake in being a nice guy. "Just make sure McDermott signs off on the installation when it's in."

"Not to worry."

Chuck stared at the camera hanging around Mark's neck.

"What's that for?"

"Going down to the track to take my weekly progress pictures."

Chuck nodded. Mark was good about shit like that. His mind was filled with little alarm clocks that went off at appropriate times.

"And you," Mark asked, "what are you going to do?"

Chuck shook his head. "Stuff around the house. Place is falling in."

Neither of these last subjects offered much of interest and so they stood, uncomfortable, yet reluctant to go their separate ways. Chuck thought about the other matters pending between them. The drafting position. Yellowknife. He noted how often their recent conversations had ended in awkwardness. This one, too.

～

As Mark drove down to take his pictures, he thought about the same matters, felt the same awkwardness and regretted them as keenly. He could see no way around the issues involved.

He still hadn't made a decision about the position up in the drafting room, but he couldn't sit on it forever. As for Yellowknife, presumably Chuck would have to fly up for an interview at some point, unless the place was so out-of-the-way that they hired mail-order engineers. Perhaps the Northwest Territory, or whatever the province was called, would finally prove too raw even for Chuck's taste, although given the man's antipodean personality, Mark didn't hold out much hope.

He parked the Caddy near the construction trailer. The site still had the embryonic look of all projects in their early stages. But he didn't mind. He enjoyed construction sites. They took him back to his beginnings in the city, so long ago, working as a project manager for his future father-in-law.

He checked to make sure he had enough film in the camera and then walked to a preselected spot near the northwest corner of the grandstand and took several shots, gradually panning from north to south. Each Friday, he would take similar pictures and thus, in a kind of time-lapse photography, capture the growth of the track.

He had been making similar recordings of job-site progress all his life, but after the pictures were developed, he never looked at them. Occasionally, when Helen nagged at him or he nagged at himself, he would promise to sort them all out, and maybe he would. "One day, one day." Yet, that prospect only made him sad. The point in taking pictures, as in anything else, was the doing of the thing. It helped bring his attention more sharply to the matter at hand.

And so he walked the site, paying attention. He talked aloud to himself, which he liked to do when alone. It was a stage of childhood that he had never quite outgrown. He stopped from time to time and turned this way and that, as if looking for a key point of view, that single vantage from which to capture the essence of the place.

Over by the kennel area, many of the piles for the foundation had been driven to refusal but not cut off or filled with concrete yet. They stuck up at different levels, like the pipes of a giant sub-terranean organ. He walked into and out of their shadows as he started back toward the grandstand, singing snatches of "A Mighty Fortress Is Our God."

In the distance, he heard the long, low whistle of a train and stopped briefly and turned to look toward the other side of the river, where a Burlington Northern freight moved slowly northward. For no particular reason, he took a picture.

"Odd, what makes you sad."

Then he continued his progress back into the center of the site, no longer sharply aware of his surroundings and so at the mercy of unharnessed thoughts.

He thought about Jack Kelley's man, Adagian. The last time he'd seen him, he'd shown every sign of being hung over. "I should go talk to him. If I don't do it, and the fellow self-destructs, how will I feel then?"

He was about to go on blaming himself should something happen when he remembered the Serenity Prayer. "Watch yourself, Mark." Know the difference between what you can change and what you can't.

At the grade beam, a black flap of vapor barrier material hung loose, the glue on the concrete behind it of a dirty mustard color. Probably that was where the confrontation between McDermott and the construction people had occurred earlier.

He took a picture.

# CHAPTER 27

~

The pool hall's back room was defined mostly by what was missing. There were no pictures on the walls, no furniture except for the battered old dining room table in the middle and an assortment of mismatched, hard-backed chairs. Empty beer cartons were piled haphazardly in one corner. The only light, hanging above the table, matched the lights above the pool tables in the other room. But the drop ceiling, which had been installed out front in a halfhearted attempt at a family-room atmosphere, hadn't been extended to the storage area, and so above the single light was a dark void, the ceiling invisible. And if the other room, with its beer and cigarette advertisements, displayed a kind of carnival barker's attitude toward its human occupants, this room remained utterly indifferent to the card players who had gathered in it.

Seven players sat in various poses around the table. Except for Cletus, Don Adagian had only learned first names. All Don needed to know about the others the game itself quickly revealed—the talkative, the taciturn, the hopeful, the victimized. They played far into the night, long after the muffled clicks of the pool balls and chatter of voices from the other room had ceased and left them alone.

Among the players, the best was a fellow about Don's age who Don knew only by his nickname—Deuce.

At first, Don won, and the others kidded Cletus about bringing a ringer into the game. The cards were falling Don's way, and he was thoroughly enjoying himself except for the lingering suspicion that, despite Clete's assurances, the game might not be honest. At first, they let you win.

Don wasn't worried so much about shaved cards as signaling. In a town like Jackson, that was the way buddies cleaned out a stranger. He watched the other players as best he could, but he found it difficult. The gestures across the table could have been hand signals, or just the way that friends will sometimes become mirrors of each other. Finally, after he really got caught up in the excitement of the game, he forgot to watch anymore for the cheating. He abandoned himself to his fate.

The player known as Deuce seemed quite off-handed, a little bored, a little hostile. When someone started talking about the meatpacking company, he said, annoyed, "Are we here to play cards or what?" He sat at an angle in his chair and dealt the cards with casual flicks of the wrist. The performance had a ritual exactitude about it, only partly undermined by his disdain.

From time to time, when an aggressive bet was made, he would glance at the player with raised eyebrow, the feigning of surprise.

He wasn't a particularly handsome man—not as good looking as himself, Don noted with pleasure—but nevertheless something about the fellow suggested that he probably had good luck with the women.

When he spoke, his voice was deep, and missed beats, like an engine misfiring. He might have had laryngitis from too much talking, although, as a matter of fact, during the game, he said almost nothing.

Don looked at him and thought how unsatisfactory his own life was.

Deuce dealt. Five card stud. An ancient game, going out of favor, but one Don liked for its simplicity.

"The ace bets," Deuce said. The ace was his, and he put five bucks into the pot. Two of the other players dropped immediately. Don had a queen showing and a four in the hole, no help. But the cards were still falling his way. He had to make it before they started to go bad on him. He stayed.

The hand continued. The next card helped no one. Deuce put another five-spot into the pot. Everybody else dropped, except Don, who hesitated, then stayed. Deuce looked at him with raised eyebrow. All that showed was Don's queen high and Deuce's ace.

The next card to Don was another queen. He smiled and bet ten on the pair. Deuce still showed nothing but the ace high. He studied Don, then casually dropped a tenner into the small pile of money in the middle of the table.

The last card helped neither one of them. Don bet twenty.

Deuce paused but only briefly. "You probably got that third queen, but I think I just gotta see for myself." He put his own twenty into the pot and then turned over his hole card, a second ace.

Disgusted, Don threw the four he had in the hole into the middle of the table and leaned back shaking his head. At once he felt a foreboding, beginning as a slight constriction in the chest.

Deuce, having raked in the pot, looked at Don narrowly. "Does your friend like to advertise, Clete?"

"Donny's just a simple country boy, ain't that right, Donny?"

Don said nothing, but the suspicion returned that maybe he was being set up, even though he had blundered in the last hand and had nobody to blame but himself.

The next went no better, and the ebullience of a few minutes earlier began to desert him. Finally, they took a break, and with relief Don got up from the table. He and Cletus opened beers and stood over to one side talking about the hand which Don had lost with the pair of queens.

"You should've got out after the third card."

"But I just had a feeling. You know what I mean?"

"Yeah, I know, but you still should've got out. Deuce wouldn't have stayed without he had that second ace."

Don asked him about Deuce.

"He's the mayor's son. Fritz Goetzinger Jr. That's where the nickname comes from."

"Plays a pretty fair hand of cards."

"He's had a lot of practice."

One of the other players approached them, and that ended the conversation.

Playing once more, Don listened to the insiders' chatter and felt isolated. At first, when he had known nothing about the others, it had been as if seven strangers had met to play together. But as the evening progressed, he sensed more strongly the bonds that held these people together, the small society that they had created for themselves.

Each lost hand seemed to separate him farther from the others. He played more cautiously now, but his stake slowly dribbled away. The cards had completely deserted him. His moods alternated among hope, the onset of despair, and resignation.

As he played, his attention funneled down until his field of vision had become very narrow. He felt strange, as if he was thinking very clearly but about the wrong things.

At the next break Deuce came over and asked Don about himself, what he did. He questioned Don with the same precision and offhandedness with which he dealt the cards. He seemed like the kind of person who didn't believe what people said, and so Don added more details than he would have otherwise. When they separated to go back to the game, Don felt like he did after he lost that first hand.

Picking up the way Cletus addressed him, Deuce started calling him "Donny." "How many cards, Donny?" "Donny's staying with the little pair." He probably didn't mean anything by it, but Don sensed dismissal, as if he had been judged and found wanting.

Whereas Don would look at his hole cards several times during a hand, Deuce glanced at his only once. Thereafter his attention was focused on the other players. He smiled occasionally, but not in a way that conveyed any useful information. He seemed rather more like a casual spectator than someone with money on the line. Don had the sense that part of the reason he was such a good player was that, deep down, he didn't give a shit if he won or lost.

Just after four a.m. and down to his last fifty bucks, Don caught a strong hand, a pair of aces in the hole, seven-card stud. Cletus had the deal. Everybody anted up and on third street, Don caught a ten of diamonds. No help.

"King bets," Cletus said. For five bucks, everybody stayed.

"Family pot, gentlemen." Cletus dealt the fourth card. "Treys bet." Deuce had the little pair. He tossed a ten-spot into the pot. One person dropped, the rest stayed.

On fifth street, Cletus said as he dealt, "No help, no help, no help, no help, no help, treys still bet." With each useless card he had received, Don's despondency intensified. Deuce glanced at all the trash showing and bet another tenner. One more player folded.

Nearly two hundred in the pot already. Don had his wired pair and a possible round-the-corner straight, Goetzinger, the pair of threes with one other showing on the board.

Cletus dealt, sixth street, and Don caught his third ace. Trips.

One of the other players caught a pair. "Tens bet," Cletus told the table. The raise was timid, five dollars, and Don bumped it another five. He looked forlornly at his stake, only fifteen left.

As the bet came around to Deuce, he nodded toward Don,

"The big dog bets ten," then saw the bet. Son of a bitch, Don thought. Two more dropped, leaving only Don, Deuce, and the pair of tens.

Clete dealt the last card. "Down and dirty. Tens still bet."

If Don could pull a pair, he'd have a full house, bulletproof against anything but four of a kind or better. He paused and took a breath, then pried up the corner of his last hole card—three of clubs. No pair. In his disappointment, it took him a moment before he realized he had caught his straight. He also had Goetzinger's last three.

The tens made another timid raise, five again. Probably he was sitting on three of a kind. Goetzinger still had shit showing, a possible flush if he had three spades in the hole, a possible full house if he had either of two pairs. Don looked at the litter of cards on the table. Most likely the bastard had been wired, too, and playing with two pair from fourth street on, looking to fill.

All at once Don knew he was going to lose. He didn't know how he knew. He just knew. Within the confusion of all his thoughts about the hands in front of him, within his own confusion of emotions—anger, desire, guilt, grief—he knew for sure that one thing. He was going to lose.

Too late, too late. He put the last of his stake in the pot, a raise of ten. Goetzinger saw the bet, so did pair of tens.

"What'cha got, Donny?"

"Straight, round the corner." His hands quivered slightly as he turned over his cards and fanned them out.

Goetzinger leaned over the table and made a great show of looking down at them and nodding his head. "Not bad. Doesn't beat a flush, though." And he laid out his own cards, five black ones.

"Or a full house," said the pair of tens, flipping his hole cards over triumphantly, a third ten and two sevens.

Goetzinger just laughed and leaned back, apparently more pleased with his losing hand than any of the many hands he'd won that night. As for Don, the fact that both of the other hands had beaten his just intensified the bleakness he felt.

"That's it. I'm tapped out."

Cletus came with him to the door. Don was shaking, like a man with a fever.

"You need some money, buddy?" Clete whispered.

"I'm okay."

"Here." He pushed a twenty into Don's hand. "This'll get you through the weekend."

"Thanks."

"You'll be okay. Hang in there. I'll see you Monday."

It was after four a.m. when Don got back to the marina. He stared across the harbor at Kate's houseboat, which rode at anchor, perfectly still, in its silence and darkness berating him for his excesses.

# CHAPTER 28

~

In any marriage that has survived as long as twenty-eight years, eccentricities are accommodated, however imperfectly. And so, as she did on particularly nice mornings such as this one, El Plowman had taken her breakfast out to the dining room in order to enjoy the view of their yard, and beyond it, from their bluff-top perch, the cityscape. The vista from the kitchen was as nice, but her husband Walter insisted on keeping the blinds drawn. He never looked outside in the morning. He told her he didn't want to see the sky before he was ready to go to work any more than she wanted to read reports from city staffers. The logic was pure Walter. He had been a TV weatherman for nearly thirty years and apparently envisioned the sky as something like a giant in-basket full of his day's work, something not to be dealt with on an empty stomach. It wasn't worth making an issue over. When she was feeling particularly pecky, El would describe the weather for him from her vantage in the other room, and he would cover his ears and sing out, "I can't hear you!"

This morning they had been sitting quietly in their separate niches, El contemplating her old rose garden through the French doors while Walter in the other room tried to decide whether to tell her about his conversation with Fritz Goetzinger the day before. A delicate matter this, for El in her years on the city council had come to share the other council members' communal hatred of the mayor. At the mention of his name, she could be counted on to make some snide comment, which Walter would take a little more personally than he should. Yet, his desire at the moment to relate the event of the previous day outweighed his reticence at the possible consequences.

"Fritz Goetzinger called me at the station yesterday," he said, his tone rather experimental, and then waited.

El was thinking she needed to find more time to spend out in the yard. The grass was brown from the drought. What little water they had bestowed on it had disappeared, like seed broadcast on sterile ground. Near El's cherished old roses crouched two inconspicuous bushes—tea roses. Many years ago she had let Walter talk her into having these hybridized in honor of the births of their two daughters, though El knew, even then, that tea roses represented a degradation of the genus, having none of the toughness and resiliency of the old roses. But once they were in the ground, what could you do? They always fared poorly in droughty weather and that summer had put out no blooms at all. El's gaze came to rest on these poor creatures. She closed her eyes at the mention of Fritz Goetzinger's name.

"Fritz wanted to talk about the weather," Walter persisted from the other room.

"Is that so?" The mayor and her husband had one of those odd little relationships that abound in places like Jackson, a special-purpose friendship that almost nobody knew about.

"He was wondering when it's going to rain," Walter said. "He hasn't got his corn harvested yet."

"Can't be much of a crop," she supposed idly, looking at the devastation outside the French doors.

"Afraid he's going to lose what he's got, I suppose."

"I see." As thoughts often diverge from words, El had only half attended to this exchange because the mention of Fritz had reminded her she hadn't heard anything recently about the crisis at JackPack. Fritz had made his proposal that the employees buy the place and then nothing. She thought about Gresham's law, bad money driving out good. Bad ideas driving out good.

So she said, "And what did he have to say about the Pack?"

"The Pack? Nothing."

"Really?"

"Not a word."

Talking from room to room required effort, which led to a certain tension in the voice, and thus to a similar tension in the mood. So even perfectly innocent conversations like this one had a way of becoming implied arguments.

Walter could smell the orange El was eating and envisioned her desultory scattering of the scraps of peel, like falling leaves.

"We talked about next spring, too," he said, bringing up the part of the conversation that he'd found particularly interesting.

"Next spring?"

"He wanted to know what the winter was going to be like. Whether he should plow this fall."

El's thoughts were still on JackPack, on Fritz's buyout scheme. Another of the mayor's grand gestures.

"He wanted to know if I expected a lot of rain next spring," Walter was saying from the other room. El, with an effort, shifted her attention.

"And what did you tell him?"

"To plow."

"You should be careful what you say to that man," El cautioned.

Walter frowned and stared up at the kitchen ceiling, high overhead, a shallow pattern of coffers, painted white, suggesting a stylized cloud pattern, like a tyrant's version of the heavens. More than once had El warned Walter about the mayor.

"What do you suppose he could do with the information I give him?" Walter asked, letting his voice rise even a little higher, to show his displeasure.

"I have no idea," El said. "I just know what Fritz is capable of."

Where the mayor was concerned, Walter thought, El was not prepared to be reasonable. But he could see no purpose in arguing about the matter, and so he said nothing. They remained for a time silent, and their thoughts returned to their separate interests, Walter's to the conversation of the day before and El's to the travail at JackPack.

She looked about her, thinking vaguely that she really ought to call Skip Peterson. Not that there was much she could do. The council had already begun to talk about renegotiating the interest rate on the UDAG loan to the Pack. They might adjust the sewer fees, too. But these were relatively minor matters.

The light had a luminous quality in the early morning, softening the edges of the sideboard and cupboards, creating a sense of seeing the invisible. The formal Victorian dining room had been so carefully restored that El always had the pleasant, expectant sense there of old pictures come to life. The room was used for progressive dinners and the other events El felt called upon to sponsor in her capacity as chairwoman of the historical society.

She fingered the half-peeled orange and stared at the spot on the floor where Walter had lain, a reluctant corpse, during the last murder mystery they'd mounted. She sighed at the thought that it was time to start thinking seriously about the next one.

In the kitchen, Walter brooded over the advice he had given to Fritz and El's warning. "Wet years follow dry," he'd said to the mayor. He mentioned the summer of '35, winter of '36. He mentioned '64 and '65. Everybody remembered those years. The possibilities excited him, but now he wondered if he had sufficiently impressed upon Fritz the statistical nature of climate regimes, the eerie elusiveness of long-term patterns. He supposed he had been a little too enthusiastic. Fritz treated him as an expert and Walter, flattered, played the role. Now he could only shake his head and decide he'd better call him back.

Finally, Walter got up and, in order to reestablish his peace of mind, took his dishes over to the sink and carefully washed and dried and stored them, leaving the kitchen as neat as he had found it.

He glanced at the weather chart on the fridge. In the dining room he kissed the top of El's head. She looked up at his kindly smile and patted him on the chest, forgiving him his good opinion of others.

"Meeting tonight?" Walter asked.

"Integration Task Force. You?"

"Going to talk to the kids at St. Columbkille's this morning. About sun spots." El smiled. They both knew what she thought of sun spot theory, lunar cycles, all Walter's precious climate speculations.

"And what did you tell Fritz, dear? Is it going to rain?"

"Not too long now. Big blocking high's beginning to move."

She nodded. "Good."

In the distance, the wail of a siren began. They paused and listened.

"Up north somewhere," Walter said.

"Toward the point."

The sound rose and faded and rose again. Then Walter kissed the top of El's head one last time.

And so they began what would be a long day for each of them, a typical day in the lives of two of Jackson's best known public figures.

Out on the porch, Walter paused and looked toward the west. The sky appeared as it had with such monotony over the past months, smudged and barren. He peered more carefully, as if he might already discern white tendrils, mare's-tails, high-riding cirrus clouds arriving far in advance of the storm system they announced. He smiled and nodded, pleased with the thought that in a few days when he came out onto the porch these portents would have appeared, just as he expected.

# CHAPTER 29

~

Patrolman Leon Sink could always be counted on to make life as pleasant for himself as possible, which was precisely what he had set about doing at the beginning of his shift on this particular midweek morning when, alas, he was all at once interrupted by a call from dispatch.

"Car six," the scratchy radio voice enjoined him, "I've got a ten thirty-three at three five zero one Bridge. Medic two is responding. Please assist."

Leon had, as usual, obtained an omelet—a western today, with all the necessary accessories, of course—from the kitchen of the Riverview and, titillated by the fervent aromas, driven the squad car to one of his favorite out-of-the-way places. Now he waited for the message to be repeated, caressing the paper sack, the bottom of which bulged like a little tummy. He was sorely tempted to ignore the dispatcher. But he liked getting calls, too. He wasn't one of those cops happy to go through a shift without incident. He liked the action.

So finally, acknowledging the message, he reluctantly put the food aside, started the squad, swung back up onto the pavement, and hit the lights and siren. At first the address on Bridge did not register, except that it had to be out toward the end of the street. The number was very high. Perhaps that was what finally nudged his memory as he jogged expertly through the neighborhood streets. Or perhaps it was the 01 on the end of the address. But by the time, only moments later, that he turned onto Bridge, he had figured out exactly where he was going—Mark O'Banion's.

The O'Banion home lay at the very end of the road, where the tollhouse of the old Wisconsin Bridge had once stood. The driveway, formerly the approach to the bridge, climbed in a long, straight incline cut into the side of the bluff, and Leon, killing the siren, accelerated up this and braked sharply, with a little fishtail for effect. A woman he recognized as O'Banion's wife stood out front. Her clothes were in disarray.

"Where's the ambulance?" she asked.

"On the way." Leon grunted as he hauled himself out of the squad. "Is it your husband?"

"Yes."

"Where is he?"

"In the master bedroom."

"Show me."

She led him along a dark, wood-paneled hallway, past large low-ceilinged rooms with fieldstone fireplaces and more paneling, and then up a half flight of stairs and into a huge bedroom.

O'Banion lay in the middle of a king-sized bed. He had the ashen gray color of a heart attack victim. He wore a shirt and tie. The sheet was pulled up so that it was impossible to tell what he had on below the waist. His eyes were closed, mouth partly open and folded down into a grimace with spittle at the corners. Bracing himself, Leon leaned toward the sick man and palpated the carotid artery. Nothing. In the distance, they could hear sirens. "How about you go back downstairs," he told O'Banion's wife, "and send the ambulance guys on up?"

"All right," she said. Despite her disheveled appearance, she seemed in control, her expression rather severe. She looked for a moment down at O'Banion, and all at once, a sad, concerned smile appeared. But for just an instant. Then she put on her sharp, businesslike expression again and left.

Leon pulled his portable out and called down to the comm center. "Advise the ambulance I'm starting CPR," he said, then tossed the radio aside without waiting for a response.

To get at O'Banion, he had to climb up onto the bed. "You gotta sleep in the middle of a fucking football field," he said to the still form while he loosened O'Banion's tie and shirt collar. As Leon bent over, his own tie hung down and he stuffed it into his shirt.

The bed sagged as he pressed down on O'Banion's chest, and so he increased his pressure slightly to compensate. The giant sack of Leon's own stomach hung down beneath him and swayed back and forth as he worked.

"Fucking ironic, ain't it," he said, counting under his breath, "me up here saving your miserable ass." Against the hoary color of his flesh, O'Banion's faded red hair appeared quite youthful. Even unconscious, his expression suggested his disapproval of Leon and Leon's unreformed life.

As he pressed down and released, again and again, Leon was aware of the feel of the silk shirt under his palms. The shirt was flamingo-colored and had white French cuffs with gold studs. He blew two breaths into O'Banion's mouth, then switched back to the chest compressions, feeling a kind of rhythm beginning. The bed moaned beneath them. Sirens, very loud now, seemed to rise up into the air about the house. The rhythmic movements had a sensual quality, and Leon felt the beginnings of an erection. "Wake up, you bastard," he said to the still form, "wake up!"

He heard a siren winding down outside. Still others were closing in. Moments later, there were footsteps on the stairs and two paramedics, carrying their equipment, came into the room.

"How long you been here, Leon?" one of them asked.

"Three minutes max."

"Christ, Leon," the other EMT said, "you fat fuck, get off, you'll smother the poor bastard."

"We've got to get him down on the floor," the first said. Leon climbed down, and they lifted O'Banion off the bed. He was naked below the waist.

A ventilator was being used now to get air into O'Banion's lungs. Leon continued chest compressions as one of the paramedics cut off O'Banion's shirt and attached electrodes to each shoulder and the lower left chest.

"Nice shirt," Leon observed.

"Not anymore."

"Musta been getting it on," Leon said. "That's the way I wanna go." He looked at O'Banion's limp penis with interest. Nothing offended him or made him uneasy, not even the image of another man's sex. The serious medic grabbed a sheet off the bed and covered O'Banion.

They all looked at the monitor.

"Flat as three-day-old beer."

Other people were in the room now. Fire department personnel. Tubing was being inserted down O'Banion's throat. An IV was prepared. The flesh around O'Banion's nipples was a smooth as a baby's and mounded, like the beginning of breasts, which for some reason saddened Leon.

He stood to one side and watched the others work. Although no one had asked, he inserted into the brief silences the story of how he had found O'Banion. He looked around the room, calculating. Gray sharkskin trousers lay crumpled on the floor, a small glitter of coins spilled around one pocket. The walls of the room were covered with pictures from ceiling to floor, signed publicity pictures and formal portraits and framed family snapshots and amateur photos of natural scenery and even of several commercial and industrial structures, probably, Leon guessed, buildings O'Banion had put up during his days as a contractor. Mrs. O'Banion's jewelry was draped over a golf trophy on her dresser.

When the medics started talking about using Isuprel, a last-ditch effort, Leon retrieved his radio and went back downstairs.

In the living room, an assistant fire chief was interviewing Mrs. O'Banion. Husband's age? Hospital he should be taken to? Was he taking any drugs? Amounts? Leon looked into her face for signs of strain. In control, he thought. Fucking lace-curtain Irish, just like her old man.

Leon had never been in O'Banion's house before, so he took a little stroll around the first floor. The furniture had the worn, knobby, slightly askew quality of genuine antiques. Leon decided that, money-wise, O'Banion's wife was sitting pretty. A glass window wall in the living room provided a panorama of the riverscape below, and, since his mind naturally turned to such matters, Leon thought, Nice place for a restaurant.

More people arrived. Everyone knew everyone else. Excitement, shock, solicitude. Voices were pitched low. People stood around in small knots, trying to think of the right things to say.

Alone in the kitchen for a few moments, Leon looked in several drawers and cabinets but found nothing of interest. He hitched up his trousers and went to find someone to talk to. Another squad had arrived and in it one of the captains, a young, absurdly serious fellow named James "Jack" Webb. A computer whiz and the youngest captain in the history of the department, Webb was, from Leon's point of view, poor material for a conversation, but in a pinch Leon would talk to anybody. Webb was striding manfully toward the house when Leon intercepted him and proceeded to tell him, in some detail, what was what.

A few minutes later, the paramedics brought O'Banion out on a litter.

"How's it look?" Webb asked.

Without expression, the medic said, "We're going to transport him." Leon understood. He watched silently as they loaded the litter into the ambulance. O'Banion looked the same as he had earlier, his face deflated and ashen, the color of soil leached of all its nutrients.

After the others had all left—the assistant fire chief taking Mrs. O'Banion with him—Leon and Webb stood by one of the squads.

Leon's mind was full of the images of the last few minutes, the unresponsive body, the feel of the man's flaccid lips on his own, the dress shirt being cut away with surgical shears, the pictures covering the bedroom walls, the riverscape, the uninteresting kitchen drawers. As they talked, another car drove up, and the city manager got out.

"He's been taken to St. Luke's," Webb said as Paul Cutler came up to them.

"What's the problem?"

"Heart, looks like." Leon watched Webb square his shoulders and puff up because he was talking to the city manager.

"Bad?"

Webb nodded.

Cutler closed his bright aqua eyes, and his face, so striking normally, lost some of its character. For a moment, he looked almost as bad as O'Banion had. But then he opened his eyes again, and life returned. "St. Luke's?"

"Yeah."

Without another word, he got back in his car and drove off, the car listing to one side and sagging on its bad springs as it reversed direction in the driveway's turnaround.

"God, that really is a piece of shit he drives," Leon thought out loud. "What the hell do you suppose he's trying to prove?"

This wasn't the kind of observation, apparently, that Webb found congenial, for all he said was, "Come on, let's secure this place and get back to work."

# CHAPTER 30

~

Chuck Fellows was late leaving the house that morning. When the phone rang, he picked it up in the front hall on his way out.

Diane, making Grace's preschool lunch in the kitchen, listened to his side of the conversation, listened to him listening, for he said almost nothing. But enough. Something was the matter, seriously the matter. She quickly rinsed her hands and dried them as she walked toward him.

He put the receiver down gently but she could see the stricken look on his face.

"What is it?" she asked.

"Mark."

"What's the matter?"

"Heart."

"How bad?"

Chuck just shook his head.

"Oh my God!"

Suddenly his face hardened and he struck out, sending the coat rack sprawling across the floor. Diane took a step toward him, then stopped.

"Are they sure?"

"Yes."

"Where did it happen?"

"At home."

Could it be? Diane asked herself, as if by doubting she might have the power to undo the thing. The question sank without a trace into the sorrow already welling up inside her. Poor Helen, she thought, and then said, "Poor Helen."

Chuck said nothing. He had become passive, but she could still sense the violence in him. He stood, his hands making loose fists, his head tilted to one side so that he appeared to be staring at the foot of the wall, as if he had just noticed the sprung cover of the baseboard heating.

Diane stifled her impulse to comfort him. But she had to do something, say something.

"What has it been, a week, since we saw them? Mark seemed fine, didn't you think so? A little tired perhaps. I just can't believe it."

On the floor the winter coats, recently taken from storage, lay scattered around the fallen rack.

"I'll check on Grace," she said softly and climbed the stairs, feeling unsteady. Their three-year-old stood wide-eyed in the center of her room, ignoring her lilliputian world of doll houses and furniture. "Oh, dear," Diane scolded gently, "you've put your dress on backwards again."

As Diane set this right, Grace swayed back and forth with the tuggings and raisings and lowerings, but she remained rooted to the spot. Diane would have to carry her downstairs. The child had begun to suck her thumb again, a habit she'd discarded except in moments of stress. Diane gently removed it, but it went right back in. Diane left it there, wishing that she had something so readily available to soothe herself. For her thoughts, even as she helped the child, ran back time and again to Mark O'Banion and to Helen. Poor Helen, what would she do now?

But mostly Diane worried about her husband. Death would bring back Vietnam, where so many of Chuck's buddies had been killed. He dealt with it in his own manner. Comfort was not sought, would not be endured.

At the same time, Diane felt a resistance to this idea. No life should be so dominated by the before and after of a thing as Chuck's was by Vietnam.

Images of her husband and her child flowed together. What if, God forbid, something happened to one of her children? Then she'd have her own before and after. She arranged Grace's wispy curls, which seemed to evaporate from her fingertips, then rested her hand lightly on the top of the child's head and smiled sadly at her.

"Do you want to take one of your dollies with you today?" she asked, but Grace didn't respond. Diane thought that maybe they should wait a few minutes, to give Chuck more time alone, but then she changed her mind. Perhaps seeing his daughter would help.

She picked up Grace's favorite doll, just in case, and then the child, grunting.

"Such a big little girl," she said. "Mommy's not going to be able to carry you much longer."

But the burden brought some relief. How many thousands of times had she carried Grace? How she would regret it when Grace, like Todd before her, had become too big ever to carry again.

As she walked along the upstairs hallway, she again thought of Mark O'Banion. At the head of the stairs, she paused. Below, she could see her discarded hand towel draped over the newel post. She tried to sense Chuck's presence. It wasn't a time to think about practical matters, but she understood that Mark's death had changed everything. For Chuck, for her, for the children. This thought crossed her mind briefly and was put aside.

Finally, she shifted Grace onto her hip so that she could use the handrail as she descended.

# CHAPTER 31

~

Jack Kelley had only reluctantly gone to Mass on Sunday. He didn't need Father Mike at the moment. At the end of the service, as the church quickly emptied, he had asked Janelle and Kitty to wait for him outside and then knelt on the hard wooden bench. Perhaps Mike would be gone by the time he left. He considered the possibility of going to confession…to reconciliation, as they called it now. But he didn't want to be reconciled. If anything, he wanted to confess. He'd have to find some other priest to hear it. On the other hand, it occurred to him, maybe confession was unnecessary after all, since he already had his penance—Tony Vasconcellos.

He rested with his rump against the edge of the pew, his forehead on his hands, and waited for the light to be turned out in the nave. Then he got up and left.

Father Mike was still there, standing in the narthex with Jack's wife and daughter. The priest seemed more upbeat than normal, and no wonder. He winked at Jack. "I'd say the patient's got some color in his cheeks, Jack."

"I see you found another specialist," Jack commented, and Mike just smiled. He had taken off his tippet and surplice and seemed in the long black cassock only half-dressed.

"What was that all about?" Janelle asked as they left.

"Mike and I are playing doctor."

When she tried to pursue the matter, Jack told her it wasn't important. Unlike Angela Vasconcellos, Father Mike was no particular friend of Janelle, and Jack didn't want to hear what she'd have to say about this latest escapade.

~

By Monday morning at nine a.m., as he drove down to the job

site, Jack had made a decision. He had been too distracted by current affairs. If they were going to finish by June 15—He stopped and corrected himself. They were damn well going to finish by June 15. The way Jack's life had been going of late, he wasn't sure of a hell of a lot anymore, but that one thing he did know. Mark O'Banion would have his track on time. Whatever it took, Jack would do that one thing.

Precast was critical; steel, critical; the roof, critical. He should have been pounding the schedule harder all along and to hell with all the personal garbage people dragged with them onto the job site. Yes, he thought. Good!

The construction trailer was locked, and there was no sign of Don Adagian. Jack walked the site looking for him. In the distance, he could see Cletus Dickey, following his belly around. If anybody would know where Don was, Dickey would, so Jack made his way over.

"Haven't seem him since Friday night."

"Friday night?"

"We played a little poker."

"Is that right?" At once, Jack felt a great hollowness. So that had been the purpose for the money he'd advanced Don, not child support but poker. He had meant to do a good deed and look what had happened.

"Let me guess," he said to Dickey. "He was cleaned out."

"I gave him a little something to get through the weekend."

"You're a prince, Cletus."

Dickey shrugged. "He didn't have to play."

"No, he didn't."

It occurred to Jack as he went back to his car that Cletus Dickey would have made a better field man than Don Adagian.

He immediately drove to the marina at the southern tip of Apple Island, his sense of violation rising as he went. In the marina office, he snapped his hand down on the call bell, the sharp ting echoing into the rooms behind the counter. He paced back and forth, unable to keep still, driven by his mounting rage.

"Can I help you?" the woman who had appeared asked.

"I'm looking for Don Adagian. Which boat is his?"

The woman gave him a canny, interested look.

"The Do-Si-Do," she said. "Slip seventeen." When Jack turned to go, she added, "You won't find him there."

He stopped, his back still to her.

"Where then?"

"What do you want him for?"

Jack slowly turned. "Where is he?"

The woman was leaning on her elbows, deciding what to say. "Gone."

"When?"

"We got up Saturday morning, no more Don."

"His boat, too?"

"Lock, stock, and barrel."

Jack exhaled, his arms dropping to his side.

Saturday morning? Good God. "Did anybody see him go? Did he leave a message? Anything?"

She shook her head. "Nothing. We're not happy about it, either. He still owes docking fees."

Jack snorted. "You're not happy?" The only thing worse than having Adagian was not having him. Who the hell was going to do all that damn work? The object of his anger being gone, however, the anger itself seemed pretty pointless. He exhaled and shook his head.

"You must be a dog track person," the woman guessed. "Don said he worked for somebody named Kelley."

"He did indeed. Jack Kelley."

"Hi. Kate Sullivan." She stuck her hand out. "I manage the marina. It looks like we've both been stiffed."

Her countenance was so cheerful despite having been stiffed that Jack smiled, if a bit grimly, as he stepped forward. Kate Sullivan had a good, strong, no-nonsense handshake.

"I know the answer, Kate, but let me ask anyway—what are the chances he's just taken a weekend jaunt somewhere?"

"Wouldn't count on it, if I were you. Boaters like him are pretty much gypsies."

He nodded, surprised at how good he was beginning to feel, how relieved, although only a fool would feel good at a moment like that, knowing what he knew. For one thing, the question about who'd get stuck with Don's duties had been entirely rhetorical. Jack would, at least until he could find someone else. So much for his dream of concentrating on the future of the project. So much for sleeping and eating, too. He leaned on the counter, pleased to have a stranger with whom to share a bitch.

"You know, Kate, the first day I laid eyes on that guy, I thought, 'Uh oh.' If I'd had a brain in my head, I would have sent him packing then and there."

"Don't feel bad. I almost made him one of my projects. Fortunately, my husband warned me off. Coffee?"

"Don't mind if I do."

And so they went into the back office and put their feet up and spent a pleasant few minutes speculating on the foibles of human beings, present and not.

As he was about to leave, Jack asked where Don's boat had been berthed. "Slip 17, you said? Which one's that?"

He followed Kate's directions and for a brief time stared at the empty rectangle of water.

~

Back in the construction trailer, he discovered a manila envelope with the single word "Sorry" scrawled across it and inside, sets of rough meeting notes, daily reports, and Adagian's phone log, too. He called uptown and informed them of this latest turn of events. He would move his operation down to the job site and start looking for a new field man.

Finally he began reading through the meeting notes, trying to decide if they were in good enough shape for one of the secretaries to type up. Very soon, however, his thoughts had drifted back to Adagian himself. A gypsy, Kate Sullivan had called him. That didn't sound quite right. Gypsies traveled in close-knit clans. Gypsies had codes of conduct, of a sort, certainly a shared loyalty. Don Adagian, as far as Jack could tell, was a man entirely alone, a cell cut from the body. Jack had had no business hiring such a person. Now the piper would be paid. More penance.

After a while, Dickey stuck his head in the door. "Any luck?"

"Go away, Dickey. Right at this moment you're the last person I want to see."

"That bad, huh?" Dickey hovered.

"Go away."

"Suit yourself." Dickey started to leave, then stopped. "Oh, by the way, did you hear about Mark O'Banion?"

# CHAPTER 32

~

As slowly as a processional, the switch engine pushed its burden across the old railroad bridge, a single car, the slanted afternoon sunlight winking through the braces of the trusswork and off the car's polished flanks. Only when it emerged on the western side of the river, sliding gracefully free of the bridge's iron mesh, did the car's impressive size and trappings become apparent—a clerestory keel running like a dorsal fin along its broad back, at either end observation platforms as ornate as opera boxes, golden filigrees decorating the paneling along the sides. Behind it followed, like a dowdy hen after a displaying peacock, the attendant engine. Slowly, this odd tandem curved toward downtown Jackson, and then more slowly still.

El Plowman, arriving late, found herself waiting impatiently at the railroad crossing leading onto the Fifth Street peninsula as the Pullman sleeper glided before her, forest green, its name embossed in a gilt cartouche—Spirit of the West.

At the beginning of the day, she had anticipated the task before her as no more than a pleasant interlude in the usual routine. But now, routine having been shattered, this ceremony of arrival survived and drew her as toward a balm.

She drove around the gate arms before they could be raised. By the time she'd reached the old Burlington Northern station and walked through the half-completed exhibit to the platform, the sleeper and switch engine had already come to a stop and Reiny Kopp gone down to talk to the engineer leaning out of his cab.

"Sorry I'm late," she said to the others and immediately went over to shake hands with Hiram and Pearl Johnson. A small path had been cleared so that Hiram might approach the car. El gave him her arm, and they immediately started forward, El on one side and Pearl on the other.

"Course," the old man was saying, "it wasn't but a few times I worked cars this old. I was pretty young in the service then. The Century, the Chief, the Dixie Flagler, those were the trains I mostly had runs on. Steamliners they were, before the diesels came in."

El had grown used to the fact that Hiram's thoughts, and therefore his speaking, were always under way and it was therefore necessary to board while moving.

"I think—" she started to say when a sudden grinding noise startled her and she looked up as the Pullman car lurched several feet backward. Reiny had moved in line with the forward steps and was using his long, bony hands as signal flags to assist the engineer in positioning the car precisely as Reiny desired.

"I think," El took up where she'd left off, "Reiny was looking for the most impressive specimen he could find." She leaned close and raised her voice, the old man being hard of hearing.

"Most likely, you got that right," Hiram said. "Trains like the Century never much went in for opulence, 'cept in the service. Nobody gave better service than what we did."

Hiram must have been a stylish man in youth. Now the remnant of that style resided in the ritual moving of his cane, which he looped and pointed as if lassoing each step.

On either side of the advancing party, photographers and reporters jockeyed for position.

The coupling between car and engine clanged once more as the car jerked forward, this time a mere foot or two. Reiny raised his hands, fingers spread, satisfied. Then he went back to the switch engine where one of the trainmen had climbed down with the necessary release papers.

Against the precipitous side of the car, Hiram appeared tiny, but he inspected the towering beast with the same imperial eye a stooped old mahout might have bestowed on a gargantuan elephant. El stepped aside so that Pearl, who had fallen back, might move up next to her husband, but she appeared satisfied where she was, arms wrapped around her purse, dividing her attention among the Pullman and Hiram and, less obviously, the people crowding around to listen.

The party moved slowly along the flank of the car, Hiram lassoing each step. Reiny had completed the paperwork, but he watched the proceedings from a short distance. He was always happy to let El handle the ceremonial end of museum business. Beyond him, the switch engine, uncoupled, backed away in the direction from which it had come.

Hiram had continued talking about the different trains he'd worked on over the years. "The Silver Meteor, now that was a nice run. Between New York and Miami. On the Pullman cars, we'd ride the best class of people, top people, people didn't jus' say 'Do this' or 'Do that' but 'Would you please,' and 'thank you,' like that."

Reiny had pulled a stool from the car's vestibule and left it for them. Spotting it, Hiram moved a little more quickly and pointed with his cane. "Now this is what I would call my stepping box."

At a request from one of the photographers, he put on the cap from his old uniform, which had a single strand of braid above the visor and a metal tag—PULLMAN PORTER—and El pretended she was a passenger about to board.

He reached out to take her imaginary suitcase, flashing a smile. "You got to put the big smile on 'em right away, see. Start working for that tip they gonna give you when you be discharging them at the other end of the line."

Pearl, who had been quiet until now, suddenly said, "What did the porters all say, Hiram? The Pullman company, they always hired the blackest men with the whitest teeth."

Hiram laughed. "Sister Pearl right. That what they said, but t'weren't so. Look at me. Got the teeth, all right, but I ain't hardly half black."

This was true. With his faded skin and narrow lips and nose, he could almost have passed for white.

The party now boarded, the smell inside musty with long uncirculated air. Reiny, in advance, threw up several shades, dust motes thick in the diagonal beams and swirling like river currents around his arms. The brocade seats were sun-faded and the carpets worn, but these long-unfashionable furnishings, El thought, still possessed a certain dignity, not unlike the old man himself.

She looked at the car's other appointments—the brass fittings and mahogany inlay and leaded windows—and said, "My husband Walter and I have been redoing an old Vic for years, and I can tell you this is wonderful work."

"What?" Hiram asked, not having heard.

"This is wonderful work," El repeated.

"That's right," Hiram agreed immediately. "Mr. Pullman, he wanted nothing but the best."

The group were jammed together in the corridor. El, becoming conscious of the heat on her back, turned to discover Johnny Pond pressing close, holding the mike of his tape recorder over her shoulder. She made way so that he could get closer to Hiram. Pond's cologne had a pleasant but odd aroma. Almonds, she thought.

Hiram was now pointing at the design on the polished diagonal wooden panels lining the walls above the seats. "That's what they call 'Bird in the Bush.'" With wings spread and an elegant forked tail, the inlaid golden creature seemed on the point of flying up toward the clerestory, where light filtered through dusty lunette windows. "That was done in the Marquetry Room. Everybody knowed about the Marquetry Room. Mr. Pullman went all the way over to Germany there, looking for the best men available. Found 'em, too."

Pearl, who had obviously appointed herself rectifier of imbalances, said, "Tell them about the nickname, Hiram."

"They don't want to hear about that."

"Makes no difference. They should hear about it."

"Well, okay," the old man conceded and then told the group a little sheepishly, "used to be, we was all called George, on account of that being, you know, Mr. Pullman's name."

"How do you think that makes a man feel?" Pearl demanded.

"After the union come in, we had a name card up at the front of our cars, and we didn't have to respond if somebody called us 'George' or 'Boy' or anything like that anymore."

"But they still did," Pearl insisted.

"Sometimes. I didn't mind, long as I saw the color of their money, you know what I mean."

Unlike her husband, who still, after all these years, possessed the pride of his job, Pearl had as keepsakes only the ancient grievances. El's heart went out to the old woman.

Through the mass of bodies, her eye was drawn to Hiram's veined, parsnip-colored hand, lying as if discarded on the backrest of one of the seats. Pearl, younger, perhaps in her mid-seventies and stout, had skin of a lustrous black, molded like glazed ceramics.

They moved slowly down the aisle, Hiram telling one story after another, old stories, oft-told stories, talking about the pride of the porters, while Pearl spoke only when she felt called to balance things out.

El began to tire, and her mood changed, becoming more burdened with the sadness of the day. She glanced back and saw that Johnny Pond had removed himself from the group and was settling into one of the seats, as if in preparation for a journey by rail. He looked so comfortable that she walked back and sat down opposite. He had laid his tape recorder aside.

She slipped out of her heels, stretched her legs out and wiggled her toes. "How you doing, Johnny?"

"Couldn't be better."

"Well," she said, unwilling to go that far, "this seems to be going okay, at least."

"Hiram's quite the old gent."

"Yes, he is, but I was particularly noticing Pearl."

While they were chatting about the railroad porter and his wife, El observed a sheaf of papers next to the tape recorder. The top sheet bore the museum's logo.

"What's that?"

"Script."

"Oh, interesting, so you're to be the narrator, are you?"

He nodded.

Reiny, of course, never bothered to inform the board what he was up to as he mounted an exhibit, so El had to snoop or just hope for accidental discoveries such as this.

"Reiny Kopp wrote it?" she asked.

"He didn't say, just asked would I read it."

Johnny had a full, soft voice with a touch of roughness in the lower register. A voice rather like Johnny himself.

"May I see?" she asked.

"Be my guest."

She picked up the pages and began to thumb through, flipping quickly past the sections dealing with Hiram's youth in the Mississippi Delta and years as a Pullman porter, only slowing where her eye caught the word *Jackson*. Then she read more carefully, looking for material that would offend local sensibilities.

The others by now had exited from the far end of the car, leaving the two of them alone. El stopped to read two sentences over.

"How is Helen O'Banion doing?" Johnny asked.

El looked up. "You know Helen?"

"We've worked together on the *Trib*'s Season of Sharing."

"Ah." El, recalling her conversation with Walter at breakfast about Fritz Goetzinger—how long ago that seemed—was once more reminded of unsuspected linkages in the city.

"Can never tell how a person's gonna react, situation like that," Johnny said, "but it'd surprise me some if she got on with the grieving process right away."

El nodded at this insight. "She's already insisted on going home." In fact, El was worried about Helen. She seemed, it was true, totally in control of herself, but who knew what was going on inside. "People will need to be with her until her children arrive."

Pond considered this and made a suggestion.

"Maybe she should be left alone."

"Eventually, certainly."

Pond's interest, as always, remained precise and cool. Like an air conditioner, he gave off both warmth and a chill, depending on where you stood. At the moment, El was aware of the coolness.

She remembered the papers in her hand and returned to the lines she had been contemplating and read them a third time:

*During the '30s when the Johnsons moved to the city, only blacks who worked elsewhere, usually for national companies like Pullman, could live in Jackson since no locals would hire them. Patrolman Francis Hogan, for many years the beat officer around the railroad station, would tell unemployed blacks getting off the train "not to let the sun set on them in Jackson."*

El crossed out the second sentence. Hogan was long dead, but he still had family in town.

She stopped to consider. Reiny, of course, would take offense at this "censorship." For such a high-handed fellow, he showed a surprising lack of appreciation for high-handedness in others. Made no difference. Delicate diplomacy wouldn't work here. A ukase was required.

"I'm removing some material," she explained to Pond, "so that people won't be needlessly hurt. This isn't an exhibit on racism in Jackson. It's the story of Hiram and Pearl Johnson."

Johnny nodded. "Well, like I said, Reiny just asked me to read it."

This response didn't satisfy El, although she wasn't sure exactly why. Too precise a statement of what was not in contention, perhaps. Pond sat blandly in his seat, in no rush to go anywhere. From the rows of half-moon windows above, the dusty sunlight drifted down into the car. El noticed that she could no longer smell the musty odor, or for that matter hear the voices from outside, either. She turned back to what she was reading.

# CHAPTER 33

~

Leaving work later, Chuck passed the spot where the previous Friday he and Mark had talked for the last time. He remembered how unsatisfying their parting had been. He wished he had that conversation back. His relationship with Mark was over but hardly complete. That was the way it had been in Nam, too, close friendships, men you'd give your life for, severed in an instant. Nam had been different, though. There, at least, you knew the guy humping with you out into the bush might be coming back in a body bag.

In his car, as he drove home, Chuck thought how ironic it would be if he ended up taking Mark's job, after all the times he'd sworn up and down he'd never put up with those assholes on the council. Acting public works director or permanent, it made no difference, it was all the same shit. "You'd like that, wouldn't you, you old son of a bitch," he said to Mark's shade.

To Diane, he said nothing about the city manager's offer.

On Thursday, at Mark's funeral, Chuck withdrew from the others and created around himself, as he was able to do when he wanted, a charged field that warned people to keep their distance. With distaste, he watched Diane fit perfectly into the ceremony of the occasion. Finally, at the cemetery, he simply turned away and walked straight into the woods, until he could no longer hear the sounds of the graveside eulogy.

Then he stopped and looked around and listened to the silence so unique to woodlands. He stood at the foot of a hill, near an old black cherry tree that had dropped its summer foliage except for a scattering of leaves at the very top, the leaves shining like fragments of the afternoon sun, although no sunlight could reach into this dark glade. Woven into its lower branches were the vines of a Virginia creeper. Several weeks ago the plant would have been flame red, but now the leaves were scattered on the ground, faded embers.

Wishing to exert himself, Chuck started to walk vigorously up the hill. After a short distance, he was breathing heavily and could feel the tension in his thigh muscles. He stopped to take a blow under a massive burr oak. A makeshift ladder had been nailed to the tree, probably by bow hunters, although he could see no sign of a tree stand. The oak's branches extended straight outward, showing that it had once grown in an open field. Now, crowded around with other trees, it was slowly dying.

In the past, when Chuck had hiked alone in the woods, he had felt an edge, just the hint of danger, which sharpened his sensations. But since his daughter's birth, he no longer had those old feelings. Now, even here, his dissatisfactions followed him.

He loosened his tie and continued on, to the crown of the hill, where he found a prairie remnant. He had hiked many of the hills around the city, although never this one, but goat prairies were often to be found. For a moment, he was pleased. The prairie wasn't very big. Firefighters had become too efficient, and these openings were quickly disappearing. This one was crowded around with cedar trees, cutting off the panorama of rolling Iowa hills that once would have been visible. From two sides, sumac invaded.

The big bluestem made a rasping sound against his suit as he walked through it. He stood at the center of the opening. The grass, head high, was extravagantly colored, in red and green and brown and purple, and topped by aggressive, turkey-footed spikes. After a time, a breeze rose and moved across the hill, a sound like rain, bringing down a shower of leaves. That was all.

With nowhere else to go except back where he had come from, Chuck lingered, until his thoughts began to ruin the peaceful scene, and then he walked back down the hill, and stood, the last of the mourners, while workmen filled in Mark's grave.

# PART IV

# CHAPTER 34

~

Homer Budge loved his family. At this time on a school day morning, the kitchen spilled over with Budges, and Homer was in his element. From the counter next to the sink, Ruthie, the second eldest acted as straw boss, overseeing the preparation of lunches. Every kid had a backpack, as if backpacks were part of God's design.

"All my scholars," Homer said, apropos of nothing except his joy. The assembled Budges were used to these little outbursts and ignored them.

Even Mother was a scholar now. Rose sat opposite, using a yellow highlighter to mark her office management text.

Homer loved to see the girls in their immaculate blouses and plaid skirts, the boys in natty trousers and school ties. He loved, it must be said, even the small ways in which they violated the spirit if not the letter of the school dress code. Their reasoning would have put a canon lawyer to shame.

Homer made a point of giving them a hard time and would manufacture a provocation if need be. Today, however, he was in luck. Veronica appeared, looking glum, and passed through without a word to anyone.

"What's wrong with her?" Homer asked.

"She's in crisis," Ruthie volunteered as she closed a lunch bag with quick, neat folds.

"I thought it was Liz who was in crisis. Where is Liz, by the way?"

"Can't more than one of us be in crisis at the same time?" Terri, the younger of the Irish twins, demanded.

"I don't know. Mother, do we have a rule about that?"

"No two kids allowed in crisis at the same time," Rose delivered deadpan, her yellow highlighter moving without pause across the page of her textbook.

"No fair! You guys just make up the rules as you go along."

"That's right," Homer admitted easily, "there's a rule about that, too. Adults get to make up the rules as they go along. That's one of the rules about rules, very important."

This declaration led, of course, to rules about rules about rules and so forth, straight to pandemonium, so that Homer didn't hear the phone ring but saw Rose take off her earring as she picked the receiver up and covered her other ear in order to hear over the din.

Homer held up his hand and yelled, "Quiet." Ruthie yelled, "Quiet." Every other kid in the room followed suit. And all that remained of sound when Rose passed the receiver over to Homer was a general tittering.

"Who is it?"

"Didn't ask. Think I recognized the voice, but I can't imagine why he'd be calling you here."

A minute later, Homer handed the phone back to Rose. "You were right."

"Who?" several small Budges asked at once.

"Skip Peterson," Rose told them.

"And what did he want?" John Michael, their eldest at nineteen, asked or rather demanded, for he was the most serious of the Budge children. He had just arrived on the scene.

"Didn't say," Homer told him. "Just a summons. There's a meeting, this morning, as soon as I can get there."

Homer was shaken. Rose had been right, Peterson never called him at home. Usually he didn't call him at all. If he had any business with the union, he left the dirty work to somebody else. And dirty work it always seemed to be.

"If he wants to see you so bad, he should come down to the union hall," John Michael said.

"We've had this conversation before," Rose pointed out at once. She became uncomfortable in the presence of her eldest's intensity. Much taller than both of his parents, John Michael had been quickly losing the softness of youth—of mind as well as body—and there were times, when Homer encountered him unexpectedly, that he seemed almost a stranger.

"All I'm saying is watch out," he told Homer now and went over and started poking around in the fridge. "You're a nice guy, Dad, but you let him walk all over you."

"You know that's not fair," Rose countered, coming to Homer's defense. She had laid her yellow marker aside.

"Well, I don't think you should go," Joey, the seven-year-old, announced. "If you don't go, Daddy, then he can't do anything."

Homer smiled. "I'm afraid Skip Peterson isn't like a process server, dear. You can't hide in the closet to avoid whatever he's got in mind."

"Well, it's not fair."

"If it was me, Dad, I know what I'd do. I'd just go up to his office and tell him no." This, of course, from John Michael.

He had done term papers on the history of the union. He had theories. He had strategies and tactics. His best friend was the son of one of the firebrands left in the union. A few remained. John Michael was, in short, a militant, born a generation too late.

"Expect I'll wait and see what he's got in mind first," Homer told him.

"Maybe they're gonna sell to the employees," Ruthie suggested, "like the mayor wants." She had paused in her work and turned to face the others. One of the cats was rubbing against her calves, like a skater practicing turns.

"Fat chance," John Michael said.

"You never know, John Michael." Homer didn't believe for a minute that Peterson would do such a thing. But no idea was so certain that John Michael couldn't make it more certain still.

"Come on, Dad, if Goetzinger makes a proposal, that's like the kiss of death."

"Maybe. Maybe not."

John Michael just glared at him. Homer sighed and smiled sadly at his eldest. "Desperate times, dear, make strange bedfellows. Anything might happen."

John Michael pointed the milk carton he was drinking from toward his father. "We make our own futures." This last idea was the great recent discovery of John Michael, the polestar by which he navigated at the moment.

"We'll see," Homer told him.

John Michael pointed the milk carton again. "Just remember what I said. Watch your ass."

"John Michael!" Rose admonished.

The boy put up his hands to deflect the censure. "That's all I got to say. I'm outta here."

And he was, taking the milk with him.

Homer wondered sometimes how he and Rose had managed to raise such a positively hell-bent-for-leather kid. They should have given him a less serious name. If they'd called him Moonbeam or something, maybe he would've been a little less inclined to take up the slack in every blessed situation.

The storm having passed, the rest of the Budges went back to what they'd been doing, Ruthie quietly preparing lunches and conducting inspections, Joey pasting the comic strips he'd been cutting from the morning paper into his scrapbook and so forth. Homer and Rose exchanged a wordless glance.

Homer barely had the heart to speculate about what the call from Skip Peterson might actually mean. Something had happened or was going to happen. The most he could hope for was that the company had finally been sold. If so, the union would have to negotiate with a new owner and more givebacks were sure to be extorted. But as bad as that was, it beat the alternative: no jobs at all.

He tipped up his mug and stared at the puddle of coffee in the bottom and thought, it was true, he'd been the perfect general to lead an orderly retreat. But each new concession took its toll. How nice it would have been if John Michael could have acknowledged the toughness of spirit required even in retreat. Alas, he was blinded by the ideals he read about in textbooks and union literature.

Had John Michael, rather than Homer, been president of the local, by now he would have led some workingman's crusade and gotten a lot of people fired. Homer told himself that that would get them nowhere, although frankly he wasn't as sure as he used to be, not even about that. Homer had never led a strike. He felt like a peacetime soldier. An enduring peace, of course, was a wondrous thing. Yet John Michael must be right about this much at least—that at some point it was better to fight, whatever the odds, whatever the consequences.

This idea was almost enough to make a man lose his sense of humor.

# CHAPTER 35

~

Billy Noel had a good day going. His knife was singing. Ever since both of Fritz's knives had gone sour on him a couple weeks back and he'd taken them to Buck Tekippe to be sharpened, Billy had been thinking he should have Buck reroll his steel. Finally he'd gotten around to it, and now the steel was working, and Billy only had to draw his knife softly across it to hold the edge.

Fritz wasn't there. Just before the last avalon, he'd been called upstairs. Maybe, Billy thought, he'd come back with good news.

Billy had nothing in common with the kid Dickie Streuer had sent over as a replacement, always the same kid when Fritz was gone, the worst of the floaters, a fellow who didn't have much going for him as far as Billy could see. Acne had left pockmarks on his cheeks and his mustache had failed to grow, leaving only a dirty black smudge above his upper lip. He talked about pride too much and lived in a trailer somewhere with a woman who had a couple of kids, apparently from a failed marriage, although Billy wasn't sure.

During the avalon, Billy had sat with the dissidents and mentioned that Fritz had been called upstairs, but nobody seemed much interested. Talk had died down about what was going on with the company. Billy hadn't heard a rumor in two, maybe three days, and it had been longer than that since anybody had talked about Fritz's scheme for the employees to buy the place. It was like people were tired and just wanted to do their jobs and go home. Billy couldn't say he wasn't tired too, just happy to have a good day going, whatever the future might bring.

Fritz had been saying less and less, too. He kept on talking to people from time to time, in the dogged way he had, but Billy could sense the discouragement in him. He could sense it by the way Fritz cut the meat—barely looking at it or with excessive care or almost savagely. He wasn't the man to go around pleading with people.

After the break, back on the floor and still no Fritz, Billy began to feel guilty that he felt so relieved that the buyout scheme wasn't going anywhere. His relief seemed like disloyalty to his friend. Fritz could read it in his face, he was sure, although nothing was said.

Everybody, it seemed, had a reason for rejecting Fritz's proposal. It hadn't been but a few years ago that Billy and Margaret had a little extra. Margaret's arthritis wasn't so bad then. The kids were starting lives of their own and doing pretty good. Now he and Margaret were getting by but just barely. What would happen if a big chunk was taken out of Billy's pay envelope and all he got for it was a tiny stake in the Pack?

Becoming aware of the meat that he'd been trimming, he paused. The best stretches, when his knife was working and only one corner of his mind keeping track, would end when his full consciousness returned to the work, like a floodlight being turned on, which forced him almost to blink, and he had to stop cutting for a few moments to keep from making a mistake.

A buzzer sounded and the line stopped.

Billy took out his steel and ran the blade feather-lightly over it.

"Been using this old Russell steel for thirty years," he said to the kid standing in for Fritz. "Tried different knives. Always came back to the 72-2 here." He held it up, with its thick heavy handle. "Once you get her good and sharp, she holds the edge."

Billy had, of course, said all this before, but with the rerolled steel and the good day going, he felt called upon to say it again. The kid wasn't interested. He had the company-issue steel. Everything he had was company-issue.

When the line started again, Billy took up his thoughts where he'd left them. Suppose the company closed, what would he do? This was the only work he'd ever known, except summer jobs as a teenager. He read stories about people going from career to career nowadays but still couldn't imagine it. Such people, without roots, tumbleweeds, why they'd be no better off than the young kids coming to work at JackPack for a year or two because they didn't have anything better to do with their lives.

Yet the work was surely hard on a man. At this thought, Billy's sciatic nerve vibrated sympathetically, and he paused to rub his buttock and then thigh, tracing the path of the ache down into his knee joint where it throbbed and slowly died away.

It was true, the work was hard, he repeated as he set himself at the cutting board again, but at least a man could take some satisfaction in standing up to it day after day, year after year. Most people didn't last. Anyway, he thought, pain was better than hopelessness.

He decided that when the shift ended he'd clean the pouch he kept his equipment in. He'd use one of the green pads, soap and water. He didn't want to get dinged by the inspectors. He'd clean his hat, too, while he was at it. Make sure everything was just like it should be.

A few minutes before the dinner break, Dickie Streuer came over to Billy's station with a replacement in tow.

"You're wanted upstairs," the foreman told Billy.

"Me? Why?"

"Don't ask me, I just work here."

"You sure it's me they want?"

"You're Noel, ain't ya?" Streuer shook his head, as if he wondered, too, how the likes of Billy Noel got to go while he was stuck doing the same damn thing day after day, never called upstairs.

Billy walked slowly at first, trying to figure out what it might be. It occurred to him that maybe something had happened to Fritz, but even if that was true, he couldn't imagine why they would have called for him. Was he being fired then? Or worse, much worse, had something happened to Margaret? He hurried faster up the iron stairs.

In the general offices, he wandered around, not knowing where he was supposed to go. He asked a couple of people, but they couldn't tell him. Finally, he arrived at the desk of the president's secretary, and she pointed down the hall, toward the big conference room.

"What's going on?" he asked her, but she just shook her head like Dickie Streuer had.

The door to the conference room was closed, and he held a fist up as if to knock while looking questioningly back at the secretary.

"Just go in," she called down to him.

After a brief attempt to tidy his clothes, he slowly opened the door. The muffled voices inside became louder, then ceased. Billy bent forward to look in, the lower half of his body still in the hall.

Skip Peterson was there, and next to him Homer Budge, and around the table, every bigwig in the company and the union so far as Billy could tell.

"Com'in, com'in, Billy," Skip Peterson said, waving him into the room. "Close the door."

Billy entered only far enough so that he could obey Peterson's order.

"What's going on?" he asked. He spotted Fritz, sitting on the far side of the table.

"Com'in," the CEO repeated. "Have a seat."

Billy noticed a lone empty chair at the table, and after a hesitation, feeling suddenly that he was holding things up, moved quickly over to it and sat across from Fritz, who nodded.

"All right, then," Skip Peterson said, "we're all here. To bring you up to the mark, Billy, what's going on is this. It won't come as a complete surprise, I expect, but after long deliberation, and in light of the current situation here, we've decided that an attempt should be made to sell the Jackson Packing Company to you and your fellow employees."

Billy's bafflement at having been summoned into the presence of all these people was too powerful at the moment for him to react very strongly to this news.

"You wanted me?"

"Fritz over there thought it would be a good idea if you were on the steering committee."

"Me?"

"None other."

"But why?" he asked, speaking not to Skip Peterson now but to Fritz.

"You're just the man this committee needs, Billy," his friend assured him.

"I don't understand. I'm no expert. I don't know about these things."

Homer Budge now spoke up. "Fritz wanted you on the committee, Billy. And a good idea, it is, if you ask me. Get somebody up here from the rank and file."

Stunned, Billy merely sat mutely and stared first at Fritz and then at Budge.

"You're not alone, Billy," Skip Peterson resumed. "We're all rookies here."

Billy started to say again that he didn't understand but caught himself. Him? On a committee to buy the Pack?

Peterson turned to the group. "If that's taken care of, let's move on."

Fritz had put on his civvies, but Billy, of course, still wore his frock and hardhat and scabbard. He held the hat in his lap as he listened, sitting up straight and conscious of the contours of the chair and conscious, too, of the high company officials on either side of him. On his right sat Mel Coyle, the corporate council, and on his left Roy Handel, the vice president in charge of operations, the very man Billy worked for, Billy and Fritz and Dickie Streuer and everybody else on the kill floor.

At first, nothing that was said made much sense, and Billy was mostly aware of his own confusion. Gradually, calming down a bit, he made an effort to pay attention to the others.

One man—Ted Bates, the human resources director—leaned an elbow on the table and casually tossed out ideas. Others appeared either involved and genuinely interested or completely the opposite, silent and withdrawn. What Billy noticed the most was the tension in the room. Except for Fritz, that is. Fritz sat comfortably, listening carefully but without visible emotion, as if he had been a neutral observer called in to witness. A couple of times Billy caught his friend's eye and Fritz nodded slightly, as if to affirm the rightness of Billy being there. Why, Billy wondered, had Fritz wanted him? He couldn't imagine. It couldn't have been just a suggestion, like Mr. Peterson seemed to say. Fritz must have insisted. But why?

Something else Billy wondered, too. The employee buyout was Fritz's idea, yet here he was, barely participating. Skip Peterson sat at the head of the table and next to him sat Homer Budge, the two of them doing most of the talking.

In all his years with the company, Billy had never taken part in a meeting with Skip Peterson, or with any of the Petersons, except at big general gatherings of the employees. He could hardly wait to get home and tell Margaret.

The vision of his wife and her imagined response and the long discussion they were sure to have over what it meant—all this helped to bring home to him the reality of his situation and to settle him down a little bit more. And then he began to attend more closely to what was being said.

# CHAPTER 36

~

Rachel Brandeis waited in the lee of the *Tribune* doorway, shielding herself against the freshening wind. From where she stood, nothing of nature remained visible, no trees, no street plantings. A red light repeatedly stepped down the neon spire atop a nearby bank building—the temperature was dropping. The warmth of summer had faded, the cold of winter not yet arrived, and the in-between felt less pleasant than either.

She had no idea what Skip Peterson would be driving, but when the red Corvette darted into view in the distance and advanced impatiently, accelerating and decelerating between stoplights, she knew it must be him. The car slid to a stop next to her and the passenger side door flew open.

"Dinner?" he asked as soon as she had squeezed herself into the low bucket seat.

"If you want."

Rachel didn't know why he'd called her, probably to complain about the pieces she'd written. Okay by her. After nearly six weeks of dealing with the snippety know-from-nothings that worked for him, she was just glad to have another shot at the man himself.

He drove with the same impatience with which he had conducted her around the packinghouse, now pointing out landmarks rather than the minutiae of hog slaughtering. In dim profile, his face was thinner than she remembered.

The seat belt pinned her against the low reclining seat. The powerful engine surged just a few inches from her feet. Traffic loomed above.

"Nice car," she remarked, not quite meaning it.

"About time to store it for the winter. City uses too much salt on the roads."

They had climbed through the bluffs to the suburbs on the western prairies. At the horizon, the sun lay huge and misshapen. The utility wires overhead glowed as if covered with ice.

Peterson parked at a supermarket and turned to her. In the intimacy of the tiny space, she imagined for a moment he meant to make an advance and flinched slightly. He paused and seemed to note her uneasiness.

"Where are we going?" she asked.

"My home."

"What's this all about?"

"I'd rather wait on that a bit, if you don't mind."

Alone with a man she hardly knew, Rachel never felt entirely comfortable. Peterson made the difficulty much worse, for reasons you could pile from here to forever. She remembered being drawn to him during their walk around the plant, a man so utterly different from others she had known, and with power and no doubt with a sense of entitlement, too. Would he keep his hands to himself? She didn't know, but she bucked herself up. This was no time to be a wuss.

"Okay," she said.

"I brought some pork from the plant, but if you'd prefer, we can get something else while we're here."

"Pork will be fine."

"Good."

Inside the supermarket, Peterson moved smartly up and down the aisles, occasionally greeting a fellow shopper or one of the stockmen, since in Jackson he was a star. As he moved, his heathery suit jacket flapped like wings around his tall, spare frame.

He went to the produce man and spoke to him privately, and the fellow disappeared into the back and returned with four ears of corn and peeled back the husk of one so they could inspect it, murmuring, their heads close together, enjoying the opportunity to make a judgment. When Peterson stood still, his clothes hung limply, deflated.

The corn in hand, he walked over to the meat section, checked out the display of JackPack products, and then complained about something to the man behind the counter.

Back in the Corvette, they continued west, out of the city. The sun had set and in the gathering dusk, they drove past black silhouettes of trees beneath a dark, luminous blue sky.

Finally he turned onto a county road, laid out as straight as the surveyor's art could make it. Out of the side window, Rachel watched the edge of the car's headlights bounce over the stalks of a harvested cornfield. They said little. The silence and the dark countryside renewed her discomfort. Peterson might be taking her anywhere. Powerful men took advantage of situations. If something happened, would people believe her or Peterson? What was she in Jackson? A nothing. She thought these thoughts, and then discarded them. She couldn't respect a person who had such thoughts.

They drove through a pair of massive stone gates and into what she supposed was some sort of development. At least there were streets and streetlights and sidewalks.

"Where are the houses?"

"This was started a few years ago by a consortium of local doctors. Supposed to be an upscale community. They got the utilities in and, bingo, the real estate market collapsed." A network of curlicue roads had been laid out and paved, with curb cuts for nonexistent driveways. The streetlights shone down on the crusty, baked-looking earth, cracked and tilted up where weeds had forced their way through it.

On the farthest dead-end street stood a single house, a rambling structure draped over the crown of a hill. Peterson parked in front, leaving the headlights on as he talked.

"Pennsylvania farmhouse. We had the main section made out of limestone mined locally, the step-down wing—over there—that's plaster, and the garage is, as you can see, wood. In the old days back East, farmers used to add to their places from generation to generation, using whatever styles and materials came to hand."

"But not here."

"No, we built it all at once. A fashion statement, I suppose you'd say. My wife and I were going to move out here. I had the cockamamie idea it would be a good place to entertain. She begged to differ." Rachel could see why. They got out and approached the building.

"But you're not married now?" she said, half statement, half question.

Inside, the house smelled of cold and furniture polish. As they passed each room, she peeked in but not much could be seen in the dimness—order, spindly furniture.

"No, we split up, but not over the house," he told her. "Because I couldn't do my job and be a decent husband, too. My fault entirely. Anyway, Lois and I have what they call a good divorce."

He paused in the hallway and adjusted a thermostat, and she heard a furnace stir deep inside the building.

"For instance," he said, looking back at Rachel just long enough to smile, "she never returned your calls, did she?"

In the restaurant-sized kitchen, he deposited the grocery bag on a counter and, his suit coat still on, grabbed pans and utensils off hooks and opened a cabinet, where he rotated a large circular shelf, pulling down condiments as it turned. Except for the veneer on the cabinets, everything was ultramodern, with a massive gas range over which hung an equally massive smoke hood, stacked ovens, long runs of stainless steel counters, and a blizzard of kitchen tools hanging from overhead.

He motioned toward a small, tiled counter, the only place in the room apparently meant for eating rather than preparation. "I'll cook, you write."

He wasted no time, and soon the dinner was well underway and Rachel had been given not a tongue-lashing for the stories already written but a new one to write, the lead for the next day's edition of the *Trib*. An employee buyout was to be attempted after all, what was called an ESOP, an employee stock ownership plan. Much depended on a consultant's report, under preparation for months, to which the possibility of an ESOP would now be appended. If feasible, money would be deducted from the employees' paychecks for stock purchases, and the employees would end up owning the company.

"Fritz Goetzinger's scheme, then," she said.

"He's on the buyout committee," Peterson said. "I'll talk about him later if you want." His tone was of impatience and dismissal. The phone rang and he answered it.

"Yes?" He listened intently for a few moments. "What did he say?" The caller spoke loudly enough so that Rachel could hear, not the words, just the intensity. A male voice. Skip told him, "I'll be down. Give me an hour."

Rachel noticed her tinge of disappointment that she was to have only a carefully meted out portion of Peterson's time. So much for her thoughts that she might have to fight off his sexual advances, too.

He went on with the food preparation, interspersing answers to her questions and his own plumping for the buyout with comments about cooking pork.

"I know we can be a profitable operation. The trick is attention to details, farm to table, nothing left to chance. That's the key. And I'll tell you what also needs to happen. The employees need to get a winning attitude. It is about winning and losing, you know, Rachel, it's not about saving jobs—excuse me, it's not *just* about saving jobs." She could sense his irritation and regret that such obfuscations were necessary. It's not about saving jobs, then. It's about winning and losing. About going head-to-head with Modern Meat.

He speared one of the cubes of meat and waved it in the air. "You see, the fat is concentrated around the muscle, so if you trim it carefully, you get virtually fatless meat."

Now he moved toward a commercial-size fridge, saying, "Pork is a helluva lot more versatile than beef." He opened the fridge and extracted a bottle of wine. "For instance, almost any wine goes with it. It can stand up to a strong red and doesn't drown out the most delicate white. I happen to like this Liebfraumilch, soft, a little on the sweet side. A glass for you? Good."

Moments later, he was back at the cutting board and back on the possibilities of the employee buyout. "There are lots of farmers who've been raising hogs for slaughter all their lives and yet have never been inside a packinghouse. Well, we've got to do something about that. Make these people our partners, help them produce better animals. Help them, help ourselves…"

And on and on he went, sowing his words as if they were dragon's teeth from which an army would spring up to save his company. Yet despite this, Rachel could get little measure of the man or the value of what he said. He reminded her of a performance artist. She liked the way he looked but in the same way she might admire a male model in a clothing ad. He did everything quickly, in flight.

Rachel couldn't have been more different. Her body dragged her down, on her best days zaftig, on her worst, a *schlump*. She felt better now that the heat of summer had passed, but even on the crispest of fall days, her nature remained phlegmatic, her impulse always to sit stolidly observant, making ironic comments upon the scene.

Peterson shoveled the stir-fry onto a pair of plates, plucked the corn from a pot of boiling water, and they ate. For a time nothing more was said. He seemed to make an effort to taste the food, savor the wine, his perpetual motion briefly in remission. She remained conscious of the dark and silent rooms all about them.

"Okay?" he asked.

"Delicious." And it was, except for the rather tasteless corn, this being much too late in the season. "But why," she asked finally, "isn't the buyout too ambitious? Why aren't you…well, like the doctors who started this development?"

Peterson abandoned his meal, half-eaten. He leaned far back and regarded her through lowered lids. He had the large, expressive eyes of a thin man.

"If we concentrate on just one aspect of the business—say, cutting costs, becoming more efficient, that sort of thing—then we fail. But we're not going to do that."

Rachel felt at ease. During her recent trial by fire, her bullshit meter had been fine-tuned, and it had certainly been registering during Peterson's smooth-talking shtick of the last three-quarters of an hour.

"I don't know," she said to him. "It all seems pretty vague to me. Is this why you brought me out here? All this could have been put into a news release."

"Yes, it could have."

"As far as I can tell," Rachel told him, "no disrespect, the Jackson Packing Company is on the verge of going out of business."

He frowned and regarded her as he had for an instant during the plant tour of several weeks earlier, a glimpse of the hostility lying just beneath his performance-artist exterior. Despite the bluntness of her last comment, Rachel wasn't prepared for him to remove the mask so abruptly, and she caught her breath.

"Okay," he said, "put your notebook away, the rest is off the record." He sprang up, his expression severe, and thrust his hands deep into his pockets and began pacing. Finally he continued.

"Len Sawyer hired you as a muckraker. That's an old term, but it certainly applies. You know about the troubles between my family and Sawyer."

"I know now. I didn't when I toured the Pack."

He nodded. "I'm not surprised. Good."

"Tell me, why the feud?"

"The beginning? Trivial. Sawyer and my grandfather got into it over nothing. Happened about 1940. They'd been friends and then had a tiff of some sort, over what, I don't know. Nothing much, anyway. After that, my grandfather bought a boat and wanted to berth it in the Ice Harbor, but Sawyer wouldn't let him do it. Sawyer was already head of the dock board. Both he and my grandfather could be pigheaded. Basically they just decided one day to hate each other. Happens. Do you know about the flood fight in the early fifties?"

"Yes, and the strike."

"Right. Well, as they say, the rest is history."

"Why haven't you patched it up?"

He thought about that and said, "Probably we should have tried harder." He thought some more. "Up until now, JackPack's been strictly a private firm, with a handful of stockholders. Our fate has depended on what we did, not on what somebody like Sawyer...or *you* said about us." He waved away an imagined protest as he paced. "But now? Well, now all has changed. We're going to have thousands of stockholders, almost all of them local people. We'll still be private, but only in a narrow legal sense. What we'll really be is a company deeply embedded in the community, like, I don't know, blood in flesh. You take a neighborhood, no matter how small, and in it you'll find people who own stock, people who have become the lifeblood of the Jackson Packing Company, so to speak. Now what you say matters."

"A prospect which doesn't appeal to you very much."

"To be flat-out honest, that's right, it doesn't. Look, Rachel, I brought you out here because I couldn't think of a better place to say what I had to say. In a way, I suppose I *am* trying to seduce you—I saw the way you looked at me in the car, I knew what you were thinking—but what I'm doing doesn't have anything to do with sex. I need your help." Abruptly he changed the subject. "Tell me, when you write a lead paragraph, is there only one way to do it?"

"Of course not."

"Right, of course not. You make choices." He grabbed the back of the chair he'd been sitting on earlier and leaned toward her and spoke softly, barely above a whisper. "And they matter, those choices you make."

Rachel had no intention of being seduced, sexually or otherwise. "Surely, you don't expect me to become a branch of your PR department."

He sat down again, quickly, on the edge of the chair, and leaned toward her. "No, of course not. But when people read your stories, they don't just read them. A little voice inside looks for the meaning underneath. You see what I'm saying? It's not even a voice maybe, maybe it doesn't even have language, maybe it's before language, that yearning thing deep inside us. You know about that. Yearning and judging and fearing. Call it intuition, call it a sixth sense, call it whatever. But it's finally what's reading your story, and it's finally what counts. And it exists in you, too, Rachel, and it guides your writing just as surely as it guides their reading."

This little speech had been as well organized as his earlier spiel about how he was going to save the Pack. But Rachel was not as unreflective as he seemed to think.

"You're wrong if you imagine I'm not aware of this."

He was up and pacing again. "Being aware isn't good enough. The stories you've written so far are stories of the death of a company." He waved away another imagined protest. "Jacksonians read your stuff and they decide it's time for the Jackson Packing Company to die...and so we die."

"I've written the stories that were there to write, and, I must say, no thanks to you."

"Yes, yes, I understand. Perhaps we should have been more up-front with you, I don't know." He gave her a quick glance and smile. "You're quite good, you know." Then he went immediately back to his pacing, hands thrust into his pockets, head down. "Anyway, it's too late to worry about what might have been. Look, for the Pack to be saved, everything has to go just right from now on, everything. And that means we have to have the support of the *Trib*."

"Maybe you should talk to Leonard Sawyer. I'm just a lowly reporter." Rachel said this, however, without her usual edge, pleased that Peterson had acknowledged her ability.

"I plan to talk to Neil Houselog," he told her. "Maybe the old man, too, if it works out. Because the union's involved, probably the paper will come out in favor of the buyout. But if you've heard a word I've said the last few minutes, you realize that I think your stories are at least as important as anything that appears on the editorial page, maybe more. You're the one who sets the tone here, you and no one else."

She resisted what Peterson was saying. He had begun to clear the plates from the table. "I'm a reporter," she told him. "I try to be objective. I try to be fair."

With his back to her, returning the wine bottle to the fridge, he said, "I'm sure you do." He didn't complete the thought until he returned to the table. "What I'm saying is that you can't be either, not really, except maybe in some rough-and-ready way. I'm serious about this, Rachel. I want you to know that if this buyout doesn't work, part of the reason will be the stories you've written. I want you to think about that. I'm not trying to make you mad, but it's absolutely essential that you accept your responsibility here."

He did make her mad, though, trying to implicate her in whatever might happen, trying to frighten her. "I'll be fair, Mr. Peterson. I promise you nothing else."

"I hope you'll be more than fair. My door will always be open. Everything's out on the table now—income statements, balance sheets, the works. No more secrets. You can get anything you want. But you've got more power than you realize. It's important that you use that power responsibly. I'm trying to speak truthfully. You want me to speak truthfully, don't you?"

Rachel understood that in bringing her out there, rather than to the company or some restaurant, he'd done more than simply assure himself of privacy. He'd made sure that what he had to say would be personal, would possess an intimacy. He had consciously breached a wall of decorum, even if, as he said, it had nothing to do with sex, although in her mind, where men and women were concerned, sex was always part of the conversation.

"Okay?" he asked. "Will you think about that for me?" He was piling the dirty dishes in one of the sinks. He didn't bother to wait for an answer, but said simply, "I've got to go back to work. Where can I drop you?"

# CHAPTER 37

~

At 2:40 a.m., Homer Budge slid quietly from beside Rose, as he did at that hour every Wednesday morning. He washed quickly in the children's bathroom and dressed in the hall, where Rose had left his clothes carefully draped over a chair. All around him, he felt the presence of the others, as if the very house itself breathed slowly in and out.

At two minutes to three, he parked in one of the diagonal slots of a small, neighborhood strip mall, before a plain commercial storefront, and let himself in the front door. Inside, all was dark except for an aura of light from the frosted glass of a doorway at the far end of the corridor that divided the building in two. Homer moved through the darkness, opened the door, and noiselessly entered what had once been an office or conference room but now was filled with rows of pews.

He turned toward the front, where a monstrance stood on a long altar table, and genuflected before settling into one of the pews, two rows behind Henry Rollins, the adorer from two to three. At other times of the day, a number of people might be found at Power of Prayer, come to pray or read the Bible or simply sit and reflect, but at that time of the night, only the person scheduled was likely to be found there.

Homer sat quietly for a minute, inhaling the fragrance of the beeswax candles and the faint odor of continuous human presence. Then he pulled out the kneeler and began his hour as adorer, saying the Rosary.

A short time later, as Henry got up to leave, Homer realized his mind had strayed. He had been thinking about John Michael's response to the news of the employee buyout attempt. All night, lying sleepless next to Rose, Homer had been haunted by the events of the day. Apparently this hour of devotion would bring no release.

He listened to Henry's retreating footfalls, slightly uncertain in the darkness of the hallway. He didn't hear the front door open, only close, then the car start, sounds that would have been masked by other noises during the day, but in the deep nighttime stillness left their trace.

He let his mind settle once more, and then continued praying. He'd forgotten his Rosary beads and so had to count out the decades of Hail Marys on his fingers. A minute, perhaps two, later, he realized that he'd stopped again. Thoughts came like temptations.

He began once more, but his mind continued to wander. Partway through a prayer, the words trailed off and scenes from earlier in the day took their place. Talking with Skip Peterson, with the union's executive committee, with so many others. The employees buy the company? Did that make any sense at all? He didn't know. He realized how desperate such an offer from the company must be. Peterson had to be telling the truth when he said the alternative was to close the place down.

Homer stopped thinking these thoughts and instead of beginning the Rosary again simply kept his eyes closed and listened to his breathing. A good Rosary, prayerfully prayed, took fifteen or twenty minutes. He glanced at his watch. He'd already been there twenty minutes and wasn't even halfway through the Joyful Mysteries.

He looked about himself. The room was as simple as a monk's cell. At the front, in the center of the long table, stood the monstrance, a golden sunburst at its heart, where a lunette held the consecrated Host. Lilies leaned in vases on either side, and smoke twined upward from the candles at the ends of the table. The weaving flames cast faint, moving shadows of the lilies.

He gazed upon these and wondered if the intention was genuine where the performance remained so lamentable. How often had he come to Power of Prayer and taken the better part of the hour to say the Rosary? Other people didn't seem to have a problem focusing, the beads ticking steadily through their fingers.

Homer understood his limitations. It might be said he had a certain affection for them, the familiars with which he had spent his life. But nevertheless, he now thought, if he was such an inadequate adorer where his commitment was so heartfelt, how could he possibly lead something like a buyout of the packing company where he was hounded by a great mob of fears and uncertainties?

For John Michael had had a point. Homer's dear but troublesome eldest son could be counted on to come up with some perfectly dreadful interpretation of events. This time, however, he could well be right. Peterson might be setting the employees up to take the fall when the company failed. They had had their chance to buy the firm, he would say, and they blew it. Homer shuddered.

Such a thought, of course, would be shared by certain conspiracy buffs among the union brethren. No matter how bizarre the possibility, a number of members were sure to find the logic overwhelming. Some would say that this sudden willingness to throw the company records open to the union proved that there were two sets of books. Many would say this was nothing but wages cuts by another name. If only, Homer thought wistfully, it were true. At that moment, he would have welcomed with open arms some devious plot. But no, alas, they were well beyond devious plots. If the employees didn't buy the place, it would fail, he was sure of it. So, the question was, would his people be willing to swap part of their pay for company stock? Homer didn't know. If they woke up to the reality they faced, perhaps. Perhaps, if something could be done about the animosity between the union and Skip's people. But all that history. And Homer, smack dab in the middle, limitations and all.

He looked at his watch. Three twenty-five.

"Dear me."

He returned to the Rosary and for five minutes said the Hail Marys and Our Fathers and Glory Be's with determination, but then he stopped, realizing the silliness of such a mechanical performance.

He arched his back and lifted and carefully replanted each knee, sore from kneeling. He tried to stop thinking, since all his thoughts were so unwelcome, but of course he failed at this attempt as he had at the others. Then he tried to remember a prayer for the situation. One started, "Inspire our actions, O Lord, by your grace," but he couldn't remember the rest. He wasn't even sure he had the beginning right. He had never had much of a memory.

He would have prayed in his own words for help, but something Father Leo Strauss, his parish priest, had once said deterred him. Father Leo had suggested that the hour Homer spent as an adorer might most fruitfully be employed in learning to be a better listener. "Too often," Father had said, "we Catholics fail to listen. We only know how to ask."

And so, everything else having failed, Homer tried to listen. But he found this as difficult as the rest. The intense silence prickled in his ears. It seemed not like silence at all, but rather filled with a white noise made up of countless words, as white light is a mixture of every color. All his discontents shouted at once.

He struggled against the desire to rise and flee.

Instead, he looked at his watch again. Time crept by. He went back to the Rosary, taking it up again in his ramshackle way. He thought about the company. He thought about his inadequacies. He did have, he reminded himself, his virtues, which Rose never tired of pointing out. He did see both sides of an issue. How else would he have known what to concede and what to hang on to when he was haggling with management? Perhaps this new situation wasn't any different, the trick being where to draw the line. This inkling gave him a little hope, but it didn't help with the saying of the Rosary.

In this manner, he arrived at the end of the hour and still hadn't finished the Joyful Mysteries.

# CHAPTER 38

~

Behind her Chuck sat at the kitchen table, wolfing down his cold cereal. Diane could hear the pages being turned as he glanced through the magazine she'd left next to his place mat. Of course, he wouldn't ignore a copy of the *Canadian National Geographic*. Probably he had never seen one before. Certainly she'd gone to enough trouble to get it, Yellowknife not being a storied community.

He laughed when he sat down. "Where did you find that?"

"I have my ways."

All around them order reigned—breakfast dishes stacked, Todd off to school, the dogs banished for the day to their run out back. Diane would drop Grace off at the day care on her way to work. From the other room floated Grace's voice, tiny, lilting, self-absorbed.

In a few minutes, it would be exactly one week since the call had come. Although Diane had respected Mark O'Banion, she believed that Chuck, if only he wanted to, would make a better public works director. She didn't have much time. He would be busy down at City Hall, each day burning another bridge.

Her approach was the soul of simplicity, even a little crude, for Chuck was the kind of person who noted subtlety but chose to ignore it. Directness was required. Deviousness, he hated above all else.

She didn't turn around immediately when she heard him toss the magazine aside but first finished packing Grace's lunch in the little plastic pail with the orange and yellow flowers. Then she poured herself a quarter cup of coffee and sat down opposite.

He had finished his cereal, replaced the bowl with his coffee cup, and leaned back, arms crossed, in a favorite pose, ready to render verdicts. "So you've been doing some research."

"Yes, I wanted to know something about the place."

He nodded and waited for her to continue.

"Did you look at those pictures? Did you really look at them?"

Chuck grinned. "Seemed okay to me. Place maybe isn't a theme park, but so what?"

"But that's just it. Yellowknife is a theme park. It's gold mines—miners, hydroelectric dam, prefab buildings, conveyers, everything you need to dig holes in the ground. And that's all, dear. There's nothing else."

"I seem to have read that it's the capital of the Northwest Territories."

"Anything with 'territories' in its title is highly suspect, if you ask me."

Chuck laughed.

Diane reminded herself not to argue with him. He'd seen the pictures. That was enough. Now was the time to switch subjects.

"You've always complained how your father dragged you from home to home when you were growing up. And now you want to do the same thing with your own kids. And a place with lousy schools, no decent library, nothing."

"You don't know that," he retorted. "Anyway, you got computers, you got satellites. It doesn't make any difference where you live anymore."

"I'm sure that's right," she retorted, using her archest tone.

"And all kids are heathens. They love places like Yellowknife."

"At least you admit it's a place fit only for heathens."

"I don't admit anything. As for my old man, the reasons he was a shitty father had nothing to do with all the times we moved."

Mention of his father always sobered Chuck.

"I can't remember how many times you've talked about how much your mother hated to move."

"We moved every year. I'm just asking you to move once."

"Only once? Is that a promise? You don't know what a comfort it is to be told that when we get to Yellowknife, we'll never leave."

"My parents had a lousy marriage from day one," he said. "If they'd never gone anywhere, they would have had a lousy marriage."

"You ask me, all the moving around had something to do with it."

"Bullshit." He spoke softly. They both spoke softly. Grace was in the next room.

Over the last several weeks, they had had many of these testy little exchanges. She didn't want to argue with him—told herself not to argue with him—but one thing would lead to another, and once they were going at each other, she couldn't afford to back down. That was almost as bad as being devious.

But bringing up his father had been a surefire way to set Chuck off. He couldn't stand the idea that he might be like him, not even the least little bit.

He sat perfectly still, holding his tough-guy pose. Diane got up and grabbed his cereal bowl and irritably began to wash it, conscious of this habitual behavior. The madder she got, the neater, too. Even with her back to him, her vision was filled with his uncompromising image.

"We are not your parents," she said finally.

"I hope the hell not."

She had said as much on this subject as she cared to for the moment. But she wasn't through. She told herself again not to argue. Chuck liked arguments too much. He called them "adjustment discussions." Okay, then, she wouldn't argue anymore, but she would make her points. And she'd make them as telling as she could.

She decided the bowl wasn't clean yet and cleaned it again.

"You know," she said, "back in the sixties draft dodgers used to go to Canada."

She said no more, letting him draw his own conclusions. To accuse him of cowardice was worse than accusing him of being like his father. But whatever he cared to call it, this was an act of cowardice, this running away to Canada. She rinsed the bowl finally and stacked it in the dish rack and then, her hands still wet, propped herself up on the edge of the sink and waited.

"Nice try," he said, "but the sixties got nothing to do with this," his words cool and deliberate.

She took a few moments to calm herself before turning to face him. "I think they have everything to do with it."

Chuck said nothing. She held his gaze and then slowly turned away, and that was the end of the conversation.

On his way downtown, Chuck mulled over the tense little firefight with Diane. What she was up to was obvious enough. He found it annoying, but it made sense. Fair enough.

Another man, in such a guerrilla war, might have endlessly rehashed his own self-justifications, but Chuck's thinking became calmer and calmer in such a situation. Time slowed. Each of Diane's moves unfolded as if predestined, and Chuck, a powerful believer in human intuition, sought for that vision of what was to happen next. He sought for his own acts in this way as well. The parts of his life he ranged in orderly ranks about himself. He acted out of that orderliness. But the act itself must always and ever, like combustion, arise out of the spontaneous moment. And so, from a distance, he watched Diane act and himself respond and waited for what would happen next.

One thing he knew. Diane was running a bluff. She and the kids would go north with him if he got the job in Yellowknife. As for the job itself, he was powerfully drawn by the idea of testing himself in a place where humans weren't such a big deal, where the best they could hope for in their campaign to control nature was a chancy truce.

And with Mark dead, what was there to keep him in Jackson? Not a damn thing.

Instead of turning off toward City Hall, he drove on, in the direction of the waterfront. Just for the hell of it, he would take a look at the dog track, Mark's pet project. He drove past the end of the dredge's pipeline. Apparently the dredge was down again, and so he thought he might as well look at that, too, as long as he was down there. He passed by the entrance to the track site, following the pipeline down and under the Wisconsin bridge approach.

The dredge, bow heavy, lay dark and silent in the river shallows. Chuck walked out along the rough, mossy-looking planking laid atop the pontoons of the floating line, noting the lack of a handrail and wondering why the local OSHA guy hadn't gotten on the dock board's case. Beneath, the river water lapped back and forth so slowly it appeared to be congealing in the cool air. Ahead of him, the spuds, on which the dredge pivoted as it stepped forward vacuuming sand from the river bottom, rose from the stern like a brace of telephone poles.

He stepped gingerly onto the deck, a narrow walkway around the dredge's engine house. All around him were littered unwound cables and come-alongs and machine casings and rusting objects of uncertain function. The sight of them offended Chuck's orderly mind.

At the bow, the cutterhead hung on cables beneath an A-frame support. Rust caked the whole apparatus, except for the cutterhead itself, a swirling basketry of metal teeth, burnished by its constant churning against the sand and gravel on the river bottom.

Below the control room window, the name of the dredge had been painted, the paint chipped and faded so that it took him a few moments to decipher it—Lydia.

He tried the doors to the machine room. Locked. Through the dusty windows, he squinted at the dark shapes within. The round top of the pump's volute reflected a faint patch of light. He could also make out the bulky shape of the diesel engine behind it. As his eyes adjusted to the gloom, he could see that the linkage between the pump and engine had been taken down, and he imagined he could discern parts scattered here and there. Chuck was no expert on pumps, but he could guess what the problem must be: the packings. Elsewhere in the large room, all seemed to be in disarray. It resembled a junkyard, tools scattered idly about, a workbench buried under discarded machine subassemblies, frayed blackened hydraulic hoses, cans of lubricant and paint with the lids left off, electrical fixtures with no covers, machinery so rusty and abused-looking he couldn't imagine it might still function.

This, he thought bitterly, was what Diane expected him to deal with. He turned away and left the dredge, marching back to his pickup without once looking behind him, and drove away.

# CHAPTER 39

~

The license tag on the pickup Jack Kelley followed the last half mile to the track site read ABN INF, which, he decided, must stand for airborne infantry. Not having been in the Army, he could only speculate on the joys of jumping out of airplanes while being shot at. The only army Jack was part of was the Church Militant, where he supposed he was some kind of NCO, between officers like Father Mike Daugherty and enlisted men like, well, Tony Vasconcellos. The world, the flesh, and the devil. Vasconcellos wasn't on the job site yet, thank God. Jack had another month or so before he had to deal with that particular example of fallen humanity. Bad enough that he was still doing Don Adagian's old job as well as his own.

The pickup passed by the track access road, and Jack, turning in, quickly forgot about it. He scanned the job site as he approached. The first of the semis with the precast had arrived. Good.

This small pleasure began to erode at once. He saw figures milling around. The sticks of the two big cranes canted idly out over the grandstand site. Jack parked and got out. Toward him came Cletus Dickey. It seemed that every day Jack arrived at the site, Dickey materialized first.

"We got a situation," he said as he neared. He had come at a dogtrot, no doubt for the satisfaction of being first to bring Jack the bad news.

"Let me guess. The truck came through the union gate."

"You got her." Jack could read the excitement in the foreman's face. Dickey loved situations.

"Are they Teamsters?"

"Yup. Makes no difference, I'm told, being as how they're delivering to a nonunion guy. That's what they're saying anyhow."

"Right." Of course Cletus knew perfectly well that it made no difference. The trucker didn't come through the non-union gate, as he should have, and so the union gate had been tainted.

"Too bad I didn't know beforehand," Dickey said. "Now I gotta pay my people show-up money."

Jack, hearing the surge of an approaching diesel engine, turned to see another eighteen-wheeler with precast—a load of concrete columns—passing the parked vehicles and queuing up behind the first. Undoubtedly, it too had come through the union gate.

"Shit," he said.

With Dickey on his heels, he hustled over to the construction trailer and let himself in and after a couple of calls managed to get through to the carrier's dispatcher and give directions to be passed along to her drivers so that the remaining loads didn't make the same mistake. If it was a mistake. Given that the drivers were Teamsters, the whole episode could have been choreographed. Probably was. Probably they'd keep on coming through the union gate.

Back outside, he was surprised to see Chuck Fellows striding toward him.

At their first meeting, following Mark O'Banion's death, Fellows had curtly informed him that he wasn't the new public works director and that the dog track wasn't his responsibility. Perhaps he'd changed his mind. If so, he was exactly the man Jack needed at that moment.

"What's going on?" Fellows asked.

Jack pulled him aside. "Come into the trailer."

Cletus, whose curiosity knew no bounds, was still shadowing Jack, eager to add to his store of wisdom. Jack told him, "Go tell your people to stick around. We're not through here today."

Dickey dismissed, Jack led the way back toward the trailer, telling Fellows, "If it isn't one thing, it's another."

This business of violating the union gate was not such a big deal. Jack had been anticipating some sort of trouble over the two-gate system. Jackson being a union town and the unions having been taking it on the chin of late, they were spoiling for a fight. So, this was not a surprise, but after two weeks as both field manager and project manager, trying to simultaneously live in the present and the future, Jack was feeling sorely put upon. "I'm trying to do two damn jobs here, and these bastards don't give a shit." He turned to Fellows. "It's not like this is just another project, you know. But all these people care about is themselves."

Inside the trailer, he continued bitching, thinking, okay, Fellows was here, he worked for the city, he could help out. He put a hand on Fellows's shoulder. This was an important project for the city, a helluva lot more important if the Pack closed. Fellows listened, saying nothing, just moving far enough away so that Jack lost physical contact with him. Precast was controlling now, Jack told him. They had to start flying it. After precast, the topping slab. Then the steel. Then the roof. If they didn't get these guys back to work—now, as in immediately—they'd never have the damn roof on by March 1.

Fellows had continued to stand with a slightly distracted air, taking in his surroundings. His glance finally swung around and alighted on Jack. "Excuse me," he said, "do I look like Mark O'Banion?"

Jack closed his eyes for a moment and exhaled. Here we go again.

"Then what are you doing here?"

"Came down to look at the dredge."

The dredge? "You plan to do something about the sand?"

"No."

"Why were you looking at it, then?"

"Shits and giggles."

"What?" Spare me, Jack thought. "Okay," he said, "never mind about that. You do work for the city, don't you? You could lend a hand. I believe Mark already had something set up for situations like this."

Fellows obviously was having none of it. "I know how this goes, Jack. One thing, then another, and pretty soon you've got your hooks in me. Not gonna happen. Call the city manager, why don't you."

The manager? Paul Cutler wouldn't have time for this. As city engineer, Fellows was the natural choice. What the hell was it with this guy?

"I would think," Jack said, "since you were a friend of Mark O'Banion's—at least I'm told you were—that you might want to help out. I promised him I'd finish this project by June 15, and I intend to."

Jack Kelley had thought about Mark a good deal since his death. He thought about his commitment, too. With Mark's death, Jack might have felt less bound by it, but in fact, the opposite had happened. It had for all intents and purposes assumed the power of a deathbed promise.

Now Fellows looked at him and said, "You seem to be under the impression that I'm a nice guy, Jack. Let me set you straight. As for Mark, I liked him all right. I respected him, too, but frankly I didn't give a shit about what he was doing."

"This project is important to the city."

"The world doesn't need another dog track."

Jack didn't know which he found more annoying, Fellows's words or the casual way in which he delivered them, as if these matters were barely worth discussing at all.

"Look," Jack said, "if I have to go through the manager's office and wait for him to contact Harvey Butts, I could lose days."

"Then call Butts yourself, why don't you? If Mark made an arrangement, I'm sure he'll honor it."

Jack gave Fellows a disgusted look, which had no discernible effect, and went to the phone. The city attorney was out of the office at the moment. Jack explained to his secretary what had happened, and she confirmed that Mark and her boss had talked about the possibility of a work stoppage. She would page Harvey, she said. The woman's crisp professional tone restored Jack's spirits a little. Fellows, in the meantime, had been poking around and stopped at the drafting board.

"Since it's not your responsibility," Jack said acidly, "I don't suppose you're interested in McDermott's solution to the methane problem," for these were the drawings and specifications that had drawn Fellows's attention.

"As a matter of fact, I am."

Jack watched as he flipped page after page, stopping a couple of times to study some detail, nodding and smiling to himself.

Rumors of Fellows's personality had reached Jack before, but not having had to deal with the man, Jack had found it easy enough to dismiss them as the typical exaggerations people were fond of nosing around. Now he'd confronted him twice and knew.

"What, no canaries?" Fellows said, finishing his perusal of the documents from the civil engineer.

"You've got a better suggestion?"

"Nope. Given the safety considerations, this seems about right." Fellows tossed the pages down, then sauntered back, crossing his arms over his chest. "McDermott's problem was underdesigning the thing in the first place. Any idiot could see that. What with the piles, no way you could guarantee the integrity of the system. He could've saved all this diddling around by doing it right the first time."

"Yes," Jack agreed. This bit of wisdom didn't elevate Fellows in his estimate. "So, tell me, Chuck, do you have anything to contribute here? Or is this all just…shits and giggles?"

"Saw people standing around with their thumbs up their asses. Thought I'd stop and see what was going on."

"In that case, why don't you get the hell out of here so the rest of us can get some work done?"

"Fine by me," Fellows said.

Jack came outside and watched Fellows walking toward his vehicle. It was the same pickup Jack had been following earlier, with the ABN INF tags. Figures, Jack thought. Fellows got in the truck and drove away.

It only increased Jack's irritation that the man had been right about McDermott and right about the whole project, too. The world didn't need another dog track. Like all things of this life, the track was suspect terrain, unworthy in itself, merely a place of testing. But both he and Mark had known full well that they weren't building a cathedral. They didn't need Chuck Fellows to tell them that.

These thoughts steeled Jack to what he must do. He didn't regret the determination of it, only the grimness. He would obtain the injunction and get these guys back to work. He would continue looking for another field man to replace Adagian. He would forget about Fellows. And he would finish the damn job by June 15.

At that moment of recommitment, the last person that Jack wanted to see was Cletus Dickey, but toward him Dickey sauntered, as if right on cue.

# CHAPTER 40

~

"Sam Turner was back asking about the drafting job."

Joyce, the public works receptionist, passed this information along to Chuck when he finally arrived at the Hall.

"Okay," he said, but her words barely registered. He went into his office and closed the door behind him. Having had run-ins already with his wife and with Jack Kelley, he was more disposed to irritability than normal.

The one with Kelley had particularly annoyed him. Kelley just assumed Chuck would take over for Mark. And when he had learned otherwise, he became offended, as if his assumption had been legal writ. He'd done it the first time they got together, and then repeated the same bullshit act this time, too. The man had an absolutely flat learning curve.

There had been something Chuck didn't like about Kelley before he ever opened his mouth, although he couldn't quite put his finger on it. He remembered liking Mark right away, despite early evidence that Mark knew how to accommodate himself to the realities.

Kelley was doing two jobs. Well, okay, life is tough, but you don't go whining about it. You keep your mouth shut and do the damn work.

In a few minutes Joyce knocked. "This just came in," she said and handed him an envelope. "I thought you'd want to see it."

Joyce did triage on incoming mail, which saved Chuck some hassles. Only occasionally did she bring his attention to some particular item. This one was from John McDermott, of all people, or rather from his office, addressed to Charles Fellows, Director of Public Works. The bulk of the packet consisted of copies of the documents Chuck had just inspected down at the construction site. The cover letter stated that if properly implemented, the changes in the design of the methane barrier were satisfactory. It was signed by one of the secretaries in McDermott's office.

"Did you see this?" Chuck gestured toward the signature, and Joyce grinned. She was no dummy. The signature had to be precisely why she had hand-carried the thing in to him.

"Okay," he said, "I'll take care of it."

When she did not leave at once, he looked back up at her.

"I was wondering if you've got a minute," she said, then immediately amended the request to "a half minute."

Without waiting for an answer, she hurried into the outer office and moments later reappeared with a file folder stuffed with papers.

"I don't mean to be a pest, Chuck. I know you have a lot of other things to do, but I'd really like to know where I stand with respect to this...you know..." Apologetically, but with a certain determination, she laid the packet of material on the very corner of his desk. "Whenever you get the chance, I'd appreciate it," she said. "Thanks." Without waiting for him to say anything, she soundlessly retreated.

Chuck didn't need to look at the folder to know the contents. It had to be at least two or three years that she'd been trying to get herself upgraded from clerk typist to secretary. Or office manager or technical assistant or who knows what other position by now. Over the years, Joyce had opened new fronts in her battle with the bureaucrats. She'd shown the same initiative in her work. Now that Mark, her champion, had fallen, she would bestow her favor on Chuck.

At the moment, however, John McDermott filled his radar screen. McDermott, like everyone else, assumed Chuck was the new public works director. Chuck remembered warning Mark—it had been the last time he saw him alive—that McDermott might try to finesse his liability on the methane system. Now McDermott was trying the same shit on him.

He called McDermott's office.

"Is he in?"

"Wait a minute, Mr. Fellows," the woman who answered the phone said, "I'll see."

It took a couple of minutes for McDermott to decide if he was in, but finally he came on the line.

"Congratulations, Chuck," he said in his best bluff manner, one professional pounding another on the back.

"What for?"

"I understand you're the new public works guy."

"You understand wrong."

"Oh, is that right? Too bad."

Chuck had no time for this futzing around. "I just got a letter from your office."

"You did? Which one?"

Which one? Give me a break. "Methane. Signed by someone named Margo Peters."

"Ah, yes. The installation was such a half-assed job, we had to do a redesign."

"Tell me, John, is Margo a PE?"

"I'll have to ask, but I believe not."

"Why didn't you sign the letter?"

"Margo's signature is as good as mine."

"All for one, and one for all, is that it?"

"Sure, why not?"

"Because it's horseshit, that's why not. Do you think I'm a complete moron? This letter isn't acceptable."

"Oh, is that right?"

"That's right, John, it's not acceptable. You're gonna sign off on the system, John, and you're gonna sign the fucking letter yourself."

"If you want some cooperation, Chuck, I suggest you change your tone. You're not talking to one of your flunkies down at City Hall."

Chuck laughed. "I give a shit. You try to jerk me around, and I'll tell you what, John. Not only are you gonna sign off on the design. You're gonna inspect the installation and certify that it's been done according to your specs. The facility will not open until I have a letter from you, signed by you. You got that?"

"Do you think I take this kind of crap…from anybody?" McDermott had started to get excited.

"You don't like it, then forget the amateur bullshit and start acting like a professional."

"Fuck you. I am a pro."

And the conversation deteriorated from there.

When it was over, Chuck sat back in his chair and, as he calmed down, stretched his legs out beneath his desk and surveyed the topo maps on the far wall, which looked more like military campaign maps than ever. He wondered about McDermott's purpose in writing the letter. Probably, the yahoo figured that he'd have to print out another one and sign it himself. It'd cost him nothing, the price of a stamp. He no doubt had such a low opinion of engineers in the public sector that he really imagined he could land this sucker punch. Chuck smiled to himself. One thing McDermott hadn't counted on—the manner of Chuck's response. He'd still been basking in the afterglow of Mark's gentlemanly approach to professional relations.

Yet, as personally satisfying as yelling at the jerk might have been, yelling left no visible record. Easily remedied, Chuck decided. A formal letter would take care of that little problem.

Chuck took out the old Dictaphone he used. While he was at it, he thought, he might as well put Sam Turner out of his misery, too. He didn't start to dictate immediately but leaned back once more and cupped his hands behind his head and considered how Mark would have handled the two matters. The place was still so saturated with Mark's presence that he could have been sitting in the chair across from Chuck, chastising him for the unnecessary scene with McDermott, inviting him to try Turner out up in the drafting room and see what happened.

"You'd like that, wouldn't you, you old coot."

Not a chance. Yet Chuck understood that in death Mark's claims on him had become, if not stronger, at least fixed, part of the constellation of his memories, like Nam. Chuck would honor the man, but not Mark's mild acceptance of situations that for Chuck held little value. In Jackson, all the problems were human problems, and people just annoyed the hell out of him. Faced with death, they made a child's game out of life: Kelley worrying about a lost day on the dog track construction, McDermott having his office girl sign that letter, Sam Turner's mediocre drafting work. What were these but different ways people diddled away their lives? As long as Chuck had the misfortune to remain in that job, he'd call people on their bullshit little ploys.

After he had completed the letters, his eye fell on the stack of papers Joyce had left on the corner of the desk. Having disposed of McDermott and Turner to his satisfaction, he found his mood improved, and he was almost tempted to take up her cause. The way he figured it, people like Joyce, who had spent a good deal of time upgrading their skills, were pretty much being screwed over by petty bureaucrats like the city manager. But if Chuck did that one thing, why not something else, for instance the dredge? He knew how he'd cut that particular Gordian knot. He'd hire somebody who could do the job right. Simple enough. But then, having once started, it would be so easy to go on and do something else. And before he knew it, he'd be doing all of Mark's old jobs and find himself trapped in that godforsaken place for another five years. He might as well kiss his life good-bye.

On the way out, he handed Joyce, along with the Dictaphone tape, her packet. "I'm not the new Mark." He stopped for a moment and smiled. "Frankly, if I was you, I'm the last person I'd want as my standard-bearer. I've been known to antagonize people."

She smiled back, a tight little smile with a parsimonious nod, the nod both accepting this small setback and vowing to fight on. Really, Chuck thought as he left, you had to admire the girl.

# CHAPTER 41

~

A letter had arrived from Yellowknife. After the temptation to throw it in the garbage, Diane did exactly the opposite, propping it up in the middle of the kitchen table where Chuck was sure to see it first thing. She was preparing dinner, dividing her concentration between the six o'clock news on the portable TV they kept in the kitchen and the small drama she expected soon to begin behind her. They'd have it out. Chuck would like that, having it out…

She listened to the sound of the letter being extracted from the envelope and unfolded and then to the sounds she made herself as she worked…and waited. She and Chuck were exactly where they'd been that morning, when they'd had their last adjustment discussion.

After a time, he said merely, "They want me to fly up there for an interview."

"A great honor, I'm sure."

"They've narrowed it down to three applicants."

She thought about that and then said, "I don't believe for a minute that they've had three candidates. I think they're just saying that." She could see the Yellowknivians—or whatever they called themselves—dancing around the office with glee at the idea that anybody at all had applied.

"You'd be surprised," Chuck said, and then added, "Pretty soon, kiddo."

Diane had decided to hold her fire for the moment. But she didn't mind giving him a hint of what was coming. Therefore she parroted him with her own "Pretty soon, kiddo" but in a minor key.

Chuck, using the remote, had begun to switch restlessly from channel to channel.

"Please," she said, "I want to see the weather."

There was a little scrap of woodland out behind the house that would have to stand in for a frontier wilderness. Diane had been reading about backyard wildlife. She had talked Chuck into teaching some survival skills to the children and their little friends from the neighborhood who were to be given a taste of buckskinning. Now, if only the weather would hold.

Chuck actually seemed more comfortable with this idea of buckskinning in the backyard, viewing it, she supposed, as a suitably degraded locale for such a degraded hobby.

If it rained, she supposed she'd have to refuse to let the kids sleep outside, although Chuck the Contrarian would probably become more interested in the activity then, an opportunity to pit himself against the elements. Diane wondered if anything was to be gained by letting them set up the tent anyway, rain or no rain. They could probably make do. The kids so wanted to wear their costumes again.

And Chuck would take care to protect them. He was a good father in that way. But he barely had a clue as to what Todd and Grace actually needed, he was so wrapped up in himself. He'd have her and the kids living in an igloo before he was through, somewhere north of Eskimos.

Anyway, Diane felt calmer than she had that morning. Fighting with Chuck would get her precisely nowhere. Another approach was required. She so hated the idea of going to Canada that she'd lost her grip for a while. She'd gotten emotional. Or rather, she'd shown her emotion. Or rather, she'd shown her emotion in the wrong way. She could not manipulate Chuck. No, she must count on Chuck manipulating himself.

Finally, the weather came on and she turned up the sound and for a few minutes put aside thoughts of the struggle with her husband. Walter Plowman had a reputation for accuracy, and so everybody watched him. Rain, indeed, was on the way. The only uncertainty, he told his viewers, was when. Friday afternoon the best bet, very early Saturday at the latest.

"After all this time," Diane said, mostly to herself, "you'd think it could wait a few more days."

Chuck was peering intently at the weatherman. In concentration, Chuck's lower jaw thrust out slightly, his chin tilted up, his eyes narrowed and even appeared to draw closer together.

"There's a man who's found his life's work," he said suddenly, gesturing at the TV.

And you haven't, I suppose, she almost said but caught herself in time. Instead, she substituted, "Do you know Walter Plowman?"

"Never met the man."

"Then how do you know? Maybe he hates being a weatherman."

"With some people, you can tell. You look at him, and you can just tell."

"Don't be too sure."

As well as she knew him, Diane couldn't imagine what Chuck might fancy his own life's work to be, probably as the member of an entirely different species. Anyway, at that moment, a conversation about such matters wasn't likely to improve the prospect of their staying in Jackson.

Plowman was talking about high clouds in the west, and Chuck got up and went out to the front porch. He had, of course, gone to look for himself. When he came back, he had an old newspaper with him and a pair of work boots and some neat's-foot oil and old rags. He settled down again and began to work the oil into the seams of the boots. For Diane, it was such a temptation to just let matters slide and hope for the best. That's what she would have done one time.

"If you've got a problem," she said, "you don't run away from it."

"I've got no problem."

She looked at him coolly and experienced a slight flush of satisfaction, knowing that this time she had him.

"You're a man who's always prided himself on his honesty, and you're telling me you don't have a problem?"

"I'm just sick of this place is all. I've had it with all the assholes."

"They don't have any assholes in Yellowknife?" she asked. "What do you suppose they do with them?"

Chuck grinned. "They have a better class of assholes in Yellowknife."

"Listen to yourself, dear," she said to him. "Is that supposed to be an argument? Leaving Jackson makes no sense. This is a good town to raise kids in. It's safe, and it's got a good educational system. How can you think of jeopardizing all that just to satisfy your own selfish longings?"

"Like hell. Jackson's in the middle of nowhere."

Diane laughed at the absurdity of it. She didn't even bother to point out that not all people thought that Yellowknife was in the middle of somewhere.

"In Yellowknife," Chuck lumbered on determinedly, "the kids can learn to be self-reliant."

"Good grief. Is that your word for it, self-reliance? I'd call it subsistence."

"They can learn to look out for themselves."

"You're on another planet, do you know that?"

She had often had to remind herself that she'd picked Chuck out all by herself. It wasn't like the old days when parents chose the lummoxes their daughters married. Now girls got to choose lummoxes for themselves.

She had figured he would eventually come around. A couple of kids, a steady job, a few years for the discontent to age out of him. Of course, she was just asking for trouble imagining any man was clay and she had the mold. And Chuck, of all men! What was she thinking?

"Mark's dead," Chuck now told her with a certain glum determination that wasn't really like him, "there's nothing left for me down there."

"Down there?"

"At the hall."

She mentioned a couple of other people whom she thought he liked, but he dismissed the suggestions.

"I respected Mark."

"You don't respect anybody else?"

"A few."

"So, there you are."

"I'm not going to play their bullshit little political games."

Okay, Diane thought, if that was what it would take, she was willing to compromise.

"Then don't take Mark's job. Stay on as the city engineer."

"Long as I'm here, I am the city engineer, period. As far as Mark's job is concerned, somebody's gotta do it. When you're in the jungle and your platoon leader gets killed, it ain't like you can decide to leave the position vacant. Somebody's gotta do it. If I stay, I'm elected."

"This isn't Vietnam."

"It makes no difference."

Chuck cocked his head to one side and regarded her. Diane wanted to sit down but feared it would give the impression of weakness, so instead, to get a grip on something solid, she reached for the handle of the refrigerator.

Chuck said, "If the Yellowknife job comes through, I'm going to take it."

"I see." She opened the door of the fridge, looked blindly inside, then closed it.

"There's nothing for me here anymore."

"You've already said that. You've said it over and over. But what about us? What about me and the kids?"

"We've moved before."

"When we had to. When we had only one baby, and you were offered a better job."

"It's time to make a decision."

His curt tone offended her. She forced herself to respond in kind. "All right. My decision is this—you can go to Canada if you want. The children and I are staying here."

"You're bluffing," he said at once, as if he'd anticipated her and already decided how he'd respond.

She made herself look him square in the face. "Try me."

"I don't believe you." His little smirk aggravated her more than anything he said.

"I mean it, Chuck. I'm through arguing. Go if you want, but you're going alone."

She turned away, the gesture meant to convey her determination. If anyone was bluffing here, he was, but she'd never accuse him of such a thing, which would just be waving a red flag. No, no, no. She'd tell him what she intended to do. Let him figure out the rest for himself.

She knew that, despite everything, he might be determined to go. She'd always been aware that there was a large part of Chuck that didn't want to be married, that didn't want to have children. Perhaps it had something to do with Vietnam, although she was inclined to see the war as mostly the occasion which had made manifest what had been in him all along.

She measured his change—or his imagined change—with the delicate counterweight of her hopes. She did hope. But their fight over Mark's job had brought them to the very frontier of the marriage, beyond which, for the first time, she could clearly see a life apart. In their separate ways, they had each set about testing that boundary. But she still loved him, and she thought in his own way he loved her. He surely loved the kids.

"You're forty-four years old, dear," she said, turning back and speaking softly, although she had started to tremble slightly. "It's time to stop running away and make something of yourself."

"I'm not running away," he said tersely.

"Yes, you are."

His expression hardened even more, his jaws locked shut. Diane was doing the best she could to hang in there against his anger. She hated how their recent fights had started out in a bantering way and then descended into this bitterness. He had never hit her, but she always feared that one day he might. Yet there was nothing to be done. She must get through this as best she could.

"Go to Canada, if you must," she said. "But the children and I are not going with you. I'll never go up to that place. Never." She clutched at the edge of the counter to steady herself and to keep the trembling, which had become worse, from showing.

All at once, Chuck got up, slammed the chair he had been sitting in across the room against a cabinet, kicked aside the boots he had been working on, then stalked out. In the distance, Diane could hear one of the children begin to cry.

# CHAPTER 42

~

Edna Goetzinger came out of the farrowing house and looked up at the thin veil of white spreading across the sky. Through it, the perfect disk of the midmorning sun burned.

She took her straw hat with the wide brim from the nail on the doorpost, planted it firmly on her head, and tied the ribbon beneath her chin. Never mind her gloomy thoughts, she could still take pleasure from this simple act.

Her kitchen garden ran along the side of the house, across what had been lawn when she and Fritzy purchased the property thirty-five years ago. Next to it were stacked bushel baskets with wire handles. She pulled off the top one and walked out to the rows of fall cabbages. She was thinking about the clouds sliding by overhead and the rain they foretold.

As she worked slowly up and down the rows, harvesting the cabbage, she would have gladly lost herself in the task. Mindful of her health, she worked slowly. The mulch in which the plants were nested had been bleached nearly white by the drought. Despite her persistent watering, the cabbages were barely worth harvesting. She picked only the largest heads, the leaves with their thick, white veins reminding her of the veins of old men's hands. Fritzy had always been proud of his hands. She thought about that. Pride. Because thoughts of eternity never were far away, she wondered what the Lord would say about Fritzy's pride. A mortal sin it was, but somehow she thought that—just as she had—God would make an exception in Fritzy's case.

Her husband looked poorly to her. He had been coughing in his sleep again. He barely ate. How strange it would be, she thought, if he passed over before she did. She felt heartsore for him, already being shunted aside in this scheme to have the employees buy the Pack. His own idea, and they were stealing it

240

from him. She wished he was out of it altogether.

She could feel the sun, as it disentangled itself briefly from the clouds, hot on the nape of her neck. This reminded her again of the rain, and she stood up and stretched her back and looked out toward the cornfield, the rows of ragged stalks, like an army of beggars. She didn't see when Fritzy would find the time to harvest the corn. In the middle of the night probably. She had tried to reach Junior, leaving a message on his answering machine, but her eldest son had the habit of not returning calls he didn't like. And certainly he wouldn't like doing something for his father.

In her hand, she held one of the heads of cabbage. She hefted it. Cabbage should feel heavier than it looks, but this head had no weight to it at all. With regret she put it into the basket and bent back down to her work.

In the kitchen, she brewed a cup of tea. Each afternoon, she took a few minutes for herself, sat quietly, and recovered her sense of balance. But today, the thoughts that had disturbed her in the garden followed her inside. Along the counter were ranged the ingredients for the sauerkraut: shredder, canister of pickling salt, peppercorns, juniper berries, bay leaves, mixing bowls and stoneware crocks, cheesecloth, the bushels of cabbage. She listened to the radio, waiting for the weather forecast, hoping it had changed. Normally, anticipation of the rain would have brought her joy. Now, it was coming too late to help either her garden or the corn, and it just seemed to pile one worry on top of another.

She listened, as well, for the phone, half expecting it to ring, half not. When the weather forecast came, unchanged, she stopped waiting, and went and called Junior again. First she got the snippy little message he had put on the machine to discourage callers. "It's going to rain, Junior," she said to the machine. "Your father's positively working himself into the grave." She paused, envisioning her son unmoved by such a plea. "Harvest the field for me, dear," she said, "if you won't do it for him."

Although it was early November, a remnant of the summer heat seemed trapped in the house, and she brushed perspiration from her brow as she washed and dried the cabbage, then shredded it and mixed it with salt in the bowls to start the pickling process.

Because her thoughts were on Junior, she began thinking about her other children as well. Perhaps the greatest sorrow in her life arose from the fact that each child seemed less able than the last, as if some vital store of energy had drained out of her each time she gave birth. Junior, the brightest. Elaine, a good enough student to get her nurse's cap—how many farm girls ended up as nurses?—and living with her husband and Edna's grandchildren in Milwaukee. Matthew, who had been in trouble with the law and had disappeared. And finally Teddy, fourteen years old now, whose birth had almost killed mother and child, leaving them both marked for life, Edna with her bad heart and Teddy with what they called nowadays a learning disability.

As she worked, she nicked herself with the knife, a few grains of salt stinging the wound. She sucked the salt out, tasting it and the blood, salty and sweet, then ran cold water over the cut and went for a Band-Aid.

When she came back to her work, she cautioned herself to pay more attention to what she was doing. But still she thought about Junior, wasting his life. These thoughts were nothing new, just the same old nagging worries, like so many trolls living under her bridge to contentment. She sighed and once more tried to concentrate on what she was doing.

# CHAPTER 43

~

At first, the two men hardly spoke. On the table between them lay the document.

Mel Coyle, the Jackson Packing Company's corporate counsel, whose desk it was, sat wondering why he didn't feel more at such a moment.

"That's it, then," he said.

His companion, Skip Peterson, who had come with the report now lying between them, roused himself from his gloomy reverie. "Is it?"

Mel paused politely before saying, "Yes."

Who knows what causes a person to give up any last remnant of hope? Mel mused over this mystery. He had no answer, only his certainty. No use, no use. After eighty-three years, it was over. The end of the Jackson Packing Company. Just like that.

He felt the poignancy of the moment, despite the accumulated exhaustion of all the plague years, all the small deaths leading to this final one. Still, he imagined, he should have felt more.

Skip, after his temporary lapse, was becoming himself again. "This company can still be saved, Mel." He tapped the report with an impatient forefinger. "There's nothing here we didn't expect."

"I don't agree," Mel told him. "It's worse." Mel felt, actually, rather relieved. He had hoped for thumbs up or thumbs down, not some weaselly middle ground, and if it was to be thumbs down, then so be it.

"We knew about the upgrades," Skip told him.

"Yes, we did. I'm talking about everything else. The price of hogs. The markets lost. The cost of the credit line. The projections. We'd be hemorrhaging money."

"I still say there's nothing here we didn't expect." Skip sprang to his feet and began pacing. "I say the equipment's most critical.

We replace that, we give the employees a reason for working smart-er, we hire a take-no-prisoners PR outfit to expose Nick Takus for the bloodsucker he is." As he made his points, he counted them out on his fingers. "We do these things, we can survive. In a couple of years, more farmers will come on line, and Takus can't overpay forever. That's the beauty of an employee-owned company, the bot-tom line isn't everything."

This was a pretty story, and Mel only wished he could believe it, he really did. "And where, do you suppose, the extra six and a half million might come from?"

"I've got two."

"And the rest?" Skip said nothing, so Mel added, "As the times get tougher, Skip, you can find money, you can scrimp, you can borrow, beg, whatever, but there comes a point when you need one dollar more and it's just...not...there."

"The employees."

"Forget the employees. They're not going to help you. Maybe they would have agreed to payroll deductions. Maybe. But forget about anything else."

If they had bought the place, Mel could see the operation be-ing dragged out for a year or two, bleeding money every step of the way, and leaving everybody worse off. But now it was academic. People weren't going to liquidate their life savings, if that's the fan-tasy Skip was beginning to entertain.

In the silence that followed, Mel remained conscious of all the words that had passed between them, a lifetime of words. All so complex and yet, when Mel thought about it, all so simple really: first success and then failure. W.F. Peterson Sr., the hardiest of old cocks, the ruler of the roost for fifty-two years, who built it up, who made it what it was. And then Will Jr., lacking the stomach for a good fight and coming within an inch of ruining the place during his twenty years at the helm. And finally William III—Skip—fin-ishing the job. No, that wasn't quite fair. Had Skip inherited from his grandfather, things might have turned out differently. Skip took direction at least.

Or there was Mel himself. He sometimes wondered what would have happened if he had had a chance to run the place. Worse came to terrible, he would have known when to let go, at least. Skip was like a child learning to ride a bike, afraid to stop once he had got going.

Mel's one last task was to help him dismount. It was ironic. Mel had spent decades as the perfect sidekick, a man with no natural constituency other than the CEO himself. Now, all of a sudden, his constituency was everybody else.

"It's time to let people get on with their lives."

That's what they should do. Liquidate the assets, pay off their debts, and call it a day. If they did, Mel guessed there'd be a little left over for the stockholders. A big if. Probably what would happen instead is they'd hang on, cutting down the workforce as they went, until one day they would walk away, leaving behind them bones bleaching in the sun. The stockholders would get nothing, the employees a few more paychecks maybe, but that was all, the inevitable merely postponed, everybody a little bit older and more ill-fitted for the world to come.

Skip paced. He was forty-six years old, his hair streaked with gray, the creases in his lanky face more deeply etched each year, yet Mel still saw in him the child he had once been. Hyperactive. Easily frustrated. Either too certain or not certain enough.

"I just hate it, Mel. Takus is a thieving lowlife. He'll pay his goddamn premium to the farmers, then screw them royally once he's driven us out of business. He's done it before. It's restraint of trade, that's what it is. The bastard should be in jail." Of late, the CEO of Modern Meat had become Skip's favorite whipping boy.

"Yes," Mel agreed easily, "all good men despise Nick Takus. But it's not just him. It's the last twenty-five years, too. It's us. It's the whole industry."

Skip merely frowned and continued to pace.

Mel wasn't unsympathetic. Skip had never had a real chance to make the company into something of his own. Since day one, it had been baling wire and sealing wax. And now, at the eleventh hour, he had had a vision. Bring farmers into the plant, explain the operation to them, make them partners. Teach housewives—if there were any housewives anymore—how to cook pork properly. Pay attention to every jot and tittle of the operation. It was like the kind of mirage of perfect health that might rise before a cancer patient in the last stages of the disease.

"You live in this town, too, Mel. Do you want to have to look those people in the eye after you've closed this place down?"

"Nobody wants to close the plant. Nobody...Look, Skip, you've done a good job. With what you had to work with, you really have." Mel would keep telling him this. He would say it until Skip believed it enough to let go. "It's simply time to get out...while there's still something left for your family." Others held stock, too. Mel did. He had no interest in throwing away his money on some utopian scheme just because Skip was still trying to become a man. Mel was tired. And after nearly four decades, to tell the truth, he was sick of the Petersons.

"You know, there's a potential upside for the family here," Skip was insisting, "if the company can survive and grow."

"There is no upside."

They lapsed back into silence. Skip continued to pace, shaking his head.

After a time, Mel said, "We'll have to take this to the board."

"Of course."

"I don't expect they'll agree with you."

"Or maybe they will. The locals, at least."

That was true. The local people—Mel excepted—would have a difficult time putting all these people out on the street, even though it was the sound business decision. Mel had counted the votes of those who controlled the bulk of the outstanding shares of stock. Skip's majority had been shrinking, but the board of directors had never gone against the wishes of the man leading the company, not against Skip, not his father, certainly not his grandfather.

There was also the matter of the buyout committee.

"Am I going to tell the committee or are you?" A phone tree had been set up, so it would take only a couple of calls.

"Let me," Skip said. "I still want to think about this some more."

Mel counted out five seconds, five taps of the end of his first finger against his thigh. "There's nothing to think about, Skip."

Skip waited even longer before he made his small concession, not looking at Mel. "I don't know. I just hate it, but maybe you're right."

# CHAPTER 44

~

Under the darkening skies, Deuce Goetzinger drove up Brick Kiln Road to the farm. Halfway, in a small hollow through which the road curved, stood a large righteously square turn-of-the-century house. Often when he passed this place, he would glance at the huge permanent sign mounted in the center of the bare, humped yard, the sign with its crude lettering protesting high taxes or Ford Pintos or the Equal Rights Amendment or whatever happened to be the outrage of the moment. Here was just the fellow to vote for the old man.

Deuce drove on and at the top of the road turned into his parents' driveway, where the vegetable stand that his youngest brother ran in the summers sat abandoned and desolate. The ridge between ruts of the driveway clipped the undercarriage of his RX-7. As he mounted the steep driveway toward the unkempt farm buildings, the scene infected him with a small bleakness.

He parked off to one side, as far away from the house as he could. As he got out into the blustery day, he heard a sharp report and froze. A gust of wind whisked the sound away, but then a second followed, lingering a few moments in a wind trough, and he realized it had had a familiar quality, hollow and tinny. Gunshot. He smiled to himself and relaxed.

He shut the car door quietly. The old man was probably at work, no chance of running into him, but Deuce didn't want to have to deal with his mother just at that moment, either. He'd do this thing for her, but that was it.

The wind shifted, and he could smell hog manure. He walked past the lean-to side of the onetime milking barn, converted into a finishing shed. Inside he could hear the scrimmaging of the animals.

Another shot reverberated, now closer, and all at once his brother Teddy raced out through the metal doors of the machine shed. The boy ran with uncoordinated abandon, swinging a .22 in one hand and the corpses of several birds in the other.

"Look," he said, holding up the birds, "starlings." He seemed not at all surprised to see Deuce. He simply accepted his presence. This was a gift Teddy had, this acceptance of the world as he found it.

"How many?"

"Four."

Deuce grabbed his brother's arm at the wrist and lifted it for a better look at the birds with their speckled feathers and stubby tails.

"What's the old man paying for these nowadays?" he asked.

"Ten cents each."

"Hell, that's what he was paying me before you were ever born."

"Yeah?"

"And a dime for pigeons. And a nickel for sparrows."

"Yeah." A blank look came over Teddy's face as his concentration turned inward, trying to calculate what this information might mean for him. Of course, Deuce knew Teddy would have been happy to shoot the birds for free.

"If the old man's gonna put you up to it, at least he ought to pay you decent. It's illegal, you know, hunting inside the city limits."

"Daddy says they got diseases."

"Oh, yeah?"

"Yeah. The hogs could maybe get sick or something." Deuce read in his brother's expression just a trace of his stubbornness. His father all over. All the kids had inherited that particular trait.

Deuce contemplated Teddy for a moment, then said in a kindly way, "Well, it don't matter. Why don't you put that stuff away? Ma tells me you're allowed to drive the tractor now."

"Daddy said I could. He's been teaching me."

"You think you can pull the feed wagon while I'm combinin'?"

"Yeah, yeah." As Deuce walked along, Teddy hopped excitedly beside him.

"Okay, but first get rid of that stuff."

Teddy ran and leaned the gun against the barn and dropped the birds next to it.

"No, no," Deuce said, "properly. Put the gun where it belongs. And the birds, too."

"Aw," Teddy complained, but he obeyed. Deuce watched him hurrying toward the house with his burden. Like any fourteen-year-old, he had trouble putting off pleasure, but Deuce thought he saw something of his disability in his enthusiasm, too, his focus narrowing down to a mere sliver. He would move like a blind man. His thoughts would rise almost to the surface, his eyes seeming to peer inward as if trying to read them, his mouth silently speaking. Of his surroundings at those moments he seemed utterly unconscious. And as for helping with the corn, well, Deuce had his doubts. But harvesting alone was a hassle, and so he would use the boy and hope for the best. Do the job quick and get the hell out of there.

In the machine shed, he checked the combine, then swung up into its cab, feeling the familiar tension on his arms. He wondered casually as he started the machine whether his father had succeeded in paying it off yet. Probably not.

It had been years since he'd harvested corn, but driving out to the field it seemed like hardly any time at all. Teddy followed on the tractor, pulling one of the feed wagons. How familiar, Deuce thought as he looked at the scene, were the arcs of the corn field, the graceful hills of Iowa, rising beside and before him, revealing themselves only a bit at a time as he lumbered along in the massive machine.

Deuce could feel his old familiar anger at his father, as well. That, too, came back effortlessly. When he wasn't around the farm, his anger lay dormant, but as soon as he came anywhere near the place, all the old resentments rose up, as strong as ever. For his father, to live was to work. He knew only work, and respected only work, and yet his work was only a kind of discontentment. From him had come, as long as Deuce could remember, only a relentless pressure to get things done.

The kids had dealt with it in different ways. Elaine, always one to do as she was told, had avoided the worst of it. Matt had simply left. And Teddy's disability seemed to protect him in some way. He lived in a world of magic charms untainted by the old man's eternal toil and dissatisfaction. As for Deuce, well, he kept everything inside. And now he had his Mazda and all-night card games and girlfriends and weekend binges in Chicago...

He climbed down and went back to give Teddy instructions. "You're sure the old man said you could do this?"

"Yeah, yeah. I've been rakin' hay to learn."

"That's not the same thing." Deuce looked up at the gathering clouds and felt the bitter, shifting wind. "Well, okay," he said to his brother. "Just remember, go easy on the end rows. And watch the spout, or you'll start spilling the corn all over the place. Got that?"

"Yeah, yeah!" Teddy's eyes glistened with excitement.

"And pay attention!"

Deuce climbed back into the corn picker, and they began. The corn stalks struggled across the field, broken and shriveled, many of the ears hanging low, the shuck fallen away, exposing blackened silk and yellow kernels with red seams between them. To pick as cleanly as possible, he ran the corn head low. That would help a little, but the harvest was going to be piddling no matter what he did. Hundred bushels to the acre max.

His father had mounted a green Deere corn head on the red IH combine because he believed there was less corn loss with the Deere head. Deuce thought there probably wasn't any difference, but the old man was always dickering with things, like with the hogs, looking for a better hybrid. The son of a bitch always thought he knew better.

Teddy's job was to position the feed wagon so that it moved down the rows side by side with the combine and Deuce could unload on the fly. As they worked, bits of chaff swirled around the stream of corn flowing from the spout of the combine's conveyer into the wagon. Deuce kept his eye on Teddy, who for all his enthusiasm still drove the tractor timidly, combining excessive care with absent-mindedness so that time after time he started to lag behind and Deuce had to open the door of the cab on the combine and yell across at him.

Deuce swung the combine wide at the headlands, counting the rows in order to get properly aligned on the next set. The machine bucked as it angled across the furrows. From the western horizon, solid gray clouds swept across the sky. The rain hadn't begun yet, but he could smell moisture in the air.

Next to the farm fence, a single red cedar stood, profuse and feathery, its green leaves tinged with a deep maroon color as if the tree had been abandoned and was slowly rusting in the landscape, like a piece of ancient farm machinery. On every pass back across the field, Deuce's gaze returned to that tree.

Time and again Teddy fell to daydreaming, and the tractor started to lag. Deuce would open the cab door and yell at him, but no matter how many times this happened, Teddy took the rebuke calmly, merely paying attention once more. His demeanor remained so accepting, so without rancor, that Deuce felt it as a reproach in some obscure way to his own outrage—against his father, against the farm, against the unremitting labor of his youth.

He swung the combine around and onto another set and watched rabbits loping between the rows, in front of the corn head nosing along with its conical green snouts. Farther on, the machine flushed a pheasant. Now that the leaves were down, there wasn't much cover.

He constantly checked his gauges, steering with his right hand, raising and lowering the corn head with his left, keeping it as low as he dared. The stalks were bent this way and that, as if a storm had already ravaged the field.

The old man liked to say that when you could see a rabbit running down the row ahead of you, the corn was standing pretty good, but Deuce could see the animals he was flushing and this crop was pitiful.

Even in the freshening wind, the stocks barely moved, their blackened leaves vibrating stiffly, waiting like dispirited soldiers at parade rest, still one moment and at the next sliding between the snouts of the corn head, seeming to pause for the briefest instant, and then disappearing, pulled down between the snapping rollers, too fast for the eye to follow, in an explosion of dust and plant fragments...the familiar smell of the shucks and chaff, which danced upon the corn head...and, behind, the heavy rumble of the drum stripping the kernels from the ears.

As he worked, his anger began to slip away. He looked toward the section of the field already harvested, checking the discarded cobs, making sure the kernels had been shelled cleanly. He liked the finished look of a harvested field. Work completed.

It was getting darker and darker. To the west, the clouds were almost black. Sometimes, when he had been out here harvesting as a youth, there had been brilliant sunsets, and he recalled the pleasure they had given him, so long forgotten. Somewhat against his will, he realized there had been good times. The old man hadn't spoiled everything.

He looked out and saw that Teddy had begun to lag behind again, and so he yelled at him, and Teddy stopped daydreaming and started to concentrate yet one more time on what he was doing.

# CHAPTER 45

~

"There's the last one, Fritz."

Billy Noel, at the opposite cutting board, had a better view across the floor and could see when the end of the line of carcasses appeared. Each day, he announced this to his friend, who would give him a nod, as he did today, and maybe a word or two. Today he said nothing. He merely stopped for a moment and adjusted his position at the board before continuing.

Billy fretted about Fritz's silences. More and more now when someone came over to discuss the buyout with Fritz, he would jerk his head toward Billy and say to the guy, "Why don't you take it up with my man over there." Fritz would wink at Billy, as if it was a joke. But he wasn't kidding. He left it up to Billy to explain whatever it was, only stepping in if Billy got completely tangled up. Seemed like Billy had done more talking in the last two weeks than in his entire life. Margaret said maybe Fritz was grooming him for something, but when Billy asked Fritz about that, all he said was, "Suppose I'm not around, Billy. What will you do then?"

"You planning not to be around?"

When Billy asked Fritz why he'd made them put him on the buyout committee, Fritz had just said, "Put everyone on it, if I could. Couldn't do that, so figured you'd be a good choice."

When Billy asked Fritz why he wasn't more upset because of the way Peterson and Budge were ignoring him, Fritz said, "Pretty much knew it would happen. No matter." Fritz, Billy had noticed, made it a point of never being surprised, but Billy figured it must hurt when he wasn't made an equal partner in the thing. And Fritz having such a low opinion of Skip Peterson and Homer Budge.

A buzzer sounded, and Billy started, his reverie shattered. The chain stopped.

"Shit!" one of the chiselers yelled.

On the post behind Fritz, the red light blinked on.

"Red," Billy said, and Fritz nodded. Probably an abscess.

Billy took off his mailed glove and arched his back and propped himself up on the cutting board to take a little weight off his legs.

It had been a tough shift. A lot of animals. A lot of stoppages. Short tempers. Across the way, Fritz stood quietly and sharpened his knife and eyed Billy curiously.

Billy was exhausted, from the meeting that morning, from all the animals in the afternoon. The meeting took more out of him than the kill floor, he thought. Trying to tell them what the rank and file thought and feeling like people were humoring him or, most likely, just impatient, wanting to get back to what they considered important. Billy hated it, but somebody had to speak up for the people on the floor. Fritz talked some, but a little less each meeting, it seemed. Skip Peterson and Homer Budge didn't completely ignore him, but it was pretty obvious they felt more comfortable when Fritz was on the sidelines. They all remembered the years Fritz was president of the union and led the strikes. Nobody ever forgot those sorts of things.

Each night Billy and Margaret would discuss the events of the day and particularly Fritz's strange behavior. Margaret ceaselessly reassured Billy that if Fritz had put him on the committee, that meant Fritz was even smarter than they thought. "You want to do what's right, love. And you have a good heart. Fritz can see that."

As much as Billy liked to hear Margaret say such nice things about himself, having a good heart seemed a mighty poor qualification for the work at hand.

Feeling the vibrations through the brick floor as a vat of inedible rolled by, his attention returned to the chain, still not moving, and he scanned the room, trying without luck to find the trouble spot. If the problem was an abscess, that meant an animal would have to be removed and the area hosed down with hot water. Billy visualized the process, as if by doing so he might speed it up.

The chiselers were screaming at one of the blue hats to "start the fucking chain again." Across the way, Fritz ignored them. He just stood waiting. He seemed to be waiting for more than the line to begin.

Finally, it did. Billy picked up his glove and knife as the first snout came off the wheel.

Fifteen minutes later Billy made the last cut, then yawned and stretched. He slid the knife into its scabbard and took off the mailed glove.

As he and Fritz walked toward the locker room with the others, Dickie Streuer came over and told Fritz somebody wanted to see him, and the two of them went off together.

"What's with hizzoner?" one of the chiselers asked, falling briefly in step with Billy. "He buddying up with the blue hats or what?"

Billy watched the retreating figures. The chiselers had been riding the foreman something fierce.

"We're gonna own this place, Streuer, and we're gonna have your ass," they told him over and over.

Billy tried to take a charitable view of the youngsters, but he figured they were just harassing Streuer for the hell of it. When the time came, most likely they wouldn't even vote for the buyout. They were interested in disposable income and didn't look kindly on the idea of money being taken out of their paychecks, no matter why.

He glanced at the one next to him and said, "I expect you best mind your own business."

In the locker room, Billy went immediately to one of the urinals and relieved himself. For what seemed the first time since he'd gotten up at five that morning, he felt his body relax. He closed his eyes and tilted his head up and let his mouth fall open, taking several deep breaths. Friday afternoon. Thank God! A couple of days for his body to heal some from the beating it had taken during the week. For a little while, he wouldn't have to live by somebody else's clock. He felt good. If he didn't quite believe the nice things that Margaret said about him, he knew at least that he was an old guy who could still hack it.

Now, however, a sadness intruded on this pleasure, for these times had also come to seem like small rehearsals for the day the Pack would close forever.

He sat in front of his locker, thinking about Fritz and Streuer, another bit of the strangeness of life lately. Three or four times now the foreman had come and taken Fritz off to "see someone." The "someone" was Streuer himself, as Fritz had told Billy. The foremen were running scared, so Billy could understand why Dickie was looking for a friend. But Fritz? The two men had no use for each other. At least that's the way it used to be, before the world got turned upside down.

As people got ready to go home, Billy chatted with them, relating as best he could news from the morning meeting. The union was negotiating with the company, but Billy didn't know how that was going, except with Peterson and Budge now in cahoots, they'd probably work things out okay. Lots of contacts were being made outside the company, with the city and state and so forth, looking for money and whatnot. Everybody seemed pretty positive that the thing could be pulled off.

Billy had finished dressing by the time Fritz got back and began to shed his whites. When Billy asked him what Streuer wanted, Fritz shook his head and said nothing, but as Billy started to leave by himself, his friend told him to wait up.

"What's going on?" Billy asked.

"Just a sec. We'll go down together."

Fritz said no more until they had walked down to the laundry and turned in their soiled whites and received chips. Fritz seemed to be dallying until the two of them were alone.

Then he pulled Billy aside, away from the stragglers.

"Come on, Billy, we've gotta go back upstairs."

"Why?"

"I don't know. But something's happened, something damn serious."

And so they hurried back in the direction from which they'd just come.

# CHAPTER 46

~

It was dark by the time Deuce and Teddy finished and the last of the corn had been augered into the silo. As Deuce came out of the equipment shed, he spotted his father talking to a woman he had never seen before. They were standing beneath the floodlight on one of the corn bins. He skirted around them and went into the farrowing house, where he found his mother.

"I ran the upper fields on out," he told her, "but there's no way I can even begin the ones down by the river before it starts to rain." She was in the midst of castrating the male piglets in a litter, the animals that wouldn't be kept for breeding stock. As always, she looked tired to her eldest son, her gestures deliberate, her hair tied back in a bun, the hair style of farm women from the days of the frontier.

"That's okay, dear," she said. "They'll have to wait. Maybe after the rain."

He frowned. The air in the farrowing house was warm and humid, filled with the smell of wood shavings and animal waste. A heating lamp had been clamped to one of the crates. That would be the last litter born. The piglets she attended went about their lives with the same single-minded determination as Deuce's father, and she would stop for a moment and watch them squabble. Yes, her look seemed to say, this was to be expected.

He told her how Teddy had done pulling the feed wagons. She held each animal to be castrated upside down between her legs, pushed the testicles down firmly against the sac, made a snip with her pliers on one side, pulled out the testicle and membrane until it snapped off, then repeated the process on the other side before painting the wounds with antiseptic and releasing the squealing animal. She would take a deep breath and then go on to the next.

"Need some help?" Deuce asked.

"Yes, you can catch the ones I haven't done yet, if you would."

And so he did that, holding the animals as she performed the brief operation.

"Have you talked to your father?" she asked. "Well, I wish you would." Snip. "I want you to see how he looks." Snip. "Please wipe that sour expression off your face. You don't have to make a demonstration of your feelings for me. I'm well aware of them. I still want you to go look at Fritzy. Just go and look. See for yourself." Snip. "I'm frightened. He barely sleeps anymore." Snip. "He's not eating. I just don't know."

"And I'm supposed to make a suggestion?"

"I wish you would." Deuce shook his head. His mother knew, better than anyone, what the relationship between him and his father was like and still she could make such a request.

"Frankly, ma, I'm surprised he ain't dead already."

She looked up from her work, tilted her head at a disapproving angle and stared at him.

"It's the truth," he persisted. "The old man's always treated himself and you and all the rest of us as if we were just pieces of farm equipment."

"Don't say that."

"It's true."

"No, it isn't." She reached down to reclaim a piglet that had almost gotten away before she was finished with it. "But I'm not going to argue with you." She shook her head. "It's not as if, deep down, you're so different from Fritzy yourself."

"I'm nothing like him."

She looked at him again, with her calm hazel eyes. "Oh no?" She held his eyes. "It's just pretend, you know."

"Pretend?"

"All this playing around."

Deuce looked away. "Not this again."

"You did say, when you were thirty. And now you're thirty-three."

"I got a job," he said lamely. "I make decent money."

"You know what I mean."

"You expect too much."

"No, I don't." She spoke very softly, so that he understood she was not arguing with him but only saying what he knew in his own heart was true. When she was through, they walked outside together.

"Who's the woman?" Deuce asked.

"Reporter with the paper."

Deuce started to walk toward his car, but his mother grabbed him by the sleeve. "Come speak to your father."

"Shit."

"Please."

Reluctantly, he allowed himself to be guided over toward the others. When they got there, Edna, a little breathless, holding her hand up against her chest, said, "Well, here we all are."

Fritz turned his head slowly and looked at Deuce from beneath his eyebrows, expressionless.

"How did it look?" he asked, obviously referring to the harvest.

"What do you think? Piss poor. Maybe eighty, ninety if you're lucky. I had her wide open and you could barely see corn coming out the spout."

"How high you run the head?" his father asked. Deuce told him. His father nodded in a way that both acknowledged and doubted the information at once. He always assumed, one way or another, that Deuce was doing something wrong.

Now the old man turned to the reporter and told her, "Like to leave as much stubble in the field as I can to catch the snow in the winter. But what with the drought, you got ears hanging down every which way and you got to skin her close. A bad year."

With the toe of his boot, he stirred the leavings on the ground next to the corn bin. "Look how white it is, floury, like damn elevator corn."

"What'd you expect, the weather being like it is?" Deuce told him.

"Ain't just the weather. Mostly, you ask me, it's the damn 3475." His father turned to the woman again and explained that 3475 was a particular type of hybrid seed. "You want a story, why don't you write that up? Last year everybody loved 3475. Record crops. Plenty of rain then. But not this year. Turns out 3475 can't stand stress."

"Is that right?" she said politely. His father hadn't introduced her, of course. In her presence, Deuce was more conscious of the spaces separating them.

"Damn right," the old man said, "can't stand stress." He shot a glance toward Deuce. Teddy had appeared from somewhere and gone around and cozied up to his father.

"How did Teddy do?"

"Junior says good," Edna volunteered, not waiting for her son to reply.

"That right?" The old man peered at Deuce, obviously wanting the information straight from him.

"Okay. He daydreams too much, but pretty good, for the first time out."

His mother's voice reminded Deuce that she wanted him to notice how tired his father was and tell him to get more sleep or something. What a joke, as if anyone could ever tell the old man anything. But Deuce did inspect him. The floodlight from the corn bin glinted off his patchy black-and-white hair, throwing most of his face into shadow, but Deuce could see enough to make out the exhaustion. Not that it meant zip. The old man was always exhausted. He wore his exhaustion like a purple heart. He liked to complain about it, to draw people's attention to it. Even in the dimness, even with just a glance, Deuce could see the calculations and resentments boiling beneath this badge of self-righteousness. And his mother wanted him to start in with a bunch of solicitous bullshit about how the old man needed to take better care of himself? She had to be kidding.

His father patted Teddy, who beamed up at him. Deuce, for his part, was waiting for a thank-you for lending a hand, thanks he knew would never come.

The small group became silent, and in the darkness, high overhead, the wind sawed back and forth.

Deuce turned his attention to the reporter. She had a dark complexion. Intelligent looking, judgmental. She lacked the covert alertness of the good poker player, and he found her gaze slightly unsettling, like that of a shopper appraising a possible purchase, something perhaps a little shoddy but within her budget.

If she was here, that meant movement of some sort at the Pack, so he turned back toward his father. "What's going on at the company?"

The old man shrugged. "Peterson got the consultant's report."

"Good? Bad?"

"According to Mel Coyle, it was sour. Buyout's dead."

"Oh, dear!" his mother blurted. "Is that right?" Her hand, which had been picking absently at the nap of her old bagged out work sweater, now became a fist and pressed hard against her chest.

The old man shrugged again, treating the news as just another typical bit of company business. JackPack had been dying for years, but somehow the end never came.

Deuce considered the best way to prick his smugness. "If Coyle said so, it must be true."

"Maybe."

"You ask me," Deuce said, choosing his words deliberately, "you've been playing a busted hand all along."

"This ain't about your damn poker," the old man snapped.

"Boys," Deuce's mother said, raising her voice just slightly in warning.

Satisfied, Deuce said no more, and the uneasy truce was resumed between him and his father. Deuce smiled at the woman reporter, who was taking all this in. Her black hair flowed thickly back from her forehead. Not bad looking, the kind of looks Deuce imagined would appeal to the men of some other country. Her manner of observing had changed slightly, a little less certain as she attempted to interpret his smile.

He felt the first drops of rain. His father looked up and around in the direction from which the storm was coming and surveyed the blackness as if he could see something invisible to the rest of them.

"I always worry," he said, "until the rain begins."

"And why is that?" the reporter asked.

He took his time answering. "Tornadoes. You get them, they come first."

"In the spring, maybe," Deuce retorted, disgusted.

"No," his father said slowly, "fall, too. You know that." The words chided his son. "Fall twisters ain't so common," he allowed, looking back toward the reporter, "but we can get them, you bet."

"Yeah, right," Deuce said sarcastically. Tornadoes this late were as scarce as royal flushes, but the old man just had to show off.

Raindrops pattered down around them, and for a time they listened to the thoughtful, hesitant sound. Deuce, when he got tired of standing there, glanced over at his mother, frowned, and shook his head, then turned and left without another word.

# CHAPTER 47

～

When she got back to the paper, Rachel Brandeis had several messages. Skip Peterson had called. Leonard Sawyer wanted to see her upstairs. She read quickly through the rest, then dialed the number Peterson had given and waited as it rang. A yoke of cold pressed against her shoulders, rainwater soaking through the coat she'd failed to get waterproofed.

For a couple of hours, she'd known about the unfavorable consultant's report but, except for Fritz, had been having trouble reaching people. Her information, all second or third hand, was consistent, however—the buyout was dead.

On the third ring, Peterson answered.

Five minutes later she was back in her car and driving toward the Pack. The guard at the main gate showed her the private entrance, and she climbed a dim stairwell into the company offices. Peterson appeared at once, in shirtsleeves, strands of his hair falling over his forehead, a document in his hand. Wordlessly, he led the way down to a conference room, where he handed it to her.

"Read."

He closed the door as he left.

As she tossed her sopping raincoat over a chair, Rachel noted the cover—a copy of the consultant's report—but didn't open it at once. Instead she sat down and, shivering, lifted the damp, sticky blouse off her shoulders, wondering about the significance of the tableau she had glimpsed a minute before as Peterson had come to meet her. Inside his office, Homer Budge and a couple of other men she recognized from the union's executive committee stared sullenly out at her. Rachel could see no management people other than Peterson, although they might have been there, out of view. Whatever he had been talking to the union guys about, the conversation couldn't have been a pleasant one.

If the buyout attempt was to be abandoned, that would no doubt explain the glum visages. What it wouldn't explain was why Peterson had been so anxious that she come up there and read the report. She resisted the surge of excitement at having her hands on the thing, at being made a party to events. But she also remembered the elaborately choreographed dinner he had staged for her benefit, his none-too-subtle attempt to recruit her to the now-lost cause. What was he up to this time? Why bother to call her at all if the company was closing?

She lowered the blouse delicately, cold against her skin, and opened the report.

~

She hadn't quite finished when Peterson returned. As she read the last few pages, he paced, carrying a rolled-up newspaper, which he slapped against the palm of his hand, against his thigh, against the backs of chairs as he prowled around the room.

Finally, she closed the cover of the report and rearranged the notepad on which she had been copying out quotable material.

"The buyout's dead?" she asked.

"Is that what the report says?" He spoke conversationally, stopping only briefly to comb his hair back with his fingers, then moving again in the loose-jointed way he had, like a man shedding excess energy.

"That's what the mayor seems to think. He's the only one I've talked to so far."

"He's misinformed."

"But he apparently got the information straight from your corporate council, Mel Coyle."

"He must have misunderstood."

"Oh?"

"People get strange ideas." He pointed at the report with the rolled up paper. "Right now I want to talk about that. Does it say the buyout's dead?"

Not knowing quite what he was getting at—for the report said many things—she read aloud the passages she thought contained the crux of the matter, a list of improvements the consultant deemed essential. Total cost: more than six million. Six million on top of the givebacks currently being negotiated with the union.

"Do you have a source for the funds?" she asked.

"Forget the money. What does the report say?" He stopped directly across from her, gripping a chair and moving it back and forth on its castors, his tone, however, still calm enough.

"Perhaps you'd better tell me," she suggested.

"Perhaps I'd better." The chair thumped sharply against the table. Again, the pacing began. "It says the buyout can still work."

"It does? Where?"

"Page sixteen, last paragraph."

She opened the report again and scanned the paragraph indicated.

"Out loud, please."

"'The Jackson Packing Company has long had a reputation for quality products. To sustain a competitive operation, this product base must be supported with adequate financing, facility modernizing, and employee commitment.'"

Peterson stopped and spun toward her, grabbing another chair. "This company can survive."

"All right," Rachel acquiesced, doubtfully. A creative conning of the document might ring a few drops of hope out of it. She could accept that. But life should be so simple.

"Am I to understand that the buyout is still on, then?" she asked.

Peterson leaned forward, over the chair, planting his hands on the table, his gaze fixed on her.

"Your grandfather," he said, "was Jakob Peretz, a socialist and labor organizer in Newark, New Jersey. Your other grandfather Irving Brandeis was a labor lawyer in New York City. On your mother's side you're related to the Rosenbergs. During the sixties, your father Morris, another lawyer, a radical, defended Black Panthers in New Haven…"

By the time he'd reached her mother's second cousin, Morty the Anarchist, Rachel had had enough.

"Excuse me, Skip, what the hell do you think you're doing?"

"A number of things. One, when the enemy of my family—that's your boss—hires an operative—that's you—you've got no right to be surprised that I've run a background check on you. This isn't a game we're playing here. Two, in your family, you've got labor organizers, socialists, lawyers, teachers, musicians, and who knows what all. Now a journalist, too, but I'll be damned if I could find anybody who looked like he knew a fucking thing about business. And liberals are apparently the right-wing fanatics in your family. Which, three, explains this." And he slid the newspaper he'd been holding all this time across the table toward her.

She left it unopened.

"Go ahead," he told her, "look at it."

"I don't need to." She knew what it contained. She'd known almost as soon as she'd seen him come in waving it like a billy club. "This is certainly a wonderful way to win me over," she told him.

"It's a shitty way, okay? But I don't have the time. There's no time here. If you're not going to look at the story, Rachel, give it to me."

With an irritated flip of the wrist, she sent the paper skimming back.

He unfolded it, then swept his hair back and took a pair of reading glasses out of his shirt pocket, which he flicked open and perched about halfway down his noise. So, she thought, he was farsighted. Perfect.

"Let's see now. Ah, here we are. 'For decades, butchers and smokehouse workers and bacon slicers have gathered at Harry's Tap across from the Jackson Packing Company to hoist a few beers and complain about their bosses. Never did they dream that one day they'd have a chance to own the company themselves.

"'But that day has come, and not everyone at Harry's is happy about it. "Might be it could work," says trimmer Clark Moseley, "if they got rid of all the deadwood. They've always been top-heavy, too many managers, too many foremen, expert at nothing but looking out for No. 1." The men gathered around Moseley nod in agreement.'"

Peterson tilted his head back as he read, which intensified the impression of distaste.

"'Francis "Deets" Fitzgerald, who works in the curing cellar, also agrees, but adds, "I figure we got no choice. Either we buy the place or the company's going down."

"'A contrary view isn't hard to find…'"

As Peterson recited, he resumed his pacing, gradually coming around the table to where Rachel sat. She listened uncomfortably, not only because of his hostility, but also because her own words sounded so very strange in another mouth.

He went on in a singsong voice, as if from the onset of exhaustion. "'Two stools down from Fitzgerald, Robert Stamm, who separates shoulders from loins on the cutting floor, shakes beer nuts like they were dice before tossing them into his mouth. "We've been working without a contract for eight months. They couldn't get the givebacks by negotiating, so they've cooked up this new scheme," he offers.'"

Peterson, standing beside her now, laid the paper down on the table in front of Rachel. "And so on and so forth." He smoothed it out with his thin, knuckly, sensitive-looking fingers. "Is this your idea of an objective story, Rachel? Is it?"

"I stand by what I've written. Not everybody is in favor of the buyout."

His voice had become almost gentle as he drew ever closer, as close as if he intended to kiss her. He placed a hand on her shoulder, on the damp material of her blouse, and she felt her flesh shiver beneath it. A current rippled down through her chest and abdomen, as if she was a pond into which a stone had just been dropped.

"But it's so easy, Rachel. It's so easy to go into Harry's Tap, the house of bellyachers, and get people to tell you what you want to hear. Is that what you're about, easy journalism?"

Rachel pushed his fingers from her shoulder. People tried to get a story written their way all the time, but never had Rachel encountered anyone quite as determined as Peterson.

"I stand by what I wrote," she repeated. "What I did was no different from what any competent journalist would have done."

"Right. Exactly. And that's what pisses me off." He still spoke quietly. "It's the same old horseshit. It's automatic writing. Some reporter from the *New York Times* could have shown up here, spent a day nosing around, and written the same damn piece. No thought. Just write what he already knew must be true."

For a moment, she thought about responding, but then decided that no, no, she wasn't going to get into a debate over how to do her job. "You didn't answer my question, Skip. The money to upgrade the plant?"

Peterson withdrew and sat down in a nearby chair and stretched out, studying her as if he might have missed something. Finally, the effort abandoned, he merely shook his head.

"There are sources."

"The employees?"

"Possibly." He idly inspected his fingernails as he said, "If you keep on writing stories like this, there's really no point in continuing." He cocked one eye up at her. "So what's it to be this time, Rachel? More of the same? First paragraph: unfavorable report. Second paragraph: desperate need for fresh capital (since you seem so fixated on money). Third: operating losses no matter what. Fourth: gloom descends on employees." With each statement, his voice seemed wearier. "Finally you put in a quote from me saying we can still save the company. But frankly, by then, it's too late. Somewhere in the second paragraph, the reader has unplugged the life-support systems. Is that what we're to have, Rachel?"

"I don't know."

"You're sure the company's going to fail, isn't that right?" he said.

"No, it isn't."

"Yes, it is."

He *was* right, she thought. The company could not survive. It was simply a fact. Of course, she wouldn't say it. She even censored the thought, telling herself that it might be true, but she wasn't in the prophesy business.

"You'll write what you want to write," Peterson now told her. "Nothing I can do about it."

He lay in his chair with his hands now clasped on top of his head. She saw in the way he kept changing his position, from one counterfeit of ease to another, the presence of his habitual motion.

"Tell me, do you believe in long shots?" he asked. "Isn't putting your money on a hundred-to-one nag more interesting then betting on a sure thing? A death foretold? The truly interesting story here, Rachel, is the story of survival against great odds...So you tell me, what's it to be?"

～

As Rachel drove back to the newspaper offices, she fumed over Peterson's assault. The fellow really was outrageous. First he ignores her completely, and now this, the bum's rush. Yet, despite all his badgering, she still found something attractive in his refusal to give up, to knuckle under, to accept the inevitable. The word *mensch* occurred to her, but that august appellation she was not ready to bestow. Anyway, he could have sold the company for parts and come away with a few bucks. Another man would have genuflected to his stockholders and done just that. Skip still had some fight left in him. She liked that. But she was still pissed at him.

Back at the paper, the night editor came over to her. "The old man keeps calling down. He wants to see you. He told me to send you up as soon as you got back."

"It's pretty late," she said. She had no desire to go upstairs. The night editor shook his head and pointed toward the ceiling.

In the elevator, she continued to ponder over the scene with Skip Peterson. In a way, he had been right about her story, but she had not the time or resources to do a scientific poll of employee sentiment. And she still believed the story gave a reasonable cross-section. People were more skeptical than Peterson apparently imagined they were.

And there was one other thing. She had not forgotten the fact that Fritz Goetzinger had been told by Mel Coyle, the man behind the scenes, that the attempt at an employee buyout was to be abandoned. What might be read into that? She didn't know, but it was certainly interesting that the JackPack management wasn't at the moment speaking with one voice.

Sawyer's personal secretary had long since gone home. Rachel knocked on his open door and went in to find the old man, as always, alone. He wore a bathrobe, the lapels falling open to reveal his thin hairless chest and sagging dugs, from which she averted her eyes. The temperature had been turned way up, the room filled with musty *alter kocker* smells and clammy from the humidity.

"Yes, yes, good," he said to himself when he saw her. "What's this about a report?" His eyes did not reveal the fear and sadness of other eyes; they betrayed only calculation.

She made her account as brief as possible.

"So what's Peterson planning on doing?" he demanded. "Is he gonna try and get his mitts on the employees' retirement money?"

"Nobody's mentioned that."

"They will."

All Rachel said was "I've got a deadline to make."

"Go, go. Tell them to hold the presses if you have to. They give you a hard time, let me know."

"That won't be necessary."

She took the stairs back down rather than the elevator.

Like a dish baking until it set, Rachel's dislike for her boss solidified a little more with each visit to the penthouse. She had chosen to remain merely civil to him, but he apparently interpreted this brusqueness as a virtue, more evidence that she was exactly the no-nonsense kind of reporter he had set out to hire in the first place. To insult him with effect would require more bluntness. One day.

She was tempted to throw her lot in with Peterson and write the story the way he wanted. How easy it would have been to become an advocate, to adopt as her own the wishes of others. While thinking these thoughts, she became aware of the workings of her mind, and an unexpected wave of sadness overtook her. She stopped on a landing, halfway back to the newsroom, and plopped herself down on a step, and stewed. Okay, she decided after a minute, so she'd put a Peterson quote near the top, that much she could do. That much but no more.

She wondered if she had time to call her parents and tell them about this new investigation of their family. Sawyer had found out who her father was, but Peterson had gone him one better, although even his efforts had been strictly amateur night. The FBI had big fat files on the Brandeis and Peretz families. They'd been hounded by the master himself, J. Edgar Hoover. Her spirits revived a little at the thought that now she had been investigated as well. She wondered if she had time to call her friend Sheila. She wanted to share with someone her impression of Peterson and his latest performance piece. No, she decided, she had better go ahead and write the story first.

# CHAPTER 48

~

Homer Budge didn't make it into the house. He turned into the bushes next to the garage and leaned over, and the vomit came gushing out. With each new surge he groaned, his mouth gaping open, his back bowing with the effort. The rain pounded on his head and shoulders, running down inside his collar. He was barely aware of the blackness of the night and the thin, watery streaks of light at his feet. Finally he strained one last time and dry heaved, nothing left, his mouth full of acid bitterness.

Head down, he made his way to the kitchen, where he got a glass of water and leaned over the sink, breathing through his mouth and sweating.

"Who's there?" Rose called from the other room.

"Just me."

He heard her get up and come toward the kitchen. She had a sixth sense where trouble was concerned.

"Look at you, you're soaked," she said. "Are you okay?" He felt her next to him and then her hand on his forehead.

"The Pack."

He grabbed the hand towel off the refrigerator door and went into the other room, trailed by Rose. He could smell the vomit lodged in his nasal passage. Seeing her homework arrayed on the dining room table, he sat down there and pressed the towel against his face, ignoring her order to go upstairs and put on some dry things.

He felt a little better. He sat up and took a deep breath and swallowed, tasting the sourness in his mouth.

In the living room, Ruthie and Veronica were watching TV. It must be one of the nighttime soaps, the only programs they watched together. Despite the vivid colors and mirrors that Rose used to make the rooms seem bigger, Homer felt the smallness of the place, the food smells left from dinner, the air thick and hard to breathe.

Rose stood with a hand on his shoulder, then sat down, on the edge of the chair opposite.

"What happened?"

"The consultant's report came." He pressed his lips together and shook his head.

"Oh." Sadness welled up in her face, and she reached out and touched the back of his hand.

"Peterson still thinks we can save the company."

To this Rose said nothing but waited for him to continue. Homer sat for a few moments, trying to decide how to proceed. Finally he could think of nothing better than to lay out the events as they had occurred.

A few minutes later, he heard a car door slam out front and momentarily John Michael came storming into the living room, stopping to give his sisters a hard time about the program they were watching and unaware of the drama unfolding in the dining room.

Just at that moment, Homer was in no mood for John Michael and his certainties.

"The retirement money?" Rose was asking.

"That's right, maybe that, maybe the 401(k) money, depending on how the legal issues play out. Could be second mortgages, too, or life insurance policies, wherever people can get something to put in."

Homer was aware of the tension around his mouth. His breathing was still labored. Rose just shook her head as she got up and went into the kitchen and returned with another glass of water, which she gave to him.

"Can this be possible?"

"Can what be possible?" John Michael asked as he came forward, having given over annoying his sisters upon spotting this more interesting subject for his attention.

Saying nothing, Homer put the glass down but kept his grip on it.

"They're talking about putting 401(k) money into the buyout," Rose told their son.

"What?"

John Michael looked at his father. Homer had to tell him something, so he gave a clipped account of what he'd just told Rose. The briefness, he intended for John Michael to understand, meant that Homer wasn't at the moment interested in whatever acerbic comments his eldest son might care to make.

"You'll have to run the company then," John Michael said at once.

"We don't know what we'll have to do."

"I wouldn't put all my money into anything unless I was in charge."

Homer took another swig of water. "At the moment," he told his son, "I'm not interested in what you would or would not do."

"What about the rank and file, what do they know about selling pork?" John Michael demanded, not so easily discouraged. Homer glared at his son, and John Michael ceased for a minute. He was thinking.

"Of course," Rose said before John Michael could start up again, "we shall contribute what we have in our retirement account."

"Just like that?" John Michael said. "Don't the rest of us have a say-so here?"

"No, you don't," Homer told him.

Whatever John Michael might imagine to the contrary, there was nothing to think about here. With as many kids as Homer and Rose had, such decisions came easily. The present mattered, the future would have to take care of itself. The two of them could give away their retirement money with a light heart. The Lord would provide.

"We might forget about ourselves, Mother," Homer said, speaking directly to Rose, as if John Michael wasn't there, "but that doesn't mean the others will put their money in." Many of the JackPack people worked merely for the day they didn't have to work anymore. They had no discernible faith, unless retirement might be one. That was a piss-poor vision of heaven, but if it was all you had…

John Michael broke in. "What will the International say?" His tone indicated at once his sympathy for the position of the Pack workers' parent union, whatever it might be.

Homer readjusted his thoughts, his irritation rising, and turned to John Michael and said curtly, "Well, they don't like what we were doing already. I expect we know what they'll think about this."

Ruthie and Veronica had abandoned their TV program and come to the edge of the dining room.

"What is it, Daddy?" Ruthie asked, and Homer repeated himself a third time. Multiple retellings were the norm in the Budge house. Homer kept a wary eye on John Michael.

"What if people don't have any money saved up?" Ruthie asked. "Is it just people who worked there a long time have to put their money up?"

"Peterson can't make anybody invest," John Michael told his sister.

"No," Homer said at once, "he can't do that. Of course he can't. But for a lot of the old-timers, the Pack's all they've ever known. If they can't see any other choice..."

"So it's just people like us?" Ruthie asked, following a line of reasoning of her own. Her sense of right and wrong was as strong as her brother's but had quite a different flavor. Veronica, for her part, still had the glazed look of someone in front of the tube.

"Others have a lot more than we do, dear," Homer told Ruthie. "Anyway, Skip Peterson's point is that if we're going to become entrepreneurs, we've got to find money wherever we can. People might put second mortgages on their homes, or sell their beloved bass boats, or hit up their rich uncles, wherever they can come up with some extra cash."

Ruthie sniffed. "Who's got rich uncles?"

"Is that it, then?" John Michael started up again. "Is that what you're thinking? Give the money to Peterson and let him do whatever he wants?"

"At the moment, I'm not thinking anything. I'm only telling you what Skip Peterson's proposing. Before we go off half-cocked, we've got to look at the thing."

"You ask me," John Michael said, "this is just another scheme to put the blame on the rank and file."

Homer had had enough. "I didn't ask you."

John Michael still didn't take the hint. "You're going to let Peterson take advantage of you, Dad, like all the other times—"

"Look, for once in your life," Homer snapped at him, "put a sock in it!"

"I just think—"

"This is not the time," Rose told John Michael.

Homer raged at his eldest, "When you're responsible for twenty-two hundred people, then you can talk! Now you can just shut the hell up!"

"Dear," Rose said softly to Homer.

He stabbed a finger at John Michael. "You got that?"

"Dear."

John Michael stood as if struck dumb, his mouth open.

Homer poked his face intently toward him and spoke again, "You don't know what the hell you're talking about, and I've heard just about enough from you."

"Homer," Rose said.

"I'm through."

She turned to John Michael. "You're only nineteen years old, dear. You mustn't forget that."

John Michael had nothing to say. Finally, Homer thought with satisfaction, he had nothing to say.

A few minutes later, Homer told Rose he was going down to Baker Street, by which he meant the Power of Prayer.

"Good."

Outside he did not start the car but merely sat in the driver's seat, watching the rainwater purl sadly down the windshield. He could still taste the bile in his mouth. He remembered, now with pain, the exchange with John Michael, how like smoke from an explosion his words had hung in the air all about them. He remembered the silence of Ruthie and Veronica. After a few minutes, he went back inside.

"Where is he?" he asked Rose.

"Up in his room, I think." Terry and Tom and Marcie and little Joey had shown up from various precincts of the house, but they said nothing as Homer made his way by.

He went up to the second floor and then climbed the narrow stairs to the attic, where a space had been sectioned off so that John Michael might have his own room.

Homer knocked softly on the door. When no one answered, he opened the door a crack. "Permission to come aboard?" He took the silence for a yes, and let himself the rest of the way into the narrow space.

John Michael's stuff was strewn about, but rooms in the house were arranged with such nautical stinginess that even the messes had a certain economy about them. The lower bunk bed, hinged to the wall, had been folded back, which gave him enough room to work at his desk, where he now sat, back to the door, bent over his homework as intensely as a possum feigns death.

His clothes hung from the rafters at the peak of the roof and could be fetched using a pulley system. Storage cubicles for underwear and such were on casters and could be moved around depending on the occasion. Homer had once joked that the space was so tight they might have to shorten John Michael's name.

For a chair, Homer rolled one of the cubicles close to his son. He would talk to his back. He reached out a hand with the intention of placing it on his shoulder but then thought better of it. The house remained surprisingly quiet considering the number of kids in it. Homer must make the first move. He didn't regret his outburst, only how close he'd come to driving away and leaving the wound to fester.

Now, peeking around the edge of John Michael's frame and seeing a chemistry book open on the desk, he said, "If you can concentrate on science at a time like this, you're a better man than me, Charlie Brown."

This lame attempt at humor brought no response. Homer sat back and looked idly around. John Michael's artwork had been hung or thumbtacked between the studs of the interior wall. Not much, an ancient picture of his maternal grandfather in his WWI uniform, complete with puttees and the other regalia of the era, and beneath the picture, hanging from a nail, the German helmet brought back as a souvenir. Bookshelves had been slotted between the studs, the studs themselves acting as bookends. The room of a serious young man. So, okay, Homer thought, only seriousness would do.

He reached out and this time did lay his hand gently on his son's shoulder. "You've got to understand, John Michael, that what we got here is a situation that's very hard on people, very, very hard." When John Michael still didn't speak, Homer continued. "I'm not saying you're wrong, dear, just that you're way ahead of yourself. Before we start coming to conclusions, we've got to see where we're at."

Homer left another small space, and then said, "I talked with the executive committee and we all agreed the best thing to do was go home and sleep on it. Tomorrow morning we'll start hashing the thing out. In the meantime, we all got to sleep on it. You see what I'm saying?"

Homer stopped now and waited. When finally John Michael did speak, it had nothing to do with the situation at the Pack.

"I've been thinkin' maybe it's time for me to find a place of my own."

Oh, dear, Homer thought, even at his age John Michael's first impulse is to run away from home. To his son he replied, "I expect, one day, we'll throw you out. But what's the rush? It's tough enough trying to get through college without having to support yourself at the same time."

"I can do it."

"Of course you can. I don't doubt it for a minute."

"I could quit school for a couple of years."

"Now why would you want to do a thing like that?"

"Lots of guys do it. Why should I be any different?"

For heaven's sake, Homer thought. "You're such an idealist, you know that? For a crust of bread and a place to lay your head, you'd leave off getting a good education…Anyway, you know, if you leave, we'll have a deuce of a time renting this room to anybody but a midget."

"Ha-ha," John Michael said. He still had not turned around, determined to present only his back to his father.

"This isn't such a big deal, you know, this little blowup between us." Homer patted his son and then took his hand away.

Because John Michael tended to discount the value of experience, having so little himself, Homer tried to avoid invoking it. Yet he couldn't resist saying, "If you'd been there today and seen Skip Peterson, you'd have realized he isn't trying to put one over on us. I know the man, and believe me, he's not that good an actor."

"But he can't believe people would put their retirement money into the company?" John Michael said, and this idea was so important to him that he finally swung around to face his father.

Homer saw with a start why he hadn't done it earlier. His eyes were red. Could it be?

"It's a terrible thing, isn't it, Dad? People worked all their lives for that money." In his voice, sorrow and determination and reasonableness all struggling to gain the upper hand.

"Certainly it's a terrifying thing." Having a few bucks taken out of your paycheck each week didn't amount to much compared to emptying out your savings. But at the moment, Homer was mostly concerned with the state of his son's eyes. In truth, he never *had* dressed the boy down in such a savage way before, and though John Michael gave the impression of being a tough and uncompromising kid, it just wasn't true. Homer recalled Rose's words to their son. "You're only nineteen. You've got to remember that." Homer had to remember it, too. John Michael was only nineteen. Underneath the hard crust he presented to the world beat a still sensitive heart. A good heart.

"We'll be okay," Homer said and squeezed John Michael's arm encouragingly.

John Michael could only shake his head.

Homer had an idea. "What is it you say, we make our own futures? Might be that's what we've got here, a chance to stop working for other people and work for ourselves for a change."

"Don't trust Peterson, Dad, whatever you do."

"I'll certainly keep my eye on him."

"Don't trust him." John Michael took a deep breath and turned to blow his nose and take a couple of covert swipes at his moist eyes with the tissue. "You know what I think?" he said. His cocksureness was beginning to reassert itself.

"What do you think?"

"Peterson just wants to keep on running the Pack. He figures if he sells to the union, he'll be able to face you guys down."

Homer felt a little of his earlier irritation resurfacing. But he reminded himself that John Michael had been raised on the hundred years' war between the union and the company. He knew nothing else.

"Well, perhaps," Homer said softly, "but if we end up owning the company, we'll decide who gets to be president, not Skip Peterson."

"Would it be you?"

"Me?" Homer smiled. He certainly had his fantasies; what man wouldn't? Even at the Power of Prayer, struggling to say the Rosary with the proper devotional spirit, his thoughts were evermore drawn to such vanities. He prayed for guidance. He argued with himself, knowing that God might speak to him in that way.

When it came right down to it, there were too many areas of the business Homer didn't understand well enough. What they should do was this: go looking for an outsider, somebody with experience that they could work with—that's what they should do. To John Michael, however, all he said now was "We'll have to wait and see. It's much too early to worry about that sort of thing."

"If you own the company, Dad, it oughta be a union man!"

"We'll see."

"If it isn't, it'll be the same old shit all over again."

"We'll see."

John Michael started to protest, but when Homer held up a hand and then patted his knee, his son quieted, remembering perhaps the upset of earlier.

"We'll see. I'll promise you this much, dear. I'll do whatever seems best. But you've got to understand—if that means working with Peterson, then I'll do it."

"Just watch yourself, Dad, okay?"

"I will."

Of course, John Michael was correct. Peterson might have been on the up-and-up this afternoon, but tomorrow was another day. There was a long history here. On the other hand, desperate times make strange bedfellows, as he'd told John Michael a couple weeks back. At the time, he realized now, he'd just been mouthing words, and suffering under the delusion that whatever might be required of others, he himself would somehow manage to endure the desperate times without the strange bedfellows.

Interesting, he thought, how we sand around the edges of a thing to make it fit. If we were more truthful, we'd realize nothing ever really fits.

"Thank you," he said to John Michael, who had been waiting patiently for what he would say next.

"Why?"

"You seek the essence of a thing, dear boy, and that makes me look for it, too."

John Michael smiled uncertainly.

"Come here," Homer said, "give me a hug."

As Homer descended from John Michael's aerie, he noticed with pleasure that the noise level below them had returned to normal. The Budge household was bedlam once more.

# CHAPTER 49

~

Through the house's heating ducts, voices carried upstairs from the kitchen, and so Edna Goetzinger, lying in bed, couldn't help overhearing the conversation. Fritzy had come in first and she'd listened to the sounds he made. A few minutes later, someone knocked and entered. She recognized Homer Budge's voice, muffled though it was by the pounding of the rain all about her. The emotions of the two men rose so clearly through the ductwork that the words hardly mattered. Homer did most of the talking.

As soon as she heard the door close, she put on her robe, brushed her hair, and went downstairs. When Fritzy saw her, he frowned. "Don't you start on me, too."

She couldn't see him clearly. They kept few lights on, for Fritzy had always been penny-wise. He had opened a beer, which wasn't like him, not on a work night, and was sitting at the table, the chair turned sideways.

She drew the robe more tightly about herself. With the house shut against the storm, the air still held a faint odor of the brine and spices she'd used to pickle the cabbage.

"I'm sorry," she said, "I couldn't help but overhear. The employees have to put more money in, is that what they're saying?"

"Yeah. Four and a half million. Peterson claims the buyout's still on despite the bum report. Anyway, that's what he told Homer and some of his people."

"Four and a half million? Could that possibly happen?"

"Probably not, but who knows? A man's worked at the same job all his life, now somebody's gonna take it away from him, who can tell what he'll do?"

Fritzy was talking about the old-timers, his people, and it was true, many of them had worked for the Pack for decades. What *would* they do?

"Did Homer just come up to tell you, or did he want something, too?"

"The three of us to work together on the thing—him, me, Peterson."

Here's something new, Edna thought. "Maybe that's a good idea," she suggested.

He shook his head.

"So you're not going to help?"

"Told Homer I'd think about it."

She took a sip of his beer and made a face at the bitterness of it.

"I wish you were out of it," she told him.

"Somebody has to speak up for the employees."

"That's Homer's job."

"Oh?" he snorted. "Might be you'd think a little different if you saw the way Budge and the others treat Billy Noel on the committee. Billy talks, but they don't listen. Used to be, Homer at least knew what it was like working out on the floor. No more. Had his nice, cushy union job too damn long, you ask me."

Edna had never known what to do about her husband's stubbornness. Or the way he had of taking half the truth and blowing it up until there wasn't room left for anything else. He was sitting hunched up in the chair. His summer tan had faded to a sickly yellowish pallor, almost like jaundice.

She moved behind him and began to massage his shoulders, and then his neck.

"You're just such a contrary person, you know that," she said, not without a trace of affection.

"Somebody's got to take the real measure of the thing. You got Homer Budge whistling in the dark and Skip Peterson looking out for the interests of the stockholders first, last, and always."

"I wish you were out of it is all," she repeated. "This isn't you, Fritzy. It's never been you. You should be worried about improving the genetics of the Berks and Chesters. You should be out harvesting the corn. That's what you really like to do."

"Junior's apparently doing it for me," he said curtly, and she realized that she'd inadvertently touched on another sore point.

"Somebody has to," she said, repeating exactly what he'd said a minute earlier about looking out for the interests of the workers at the Pack. Somebody had to.

"Don't you have him harvesting the Fish and Wildlife fields behind my back, too."

"Behind your back? Bosh. I'm not doing anything behind your back, except giving you a bit of a rub." She dug her thumbs sharply into his flesh, and he flinched. "The fields have to be harvested. It's been a bad enough year as it is. We can't just leave the corn to the deer and raccoons."

He grunted.

Slowly, her fingers moved round and round, kneading the rough flesh, the knotted muscles. The kitchen chair creaked in rhythm.

She looked about herself, conscious of the modesty of the place. The old appliances, the splay-legged table and chairs of too-shiny plastic and pitted metal. The graying walls with nothing on them except a calendar, and next to the back door, her one extravagance, her life list nailed above the container of birdseed, handy so she could feed and identify the birds. She and Fritzy had always been practical people, but the birds added a touch of color about the place. They were seasonal, like the vegetables she raised, and so she used them to measure the passing of the years. No matter how bad things got, she would always manage to feed the birds.

Finally, she tried one last time. "Why not, just for once, help Homer and the others? I mean, if you're bound and determined to do something..." He would be involved. It was too much to hope otherwise.

Beneath her fingertips, she felt him tighten. She rested her hands on his shoulders.

"This isn't like anything else, dear. Think of all the jobs at stake. What would happen if the plant closes and you could have prevented it?"

"If it's gonna close, there's nothing I can do about it."

"Are you sure?"

"Maybe the company *should* close, you ever think of that? Maybe that's what's best for people. I'll tell you one thing, they stand to lose whatever money they give Peterson."

Edna supposed this might be true, but at the moment, that wasn't what worried her. "My fear is the company will fail and you'll get the blame. If that were to happen, it would be a terrible thing." Could they even continue to live in Jackson then?

"I suppose you'd blame me, too."

"No," she said at once, then more slowly, "No, dear, but people listen to you. I'm afraid you'll do something you'll regret."

She stopped. That was it: regret. Most people didn't understand Fritzy. They didn't understand the power of his own blame, his self-blame. The blame of others was only part of it.

"Don't you worry about me," Fritzy said.

"But I do, dear. How can I help it?"

"I can take care of myself."

"You only think you can."

"Don't you worry about me," he repeated.

The phone had begun to ring, and he gripped his thighs and rose from beneath her hands.

As he spoke to the caller, a stranger by the sound of it, Edna's thoughts remained with what had preceded. She would worry about him, no matter his farmer's sense of standing one against the world. Nor had she forgotten that the buyout idea had originally been his, even if others no longer honored him by remembering.

For many years, she had watched the cycles in her husband's life, the rise and fall of his schemes that never quite ended up where he was aiming at. Fritzy didn't have much luck, but somewhere inside him there had always been an optimism he could draw on. Used to be. Now, what with her own vitality rapidly giving way, she feared he might be exhausting his last little store of hope. He was not a young man anymore. He had not so many good ideas left…and to have them stolen…

But the world would not change for Fritzy's sake.

When he finally hung up, Edna watched him looking off into the distance as he considered. She asked who had called.

"Said his name was Richie Chinn. Said he was from Los Angeles, owns a string of Chinese restaurants." Thoughtfully Fritzy rubbed along his jawline. "Had a proposition to make." He took a swig of beer and held it in his mouth for some time before swallowing. "Might be, Edna, we don't need to come up with this extra money to buy the Pack. Might be we don't have to buy her at all."

# CHAPTER 50

~

Skip Peterson had gone home to get a few hours of sleep with the idea that maybe then the world would look a little brighter. But sleep wouldn't come. He lay awake, listening to the rain. The violent drumming made the house seem even emptier, a clotted silence that cut him off, swaddled him. He felt the return of the loneliness of the only child.

In his phone conversations with the company directors, he had given each a situation report and struggled to keep the idea of an employee buyout alive. They asked their unhappy questions. He could feel their loyalty slipping away, not gone yet but any day now.

On every hand he met disbelievers and the weak-willed. How nice it would have been if one of his friends in the industry had simply taken a tour of the facility, the books been opened, a deal struck. It hadn't happened; it wouldn't happen.

He had cornered Homer Budge and his people and practically pleaded with them. But whatever Budge's virtues, they weren't the virtues of the new day aborning.

He'd even blitzkrieged Rachel Brandeis. Maybe that would do some good, but he doubted it. The surface waters could be stirred, but in the depths she remained passive, in her own mind not a player and so distrustful of people who were. And what a background!

Finally, there was the problem of Mel Coyle; Mel, who had been corporate counsel since the days of Skip's grandfather, Mel, who still thought of him as Skippy, the four-year-old riding his grandfather's shoulders through the plant. Skip regretted that he hadn't tried harder to get rid of the nickname, but more he regretted that he'd never managed to shuck off his habitual deference to the older man. Now, saddest of all, Mel had decided that the company couldn't survive and would, no doubt, exercise his considerable influence on the board.

To all these people Skip said what he'd said before, but the words weren't good enough, not anymore. New words were required. When he tried to think what they might be, his mind became mulish, refusing to budge. He flopped this way and that on the bed, his thoughts paralyzed even as his body thrashed obsessively about.

His recurrent fear returned. He should never have gone into the company. He had been too weak to make a life of his own. Instead he'd taken the one offered. He'd seen the trap, knew it for what it was, and still he'd stepped beneath the deadfall. What a goddamn coward he was.

Finally, he gave up and lay back, his hands clasped behind his neck, listening to the surges in the intensity of the storm and wondering what was the use.

The phone rang. He rolled over and looked at the luminous dial of the bedside clock: 12:37.

"Skip, Skip, Skip," the caller said without preamble, "what the hell do you think you're trying to prove?"

Skip knew the voice but couldn't quite place it. "Do you know what time it is?"

"What the fuck difference does it make?" the voice demanded, and then Skip knew, a person for whom time was irrelevant: Nick Takus, the CEO and chief son of a bitch at Modern Meat.

"That's right, Nick, I'd forgotten, you never sleep."

"Three hours a night," Takus boomed. "When you get up at two a.m. to take a leak, you should think of me, hard at work, making myself useful."

"I'm sure that's wonderful, Nick. Did you call to tell me you're still awake?"

"Hell no. I called to tell you not to make an ass of yourself."

"Am I making an ass of myself?"

"You sure enough are. All this business about selling out to your employees. Good God, man, what do they know about anything? They don't know diddly. This is a tough goddamn business we're in, and you want to make it amateur night. Jesus H. Christ, give me a fucking break." Takus apparently had been born on speed and never come down.

"Employee buyouts have worked before," Skip pointed out.

He found something strangely calming in Takus's scorched-earth approach to the Socratic method.

"Employee buyouts have worked before?" Takus mocked him. "Not when the friggin' consultants are telling you to pack it in. Not when you're coming up for air the goddamn last time."

So that was it. "Good news travels fast."

"Damn right it does," Takus yelled. "Some people over there ain't lost their marbles yet."

How the hell did the bastard find out so fast? "And who might they be, these people still in possession of their marbles?"

"Who?" Takus laughed.

"Yeah, Nick, how did you find out?" Skip's anger was just beginning to kick in. Mel Coyle? Would Mel have talked to Takus?

"Hell, let's face it, Skip, my people are talking to your people, your people are talking to mine, it's a regular friggin' hen party. You think you got a problem? I got people out here slipping info to reporters all over the place. I'm runnin' a fucking sieve. Ya gotta love it. These sons o' bitches got balls. Of course, I'd fire their asses like that if I could figure who they were. Figure maybe I'll deep-six all my product development people, just on principle. Kill-them-all, let-God-sort-it-out kind of thing. Got to steal me some good people from somewhere else first."

And again he laughed and laughed. The bastard was having entirely too much fun with all this.

"Well, this is a fascinating conversation, Nick—"

"Look, Skip, let's lay our cards on the table," Takus stormed on without a breath. "My people are having a helluva tussle out here about how we go about getting into the high-end stuff, but I've been thinking, maybe we could do something with your trademarks. Your people've done a nice little job bringing the Jack 'n' Jill label along. Too bad your granddaddy didn't see that the chains were the coming thing."

"I'm sure you weep every night, Nick."

Takus ignored this. "No matter. Water under the bridge and all that. Now wha'd'ya say you give the brands to somebody who can run with 'em? Wouldn't that be nice, to see Jack 'n' Jill right up there alongside Hormel and Oscar?"

"It'd be wonderful, Nick, but the trademarks aren't for sale."

"Skip, Skip, Skip, listen to what I'm saying. You're up shit creek without the proverbial paddle. The market value of the

Jackson Packing Company is zilch. Synergies, that's what you gotta have. You ain't got synergies, my friend. I, on the other hand, got 'em up the wazoo."

"Mr. Synergies."

"Damn right."

"You can't know what a comfort this is for me, Nick." If Jack-Pack was worth zilch, he and Takus wouldn't be having this little conversation, so except for the depressing fact that Skip had a mole in the company, somebody talking to Takus on the side, he found all this quite bracing.

"Listen to me, Skip. I can't believe you're serious about the employee buyout thing." Takus was suddenly speaking calmly. "But maybe you are, maybe you're just determined to keep on going until there's nothing left. What a shame. Nobody wants to see that. Son of a bitch, I don't want to see it. So here's what I'm gonna do. You're trying to save the company. Fair enough. Tell you what, I'll buy the whole shebang, how's that? You give me the assets, I'll give you eight mil. Eight million. You hear me? More than fair, considering. Damn sight more than fair. Hell, I'll throw in a little sweetener, too, just for you. How's about a consulting contract for the next couple years, let's say two hundred grand per, perfectly reasonable considering your lifetime in the business. Fuck, I can't believe I'm saying this. But what the hell, let's do it, let's cut the crap and get this done!"

What was eight million to a high roller like Takus? Chump change, well worth it to see somebody like Skip squirm. It was an insult, too, a bare fraction of what the company was really worth. And it wouldn't save a single job.

"Tell you what, Nick, make it twenty million and buy the stock, and I think you might have a deal."

Takus howled. "You kill me!" When he finally managed to bring his mirth under control, he said, "No, the deal's the deal. Eight mil for the assets, debt free, and I'll throw in the little sweetener for you. Probably be able to find a place for some of your people in my operation, too, who knows? But that's all. Wha'd'ya say?"

Skip considered the situation. The proposal was an insult, but that didn't mean Skip's board wouldn't jump at it. The jobs would be gone, but at least there'd be some money for the stockholders. He'd have to jawbone like hell if he wanted to keep the employee buyout alive.

"Well, this is a lovely offer you've made, Nick. I'm going to have to think about it."

"Of course you do. Tell you what, I'll give you forty-eight hours."

"Not much time."

"Oughta be more than enough, you ask me. Look, Skip," Takus pushed on, now the soul of sincerity, "this is a nice little piece of change for your family, but if you wanna go it on your own, no skin off my behind. Forty-eight hours. You tell me 'Forget about it, Nick' and I'll say, 'Okay, no hard feelings.' But one way or the other, up or down, I gotta know. Forty-eight hours."

Skip hung up and fell back on his pillow. A minute later, unable to lie still, he rolled over and turned on a light and sat on the edge of the bed. Then he got up and started pacing, first in the room, then in the upstairs hallway, then all over the house, turning on lights as he went. He threw open the front door and stood watching the rain cascading in pulses through the globe of the nearby streetlight. Rainwater spattered against his face and pajamas. He barely noticed.

# PART V

# CHAPTER 51

~

For a week, the rain had fallen, mostly at a walking pace but from time to time in brief wild surges. Afterward, the storms would pause, as if to take their bearings. Now a mist hung in the night air. In the darkness, the wet polished flanks of the Pullman sleeper caught and reflected streaks and patches of light from the windows of the old Burlington Northern railroad station.

Inside the station, bathed in the cool humid air and the odors of freshly cut wood and glue and paint, El Plowman bent to her work on the mural of cotton fields that would serve as a backdrop to the Mississippi Delta displays, scenes from the boyhood of Hiram Johnson. Behind her, people labored over other parts of the project, and she listened to the rustle of their voices. Time had grown short, much remained to be done, almost nothing completed.

She worked steadily but with little of her usual joy. She had slipped into another of the long, shallow depressions that characterized periods of her life. She told herself that the death of Mark O'Banion had led to this descent, but in truth she didn't know. She never knew what caused these dreadful periods, only that they came and went according to a logic of their own and must be endured with the good grace that a life in public demanded. She refused to take pills. She just tightened the stays on the corset of her willpower and did whatever had to be done next, although at the moment each fresh application of paint seemed only to make the mural worse.

Someone entered from the parking lot side of the building, and she felt a wisp of cool, damp air at the nape of her neck. She added a touch of color to the head cloth of a picker, and as she backed away for a better look, became aware of a presence behind her and glanced over her shoulder to discover Johnny Pond, a little closer than was polite, his head tilted at a professorial angle as he inspected the mural.

"Old Hiram picked cotton."

"As a boy, I know." She turned back to her work. "No doubt like everybody else in the Delta."

El's cotton pickers were stooped over in the field, bulging white sacks dragging from their shoulders, their long starved shadows slanting across the foreground. They looked like she felt.

"I suppose that's one advantage of growing up in the city," she suggested, Johnny being a Chicago native.

"That I didn't have to pick cotton? Yup, no cotton fields in the projects." He paused. "Probably just an oversight."

She added another dollop of color to the headdress she couldn't get quite right. She'd been unhappy with everything she'd done that night. She would have quit long ago, except that time had become precious. Less than four weeks to the exhibit opening. All hands were shanghaied into service, even board members of questionable talent, gloomy Guses or not.

She stopped again and stepped back and tilted her chin up as Johnny had, sighting along the ridge of her nose.

"Mostly I paint roses," she said. "Reiny convinced me I could expand my horizons." She pointed to the right. "That chinaberry tree over there, that's my masterpiece."

Johnny moved along the mural to examine it. Beneath his long, brown leather coat, he wore a shirt in a bright, slanting patchwork of primary colors, like a poisonous creature's warning to predators. His trousers were of some rich alpaca-like material. Johnny's success as a black man in Jackson had not been based on the principle of fitting in, although, as a matter of fact, it hadn't been based on the principle of not fitting in, either, for he seemed to take nothing personally and possessed the agile kind of mind that could always see the other fellow's point of view, certainly one of the cardinal virtues for anyone who emceed a radio call-in program called "Sound Off."

"Speaking of Reiny," he asked, "where is he? Got something for him."

He held up the satchel he was carrying, and El, remembering their encounter on the Pullman coach on the day of Mark O'Banion's death, guessed what must be in it—the audiotapes Johnny had made from Reiny's written narrative of Hiram's life.

"Taping go okay?" she asked.

"Couldn't be better."

What was the chance, she wondered, that Reiny had managed to put back the stuff she'd edited out? He hadn't liked it one bit when she told him what she'd done. They'd had one of their rows. It didn't matter to Reiny that a racist police officer, though long dead, still had relatives living in the city. If anything, it pleased him.

"He around?" Johnny asked.

"On the other side, working on the Jackson displays. You can't get there directly. You have to go outside, past the Pullman."

Johnny lingered, inspecting her work. "Nice tree," he said.

A minute later, he nodded good-bye. She saluted him with her paintbrush and watched him go, rambling from display to display, inspecting them in the intimate and detached way he had. She looked at the bag he carried and supposed that she should contrive a way to review the tapes, just to be on the safe side. He stopped before the painting of a shotgun house, Hiram's birthplace, from which in a kind of 3-D effect a section of a wall extended, papered with pages from an old Sears catalog. Before it stood an iron bed and an open keepsake trunk. Two women, a museum staffer and one of the young blacks recruited to help with the exhibit, arranged and rearranged the items in the trunk. Johnny directed a comment at the young black woman before moving on.

After he disappeared from sight, El tried to return to the mural, but it was no use, she could do nothing but make it worse, and so she abandoned the effort for the night and began to clean up.

She didn't get home until after ten. Another full day had left her exhausted, but that made no difference. She knew she wouldn't sleep. She never slept well, even when she was feeling good, her vaunted willpower helpless in the face of insomnia.

On the table in the front hall, the mail had been separated into four neat piles, one for Walter, one for her, one for both of them, one to be discarded. Discarding was her job. Walter never threw anything way. The letters in her pile promised nothing interesting and so she left them unopened.

She wandered into the kitchen and was pleased to find dirty dishes in the sink. Something to do. On the table, the morning paper lay, folded back to the page with the crossword puzzle on it, the puzzle abandoned only half-completed. The window blinds were still drawn. Often El and Walter's paths barely crossed during a day, the only signs they had of one another these small bits of archaeological evidence.

She debated whether she should but then went ahead and poured herself a glass of wine. Maybe it would make her feel better rather than worse. She turned on the TV and listened to what was left of the ten o'clock news as she did the dishes. After a while, the weathercast came on. Walter could have been in the room with her, his TV voice as relaxed as if he had just put the crossword down for a moment to say something.

She didn't at first hear the doorbell ring. She looked at her watch, then sighed and dried her hands.

On the front porch she found Johnny Pond. "Got a minute?" He stood solidly before her, seemingly impervious to the cold air, which, trapped beneath the porch roof, prowled around them. Her damp hands tingled as she held the door open for him.

Back in the kitchen, he declined the offered drink and sat at the table while she turned off the television and went back to the dishes, conscious of his presence behind her, as she'd been conscious of Walter's a few minutes earlier.

Though his manner at the door had given the impression of some urgency, he began chatting quite casually, and El waited for whatever was to follow.

If a large percentage of the black population in the city seemed there almost by accident, Johnny gave that impression not at all. He was one of those men who had chosen to live among his enemies. And he always had something on his mind.

Yet El, finding that she was glad to have the company, let him rattle on. And in due course, he paused, a signal that the serious matter had at last come to hand.

"You know what I found most interesting down at the exhibit?" he asked.

"Not my chinaberry tree, I imagine."

"No, afraid not. It was something Sam Turner told me. Ran into him in the other room. You know Sam?"

"Just to say hello to." The mention of Sam Turner called into El's mind the image of a short, skinny, talkative, rather humorous but somewhat vague man. She reviewed what little she knew about him. Worked for the city, of course. He'd acquired something of a reputation, never seeming to quite fit in. Perhaps his fault, perhaps not. The life of a black man in Jackson couldn't be easy. On the other hand, it was a two-way street, and look at Johnny, look at his skill at getting along.

"Did you know that Sam has bid on a job in the drafting department?" Johnny asked.

"Has he?"

"Yup. It's entry-level, and he's got the necessary training."

"Is that right?"

"Yup. And one more thing. He's not gonna get it. Got the training. As a matter of fact, he was an A student, straight As. Makes no difference. You people aren't gonna give it to him."

"Oh?" Why, El wondered, hadn't she heard about this?

She waited for Johnny to continue, but he said nothing more, and the silence stretched out between them.

She put away the last dish, and sat down across from him with the remnant of her wine, taking her time and trying to figure out just why she felt so odd.

"There's a freeze on hiring," she finally said. "If JackPack closes, that has an impact on the city budget."

"Sam Turner isn't a new hire. He's already working for the city."

"That's right, but..." She didn't know how she was going to finish this thought.

"According to the city engineer," Johnny forged ahead, "it's got nothing to do with any job freeze." He extracted from the pocket of his coat a letter, which he passed over to her.

El thought, dear me, as she read the brief communication from Chuck Fellows to Turner.

Dear Mr. Turner:

I have reviewed the documents you submitted and find them not up to the standards required by the city's drafting department. I would suggest that if you are seriously interested in obtaining drafting work somewhere in the future, you try to master the traditional skills still called for by many firms. Knowing CAD isn't enough. Until CAD becomes universal, there will still be a need for those who have taken the trouble to become proficient in traditional drafting methods.

Sincerely,

Charles W. Fellows, P.E.

A copy had been sent to Paul Cutler, the city manager, so he knew what was going on. El wondered again why she hadn't been told.

"Your man Fellows isn't much when it comes to diplomacy," Johnny said.

El handed the letter back. Fellows certainly did lack the common touch. But that was not news. "What makes you so sure Sam Turner's qualified to do the work? Chuck doesn't seem to think so."

"I know because Sam told me. He told me, and I believe him."

El repeated these words silently to herself. Her first impulse was to reject them as utterly inadequate to the situation. What a man says about himself, without corroboration, simply can't be trusted. But in thinking this, she immediately felt the coldness of its pure objectivity. What about women who had been rape victims? Where would they be if they weren't believed? But, she reminded herself at once, the situation here was hardly the same. This was no crime without witnesses. This was a bureaucracy. If anything, there were too many witnesses.

These contrary impulses led her to say, softly, "Do you really expect us to give someone a job just because he says he can do it?"

"He went to school for it. Was an A student. Got his degree. Just how difficult can it be?"

"I'm not qualified to judge. I imagine that in drafting, experience is important, too. Not only what you get in the classroom."

"Experience," Pond said with great disdain. He cleared a space for himself on the table so he could press his big forearms down on it as he leaned toward her. "Experience is like what the poll tax used to be down South, nothing but prejudice dressed up in a coat and tie."

All at once, El understood what seemed so odd here. A possible explanation, at least. This was really quite unlike Johnny Pond, this aggressiveness. She had never heard him talk in this way. She couldn't remember once, not when she'd been with him or heard him on the radio or read quotes from him, not once had he ever broached racial issues like this. She had heard him discuss such matters, of course, but only in reaction to what someone else had said.

At the moment, this insight didn't make much difference. Johnny *was* talking now, and she needed to respond carefully.

"I believe," she said, "that Chuck Fellows is a competent civil engineer, and I have no reason to think he's prejudiced." El didn't know the man well. He had an abrasive personality, it was true, but Mark O'Banion had sworn by him.

"That's your opinion." Pond had leaned back and resumed his relaxed posture.

"If he's a racist, I think Mark O'Banion would have known. And if Mark had known, he wouldn't have respected Fellows as he did."

Pond was obviously not convinced. He looked at her and chewed on his lower lip as he thought. He had the black man's features, a broad flattened nose, thick lips, smooth skin the color of—she wasn't sure, cedar perhaps—a good looking man, she thought. She remembered, too, how these features had made her uneasy when she first met him, before he'd set about fitting himself into the community, if only in the admittedly rather odd way he had.

"Look, Johnny, what we're really talking about here is the professional opinion of Chuck Fellows, and he's in a better position to judge than you or I...or Sam Turner."

"So," Pond said, with the look of a man who had known it all along, "that's that." El couldn't mistake the accusation. The two of them were on the Integration Task Force together. He'd never approached her with a request like this before, and now he does and see what happens?

"I'll talk to Fellows, okay? I'll certainly do that much, but if he tells me the man isn't qualified, then I don't know what else I can do. From what little I know of Turner, I can't say I'm filled with confidence. If he was a bit more, I don't know, a bit more like you, I suppose, that might make a difference."

"What do you mean, like me?" he challenged her.

Pond held his arms out, the labels of his coat folding outward, exposing his massive frame.

"The good Lord gave me this. Gave me the gift of gab, too. I've got a lot to be grateful for. But that's me, that's not Sam Turner. And let me tell you, El, Sam's like a lot of the brothers and sisters still trapped back there in the city, in Cabrini-Green or the Robert Taylor Homes or one of those other projects. They're just average, okay, just like most white folks. Nothing special. Excepting for one thing. You understand what I'm saying? Well, let me tell you, giving these people a chance, that's the real test of people like yourself, who think you're decent folks. You got to give the Sam Turners of this world a leg up. Then you can start talking about who should be like me. You don't, then all this bull-jive about how important experience is and whatnot, why it...ain't...worth...shit. You understand what I'm saying?"

El listened to Pond's sermonette with increasing impatience. She understood her own limitations in this situation. She did believe she was a decent person, a person of goodwill, but along with just about everybody else in Jackson, she had had little experience with blacks. She might try to see parallels between their lives and those of women like herself, to seek empathy that way, but all that did was reinforce the sense of difference. Yet she still wasn't ready to accept that in each and every situation like this what you had was a white problem and nothing else.

"I understand what you're saying," she told him, "but Sam Turner, so far as I can see, is hardly average. He lives in a world of his own. He makes almost no attempt to fit in."

"People who are black got to fit in any which way they can, sometimes by not fitting in at all."

This Zen-like pronouncement did nothing to improve El's souring mood.

"I'll talk to Chuck Fellows," she told him. "I'll see what he has to say."

"Call me."

"I will."

"Fair enough." He settled back, satisfied, and just like that, the confrontation had ended and El seemed to see him transforming before her eyes back into the Johnny Pond she had always known.

"I can't promise anything," she warned him.

He smiled. "You're a tough lady. You set your mind to something, it gets done."

This comment—El supposed he meant it as a compliment—served only to remind her of how different she looked from outside than from in.

She smiled disconsolately at him. "How little we know each other," she said.

# CHAPTER 52

~

The next morning, El set up a meeting with Chuck Fellows and went down to City Hall. He was waiting for her in his office, looking out at the rain, which had once again become heavy. She closed the door and walked over beside him, and the two of them stared down at the street a story below.

The air was filled with the luminous gray color particular to certain rainy days, and the wind having died away, the rain plummeted straight toward the earth. Her skin prickled as if she could feel the drops, but this tingling sensation barely touched the inner El, the strange, oppressive mixture of anxiety and indifference and determination that crouched in the center of her chest. Fellows's reputation preceded him. With Mark gone, she would have to deal with him directly, and she felt as if a myelin sheath had been removed and a bare, raw nerve exposed.

"We get no rain for months," Fellows said, "and now this." His tone was less of wonder than of interest, as a man might sound who had just added another fact to his store of information about the world.

El thought about one of Walter's pet theories. "My husband's already talking about a flood in the spring."

"Oh? How does he know?" Fellows's tone had immediately flipped from interest to skepticism, although something of interest remained.

"You'll have to ask Walter."

"Something to do with El Niño, maybe? I haven't heard anything about next year being an El Niño year."

"You'll have to ask Walter."

"Mm," he said. They resumed staring out of the window. El, who took Walter's long-range predictions with a grain of salt, didn't know why Chuck Fellows should be so interested.

Perhaps it was an engineering thing.

"Anyway," she said, "I didn't come here to talk about next spring. I came to talk about Sam Turner."

Fellows said nothing. El regarded him out of the corner of her eye. She had always dealt with Mark O'Banion in the past, and Mark was a sweetheart. That Mark had by all accounts been quite fond of Fellows just signaled another of those strange alliances in which the city abounded.

"Some concern has been expressed," El told him.

"So Turner's decided to raise a stink, has he?"

"No. I was approached by someone else."

Fellows didn't ask whom. And in spite of the harshness of his comment, she thought she detected some sadness or disappointment in him over the business. It was hard to tell, for he was the kind of man whose emotions were all, it seemed, refracted through his anger and impatience, as hers were through her depression.

"I read the letter you sent to Turner. It was—how shall I say?—a little brusque."

"I like to think it was to the point."

"Perhaps. I understand he has the necessary educational background for the job."

"He's got no experience."

"Did any of the other current city employees bid on the job?"

"No."

"So it was just Turner. You do know about our affirmative action policy?"

"Of course. Two people equally qualified apply for a job, the black guy gets it."

She listened to this astringent description and said, "I suppose you're trying to say this issue has nothing to do with affirmative action."

"I'm saying he can't do the work. I put him up there, not only doesn't he contribute, but I've got to pull somebody else off their own work just to nursemaid him. I don't gain a man, I lose one."

"I see." El had some sympathy for this argument, but no argument stands entirely free of the man uttering it. "Why didn't I know about this?" she asked. "Why did I have to find out about it in a roundabout way?"

"Turner dumped his portfolio on Mark's desk one day. Mark and I were thrashing the thing out. Then we were gonna tell whoever had to know."

"Is that right? So Paul wasn't in on it, either?"

"Correct."

"But he is now?"

"If he reads his mail."

"And what was Mark's thinking on the matter?" she asked.

"Mark's dead."

"That's not an answer to my question. What was he going to do, Chuck?" Fellows didn't say anything immediately, so she suggested, "Perhaps you didn't know."

"I knew."

"What then?"

"He was going to give him the job."

"So he believed Turner was qualified, even if you didn't?"

"I suppose."

"You suppose?"

"He thought he could be brought along. Look, Mark was on the Integration Task Force. He'd lost his objectivity."

"I'm on the Task Force, too."

Fellows looked at her sharply, and said, "You're both on it. End of story."

"No, it's not the end of the story," she retorted, turning for the first time to face him squarely. She could see, more clearly than ever, why Mark had been careful to shield this guy. He wouldn't last ten minutes on his own.

Fellows turned, and they stood toe-to-toe.

"Was Mark competent?" she asked.

"He was too nice a guy."

"A terrible failing, I know. But you didn't answer my question. *Was he competent?*"

"Yes."

"Presumably, then, he would not have been willing to hire someone who was clearly unqualified for the work."

"If Turner could do the work, I'd hire him in a heartbeat."

"Is that right?"

"Yes, that's right."

Her impulse at the moment was to end this uncomfortable interview as fast as she could. She had no PE she could attach to the end of her name. Cocksure people like Chuck Fellows brought out all her insecurities. Yet despite this, he'd gotten her goat, and she wouldn't leave until she was satisfied.

"But you said," she told him, "that he might be brought along."

"Mark said it. I'll tell you what, you want to look at Turner's work? I'll show you." He stepped across the room, yanked open one of the wide, flat drawers in which plans were stored, grabbed a sheaf of papers, and tossed them onto the drawing board.

El stared at him.

"Look, if you want," he told her, gesturing impatiently at the material, but his brief flare-up had disappeared, replaced by the simple bluntness that seemed his normal manner.

"What's the matter with you? Put them away." She had no intention of making judgments about somebody's drafting skills. "I came here asking you to explain this matter to me, and you behave like this?"

El studied Fellows and let her irritation simmer. He looked like a fighter that had started to run to fat. If he lost some weight, she imagined that he'd be quite a good-looking man, although it probably wouldn't do much for his personality.

At that moment she had another idea. Why be mature about this thing? Why not have Chuck Fellows and Johnny Pond—who were obviously both physical specimens—fight it out, the winner to choose? A good old-fashioned fistfight? Pond, the ex-footballer, was considerably bigger, but he also had a gentlemanly side, as if conscious of his prowess and a little hesitant to take advantage of it. That, she imagined, would give Fellows the only equalizer he needed, for she saw something in his eye, something in the slight sideways twist of the jaw, that suggested he was not the man to pay scrupulous attention to the Marquess of Queensberry Rules.

Well, this was all a nice fantasy, she told herself, and wasn't it a shame, but she'd have to find another way. "I understand you're leaving the city," she said.

"What about it?"

"Perhaps under the circumstances, the decision about Turner ought to have been made in consultation with the manager. At the very least, you should have told him what you were doing *before* you did it, so that the information could have been passed along to the council in a timely manner. I don't appreciate getting blindsided."

He pressed his lips together and nodded in a tacit acknowledgment that there, at least, she might have a point. For all the good it did. The cat was out of the bag. And now that it was, Fellows looked to be part of the problem, not the solution. But she was still mindful of the PE after his name. She wasn't about to tackle him on her own, as much as part of her might want to. She'd have a word with Paul. Since a suit was always a possibility in such a situation, the city attorney should be involved, too, so she and the manager probably ought to talk to Harvey Butts.

"Well, I've heard what you had to say," she told Fellows. "It might be the end of it, it might not. We'll just have to wait and see."

# CHAPTER 53

~

Walter Plowman glanced about himself, a little distracted. "I'm afraid it's not much to look at. Absentee owners, you know. Small market. Old equipment." He made a vague gesture toward all the stuff crowded into the tiny cubicle, then swung back around to the color monitor. "Hope you don't mind," he said to his guest, "I've got a cast to prepare."

"Go right ahead."

Walter checked the clock above his head and then cozied up to Hazel, his computer, and continued customizing the weather graphic for the six p.m. news. Plenty of time yet. Twenty-five minutes to the teaser.

"So El told you to come see me, did she?" he said as he worked.

He had never, as far as Walter could remember, actually met Chuck Fellows before, but he had certainly heard about him.

"She said you expected a flood come spring. Is that true?" Having done with the formalities, Fellows wasted no time getting down to brass tacks.

Walter cocked an eye briefly up at him, standing inside the door, a stocky man, alert and impatient, his slicker shiny with rainwater.

"I'm certainly not predicting water high enough to go over the wall, if that's what you're worried about," Walter told him. This, he assumed, was the only thing that would interest a city engineer in Jackson. The next question, therefore, surprised him.

"What about above normal?" Fellows's attention moved quickly around the room, like a man accustomed to gauging a place and his relationship to it.

"Could be," Walter said.

"How far above?"

Walter paused and cautioned himself to have a care here.

"Can't tell you. Could get a flood of record without water going over the wall."

"I don't care about that. I'm only concerned about high water. You're saying that's a real possibility?"

"Yes," Walter said slowly, dragging the word out. Here was an interesting turn, he thought. If Fellows wasn't worried about water going over the wall, what then?

"Well above normal?" Fellows asked.

"Maybe."

"How do you know? What's your evidence?"

Walter, in his growing excitement, had stopped working. "How do I know?" Fellows was not the kind of man, Walter suspected, who would give much credence to mud daubers. Or the width of the stripes on woolly bears, or the color of the dorsal fins of perch. "Of course, I *don't* know," he said, deciding that was the safest response for the moment.

He turned back to what he had been doing, typing the data from the remaining weather families into Hazel. From the McCrae Family in Peosta—0.79 inches of precip over the last twenty-four hours; temp at five o'clock, 41 degrees.

"But you think there's a good chance," Fellows persisted. "You must have some reason."

Walter typed in the last reported data—1.02 inches precip, 39 degrees Fahrenheit—from Fred Herrig out on the highway south of town. Walter always saved Fred and Mary until last, his private way of honoring them as his very first weather family, many, many years ago.

He paused and laid his hands in his lap and glanced back up at Fellows. "Well, yes, that's a different matter."

Pivoting around on his stool, he wheeled himself over to the PC that he used in his work on the database. He turned the machine on and, while he waited for it to warm up, searched through his files of DIFAX charts from early summer.

Then, as the PC printed out the sheets he wanted, he reached up and pinned several of the old weather maps from the National Weather Service onto his pegboard. Walter loved the maps, with their patterns of isobars, loops and ovals and swirls, like fingerprints.

"See these westerlies here," he explained, pointing at the first map, from late June, "see how they loop up, just like an oxbow in a river. We call this an extreme meridional flow." He moved to the next map. "It's even more extreme here, barely connected to the main west to east movement." At the next map, from the first of July, the large region of clockwise flow had separated entirely. "What we have here is a cutoff high, what you probably know as a blocking high. It formed in early July and didn't break up until last month. Our drought, okay?"

"Yeah, okay, and your point is?" Fellows had come right up to the map, poking his face aggressively at it, interested and suspicious.

"Extremity. For several years now we've been seeing increasing swings between extremes. This year it's got worse, a whole helluva lot worse."

"Global warming?"

"Might be part of it. Probably more complex."

These were the moments Walter cherished. On top of the DI-FAX charts he pinned the PC printouts. "Here we have rainfall in Iowa during the twentieth century."

As Fellows was looking at these, Walter scooted on his stool back over to Hazel and resumed working on his cast, dialing into the service to get the latest national and regional graphics.

"Look at 1937 and '38," he said over his shoulder. "Then look at '64 and '65. What do you see?"

"Dry years, then wet."

"Bingo!"

"This is your evidence?"

Walter smiled to himself at Fellows's doubt. "It *is* evidence. Maybe not conclusive. But I've compared the pattern from year to year with what you'd get randomly. The results are statistically significant."

Walter looked back at Fellows, down on his haunches now, intently studying the tables.

"If it isn't random," the city engineer asked, "what's the mechanism?"

"Ah, yes, good question. Don't know, not for sure. Got some ideas."

Walter hesitated. Each new subject led him into deeper waters. Did he dare to talk about possible causes? For some people, they were hardly more scientific than the mud daubers. And Fellows being a technocrat…But suppose he turned out to be genuinely interested in the climate? If so, it was like meeting a friend Walter didn't know he had. What the heck, he decided, he'd take a chance.

"You know anything about sunspots?" he asked, and without waiting for an answer he launched into a quick description of lunar and sunspot cycles. He talked about perturbations of the earth's annual path around the sun, and their possible effect on climate. He mentioned the possible exacerbation of such cycles by global warming.

Fellows had abandoned the charts and printouts and was reading a sheet scrolling out of the weather wire machine. Walter rolled over and ripped it out of the machine and glanced at the updated forecast. "This is from the weather service office in Des Moines." It didn't tell him anything he didn't already know. He pegged it on the board with the earlier bulletins, which would all be pitched at the end of the day, not worth saving.

"Okay," Fellows said, "for the sake of argument, let's assume this isn't all a crock. But even so, a flood's not a sure thing."

"True," Walter agreed.

"Give me a probability, then. A number."

Fellows's eyes were dark and alert. His attention moved crisply from object to object, locking on each as if with a little click. And as Walter returned to Hazel, to finish customizing the regional graphic, his uneasiness about trusting this man returned. Whatever he told him, he imagined, would have consequences.

"Perhaps, first, I'd best outline for you the sequence of events leading to a big spring rise." He did this, starting with rains in the autumn, which would saturate the ground. Then a spell of very cold weather, driving the frost deep. Come spring, even when it got warm there would be frost below the surface and no place for water to go but into the river. After the frost formed, there would be a series of winter storms, ice followed by snow, trapping and holding massive amounts water. Come spring a sudden break in the cold weather, the temperature above freezing day and night, meltwater sloughing into the river continuously rather than in pulses. And finally heavy rains, a series of storms migrating out of the Four Corners area of the desert Southwest and picking up loads of moisture from the Caribbean. "That," Walter told him, "is what would give us the big one. But, as you can see, a lot of things have to happen first. As for putting a number on it…"

"We're having the fall rain," Fellows said.

"We're having the rain. Another storm has just passed over Washington and Oregon, and I expect it to reorganize on this side of the Rockies and head our way. And another one is just now coming out of the Gulf of Alaska. If the cold settles in later—and the long-range forecast suggests it might—then the second condition will have been met. But even if that happens, it's still only a beginning."

Fellows nodded two, three times. "And you really have no way of knowing about the rest—severe winter, rainy spring—your *evidence* notwithstanding." Obviously, the current volatility of the weather and the historic pattern of wet years after dry hadn't much impressed him. Walter was sure glad he hadn't brought up the mud daubers.

"That's correct," he admitted.

"So this is all pretty damn hypothetical."

"Maybe."

Walter could have left it at that and let Fellows walk. Probably, given his rep, that was the smart thing to do: let the sleeping dog lie. But this stuff was important to Walter, and despite his uneasiness, he was loath to let it go at that. "Look, Chuck, might be I'm wrong. Might be. But when you've been in this business as long as I have, you begin to get a sixth sense. Do you believe in that sort of thing?"

Fellows looked at him intently, and Walter saw that this last arrow had struck home.

"I collect data, Chuck. I look for patterns. But where the climate is concerned, there are profound truths we simply don't know. I don't expect to ever know them. Maybe another man a hundred years from now will look at my data and see what it says clear as day. Or maybe it'll take a thousand years, who knows? But for all of that, I'm not just plain ignorant. I've spent a good deal of time developing the ol' sniffer." He tapped the side of his nose for emphasis.

"Okay, okay," Fellows conceded, once again nodding several times, intense. "So give me a number. Give me something to hang my hat on."

Walter sighed. He remembered an unfortunate incident earlier when he had made a forecast to the wrong person. Probably, he again warned himself, he should say nothing. Probably so. But to say nothing, why, that seemed like a cowardly act. Why had he studied the climate all these years, then? To remain mute when someone asked him a really important question? And wasn't it true that in his soul he felt that the chance for high water was great? He did.

Thus, after long hesitation, he said, "Fifty percent."

The figure had a consoling randomness about it, just the toss of a coin, a who-the-hell-knows-what's-going-to-happen figure. But where climate was involved, where flood events were measured in the tens and hundreds of years, the matter was not quite so simple as Walter for an instant wished it might be. And Chuck Fellows here would understand that they were talking about no mere coin toss.

"Fifty percent," he said, latching onto the figure. "You'll stand by that?"

Sensing he had perhaps gone too far, Walter now set about softening the thing some. "Maybe. But even if we get high water—I say, if—that's not to say what kind of stage we're gonna be looking at." Walter remembered the height of the dauber nest he had found in the abandoned cottage. Should the wasps' prediction be his, too? Did he want to start talking to this guy about twenty-seven-foot stages? No, no, better not.

"The wall and levee system is designed to protect the city against a two hundred-year event. I have no reason," he said, repeating what he had told Fellows at the beginning of the conversation, "to believe water is going to get anywhere near the top of the wall."

"I hope the hell not," Fellows said. "Anyway, I've got what I needed. Thanks."

"You're welcome. Do you mind if I ask why you're so interested in this information?"

"Nope. The dock board's dredge is supposed to provide sand for the dog track. The dredging season is almost over, and barely half the sand has been placed. If we get high water next spring and the river stays up, then no more sand will be pumped before the track's scheduled to open."

"Ah," Walter said. "And the track itself could be threatened if the water gets high enough."

"It could."

"Interesting." Up until that very moment, Walter had barely given the track a second thought.

"Anyway," Fellows said, "thanks." He looked at the clock above Hazel. "Hope I didn't screw up your weather forecast."

It was four minutes to six.

"Naw," Walter said, "I got plenty of time."

"You'll be hearing from me."

"Always happy to talk."

~

Later that night, after the ten o'clock cast, after the rest of the news team had gone home, Walter sat thinking about the exchange with Fellows. He regretted the 50 percent prediction. He regretted that Fellows had seemed to believe him. Sometimes it was better not to be believed. Once a banker had come to him asking about the long-range weather. Only later, quite by accident, had Walter learned that the information he'd given had been used to deny a bank loan to a local farmer, who had been driven into bankruptcy. Walter could never remember that without pain. It was even more painful than it might have been, for his forecast had turned out to be wrong.

He shook himself free of this sad recollection and made his last call of the day, always the same, not to a person but a machine, interrogating his data collection platform, the weather instruments he had installed outside the city. He logged in the information, making it part of the long-term data record that he had been accumulating for more than a quarter century. Doing this helped to soothe him, to set the compass of his life right again.

He checked and double-checked each step in the procedure, although he had done it thousands of times. Walter intended that this data would outlive him, that after he had been long forgotten, this trace of his essential self would still survive, still, with luck, be aiding the researchers of the future, the ones who would finally unravel the mystery of the climate.

This done, he closed up and walked down to the street. Outside, standing alone in the squally rain, which was mixed with a little sleet and even a few snowflakes, he listened to the cold wind high above and the sharp clicking, like ice breaking, of the time-temperature instrument hung off the corner of the Jackson National Bank. He shivered and felt for the first time a twinge of fear at the prospect of a big spring flood. And as he began the long climb up the bluff to his home, he wondered—knowing that the human mind is filled with fearful and untapped powers—whether thinking and talking about a thing might, indeed, make it so.

# CHAPTER 54

~

Early the next morning, Chuck parked his 4x4 in the turnout near the dredge and walked out along the planking laid along the discharge pipe, retracing his steps of two weeks earlier, even stopping for a moment to read the faded name Lydia. Nothing had changed. Finally, he stood at the bow and stared at the cutterhead, dulled by the rain.

He was troubled. He still hadn't responded to the request from Yellowknife officials that he fly up there for a job interview, trying instead to gauge the seriousness of Diane's threat to stay in Jackson with the kids. And to decide, if she wasn't bluffing, whether he was prepared to leave by himself. Applying for the job in Canada might have been a spur-of-the-moment thing, his gut reaction to the odious weekend with the buckskinners, but it, or something like it, had been coming on for a long time. The engineering work bored him, and now, with Mark's death and the prospect of being loaded down with his work, too, of having to deal with the El Plowmans of this world, a bad situation had grown worse, a lot worse. But Yellowknife was different. He was drawn to the harshness of such a place, where the natural world remained alive in men's consciousnesses, where life was never routine.

Despite what she was saying, Diane might come with him. The trouble was that some of himself had rubbed off on her over the years. She still looked like the sweet, reasonable thing he'd married, but she'd become in certain ways quite as arbitrary and one-way as he was. She'd learned from the master. So Chuck couldn't be sure she was running a bluff. In fact, he suspected she probably wasn't.

But he just hated the idea of staying.

And if he did stay, what then? He'd been busting Mark's hump for not doing the dredge work himself and to hell with the dock board. But finding a pro at this late date wasn't going to be easy. And this new threat, that there might be high water next spring, assuming Walter Plowman knew what the hell he was talking about, well, it introduced another variable in what was already a totally fucked up equation.

What he remembered most vividly from the conversation with Plowman was the man's enthusiasm. If you just listened to the meaning of the words, all the appropriate disclaimers had been provided. But it was clear Plowman believed in his long-range mumbo jumbo. Chuck's technical mind told him, yes, long-range forecasting was a crock. But suppose, just suppose, for whatever reason, Plowman happened to be right about next spring?

Chuck had liked the man. Unlike El Plowman, just another pol, her husband clearly had his own life, and he seemed like the kind of guy who would go about it with a minimum of bs. On top of that, Chuck did, as a matter of fact, believe in intuition, some people's at least. Could it be that a weatherman like Plowman, who had been in the business for a good long time, had antennae for these sorts of things? Maybe. Anyway, he'd liked the man. With Chuck that counted for a lot.

~

John Turcotte, the dredge master, lived in Little Wales on the north side of town. When no one came to the door, Chuck walked around to the back and could see a light on in the depths of the garage. Around the building, catfish traps had been piled, and on the side, fishing nets hung to dry. Behind, the bluffs pinched down toward the river and cut off the gray western sky. The cold rain continued to fall.

He could see a man working in the garage. Turcotte. Chuck knew almost nothing about him. In his spare time, he fished commercially, Chuck knew that much. Moonlighting was against city policy. But according to Mark, old Len Sawyer remained in thrall to the man, thinking him apparently some sort of living legend, one of the few surviving river rats of yore. So Sawyer didn't say boo when Turcotte did what he damn well pleased.

At the moment, he was puttering around a workbench that ran the length of the building. The bench, to Chuck's eyes, appeared about as messy as the dredge. On top of it were piled empty soybean meal sacks, sections of rebar, boxes filled with four-pronged hooks, dirty rags, empty spools, various other debris, and a bunch of long narrow strips of wood, one of which Turcotte had picked up and was inspecting. Chuck surveyed the mess calmly, with even a trace of satisfaction, as a scientist might enjoy a piece of data which confirmed a pet hypothesis.

He could imagine what was coming, but just for the hell of it, he decided to try a little tact. At his approach, Turcotte looked up. Where another man might have asked him what he wanted, Turcotte instead motioned for him to come closer, and held the wooden strip out toward him.

"Lookee here."

Chuck stared down at it but could see nothing unusual. "What?"

"Knots." In the middle of the strip lay a hard little plug with the grain flowing around it. "I told him, it's gotta be clear. This ain't worth a damn." In a single motion, Turcotte raised the board and brought it sharply down, right at the point of the knot, against the jaws of the workbench vise. Chuck heard a crack. "See," Turcotte said, and then slammed the board down twice more, until it split in half. He dropped it at their feet and picked up the next one from the small pile on the workbench. "Gotta be clear, I tells him. My own fault. Shoulda been here when he brung 'em."

"What are they for?"

"Fishin'."

"To make traps?"

Turcotte smiled, a sly little smile. "Not hardly. This here's for fishin' in the winter, through the ice, you bet. You take these"—he picked up another board and held it and the first end-to-end with an overlap—"and nail 'em together. Then another. Do it until she gets maybe fifty foot. Use her to pull your net under the ice." Chuck, who was always interested in technique, tried to visualize the process and decided it must work on the same principle electricians use to pull cable through electrical conduit. "But they gotta be strong," Turcotte said, "else she just snaps on ya. Good way to lose a one o' your nets."

"Yeah. I see."

"You fish?" Turcotte asked.

"Once in a while."

"Ice fish?"

"Nope."

"Oughta."

And immediately, Turcotte started talking about winter fishing. Close up he seemed softer and heavier than Chuck, for some reason, would have expected. Chuck smelled the cold, oily air of the garage and Turcotte's acrid body odor. He wore greasy, industrial-blue coveralls and a baseball-style cap. His forehead had blotches of red across it. As if living up to his reputation as a river man, he had a muskrat-like alertness. Chuck introduced himself.

"I know who you are," Turcotte said, taking in Chuck briefly, and then, with hardly a missed beat, continuing to talk about fishing. "Used to be you could bring up three, four hundred pounds of buffalo and carp at a single netting. Them's what you call rough fish. The colored in Chicago love them buffalo. The market for 'em goes up in the fall, stays there till spring." He talked as if under some sort of compulsion, like a man who spent too much time alone.

"Panfishing is still pretty good, but fishing for rough fish ain't so good no more. Nowhere near as good as it used to be, unless you got a smoker." He started talking about the contract truckers who covered the Mississippi from Prairie du Chien to Burlington.

Chuck had had enough of this one-way conversation, so he said, picking up one of the strips of wood himself and pretending to inspect it, "I take it you're planning to go fishing. I guess that means you've giving up dredging."

Turcotte found another knot in a board and smashed it against the vice until it splintered.

"My oldest boy, he still fishes. Outta Santa Barbara, you know, way out there in California. For them sea urchins. He does it for the Japs. Uses an aqualung, don't you know. They give him thirty-five dollars a hundred for 'em." He shook his head as if at the strangeness of the world.

"The dredge," Chuck said again. "What about the dredge?"

Turcotte seemed to think about this for a time, and then said, "Gettin' late. Think I'm gonna shut her down for the winter."

"You're two months behind schedule."

"Once ice starts coming, that's all she wrote. You keep on dredgin', your floatin' line will get all tore up."

"So you just stop."

"Yup. That's about the size of it."

"And start next spring."

"Yup."

"I hear some people are predicting high water for next spring."

"That right?"

"That's right."

Turcotte rubbed his chin with fingers surprisingly long and delicate. "Well, ya know, since the Corps put in them lock and dams, the river's been siltin' up terrible bad. Ain't nothin' for the water to do anymore 'cept spread out. Ain't got no other choice." He nodded slowly. "Yup, I believe you've got yourself a point there. Could have us some high water. If not next year, sometime, you bet."

"How would you complete your dredging contract before the track opening, then?"

Turcotte considered that dilemma. "Don't expect we would." He seemed not the least bit concerned.

"No?"

"Expect not."

"If it was my project, I'd make damn sure I finished. One way or another."

"You would, would ya?"

"Yes, I would."

Turcotte surveyed Chuck, then reached into his pocket, took out a set of keys, and tossed them over.

"What are these?"

"Dredge."

"What are you giving them to me for?"

"You're so anxious but what enough sand gets pumped, how about you do it yourself?"

Chuck snorted. "Like hell." He tossed the keys onto the workbench. They disappeared, clattering down into the junk Turcotte had accumulated.

Turcotte shrugged and said ambiguously, "Never asked for the work."

"Your boss asked for it."

Turcotte just smiled. "Hear its going to get mighty cold," he said. "That what you hear?"

Chuck didn't respond to this feint, but merely considered the situation and looked at Turcotte, who was just too damn composed. Probably he had been waiting for the day Mark got too insistent. Probably he figured that Mark would never take the keys.

Chuck visualized himself rooting through Turcotte's junk looking for them.

"You don't want me to take over the dredge operation," he told him.

Turcotte waggled his head from side to side. "The thing of it is, I don't much care. You think you can do a better job, have at her. Course, you're gonna have ice in the river mighty soon now." Clearly, Turcotte thought he had him by the short hairs.

And for a moment Chuck thought so, too, thought that, yes, the son of a bitch was right, he'd forced Chuck's hand, and there wasn't a damn thing Chuck could do about it. But this unaccustomed sense of weakness quickly passed, and for the first time that day, Chuck felt, all at once, a real clarity.

"If I take those keys," he said, "you're through with the city."

"It'd sure be a shame," Turcotte answered, still cocksure of himself and as casual as could be.

"Suit yourself."

It took Chuck some time to retrieve the keys. He weighed them in his hand, then closed his fist around them.

"Okay," he said. "So be it."

~

When Chuck got back to City Hall, there was a note on his desk from the city manager asking him to step into his office before he left for the day. Chuck went over at once.

Paul Cutler sat tapping on the edge of his desk with one finger.

"Close the door," he said.

What was it this time? Chuck wondered. Yesterday, they'd had a little talk about Sam Turner. With Mark gone, Chuck and the manager were getting to know each other better. Earlier there had been the matter of John McDermott and the methane problem at the dog track. McDermott, of course, had gone whining to the manager.

"Len Sawyer wants his keys back," Cutler now informed him.

Chuck laughed. "That didn't take long."

"I got off the phone with him fifteen minutes ago."

"You did, huh? And he wants his keys back, does he?"

"That's right."

Chuck smiled broadly. "No friggin' way." He loved this shit.

Cutler's finger stopped tapping. The next thing he said surprised Chuck. "Tell me, does this mean you actually plan to stay?"

Chuck took a deep breath and paused. Cutler was no fool. If Chuck was going to Yellowknife, why take possession of the dredge? Made no sense. Chuck knew that, even if he'd only half acknowledged it to himself. He had made his decision. He'd made it by acting. He'd made it while he was standing face to face with Turcotte, not even acknowledging to himself that that was what he was doing. Now it had been done.

To the city manager, he said simply, "Looks that way." Good. He'd been diddling around with the thing too damn long. But then again, he supposed the outcome had been a foregone conclusion for some time.

"What changed your mind? The dredge?"

The city manager had very pale eyes, which suggested some extremity, blindness or x-ray vision. He possessed the mind-set of a courtier, his overlords the local movers and shakers, and of course, Mark had known very well what he was doing when he kept Chuck out of the man's way.

"Not the chance to do more damn budgets, I'll tell you that." If he became the acting public works director, he'd have budgets up the ying-yang—dog track, engineering, public works.

"They're essential, of course," the manager pointed out mildly. His finger had begun tapping again.

"Budgets are the goddamn price you pay to get to do something interesting."

"I must say that *interesting* is not the first word that pops into my head when I think of the dredge."

"At least it's not more of the same," Chuck told him.

Cutler nodded deliberately. "Len said you demanded the keys from Turcotte."

"He's a liar."

"Perhaps. More likely, he was just repeating what he'd been told...Tell me, exactly what do you know about running a dredge?"

"Nothing."

"I see. That certainly fills me with confidence."

"I'll find out what I need to know. Basically, I think the city's dredge is past its useful life. We need to get a commercial outfit in here, or maybe even the Corps's big dredge. Should be no problem. Get the job done right."

"Money?"

"I'll look at the dog track budget, see if there isn't some fat there." As Chuck said these things, laying out one crisp sentence after another, his commitment to stay solidified.

Okay, he thought, good. Diane would have her little victory. He'd stick around for a while. But he wasn't going to take anybody's shit. "I plan to fire Turcotte. I told him if he gave me the keys, he was through."

"But you've just said," Cutter cautioned him, "that you don't know a thing about dredges. Suppose you can't find somebody to do the work. Suppose you can't get the thing up and running. What then?"

"I'll deal with that when I get to it. But no way I'll use Turcotte again. No damn way."

Cutter closed his eyes, as if saying a silent prayer.

When he looked again, Chuck smiled at him. The manager shook his head. He was not pleased.

Nevertheless, he said, "Well, we've got the keys. Let's keep them."

# Chapter 55

~

Rachel had never seen Fritz so carefully turned out—sports jacket, slacks, his patchy white-and-black hair slicked down, leaving just the trace of a cowlick in back. Too restless to wait in the terminal, he went out on the tarmac despite the frigid weather.

Rachel huddled in the wind, holding the back of her skirt to keep it from flying up. After nearly two weeks of rain, the city lay in a seam of clear weather between storms. The temperature had dropped into the low thirties and across the watery blue sky, cumulous clouds drifted like icebergs.

Finally, the small chartered plane appeared, coming from the west and yawing in the wind as it looped around and dipped toward the runway. As soon as it had taxied to a stop, the *Trib* photographer began to move here and there, seeking interesting angles from which to shoot.

The hatch swung upward but at first remained empty. Fritz in his anxiety started up the accommodation steps, then hesitated. The photographer had stopped and raised his camera. For several moments, the scene remained perfectly still, the only sounds the unwinding lament of the plane's engine and the bluster of wind.

A young man appeared, ducking his head beneath the hatchway. Very tall. Young. His eyes fell on Fritz, and he smiled. This, Rachel realized, must be Richie Chinn.

He came quickly down the stairs and seized Fritz's hand. Behind him materialized two older men, one white, one Chinese.

"You're late," Fritz said.

"Couldn't avoid it."

Chinn had only scheduled a few hours in the city.

"You're going to stay longer then?" Fritz asked, more a demand than a request.

"I don't have time." Chinn's look, so open as he descended to greet Fritz, closed when he realized he might have a problem. The two men seemed to have forgotten that they were still shaking hands.

"You've got to stay longer," Fritz insisted. "We've got things to do."

"Alas, cannot," Chinn said. For a moment, Rachel thought there was going to be real trouble. The mayor wasn't the kind of man to accept disappointments with grace.

Chinn eyed him and then, his expression betraying nothing, said, "Maybe a little while longer. Don't worry, I'll put on a good show for you."

"All right," Fritz said.

"All right," Chinn repeated, grabbing Fritz's forearm with his free hand and grinning down at him, a sudden grin. "Very all right. I am most glad to meet you, my friend. I've looked forward to this."

Fritz made the introductions.

"Good, good," Chinn said as he looked frankly at Rachel. "We'll go now. Not waste time."

Chinn's smoky gray suit matched the color of the suits of his assistants. The little party hurried toward the city van, the wind lifting the flap of Chinn's jacket and exposing its Chinese red lining. Eyeing his clothes, his retinue, his confident demeanor, Rachel found it difficult to believe that here was a man barely older than her.

As they bustled along, Chinn asked, "My man, he get here all right?"

"Came in yesterday," Fritz assured him.

"Everything all set?"

"As far as I know. I set him up at the Wayfarer Inn. They cater a lot of big affairs."

"Okay, okay." Chinn turned to his Chinese companion and spoke to him rapidly in Chinese.

"We'll drop off at Wayfarer Inn," he told Fritz.

In the van, Rachel interviewed Chinn as Fritz drove. The mayor said little, but cast many glances toward his visitor.

At the Wayfarer, they left his Chinese assistant, then went on to JackPack, where a tour had been arranged. Chinn's Caucasian associate produced a press kit. Rachel flipped through it—history of Richie Chinn Restaurants; several color photos of fast-food restaurants, before and after; highlights of a business plan; laudatory press clips. "Got fifty-four restaurants," Chinn said as he watched her. "Just a start."

They toured the Pack, Skip Peterson and Richie Chinn in the lead, Chinn attentive, firing off one question after another, moving double time, a pace that seemed to suit each of them. Rachel hustled to keep up. Fritz lagged behind. Here and there he stopped to exchange a few words with people on the floor whom Rachel assumed were his loyalists.

"The supply and demand sides of the industry have virtually no relationship," Skip told Chinn. "JackPack is paying 48.50 and cutting out 46.75. So we kill 7,500 animals today and lose 22,000 dollars."

"Need more value added," Chinn said.

"Precisely."

"Precisely."

The photographer bounded nimbly around the little group, stopping dead still every once in a while to squeeze off another picture.

Chinn wasn't a particularly handsome man. Even for a non-Asian, he would have been considered tall, and as was common with abnormally tall people, his appearance suggested the equine. But his features were unlined, and so the joy, sorrow, concern, determination that filled his expression in rapid succession left no trace of their passage.

She noticed that he had had hardly any accent when he got off the plane, but as his visit continued, his accent became more marked. Yet, when he spoke, he no longer seemed a young businessman on the make, but someone substantial, fully formed, and Rachel recognized, along with her suspicion, her envy as well. She had come from a family of activists. True, they wouldn't think much of Richie Chinn. But one thing they did share with him: this intense drive to mold the world according to some inner vision. People like herself—mere observers—lacked that essential human spark, that drive to change the found object, to make it over in her own image. She both rebelled against such a notion, and, at the same time, felt the lack of it as a weakness in herself. She respected and disliked and envied Chinn all at once.

The breakneck tour continued. Skip talked about the improvements they'd made in their fresh-cut operations.

"Overcapacity," Chinn said. "Too much fresh-cut meat."

"That's right," Skip conceded. "That's the killer."

"Richie Chinn Frozen Stir-Fry Gourmet. Quicker than quick."

Fritz continued to lag behind. Chinn seemed to have forgotten about him.

By the time they arrived back at the Wayfarer Inn—a low, modern structure out on the highway, with a marquee out front for motel promos, today reading, "A Wayfarer Welcome to Richie Chinn"—it was after twelve noon. Few of the invited guests had arrived. Those who had cast curious glances toward Chinn but showed little inclination to add to the Wayfarer's welcome.

"Need to get show on road," Chinn said to Fritz.

"Nobody's here yet."

"No time, no time."

"You said you would."

"Okay, okay, few minutes only."

Chinn conferred with his lieutenants, then disappeared through a swinging door at the far side of the banquet room, only to reappear a minute later.

"Is everything all right?" Fritz asked.

"Could be better, but make do."

Finally, Chinn said, "Now, got to start now," and after another brief verbal scuffle with Fritz, those who had arrived were ushered through the swinging door and into the banquet room kitchen, where stood the associate of Chinn who had arrived the previous day, now wearing the whites of a chef. As soon as Chinn appeared, this man moved respectfully to one side, and Chinn doffed his suit coat and put on a white smock and mushroom-shaped chef's cap. A row of woks stood atop a large gas range, and an assortment of ingredients stood, neatly ordered, along the cutting board before the woks.

"Everybody gather round so can see," Chinn instructed the guests.

"Can you make cheese soup?" someone asked Chinn.

"Make cheese soup," Chinn said, not missing a beat. "Stuffing sandwich, too." Rachel listened to the appreciative laughter and wondered where he'd learned about the notorious local tastes. "Not today. Today do little Chinese stir-fry. You like."

He picked up a cleaver, inspecting the lethal-looking implement, then quickly reduced a slab of meat to thin slivers. As he worked, he talked.

"When Chinese say 'meat,' mean 'pork.' I am pig. Born in Year of Pig. Parents name Chu. Chu Chinn. Mean pig in Chinese. For good luck and so evil spirits would think I just lowly animal, not worth bothering. Now I in America, no longer Chu. Now I Rich." He smiled at his joke. "You Americans, you cook meat too long. Too afraid of trichinosis. Also use too much seasoning. One hundred percent soy sauce. Shame."

He scooped a handful of mushrooms out of a bowl where they had been soaking and squeezed the juice out of them. "Dried Chinese mushrooms concentrate taste, strong, smoky. Can use fresh depending on season, maybe morels in spring."

Score another point for Chinn, Rachel thought. Under his sharp knife, the mushrooms were slivered in an instant as he gave hints on where to find morels in the nearby woods.

"No need truffle-smelling pigs," he joked. He moved quickly down the row of ingredients, chopping as he went—ginger, scallions, much that Rachel couldn't identify.

"Root of ginseng. Found around Jackson, too. Big demand in China. You can make a lot of money exporting ginseng. Only problem, it's illegal. Chinese believe, eat ginseng, live long time." He poured oil into the woks, and turned on the flames under them.

"Secret ingredients," he said as he chopped several more small piles of variously colored substances. "Eye of newt, toe of frog."

These and the rest went quickly into the wok. With a long-handled wooden fork, Chinn stirred the mixtures, hopping back and forth between them, his long lean body arching over the wok, his eyes half-closed as if his nose was the only sense organ he used to test the results. Almost immediately, he started to spill the steaming food out onto serving dishes.

"Here, Mayor Fritz, you try." Chinn motioned for him to come forward and sample the dish. Rachel watched as Fritz took a forkful and chewed thoughtfully, with the same intensity a connoisseur tastes wine, except that Fritz couldn't quite pull it off. He took a second bite and chewed thoughtfully again. Finally, he rendered his opinion. "Delicious." Not a Fritz kind of word, Rachel thought, delivered rather too self-consciously, adding to the comical effect of the whole performance.

Chinn smiled broadly. "Not like usual Chinese foods. Not all soy sauce and MSG, you bet."

"Tell you what," Fritz said. "You better let somebody else take a bite. Some people here been known not to take my word on a thing."

Chinn laughed. "Tough being politician in America. Here, you try." He waved his long-handled wooden fork at El Plowman.

"I usually insist on chopsticks," she said as she came forward.

"Ha!" Chinn put down the fork and patted his breast pockets, his pants pockets, performed a brief tap-dance-like step and suddenly produced from some hidden compartment in his clothing a pair of chopsticks, sheathed in a protective paper wrapping.

Plowman acknowledged the little magic trick, then unwrapped the utensils, lowered her face to the plate, and adroitly scooped up a mouthful of the still-steaming vegetables and meat.

"Very good, very good," Chinn said as he watched her. "You eat like real Chinese." Unlike Fritz, she immediately rendered her verdict.

"Wonderful!" she said. "Absolutely wonderful! I've never tasted food quite like this." She reached for the napkin he offered. "You don't happen to provide recipes, do you?"

Chinn laughed delightedly. "No recipe, no recipe. Richie Chinn secret ingredients."

"Well," she said, "like our mayor, not everyone here always believes me, either. Surely, you've got enough so we can all have a taste."

"Got plenty." He motioned for his assistant to come forward. "Why not we go into other room, sit down? Yang Chao, he cook now. We all eat. Then I talk to everyone about Richie Chinn Restaurants."

And so, out in the banquet room, Rachel got her chance to sample Chinn's fare. Each bite left some slightly varied combination of tastes, sweet and sour, salt and bitter, which lingered in different parts of her mouth. She paused and noted a faint earthiness as well. An herbal scent, too, a suggestion of the medicinal. As impressive as Chinn himself was, she decided, he couldn't match his food. In that food, with its wonderful bouquet of tastes, some magical essence seemed to reside, which might really promise the salvation of the Jackson Packing Company and the elevation of Fritz Goetzinger to a man of genuine stature in the city, the Man Who Saved the Pack.

After the meal, as Chinn prepared to speak, Rachel slipped her tape recorder onto the head table, turned it on, and then moved to the back of the room where she could observe the listeners as well as the speaker.

"This is true story," Chinn began. "Happen in China many, many years ago. China called the Middle Kingdom. You know that? Middle Kingdom. Just like Jackson. This true story. You look it up. Once lived in China man named Yu. Patron of agriculture. Live in valley of great Yellow River. River of plenty, like Mississippi. One problem. River untamed. Only one year in seven good for growing. Many years great floods sweep land. Yu have vision. Yu have determination. He struggle mightily against river, year after year, year after year, against monsters and evil spirits, against natural forces. He divert water. He build canals. He raise walls against water. Is said that for thirteen years he not see his own home, his determination so great. Is said that three times even he passed by his door and hear children crying but not enter. True story."

As Rachel listened and surveyed the assembled grandees, she became conscious of another presence, a person, like herself, observing the scene from a distance. The man stood in the main doorway to the banquet room. She had seen him somewhere before but couldn't quite place him. When he noticed her gaze, he nodded slightly but made no move to approach. Instead, he coolly continued to study Chinn. Rachel stared at him, trying to remember just where it was they had met. Quite recently, she thought. How odd.

"That's where success come from," Chinn was saying, "vision plus determination. You got that, you okay." The lights suddenly dimmed, and on the screen behind him, a picture appeared: an abandoned, decaying fast-food restaurant on a commercial strip. "Look carefully," he admonished the Jacksonian leaders, "first Richie Chinn Restaurant, on day I buy. Later, on National Register of Historic Places. Guaranteed." And so he launched into a discussion of the Richie Chinn Restaurant chain and his plans to market nationally Richie Chinn brand-name foods and his need for a major source of fresh-cut meat. Maybe they could arrange something, he said, a strategic alliance, Richie Chinn and the Jackson Packing Company. "Maybe, who knows? Sounds like good idea to me. Sound like good idea to you?"

At the conclusion of the talk, Fritz came over to Rachel. "Time to go to the airport," he told her.

"I think I've already got enough material."

"No, no, come. Ask Richie some more questions."

Rachel had no desire to return to the airport. She had more than enough. Nevertheless, it was clear that Fritz very much wanted her to go, so she sent the photographer back to the *Trib* to develop his film and reluctantly went off once more with the Chinn party.

Later, on the way back from the airport, when just the two of them were in the van, Fritz wanted to know what she thought. Despite Chinn's virtuoso performance, he needed reassurance. She found this vulnerability rather attractive in the mayor, a pleasing change from his normal dogged and distrusting nature. For the moment, she almost liked the man.

"I thought," she said carefully, "Chinn was very impressive."

Picking up the doubt in her voice, he asked what she hadn't liked.

"Oh, I don't know…Did you notice how his accent changed?"

To this Fritz said nothing. Chinn's pidgin English had all but disappeared again when he said good-bye to the mayor just before rushing up the accommodation steps, "See, I put on a good show for you, just like I said I would." Perhaps he meant it—this partial unmasking—as a mark of respect for Fritz, but she couldn't imagine Fritz would see it that way.

"By the way," she added after the two of them had driven in silence for a time, "I saw your son there, at the presentation."

"What?" Fritz looked at her, unbelieving.

"It's true. Standing in back, near the door. At first I didn't know who it was, but then I remembered him from the farm, the day the rain began."

"What did he want?"

"We didn't speak."

Fritz frowned. When he didn't seem inclined to continue the conversation, she said, "I guess you two don't get along all that well."

A severe glance in her direction told Rachel that he didn't much care for the comment. They drove silently again, until Fritz said, "Junior's as smart as Richie Chinn."

"That right?"

"Yup."

And that was the last statement he cared to make on the subject of his son.

# CHAPTER 56

~

R ichie Chinn isn't going to save the company," Mel Coyle said.
     The pavement sizzled beneath them as Skip accelerated
into traffic. Since the bum report, Mel had changed, and he was
getting on Skip's nerves.

"No," Skip agreed, "but he might be a piece of the puzzle."

"Perhaps. Anyway, you can bet he's no great friend of employee ownership. He's just looking for cut-rate meat."

"He may get it, too. Right about now, I'd be happy to sell
at cost."

"I imagine he's got a somewhat better deal in mind."

"Maybe." Skip didn't want to sell below cost, but it might come
to that. "We'll have to wait and see." He had a vision of thousands
of Richie Chinn restaurants, all over the country, all serving stir-fry
pork made with JackPack meat. He'd be willing to sign almost any
kind of deal now, whatever it took to drive in the thin end of the
wedge. Later, they could renegotiate. To Mel he said, "Hey, we'll
get him to open his first restaurant out here right in Jackson. El
Plowman will never have to worry about MSG again."

Skip's world was coming down around his ears, but at the
moment he felt okay, still jazzed by the demo. Boy, if he only
had a slew of Richie Chinns working for him and not all these
funeral directors…

"But you do admit that Chinn *was* impressive, that much
at least," he said to the dour figure next to him. It was rather an
understatement to say that Mel hadn't entered into the spirit of
the enterprise. He had, Skip understood, given up. He would go
through the motions, nothing more. At the moment, he sat perfectly motionless except for a slight pursing of the lips, as if conscious of being watched.

Suddenly, his arms shot forward. "Watch out!"

Skip looked just in time to see the rear bumper of a pickup truck, closing fast. He jumped on the brake and the Corvette slithered to a stop, its nose tucked under the ball hitch on the back of the truck.

"Damn it, Skip, watch where you're going."

Ahead of them the light at the intersection of Kennedy turned, and the line of vehicles began to move again. Skip discovered he was unperturbed by the near miss. Ha! he thought, he might not be as young as he once was, but his reflexes were still good. He drove on.

From The Wayfarer, Waterloo Road took them back downtown. It was barely midafternoon, but already dusk had begun to gather and cars to turn on their lights.

"I suppose you'd have us just forget about Chinn," Skip prodded.

"No. We've gone this far."

At the bluff top, where the road crossed Grandview Boulevard, the nose of the sports car dipped down, and they began their descent through the limestone outcroppings toward the floodplain below. Skip touched the brake.

Partway down, an accident had occurred, and the lights of emergency vehicles pulsed off cars and buildings and trees.

Panning the scene as they edged by, Skip noted that Mel continued to stare straight ahead, ostentatiously ignoring the damaged cars and the empty stretcher.

Skip turned back to the road and, as they continued their descent, brooded about the corporate counsel. Mel had become even more of a pill since Skip convinced the board to reject the offer from Nick Takus. Mel hadn't gotten exercised over the pittance Takus put on the table. Oh, no, not Mel. He never got exercised over anything. He'd merely argued in the irritatingly oblique lawyerly way he had. The paragon of objectivity, as always. Very annoying. He also had the equally annoying habit of being right. He might be right this time, too. Skip shook his head and thanked his lucky stars that most of the key board members still lived in the city and weren't so coldly rational as Mel Coyle. He wondered if they had really believed his own assurances that Takus was sure to sweeten the pot later. No telling. They'd accepted it, that was what counted. If Takus did up his offer, that was all she wrote. But would he? The son of a bitch had the soul of a freebooter. No doubt nothing but theft and warfare got his juices flowing. If he couldn't steal JackPack, he'd try to destroy it. Skip, as a matter of fact, counted on that.

His mood darkened even more as he remembered not the substance of the board meeting but the tone Mel had managed to create, the little-boy-being-put-on-notice style of it. Still, like it or not, he could feel the force field of the man sitting next to him. And there was always the possibility—hell, the probability—that Mel was right. When had Skip ever acted in the teeth of opposition from Mel and eventually been vindicated? Never, that's when.

Near the bottom of the hill, he realized that his shot of adrenaline from Richie Chinn's demo had vanished completely. He seemed to have stopped breathing. Black spots began to appear before his eyes, and he felt a prickling sensation beneath the skin along his jawline and at the nape of his neck.

As he drove, the numbing sensation spread to his forearms, wrists, the backs of his hands. He took several deep breaths and blinked, and gradually the spots dissolved and the tingling faded away, leaving him feeling drained.

Downtown, he parked in the small lot of the Jackson Bank and Trust, where he and Mel were to meet for the second time with a consortium of local bankers. He had no hope that a bridge loan might be arranged, but the meetings had to take place. Even remote possibilities must be explored. Relationships maintained. Skip looked at his hands. They didn't appear to be shaking, although he felt as if they were.

He and Mel got out. Mel paused and spoke to him across the roof of the car.

"Yes," he said, "Chinn was impressive."

This admission, as slight and grudging as it might be, encouraged Skip for a moment. "Perhaps, Mel, he really *is* part of the answer."

Mel considered this, something lawyerly in even his silent deliberations. Skip was conscious of his former mentor's tidy good looks, slim, no beard or mustache, hair cropped close and with surprisingly little gray in it, a man who would fit in anywhere.

"I doubt it," he finally delivered his verdict. "But he will accomplish one thing at least." Mel fixed Skip with his judging eyes. "He'll give the employees another excuse not to risk their own money."

To this Skip had nothing to add, and so they went inside.

# CHAPTER 57

~

The last place in the world that Joe Wheeler, director of the packinghouse division of the international union, wanted to be at that moment was in Jackson, Iowa. Joe had grown up in Jackson. He'd gone to work in the packinghouse there and joined the union there. He'd known many of the union people all his life and counted them among his friends. And it had been a sad day when he'd left the local and gone to D.C. But it had been a grand day, too, one of Jackson's own moving up in the ranks of the union hierarchy. He'd been Jackson's man in Washington then, although perhaps they had all known in their hearts that one day, he might become Washington's man in Jackson.

In the spartan motel room, a depressing little room, he unpacked his overnight bag with undue care. It didn't take long. This was to be a short stay.

Most of all, he didn't look forward to seeing Homer Budge, whose wife Rose Joe had once dated, whose eldest son John Michael was Joe's godchild, and whose family was as close to having kids of his own as Joe was ever likely to get. He felt guilty that he hadn't contacted them. But what could he say when they asked why he had come?

Having finished putting his clothes away, he called his wife to tell her he'd gotten in safely. Then he sat on the edge of the bed, wondering what he should do next.

He turned on the TV and watched the local news, hoping for a story about the Pack. The reporters, even the anchor, were all young kids, nobody he recognized from the old days. Everything had changed. Each time he came back, he recognized fewer people and fewer recognized him. It was easy to wish he'd never left, that he still worked for the Pack and knew that soon he, too, would be out of work and suffering along with everybody else. How much easier that seemed at the moment.

Anyway, he'd come. He'd say what he had to say, and that would be that.

The weather came on, and he saw a familiar face: Walter Plowman, who'd been doing the forecasts on KJTV as long as Joe could remember. He smiled and leaned back, pressing his hands against the rough fabric of the bedspread, and gave himself up to the pleasure of this brief return to the way it used to be.

Someone knocked.

"Who the…" Reluctantly, he got up and turned down the TV and answered the door. Outside stood the familiar stocky figure of Homer Budge.

"Homer!"

"You didn't think you could sneak into town, did you? Rosie's sent me to bring you to dinner."

"I wasn't sneaking into town, Hom. It was a last-minute trip—"

"You come to town, you don't tell Rosie and me you're coming, I call that sneaking."

"I'm sorry. I didn't want to bother you. I just wanted a word with the executive committee."

"He didn't want to bother us, the man says. Who ever heard of such a thing?"

Having tried to avoid Homer, Joe now discovered that he was grateful that he had been found out and that Homer had come to collect him. His friend, scowling in the mock-gruff way he had, brought life to that dreary room. But Joe was still mindful of the unhappy reason for his visit to Jackson.

"Frankly, Homer, this isn't a trip I would have chosen."

Homer raised his hand to forestall such talk. Serious matters later. "Come on," he said, "put on your coat. We're going."

When they arrived at 18 Shake Rag Lane, it became apparent almost immediately that all the assorted Budges had been warned. Whatever the reason Joe had so unexpectedly turned up, it was not a subject likely to make anybody happy. No one asked the question, not even John Michael, Joe's godson, who had never before shown a reluctance to launch his little craft into stormy waters.

Dinner was already under way when Joe and Homer arrived, and after the muted greetings, they sat down at once. Even Rose, whom usually nothing fazed, seemed a little put out by the circumstances. Joe seated himself where he always did, at the place setting left empty each and every night, despite the crowded conditions, ready for the unexpected guest.

Rose had prepared ham loaf fried in brown sugar, macaroni and cheese, and peas. Joe still relished the foods of childhood, a secret pleasure he could count on indulging at the Budge table. Today, however, though he could taste the ham and brown sugar, the sweetness died on his tongue.

No one had much to say, not even Homer, so the conversation was left to Joe and Rose. They talked about family. Joe managed to pry a few sentences out of the kids. But after his pleasure at Homer having come to fetch him, now it seemed like a mistake.

Through the meal, Joe kept an eye on his friend. His impression at the motel that Homer was the same old Homer was not confirmed. In fact, he didn't look good at all. He ate nothing but a bowl of soup. In the past, Joe had always been impressed with Homer's golden glow; Joe could think of no better way to put it. Though not a conventionally handsome man, the color of the long bald ridge of his skull reminded Joe of sunlight at dusk, and around the edges of this, his sandy hair clustered in a thick, pleasing manner. Homer's features were generous, seeming almost to spill over the edges of his face, his large eyes and mouth always alive with light and movement, his mouth particularly, stretching practically from ear to ear, with little twitchings at the corners, as if he was trying, but not very hard, to suppress a smile. Now, however, he had become pale, his eyes still alert but a little dulled, his mouth quiet. He ate his soup and listened to the strained exchange between Joe and Rose.

Over coffee, things picked up a bit. Seven-year-old Joey, obviously aware that things weren't exactly all right, but a little hazy on just why and determined to share his latest enthusiasm with "Uncle" Joe, brought out his scrapbook, in which he'd been pasting stories from the *Jackson Tribune* and *Des Moines Register* about the buyout attempt. As Joey turned the pages, Joe read bits and pieces of the stories, trying to fill in some of the missing details of recent events, which had so spooked International's leadership.

Discovering that the buyout might be discussed without referring to the reason for Joe's visit, talk became a little more animated among those who had lingered around the dinner table, and some of the old Budge exuberance returned. Joe noticed, however, that as soon as John Michael could, he had excused himself and disappeared.

The worst moment came in the kitchen, when Joe and Rose found themselves alone for a minute.

Rose often seemed a little distracted, a little not-there, but Joe had always figured it was just the way she distributed her attention across the field of her children. Of all the Budges, she had the sharpest tongue. She'd bring you up short with it. Joe had seen more than one kid snap to when Rose had had enough guff.

And so he was hardly surprised that, when they were alone and after she'd asked a couple of questions about Joe's wife's cancer, the kinds of questions she didn't want to ask in front of the boys, and satisfied herself on that score, she'd turned to the reason for Joe's trip to the city.

"Have you come here to help, Joe?"

"I hope so, Rosie."

She judged the evasiveness of this response. "Remember, you're from here."

"I know that. Don't you think I know that?"

"You're one of us. And don't you forget it."

"Not a day goes by I don't think about you, Rosie, and about Homer, and about all my old friends back here."

As a kid entered the kitchen, she held a warning finger up to Joe and lowered her voice. "You're one of us. Enough said."

Later, Homer took Joe back to the motel. They rode in silence. Homer, unlike Rosie, still had made no reference to the purpose of Joe's visit. The local had already called International and been told there wasn't a lot the parent union could do to help, not under these circumstances, so Homer already knew that much. But about the rest, he no doubt guessed.

Something had to be said. They had known each other too long to slink around like this. Joe suggested that they stop in the bar of the restaurant next to the motel, and they did that, each ordering a draft and taking the beer back to a booth where they could have some privacy.

They settled themselves. Homer remained quiet, and Joe hardly knew where to begin. "Are you okay, Homer?"

"I'm okay."

"Because, I've got to tell you, you don't look so hot."

Homer frowned and gave a slight dismissive toss of his head. Then he leaned forward and settled his elbows on the table, forearms crossed.

"So, Joey, is International planning to put us into receivership? Is that why you've come?"

"Good grief, no, of course not. Why would you think such a thing?" In fact, the idea of taking over the local had been batted around in Washington, but not really seriously. There wasn't enough time, even if they had been serious about it. The Jackson Packing Company was going down. Everybody knew it, even if some of the people in Jackson weren't ready to accept the fact yet.

"Can't think why else you'd come," Homer said. "Except, I guess, to jawbone us."

"Well, I won't pretend—"

"No doubt you think we're going to give the ranch away."

"To be honest, some people back East suspect this is just wage cuts by another name."

"Well, it isn't," Homer said curtly, the first sign of real fire that Joe had seen in his friend all night. Now they were joined.

"Maybe not," Joe said, "but that's what they think. They're afraid you're going to agree to work for practically nothing. They're afraid...well, you know."

"That we'll spoil it for everybody else?"

After having said nothing, now Homer all at once appeared intent upon speaking as bluntly as he could. Joe tried to soften the thing. "We're having enough trouble negotiating contracts as it is."

"What about you? What do you think?" Homer lowered his voice further, but still spoke with an intensity that would not allow evasion on Joe's part, although Joe would try evasion anyway. He was finding the conversation even more painful than he'd imagined.

"I know you're a good union man, Hom."

"The people in D.C. have never had much respect for me." Homer was such an easygoing gent most of the time that Joe had almost forgotten how blunt he could be when he got his blood up.

"I know that nobody could have negotiated better contracts than you have. You've done as well as anybody could have...under the circumstances. But we can't give these damn companies more excuses to demand cuts. That's why I came."

"In the expectation, I suppose, that once you've told me the damage I'm doing to the movement with these givebacks, I'll come to my senses."

Joe rubbed his face and blew out a big wad of air. "No, I didn't mean that." Not exactly. Joe was tempted to tell Homer that the International wanted the wage concessions kept under five percent, but he supposed he'd better save that for the executive committee.

"Is it all really worth it, Homer, just so people can take home paychecks for a few more months?"

"How do you know it's just for a few months?"

Every statement now seemed to drive Joe into another box canyon. He sagged back against the hardwood bench. Homer was not speaking angrily, just with the intensity of a man intent on cutting off all routes of escape.

"You really think you can save the company?" Joe asked.

"I don't know. But apparently you're convinced we can't."

Joe looked down at his hands and tested several responses before he settled on "Me, Homer, I don't know. But, yes, nobody else in D.C. believes you have a chance, not going up against the likes of Nick Takus and Modern Meat."

"You don't think so, either. Or are you just an errand boy here?"

Joe winced. "Homer!"

"I'm sorry, Joe. But I'm getting no help from you people. Now you're gonna be less than no help. How do you expect me to feel?"

"Isn't there any room here for an honest difference of opinion? This isn't like you."

Homer relented a little. "Yeah, sure, okay. I don't mean to hurt your feelings, Joey. And you're right, it isn't like me. But if we're going to make this buyout work—this thing you don't believe in— then I can't afford to be *like myself* anymore."

Joe shook his head. "How do you do that, not be like yourself?"

Homer laughed. "It ain't easy. But as you can tell, I'm practicing." He leaned back and became a little more comfortable. He hadn't touched his beer.

"And what about the other members of the executive committee?" Joe asked, mystified. "Can they start acting not like themselves, too?"

Homer considered this, and said only, "I expect that, come tomorrow, you'll find some of them are trying. But you won't be alone. Some of the old-timers will agree with you, right down the line."

So the local itself was split. "I see. And still you're going to try to do this thing, buy the company, give half your wages away for stock that might be worthless." That was worthless.

"It's not half our wages. Probably we'll be getting more or less what the Modern Meat people are getting by the time we're through. A lousy deal, but I don't see how we've got much of a choice. Certainly, you're not offering us anything. You're concerned about the movement. Fair enough. You've written us off. Okay, I guess I can understand that, too. But being as how that's the case, then we're gonna do for ourselves."

To these comments Joe could think of no response that might change Homer's mind. So, that was it, then. International and the local were to be at loggerheads on this matter. Joe had figured as much, but he had to try. International would stand back and hope that whatever concessions the JackPack rank and file made, they didn't infect the rest of the union movement.

Joe also understood that Homer's silence earlier, at his home and during the car rides, hadn't been the silence of a man who didn't know what was coming. He'd known only too well. He had been preparing for it. A gap had opened between them that would perhaps never be closed. Joe felt a sudden flaring of anger, a desire to hurt his friend.

"It would be unfair of me, Homer, not to tell you what they really think in D.C., so that you know the worst."

"Okay. Shoot. Let's have it."

"International believes that you can act in the demeaning manner of a condemned man begging for his life if you want. But it won't get you any respect, and it won't save your jobs."

"And that's what you think, too?"

"We've been friends too long for me not to be honest with you."

"I thank you for it," Homer said, looking squarely at him.

"Just between you and me," Joe said, the anger replaced by a sudden urge to justify himself, to show that he was doing more here than merely trying to convince Homer to fall on his sword, "we're going to organize Modern Meat."

"Oh?"

"Yes." Almost anything he said would imply a criticism of Homer, given the recent sorry history of the union, but it couldn't be helped. Anyway, it was really a criticism of them all. "We've decided it's no good anymore just to circle the wagons."

He went on and talked about how in D.C. they'd been discussing the new plant in Maquoketa. Nick Takus didn't like hiring people with any union background, but he was having a hell of a time getting people at the shitty wages he paid. Most likely he'd end up with some of the old JackPack people. Not Homer. Takus would never hire a known labor leader, not even one as compromised as Homer. And anyway, even if he did, it wouldn't be Homer that International used to lead the organizing effort. Homer didn't have the sand to run the kind of campaign they were thinking about—in your face stuff, a lot of exposure in the media, stockholder actions, house calls on every single employee, the whole nine yards.

As Joe talked about the union strategy, however, Homer's interest perked up. Joe continued, encouraged that perhaps a spark of loyalty for the union movement did, after all, survive in his old friend, that perhaps the next morning, in the presence of the executive committee, some sort of compromise might be struck. If the concessions could be kept to a minimum, that would at least be something for Joe to take back to D.C.

"We've decided that traditional campaigns—leafleting at gates, mass meetings, mailings, that sort of thing—aren't good enough anymore. It's got to be real grassroots organizing—house to house, small meetings where we can start to build leadership right away, acting like it's a union right off the bat and not just some kind of wannabe."

Homer had taken an envelope out of the inside of his sport coat and made some notes as Joe talked.

"I'm telling you, Homer, we're going to bring Takus to heel."

"You got people who can speak Spanish?"

The genesis of this question was obvious. Mexicans had begun to move into the Midwest.

"We're prepared to deal with any situation."

Homer nodded. "Good luck to you." He was rubbing his fingers across his forehead and thinking.

Emboldened, Joe said, "So, you can see, I'm sure, why I've come. Now's not the time..." Joe stopped, leaving the thought uncompleted.

"Yes," Homer said. "I understand." Then he smiled and added something, in the way of a small joke, that extinguished the flame Joe had lit. "Maybe, after all, we won't be making as much as the people at Modern Meat."

Since Homer hadn't touched his first beer, Joe didn't bother to suggest they have another.

When, a few minutes later, Joe arrived alone back at his motel room, he found John Michael waiting for him.

# CHAPTER 58

~

"What about Chinn?" Homer asked.

"We've got our marketing people working up the details of a proposal. I've written a letter to him confirming the points we discussed when he was here."

Skip Peterson seemed wary. He must not take part in many meetings whose purpose remained mysterious. But Homer wasn't prepared to reveal the reason for his visit just yet.

The rain had returned, the outside gray with it. In Peterson's office, a desk lamp, a table lamp, a floor lamp, a reading lamp on the middle shelf of a bookcase had all been turned on, creating islands of light and a kind of cozy fireside atmosphere.

Homer continued questioning him about the Richie Chinn visit.

"Chinn mentioned contacts he had, Skip, people with money to invest. Have you done anything about that?"

"It's in the letter. I'll wait a few days and then call."

At once there was a knock and the door opened. Mel Coyle, the corporate council. "You have a call," Coyle told Peterson.

"Tell him I'll call back."

"It's Karl."

"I'll call him back," Skip repeated.

"I think you'd better talk to him now," Coyle said.

They spoke quietly, creating the sense of a private conversation although Homer could hear perfectly well what was said. The Karl under discussion must be Skip's cousin, his nemesis in the Peterson family.

Peterson turned to Homer. "How long's this going to take?"

"A little while."

"Perhaps you'd like Mel to hear, too," Peterson suggested.

"No." At this, Coyle smiled blandly. Homer, who liked almost everyone, did not like Mel Coyle.

"Okay," Peterson said. He turned back to Coyle. "You heard. A few minutes."

The corporate council withdrew, closing the door behind him.

"Where were we?" Peterson asked.

"Chinn."

"Ah, yes, Chinn." Peterson, up to this point in the conversation, had been uncharacteristically still, leaning way back in his chair, his body twisted slightly to one side, but now he leaped to his feet and began pacing. "So tell me, Homer, what are the rumors on the floor? Do people think Chinn's going to ride in on his white horse and save the day? Is that the idea?"

"Well...is he?"

"Don't count on it," Peterson said.

"Because," Homer went on, now close to the crux of the matter, "if you start getting your markets back, and if maybe you can find some money—you know, some conventional money—for the upgrades somewhere, then maybe..."

"Maybe we could forget about the buyout?"

Homer let this possibility linger for several moments. When he did speak, all he said was, "It would solve a lot of problems."

"Yes, it would," Peterson agreed. He paced more quickly, appearing and disappearing as he moved around the room, into and out of Homer's field of vision. Homer crossed his legs and settled himself more firmly in his seat. "Tell me, Homer," Peterson said, a sudden veering in the conversation, "are you a movie buff?" He seemed to be getting the hang of not knowing what the meeting was about.

"My kids are."

"Myself, I never see movies, but I know something about how they're made." Peterson had moved back into view and was peering intently at Homer. "Or rather how they don't get made. For every success, a hundred failures. I understand that in Hollywood there are actually people who make a living writing screenplays for movies that never get made."

The point of this short speech being obvious, Homer said, "And so you're telling me to forget about Richie Chinn."

"No. I'm not ruling out anything. But we've got to be realistic."

Skip, who apparently underestimated Homer's grasp of the situation, had resumed his pacing, disappearing once again from sight. All this movement was beginning to get on Homer's nerves.

"All right," he said, "so maybe Chinn won't come through. What about other markets? What about conventional loans?"

"We're still trying. Maybe we'll get lucky."

"And the buyout? It's still on."

"Of course. I don't understand what you're getting at here, Homer. You know the buyout's got to go forward."

"Okay, good, I just wanted to make sure." Which brought Homer to the purpose of his visit. "The buyout might be necessary—we all realize that. But you do know that my people don't really want to buy the company? You do know that, don't you?"

"Yes, of course, what's your point?"

"Skip, damn it, sit down."

"What's your point?" Peterson had swung back into view, but he didn't sit down.

"Just this. We want control of the plant."

"You're kidding."

"I'm willing to go to the wall with you on this thing. I'm not talking about marketing, I'm not talking about buying, I'm not talking about finance or any of that stuff. I'm talking about the shop floor. There I want absolute control, period."

Peterson now took up a post at the window, from where he stared out at the rain. "I can't do that, Homer. You're asking too much."

"I'm not asking, Skip." Homer paused a beat. "I'm telling."

Aside from a slight rigidness, a slight drawing up of the body, Peterson didn't react to this blunt statement. No doubt, he'd had to accede to many imperatives in his life. No doubt, he'd have to learn to live with many more. But to have the president of the union march in with such a demand as this, well, Homer understood it would be the bitterest pill to swallow of them all.

After Joe Wheeler's visit, Homer had laid awake most of the night thinking. At 2:40, although it wasn't his night to be an adorer, he got up and went down to Baker Street and sat in one of the pews thinking about many things. He didn't say the Rosary, but he remembered how easily his mind drifted when he did. He had told Joe he was trying to become "not like himself." A different self, hopefully a better self—someone, anyway, fit to lead this buyout attempt. He reflected for a long time on exactly what that meant.

And then he returned home and climbed back into bed beside Rose and clasped his hands behind his head and continued pondering over the matter. Tactics now. Joe had given him the idea for an effective campaign to convince the employees to buy the company. They had almost no time, so it would be very, very difficult, but Homer thought it could be done. Joe, of course, would be horrified at the thought that his nifty new union organizing tactics were to be put to such a heretical use, but Joe and the International were to be discounted. They wanted to sacrifice the local to their larger purposes. That being the case, Homer would use whatever tools came to hand and the International be damned. And he'd get what he wanted from Skip Peterson, too.

Peterson continued to stare at the rain.

Homer said, "You can't ask a man to buy a company without giving him authority over what he does. It's no longer your job, it's his." When Skip still didn't respond, Homer went on. "Nobody wants to tell the marketing people what to do or the buyers or the accountants *or you*. All we want is control over what *we* do. And we're not asking. We're not coming hat in hand, not anymore. This is going to be a fifty-fifty deal or it's not going to happen."

Homer stopped and waited. There came a knock on the door, and Mel Coyle stuck his head in again. Peterson looked at him and snapped, "One more minute, for Christ's sake." Coyle withdrew.

Homer heard people take the Lord's name in vain. It happened all the time. But he never got used to it, and now he set his heart even more firmly against whatever opposition Peterson might choose to offer. The interruption had galvanized Peterson, who turned to Homer as soon as they were alone again.

"Look, Homer, to run the operation full bore, we need a twenty-million-dollar line of credit. You know the local banks aren't big enough for that. We're going to have to go to Chicago or Minneapolis or someplace else. And frankly, nobody's going to give us a red cent if they think the inmates are running the asylum."

"Maybe so," Homer conceded, "you might be right." Peterson's argument had force. Homer knew—everyone knew—that the farmers had to be paid for their animals within forty-eight hours, and it took two weeks or longer, longer most of the time, for the packer to process and sell the meat and get paid by his wholesalers and retailers. Without the credit line, he was out of business.

It made no difference. Homer would have his way.

"Look, Homer," Peterson had continued, "I hear what you're saying. Your people have to be involved. I want you to be involved."

"Do you?"

"Of course."

Peterson held his hands out, a few inches apart, as if offering Homer an invisible box within which might be found all the promises that he had made over the last few weeks.

They'd been talking about this all along. *Participation* was the word they used, a word that to Homer's ears sounded like nothing more than a half measure. The way he looked at it, half measures had a way of becoming no measures at all. People got used to doing something a certain way, and they became adept at figuring out how to keep on doing it that way, no matter what. Homer knew all about it. When it came to inertia, he'd written the book. And on top of that, being as how the management at JackPack had always looked down their noses at the rank and file, it took a good deal of imagination to accept these promises of Skip's as anything different from the fervent kinds of protestations that young boys make to young girls in order to have their way with them.

"If you *want* us to be involved, that's good, Skip, but I've come to tell you we *will* be involved, whether you want it or not. You say that without the credit line, we're going down. I say to you that without the employees get control of their jobs, we're going down, too. Maybe outsiders can kill us. Maybe so. I expect that's always true. And if that's the way it's gonna be, that's the way it's gonna be. But if you want us to buy this company, you'll give us what we want."

In the silence that followed, Homer could find no trace of acceptance in Peterson. Homer imagined him to be doing nothing more than searching for the most effective response, concerned only to maintain the course he'd determined upon all along.

"You understand, Homer, that this can't work if it's based on one demand after another."

"Nope, it can't," Homer agreed.

"And I must say," Peterson went on, trying to press whatever imagined advantage this fact gave him, "that since all this began, you've spent a helluva lot more time milking the situation for all it was worth than worrying about what we need to do to save the company."

"That's right, and who taught us that?"

Homer realized that it wouldn't take much to create a bitterness that would erase whatever of value was happening at that moment. The two of them might not be able to make the buyout happen, but surely they could destroy it. Made no difference, no earthly difference. If they were going to fail, so be it. Certain things had to be said. For once in his life, Homer would say them. "Who taught us to worry about wages and fringe benefits and working conditions and nothing else, Skip?"

This apparently was not a discussion Peterson intended to get trapped in, for he returned immediately to the question of demands. "So we're to get rid of the foremen, is that the idea?"

"If that's what it takes."

"Many of these men have given their whole adult lives to this company. It's all they know. You do understand that?"

"I do."

"So you'd have me do right by your people by treating them like shit? Is that your idea of fairness?"

"We didn't create this situation, Skip."

"But is *that* your idea of fairness?"

Homer paused. In thinking about the rest, he'd thought about this, too. He'd given it a great deal of thought. He wished misfortune on no one. Some of the foremen were decent enough fellows. And he felt heartsick at the unchristian pleasure he knew many of the members would take in the downfall of the blue hats. Yet, what simpler way to proceed? Somebody more ruthless than Homer would have done it without a second thought. Perhaps someone simply more realistic would have done it, too, someone willing to take on the burden of guilt that would come from acting for the greater good.

"Maybe we can devise some other way, Skip. But maybe not, too. One way or the other, though, my people must, *must* have control over the job floor." Having made this small concession, Homer said the last of what he had come to say. "Is this a new day or isn't it? That's what *you* have to decide. If it isn't, then okay, we can all go home. But if it *is*, then like it or not, you've got to start acting like it." Homer got up. "That's all I have to say."

As he was about to leave, Peterson held him up for a moment, "You know, Homer, you're not the only one who could pull the plug here."

"That's right," Homer agreed, glad to have the opportunity to say what he next said. "But neither one of us wants to do that, Skip. We both care about this company too much to do that."

# CHAPTER 59

~

As Homer Budge left, Mel blew by him and back into the room. Skip, still powerfully under the influence of the exchange just ended, had no interest in talking to Mel, or to anyone else. The phone rang at once. Mel answered and spoke briefly and then transferred the call to the speakerphone.

"Skip, are you there?" Karl's voice wheezed from the little box on the desk.

Skip remained standing where he'd ended the confrontation with Budge, in no clear alignment with anything in the room, a step away from the side of his desk, his back half-turned to the window, near the corner of the coffee table. Could Homer, he wondered, have really changed that much, so quickly? Could it be possible? Or was this just some momentary aberration and tomorrow he'd be back to his old pliant self?

"Skip?" Karl fretted, his voice for an instant uncertain. Skip sighed.

"Yes, Karl, I'm here."

"What the hell's going on out there?"

What's going on? Skip considered and at once dismissed the idea of mentioning the business with Homer. What else could he tell his cousin? He didn't want to tell him anything. "Like always, Karl, trying to keep our heads above water."

"Mel tells me you're going to start giving meat away."

"Is that what Mel says?" Skip looked quizzically at Coyle, who had taken his usual chair, where Homer had been sitting not two minutes earlier.

"What do you know about this Richie Chinn?" Karl demanded from his prison on top of Skip's desk.

Skip sighed again. He went over to the wall covered with photographs and stood before a twenty-five-year-old snapshot taken at one of the Peterson clan gatherings, his grandfather's eightieth birthday. In the picture, he and Karl were side by side, still friends, Karl so very youthful then and earnest and unkempt. With effort, Skip could remember why he had once been quite fond of his cousin, the young Karl, however, a person so very different from the Karl of the speakerphone, who having lived for many years on the West Coast considered himself to have become a sophisticate, a world citizen. And, as a corollary, Skip still a rube.

"Skip? Goddammit!"

"I'm still here, Karl. I don't know what to say. Chinn came, he made a presentation. At this point, anybody has a proposal, we listen. You do expect us to listen, don't you?" But Skip knew that Karl didn't expect that. Karl had stopped listening years ago, so why should he expect anybody else to?

"Are you planning to sell him meat under cost?" Karl demanded.

Skip again looked at Mel, who of course betrayed nothing, content to doodle on the arm of his chair as he listened to the cousins. Turning back to the family photo, Skip peered closer at the ancient images. Neither looked directly at the camera. Karl always appeared distracted, like a scientist whose experiment had just started to go wrong. Skip's younger image remained illegible, even to him, as composed and formal and frozen-in-place as a nineteenth-century studio portrait. He was, he thought, more like the camera than the image it made.

"Well?" Karl demanded behind him.

"We haven't gotten that far yet."

"When you do, don't sell below cost."

Skip pondered several of the other cousins in the photo before he answered. "It's not up to you."

"I am on the board, and that's my goddamn money you're giving away."

"Marketing agreements aren't a board decision."

First, Homer Budge lobs mortar rounds in from the union's bunker, and now here comes Karl, sniping at him from the other side. Given the choice, Skip would have ignored his cousin altogether. That option not being available, he attempted flippancy, which of course shared a border with anger. "Would you like a sign-off on purchase orders for paper clips, Karl, would that make you happy?"

"This isn't goddamn paper clips."

"Maybe not, but it's still not a board prerogative."

"Like hell it isn't."

Skip tried to imagine Karl as he must be at that moment, the laird in his hilltop mansion overlooking Monterey Bay, surrounded by the English gardens he so adored, a naturalized Californian and the family's self-appointed gadfly.

"I say we go back to Nick Takus and tell him we're ready to accept his offer," Karl had gone determinedly on.

"The offer's no longer on the table. We crawl back to him, he'll cut it in half and stuff it down our throats."

"You don't know that."

"You're wrong, I do know it."

Karl paused, then changed course. "Look, Skip, this buyout scheme of yours makes no sense at all. Buyouts take time. A company's got to be at least marginally profitable and up-to-date even if it has a shitty return on investment. You've got to do a full-blown feasibility study, for Christ's sake. Does even one of these conditions exist at JackPack? I'll be damned if it does."

Skip knocked down Karl's points one by one. Another feasibility study wasn't going to tell them anything they didn't already know. If the employees owned the place, the ROI wasn't so critical, either, and anyway it hadn't really been adequate for a long time, so what was this but more of the same? On and on he went, but Karl wasn't buying.

"I don't believe this," he muttered. "Okay, Skip, I'll tell you what, you want to do this thing, fine, but buy the rest of us out first. Then you can do any damn thing you want."

Karl's bottom line, the point he had already raised on several occasions. Skip answered as he always had. "If the employees buy outstanding stock, Karl, all we'll be doing is moving money from them to the current stockholders. It does nothing to help the company." Without using the unissued stock, they'd get no relief for current operating expenses.

"Buyers pay sellers, Skip, that's the way it works."

"But we're not selling."

"No, what you're trying to do is water the stock until it's absolutely worthless."

"We're not doing that, either. The problem is, Karl, you've given up on the company." Karl and Mel, they both had, birds of a feather.

There was a pause here, and when Karl spoke again, he had calmed down a bit. "That's right, Skip, I don't think you can save the company. I don't think anybody can. Maybe Grandfather, maybe, if he was still alive. But let's face it, let's be honest here, you're not him, and you're not man enough to do the job."

"You're wrong." Karl, of course, knew exactly where to stick the knife in. But as much as this crack pissed Skip off, he wouldn't push the matter further. He didn't care what the provocation was. Mel sat mutely in his chair, no longer doodling, merely sitting passively, his hands folded in his lap.

"I want out, Skip," Karl persisted. "Based on Takus's last offer, I figure my stock's worth sixty-five thousand dollars. It isn't much, but I'm damn well not going to throw it away on a lost cause."

"Just you, Karl? What about the rest of the cousins?"

"I'm speaking for all of us. And just so you know, I've been talking to my lawyer."

"I should consider that a threat?"

"Call it what you want. I *do* care about the family even if you *don't*. Some of us have gone on. Some of us have lives. Maybe the stock isn't worth much, but it's worth something, and I'm not going to sit still while you turn it into toilet paper."

If Karl did put the matter into the hands of his lawyer, that would be it. The family sundered. They'd talk through their legal representatives from then on. Skip would no longer have the pleasure of these exchanges with his cousin. But at what a cost.

"Not all of the cousins think as you do," Skip reminded Karl.

"If they don't, it's just because they've bought into your line of baloney."

"This is getting us nowhere." Skip felt totally in control for the moment, his anger tempered by the grimness of the possible consequences. "I know what you think, Karl, you've made your feelings abundantly clear, but I still say the company can be saved. So what do you say, shall we call this round a draw?"

"A draw? Hell, no, I'm coming out there. I'm tired of trying to deal with all this shit over the phone."

And the line went dead. At once, Skip wheeled on Mel. "That was the call I had to take? Wonderful."

"I just want to make sure everybody's heard."

"You told him we were going to sell meat under cost?"

"I discussed what's been happening, that's all. He certainly has a right to know."

"He's just out to get me. What's the matter with you?"

Mel never got rattled. He never blew up, his anger instead an implosion, leaving only a shuttered impression. Skip found this habitual calm so distasteful at the moment that he turned away and stared blindly back at the family picture.

"You *are* vulnerable to a stockholder suit," Mel said, or rather repeated, since he'd already reminded Skip several times of his fiduciary responsibility.

"Right, I am, Mel, and you know what? I don't give a shit."

"Well, you should. Look, Skip, you've done a good job. You've done a better job than Karl would have. I mean it. But this time he's right…And I've got to tell you, what you're trying to do just gets more bizarre by the minute." He spoke softly, and when Skip turned back toward him and began to protest, he held up a hand. "Let me finish, please. If you keep on with this, and it fails, a lot of folks will get hurt. What *are* you thinking about? The buyout can't work. These people aren't entrepreneurs. Maybe once a few of them had some idea about starting a little business of their own, some mom-and-pop operation somewhere, I don't know, maybe. But for most of them, it's just daydreaming, something to help them get through another shift on the floor. Don't go tinkering around with their illusions, Skip. Let them get on with their lives. Let them blame us if they want. If that's the way they keep their pride, then let them, it's okay. Because you're not going to save the company. All you're going to do is raise a lot of false hopes, and in the end they're going to leave people worse off, not better. Do you want to do that, Skip? Do you *really* want to do that?"

Skip thought about these words as he went around to his desk and sat down and took a deep breath. He wavered. Karl was an outsider, just like Nick Takus, for that matter. He didn't care about Jackson. No outsider did. Not Karl, not Takus, not anyone. They just didn't give a shit. But Mel wasn't one of them. He might be a hard-nosed lawyer and businessman, but he'd worked among these people for nearly four decades. They were his neighbors. How could he not care?

Mel sat, as neat as a pin, waiting for Skip to capitulate to his superior logic, as always. He seemed so very unchanged, as if none of this really *had* touched him. And wasn't it true, Skip thought, wasn't it true that in his own way Mel was an outsider, too? A consummate professional, and like all such people, only imperfectly moored to the community in which he lived.

"You're probably right, Mel. This is dangerous. People could get hurt. But is that what we're here to do, protect them from the consequences of their dreams?"

"From their folly, at least."

"Their folly? How do you know what they're capable of? This is a completely new situation. Maybe they'll work as hard as you and I know they'll have to. Maybe they will. Maybe they'll work their asses off and save the Pack."

"That's certainly a pretty thought," Mel said. Mel liked the expression "pretty thought." He had used it any number of times, and always to good effect.

Skip, for the moment, ignored him. As they had been talking about his employees, he had realized something about himself. If he really did expect them to work their asses off, he'd better be prepared to do it, too, and despite all the time he'd already put in, too damn much of it had been spent in all this petty squabbling. In situations like this, you imagined you were doing things all the way up, but mostly you were wrong. What you had to do was get outside yourself, then look back and make a flat-out, cold-blooded assessment of the situation. You didn't cut yourself any slack, not an inch. Then you could start expecting something from somebody else.

Okay, Skip thought, good. A lot he still didn't understand. But he knew that one thing at least. He turned back to Mel.

"'A pretty thought,' you said."

"Yes. And believe me, I wish it were true. I really do."

What they were engaged in here, Skip realized, was a kind of high school debate. Nobody's mind would be changed. And with this realization, he understood that he knew two things, not just that he had to work harder and more effectively but one more thing, too.

A necessary task had been left undone far too long. He didn't know why he hadn't understood it earlier. Still trapped in the old way of thinking, probably. Well, no more.

"For many years, you've meant a great deal to this company, Mel. And to me personally. You really have. But I'm afraid I'm going to have to ask for your resignation."

"What?"

"You heard me."

"You can't be serious."

"Oh, I'm serious all right. If I'm going to get anywhere, I've got to cut the anchors free, and you've become an anchor. You don't believe in what we're trying to accomplish here. If you stay, you'll just try to destroy it. And I won't have that."

"You can't know what you're doing," Mel told him. This turn of events had almost gotten a rise out of him.

"I think I do. I want your resignation. We can call it retirement, if you want. I'll fire you, if I have to. But one way or another, that's it."

Mel didn't speak for a time. Finally, when he did, all he said was "Okay. But you can't remove me from the board."

This statement pissed Skip off. It was so fucking typical of Mel. "Oh, I think I could, but frankly I've got more important things to do with my time at the moment. No, you'll still be on the board." Giving vent to his anger, he added, "That should make you happy. It's the board you've always cared about."

"It's not the board, it's the stockholders. And it's the stockholders you should care about, too, just as Karl said."

"You think Karl gives a shit about the stockholders? What are they going to get, a few pennies on the dollar, maybe not even that. Karl could care less. He's out to get me, pure and simple. All this talk about the dear cousins is nothing but pious bullshit."

"I don't think so." Mel, unflappable to the end.

After this exchange, Skip mastered his anger long enough to say, "I want to thank you again for all the years of service you've given to the company."

"You do?"

"Yes. Despite the situation now, despite whatever you might think, I *am* grateful for everything you've done in the past, for me personally and for my family."

Mel nodded slowly, still thinking. "And so," he said, "that's it."

"Yes." Nothing more.

When he was alone, Skip began to shake, and it took him some time to calm down.

It had been done quickly, but he had no doubt about the act. A curious realization came over him. Although his parents had been dead for years, he had never been an orphan, not really. Mel had been pleased to act in loco parentis. The fate of an only child raised among adults. Well, no more. He was on his own now. Good. Good!

Suddenly, he felt ravenously hungry. He picked up the phone and told his secretary to order in some food. She hesitated, apparently confused. Skip guessed that Mel had already informed her that he no longer worked for the company, and so she found the mere request for food at such a time rather odd. "And," he added, "contact Homer Budge for me, will you? I want to have a word with him." Skip held her on the line as he thought.

"Are you sure, Mr. Peterson?"

Skip laughed. Carole never called him Mr. Peterson except in front of others, when a little formality was in order. She must be afraid he'd lost his marbles. "Yes, I'm sure. I need to speak to Homer, PDQ. And I want to see some people in the conference room, too." He listed key members of his management team. He'd give anyone who wanted one last chance to jump ship. And he'd decide who else besides Mel had to be pushed. "You might as well order up enough food for them, too, Carole. We're going to be here for a while. Pizza, why don't you? Different kinds. I'll take mine with anchovies." He hated anchovies.

"Anchovies," he repeated, and laughed. Yes, indeedy, from now on, *that* was his life, anchovies all the way.

# Chapter 60

~

John "Ole" Olson, retired master of the U.S. Army Corps of Engineers dredge *Thompson*, just shook his head. Chuck Fellows, the Jackson public works guy he had talked to on the phone that morning, now stood behind him, making notes as Ole picked his way through the debris scattered around the machine house on the city's dredge and ticked off the deficiencies, one after another. Compared to the *Thompson*, with its twenty-inch discharge, this little twelve-inch dredge seemed like a toy. An old-fashioned toy at that, with its chain-link drive and ancient Detroit diesel. Hydraulic hoses cracking with age, frayed cables, corroded electrical contacts, filth, filth everywhere. And this was only what Ole could see. "If you manage to get her up and running," he said, "she'll be a noisy old gal."

He glanced at Fellows from time to time, trying to size up the man. Seemed like a decent enough chap. Rather too abrupt for Ole's taste. And what was a city engineer likely to know about dredge work? He'd be good at sizing catch basins and doing estimating for road reconstruction, that sort of thing. But dredging? Technical expertise aside, he didn't seem to have the personality for the work. Dredging took patience. It was hurry-up-and-wait kind of work. Work at a distance. A good dredge man had almost a sixth sense about his equipment and the natural world around him. His knowledge came through his fingertips as he manipulated his panel of controls in the lever room, in the medley of noises engulfing him, in the vibrations rising through the soles of his feet. Experience, not textbooks, bestowed such wisdom as he possessed. And none of this, Ole guessed, boded well for Mr. Fellows.

They went back onto the deck and then walked through the rain out to the end of the discharge line. When she was up, the dredge was pumping about as far as she could manage. Fellows pointed out the area yet to be covered, several acres choked with brush and the remnants of a dump. Two makeshift dirt roads, patched with stone, approached from east and west, joined and then mounted the sand already in place, which had been shaped into low platforms on top of which the city of Jackson was building its dog track. Ole, who all his life had read the *National Geographic*, was reminded of a Mayan temple site in the middle of jungle wilderness.

He looked at the sweep of land yet to be covered and then back along the fragile-looking twelve-inch pipeline. "A little like trying to put out a fire by pissing on it, ain't it?" he said.

Fellows hadn't said yet precisely what he was after, but Ole could guess. As they walked back, Fellows asked about winter dredging, and Ole shivered and shook his head.

When they were all through and standing next to their vehicles and looking back toward the sad little spectacle the dredge made, sitting at anchor, bow-heavy so she seemed almost on the point of foundering, Fellows laid out his cards. "Do you think you could complete the contract to pump the sand?"

"With your equipment?"

"Yes."

Ole thought about his career on the *Thompson*, a first-class operation. He had reached the peak of his profession. And he thought about retired life. In two weeks, the Wisconsin deer season started. And he and his wife were thinking about maybe driving to Arizona in February.

"My suggestion to you, Mr. Fellows"—reverting from Chuck back to formal address for this, the difficult part of the conversation—"is that you contract this work out to a commercial outfit."

"Yeah. But as I said over the phone, nobody's available. Not until next fall at least."

"Yup," Ole conceded, "I remember. Can't say I'm surprised. People like to get their contracts lined up maybe a year in advance. There's gotta be a lot of work out there now, too, what with the drought and all the low water. But still, my suggestion holds. You best wait. Wait and do it right."

"I can't."

Ole shook his head. "In that case, all I can recommend is you hire back—Turcotte, did you say his name was? Hire back Mr. Turcotte to finish what he started. Old equipment like this is awful cranky. Not so different, it ain't, from an old fellow like myself. Can't imagine anybody but my wife putting up with me after all these years. As for that little dredge, probably, you ask me, nobody but Mr. Turcotte will be able to coax that old gal into supplying you with the sand you need."

"Would you consider doing the work yourself? The Corps tells me you're the best."

Ole sloughed off the praise. "I ain't that special, Mr. Fellows, but I'm smart enough to know when to say no."

He rather expected an argument at this point, an attempt to coax him, perhaps an appeal to his pride, but it didn't happen. Fellows merely thanked him for coming and climbed into his 4x4 and drove away.

Thinking about what had just happened, Ole felt a little disappointed in himself, a little sad. He wished Fellows had tried harder to recruit him. The outcome would have been the same, but somehow that would have made the trip down here seem more worthwhile.

Maybe, he thought, Fellows had taken to heart the words about getting Turcotte to finish the work. That, Ole told himself again, was the only way it was going to get done. If at all. He tried to envision what Turcotte must be like, what the man would be like who ran such a piss-poor operation. Finally, he climbed into his vehicle and drove over the bridge to Wisconsin and turned northward onto the Great River Road, glad to be heading home.

# CHAPTER 61

~

Rachel Brandeis was back up in the penthouse. She'd continued to have her audiences with Leonard Sawyer, but he had lost his power over her. At least she told herself he had. As she gave him her updates, she would wander around the office he had paneled off from the rest of the attic-like space. At the foot of the panels stood various mementos, many attesting to the old man's fixation with the river. Just as he had been physically whittled down in old age, his focus on the world appeared to have been reduced to his few obsessions: the newspaper, the river, the Petersons. Rows of knots and splices were displayed in a vitrine before one of the panels. From a small bookcase before another she might take an old, cloth-bound volume and leaf through it while he bragged about himself by bragging about the locally famous author who had written it. Always books about the river, often signed, sometimes with appreciations for the help Sawyer had provided. Such evidence that the publisher had had a life with other humans Rachel found rather curious, like speculations on alternate realities. Except for her first day in the city, she had never seen him with another living soul, other than herself, of course. Lucky her.

On a small antique writing desk, where she stood at the moment, various curios were arranged—several miniature books puffed up with water damage, etuis, a bud vase with no bud, and other Victorian sundries. She had been telling Sawyer about the energetic campaign that Homer Budge had begun mounting to persuade the union members to buy the Pack. Sawyer seemed less interested than normal.

From the small desk, she picked up a jointed wooden figurine, like a puppet, and fingered it idly as she talked. She didn't ask Sawyer about it. He had long ago told her the macabre story of the figurine and the other objects, recovered from the trunk of an unidentified woman, a drowning victim of a famous nineteenth-century stern-wheeler that exploded and sank.

"Budge's people are going house to house. He's holding small-group meetings, very hush-hush. The only accounts I hear are pretty vague. I haven't managed to crash one yet. He's also formed a large committee made up of rank-and-file people from different departments of the plant. All stuff straight out of your thoroughly modern union organizer's handbook."

"Was this Skip Peterson's idea?" Sawyer wanted to know. He was wearing a bulky cardigan the color of an animal pelt. Naturally, whatever the scene in the JackPack drama, he suspected Peterson was hiding behind a pillar in the background.

"No, Peterson's got nothing to do with it. In fact, it appears he might have gotten more than he bargained for when he proposed the buyout. The union, I understand, is demanding absolute autonomy on the shop floor. I'm working on that story, too."

She found her skepticism in temporary remission and herself writing fairly upbeat articles, which she didn't mind doing, up to a point. And she had begun to think that something Skip had told her could possibly be true—the real tale here might be of a genuine alliance between labor and management and the saving of the Pack against extremely long odds. Might Skip, Homer, and the others actually pull it off? Hard to think so, but for the moment, news from the front was encouraging.

With the report of all this frenetic union activity, Sawyer seemed to have been thrown off balance and could do no more than repeat his dark warnings about Skip Peterson's motives. Rachel listened without emotion, sheathed in the brusque coolness she now brought to sessions with the old man. Sawyer studied her as if he could for the first time detect signs of apostasy.

"Well, okay," he said at last, "you keep at it." He cocked his head to one side and gave her one of his beady little looks. "Anyway, that wasn't why I called you up here. Got something else for you to do."

Immediately, Rachel was on her guard. "You're pulling me off the Pack?"

"Nope. You still do that. It's something else. You're going to like it."

Something else? That she'd like? Uh-oh.

"Said you were interested in racial stuff."

It took her several moments to identify the source of this comment—her first day in Jackson, when Sawyer had been driving her along the waterfront in his ancient Jeep, wearing his safari gear, and she'd asked why there were so few blacks in the city.

"Yes, I am," she confirmed, asking herself what this might have to do with Sawyer's small hoard of interests. She remembered what he'd said that first day. "There's a story, we run it." Not the sentiment of a man who took much of an interest in civil rights.

"Okay, here it is," Sawyer told her now. "City's got a policy. City employees get first dibs on job openings." He paused and inspected her like a scientist with a lab rat and a new experiment. "Turns out they're gonna hire a draftsman. Employee bid the job, but he isn't gonna get it. Got all the necessary qualifications, and they don't intend to give it to him."

"This is a black man you're talking about?"

Sawyer smiled. "City's been all hot to support the Integration Task Force there, been pushing the museum exhibit on the Pullman porter, too, but it looks like they're not so keen when it comes to promoting from within. It's okay if somebody else's horse is getting gored."

"How do you know this?" Rachel asked suspiciously. Plummy assignment or not, a chance to reestablish her hard-nosed bona fides or not, she had to figure the old man was up to something. Her sense of invulnerability where he was concerned had disappeared like the insubstantial thing it was.

"Got friends in the black community," he told her, his eyebrows jumping up as if at the joy of surprising her with this fact. "They let me know what's going on. You bet."

Could this be true? Rachel found it difficult to believe. But the story seemed straightforward enough, and certainly she felt the draw of it. "So I'm to do this story, and keep following up on JackPack."

"Expect you can handle both. Can't ya?"

"Of course."

"There you are, then."

Could this really be on the up-and-up? She opened her notepad. "Tell me what you've got," she said. "Who's the guy? What job did he apply for?"

A few minutes later, she stepped outside the newspaper building and stood, momentarily uncertain. A spritz of cold rain fell. Even at midday, the temperature seemed to be falling. Far down the street, barely visible from the steps of the paper, the facade of KJAX was visible as a narrow column of light. Her first impulse was to walk down for a chat with Johnny Pond, who was the only black she knew in the city. An absurd idea, of course, talking to a rival and throwing away an exclusive. She wouldn't do it. But not trusting Sawyer and feeling slightly off balance, she surely wished she had a source, someone with whom to have a quiet chin-wag.

And yet...she was a reporter and destined to deal with schmucks from now until the end of time, schmucks and their tips. What was Sawyer but one of those? Practically a type specimen. Not only that, but a man's man to boot, totally hung up on the trappings of manhood. As he lived out the remnant of his life, he seemed to have put aside all dissembling and dedicated himself to the service of his emotional needs. That was it, emotional needs. As far as Rachel was concerned, men were at least as emotional as women; her father, for example, was just this side of hysterical with all his invective against the right-wingers he found on every hand, his powerful manipulation of logic not the evidence of a determination to live by reason alone but merely the sublimation of his rampant emotional convictions. Her brothers, in self-defense, had developed their own convictions and their own sublimations.

And women, if anything, women were the other way around, their manifest emotions the artifices of basically reasonable minds. Perhaps that was true, perhaps it wasn't, but either way she didn't plan to waste a lot of time worrying about it. She intended to be reasonable. That was the way she'd deal with all this covert male neediness.

So whatever Sawyer had up his sleeve, it had nothing to do with her, right? And the story he'd just given her certainly came without apparent complications. A modern tale of prejudice. Of innocence and guilt. The simultaneous presence and absence of racism, which was the way it was done nowadays. It was what came after gentlemen's agreements.

Okay, she thought, so what's to worry about? Just do it.

And she set off to find this Sam Turner person and follow up on what was, after all, as Sawyer himself had observed, the kind of story she had wanted to write all along.

# Chapter 62

~

Chuck didn't get back to his office until after five. Waiting for him was a *Trib* reporter, not the guy assigned to city hall but the hotshot chick the paper had hired to cover events at the Pack. Chuck had seen Rachel Brandeis at city council meetings but hadn't had any dealings with her. Just fine, so far as he was concerned. Reporters he lumped in the same category with politicians: bottom feeders.

"I've been waiting for you," she said. In fact, she had her stuff spread around her in a way that suggested she had been there for quite some time.

She followed him into his office.

"No time to talk," he told her. "I'm on my way back out."

"If you don't mind, then, I'll walk with you. I've only got a couple of questions."

"Suit yourself."

He knew what she wanted to talk about. Had to be something that concerned both himself and the Pack, which could only mean the break the company was looking for in their sewer rate. The treatment plant had been designed to handle the heavy load of organics the Pack dumped into the system and so now Peterson was crying poor. Another chance for Chuck to be the villain of the piece.

As they walked toward the stairs, Brandeis's heels ticktacked across the tiles. She was a sharp dresser, Chuck noted, a point in her favor. Good figure, too.

"I understand," she said, "that one of the city employees who applied for an opening in the drafting department has been turned down. Is that correct?"

Surprised, Chuck didn't answer immediately.

"His name is Sam Turner," she added and then waited.

Chuck stopped at the head of the stairs. "How did you find out about this?"

She shook her head. "Sorry."

Chuck gave her a look, then turned and took the stairs quickly. Halfway down, he stopped.

"It didn't take Sawyer long, did it?"

"What do you mean?" she asked behind him.

He resumed his double-time pace down toward the first floor without bothering to react to this show of ignorance. He could challenge her, but she'd just stonewall, and they'd get into a bullshit little duel. Wasn't worth it. If she wanted to do Sawyer's dirty work, that just proved Chuck's point about reporters.

At the foot of the stairs, he stopped again and let her catch up. "Okay, this is the situation. Yes, Sam Turner didn't get the job. You want to know why? Because he wasn't qualified."

As they walked along the first floor corridor, Brandeis asking her follow-up questions, Chuck wondered: who had talked to Len Sawyer? El Plowman? Unlikely. Perhaps the same joker who had passed the good word along to Plowman and sent her scurrying up to Chuck's office the other week. Not that it made a helluva lot of difference. Sawyer had lived in Jackson forever and had his antennae out. It couldn't have been hard.

Brandeis's heels beat a furious tattoo as she hurried to keep up. She made her notes with a few quick strokes—a lefty, her hand curling around the pen as she wrote.

"So it has nothing to do with the situation at the Pack?" she persisted.

"What? Who said it did?"

"I spoke with Aggie Klauer."

"So?" The personnel director wasn't a player here.

"She told me that all promotions have been frozen. She mentioned the fact that the Pack might close and the impact that would have on the city budget."

Shit, thought Chuck. "Turner's not getting the job because nobody's being promoted? That's what Klauer said?"

"That was her understanding," Brandeis told him.

"There is a freeze, but I made the decision about Turner before I knew about it."

It was amazing how people could take a basically simple situation and turn it into a clusterfuck. He pushed through the door,

Brandeis right behind him. Outside, the frigid November darkness engulfed them.

"But he does have the associate's degree," she persisted, speaking louder as the wind whisked her words away. "I spoke with one of his instructors at Jackson Tech, who told me that Turner was an A student and took every drafting course taught at Jackson Tech. He was surprised to learn that he hadn't gotten a position yet."

"Sam Turner's education is beside the point. He lacks the necessary experience."

"Isn't that a catch-twenty-two? No work experience, no job. No job, no work experience." Exactly what Mark had said when he had been trying to wheedle Chuck into taking Turner on.

"Yeah, that's right, life is tough. But I'll tell you what, if you want him to fail, then fine, we could give him the job."

"I see..." Brandeis replied. Chuck had stopped next to his 4x4. Brandeis held her ground, the wind beating against her, the leaves of her notepad flapping violently. "And so you told him he wasn't qualified?" she asked again.

"Yes, I did," Chuck said impatiently.

"Then I don't understand this business about freezing promotions. It seems to me that telling him one thing and the public something else is hardly fair to Mr. Turner. Would you say that's fair to Mr. Turner?"

"No, I wouldn't."

"So there seems to have been some miscommunication here."

"What a surprise."

They remained standing next to his pickup. One side of Brandeis's face was lighted, the other in shadow. She looked intelligent. Looked like she didn't mind getting in people's faces, either. Too bad she'd chosen such a bullshit career.

"I have one more question," she said.

"Which is?"

"What did you mean, it didn't take Sawyer long?"

Chuck paused and studied her expression. Maybe she wasn't in on the thing. "Do you know about the dredge?"

"Sure. It's pumping sand for the track. It belongs to the dock board, and Sawyer's been the chairman of that forever. He's got this thing about the river."

"Mostly true. Except that he no longer happens to be in possession of the dredge."

"Who is?"

"Me."

He waited for this to sink in. It didn't take long.

"I suppose we can assume," she said with no attempt to hide her disgust, "that he's none too happy with the fact."

Chuck smiled at her. "Apparently not."

They stared wordlessly at each other, and then Brandeis closed her notebook. "Thank you for your time," she said.

Scooped your ass, didn't I? Chuck thought with satisfaction. Still, he had to admit, at that moment he rather liked Rachel Brandeis, reporter or not.

# CHAPTER 63

~

Chuck drove down to the Jackson Building, where he'd been heading before the encounter with the reporter. Brandeis didn't impress him as a woman who pulled her punches, so probably there'd be a stink about Turner. They'd make Chuck look like some sort of closet racist. The typical bullshit. It ticked him off. The more he thought about it the more ticked off he got. Finally, as he parked and got out, he said, "Fuck it," and forced himself to think about something else, the reason for this little side trip. The dredge wasn't much of an improvement over Sam Turner, but at least it was a problem he could do something about.

The KJTV reception area being deserted, Chuck showed himself back to Walter Plowman's tiny cubicle crowded with his weather forecasting gear.

Plowman, hunkered down before his computer, working on a graphic of the Upper Midwest, didn't realize at first that he had a visitor. Something in the way he leaned forward, his chin canted upward, his lower lip laid over the upper, suggested a man perfectly absorbed in his work, and Chuck thought of withdrawing and leaving him in peace.

The screen of the monitor showed areas of clouds and precipitation. To this he was adding various symbols by drawing with a stylus on a white tablet tilted up beneath like a small drawing board.

He paused for a moment and glanced at the clock overhead, and that's when he became aware of Chuck's presence. Chuck looked up, too. Quarter to six.

"Don't you ever show up except when I'm on deadline?" Plowman asked.

"I'll come back."

"No, no, never mind." He waved Chuck in.

Plowman's mood of utter concentration vanished. But he wasn't angry. His delight at Chuck's arrival, despite its untimeliness, was so spontaneous and natural that Chuck realized how seldom people were really pleased to see one another.

"Just a few minutes ago I was thinking about you," Plowman said at once, dispensing with further formalities. "Remember what I said last time?"

"You said a lot of things."

Plowman held a finger up, waggling it and smiling like a man who had just won a bet. "The ground is saturated, the cold is on the way. Look here."

He swung back around to his computer and beckoned Chuck closer.

"Here's your problem," he said, nodding toward the monitor as he marked a smooth arc on the white graphics tablet. On the video screen the line appeared as a curve through a massing of clouds bearing down on the city. "Cold front," he explained and made a series of marks on the tablet, which appeared on the screen as small blue triangles along the leading edge of the line. "A humdinger, too, not much snow, but the temps are going through the floor. Single numbers tonight, subzero after that."

"Okay. Step two. But a lot more's got to go wrong before we get your flood."

"Well, true enough. I heard something else, too."

"Oh?"

"Heard you seized the dredge from old John Turcotte. Heard you were thinking about maybe dredging in the winter."

"You hear a lot." Chuck hadn't made his plans public. Rachel Brandeis had heard about Sam Turner, and now Plowman about the dredge. News got around. He was about to ask Plowman where he got his information, but that proved unnecessary.

"Frank Duccini told me. Said you'd been down to see him about leasing one of his little harbor tugs."

"You know Duccini?"

"Yup. Know John Turcotte, too."

Of course, Chuck realized immediately. Walter was a native, had been in this business for decades. He must know everybody.

"Yup," Plowman confirmed, "John and I go back a ways."

No doubt Turcotte had been bellyaching up and down the river. "I suppose you think I screwed him."

"If you did, no doubt he deserved it. John Turcotte has a long history of being a horse's ass."

This intelligence immediately raised the weatherman another notch in Chuck's estimate. "Can't say I care too much for Frank Duccini, either."

"Frank's okay. Just a little set in his ways."

There was, Chuck supposed, some sort of philosophical distinction between a man set in his ways and a horse's ass, but he wasn't interested in pursuing it at the moment.

"Anyway, Walt, you're right, I came to ask you about this cold snap." Chuck already knew about the approaching front. "Really heavy duty, huh?"

"Gonna sock in pretty good. Last a while, too." Plowman squinted at the monitor and, not quite satisfied with what he saw, began some touch-up work as he continued. "Till spring, maybe. Could be. All the National Weather Service's computer models agree, anyway. The next thirty days will be a good bit below normal."

Given his recent run of luck, Chuck was not surprised. "Okay, assuming that's the case, how long's the river gonna stay open?" The nut of the matter.

"She'll lock up fast. You got anything in mind, you better do it in the next couple of weeks."

Chuck swore under his breath.

One of the machines in the room turned on automatically, a teletype-like clatter as a sheet of paper scrolled out of its bowels. Plowman ignored it.

He squinted judgmentally at his artwork. "You figure to use the backwash of one of Frank's harbor tugs to keep the water open around the dredge, that the idea?"

"I'd use bubblers, if I could get away with it, but they wouldn't even begin to give me enough room to maneuver."

"No," Plowman said, "expect that's right."

"Trouble is, I give Duccini what he's demanding, he'll retire a rich man."

Duccini knew he could sit tight and wait until he got his price, but Chuck would be damned if he'd just roll over and spread his legs for anyone.

"Frank isn't keen on being out on the river in the cold…There, done!" Plowman tossed the stylus down and swung his chair around to face Chuck. "All the old river rats like Frank are pretty long in the tooth now. Frank takes it easy after he lays his boats up. You start getting along in years, the blood begins to thin out. When it comes to sitting in front of a nice warm stove and maybe playing a little euchre or freezing your butt off to make a few extra bucks, well, that stove's mighty hard to beat."

"Yeah." Chuck saw the point, but it didn't make any difference.

"You really intend to do this?" Plowman asked. "Dredging in winter? Never heard of it." Plowman was now threading his tie through the button-downs of his shirt collar.

"One way or another, it gets done," Chuck said.

"More power to you, that's all I can say. I suppose you won't mind if I come down now and again, just to see how you're making out."

As Chuck left the office, Plowman was warming up his lips by blowing between them and making underwater sounds.

Next Chuck drove down to the dredge. His mind remained filled with images of Walter Plowman, the weatherman's wonderful concentration as Chuck had entered his cubicle, the ratty equipment that nevertheless seemed so natural to Chuck's sense of the man, the way the invisible figures he drew on the tablet with the stylus would spring, as if conjured from thin air, onto the monitor above. Plowman seemed like an animal perfectly adapted to its niche in the ecosystem.

By the time Chuck reached the dredge, everyone had gone home for the day. His flashlight barely penetrated the cold, black water. Inside the engine house, he switched on an overhead bulb, which swung back and forth on its cord for some moments, sending light and shadow ricocheting around the room.

Parts lay scattered about the machinery being reconditioned. Unable to entice any experienced dredgemen yet to help with the work, Chuck proceeded as any competent engineer would have. Systems, subsystems, sub-subsystems. With the pump guy, he talked about pumps; with the diesel mechanic, prime movers. Where he had no expert, he read and on the dredge patiently traced out the system components, the hydraulic hoses snaking from lever room to the winches of the spuds and swing wire and ladder, the voltage and current wires connecting gauges to electric motors, the valves, the pipe connections. Slowly, he was becoming familiar with the tangle of components.

The place still looked like hell. He didn't have time to perform triage on the litter—the immediately usable, the salvageable, the rest. John Turcotte apparently saved everything, just in case. That wasn't a problem Chuck had. Anyway, something had to be done to bring order into the place, but he didn't know when he'd find the time.

He checked progress on the pump and diesel projects, then went up to the lever room, where, to someone observing him, it would have appeared as if he was doing nothing, just standing and staring at the controls, his head moving the slightest bit left and right, the fingers of his hands closing slightly, opening slightly, as he began to operate the dredge in his mind.

He heard a car door slam outside but ignored the sound and continued his mental exercises.

Somebody entered and called his name…

⁓

"I recognized your vehicle," Jack Kelley said.

"Too bad." Chuck had come back down from the lever room. The manager of the track construction was inspecting the disassembled machinery.

Kelley looked up, smiled, and said, "It's nice to be loved."

Chuck made a small conciliatory wave of his hand.

"By the look of you," Kelley said, "I'd have to guess everything's not exactly A-OK."

Chuck cast a baleful glance toward him. "Got too many people in my face."

"I can imagine."

If Chuck wasn't exactly A-OK, Kelley didn't look so goddamn hot himself. He obviously hadn't been getting much sleep of late, his eyes ringed with shadow as if he had a pair of shiners.

He thrust his hands deep into his pockets, looked at his feet, and rocked slowly from side to side.

"There was a matter I thought I might alert you to," he said, "now that we're friends."

Since Chuck had officially become the acting PW director, the relationship between them had changed some. Kelley could pretend it had improved if he wanted to.

"We have a small problem brewing."

Chuck snorted.

"Not such a big one this time," Kelley pressed on. "Tom Sharkey's started hinting he might ask for a change order."

Chuck opened the dog track file in his mind—Sharkey, concrete contractor, topping slab.

"A change order?" he asked. "Why?"

"The weather. Sharkey claims it's gonna be too cold to pour without using hot water, maybe enclosing the pour and heating the concrete until it cures."

"So? It's November. What does he expect?"

"Sharkey always assumes he's going to be pouring in July."

"He can assume any damn thing he wants. That doesn't change anything."

"There's standard language in the contract that's supposed to cover situations like this," Kelley explained. "Trouble is, the weather's a big gray area." As Chuck listened to these words, what he heard was Kelley getting a head start on covering his own ass.

"Like I said, it's practically the middle of the damn winter. Any responsible contractor would have made allowance for that."

"Yes," agreed Kelley thoughtfully, "that's the position we ought to take."

"The point here, I suppose, Jack, is to give me something pleasant to look forward to."

Kelley had shifted slightly, the light falling more directly upon him and throwing deep shadows down across his face, revealing his exhaustion more vividly. But a faint smile had appeared, perhaps at the thought of giving Chuck something pleasant to look forward to.

"When the time comes, Jack, I'll deal with it. Until then, I don't want to know about it."

"Okay, fine. But it would be nice, Chuck, if we could move a few fans, you know, before the shit hits them."

After getting rid of Kelley, Chuck tried to go back to what he had been doing, but for the moment his heart just wasn't in it. He shook his head. Pouring cement in July. The damn concrete contractor had lowballed the city. Another asshole thinking he could rob them blind. Just like Frank Duccini.

Chuck looked up past the running crane, into the dark rusted and cobwebbed recesses of the machine house. "O'Banion, you son of a bitch," he said, "you knew there was going to be one huge god-

damn shit storm. You croaked just to spite me, you old bastard."
An idea occurred to him. "I suppose you think these little exercises
are gonna make a difference." He knew how Mark would handle
the Sharkey thing when it came up—a little for you, a little for me.
But Chuck was different. "You want to come along for the ride, be
my guest," he told the shade of his old boss. "But you think I'm
gonna change, you've got another think coming. It's my fucking
party now, and we're gonna play by my fucking rules."

# CHAPTER 64

~

At the appointed hour, Rachel arrived at the radio station, and in a short time Johnny Pond had appeared and conducted her back to his office. He settled himself behind his desk, showing a certain curiosity but no apparent surprise at this sudden request for a face-to-face.

On one wall hung a large clock (radio stations being time-haunted places), and around it, framed citations and pictures from Johnny's football-playing days. Pictures of an attractive woman and two little girls stood on his desk.

"Your family?"

"Chloe, my wife. The imp on the left over there, now, that's Angelina. She's five. Her companion in mischief is Celestina, aged almost three and three-quarters, I'll have you know." He intoned this last phrase with the seriousness of a little girl determined to be as old as she could possibly be.

"Cute kids." The photographer had done a good job. The grinning little girls looked as if they'd paused for an instant amid some delicious game.

It seemed odd to find Pond among these accoutrements of a normal life—husband, father, football player. An entirely empty room would have been more appropriate for the man she had known—aloof, self-sufficient. Even squeezed in beside her at the reporter's table at city council meetings and bathing her in his football player's heat, Johnny retained that aura of separation from his surroundings, as if he watched the world from deep within himself. How strange to hear him speak with such disarmed, fatherly love.

He sat still, waiting, a man as always who would let the game come to him. When she heard his interviews, or his style with the call-ins on *Sound Off*, he asked very few questions, sometimes using no more than a word of encouragement or even the tension of dead air to draw responses from people, to get them to say one more thing than they had intended to say.

"Do you know a man named Sam Turner?" she asked. "Works for the city."

He kneaded the palm of one hand with the thumb of the other and nodded slowly.

She told him what she had, although for the moment left out the part about Len Sawyer. The story remained unwritten. Perhaps it would never be written. She had no stake in it anymore, and even felt liberated in a queer sort of way, finding herself in possession of a good piece, an exclusive, and not giving a fig whether it ever saw the light of day. The *alter kocker* had done it to her again. So what else was new? She wasn't going to do anything different than she had the first time. She'd make damn sure this new story was truthful, that it didn't cause harm except where harm was due. If she ended up in the eyes of her associates at the *Trib* as the old man's accomplice, that was just tough, the price of doing business. After the interview with Chuck Fellows, it had taken her five minutes, no more, and she had accepted her complicity and set her course.

"The last time I looked, you and I were competitors," Johnny observed when she had finished outlining where the situation stood with Sam Turner. "Why're you telling me this? I could have it on the air before you're hardly out the door."

"And you'd be welcome to it."

He leaned back and once again massaged palm with thumb.

"In fact," Rachel told him, "I've even got another story for you."

"My lucky day."

"As you know, the dock board has a dredge that's been pumping sand for the dog track project."

Again, the slow nod. She told him the rest.

After she finished, he took even longer before he spoke. It was hard to tell with Johnny, but this latter half of her story seemed to have had some sort of impact, and she studied his expression. Johnny was the kind of man who, when you looked at him, you just naturally wondered what was going through his head. The thumb paused in its kneading and then continued. "And so," he said at last, "you're telling me what we got here is Leonard Sawyer fixing to take his revenge on Chuck Fellows, and he's gonna use Sam Turner to do it."

"That's what it looks like to me."

He took a deep breath and then said nothing more. The impression of disquiet remained. It was as if a slight rift had opened.

"I'll write the story, Johnny, but I don't want to do it if there's any chance at all that Sam Turner doesn't really want the job."

"But he told you he does."

"Yes, he did." She wasn't sure exactly how she wanted to express her doubts. Sam Turner hadn't impressed her. "He told me, but people lie all the time, even about strange stuff you'd never think they'd lie about."

"Expect if he told you, you can believe him. Sometimes, you've got to believe what a man says."

Rachel understood that Pond wasn't inclined to become involved. Something in his demeanor suggested that he had little interest in either story, which was strange. Yet the business about Sawyer's duplicity had bothered him, she was sure of it.

She got up as if to leave but didn't, merely stood in the middle of the room, thinking.

"Tell me, Johnny, how well do you know Leonard Sawyer?"

With his right hand he now reached over and delicately scratched his left temple, looking at her from below the arch his arm made.

"Mr. Sawyer's shown me a number of kindnesses over the years." He paused, as if deciding whether to continue. "He's a trustee up at the U., perhaps you didn't know that. I played my college ball up there, was on the only undefeated team the school ever had. He always appreciated that. Saw that I had the gift of gab, too, so when I blew out my knee in my second year of pro ball, he got me a sports talk show back here. That's how I started in this business." He spoke carefully, as if intent upon laying out every particular, since he had started. "And come Christmas each year I help Mr. Sawyer out with the *Trib*'s food and toys drive. About time to get going on that again, matter of fact." Something about the completeness of this recitation and the determined manner of his delivery told her what she wanted to know.

"So it was you then," she said. "You're the source." Johnny had to be plugged into the city's black community. It only made sense that he'd know about Sam Turner if anybody did. How ironic, she thought, her bringing Pond's own story back to him.

He smiled, the slightest of smiles, and dipped his head in the kind of gesture that confirmed without confirming.

"But why? It's your story, it's a good story, why not just run it?"

"I'm sure I don't know what you're talking about…But if I *did* know, suppose I'd say something like…" With his large meaty hand he gripped the top of his head, as if it was a football and he was about ready to tear it off his shoulders and fling it as far as he could. "Question is—question you got to keep in the forefront of your thinking—do you want to make a point or do you want to get something done? That's the question." He nodded. "Suppose that's what I'd tell you…if I knew what you were talking about."

Okay, Rachel thought, so now she understood. Pond could have stonewalled, but he'd been honest with her. A little elliptical, maybe, but honest enough. She supposed she could leave it at that. Except that Sawyer's mean-spirited manipulations still stuck in her craw, and it irritated her that Johnny appeared to hold the old man in something close to esteem.

"But you didn't know about the dredge, did you? You didn't know Sawyer was planning to kill two birds with one stone."

Of course he refused to acknowledge this, revealing nothing except in the thin thread of emotions, bare traces of irritation and disgust and resignation that her words seemed to call up from him. "I'll tell you what," he said. "I'll talk to Sam Turner. See what he has to say for himself. Give him one last chance to decide he doesn't want the job. How's that?"

"Thank you."

He was rocking back and forth, just the slightest movement, a trace of agitation. Pond was an interesting character, as self-contained, she thought, as any man she had ever known, and no doubt this slight fissure in his armor would quickly be mended. They looked at each other and she felt the mute understanding that had arisen between them. And she saw the special circumstances under which he operated. He would take steps to bring the Sam Turner matter to the public's attention, but in his own way, for his own reasons.

"I appreciate it, Johnny."

He nodded. "No problem."

∼

She went back to the paper and wrote up both stories. Maybe the dredge story would get spiked, but either way, she was determined to write the piece. She even called upstairs to Sawyer and got a quote out of him, although he wasn't particularly happy about it and told her to make sure she mentioned that he owned the paper.

"Thank you for warning me about that," she said.

So the stories were written. She knew what would happen if they were published. Her relationships with the other *Trib* staffers had become cordial enough, but they didn't really trust her. She was still Sawyer's girl. Now they'd read the pieces, put two and two together, and decide she was at it again, Sawyer's willing cat's-paw. All she wanted was to become a good journalist, and these people dismissed her as a moral bankrupt, just another East Coast carpetbagger come to make her mark any way she could. Was she? Certainly she intended to add to her clips and then get the hell out of there. Did that make her a carpetbagger? Maybe it did.

Several hours later, Johnny called and told her that Sam Turner wanted the job.

# CHAPTER 65

~

The Greyhound Bus was just pulling in as Chuck arrived. He parked, got out, and watched a number of people disembark who were obviously not his man. He'd arrived at the bottom of the list of potential dredge operators he'd obtained from his contact with the Corps of Engineers. Olson, the ex-master of the big Corps dredge, had been the obvious choice, but the fellow had gotten a little too comfortable running the Corps's white-glove operation and didn't have the stomach for the Jackson dredge work. Maybe he could have been pressured, but Chuck wouldn't beg anyone. He went to the next name on his list. And the next. As each successive person had turned him down, he'd been almost pleased. Let's just see how tough this damn job can get.

The fact that this last guy had to come to Jackson by bus didn't exactly fill Chuck with hopeful anticipation, either. Only the incompetent, he suspected, rode buses. The bottom of the barrel. He sat on the hood of the 4x4 and watched as the last rider got off and the bus pulled out, and he was left all alone. "Well, that's that," he said to the empty parking lot. He was on his own.

He drove back up to the Hall, contemplating his fate. The guy he knew in the Corps—the one who had supplied him with the list of names—had also passed along a bit of wisdom. Dredging, he told Chuck, was like working in a medieval guild. Good dredgemen learned their trade by apprenticing themselves to those with years of experience. Swell, Chuck thought. As if the fucked-up condition of the dredge wasn't enough to have to worry about. And the fact that almost anytime now, there'd be ice in the river.

He thought about all the other problems he had, the paperwork for three budgets sitting on his desk, the fact that the city manager had, after all the bad publicity, decided to pull rank and give Sam Turner the job in the drafting room, the rest. A truly fucked-up situation.

Okay, Chuck thought, now things are starting to get interesting.

# CHAPTER 66

~

The field lay across the wedge of land where the Little Mesquatie joined the Mississippi. Throughout the summer, in the droughty conditions, it had been baked hard, but now, after all the rain, Fritz Goetzinger stood staring down not at the earth between the corn rows but at the reflection of the sky from skim ice. Water had backed up from the river. Most likely the Corps of Engineers had raised the gates at the lock and dam downstream, holding back the water so the barge companies could move as much product as possible before freeze-up. The Corps had their clients. They didn't give a damn about the small farmers along the river.

He fetched a pair of waders out of the back of the pickup and put them on, then walked out through the corn rows, breaking the thin ice as he went. He moved slowly against the pressure of water and ice. Most of the ears were high enough on the stalks to be dry. He picked one and peeled back the brittle yellow husk, exposing rows of kernels imperfectly filled out. He ran one finger across the waxy kernels and pressed down on the soft cob where no kernels had grown, contemplating the softness a few moments before casting the ear away and moving farther down the row.

Through his waders, the water made two cold rings around his knees. He picked more ears at random. Most were still okay. As he moved, he flushed a small flock of wood ducks, which rose and wheeled and made a long transit across the sky. Fritz watched them and then, as the birds evaporated in the distance, he heard behind him an engine and turned to follow the approaching sound, invisible until a small, red sports car appeared from behind the spur of the bluff that cut down between the two rivers.

The little car stopped some distance from the pickup, and Fritz waited, expecting it to turn around and leave, but after a long pause it came on again, gliding slowly to the lip of the field.

This pleased Fritz, for he had a question he wanted to ask his son. Yet he turned his back and continued walking, as if the arrival was of no concern to him. He listened carefully to the slight metallic rubbing of the car door opening. He didn't hear it close. At the headlands, he turned and walked slowly back along the corridor of black water he had opened through the shell ice.

He drew near. Junior stood on the low embankment. Even without looking directly at him, Fritz was conscious of the way he stood, as Fritz himself stood, feet spread a little wider than another man might have, as if to gain an extra purchase on the ground. His son idly twirled the blackened floret he had snapped off a stalk of velvet leaf. His camel hair coat flapped open in the cold, gusty air, and Fritz could see that he was dressed up.

For a time, neither spoke. Fritz picked an ear of corn that had slumped and hung half in the water. Such corn, its nutrients leached out of it, was worthless. With a flick of the wrist, he tossed it away.

"Damn Corps of Engineers," he said.

His son said nothing. Fritz squinted up. Despite the cold, Junior wore no hat, his hair mussed by the wind. Beneath the coat he had on a V-necked sweater with a fancy collar, folded like the lapel of a suit coat. His slacks were sharply creased. Shoes shined.

"Guess you ain't going to work," Fritz said.

"Guess not." After a silence, Junior said, "Looks a little damp."

"Bit."

"Shoulda planted rice."

Fritz didn't react to this crack.

"Corn okay?" Junior asked.

"Better'n up above."

"Gonna be a while before you can get the picker in there." His tone had gotten a little less flip.

"Wait until she freezes. I told your mother you're not to harvest this field. I'll do it myself."

"Fine by me."

Between each statement and response lay a pause full of calculation. Junior's eye roamed, taking in this and that, like a man waiting for someone who might come or might not, but one way or the other, it didn't make much difference.

Fritz's legs had started to go numb from the cold water. He struggled back up the short embankment, reaching out so Junior would lend a hand. Their eyes met for a moment. Junior's were as noncommittal as everything else about him. He started to look away, then caught himself, and for a moment more held Fritz's gaze, and the father imagined that he saw a question beginning to form beneath the feigned indifference. Then Fritz got his footing, and they turned away from each other.

Back at the pickup, Fritz folded down the waders and stepped out of them. One of his ankles throbbed from where he'd banged it against a piece of machinery that morning. Junior was still looking out across the field—toward a strip of willows in the distance, willows and cottonwoods, and beyond, the mists drifting down the Mississippi.

"I see where Skip Peterson's decided to go after the employees' savings," he said without turning.

Fritz looked the other way, up the valley of the Little Mesquatie with its steep limestone cliffs, ridges covered with hardwoods, and farther to the north, the opening of another valley, once the course of the Mesquatie, but long ago abandoned by the river.

He didn't want to talk about this latest wrinkle in Peterson's buyout scheme—the 401(k) money.

"Even if the IRS okays it," he told his son, "the employees aren't gonna remove that money from safe investments and plow it back into the company, and Peterson's a damn fool if he thinks they will."

Junior allowed as how that was probably true and they lapsed back into silence. Fritz hesitated. The relationship between him and his eldest son had been bad for so long it was hard to see how it could be any different. "Heard you were there," he said when he'd finally gotten ready, "at Richie Chinn's demo."

Junior stared down at the dead velvet leaf, which he still held. "Yup."

Fritz didn't know where to go with this…trying to reach out to his son. "Hardly ever see you at get-togethers on city business."

Junior snorted. "Who'd go if he had a choice?"

"Not you."

Junior said nothing.

"So," Fritz asked, "why did you?"

"What difference does it make?"

This stopped Fritz. Perhaps Junior was right. Perhaps, after all the bad blood, it didn't make any difference. Yet he couldn't help but seek for any sign of a change of heart. He had never given up on the idea that his son might finally come around, for his mother's sake if not for Fritz's. So much potential, and look what he'd turned into. A damn shame.

"You came," Fritz said. "Something must have brought you."

Junior shrugged. "I don't know. Chance to check out a fellow bullshitter, I suppose."

"I'd appreciate a straight answer for once," Fritz told him.

Junior shrugged. "Chinn had a snappy routine."

"And what's that supposed to mean?"

"Nothin'. It was a well-honed spiel is all. Expect he's used it before."

"So?" Was a time when Junior's snotty attitude would have set Fritz off, but that time had long passed. Still, it rankled. It did something more. He felt the pain of it.

"Sometimes people are just too good," Junior said. "Chinn, you ask me, was just too damn good."

"That makes a lotta sense."

"Chinn call you first, did he?"

"He did."

"Did he just come here, or was he going around putting on his dog and pony show for other packers, too?"

"I don't know."

Junior nodded. "I figure if he's for real, he'll want to deal with a company that's going to be around awhile. Either way, it's not gonna help you."

"We're not going to be around awhile?" Fritz stared at his son. "Is that what you think? Where did you find out? While you were playing cards? While you were chasing women? Look at you, standing there dressed like a damn pimp. Where do you come off telling me what's gonna happen?"

Junior tossed away the weed, smiling and shaking his head. He looked back over his shoulder toward Fritz. "We're alone, Dad, you don't have to bullshit me. One way or another, JackPack's going down. Maybe Chinn was gonna be your last big chance to save the day. Maybe, but no way it's gonna happen."

"You don't know that. You got no right to know that," Fritz snapped at him, but Junior simply went on with his thought.

"Whatever's done now, Peterson and Budge are gonna have to do it. But I'll tell you what I think. Even if they contrive to put something together, sooner or later, you'll screw it up. You'll find some reason to be against the thing, you always do. That oughta be enough to kill it."

Fritz should have figured that this was the kind of garbage that would come out of his son's mouth. "I don't know why I bother to ask you anything," he said bitterly.

"Beats the hell out of me, too."

Fritz turned away and flung his waders violently into the back of the pickup and climbed behind the wheel.

"Goddammit," he said as he turned the ignition.

He swung the truck around the sports car, barely looking where he was going, and heard the back end clip something. In the rearview mirror, he watched Junior run over to inspect the door that had been left half-open. Serves him right, Fritz thought. God-damn kid. Never again, he promised himself, never again.

# CHAPTER 67

~

Skip moved quickly, the same double-time pace he'd used as tour-guide at JackPack, but this time, in the family manse, giving a rapid-fire disquisition on Italianate architecture. Not as interesting as dissecting hogs, Rachel decided. Her attention lingered on him, anyway, not on the inlays and imported marbles and hand-carved finials. For the Peterson Thanksgiving dinner, he had turned himself out. She liked the informal way the elegantly tailored suit hung on his spidery frame, his long hair combed straight back. Up in the square cupola atop the mansion, she became conscious of his aftershave lotion, mixing with the dusty, neglected odor of the tiny room. Through the arched windows, the city spread around them, like a 360-degree panorama in a set of old lithographs. They went from window to window, stooping down slightly as with one hand he pointed out the sights, the other resting lightly on her back.

When they returned downstairs, descending the long, wide staircases to join the others, it occurred to her how very often he had, in his schoolmasterish fashion, told her more than she wanted to know about one thing, and less about something else.

"Now the introductions," he said.

He swept through one room, poked his head into another, greeting each person he encountered but passing on without taking the time to introduce her. "Most of the family is scattered, but we still get a good turnout for Thanksgiving." Rachel had noted all the out-of-state tags outside—Illinois, Wisconsin, Minnesota, one even from Ohio. Many of them would belong to people who had once lived in Jackson, where the Petersons were a dying family.

Finally, Skip found the person he was looking for, an elderly woman seated in a drawing room of the old house with one foot resting on a needlepoint stool.

"Aunt Louise," he said, raising his voice, "I want you to meet Rachel Brandeis. Rachel is the one whose stories you've been reading in the *Trib*."

Aunt Louise grabbed Rachel's hand and pulled her close. "You're the reporter?"

"Yes, ma'am."

"I like your stories. Thank God for them." Rachel leaned awkwardly forward, staring into the old lady's face, at once keen and vague. "My nephew never tells me anything."

"He never tells me anything either."

Aunt Louise was delighted. She kept on pulling on Rachel's hand, in a kind of rough camaraderie. "Good, then we understand each other."

Skip laughed. "Pish posh, auntie."

"Pish posh yourself," she said to him, then to Rachel, "You keep it up."

As he led Rachel away, she said, "See, someone appreciates my writing."

"We all suspect that auntie's beginning to lose it."

Rachel knew about Aunt Louise—Louise Nevins, the doyenne of the family, the last surviving member of her generation. That she approved of the stories surprised and pleased Rachel. Could it be true that she knew things that Aunt Louise didn't? Was Skip that tightfisted with information?

The next introduction hardly matched the triumph of the first. Skip led her to a very tall personage standing somewhat apart in the next room. He reminded Rachel a little of Skip, a Skip who had been stretched upon the rack.

"Rachel, I'd like you to meet my cousin, Karl Nevins. Karl is Aunt Louise's son."

Nevins extended one long hand toward Rachel.

"And this, Karl, is Rachel Brandeis," Skip informed his cousin.

Nevins's courtly expression changed at once. He turned sharply toward Skip. "The *Trib* reporter? Is this a news conference?"

"Since Rachel decided not to go back to the East Coast to be with her family," Skip explained blandly, "I thought it would be nice if she could have Thanksgiving dinner with us."

Karl Nevins's clothes hung upon him in an even more drapey fashion than Skip's. From his wide shoulders and the beginnings of a widow's hump, an enormous sports jacket descended in great lappets like a tweed waterfall. He withdrew his hand, gave Rachel a perfunctory nod, said to Skip, "I'll see *you* later," and stalked off. In her plumbing of the Peterson history, Rachel had learned a little about Nevins. He and Skip were the family representatives on the company's board of directors. That was one thing. The other was more interesting if somewhat less specific. She understood that within the family orbit, the two of them had long vied for hegemony.

"I apologize for my cousin," Skip said, distracted, glancing to the side. "Ah, we seem to have hit the mother lode, here's somebody else you'll want to meet."

Karl at once forgotten, he guided Rachel by the elbow toward a woman standing at the French doors between that room and the next.

"This is Lois," he said. He didn't bother to identify Lois further, since that was hardly necessary.

Lois shook hands firmly, her fingers cool, and said, "Well," her head held back slightly, as if to get a better look.

"I've talked to your answering machine," Rachel said. It hadn't occurred to her that Skip's ex might be at the party.

"Yes, you have," Lois said, clearly interested in this sudden encounter, if only in a kind of taxonomic way. And so, her look said, what do we have here—a mere business acquaintance of Skip's? Or something more?

This unexpected intimation of possibilities startled Rachel, yet she discovered that she was not displeased. Lois's trim figure didn't quite jibe with her plump face. She wore a long, black dress with vivid bead earrings and a gypsy scarf. Part sophisticate, part fortuneteller.

A large, soft-looking man stood a pace away with his back turned. "And this," Lois said, pulling him by the coat sleeve, "is my friend Larry." Larry turned around and grasped Rachel's hand in both of his own, his palms warm and moist, nodding as Lois explained to him just who Rachel was.

Skip had disappeared, introductions completed. As her boyfriend peppered Rachel with friendly questions, Lois linked her arm through his and listened, her eyes resting on Rachel.

After a while, Skip came back, and they all went in to dinner, served in the ballroom.

"The place cards are my aunt's idea," Skip explained as he

seated Rachel in the middle of the long refectory-like table. "She got tired of the same people sitting together all the time." Around the room stood satellite tables where the children were gathering, while along one wall the caterers stood at attention. Skip left her, went to the head of the table, behind the turkey, and picked up a carving knife and sharpener. Aunt Louise was already installed at the other end.

When Cousin Karl appeared, a brief drama ensued. He walked slowly, seeking out the card with his name, exhausting all the other possibilities before deigning to approach Rachel. She glanced down and saw his card next to hers at the exact moment he arrived and spotted it himself. Reaching out with one long arm, he plucked it up, and she imagined he was about to make off with it.

"We seem to be sitting together, Mr. Nevins," she said.

He stood silently fingering the card, not looking at her, thinking. Then he replaced it and stood behind the chair. "Yes, we do."

When Lois took her seat opposite, Rachel decided that Aunt Louise hadn't been the only one involved in the seating arrangement. Lois immediately set about introducing Rachel to her neighbors, including Karl Nevins.

"Mr. Nevins and I are old friends," Rachel said.

The dinner began.

Waiting for her plate to be filled, Rachel looked from face to face and observed a certain inward-turning vision in the standard Peterson physiognomy, as if there existed some small flaw in their connection with the world, something gone slightly awry, which they continually fretted over yet could never make quite right. Peering down to the end of the table, where Skip carved the bird with fluid strokes, she made it out in him, too, and wondered why she hadn't noticed it before.

She glanced up at Karl Nevins, intent upon identifying it in his features as well. Even sitting down, Nevins was absurdly tall, his head somewhat small for the long stalk of his neck, his Adam's apple so sharp and prominent it made her uncomfortable. Looking up created a sense of foreshortening, like a figure seen at an extreme angle. She wondered what question might draw him out. Hard to tell, for though Nevins had condescended to sit beside her, he showed no signs of making himself agreeable. Anyway, she decided, questions would be too much like a news conference. Better to wait.

She turned to Skip's ex-wife. The scarf Lois wore turned out not to be of Romany origin at all but a batik design from Indonesia, which Lois imported and distributed in the Midwest, so they chatted about this, talking about Java and manufacturing techniques and the problem of finding reliable suppliers. Lois supposed that as a young workingwoman Rachel didn't have a huge clothing budget, but batik wasn't expensive and could do wonders to spruce up a wardrobe.

Budget, smudget, Rachel thought. "Mostly, I buy separates at Sears."

"All the more reason. I could show you my patterns."

"Yes, you could." Rachel wasn't above using an opening when one was provided. "And we could talk about Skip. After all, you never returned my calls."

Lois stopped eating and clasped her hands above her plate, regarding Rachel cannily.

"No, I didn't." Compared to the Peterson family members, she appeared outgoing and self-possessed.

As the two of them had been talking, the question of Rachel's relationship to Skip—Rachel as the new Lois in some latent way—remained implicit in the looks they exchanged. And now that Rachel had brought his name up, that sense of possibilities intensified.

What was it to be then, this relationship she might or might not have with Skip? So okay, in the presence of a man, any man, she felt sexual tension. Skip, too, he had a roving eye. A lot of older men did, and after her experiences with the males of her own generation, who didn't know from sex, she was almost tempted. Older guys were supposed to be superior *shtuppers*. Maybe, although she had her doubts. But even assuming the sex would be a complete bust, hopping into the sack with Skip had its attractions. Consider the pillow talk. Of course, she'd be totally compromised. So much for little Rachel, the hard-hitting, strictly objective journalist. Then again, in her heart of hearts, wasn't she beginning to believe in the buyout? Skip and the others were trying to break the mold, they really were. Wouldn't it be wonderful to be part of that? She considered these rogue thoughts and then cast them into the heap with all the other unbidden, outrageous possibilities her mind had always been perfectly happy to entertain without her consent.

To Lois, she said, "We could talk about batik, we could talk about Skip, we could talk about other things. As a matter of fact, I'm writing a piece about the women involved in the buyout, the wives of the employees, and it occurs to me that your perspective might be very interesting."

"I don't see why. Skip and I aren't married anymore."

"But isn't that just the point? Wasn't he married to the Pack as much as he was to you?" Rachel became at once aware that several heads had turned in their direction. "Excuse me, I didn't say that quite the way I intended."

Lois snorted. "You didn't?"

Rachel laughed. "I meant to be more politic. I'm sorry. But wasn't it true? I think it's important. Skip's idea, so far as I can tell, is to make all the employees as obsessive as he is."

Lois shifted in her chair in a way suggesting that she was very conscious of the Peterson eyes upon her. But she squared her shoulders and said, "Since you put it that way, yes, I think there's always a problem when the husband's away from home most of the time. But my experience was hardly unique."

"No, but it's not an experience that most of these women have had. You know the pressures, you know what can happen. Nobody's more qualified to talk about this stuff. The employees are going to have to work their tushies off. What happens when their enthusiasm wears off? What happens when they become disillusioned and start taking their frustrations home with them? Think of the strain on their families."

"Now that's interesting." These words came not from Lois but from Cousin Karl.

Well, well, what have we here? Rachel thought. She hesitated for an instant, then thought, No, no, talk to Lois. "It would be really wonderful, Lois, if I could interview you. You'll be the employees' reality check."

Lois smiled, and shook her head doubtfully. "I don't know."

"And they would certainly be interested in what you'd have to say, that's for sure."

Lois still refused to commit, and Rachel made a mental note to talk to Skip about it. And *now*, she thought, for Karl Nevins.

"You said 'very interesting,' Mr. Nevins. Do you mind if I ask what you meant?"

But even as she said this, Rachel realized that she really had ceased to be the guest and become the reporter, not that she was ever anything else. "I'm sorry," she said at once, "I am turning this into a news conference, aren't I?"

"But the point you bring up *is* interesting," Nevins told her. He had stopped to take a mouthful of wine and then pat his lips with his napkin. "Yes, it's *very* interesting, the whole situation. The employees are being given a wonderful opportunity."

"So you support the buyout then?"

"Of course I do. We all do."

"We? The family, you mean? Or the company's board of directors? I understand you're on the board."

"Everybody, isn't that right, Karl?" Lois prompted him.

"Yes. The Jackson Packing Company has meant a lot to this town, still does. So, whatever the odds, we're behind the thing one hundred percent. The family, the board, everybody."

"But the odds are long?"

"Well, of course. Wouldn't you agree?" The change from his annoyed dismissal when she first met him to the pleasant, speculative countenance he now bestowed on her was really quite remarkable. He patted his lips with the napkin again, then unfolded and folded it before laying it back in his lap. "But I'll tell you one thing—Skip's doing it the right way."

"What do you mean?"

"This business with the 401(k) money. You said it yourself, if the employees are going to make a go of this, they're going to have to work their fannies off. No more 7-to-4 and then back home to the wife and kiddies. No, sir. No more forty-hour weeks. No more lazy weekends fishing in the sloughs in their bass boats. So, that being the case, look at the wage concessions and ask yourself if that's enough. I mean, really, giving back wages is pretty commonplace now, isn't it? Take home a few less bucks, keep your job. What kind of motivator do you think that is? Not much, if you ask me." He used his knife to emphasize his next point before neatly cutting himself another mouthful of the bird. Like his cousin, he was very comfortable with a blade in his hand. "But putting your retirement money at hazard, well, that's something else again. Now you're starting to get serious. Now you're starting to separate the goats from the sheep."

"I suppose you're right, Mr. Nevins, but my understanding is the money might not be available. The IRS has to approve, and the union has to vote before individual members can choose to reinvest the money in the Pack."

"We're talking to the union, we're talking to the feds, too. I believe we'll get it done."

"And if you do, what then? Do you think that the employees are, to use your own word, *goats*?"

"I don't know, but we're going to find out."

And that was that. The conversation ended as abruptly as it had begun. For the rest of the meal, he had almost nothing to say to her, and Rachel's attempts to get anything more than pleasant chitchat out of him were to no avail.

~

Skip, intent upon a debriefing and determined to find out what Karl and Rachel had talked about, went in search of her as the party began to break up. She already had her coat on. "I was just coming to find you," she said. "I wanted to thank you for inviting me. I had a good time."

He couldn't talk to her there. "I'll give you a ride home."

"I don't mind walking. It's only a few blocks."

He took her elbow. "I'll give you a ride."

She didn't resist and in a minute they were outside in the cold and heading for the old Volvo he drove in the winter, the 'vette in storage.

The car started reluctantly, and he let it warm up, rubbing his hands together.

"You should have a coat," Rachel said.

"I'm okay." He cupped his hands and blew into them. "So, you had a good time."

"Yes, I did. I liked Lois. We talked about batik."

"I'm sure you did."

"She thought you and I might be an item."

"Really?" A little startled that Rachel would volunteer such information, he wondered if it could possibly be an invitation. "What did she say?"

"She didn't have to say anything."

He switched on the headlights, slipped the car into gear, and started slowly off, peering into the dim afternoon light through the small hole the defroster had managed to make in the fogged windshield and thinking about the possibilities.

"She's still interested in you," Rachel said next.

"Lois?" Slightly deflated, he told her, "We'll never remarry."

"I didn't mean that. I meant she still cares about what happens to you."

"I see. Yes. Well, as I once told you, Lois and I have a good divorce."

Any discussion involving Lois always left its residue of dissatisfaction. He blew into his hands again, one hand at a time. Damn, it was cold! The Volvo slid along the nearly deserted streets. Every once in a while a house appeared surrounded by cars and pickups.

"I asked if I could interview her for the paper," Rachel said and then described a feature she was preparing on the women behind the Pack workers and her idea that Lois could provide a needed cautionary note.

"As if everything you write doesn't come with a cautionary note," Skip observed, regretting the observation at once, a tic of irritation left over from the old days of direct confrontation, not the new, agreeable face he was determined to present to her.

Would it help, he wondered, Rachel interviewing Lois? A cautionary note? What good was caution to the employees now? Skip could see the point of a story about the wives, if only somebody besides Rachel had been writing it. Old Len Sawyer certainly knew what he was doing when he hired her. Bring in somebody with the soul of an outsider.

No matter, no matter, he was bound and determined to be pleasant. He was doing this thing all the way up, right? As for the employees, well, it was certainly true that he needed more than naive enthusiasm here. People better damn well understand what they were getting themselves into.

"I'll talk to her," he told Rachel.

They had already arrived outside the apartment building where Rachel lived. He parked, leaving the car engine running, and shifted in the seat, propping a knee on the console, and looking at her, studying her silhouette. He slid his hands under his suit jacket, one in each armpit for warmth and clutched his elbows to his chest, trying to quell the bursts of shivering.

"I should go," she said, starting to open the door, "look at you, you're freezing."

"No, no, stay. Let's talk."

Reluctantly, she closed the door.

"And what about Karl?" he asked. "What did you think of him?"

"I don't know. He was certainly pleasant enough."

"Pleasant?"

"Yes, it was quite remarkable really. I expected him to bite my head off, I mean, after the way he reacted when you introduced him. But we had a perfectly civil discussion. We even talked about the buyout."

Skip listened, rather gloomily, as she described the exchange. In the dim light, Rachel's voice seemed lower. She hadn't quite gotten back in the car. The door was closed but she remained pressed against it. He remembered her edginess the night he'd taken her out to his home.

The dimness made her appear formidable and aloof, fortified in her thick winter coat and big floppy knitted cap. The glow from a nearby streetlamp frosted her cheek, like a spotlight on a blackened stage. A handsome woman, Skip thought. But part of her had gotten out when she opened the car door, certain possibilities been foreclosed.

She had reached the end of her account of the conversation with Karl, and Skip put aside these ruminations and reluctantly returned to the subject of his cousin. So, with the reporter, Karl had decided not to be himself. It made sense.

"Interesting. He said that going after the 401(k) money was *my idea,* did he?" Of course, this was just the sort of stunt a mole rat like Karl would pull. "Perhaps you misunderstood. Actually, he was the one who brought it to the board. This is off the record, of course. Board proceedings are privileged."

"Why would he claim it was your idea?"

How much could he tell her? How much did he dare tell her? "I don't know, Rachel. I don't pretend to understand the way my cousin's mind works."

"Is it true that you two don't get along? That's what I've been told."

Another question inviting disclosure.

He wanted to tell her. He wanted to tell her that Karl was out for revenge, that he thought the buyout was doomed, teetering right on the edge, and that he was scheming—thinking what could he do to give it the teensiest of shoves? Suppose he brought the employees' retirement money into play, what would that do? Would they invest it in the company? Fat chance. The whole project to save the Pack would just become that much shakier. Even the wages-for-stock plan would be threatened. Of course, Karl was a mole rat, his mind full of tunnels, and maybe Skip had picked the wrong one to crawl down. But it was something like that. Go after the employees 401(k) money, fuck with their minds.

That's what Skip *wanted* to say to Rachel. Did he dare? Sure, he was talking off the record, but what exactly did that mean aside from the fact that he wouldn't be quoted in the *Trib* tomorrow? Rachel was schmoozing with everybody, and loyalties existed on sliding scales. So who had become her familiars? Homer Budge? Given Rachel's family history, that was a good bet. Or what about Len Sawyer? Or even Fritz Goetzinger?

Good God, two months ago, he wouldn't have told her a thing, absolutely nothing, and here he was, ready to spill his guts. Was he crazy? He couldn't do it, he just couldn't do it.

And so, about his relationship with Karl, he said merely, "What's that old Chinese saying—you never find two tigers on the same hillside."

Rachel didn't react to this. Skip understood that such evasions accomplished nothing except to drive them farther apart. Instead, she asked, "Do you really believe, Skip, that the employees will reinvest their retirement money in the company?"

Yet another question that invited one answer and would be given another.

"Yes, I do. You've been studying the campaign Homer's put together. Every day I see more enthusiasm. The employees are going to surprise some people. Maybe you, too. That's one thing. The second is, I'm still looking for money from other sources. It's out there, I just have to find it. A lot of people understand the profound significance of what we're trying to do, Rachel."

He hated saying these things to her. He wanted to tell her he had no hope of finding money anywhere else. He wanted to say he'd get some from the employees but not nearly enough. He wanted to say that the board of directors wouldn't dare throw the company into bankruptcy, not if the employees voted to swap wages for stock, no matter what Karl thought or said or did. He counted on that. The board wouldn't have the balls to shut the place down, but he had to be careful, for if they caught on to the game he was playing, if that went public, he was finished. Karl would have his way. Then the employees *would* have to act like real entrepreneurs. To Rachel he wanted to say all these things, and yet he dared say none of them.

A car stopped beside them and backed into the space immediately behind. They remained silent as the driver got out and went into the apartment building.

Skip's thoughts had returned to his relationship with Rachel, the sad, stillborn quality of it. From the other shore of the darkness separating them, she watched him, chips of light in her dark eyes. Lois had suspected they might be "an item"? Well, Lois had always had a good imagination. Even if he somehow managed to leap across the gap between them, even if by some stretch of the imagination they ended up in bed together, sex with Rachel would be a tricky business. He'd be performing for a score. But at least then the barriers would be down and afterwards they could talk.

Awkwardly, he reached out and grasped her hand. She didn't resist, but her fingers remained passive in his grip.

"Rachel," he called out to her, his voice low, intense. "Rachel." With each exclamation, he squeezed her hand and then continued to hold it.

After a time, slowly, gently, she freed herself.

# CHAPTER 68

～

On the second and forth Friday of each month, Fritz Goetz-inger would stop down at City Hall to pick up his agenda packet for the following Monday's city council meeting. Then on Saturday morning, after he finished his chores at the farm, he'd take the packet and drive around investigating whatever agenda items attracted his attention. First, however, he stopped off at Poor Man's Café, on the road toward Kleinburg, and sat with the other local farmers in Harley Grant's converted milking shed and drank the extra cup of coffee he could never allow himself on weekdays.

And so, two days after Thanksgiving, as always, he parked the old Ford pickup outside Poor Man's and went in. Today, the special on the little chalkboard standing on the easel inside the door was a turkey scramble. Mary Beth must be using up her leftover bird. A handful of the regulars were sitting at the big, round table in the back, convenient to the coffee pot.

Nobody rested on ceremony at Poor Man's, so Fritz poured himself a cup, dosed it with cream and sugar, then settled down among Harley and the others. A light turnout today. Some people were probably still dealing with relatives come to visit over the holiday.

As soon as Fritz sat down, Harley leaned over and tapped him on his sleeve and wanted to know what the hell was going on at the packinghouse with all this business about the employees kicking in their retirement money.

"You don't mind, Harley, I'd like to enjoy my coffee and take a breath or two before I got to talk about the Pack. Seems like that's all I do anymore."

With a single downward jerk of his head, Harley acceded to the request. Everybody sat quiet for a bit, watching Fred Knapp eat his pancakes.

"What's your corn look like, Fritz, got a lot of husk, does it?" Harold Till asked, starting up a round of comments.

"Hasn't got a lot of anything," Fritz told him.

"A lot of husk means a bad winter."

"What's the Old Farmer's Almanac say?"

Nobody knew.

"Corn looks better in Wisconsin. Jim Yoerger was driving up there last week. You know, up there, hardly no beans. Once in a while a little alfalfa."

"Alfalfa? A dairy operation most likely."

"They probably rotate."

"Yeah, corn and corn."

Harley had been observing Fred as the conversation rebounded around the table. "That's the way to do her, Fred. Eat all that syrup and sweet stuff and then put diabetic sugar in your coffee. Real smart."

"You my wife?"

"Real smart, I'd say."

"You my wife?" In Fred's frustration, half of one of the packets ended up in his mug along with the sugar. He fetched it out and slapped it down on the table. "I ain't come in here to put up with the kind of shit I get at home."

"Easy, Fred, take her easy, or you'll get high blood pressure, too."

Fritz joined in the laughter.

"Ol' Fred, he'll never change," Harley said, speaking to Fritz. "If he's what you got for raw material, I expect the buyout's in a mighty hard way."

Fritz looked at Fred Knapp, staring sullenly into his coffee, and figured Harley was probably right. If the JackPack people were all like Fred, they were in a mighty hard way.

Five minutes later, Merle Dolan came in and got himself a mug of coffee and sat down next to Fritz.

After he greeted everybody, he turned at once to Fritz. "The people at the Pack know what Modern Meat's gone and done out in Kleinburg?"

"Fritz doesn't want to talk about the Pack," Harley warned Merle. "He's sick to death of talking about the Pack, isn't that right, Fritzy?"

Fritz ignored this sally. "What have they done, Merle?"

"Well, you know the JackPack buying station out there, at the S-curve just this side of town. You familiar with the Rose place, right across the highway? No? It's right across the road, could throw a stone and hit it from the buying station. Used to be Pete and Thelma Rose's, you didn't know them, huh? In California now. Anyway, it's been on the market quite a while. They won't lower the asking price. Pete was always stubborn that way. I think Joe Hess—he's the one trying to sell it—pretty much gave up on showing it to people. Not much of a place to begin with, and what with the market being like it is…Anyway, I was talking to Joe the other day. Seems like, out of the blue, he's got an option on the property." He gave Fritz one of those looks you give a person just before you deliver the zinger. "Modern Meat."

Fritz regarded Merle, sensing at once that this information was interesting, although he couldn't see just how right off. "Well," he said, "they're opening up that plant down in Maquoketa, got to be not more than a couple of months from now, so they're gonna need buying stations. Gotta get their animals from somewheres. Must be setting up buying stations all over the place."

Merle was leaning toward Fritz and speaking low, but not so low the others couldn't hear. He'd obviously been thinking about this some. "But right across the road, Fritz. It's almost like they're flipping you the bird."

"Yup," Fritz agreed, seeing the logic, "wouldn't be surprised." Another aspect of the thing had become at once apparent, as well, although it was one that might work in the Pack's favor. "A farmer wants to sell to Modern Meat, he's gonna have to do it right under the nose of the guy he used to sell to, guy who's probably not just someone he does business with, either, probably a friend or neighbor or maybe even a relative."

"Or all three."

"That's right. He hauls his animals in and maybe it's his wife's brother standing there across the street and watchin'."

A couple of the others clucked at this. Tough on a man.

"Can't say I'd mind a little more competition for my hogs," Fred put in, his first words since the pancake and dietary sugar incident, still staring at his mug, but his sullenness beginning to lift.

"You'd sell to Modern Meat, Fred?" Harley asked incredulously. "Here you are, you work for the Pack and you'd go sell to the competition if they gave you a couple more bucks?" Harley was so amazed, he'd forgotten the jokey tone he reserved for Fred.

"That's the free enterprise system, ain't it?"

Fritz didn't say a word. No need.

"I guess when God passed out survival instincts," Harley said, "Fred must've been at the back of the line."

Merle had gone on talking quietly to Fritz. "But why the option, Fritz? That's what I keep on asking myself. Why not buy the place outright? Then they could go ahead and throw up their fencing and a loading chute, and whammo, they're in business."

Fritz didn't know. He'd have to think about it. "Probably a just-in-case. Probably Nick Takus expects the employees ain't gonna buy the Pack after all, and he can pick up our buying stations for next to nothin'."

"Think so?"

"Sure. Makes sense."

Did it? Fritz didn't know. He'd have to give it some more thought.

"Well," Harley said, "I guess this means it's okay to talk about the Pack now. So tell me, Fritzy, I've got a question I've been meaning to ask you. Now that Peterson's decided to go after the retirement money, are you gonna invest your slice of the pie back into the company or what?"

Fred's head came up and looked around at Fritz with interest.

"I expect that's the idea, ain't it?" Harley said when Fritz didn't respond right away. "And being as how you're the mayor and all, and work at the Pack..."

"You think I got a responsibility, Harley, that what you think?" Fritz didn't much like the question. But he knew a lot of people would be thinking it. Harley had always been the man to ask right out what the others were just thinking.

A lot of people would be expecting him to set an example. Fritz knew it. And he carried the burden of what Junior had told him down at the lower field, that the company would fail, and one way or the other it would be his fault. He remembered Edna's fear that they'd be ostracized if people thought he had killed the buyout. He didn't have as much influence as people seemed to think, but that wouldn't stop anybody from blaming him. That was the thing of it—blame, which always got to be heaped up on someone. People thought it didn't matter to him, that he took the measure of a situation and did whatever he figured was right and if somebody didn't like it, that was just the way it was. People seemed to think that doing the right thing made it all easy somehow, as if having lots of enemies was the most natural thing in the world. He noticed that they hadn't tried it themselves.

"Well, I'll tell you what," he said to Harley. "This is the situation. Edna and I owe money on the house, owe money on the picker, owe money on the land I bought way back in the seventies and can't sell and can't pay off, either. Hell, I owe money on the money I borrowed to pay off money I already borrowed. So I guess you could say I need every cent I can get my hands on, if you get my drift."

Harley had to know this was just Fritz's way of not quite answering the question, but he shook his head and grinned and said, "Ain't that the truth. Ain't it, though."

When Fritz left Poor Man's Café, his mood had not improved. Looked like he couldn't go anywhere to escape anymore. He remembered again what Junior had said. He remembered Edna's fears. But most of all at that very moment what he carried away with him was the image of Fred Knapp eating his pancakes loaded down with syrup and drinking his coffee with dietary sugar.

Was there any conceivable way all this business with the Pack could turn out all right?

Well, he thought, looking down at the council's agenda packet lying on the seat of his truck, he didn't know, but right at the moment he might as well go and attend to other people's problems for a bit.

# CHAPTER 69

~

Fritz Goetzinger was the city council's nigger. Didn't matter how low the rest of them got to feeling, they could always think, Well, maybe I ain't much, but at least I ain't him. Hell, Johnny thought that way himself when Fritz had gone and staged one of his hopeless charges in the teeth of the way things were. At least I ain't him, Johnny would say, and then catch himself and think, "Shee-it."

Fritz could be counted on. Do it every time. Now he wanted the city to buy the Pack and lease it back to the employees. Damn fool idea. Never happen. But it was just like Fritz, everybody else going right, he'd go left, the world going up, he'd go down or sideways or slantwise in a corkscrew, anything but up.

Man couldn't live like that without thinking like one of the brothers. Had to have that extra layer of consciousness, the one where he made his private arrangements. His strategy. Got to have a strategy if you wanted to survive in this world.

Fritz talked, and the other council members sank into the recesses of their high-backed leather chairs and swiveled around like guns on an aircraft carrier. El Plowman's gaze swept across Johnny, returned, and paused. Not hard to tell what was on her mind. Same thing that had been on Johnny's, weighing it down since the Sam Turner decision came down. She hadn't said anything, but she knew. Didn't take a genius to figure out that Johnny had been the one orchestrating the publicity campaign that got Turner accepted in the drafting room. Her look said, Okay, you got him the job, I'll remember that.

He looked boldly back. A bold look didn't cost anything. Then he moved his gaze away, as if he'd seen as much as he cared to see.

He wished he could get Turner off his mind. Bad enough he kept on worrying about putting the man in a situation he couldn't handle. Now every time Johnny turned around, there was Sam in person. Ran into him in the convenience store muttering at the displays. Went to the library, there was Sam in conversation with a magazine in the reading room. Used to be every once in a while as Johnny was leaving the house in the morning, he'd see the trash collectors work their way down the street, and there'd be Sam Turner, a skinny shambling fellow, dawdling behind the others and talking to himself. Occasionally Turner would interrupt his monologue with a vague wave and a "Yo, brother," but mostly not. Now seemed like every time Johnny left the house, there were the trash guys and there was Sam, barely visible in the predawn darkness, ambling behind the massive hump-backed truck. Turner must have his strategy for living, too, although damned if Johnny could figure it out. Soon the man would be gone to take up his new life in the city's drafting room. Johnny had argued with himself, argued with his feelings. Getting him the job had seemed exactly the thing to do before it was done, and exactly the wrong thing afterward. Strange how the aspect of a thing could change so fast. Like suddenly seeing the dark side of the moon.

Fritz finally finished saying what he had to say. Nobody spoke, the room as quiet as if somebody had died. The mayor looked right and left at the other council members, who must have been mighty glad right about then they weren't him. He added another couple of sentences to what he'd already said, hoping maybe to encourage others to speak up. Nobody was encouraged.

Johnny glanced at Rachel Brandeis, squeezed between him and Bruce Moss, come to the meeting because the mayor promised to say something that would interest her. Looked like her interest had waned some. She'd stopped writing along the way, then abandoned her notebook entirely.

Finally, from his small table across from the council, Paul Cutler, the city manager, stirred. "If I might," he began, and then, after a pause, "as the mayor spoke, I made a list of some of the pluses and minuses here. Certainly we all want to help the Pack..." He took a few moments, like a man who figured he'd give his listeners a little time to prepare for the bad news. "The only way the city could even consider such a course would be as bridge financing for some private buyer. But even then, even with safeguards to protect the investment, it probably wouldn't be enough. I certainly appreciate what Fritz is trying to do here. I just don't see how we could possibly justify it."

Normally, the manager didn't use Fritz's given name at the council table, so Johnny understood that this was his small way of softening the blow, of pretending this wasn't just another of Fritz's pissant, tilting-at-windmills ideas, not even worth kicking back to staff for review.

But Fritz wasn't the man to back down without a fight. He hunkered close against the council table and took the measure of his adversary.

"City's building the dog track, gonna lease it to the racing association. We justified that all right. No jobs at stake either. Nobody can lose a job that doesn't exist yet. At the Pack, you got twenty-two hundred people about to be out on the street. And you're telling me we can't do it, that it isn't proper?"

The manager again paused before he spoke. Cutler always spoke after deliberation, always used complete sentences, always wanted to make sure the peckerwoods on the council had no doubt of his meaning.

"As you'll remember, Mayor, a bond referendum for the construction of the track was placed before the voters and passed. We hardly have time for that sort of thing here even assuming it would make sense."

But Fritz wasn't done. Cutler could strip him naked, and he'd keep on charging.

"We got a crisis, and I don't appreciate it that people seem to think it's all business as usual. I'd like to see your list of pluses and minuses, Paul. Perhaps they're not so one-sided as you seem to think."

This wasn't what Cutler wanted to hear, but he swallowed his irritation and told Fritz he'd submit a letter to the council at the next meeting.

"Because," the mayor forged ahead, still not done to his satisfaction, "now we've got Skip Peterson talking about the employees putting their retirement money back into the company, too. First the wage cuts, now this. But the employees aren't the only ones with a stake here, folks. What I'll ask you to do, Paul, is add to your list of pros and cons. If the company fails, what do we lose, what does the community lose? How many other jobs will be lost? What about property taxes? What's the shortfall likely to be there? And what about the extra burden on social services, what's that gonna be? Let's look at all the pluses and minuses of the thing. Then we can talk about what we can and cannot do."

To this, the manager assented. He had little choice. Fritz would score his points, win his skirmishes. But the city would never buy the company and lease it back to the employees. Johnny knew it. Everybody in the room knew it. Fritz, too. But he didn't feel beholden to the realities. They, like everything else, had to measure up to his standards. If they didn't, well, then, he'd damn well try to change them until they did.

The council returned to its normal order of business. Johnny felt the sense of relief in the room, another Fritz episode behind them.

For Johnny, there was no sense of relief. He thought about the Pack, and he thought about Sam Turner, about all the coverage Sam had gotten in the media. Two thousand jobs and one job. He was not fool enough to think there was no connection. Oh, no. Not half fool enough. No one had called *Sound Off* to complain, not yet, but after Fritz's performance tonight, it was only a matter of time.

~

At the break, before she went to find the mayor and talk about this latest cockamamie scheme of his, Rachel turned to Johnny. "You've been here a lot longer than I have. So tell me, what does Goetzinger think he's trying to prove?"

"Why don't you ask?" Johnny suggested. "Be interested in what he's got to say for himself."

Rachel went off to talk to Fritz, and Johnny went over and chatted up El, gave her the chance to bring up Sam if she had a mind to. Turned out the matter was closed, nothing to discuss.

Rachel returned to the reporters' table for only a moment. "I'm outta here," she told Johnny and Bruce.

"Wait a sec," Johnny said. "I'll walk down with you."

On the elevator, he asked her what Fritz had said when she put the question to him.

"He told me why he's right."

Johnny chuckled. "Once Fritz's got it into his mind what ought to be done, he doesn't spend a lot of time second-guessing himself."

This obviously cut no mustard with Rachel. "Well, I'll tell you what, if Goetzinger's trying to kill the buyout, his little performance made perfectly good sense. He'll certainly stir up more resentment among the disaffected, playing the tin-pot demagogue like that."

Johnny didn't remember seeing Rachel quite as disgusted as she appeared at that moment, not even when she was talking about Len Sawyer's revenge against the city for taking his precious dredge away.

Johnny said, "Guess that means you've enlisted in ol' Fritz's army of detractors."

They stepped outside. The cold knocked the breath out of Johnny, like a punch to the solar plexus, and he rubbed his hands vigorously together and hunched his shoulders. But even as Rachel put on her gloves and turned up the collar of her coat and tugged down the oversized beret she wore over her thick mane of hair, she seemed to hardly be playing attention to the brisk, icy wind.

"I'll tell you what, Johnny, all my life I've had to listen to that kind of dreck in my own family. My father's a courtroom lawyer. You've never met a man more self-righteous than he is, although the mayor would give him a run for his money. But what I really dislike is this attempt to manipulate people's emotions. That just totally turns me off."

Ah, Johnny thought, so that's it. Her father. He used his voice and measured his words. "One thing you've got to understand about Fritz, Rachel. Maybe your father is that way, but Fritz isn't. I don't believe he ever gives it a thought how people are going to react to what he says. And he knows something, he sure enough does. He knows what's going on here. People like Paul Cutler, why, they might suspect it's not business as usual, but they're not quite sure. Pack's been sick a good long time, they're thinking, maybe its time has come. Anyway, Cutler wasn't hired to change things all around, except by building dog tracks and such. Add a game room to the house, okay, tear the whole place down and start all over, uh-uh."

He turned his back, shielding himself from the wind so he could light his cigarette before he continued.

"I'll tell you what I worry about. I worry about what happens when people don't have jobs. If the company just closes, just like that, you've got twenty-two hundred folks out looking for work. Think about it. One day, twenty-two hundred are working, next day, out on the street. Best they find a way to keep the place open. Best let it die a little bit at a time if it's gotta die. That would be the thing to do. It would be a small mercy. Give people a bit of time. Soften the thing. Otherwise, there's no telling what might happen."

The wind soughed ominously overhead.

"Fritz knows all these things, Rachel. And he's trying. So you give the man his due."

# CHAPTER 70

~

B illy had had enough.
   "Well, let me explain it then!" he said sharply.

"Hear the man out, Collie!" someone called out, and several others joined in a chorus to let him speak, and in this way Billy found that they weren't all against him.

A tall kitchen stool had been set for Billy on the landing, two steps up, where the stairs turned and began a steep ascent to the second floor. Below him, in the host family's living room, the Pack workers from the neighborhood sat on just about anything that was sittable—chairs, sofa, hassocks, the corners of tables, a magazine caddy, a cat's scratching post. Others remained standing, lounging at the back or leaning against doorposts with their arms crossed. The room was close, with odors of cigarettes and cooked fish and pets. Two large, old, black dogs, their tails swishing, wandered around as if unable to get their bearings. This was, by Billy's reckoning, the eleventh of these sessions he'd led over the past two weeks, since Homer Budge came up with the idea. Billy wasn't the same Billy anymore, either. He didn't take people's guff the way he used to.

"If you're not gonna believe me, nothing I can do about it," he told Collie, who'd been giving him a hard time all night. "I'm just telling you the way we're setting the thing up. It's not gonna be top down anymore. It's gonna be bottom up. The work teams can change things, don't have to wait for someone else to tell them what to do. Long as the changes don't affect nobody else, you don't need nobody's approval, neither. Teams can get together and decide things, too. Nothing's nobody's business except those that got a stake in it."

"Bull," Collie said. He'd positioned himself right up front, on a footstool he'd pulled over, and at once had set about peppering

Billy, not believing a thing Billy said. "What about the speed of
the chain, Billy? Suppose the people on the floor decide it's going
too fast. Suppose we decide to cut it in half, Billy." Collie had been
putting Billy's name into practically every sentence, which made
Billy uncomfortable. "You think they're gonna let us do that, do
you, Billy?"

"Yes."

"Come off it!"

"We can do it, but nobody would!" Billy was off his stool. He
clipped the low ceiling and stumbled from the landing down to
Collie's level, rubbing the top of his head. "Look, it'd be stupid!
We'd be cutting our own throats." He was leaning down, still rubbing his head, and staring Collie square in the face, Collie sitting,
short and stocky, hands on thighs, fingers turned inward, elbows
sticking out, shoulders hunched forward, sure of himself.

"Anyway," Billy said, "the speed of the line affects everybody.
We all got to agree before we can change that. Don't mean—"

"That's the friggin' point, Billy!" Collie interrupted, leaping to
his feet and turning toward the others. "They chop the jobs down
so we're all doing the same little bitty thing over and over, they
speed up the line, and Billy here tells us everybody got to agree
before we can do anything about it. Peterson ain't gonna agree. He
likes it the way it is. So how's anything gonna change? I'll tell you.
It ain't."

He was standing between Billy and the others, and Billy spoke
to his back. "We got to compete. Okay? We got to compete. But I
don't disagree with you all the way. I mean, you're right, 950's an
awful lot of animals."

"Oh, 950's an awful lot of animals," Collie said. "Is that
right, Billy?"

Billy moved so he was standing beside him, as if the two of
them were leading the meeting together.

"You got a point, okay?" Billy said. He wanted to be fair.
Seemed like there was always a few people like Collie at these meetings Billy had been leading, people already made up their minds
to vote against the givebacks and wanted to make sure everybody
knew. Billy talked to them, but they didn't hear. But he wanted to
be fair. He knew they had a point. Wasn't no way this could ever be
a 100 percent good thing. "Maybe we can figure a way to cut the
speed down some. Maybe nine hundred, I don't know."

"Nine hundred? Whoop-dee-do."

A hand went up in the back, a sarcastic kid named Ray, one of the chiselers who worked only a few feet from Billy on the kill floor. Billy had been waiting for him to make some sort of snotty comment all night, but so far he'd been satisfied to let Collie do all the mouthing off. Billy looked around to see if there might be somebody else wanted to speak, but the kid didn't wait. He pulled his hand down and started to talk.

"You want me to work this hard, Billy, I wanna get paid for it. For the kind of money you're talking about, I might as well be flippin' burgers at McDonald's."

Billy looked across the room at the young man he'd never liked but who had now surprised him, not with his words but with their quiet, respectful tone. He wasn't trying to be a wiseass for once.

"Might be, you're right," Billy said to him. "I don't know. I keep asking myself, are these jobs worth saving? I wish I knew…"

"Are these jobs worth saving?" Collie interrupted again.

"For Christ's sake, Collie," someone called out, "we know what you think. Let the man speak."

Collie just raised his voice. "Does anybody here think these damn jobs are worth saving? I sure as hell don't. I'll tell you what, they want me to buy the company, they damn well better go back to the way it used to be."

When Billy tried to say this was impossible, Collie merely spoke louder, but more voices rose against him.

"Shut the hell up, Collie!"

"Let the man speak!"

"Sit down!"

Collie put his hands up, in a kind of surrendering gesture. "If you want to buy this line of bull, fine, be my guest." He sat back down on his stool, back to Billy.

The room had suddenly become perfectly still. Billy took a deep breath.

"I look at what I'm doin' now and try to figure how it's gonna be different. What with rotating jobs and so forth, that might make a difference, make things a little easier." Billy moved into their midst, in the center of the small crowded living room, away from Collie. "Maybe, like I said, we can slow the line down some. But most likely I figure to be working harder than what I am already. Maybe it ain't so bad if I own the company. We're gonna cut the blue hats down to size. They'll be working for us now. We won't have to take their crap anymore. And, you know, if we can make it work, why, other companies are gonna be looking to us, taking the measure of what we're doing. That's what I think. So I figure I'm not just taking home a paycheck anymore."

"A worthless paycheck!" muttered Collie behind him.

"Let him finish," someone spoke up at once, and Billy continued, encouraged, feeling more comfortable with people all around him, close enough to touch.

"It's not just the paycheck. It's not just the job anymore, neither. I've been working all my life, just like you. Put in an honest forty hours and got no thanks for it, just what pride a man has doing a decent job. People been working these terrible-type jobs forever and getting their noses rubbed in it to boot. And I gotta tell ya, you ask me, work like this ain't gonna go away anytime soon."

He paused. He could feel people waiting to hear what he'd say next. The kid, Ray, stood only a couple of strides away, and Billy talked directly to him.

"I got no illusions. I'm not an educated man. No way I'm gonna start pulling down big bucks by learning all about computers or anything like that. I lose this job, I don't know, I'll be selling pencils on the corner or something. Or flipping burgers for minimum wage, like you say. Whatever. Doing something takes away all the pride I got left. That's for sure.

"But we buy the Pack, we put in all these changes we're talking about, maybe we'll be able, you know, to outcompete all the companies that treat their employees without respect. Think of what a big difference that could make. A big difference, you ask me. Real big. Nothing you'll ever accomplish flipping burgers, that's for sure.

"We do it, though, we're probably gonna be working harder than ever. Yes, sir. But I figure that's okay, too. I mean, a man got his pride, what difference does it make how hard he works?"

The room was quiet, the only movement the pen of the reporter as she took her notes. Even Collie had shut up for a minute.

Yes, Billy thought, that was pretty much the way he felt about the thing.

# CHAPTER 71

~

From the neighborhood meeting, Rachel drove over to the Budges' home, carrying with her the vision of Billy Noel, hair combed, brown-on-brown checked shirt, creased trousers, neat with a wife's care, standing in the midst of the other Pack workers, his hopes flowing out and embracing them.

She parked on the street in front of the bungalow at 18 Shake Rag Lane. In outline against the night sky, the roof, with its molded gable ends, appeared to be made out of thatch, while below, lights glowed in each window of the trim little dwelling, lively as a jukebox.

Rose Budge proved to be as trim and compact as her house, her hair cut short and thatched like the roof, wearing a blouse with tiny blue stars and a denim jumper and tennies.

"Shake Rag? Yes, a lot of people comment on that. Way in the last century, there was a lead mine nearby. Called the Gobaith. Biggest mine in the city, so I'm told. The Welsh miner's wives used to wave handkerchiefs to call their husbands home to dinner."

Rachel scribbled this down. Maybe she could use it as a hook. Probably not, probably just another odd piece of information to store away higgledy-piggledy with all her other odd bits of this and that.

Rose asked Rachel if she'd like something to drink.

"Tea, if you have any. It's been a long day." From the women of the Pack, Rachel got less hard information, some never really opening up at all, but whatever happened, it usually came with refreshments.

"I think I have some somewhere."

"If it's a bother..."

"No, I just have to find it." Rose was rooting around at the back of a cabinet. "I'd enjoy a cup myself. I never think to make it."

Her tone, however, hinted at disapproval. "Aha! Is this okay?" She held up a box of English breakfast. Rachel said fine.

The interview took place at the dining room table. At first, they talked of inconsequential matters. Children came and went, flybys to check out the lady reporter. The Budges, good old-fashioned Catholics, had been fruitful and multiplied. Old-style Jews were that way, too, and got the injunction from the same place. Children were supposed to be a blessing. Rachel couldn't see it. The house was a bedlam of TV and rock music and other kid noises, which, like a brush fire, would be quelled in one place only to break out somewhere else.

She brought the conversation gradually around to the matter of the buyout. They spoke of women already talked to. Rose was fascinated that Rachel had managed an interview with Skip Peterson's ex-wife. She gave Rachel a couple of more names to add to her list. "Tell them I told you they'd be just perfect for your story."

"Thank you."

Rose settled herself a little more comfortably behind her cup of tea. "But you came here to talk to me. You want to know what I think."

"Yes, I do. As I've talked to women," Rachel started and then, realizing she needed a short preamble, she stopped and started over. "I mean, many women have gone into the workforce, we all know that. But it's no secret that their husbands haven't exactly fallen all over themselves trying to help out at home." Rose smiled and nodded in agreement. "Now women get to have it all, the joy of doing everything if it doesn't kill them first. Still, despite their wonderful careers as realtors or junior execs or whatever, when I talk to them, it's clearly their families that remain uppermost in their thoughts. They're worried about what's going to happen to their kids now that a lot less money will be coming into the house."

"A terrible dilemma, I know."

"And then I mention the 401(k) money!"

"Just awful," Rose agreed, now shaking her head and frowning.

"One woman told me that she had nightmares about it, that she wandered around her mortgaged house thinking, 'Oh my God, what if we lose this, too?'"

Rose shook her head a few more times and then gathered herself together. "My husband is fully aware of this, you know, Rachel. He understands that every family will have to struggle with these issues which are all so…so heart-wrenching. He doesn't want to tell anyone what to do."

"Yes, yes, I'm sure," Rachel said impatiently, "but I want to know what *you* feel." The danger here was that Rose would decide at some point to start referring everything to Homer. "As a woman, how do you address such issues?"

"Yes, I see," Rose said. "But it is so difficult…I hardly know what to say…"

As Rachel waited for a response, she began to feel slightly odd, a queer sensation crawling up her back, and she looked around and flinched. Behind her, in the doorway leading to the kitchen, a young man stood frozen in place, staring at her, something hostile in the stare. His face seemed to harden when he saw himself observed.

"Yes, dear?" Rose said to him, and Rachel caught a warning in her tone, or imagined she did.

Although he was taller than his parents and certainly lacked their composure, he was clearly a Budge.

"This is Miss Brandeis of the *Tribune*. She's here to interview me. I'm sure she wouldn't mind if you listened in."

The young man ignored all this. "Where's Dad?"

"At one of his meetings."

For some reason, this bit of information seemed to upset him. Wordlessly, he disappeared, and in a few moments, Rachel heard the back door slam shut.

"An intense person," she said to Rose.

"That was John Michael, our eldest."

"Why was he so angry?"

Rose drew her mouth out in a slight frown and shook her head.

"Everywhere I go," Rachel said, "I find at least some people who aren't happy with what's going on."

"I suppose that's to be expected," Rose answered.

She clearly had no intention of talking about her son's hostile attitude, whatever its cause might be.

"Anyway…" Rachel said.

"Yes, anyway…"

Rachel waited. In her earlier interviews with Pack wives, she had quickly learned to adjust her usual interviewing technique. Some of them talked a great deal, shaping and reshaping their thoughts as a ceramic sculptor might shape and reshape clay.

Others, and apparently Rose was one of those, would do the work internally, requiring long pauses in the conversation. And so Rachel had learned to wait.

Rose had a squarish, settled face, a slight sadness having taken possession of it. She wore pale red lipstick, not recently attended to, and just a trace of eyebrow pencil and a little color for her cheeks, just a little, but she had left untouched the crinkly look about the eyes. No young girl effect here. A realist, then, like her husband. No doubt a person careful not to say the wrong thing to a reporter. Also like Homer. Rachel had noticed that the maturity in such people, in which they took evident satisfaction, was hardly a simple thing, and if you broke it down, one of its parts, she suspected, would turn out to be resignation.

"When Homer first came home with the news that the consultant's report hadn't been favorable," Rose said at last, "we talked about what we would do if the buyout went ahead anyway. We immediately thought about the 401(k) money. We decided—it wasn't even a decision really, just something we knew we'd do—we knew we'd reinvest the money in the Pack if it came to that. It's not a great deal. Homer didn't work for the Pack as long as a lot of the others, but it's a fair amount. Anyway, by the look of it, the time has come around, and so we're going to go ahead and do it. I guess that's the best way I can answer your question."

"Suppose you do that and the company fails. What will happen then? You've got all these kids, you live in this tiny house. It must be tough to make ends meet as it is. If that money is gone and the union collapses…"

Rose gave Rachel a shrewd look, but then visibly exhaled and settled back and gazed frankly across the table, as a person will who has committed herself to some particular response. She said simply, "God will provide."

Rachel stifled an impulse to make a flip response.

"We must try, too, of course—this isn't a one-way street," Rose continued, more confident now. "Having so many children is a blessing in many ways. One might not occur to you, so I'll mention it. Because we can't provide our kids with all the material advantages that parents with small families can, we've learned to do without certain things. So that's one reason giving up the money is not so difficult as you might imagine. At least for us. As for other people, well, I just don't know. Each family, I suppose, will have to deal with the thing as best they can." She smiled wanly at Rachel. "You don't happen to have any easier questions, do you?"

"I believe I do," Rachel said as she finished jotting down the last quote, thinking she might be able to use it—the advantages of deprivation. "I'm very interested, Rose, in what you think the buyout might look like if women were running it instead of men."

And so they moved on to a discussion of the ways a woman's perspective might be incorporated into the changes being contemplated for the Pack.

As they talked, one of the Budge children, a small boy in pajamas, appeared several times and hovered silently, but with growing agitation, under the proscenium arch separating the living and dining rooms. Finally his mother said, "Yes, Joey?"

He didn't speak but advanced a half step forward, as if poised to beat a hasty retreat.

"This is Miss Brandeis, Joey."

He was bouncing on the soles of his feet, like water coming to a boil.

"Can I show her, Ma, can I?"

"Joey has something he'd like you to see, if that's all right."

"Sure, I suppose so."

Mystified, Rachel looked at his mother, but she just smiled.

The boy dashed off and returned a moment later with a scrapbook, which he carefully placed on the table before Rachel, then aligned with the care of a land surveyor, and finally when satisfied, opened, the big cover swinging up and over to reveal one of Rachel's own *Trib* stories, carefully trimmed and pasted onto the thick, manila pages. He handed her a pen.

"Could you please sign your name, please?" he asked.

"An autograph. Good grief." She laughed awkwardly and looked again at his mother.

From the kitchen came the sound of the back door opening, and moments later Homer Budge appeared in the doorway to the dining room.

"Joey has decided he wants to be a reporter when he grows up," Rose explained to Rachel.

"You do, huh?" Rachel said to the boy.

"Yes, ma'am."

From the door, Homer said, "A month ago he wanted to be a cartoonist. Now, thanks to you, he has a higher calling."

Self-consciously, Rachel signed her name where Joey indicated. "I'm sure," Rachel said to Homer and Rose, "if you're patient, he'll end up in medical school yet." She swung the book around so that Joey could check out her signature. The boy, however, quickly realigned it, turned to the second page, and handed the pen back to her.

Rose, seeing what was about to happen, said, "No, no, Joey, only once."

Joey hesitated. Rachel handed the pen back, relieved. "Your mother's right." She leaned closer so that she could speak *sotto voce*. "You wouldn't expect an author to sign every page of his book, now would you?"

Reluctantly, he accepted this rationale, although it clearly didn't sit well with him.

He wasn't, however, done. Lovingly, he began to turn the pages, one after another, unfolding the sheets which had been too large to paste in flat, his fingers manipulating the pages as delicately as if they had been the wings of butterflies. Rachel, attending this exhibition, felt like an artist who, when wandering idly through a museum, had suddenly stumbled upon a room filled with her own work.

"Okay, Joey, that's enough," Rose said. "Your father and I have got to talk with Miss Brandeis now."

"No, no," the boy protested and speeded up. Turn, unfold, press down, display for an instant, fold, turn again…

"He's not like this with other people, I can assure you," Rose said to Rachel.

"Come on, Joey," Homer told him, approaching, "that's enough." And Joey went even faster, and all at once, one of the pages ripped. Joey froze.

"Oh, dear," Rose said.

"That's okay," Rachel said, rescuing the moment. "What story is it?" She looked at the date on the paper. "I'll send you another copy."

"Isn't that nice?" Rose said. Seeing her son's distress, she came around the table, leaned down, brushed his hair back from his forehead, and patted him. "You should thank Miss Brandeis," she said softly.

But Rachel could tell he wasn't at the moment quite able to speak, and she quickly put in, "That's all right." An awkward silence followed, until Rachel thought to say, "You know, Joey, I keep a scrapbook, too." He looked at her through his shiny eyes. "Reporters all keep stories we've written. We call them our clips. We use them when we apply for jobs at other newspapers."

"Really?" he managed.

"Really."

"Okay, dear," Rose said to her son, patting him again. "Now we really must let Miss Brandeis finish her business."

Reluctantly, Joey patched the rip as best he could and closed his scrapbook, and then, covertly wiping his eyes with the back of his hand, he left the room.

"If you don't need me," Homer said to Rachel, "I'll be off, too."

"Actually, Homer, I do have a couple of questions I'd like to ask when Rose and I are through."

"All right." He tossed his coat over the back of a chair and sat down.

In the presence of her husband, however, Rose became much more reticent, and it quickly became apparently that the interview was for all intents and purposes over. Rachel would have to make do with the material she already had.

"So *I'll* be off then," Rose said with relief.

"No need," Rachel told her. "I'd like you to stay." But Rose had already gone, returning briefly with more hot water to pour into Rachel's mug.

Homer, in the meantime, had moved over to where Rose had been sitting earlier, and Rachel became, in turn, conscious of the wife in the husband—short, stocky, self-contained. His face, a more public face, seemed to reflect the question he was about to ask.

"You had something you wanted to talk to me about?"

Rachel meditatively dunked her old tea bag into the hot water, and then sipped the weak, hot liquid, finding herself reluctant to bring up what would be an unpleasant subject. Since unpleasant subjects were her business, however, she quickly breached this obstacle.

"I've learned that two members of the union's executive committee have quit."

As she waited for a response, she flipped to a new page in her notebook.

"Yes," Homer said, then fell silent. She sensed his withdrawal.

She listed the names she had, and he confirmed them.

"I know this is something you'd just as soon keep out of the *Trib*, Homer, but you must understand that's not possible."

"I suppose."

"I know," she told him, "it's painful when old comrades fall out." Hearing herself use the word *comrades*, she realized that the union defections had brought to the surface recollections of the many stories in her own family about their radical past, all the conniving and infighting.

Homer remained silent as she related her understanding of the situation. Before union members could choose individually to invest their 401(k) funds in the company, the union would have to approve. There would be a vote, and a fight had broken out over what the executive committee's recommendation should be. The defectors wanted to tell the rank and file to vote no. Then it wouldn't make any difference what individual members wanted to do. They couldn't reinvest that money in the Pack.

"Yes, yes," Homer said, rousing himself, "but before we get into that, I want to say something." He adjusted the chair so that he faced more directly toward her. "This is a very difficult time, Rachel. Not just for me. For everybody. Okay, there are different points of view, I respect that." As he spoke, he pressed his forefinger repeatedly against the table, like someone typing the same letter over and over. "But what we've got to understand here is that relationships are more important than issues. When this is over, the issues go away, but the relationships remain. You see what I'm saying?"

"Yes, of course. And I'm sure that's very generous of you." By which she meant, Homer's opponents were unlikely to reciprocate, viewing this as a zero-sum game. Homer smiled painfully. But he forged onward.

"I mean it. When this is over, the relationships *will* remain. We all need to remember that."

Out of respect for this sensibility, Rachel paused before delivering her next question. But she thought, so relationships were important, so who didn't know that?

"This split has been a long time coming, is that right?"

He took a deep breath and expelled it slowly, looking at her, a disappointed look, but then he nodded.

"The union's a democratic organization. There have always been splits of one sort or another, so I'm not sure what you're getting at. I can tell you one thing, everybody on the committee is a good union man. But the thing of it is, you won't find what we're doing now in any union manual of arms. So it's only natural, people disagree. In a way, it's not about the union at all. We're trying to get our people used to the idea of running the darn company. So you tell me two of my people have quit and ask what does this calamity mean, and I say, isn't it wonderful it's only two? We must be doing something right."

Of course, he hadn't really answered her question, determined, apparently, to keep the conversation as fuzzy as he could. She pushed on, extracting shards of hard information, from which later she'd try to piece together a whole pot. Homer remained doggedly charitable to all his fellow unionists.

During the exchange, Rose Budge reappeared in the doorway of the kitchen and leaned against the jamb, listening. Rachel supposed she'd been listening all along.

"Why don't you take Rachel over to Power of Prayer, Homer?" she suddenly proposed.

Homer's expression showed clearly that this idea was as distasteful as it was unexpected.

"Power of Prayer?" Rachel asked.

"It's awful late," Homer said to his wife.

His wife smiled. "You think maybe they won't be open?"

"Rachel wouldn't be interested in that sort of thing."

"That sort of thing?"

"You know what I mean. It doesn't have anything to do with the company."

"Oh, I think it does, dear. I think the Power of Prayer has to do with everything." Rose spoke softly, turning her attention toward Rachel. "I understand Homer's reluctance here. But he wants to do what's right and proper. People don't give credit. Maybe you won't either. I can see that you're a very skeptical young woman." She turned back toward her husband. "I think Miss Brandeis is so concerned with the specifics of the thing that she's missing something more important. You do want her to understand, don't you, dear? She never will if all you ever do is talk about the buyout."

As she spoke, Rose had laid the palm of her hand against her breast. The gesture seemed unconscious and lent persuasion to her words.

Homer sat stony-faced as he listened.

But a few minutes later, dutifully driving Rachel to see the Power of Prayer, he explained, "Rose takes all this stuff at the Pack pretty hard. Harder than you'd think. Looking at her, she seems to be such a tough ol' gal. Used to be, I'd get pretty upset, too, but after a time you build up, you know, calluses. Not Rose, though. She isn't the kind of woman ever gets used to it."

"What exactly is the Power of Prayer?"

"I'd better show you."

As they drove down through the bluffs, Rachel thought that perhaps Rose was right about her husband. Perhaps he only wanted to do what was "right and proper." In the absence of the necessary drive—the willingness sometimes to be not nice, sometimes even downright nasty—propriety seemed to her, however, like pretty small beer.

Downtown, Homer pulled into a parking lot next to a one-story commercial building, a structure like a thousand others Rachel had seen, strictly utilitarian, devoid of any trace of the interest or quaintness Rachel had, for instance, glimpsed in the design of the Budge's crowded little bungalow. Darkness hooded the building's front rooms, but from deep inside came a faint, wavering glow, and this served to light their way as Homer opened the front door and walked softly down a narrow central corridor.

Approaching the end, Rachel became aware of the odor of burning candles. They entered a room, and at once the merely functional aspect of the building gave way. At one time, no doubt, the place had served some mundane purpose, for conferences or the like, but of its former use, no trace remained. Although window-less, stained glass pictures, like windows, had been hung around the walls. Pews were arranged in a neat series toward the front, elaborate edifices of polished wood with saintly figures carved in their armrests. An old woman sat in the foremost pew, the only other person in the room, praying. Before her stood a long table, on the ends of which flickered candles. In vases, on either side of a tall case in the middle of the table, nodded roses and lilies. The case itself contained a sunburst mounted on an elaborate pedestal. In the middle of the sunburst shone a translucent white disk and on top of it, a small cross.

The deep silence in the room, such a contrast to the hubbub in the Budge's house, seemed to crackle in Rachel's ears. Homer genuflected, sat down, and bowed his head briefly before getting back up and taking Rachel out into the hall, where they could speak without disturbing the woman in prayer.

He spoke barely above a whisper, telling Rachel that always someone was praying in the little chapel, that Power of Prayer had been founded twenty years before as a devotion to Mary, the Mother of Jesus, whom Homer referred to as the Blessed Mother. The object in the case was called a monstrance and contained wafers—the Host—that had been blessed by a priest.

Rachel had known that Homer was Catholic, but like many facts that are learned secondhand about a person, this one had made no particular impression on her, not until now, in that quiet sanctuary, filled with the scent of beeswax candles and gently wavering light and silence.

Yet he spoke simply, providing a description rather than a testimonial. Expressing one's beliefs, after all, was always something of an imposition, as he undoubtedly understood.

The people praying, he whispered, devoted themselves to the Adoration of the Blessed Sacrament. They believed in the power of prayer to bring peace to the family, to the world, within the human heart. It was vitally important, Homer said, that someone always be present. "We need to be constantly at prayer," he continued, "to always be speaking with the Lord. How else can we achieve this peace we all want?" His enthusiasm had begun to peek through his reserve.

As they were talking, another person came along the hall, and passed into the chapel, briefly illuminated, a man this time, quite young, carrying a Bible. People come for an hour at a time, Homer said, the same hour each week.

"And when do you come?" she asked.

"Wednesday, between three and four a.m."

She groaned. "Self-flagellation."

She meant it as a joke, but this subject was obviously not one Homer joked about. "You get used to it" was all he said.

"And this is what Rose wanted me to see? It's all the business about wanting peace, I suppose." Rachel was being more cavalier than she intended, but places like Power of Prayer gave her the willies, not that she'd ever been in a place quite like that before. But some situations just came with the willies attached. And all this business about peace and the sincere differences among loyal sons of unionism got on her nerves. "Peace is all well and good, but it seems to me that sometimes you better be prepared to fight for it."

Rachel had bent her head near Homer's, the light drifting like dust through the frosted glass of the door.

"I think," Homer said reflectively, "it's not so much a matter of peace. That's the goal, yes, but you're right, sometimes it's necessary to fight. Human beings leave a good deal to be desired." He chuckled, the first sign of humor she seen in him since his young son had been sent off to bed. "The reality of the thing is that, fight or not, the buyout's a long shot." He quickly told her that that last remark was off the record, but repeated it anyway, as if to underline his awareness of the fact. "When I talked about the importance of relationships earlier, Rachel, this is what I meant. This is why I think Rosie wanted me to bring you down here."

"Relationships?"

"Here at Power of Prayer, I'll grant you, it's a little different. I wouldn't expect you to understand the nature of the relationship that a Catholic has with the Blessed Mother. But what are human relationships if not an attempt to live up to our ideals, whatever they happen to be?"

"Ah," Rachel said, thinking at once of that old Hasid, Martin Buber. I and Thou.

"The buyout," Homer said, "really isn't all that important, you see."

As they were leaving, he requested that she not put anything about the Power of Prayer into her story.

"Frankly," she told him, "I don't see how it would fit…But I'd imagine you'd want me to use it if I could."

"Yes, but…well, there are quite a few people in Jackson that would—I don't know—would just take it the wrong way."

"Yes," she said upon second thought, "I can see that might be the case."

"Thank you."

The first few blocks on the way back, they drove in silence. But then Homer, perhaps as a matter of simple politeness, perhaps of genuine curiosity, asked about her religious experience, "if you don't mind. I have to confess that I don't know much about the Jewish faith. The Old Testament, of course."

"Nice Jewish girls are more dutiful than religious," she told him at once, but this selection from her store of cynical epigrams seemed a little too harsh given the obvious sincerity of the question, so she added, "I come from a line of socialists and other nonbelievers. Gentiles seem to think that Jews are this pious lot, but most of us aren't. Although, it *is* true, my parents and their generation did go back to the temple after the Six-Day War. That was 1967. The Israelis routed the Arabs, and suddenly everybody was wild for all things Jewish. I was just a little kid. What did I know? Anyway, I went to temple and the idea, I guess, was that I'd be Bas Mitzvahed, which is a kind of coming-into-womanhood ceremony for girls. I even learned some Hebrew, but it turned out I liked the bits and pieces of Yiddish I picked up a whole lot better. I met my best friend Sheila in temple. But after a time, it all seemed pretty dull. Who wanted to bake cookies and sit around all day talking about what it meant to be Jewish? So I kept Sheila and forgot about temple."

He didn't say anything for a while, and she listened to the car's laboring heater and felt the thin stream of half-warm air against her calves.

"And what about your parents?" he finally asked. "Did they continue to go to temple?"

"On the High Holidays—Rosh Hashanah, Yom Kippur. Like Christians going to church just on Christmas and Easter."

Since a note of sympathy had been struck between the two of them, Rachel hated talking like this, but what was she supposed to do, lament for her lost faith just to be polite? She felt the barrier going back up. It was too bad, it really was. And it was true, she lived with the incompleteness of her parents' attempt at belief and with her own complete disbelief, but so what? Everybody lived with all kinds of limitations.

"Thank you for sharing that," Homer said. "Yes, I'm sure it is a lot like many Catholics nowadays. I appreciate your honesty." He thought about this for a time, and then he added, "There are, after all, many ways of keeping faith."

~

Finally, back at the paper and on deadline, Rachel dashed off the story on the two men who had quit Homer's executive committee, a standard piece of journalism. After that, she carried one of her own tea bags down to the caf and got a cup of hot water and walked back with the tea steeping. In front of the computer terminal once more, she jotted down some ideas about the story on the wives of the Pack workers. That done, she riffled through her notebook until she got to Billy Noel.

She opened the story, slugged it with NOELPROFILE, and sat back, staring at the mindlessly blinking cursor. This wouldn't be a piece of standard journalism. This would take some time. She was glad she'd found Billy. He was clearly Everyman, her Willy Loman. He deserved the best.

She sipped her tea. For important stories, reporters had different techniques. Some began in the middle. Others wrote down any old thing as a first approximation to the opening lines, then went on to finish the rest of the piece before returning to deal with the beginning. But Rachel couldn't do that. She would practice openings as she drove around or took a bath or ate, discarding one after another until she had to abandon the whole enterprise for a time and try again later.

But every once in a while, she would experience a moment of grace, and the lead would magically appear, to be snatched from the ether and transcribed before it could slip away. Now, sitting in the nearly deserted newsroom and leafing through her notes from the first interview with Billy, her glance passed over a certain quote, stopped, went back. She read it once, twice, then took a deep breath and began:

> "I'm not a very good knife man. But I make the standard. There's more days I'm plus than I'm minus. But it's fast now. We do 950 hogs an hour. And that chain has a tendency to crawl on us. One day, someone yelled at the steward to go check. They were coming off like bullets. The line was going 976."
>
> The speaker is Billy Noel, one of the headers at the Jackson Meatpacking Company. Noel trims jowl meat off the hog carcasses, another hog every four seconds. He has worked for the company for 34 years, and it's in his hands, and those of long-time employees like himself, that the fate of JackPack now rests. But the relationship between the employees and the management at the firm has for many years been strained, never more so than recently, and so while no one wants the company to close, while many speak bravely about the future, it is the past that haunts most conversations.

*"Sometimes," Noel, who represents the rank-and-file employees on the buyout committee, says, "I get to wondering if a job like this is worth saving."*

At this point Rachel stopped and looked back at what she had written so far. Yes, she thought, this will do.

A moment of grace.

# Part VI

# CHAPTER 72

~

Sam Turner was talking to a bunch of birds holed up in a pine tree at the corner of Langworthy and Milk, saying his good-byes. The invisible flock chirped away, announcing the dawn, although there wasn't much dawn to announce.

"Sounds like you got a party going on in there. Bunch of party animals, are ya?" Sam didn't know what kind of birds they were, maybe a mixed flock like you got this time of year. He wouldn't mind sitting on a branch, twittering away and seeing the world bird-fashion. Birds must know something people didn't, or why sing like that?

He knew what kind of tree it was, a Scotch pine, not much more than a dark, scraggly shape in the bad light, branches going every which way, some short and dense with needles, others long and clumpy. Every Scotch pine had a different idea what shape it should be.

Sam was sorry he wouldn't be coming by that corner at dawn anymore and hearing those birds and seeing that funky tree.

He turned and trotted after the others. He was picking with Casey while Daryl drove, the grainy dawn light overhead trying to roust out the night, but the night not in a rush to go anywhere. Cold. When Sam jogged and his breathing came quicker, he felt the needles in his lungs.

He was trying to concentrate on what he was doing. Each step the last. Last time he'd pick up the garbage at 451 West Langworthy. This time tomorrow he'd still be laying in bed, thinking about getting up and going down to City Hall and starting his new life. At the moment, it seemed easier to be up and doing rather than lying around worrying about what was gonna come next.

The truck bucked in low gear. Daryl drove for shit. Casey was already jogging toward the next island of refuse. Sam lagged behind, alone, tailending like he always did, catching up just in time to upend cans and sling bags.

Last time he'd pick up the garbage at 499 West Langworthy.

"Gear it!" Casey yelled up to Daryl and then impatiently ran the blade through its cycle, sweeping the rubbish up from the hopper.

"Let's go! Let's go!" he yelled as soon as that was done.

Casey was one driven dude. Worked two jobs, sometimes three, anything that would bring in a few more bucks. Crazy to make money, didn't matter how, it seemed like.

They loped from house to house, dumping the garbage cans into the hopper, tossing in the bags of trash. Sam's skin burned. So cold it might be hot.

He kept on trying to concentrate on what he was doing, even though it was only picking, the kind of job people were putting down all the time. But there were worse jobs than hauling trash, a lot worse.

The dawn came slowly, not rising into the deep blue-black of the late night sky but flowing like colored water along the rim of the sky.

They passed the big Catholic cemetery. They passed the historical marker where there used to be a lime kiln. Sam knew all about the lime kiln. They passed the dirt turnoff where kids dumped the cars they took for joy rides. Last time, last time, last time.

At 814 Highland, he paused a few extra moments at the house where a woman used to put out milk and cookies for him and Casey and Daryl. "Like we was Santa Clauses." Reverse Santa Clauses, come to take away what nobody wanted no more. Old lady died or something.

And then it was Sam's turn to drive. Sam and Daryl were the pickers, Casey the driver. Case could have driven all the time, but he was a good guy and divvied it up. Sam concentrated on the smooth operation of the machine. He never drove as fast as Casey wanted, even slower today, figuring the chances of having an accident went way up the last time you were doing something, like soldiers killed just before they were supposed to go home.

"Gear it!" Casey yelled up to the cab, and Sam engaged the PTO and shifted into neutral so Case could run the blade through its cycle. They almost had their first load, and Sam could imagine Casey back there feathering the blade or maybe air hoppering it as he tried to pack in that last little bit of shit. Packing a load tight was a matter of honor for Casey.

When they had the truck filled, all three of them climbed into the cab. Casey drove, Sam sat in the middle, and Daryl rode shotgun.

"Last day," Sam said after they got settled and Casey started toward the landfill hell-bent for leather.

"So you're really gonna do it?" Casey asked.

"Expect so."

"No more getting up at four thirty and freezing your ass."

Sam shrugged. "Pickin' ain't so bad. I don't mind." A little hard on the legs. But he got $9.26 plus benefits, and once they finished their two runs, they was through for the day, didn't make no difference when it was. Bust his hump, get through at noon, go on home. He could've kept on doing it. Given a choice, he would have. But he figured he didn't have a choice. It was time to move on.

"I've been keeping track," he told them.

"Of what?"

"Lots of times, you don't know when it's the last time for something. The last snow of the winter, a little thing like that, or maybe the last time you see your friend before he gets killed or something."

Casey laughed.

"I want to remember it is all," Sam told him. "I don't want it to be just another day picking."

"Ain't much memorable about hauling trash, you ask me, last day or any other day."

They were silent for a time, and then Sam said, "I remember my brother Raymond. Last day I saw him, I never knew. Me and Raymond was fighting at the breakfast table, you know, like brothers do, nothing to it. Then Raymond left, supposed to go to school. And we never saw him again, just like that, got no idea what happened to him or where he got to or anything."

"I got a brother I wouldn't mind that happening to," Casey said.

The vacant lot at Asbury and Lime had a temporary orange fence around it and Christmas trees trucked in to sell, which reminded Sam of the scene at the corner of Langworthy and Milk. Most Christmas trees were Scotch pines, that was something Sam knew. The little trees were nice and symmetrical, just like people wanted. Only later, if they were let alone, did they grow this way and that, each becoming its own self. Sam told this to the others.

Casey laughed. "You certainly know a lot of odd shit, Sammy. Who's gonna keep me informed after you're gone? Sure as hell won't be Daryl." Daryl never had much to say for himself. He had a hernia. Talked about that sometimes.

Casey swung the rig onto University.

"So, tell me, Sammy, you nervous about going up there to City Hall?"

Sam was conscious of the three of them swaying back and forth in the cab as the truck leaned on the curve and then righted itself and began the run down toward the OkyDoky convenience store.

"I ain't nervous," he said. "I figure it's like athletes before a big game, gettin' an edgy feeling, something like that. If they don't, then probably they're gonna play for shit. I figure it's like that."

"So that's how you feel, edgy?"

"Yeah." Matter of fact, Sam felt a good deal more than edgy, although he wasn't about to admit it to these boys. Hardly admitted it to himself. Looking back he could see how everything fit together, but he sure hadn't scoped things out when he spotted the job opening and took his old drawings up to City Hall. Pretty much did it on the spur of the moment. Seemed like a good idea at the time, as they say. Then things got out of hand. And here he was, like it or not.

To Casey and Daryl, he said, "A guy once told me anything worth doing wasn't easy. It wasn't like climbing a ladder or nothing, he said. You climb a ladder, you always got one hand holding on. You really want to get something done, you gotta have both hands free. Try climbing a ladder that way, both hands free."

"Wha'd'ya think about that, Daryl?" Casey asked the silent figure next to them.

"Like I care."

That was Daryl's favorite expression, "Like I care." Some people are quiet and it's because they're deep in thought, but not Daryl. He wasn't a bad guy, though. He never gave Sam a hard time. Right at the moment, Sam envied him the way he didn't think too much. Get in less trouble, you didn't think too much.

They went inside the OkyDoky and got donuts and coffee. The cashier that wouldn't touch Sam was on duty. She placed the change he had coming on the counter so that he had to pick the coins up.

Back in the truck, Sam could feel needles of pain in his chest from breathing the super-cold air. He sipped the coffee through the tiny hole made in the plastic lid, his hands wrapped tightly around the cup.

Out at the landfill, they weighed in and drove down to dump the load, the truck rocking in the icy potholes along the access road. They weren't the first city crew there. Beernuts had beaten them, his ejector forcing a great wad of garbage out the hopper of his truck.

Casey backed up next to him and got out to run the ejection blade, while Daryl went on around to keep an eye on the garbage as it was pushed out. Sam stayed in the truck.

As he listened to the two crews joking, he caught some movement out of the corner of his eye and looked over toward Beernuts, who was motioning for him to roll down the window.

"Stayin' warm, are ya, Sam? Practicing up for that nice, cushy, indoors job? Sit on your ass all day drawin' pretty pictures."

Beernuts was another bad one, but different from the girl at the OkyDoky. He liked to give Sam a hard time. For Beernuts, that was like some kind of recreational sport. So Sam would shuck and jive, and the two of them pretend this was just good, clean fun.

Sam stuck his arm out the window, as if he was driving through the countryside on a fine summer day. "Cold don't bother me," he told Beernuts. "Just a little airish."

Beernuts ignored this comment, having something in his mind to say and not giving a shit about anything else. "You black guys got it made. Well, what the fuck, that's what I say. Go for it. Just because there's some poor white bastard out there can actually do the work ain't no reason he should get the job."

Most whites think all the bad things they say about the black man are true, and somehow that means they ain't racists. Beernuts, though, he was different. He knew his own mind. He was content in himself.

"You got that right, Beernuts," Sam agreed breezily. "It's like I say about you, just because there's lots of the brothers back in the projects would be glad to come out here and haul garbage for half what the city's paying you white boys don't mean you shouldn't get the work."

As he talked, Sam was checking himself out in the side-view mirror. His skin always got an ashy color in the cold and wind. His old acne scars stood out more. His face looked skinnier than ever. An ugly motherfuck. But he'd done okay, made it out of the Robert Taylor Homes, got himself a decent job in this here white town, and now he was moving his skinny ass on up. There were lots of pretty boys back in the hood got themselves nothin' but dead in their short time on this earth.

"We was just discussing Sam's new job," Beernuts called out to Casey and Daryl as they walked back up toward the cab. Beernuts's own pickers were already sitting next to him. "Not gonna work with your sorry asses anymore." Beernuts pulled a long face. "Sam's on the way up. Gonna get himself into the middle class, he is. Be a regular Afro-Saxon." He jammed his truck into gear. "That's a laugh. Afro-Saxon." He howled as he drove off.

"I got my doubts about Beernuts," Sam said to Casey as soon as they were rolling again, heading out to start the second run. Casey smiled. It was an old joke, something Sam always said after Beernuts had been at him again, laying on all that racist shit of his.

"But you boys are okay. I'm gonna miss you guys." Daryl frowned. He didn't like to hear that sort of mush. Didn't mean nothing. But Sam had reached an understanding with these boys, the way you do.

"Still not too late," Casey said. The truck was tracking down the long highway grade leading back to town, Casey pushing it, anxious to start picking again. "Ain't like you're gonna be making that much more money."

"Money got nothing to do with it."

"What then?"

"Just something I gotta do."

Sam was no race man, but he figured you got to have some reason for living, and if a black man like him was satisfied with nigger work all his life, then what had he accomplished? But this was something else he couldn't tell these boys.

And so he said instead, "Already told my momma. Made her real happy. She's had a lot of misery in her life."

"Well," Casey said, "if we can't talk you out of it, then good luck."

"Expect I can use all the luck I can get."

They were rolling headlong down the highway, Sam's ass bouncing on the slippery seat, Casey leaning out over the wheel, driving like a maniac as he talked.

Sam braced himself as best he could as they swung back and forth, the truck swerving in and out of traffic. The world rushed toward him, faster and faster.

# CHAPTER 73

~

The early afternoon sun stood well above the western bluffs, but darkness seemed already to be gathering, distilled from the thin, cold air as El Plowman and the city manager, Paul Cutler, a few minutes early for the museum opening, moved in and out of the old Ice Harbor buildings.

Paul inspected the Christmas decorations and looked in one shop after another, as curious as an otter.

"I like seeing these people here," he said. Once upon a time they'd envisioned crowds throughout the off-season, not just during special promotions like The Prelude or the Winter Carnival in February or, six weeks ago, Oktoberfest.

At the former boat and boiler works, inside what had been a construction shed, they stopped to watch climbers scaling the artificial rock wall.

"Speaking about hard climbs," Paul asked, "when was the last time you talked to Skip Peterson?"

"Few days."

"Why don't you give him a call?"

She hesitated—would it make any difference?—but then said okay.

"Good."

Paul could have called himself, of course, but she knew Skip better, and he was likely to be franker with her. Like Skip, she and Walter were Old Money, or at least would have been if they'd had any money.

As they continued their walk, they discussed what else the city might possibly do to help the Pack buyout along. Not much. A little.

She prayed for its survival. If it went down, City Hall wouldn't be immune from the consequences. They'd suddenly find themselves with a million-dollar shortfall. They'd have to wring that money out of the budget somehow.

From this imagining, others followed, a cascade of melancholy ideas. She remembered when Paul had come to town, the young hotshot city manager on his way up, a sure bet to turn Jackson into an All-American City. Almost happened. Almost. If events had turned a few degrees in their favor, Paul could have ridden out of Jackson triumphant, moved up to the next rung, maybe even one day made it to the top, to one of the famous city manager towns like Cincinnati or Dallas. But he'd stayed and now must suffer the consequences along with the natives like El.

She noticed that he was leading them closer and closer to his favorite building in the project, the old tool-and-die company they'd converted into an arts and crafts pavilion.

Once he got in there, she could forget about the private little discussion she required, so she tugged on his sleeve, drawing him to one side.

"Chuck Fellows," she said.

The manager cocked a quizzical eye toward her. "What about him?"

"Last night I had a call from Tom Sharkey. He's got the concrete contract down at the dog track. Seems he met with Fellows yesterday, about extra costs because of the weather. He claims Chuck treated him in an insulting way."

"At least, so says Tom Sharkey."

"So he says. Perhaps it's not true. After all, Chuck would never say anything to hurt somebody's feelings."

"Okay," Paul conceded. "I'll talk to him."

"Please." That was one thing, but it wasn't all. "And what's the situation with Sam Turner? When does he start in the drafting room?"

"Tomorrow, as a matter of fact."

"Tomorrow? The middle of the week?" That seemed a bit odd.

"Chuck said he was ready for him. Could put it off, I suppose, the first of the year maybe, but if Chuck says he's ready..."

Being of a suspicious nature, El wondered whether Fellows, after all his bitching and moaning, was actually prepared to toe the line here. Hard to think so. But then again, she supposed there was no law against things going right every once in a while.

"Let me just say, Paul, the last thing we need is more unfavorable stories in the press about how we handle our affirmative action program."

"Yeah. But no guarantees, not as long as Chuck Fellows is around. I'm certainly not going to start micromanaging. And if it turns out that Turner can't hack it…"

"There are such things as self-fulfilling prophesies, you know." She looked at him narrowly. "If you ask me, I think you rather like the idea, Fellows riding roughshod over people, in the name of, oh, I don't know, generally accepted engineering standards."

Paul didn't deny it.

"I still expect him to do right by Sam Turner," she said, intent upon driving her point home. "If Turner isn't quite up to snuff, then he must be given every chance to come up to it. And if you have to sit on Chuck Fellows, I expect you to do it."

Paul tilted his head to one side, his lips pressed together, a familiar expression of frustration and disgust.

"I know," she said, "the pits." On an impulse, she added, "Come here," and gave him a big hug, one so firm that when she held him at arm's length, he looked like the breath had been knocked out of him. "I'm depressed, you're a gloomy Gus, but what the hell, somehow we'll muddle through."

"You're the boss," he said.

Since the conversation about Fellows had used up what little time they had left to themselves, they forgot about the arts and crafts building and turned at once toward the museum.

~

The outside doors to the old railroad station's waiting room had been sealed, and patrons would enter the black history exhibit from what had been the stationmaster's office. El and Paul joined the other officials and media people in this outer room, where tickets to the exhibit would be sold and self-guided tour tapes rented and docent-led groups marshaled, all this activity to begin at the official opening on Saturday. First, the VIP walk-through.

The old Pullman porter Hiram Johnson and his wife Pearl arrived late. Museum director Reiny Kopp, sharp-boned and hawk-like in his vigilance, perched on the edge of the scene and showed increasing signs of fidgetiness until finally the outside door swung

open, and after some little confusion, Pearl Johnson entered, leading a small processional. Behind her came Hiram in his wheelchair,
pushed by a middle-aged black man El had never seen before. Another stranger carried a walker. Apparently the old Pullman porter
used various modes of travel. Several more blacks, men and women
and children that El didn't know, followed along. She understood
these must be children and grandchildren, perhaps even great-
grandchildren, come to Jackson for this special occasion. They were
all turned out.

Pearl approached Reiny. In her hands, as one would hold an
offering, she carried a large, carefully wrapped bundle.

She might be short and stout, but Pearl held herself erect, her
shoulders thrown back, her pace measured. The others in the small parade came solemnly forth. All the chatter in the room had died away.

Pearl stopped in front of Reiny but said nothing.

"May I?" he asked.

She nodded and held the package toward him, each gesture
barely perceptible.

"You finished," he said.

"Wasn't but a few minutes ago. Would've been here sooner
otherwise." She spoke with her customary tartness.

Reiny carried the package over to one of the tables, where on
Saturday they would be serving soul food, and began gingerly to
unwrap it.

"Johnny," he said as he folded back the last of the wrapping,
"you're tall. Give me a hand here."

Johnny Pond slid lithely through the crowd and up next to
Reiny, and the two of them lifted up the object inside, which, to
oohing and aahing, gracefully cascaded open, revealing itself to be
a large, ornate quilt.

"Thank you," Reiny said to Pearl. She once again nodded,
still solemn.

"This," Reiny explained for any who might not understand the
significance of what was happening, "is Pearl's history of her family
in Jackson."

Each patch of the quilt portrayed a scene in vivid colors and
intricate detail. Some were stitched with dates: 1934, with two
men shaking hands and a railroad engine in the background; 1953,
a montage of infant, graduation cap, house. In one, a picture of Hiram Johnson in his porter's uniform. In another, a family portrait.

At the center, a large diamond, labeled Jackson, Iowa, depicted a cityscape of downtown and bluffs.

Reiny asked Pearl to come forward and explain the significance of the abstract designs at the four corners.

"This one," she said, pointing to a patch with inward-turning triangles and an open square in the center, "is from a Monkey Wrench quilt. It was a secret code during slave days telling the people to get their tools and other things together and be ready to escape." She went from corner to corner, her voice insistent, as if she imagined her listeners to be skeptical—the Drunkard's Path design warning escaped slaves to follow devious routes, the Evening Star patch reminding them to follow the polestar. The last corner contained a design of variously colored strips radiating outward toward the four sides of the square. "This is from a Log Cabin quilt," Pearl told everyone. "It was hung outside a home on the Underground Railroad as a sign that that was a safe place to stop."

"Thank you, Pearl," Reiny said and then added, "One day I hope Jackson will be a town where we can hang a Log Cabin Quilt."

He moved his hand slowly upward and downward, as if to draw the eyes of the onlookers to each panel. "Quilting is without doubt the finest craft tradition in African American families. What better crown for our history of the Johnsons than this magnificent work?"

Although El could appreciate the symbolic power of the four corners, she found the other patches more compelling, as if, in the brilliantly colored bedcover, Pearl had revealed her truer self, not the dour, restrained image she presented to white folks, but the homey, joyous, even sentimental person that her own family must know.

Someone began to clap. In a few moments, others had joined in, and an instant later the solemnity of the occasion was shattered with whoops and amens and back slaps and hugs.

El went over to Pearl to thank her in person. "Reiny's been talking about your quilt for weeks," El told her. "I can't express to you how much it means to him, to me, to all of us."

"I did it," Pearl explained, not to be misunderstood, "for the sake of my husband."

Next, several persons spoke, El starting things off by welcoming everyone on behalf of the museum board.

And finally, the tour of the exhibit itself began. The moment was Reiny's as well as the Johnsons', so El hung back and let the others go first. It took a little while for everyone to enter. Several stopped at the door, gawking, before they thought to move on and make room for others.

El had been there only a few days earlier, but even at that late date, nothing had been moved over from the workshop, and the rest was chaotic, so the final form of the exhibit still lay hidden in Reiny's inner vision. His secretive nature had given El anxious moments in the past. Their biggest fight this time had been over the labels, which all exhibits had, which made the visuals legible, but which Reiny insisted on leaving out, believing they would spoil the effect he was attempting to create.

"There are always people who don't want to rent a headset or to go around with one of the docents. What about them?" El had asked him. He was unimpressed with this argument. Reiny ignored what didn't please him. At moments such as that, she had to remind herself how good he was. Allowances had to be made.

Finally, they compromised on handheld labels, a booklet describing each display, which people could carry around with them or not, as they chose.

Now, as El stepped into the old waiting room, the Mississippi Delta room, her first surprise—not something seen but rather felt—was the heat, as if she had stepped directly from a cold Iowa winter into a steamy Mississippi Delta summer. In front of her, people with glasses had removed them to wipe off the condensation. They stared about themselves as if stunned, nobody looking at precisely the same thing, for whatever way they turned, there was something to see.

They stood on a path winding through a Delta village, in the midst of the tall panels encircling the room and painted with distant vistas—cotton fields on one side, an antebellum mansion on another, sloughs and a levee and the Mississippi River on a third—all as if seen from quite far away. A number of the panels were new to El.

From the paintings, buildings projected in high relief, partly painted and partly real, creating a striking three-dimensional effect, the first a general store. Somewhere Reiny had found the hood and front fenders of an old touring car, a Packard, along with a Mississippi license plate. A mannequin stood with its foot raised on the bumper of the car, obviously meant to be a white overseer, while on the porch of the store, three other figures represented black men, each positioned to suggest a different attitude toward the white man—obsequiousness, resignation, disdain. As El passed slowly by this scene, she was startled to realize that playing softly in the background was the conversation taking place among the four men. El paused and listened. The exchanges contained nothing unusual, just men passing the time of day, and would have signified little if it hadn't been for Reiny's artfully arranged tableau—the banal face of racism. She was hardly surprised he hadn't told her about this. He loved his surprises, and what better person to surprise than the chair of the museum board. Perhaps he had also been concerned that she would decide he'd stepped too far over the line. He was wrong. She loved it. What she didn't love was the heat and humidity, which was carrying this verisimilitude thing just too far.

The group had gathered at the point where the path through this part of the exhibit widened to provide the docents space to give their recitations.

"We have headphones for museumgoers," Reiny explained, "but for the purpose of this first tour, we've rigged up a public address system. The voices you'll hear belong to Hiram and to Johnny Pond, who I'm sure all of you know as the host of *Sound Off* on radio station KJAX. Take a bow, Johnny." Pond, standing behind the others, gave a perfunctory wave. "Are we ready?" Reiny asked nobody in particular as he stepped up to the first tape player. He pushed the play button.

"Hello," Hiram's voice, surprisingly strong, filled the room after a pause, "my name is Hiram Johnson. I was born in eighteen and ninety-eight in Stringtown, Mississippi, and there I was raised up, a black man in the heart of what they call the Mississippi Delta. If you got a few minutes, I'd be mighty pleased to tell you my story..."

As she listened, El surveyed the rest of the room, which contained fewer surprises. On one side stood the front portions of two shotgun houses, and on the other, a country church with its amen corner. Next to one of the houses, the front half of a large pig extending from a panel, the back half painted using extreme foreshortening. She looked closely at the animal, an example of the taxidermist's art. There was a small vegetable and flower garden, complete with weeds being weeded by another of his mannequins.

The place was peopled—little girls playing hopscotch, women gossiping as they sewed, men tossing horseshoes. Reiny had even contrived, using a ground cloth or canvas, imitation hardpan, but when she knelt down and touched it, she found that it wasn't cloth at all but dirt hauled in and tamped down, and it, too, reached all the way to the mural panels where it mingled with painted earth, creating a vivid sense of closeness and distance all at once.

On the tape, Johnny Pond provided the historical background while Hiram related personal anecdotes. As the others listened, El moved quietly among them and took Reiny aside. He still had the quilt, refolded, in his possession.

"You've got to do something about the heat," she whispered.

"It's only seventy-four. The humidity makes it seem hotter is all."

"I don't care. I'm not going to have everyone catching pneumonia when they go back outside. Turn it down."

Next, she went over and whispered to Pearl to make sure Hiram was bundled up when they went out to the Pullman coach. Pearl pursed her lips and nodded, the gesture acknowledging the advice and indicating she'd been taking care of Hiram all these years and supposed she knew what she was about. Hiram in the meanwhile was busy expatiating for the benefit of those around him on what he was saying on the tape, Hiram on Hiram.

Finally, Johnny Pond's voice returned and told the listeners to turn off the tape player and wait quietly for a moment before proceeding out to the railroad car.

As his voice disappeared and the incidental chatter died away, in their place came a suite of sounds that Reiny had created as a background, not just the men at the general store talking, but much more—bird calls, a boy shouting in the distance, someone digging, perhaps in a garden, women's conversation and laughter—creating an eerie sense of activities seen and unseen at once. A whiff of the dirt reached El's nostrils, and she felt the prickly moisture on her skin. Of course Reiny hadn't wanted labels, she thought. Of course.

As people moved toward the exit leading to the station platform, they passed the old ticket booth, still a ticket booth, complete with a mannequin ticket agent behind the grille and above it the word "Greenville." El glanced back, to take one last look at the scene. Johnny still lingered there. And so, remembering the day when the Pullman coach had arrived and the two of them, separated from the others, had sat in the coach talking about Mark O'Banion's death, she returned and stood next to him.

Neither spoke. They simply listened to the birdcalls and other background noises and stared at the deep landscape contrived in that small space. El had been so startled by the transformation of the room that she hadn't even thought to inspect her own panel, the cotton pickers and cabins and chinaberry tree. Melded into the rest now, it seemed barely her own work.

"Quite something," Johnny said.

"Yes, quite something."

As they walked out together, El told him, "By the way, you'll be happy to know that Sam Turner begins work in the drafting department tomorrow."

"Is that right?"

"Yes."

He nodded slowly but didn't seem nearly as pleased as she would have expected.

# CHAPTER 74

~

After Walter Plowman finished the ten o'clock cast and performed the daily ritual of logging in the weather stats from his data collection platform, he drove out to the lock and dam, where Corps of Engineers personnel were struggling to lock through the last tow of the season.

Walter's life was embedded in the seasons of the year, each with its own markers: in winter, the January thaw, no less mysterious for its commonplaceness; the moment, and it was barely more than that, when ice went out of the river in the spring; the summer hatches of fishflies; the first killing frost; and at the threshold of winter, the last commercial tow on the river just before ice-up.

He parked his car behind the lockhouse and went up to the chain-link fence separating the public area from the workspace around the lock. The sleet, like shotgun pellets, came in intermittent blasts.

Barely a hundred yards upstream stood the towboat with her name "Dixie Darlin'" painted below the pilothouse window and clearly visible from where Walter stood. He had been following her progress downriver. Her home port was Hannibal, and she was hauling grain from the Twin Cities, bound for St. Louis. That morning, she'd passed Guttenberg and had the dickens of a time locking through up there. Now the same struggle was underway here at Lock and Dam 11.

The tow's nine barges, three rows three abreast, were angled toward the long guidewall that boats used to align themselves as they approached the lock. Beyond, as tall as a three-story building, the Dixie Darlin' herself rose and seemed to peer down, almost with a motherly concern, on the brood of barges she was attempting to push down the river. The floodlights from the lock reached as far as her foredecks, her stern in blackness and beyond, the night closing in. Walter could hear the tow's diesel engines as she jockeyed against the encroaching ice. Her powerful spotlight, which would swing from shore to shore as she moved down the river, now remained perfectly still, the brilliant beam trained on the upper gates of the lock, where the Corps crew worked with pikes and chainsaws.

Wedged against the upriver side of the gates, the massive slabs of ice were ragged and full of hummocks and tinged here and there with yellow-green algae or duckweed. The sounds of the chainsaws rose as the men wheeled them against the slabs, spewing sprays of ice shavings, like the sparks from acetylene torches. Out in the small patch of still-open water, a workboat maneuvered, the men in it cutting and prying at the upstream edge of the ice. Nearer the gates, the lockmen stood directly on the ice as they worked.

On the catwalk that crossed the top of the gates stood a large man observing the work and occasionally yelling orders and pointing here or there. Probably Vern Gunderson, the lockmaster, Walter guessed.

After a time, the man started walking back along the catwalk toward the sidewall and, spotting Walter, changed course and came over. As he neared, Walter saw that, indeed, it was Gunderson. Only the circle of his face was visible, surrounded by the hood of his parka and red from the frigid air sweeping down the river.

"Got yourself a little problem, Vern?"

"You could say."

"This is one of those times, I bet, when you wished the gates opened downstream, so you could just lock the ice on through."

Vern sniffed. "This is a time when I wish the damn barge lines would lay up their boats while the river's still open." As he spoke, the wind whisked his breath away in a thin, white stream.

He turned and looked out toward his crew. "I'll tell you what, Wally," he said, "I sure as hell don't like putting my people out there in conditions like this."

A sudden spray of sleet peppered them. Walter stamped his feet and pulled his old favorite watch cap far down over his ears. "It's pretty ugly," he agreed, although, secretly, as any meteorologist would, he couldn't help but take a certain pride in really filthy weather.

The work proceeded almost in slow motion, the lockmen gingerly prodding here and there in the ice pack. In the distance, the diesels of the tug became audible when the whining of the chain-saws subsided into a low murmuring idle as the sawyers stood up and scanned the ice pack looking for weak points.

"How long are you going to keep at it?" Walter asked.

"Everybody's here. Runnin' two crews. Half hour on, half hour off. I wouldn't put my worst enemy out any longer than that."

"What's the temperature down here?"

Vern smiled at him, his smile distorted by the cold. "You're the weatherman. You tell me."

"Let's see," Walter said, delighted at the challenge. "Up at the airport, they were looking at nine below when I did my forecast. Now it's probably a degree or two colder. It'd be a few degrees warmer downtown, of course. But here? Well, you've got yourself a little microclimate. It's low lying, a natural sink, and there's the wind chill." He craned around. "All them floodlights maybe add a degree or two, no more. Probably, I'd say, it's minus fifteen with a wind chill of, oh, minus thirty."

Vern nodded. "Close enough."

"What is it?"

"Last time I was inside and looked, it was thirteen below."

Walter, who had never bothered to collate the temperature at the lock with those that he recorded elsewhere, nodded and filed the information away.

"Well," he said, "it could be worse. In fact, it will be. You just wait a couple days and that Alberta Clipper's going to be on us full bore. Then we're going to be looking at wind chills of sixty, seventy below."

"No concern of mine. One way or t'other, we'll be through here long before that." Vern started to move away, then turned back briefly. "If you're going to stay until we lock the Dixie Darlin' through, you're in for a long wait."

"Guess I'll hang around a little longer."

"Suit yourself."

At the lower end of the lock, the Leprechaun, one of Frank Duccini's harbor tugs, was tied up, waiting for the upper gates to be opened wide enough to start forcing the ice through. The Leprechaun would then use its backwash to flush the ice out of the lock.

Seeing the little tug reminded Walter of the conversation he'd had with Chuck Fellows a couple of weeks back. He wondered if

Chuck had managed to cut a deal with Frank to keep the water open around the dredge. Walter had his doubts. Frank surely loved to close down his harbor service and head south after the last tow went through. Didn't need the money. Yup, Walter thought, Frank would drive a mighty hard bargain. If Fellows suspected he was being held up, probably he was. Only a highwayman's wages would keep Frank Duccini in Jackson when the snow flew.

Walter looked back toward the Dixie Darlin', towering in the background, its white paint and dark windows seeming less maternal now and more like a sad clown face. Walter thought about waiting until they either locked the tow through or gave up the effort, but as one shift of lockmen went inside and the other came out to continue the work, he decided that the idea of staying was sufficient. So he got in his car and went home.

# CHAPTER 75

～

The next morning, determined to find out whether the Corps of Engineers people had finally managed to lock the Dixie Darlin' through, Walter drove back out to the river.

The day had dawned brilliant and clear. From the open water below the lock and dam, a thick curtain of mist rose into the frigid air. All that remained of the sleet storm lay scattered along the roadside like salt stains.

As he approached, Walter could see water rushing in thick, black, ropy strands through the bays of the dam. He drove around the lockhouse, as he had the night before, and parked and looked at once upstream, expecting to see an empty riverscape where the night before the Dixie Darlin' had been jockeying in the encroaching ice. But the river was not empty. The towboat and barges lay almost exactly where they had been nine hours earlier, except now alive with the blindingly bright sunlight.

Above the dam, the Mississippi spread in a broad reach, more lake than river, choked with the floes from the north, a vast sweep of white and gray and organic yellow. Yesterday, the towboat had pushed its barges along the narrow open channel through the ice field, but now that river within the river had frozen, leaving a gleaming gray track winding upriver from the stern of the towboat.

Walter got out and stood in the cold. All around him the world lay in silence, except for the chafing of the wind and the occasional cracklings of the ice as it froze and expanded, locking the tow into an ever-tightening prison. No one was around. The workboat had been lifted back onto the top of the lockwall. The jumble of ice pinning the upper gate shut lay crisscrossed with sutures. Walter wondered when they had given up.

He stood there for a minute, then took one last look at the Dixie Darlin' and realized that he was pleased. Yes, that was the only word to describe how he felt at the moment. The elements had won. Standing there alone, the sole human representative on that arctic shore, last night's battlefield, he imagined he could hear the wind whispering to him in its secret language, explaining everything.

The Leprechaun was long gone, of course, back to the Ice Harbor. Frank Duccini would be laying up now for the winter unless, of course, Chuck Fellows finally gave in and agreed to pay his king's ransom.

Well, Walter thought, since he was down there, why not go take a look at the dredge, see what was what, and so he got back in his car and drove in that direction.

As he passed the dog track construction site, he could make out tiny figures in the distance moving around on top of a foundation structure of some sort. Cold work, he thought. A pair of cranes swung panels gracefully above the site.

Two cars were parked at the dredge. Holding on to the makeshift wooden railing, granules of sleet crunching beneath his shoes, Walter delicately made his way out along the gangplanks. If Fellows had already talked with Duccini, there was no sign of the harbor tug. Or of Fellows either, for when Walter gained the dredge and stuck his head inside the deckhouse, all he found were repairmen reconditioning pieces of machinery. Since he was out there, he looked around and chatted up the two machinists, one working on the engine that drove the pump, the other on the pump itself. Space heaters glowed red hot but barely disturbed the cold, dense, still air. The mechanics bent to their tasks.

Finally Walter went back outside, figuring there was no reason to stick around, but as he was about to step off the dredge, who should pull into the little dirt parking lot opposite but Fellows himself.

Walter waited. Chuck was not alone but was followed along the gangplank by a small figure wrapped in a hooded parka, who turned out, upon closer inspection, to be a black man, and not a very happy black man.

"You come down to see my operation, Walt?" Chuck asked. "Let me take care of this guy first, and then I'll show you around." He hooked a thumb back toward his companion.

Next to the stocky Chuck, the other man appeared insignificant, indeed, thin and runty, as if he consisted of little more than the clothes piled on against the cold.

Once inside, he looked about himself. "This the dredge? Never been on a dredge before." He squinted suspiciously at Chuck.

"Over here." Chuck took him across to a workbench that lined most of the far wall, although with all the stuff piled on it, precious little room remained where somebody might work.

"You can start here, Sam. I want you to GI this place. It's a goddamn mess."

"Man, you don't have to tell me." The person named Sam stared down at the workbench. "People on my trash routes throw away better looking stuff than this." Walter had by this time figured out just who this fellow was.

"I want you to triage it, Sam," Chuck told him. "You know what that is? Three piles—stuff that's good as is, stuff that's salvage-able, stuff that's worthless."

"No problem. We just back a truck in here and fill her up. Gimme an hour, I'll have this place spic-and-span."

Chuck picked a small object off the bench and held it up for Sam's inspection. Turner, Walter suddenly remembered. That was his last name. Sam Turner. Walter thought he was supposed to be up in the drafting room. Ellie had been working on that.

"What's this?" Chuck asked him.

"It's a screw."

"Still usable?"

Turner gave Chuck a wha'd'ya-think, I'm-a-moron? look.

"Right," Chuck said. "So we save it."

From among the objects on the bench, he picked a pipe wrench and gave it out to Turner, telling him to open the jaws. Turner held it with distaste and made a halfhearted attempt to do as he was told. The jaws were frozen shut.

Chuck looked at him suspiciously. "For a trash collector, Sam, you're mighty damn fastidious."

Turner dropped the tool onto the bench.

"Man, this is the kind of work people putting on me all the time. The ass end of things."

"I told you once, I'll tell you again, everybody in the drafting room is a jack-of-all-trades. You want to work for me, you better be prepared to make yourself useful."

Chuck handed the wrench back to Turner and told him, "A steel brush, a little liquid wrench, and it'll clean right up. You focus your attention on the stuff that can be saved, Sam.

Don't waste your time on the rest. What's this?" He held up another object.

"Mess of wire, all scrunched up," Turner suggested.

"*Copper* wire. Save it. And this?" Chuck was now holding a metal contraption, a subassembly of some sort by the look of it, but badly rusted and staved in on one side.

"You got me, boss. Expect you're gonna tell me it's a whiz-bang doohickey every machine gotta have."

"I have no idea what it is," Chuck told him. "Junk. Pitch it."

"Don't look any worse than all this other shit," Turner said, more or less under his breath. "How you expect me to decide which is which?"

"Use your head. If you're not sure, ask one of the other guys." Chuck pointed at them in turn. "That's Phil, that's Howie."

Turner continued to mumble imprecations against the task he had been assigned as he started to poke among the various objects on the bench. Chuck stood back a step and watched him for a minute, and then said, "Okay, Walt, now for you."

They walked about the dredge, climbing up into the lever room and back down, stopping to converse with the fellows working on the pump and the diesel engine.

"How goes it, Phil?" Chuck asked the pump guy.

"See for yourself."

Chuck walked along the drive shaft, which linked the engine to the pump. Lubricating oil glistened on all the joints. "Looks pretty good."

"Packings are okay, time being at least," Phil said. "But come over here, something I wanna show ya."

He led the way up to the front of the pump, where a pipe opened out into a metal box. "This thing's called a stone box," Chuck explained to Walter. "The idea is that debris too big to pass through the pump will get trapped here and can be removed." The cover had been hoisted by a traveling crane and was hanging at an odd angle, like a doffed hat. Phil reached through the opening and up into the pump itself. When satisfied, he withdrew his hand and said to Chuck, "Feel up in there."

"That there's the throat piece," Phil explained when Chuck had managed to locate the part, groping blindly up into the machine. "Seals the discharge. Or at least it oughta. This one's worn real bad."

"Which means?"

"Lose your efficiency."

When Chuck withdrew his hand, Walter said, "May I?"

"You'll get dirty," Phil warned him.

"Don't mind."

"Suit yourself."

So Walter reached up into the pump, as the other two had.

He inhaled a cold, muddy, metallic odor. His fingers felt numb against the metal. Phil gave instructions, telling him what he should be feeling for, until he managed to locate an open seam in the casing, large enough to side his fingers into. He described it to Phil.

"That's it."

Walter stood back up, satisfied, and used the rag Phil offered to wipe off his hands.

"How long's it gonna take you to get a new one?" Chuck asked.

Phil shrugged.

"Do it," Chuck told him. "Have them second-day air it if you have to."

A few minutes later, as Walter and Chuck went out onto the deck, they passed through Sam Turner's air space and heard a patch of his ongoing monologue. He held up what appeared to be a vacuum cleaner attachment and inspected if from various angles. "Triage, the man says. I don't care how many piles you got, this don't fit in none of 'em…"

Outside, Walter and Chuck stood talking. The view down here, on a reach of the Mississippi, was a good deal different from that above the lock and dam. The river had dropped a foot or so over the last few days, leaving shell ice scattered along the shore. New ice skimmed the shallows around the dredge. Farther out, however, where a few days ago heavy floes had been moving steadily downstream, none were visible now, as if the river were opening up. An illusion.

"She's frozen solid above the dam," Walter said. "Won't take long for the same thing to happen at Lock and Dam 12 down in Bellevue. Then the icepack will back upstream. Mighty quick, too, given this weather."

They walked up onto the foredeck and stared out at the basket of blades used to cut the sand free from the bottom of the river. Walter asked him about the situation with Frank Duccini.

"Bastard's got me over a barrel. Probably I'm going to have to pay his price."

Walter wanted to help Fellows out. The idea of dredging in midwinter excited him. Only a crazy man would attempt such a thing, of course.

He mused over the possibilities. He had a friend, another of his many friends of long standing, who just might...

Walter waited a few beats, enough time to ask himself one last time if what he had in mind might work, and if he really wanted to do it.

"I know a guy," he said.

"Yeah?"

"Got a boat. An old harbor tug. Decommissioned, you might say."

"Still in the water?"

"Yup."

"He might be interested?"

"Not sure. Maybe. Orville's another old river rat. Retired."

"Decommissioned? Retired?"

"Well, yes. And maybe he won't be interested. But you've got one thing going in your favor."

"What's that?"

"Orville and old John Turcotte go back a ways. When Orv learns you've taken the dredge away from him, he'll be mighty well disposed toward you is my guess."

"How come you didn't tell me about him before?"

"Is this the kind of work you'd wish on a friend?"

"No, I guess not."

"There you are. And Orville's not a young man anymore."

"How old *is* he?"

"That's a matter of some speculation."

"Too old to do the work?"

"Not for me to say."

"I see. Anyway, he might be willing, this Methuselah of yours?"

"We'll have to ask."

"Not much time."

"Orv has always been a man knows his own mind. I'll put the question to him. You'll have your answer in short order, I expect." Walter cocked a quizzical eye toward his new friend and wondered whether he was a man of a proper liberal temperament.

"In a situation like this, you understand, what you get might not be exactly what you're counting on."

Chuck looked back at him suspiciously, but didn't ask. They let it go at that.

# CHAPTER 76

~

A dvent. A time of waiting.

A small storm had passed over the city earlier in the day, bringing squally snow, the second storm in less than a week, neither amounting to much. At eleven a.m., the wail of sirens rose and gradually subsided, not an emergency, only the normal monthly test, always the same day and time, causing a few people to pause and check their watches, but nothing more. City workers were putting up the last of the wreaths and swags and other Christmas decorations along the blocks of the Main Street pedestrian mall, the decorations somewhat dull against the pallid sky. Beneath them, shoppers passed quickly in the cold.

Late in the afternoon, the meatpacking union held its last membership meeting before the vote, to be taken at the end of the week, on purchasing the Jackson Packing Company.

Homer Budge had intended to drive straight from the labor center, but at the last minute detoured past Shake Rag Lane, looking for John Michael. His son's ancient VW Beetle wasn't parked in its usual place at the curb. No one seemed to be home. Homer stood in the empty kitchen and listened to the silence. He went up to check his son's attic hideaway, walking through empty rooms and along empty corridors. Back downstairs, he lingered in the kitchen and wondered when he had ever been alone in the house. He ran down the roster of his family, trying to figure where Rose and all the little Budges would be at that moment.

Then he got back into his car and drove toward the Reinert College field house. The remnant of clouds from the earlier storm caught the last light of the sun, which had already set, darkness quickly settling in along the streets.

At the school, instead of following the road to the meeting site, he turned into the parking lot next to the library. Inside, the staff member on duty knew John Michael, but hadn't seen him. He usually studied downstairs in the stacks, she said.

Homer went from carrel to carrel in the basement until he found a desk with John Michael's stuff on it but no John Michael. Fruitlessly, he looked for him in lounges and opened the doors to lavatories, calling his name. Finally, standing outside once more, on the broad, marble entrance stairs, he reminded himself that he should be at the meeting. But the desire to take his son along with him, a casual, spur-of-the-moment thing earlier, had grown in urgency. If John Michael could be made to experience, however briefly, the flesh and blood of the buyout attempt, if he could be touched by the energy of it…

Back inside at the circulation desk, he asked the staffer the way to the school cafeteria.

With no time to lose, he cut across the quadrangle, walking double-time, then jogging a few steps, then double-timing again. Seedballs hung in the gloom like Christmas tree ornaments from the rows of leafless sycamores, reminding him of the coming holidays. Yesterday had been the second Sunday of Advent. John Michael hadn't gone to Mass again. Yet Homer realized that he was less upset about this scanting of his son's faith life than the boy's antagonism toward the buyout. Everything took a backseat to the buyout, even Homer's religion. He would have to make amends, but right now he didn't have the time, and he began to jog again.

He spotted John Michael coming across the plaza in front of the cafeteria. At that distance, he still recognized his son at once, stocky and purposeful, upright, as if walking at attention. John Michael wasn't alone. Lyle Wauters was with him, which figured. The annoyance this caused, added to the difficulty Homer had had finding his son and his lateness to the meeting, made him sharper than he meant to be.

"Come hear for yourself what's going on," he demanded.

John Michael glanced at his friend, the brief, knowing glance of people who shared an understanding.

To Homer he said, "I've got to study for finals."

"You can afford an hour. What are you afraid of, that you're going to change your mind?" This abruptness and sarcasm, though unintended, had their effect.

"You wanna come, too?" John Michael said to his friend.

"No way."

"I'll see you back at the library." Without another word, John Michael set off beside Homer.

They walked in silence, through the darkness. Homer, who had, minutes earlier, been so intent upon finding his son, now quailed slightly. Would this really help? He wanted to say something, to make some telling observation in this brief time he had, although the whole point of hectoring John Michael into coming was to accomplish something for which words were futile. To get him away from his books and the kind of bull sessions he would be having with the likes of young Wauters. To put him amid the men whose livelihoods rode on the outcome of the buyout attempt.

They progressed quickly along the network of sidewalks, laid out across the campus like some intricate geometry problem. No one was outside in the bitter cold, but students could be seen in dorm rooms, studying or moving about, intent upon their personal matters.

"I don't want to make this into a contest," Homer said to his son.

"But you want me to believe in the buyout," John Michael responded at once.

"Of course I do. But I understand. You do your own reading. You talk to the people you talk to."

"You mean Lyle," John Michael retorted. "I've been friends with Lyle for a long time."

"I know."

"We agree on a lot of things."

"And Lyle listens to his father, and his father made his mind up a long time ago." To forestall any response from his son, Homer added quickly, "All I'm saying, dear boy, is withhold your judgment, please. Have a doubt. If we fail, then I'll be glad to admit you were right. But at least give me a chance to be right."

"And what if you do buy the Pack and people are trying to live on practically nothing and it gives other companies an excuse to drive down their wages. Wages are already way too low. You've got all these people living below the poverty line. What will you accomplish except make rich people richer and poor people poorer?" His son's talk often had whiffs of union pamphlets and textbooks about it.

"Yes, all these things might happen, and yet who knows, maybe they won't. And maybe one day all these bitter fights between union and management will be a thing of the past."

They were nearing the rear of the field house. At the front and along the far side, cars were parked row upon row and people still arriving and milling around under the floodlights. Homer understood it had been a mistake to engage John Michael in debate on these matters. Each time they spoke, the grooves in his son's thinking were etched a little deeper.

And now the boy said, the words praise and criticism at once, "You're a nice guy, Dad. I just think you're making a big mistake here." They walked along the near side of the brick building, where a ribbon of sidewalk clung to the concrete footings, and low-wattage bulbs cast just enough light to see by. "Sometimes they leave the side doors open," his son said, and the second one they tried proved to be unlocked. "I'll go to your meeting, Dad," he told Homer, the last thing before entering, "but let's leave it at that, okay?"

The strange quiet of the secluded entrance immediately gave way to the clamor of the crowd inside. As Homer worked his way through the thronging membership, greeting people as he went, he quickly lost contact with John Michael. The hundreds of simultaneous conversations created an electric buzz that hovered in the air overhead, and he had to move close to people to hear what they were trying to tell him, smelling the beer on the breath of those who had stopped for a quick one on the way over. But his thoughts remained with his son.

Near the far end of the cavernous building, where a low platform had been set up with a podium and a row of folding chairs for the executive committee, Homer encountered a retiree named Smokey Neyens.

"I crashed your party, Hom, hope you don't mind."

The long, narrow fissures that looped out of Neyens's eyebrows and descended to his chin had deepened in the years since he worked his last shift in the curing cellar, and his nose seemed more starkly beaked now, but the expression in his eyes and the half smile remained and his hair still curled thickly upward, the gray now streaked with white, more like smoke than ever.

"You're not the only one who's crashed the party, Smokey. John Michael's here, too."

"John Michael?"

"Mikey."

"Oh, Mikey! I haven't seen him in ages. So he's John Michael now, is he?"

"And a very serious young man, too."

"Is that right? Well, I'm not surprised. He always was an intense little tyke."

"He's not so little now. Do me a favor, Smoke, go find him, talk to him about the buyout."

"Sure, glad to. Suppose I can recognize him after all this time?"

"Don't worry, you'll recognize him. Nineteen going on forty. Don't tell him I sent you, okay?"

Homer watched Neyens move away, disappearing quickly in the crowd. How providential, he thought, that the very man who had first befriended John Michael at union functions all those years ago should be here now, almost as if he had come out of retirement for this one last task.

Homer stepped up onto the makeshift stage and craned in a futile attempt to look over the others and spot his son. Maybe Smokey would succeed in chipping away at his infernal certainty. Maybe this meeting would, too, seeing all these men ready to seize this opportunity to work for themselves.

Others were already talking to him, so Homer couldn't dwell on these possibilities, and he put them aside with one last prayer that they might sway the boy whom he loved so well but feared was slipping, slipping so steadily away.

~

Skip Peterson paced back and forth, alone, silent, letting the tension build in the room and in himself. He glanced back toward Homer, who had returned to his seat after the two of them stood together at the podium and explained one last time the mechanics of the buyout. The other executive committee members sat with their carefully manicured expressions, waiting for Skip to finish and leave so the real discussion could begin.

Skip panned the hundreds upon hundreds of union members, the ones along the front row with their legs crossed or squarely planted in show-me postures, the decades of mistrust there for anyone to see.

A banked track encircled them. The frameworks holding basketball nets had been folded up into the roof trusses, climbing ropes tied back, pommel horses and other gymnastic apparatus pushed to the periphery. The ranks of folding chairs were filled, but that still left many standing along the sides and in the back, come to hear what Skip had to say.

He stopped and turned toward them, lifted the mike to his lips, and spoke. "It's up to you now."

That was it; that was his curtain speech.

"Questions? Anything you want to ask me before I leave, anything at all?"

Caught off-guard, no one raised his hand. Skip resumed his pacing, satisfied.

Keep it simple, he thought. Ask for a lot, expect little. By hook or by crook, they had to make it to next Saturday, get the vote for the givebacks, get some of the upgrade money, enough to appease Karl and Mel and their friends on the board. When the company started percolating along again, then they could talk about religious conversions.

"Questions?" he repeated as he reversed direction and started back along the lip of the platform. Finally a hand went up.

What about buying hogs? the man wanted to know. What bank was going to give them a fifteen or twenty million dollar credit line so they could purchase animals?

"That's right," Skip answered briskly, "that's a problem, we've got to get a credit line. We might have to go to a factor. The interest rate will be way over prime, and they'll take possession of our inventory. They'll have us by the short and curlies. But if we have to do it, by God, we will." He leaned out over the edge of the stage. "Whatever it takes. Next!"

The pace picked up. Men roamed with cordless mikes for the questioners. Skip prowled back and forth, took a question, answered it rapid-fire, moved on, took another.

"No, not two years, I don't know where you heard that. We *will* lose money at first, but for how long, who knows. It depends on me…it depends on you. Can you make that old plant sing? I'm betting you can. Okay, the woman in the back there, the one in the Chicago Cubs jacket. Yes, ma'am?

"Richie Chinn? I'm glad you asked. I just heard this morning. Chinn has signed an agreement with Modern Meat. We offered to provide him fresh meat at cost, Nick Takus is apparently giving him a somewhat better deal. Next."

As Skip paced, he kept one eye out for Fritz Goetzinger. He was there somewhere. Did Skip want to ask him a question, flush him out into the open?

"No, there's no money from the feds or the state. Look, if you people are waiting for some outsider to save your butts, forget it, ain't gonna happen. It's you and me, nobody else. It's not gonna be a bed of roses. Everybody's written us off. Okay, fine, to hell with them, that's what I say. Since when have you people given a damn what some outsider thought? The question is, what do you think? Have you written yourself off?"

Skip stared straight at the man who had challenged him, but out of the corners of his eyes he saw several people nodding in agreement.

"Next!"

He walked and walked, telling himself, don't pull your punches, we're doing this all the way up, right? "And a lot of you don't trust me. This is not a secret." He stopped dead in his tracks. "We all know the history here, folks. And I'm not stupid. You won't forget it any time soon. All I'm saying is this—look at the situation! Look at what's in your interest! Look at what you hold in your own hands! How many times have I heard somebody in the plant say, 'We know a thousand ways to improve the place, but nobody ever listens to us.' Well, hell, now nobody has to listen to you. *You've* got the power. *You* make the damn changes."

Skip stopped in his tracks and scanned the back of the room.

"Fritz Goetzinger! I know you're out there somewhere, Fritz! Show yourself!"

Somebody raised his hand, not Fritz but apparently standing in the cluster where he was to be found.

"Come on up here, Fritz," Skip called out, still unable to spot him. "Take Fritz a mike, somebody."

That was done and Goetzinger emerged, but he made no move to come forward, just stood slightly apart from his immediate companions, although even at that distance his patchy white hair and severe expression could not be mistaken. He held the mike loosely at his side and waited.

"What's it to be, Fritz?" Skip asked. "Are you with us? One hundred percent, balls to the wall, let's get this thing done? That's the way it's gotta be, Fritz. Anything less just doesn't cut it. So what's it to be?"

Goetzinger waited and then slowly raised the microphone.

"What about the 401(k) money?" As soon as Skip heard the bass of Goetzinger's voice, its flat Midwestern tone filled with its Midwestern certainties, he regretted calling on him. But, shit, he'd done it because he knew Goetzinger would ask the question, right? He wanted him to ask it.

Skip turned first to the membership. "You voted to allow individual members to decide to reinvest in the company. Good. So each of you can choose for yourself." Next he swung back around to Goetzinger. "We need that money, Fritz. We need the upgrades."

"You really expect us to give it to you?"

"Yes. Some of it, most of it."

"For a lot of folks here, that's pretty much all they got. You take away that, you take away their future."

Goetzinger was advancing slowly up the side aisle.

"I'm not asking for it all, Fritz. I'm asking for 4.5 million." As he said these words, Skip sensed their inadequacy. This was no time to start backing off. "But you're right, Fritz, this is dangerous stuff. People could get hurt." He turned away from Goetzinger and back toward the others. "The question is, how much faith have you got in yourselves? I'm asking you. Are you willing to put your money on the line? Are you? If not, then what's your faith really worth? You tell me."

Goetzinger had come to a halt halfway up the aisle and stood stolidly among another group of standees.

"What say, Skip, you pledge never to demand the retirement money? You do that, I'm behind you, balls to the wall, like you say."

"Look, Fritz, I have no intention of demanding the money. But you've got to understand we've thrown the rulebook away here. I can tell you what the situation is today, but tomorrow, who knows?" Skip turned once more toward the others. "You want guarantees, forget it. This company is in trouble. You vote to buy the stock, you give me the upgrade money, then I think we can make it. But I'm not telling you what to do. This Friday you vote the stock plan. You vote for that much, then we'll see where we're at."

And finally back toward Goetzinger.

"So I ask you again, Fritz, are you with us? Are you?" Goetzinger said nothing. "If not, then understand that there are a lot of people in this room trying to make the thing work, so please just stay the hell out of our way!"

Good, he thought. Good! *Good!*

~

Outside the field house, Rachel Brandeis had crowded into the KJAX van with Johnny Pond and the other members of the local press corps, waiting for the union meeting to break up. More than an hour had passed. Who knew how long they'd have to wait. She kept her eye on the building.

Conversation inside the van had meandered from issue to issue—a local man who had sunk all his money into the lottery and then committed suicide; a stag party, complete with strippers, which had been hosted by lobbyists for state legislators and gotten out of hand; a polygamy case in Sioux City—the oddball stuff reporters liked to gossip about among themselves. Rachel was the only woman present and finally, when the men got off on sports, she became bored.

The last few days, she had noticed her interest flagging in general. The Pack buyout had entered the endgame, everything that needed to be said, said, and said again and again. Nothing remained except busywork, the typical end-of-campaign stuff, all fairly routine absent an October surprise of some sort, which seemed unlikely. And so she listened to the sports arcana being exchanged by her companions and let her mind wander.

Something outside the van caught her attention. A figure had come from behind the field house and begun to move away, head down. At that distance, she couldn't be sure, but something about him seemed familiar.

"Gotta run," she said to the others at once, sliding the van door open, hopping out and going quickly after the man, trotting finally as he appeared to shake off some indecisiveness and lift his head up and set off in a determined fashion.

"Excuse me!" she called, and the man stopped and waited for her. "You're Homer Budge's son, aren't you? I met you when I was interviewing your mother."

He didn't acknowledge this, only stood looking at her.

"I'm sorry, I don't remember your name," she said.

"John Michael."

"Hi. I'm Rachel." She stuck out her hand, and after hesitating, he reached out and took it.

She glanced back to where Johnny Pond and the others, their curiosity aroused, trailed after her, coming to see what she'd treed.

She had John Michael to herself, but not for long.

"Were you in the field house?"

He nodded.

"What's the sense of the meeting?" she asked quickly. "Are they going to vote for the buyout?"

"What do you think?" His apparent bitterness surprised her.

"They are, then?"

"Peterson's got them so buffaloed they'd vote for anything." John Michael wasn't looking at Rachel as he spoke, but over her shoulder toward the other reporters advancing on him.

He had stuffed his hands into the pockets of his jeans, his shoulders hiked up and tense inside the letter jacket he wore, a large R sewn on it. Rachel didn't know how savvy he might be, but he *was*, after all, Homer's son. Why the bitterness? she wondered.

She had only moments before the others arrived.

Lowering her voice, she asked, "What choice do they have? Don't they have to buy the company?"

Momentarily, his eyes left the others and returned to Rachel. Perhaps he was just shivering from the cold, but he seemed to pulse as he stood before her, like a bomb ticking. "A man's always got a choice," he said.

"What do you mean?"

He shrugged but did not answer.

"You don't approve of what's going on?"

"That's right."

In the cold air, sounds carried, cutting through the concussions of the frigid wind, and she heard the footsteps of the others.

John Michael looked toward them again. Rachel had only an instant, one more question, something short, cutting to the bone.

"Do you blame your father?"

"I blame you all," he answered at once, continuing to look over her shoulder.

"Perhaps we can talk. Can we meet?" She was practically whispering.

It made no difference. Without uttering another word, he had pivoted and started walking away as fast as he could.

"Who was that?" Johnny asked as he and the others came

abreast of Rachel. She watched John Michael, leaning rigidly into the wind and quickly receding.

"Nobody," she said to Pond. "One of the students. I thought I saw him leave the field house, but I was mistaken."

Johnny looked at her with raised eyebrow, and in return Rachel gave him one of her best deadpan expressions.

As they moved back toward the van, she considered the significance of what had passed between Homer's son and herself. Back in the car, she took an informal poll among her brethren. Not one of them believed the company could survive, although Johnny reiterated his hope that it would die by stages, not all at once. She listened to their reasons, ticked off as readily as a child recites the definitions of words she has memorized, and realized that as the buyout attempt had heated up, this most fundamental of questions might have been asked less and less often, but no one had forgotten it. Or changed the answer he would have given months ago.

"And what about you, Rachel?" Johnny asked. "What do you say?"

"I'm not sure."

She felt her own reluctance to answer, despite all the evidence screaming at her that they were right: the project to save the company was *meshugge*. It had failure written all over it. And yet…

Perhaps she'd been co-opted by all her own stories about the Pack. Say something enough, and you begin to believe it. Perhaps that was it. Or, she supposed, it might have been something as simple as the fact that she found the people leading the buyout—Skip Peterson and Homer Budge and even such minor players as Billy Noel—so much more sympathetic than doubters like Leonard Sawyer and Fritz Goetzinger…and even her own father, who possessed a true belief about the tenacity of class animosities and who, if she happened to catch him at home when she called, would cluck-cluck over this Midwestern utopian fantasy she was chronicling. But her father wasn't the real issue here. Goetzinger, either. It was Sawyer. She didn't want the old man to win, that above all else.

When she hadn't answered, the others had gone on chatting among themselves, and by the time she decided what she wanted to say, the conversation had strayed well beyond the matter of the Pack.

"Of course, the company can't survive," she told them. "But who knows, maybe it will anyway."

Only later, after their vigil had ended with Skip Peterson prancing out of the meeting, bursting with self-confidence, and she had become conscious of her own pleasure that this should be so, did Rachel recall the last words that Homer Budge's son had said to her.

# CHAPTER 77

~

At hog call the next morning—after the usual reports on the market conditions, margins, kill and cut numbers, yields, and so forth—the conversation, as it always did now, quickly turned to the buyout, the chatter about disciplining the marketplace and resistance from the producers replaced by the search for more retailers willing to stock JackPack products and the priorities for refurbishing the plant.

Skip loved these skull sessions. An afterglow of mellow satisfaction still lingered from his performance at the union meeting the day before. The account in the *Trib* that morning had even been fairly upbeat, Rachel Brandeis's vaunted objectivity showing cracks in the face of the momentum for the buyout. He almost laughed out loud.

And that wasn't all. According to Homer, a couple more of his people had told him they would sign pledges. Another twenty grand. Seventeen pledges so far. Dribs and drabs, but come Friday, with the favorable vote, he expected a lot more. He wasn't worried about that. The credit line was key now. He'd use a factor if he had to. The important thing was to keep going any way he could, keep going.

Yes, he thought, this just might work. He rubbed his hands briskly together.

"And so, Harry," he asked the head of marketing, "we're ready for Saturday?"

"We've increased deliveries to a number of existing accounts, particularly the local ones, others, too. The trick will be to sustain that spike of interest."

"Jack 'n' Jill products are gonna be flying off the shelves. What about your friend at Empire?"

"He's still interested. I'm talking to him a couple times a week."

Skip liked Harry Long. Too inexperienced to be marketing head, of course, but coming along. And what a nice add-on that one of his old college chums was a buyer for the biggest supermarket chain in the Upper Midwest. Harry had some gumption, too. He wasn't one of the crepehangers in the company.

"Good, good, keep the pressure up," Skip told him. "And what about Grand Superette?"

"Still waiting for a callback."

"Is that a problem," Skip asked, "getting these people to call you back?"

"Not a problem. Everybody I approach is intrigued with what we're doing. They can see the possibilities. The idea of employee ownership carries a good deal of moral weight in this part of the world. It's a little bit like the family farm thing. But everybody keeps on asking, 'Where's the ad campaign?' We can't count on free publicity forever. People need to be more conscious of what we're doing here. Then they'll start asking for us by name. But until then it's hard for my guys to justify the shelf space. They want to, but they just can't do it."

Homer Budge now roused himself and put in his two cents. "I think Harry's right. Employee ownership separates us from everybody else. It *is* a moral thing. And it cuts both ways. It's not just something we talk about to our customers, it's something we make a reality in the company. The reason buyouts like this fail is that there's a lot of talk about employee empowerment, but that's all it is, talk."

Skip didn't mind Homer sitting in on these meetings. It even made some sense, although he could have done without the whiff of union negotiating atmosphere that Homer dragged in with him.

"You're right, Homer. I'm not arguing with you," he agreed. He could have told Homer a thing or two that might have cooled his jets. Skip had been working the phones as well, it wasn't just Harry, and he could tap into organizations at a higher level. Unfortunately, enthusiasm for employee ownership seemed to be inversely related to where a man stood in a company's hierarchy. Skip could have pointed that out, but what purpose would be served?

Instead, he turned back to Harry and asked if he'd made any progress with the convenience food chain he'd been negotiating with.

As the conversation continued, Skip heard a soft knock on the door, and his secretary Carole slipped into the conference room and came quickly and noiselessly around to his chair. Whenever Carole appeared unexpectedly, it always meant that something had occurred that wasn't part of the plan. Being the pro she was, nothing could be read in her expression, although Skip did imagine at such moments that her habitual seriousness seemed to deepen with the weight of the message she carried.

Now she leaned over and whispered in his ear, "You have a call from Modern Meat. Mr. Nick Takus."

He didn't move, but something inside him let go. He hadn't heard from Takus in so long that he'd managed to convince himself that he wouldn't hear. His first impulse was to ignore him, to wait until next week and then call back, when it would be too late. In the quiet that had descended around the table, he weighed this enticing thought. So very enticing, but he supposed he'd better talk to the fellow.

He excused himself and followed Carole out.

Walking down the corridor, he felt a tingling sensation squeezing him from both sides and his peripheral vision went black. His legs became uncertain under him.

"Hold on, Carole."

"Are you all right?" He heard the sudden concern in her voice as he bent over, staring down at the carpet runner, his hands on his knees. "Should I go get someone?" she asked.

"No. Just wait."

He took several deep breaths. Easy, he told himself, easy, this is no time to start hyperventilating.

Slowly, his vision cleared.

He stood up. "Okay."

"Are you sure?"

"I'm fine. Don't worry." He leaned close to her and cupped her elbow as they continued along for a few paces. "This is what I want you to do. Go tell Nick Takus that you couldn't find me. Tell him you looked all over the place, but I'm not to be found. Tell him you'll leave a message that he called. You understand?"

"Yes, of course," she said doubtfully, then more strongly, "and is there anything else?"

"No, that'll be enough for now. Thank you."

He watched her walking on without him. Takus wouldn't believe her. What would he do? Skip didn't know. At that moment, he didn't much care, either. He had no control of Takus. He had no control over anything, just what he did. And he'd be damned if he'd go like a lamb to the slaughter.

He went back into the conference room and sat down with the others.

"Okay," he said, "where were we?"

~

It didn't take long.

At two that afternoon, when he returned from a plant walk-about, Carole regarded him dolefully. "I'm sorry. There was nothing I could do."

What she meant became clear as soon as he opened the door to his office, for inside he found none other than Mel Coyle, once again sitting in the chair he had occupied so often, for so many years.

"Close the door," Coyle told him.

Skip complied, and then went over and sat behind his desk. The two of them regarded each other silently.

Almost immediately, the phone rang. Skip understood that Mel had instructed Carole to put the call through as soon as he returned. He did nothing, however, merely sat there and continued to look at Mel.

"Pick up the damn phone, Skip."

For several more beats, Skip still did nothing. When finally he picked up the receiver, he spoke at once, without bothering to wait for the caller to identify himself.

"Hello, Nick. It's not 1 a.m. What are you doing calling at a time like this?"

Takus laughed.

"I thought maybe you'd make more sense in the daytime."

"Well, we'll have to see. What's on your mind?" Mel jabbed his finger toward the speaker. "Wait a second, Nick. There's somebody here that wants to listen in. Mel Coyle. He's on our board." As if Takus didn't know.

"Okay by me," Takus said, and Skip switched the call over to the speakerphone.

"So, as I said, Nick, what's on your mind?" Now that the miserable business had begun, Skip wanted nothing so much as to get it over with.

"What's on my mind? Lots of things, Skip. My mind's always occupied."

"I'm sure it is."

"You know I'm about ready to open my new plant out there in Maquoketa. Just a few weeks now. A nice little operation, if I do say so myself. I'll have to show you around it one day. Anyway, I'm opening up shop, and since I'm the new boy on the block, and it'll take the farmers a little while to gear up their production, I'm gonna have to work real hard to convince them to sell their animals to me instead of you. I'll do it, of course, if I have to. I'm gonna do whatever I have to. You better believe it."

"We all do what we have to, Nick."

"Now, I made a nice little offer to you some time back, but you just couldn't see your way clear to take me up on it. I figured your board would, but apparently you're mighty persuasive."

"What makes you think that I had to convince my board of anything? Frankly, Nick, your offer wasn't adequate. Any board would have refused it."

Takus laughed. "That's rich. You kill me, Skip. There you are, you barely got a pot to piss in, and you're talking like…hell, like me."

Skip couldn't stand this guy.

"I keep trying to get a grip on the thing," Takus roared on. "Just what are you trying to prove with all this Ted Mack's Original Amateur Hour stuff? Are you trying to give people a paycheck to take home for a few more months? Is that the idea? Or maybe you really do believe you can pull the thing off. You can't, my friend, believe me. Or maybe—now here's a thought—maybe you're putting this little dog and pony show on strictly for my benefit. Trying to wring a few more bucks out of ol' Nick Takus. Maybe you think Nick stands for Saint Nick and being as how Christmas is on the way—"

"Now that *is* an idea, Nick. But I have to confess, I've never confused you with Santa Claus." Old Nick was more like it. Skip saw no reason to continue Takus's charade of puzzlement. "So what's it to be, Nick? Did you call to put something else on the table?"

"Right! Let's cut to the chase, shall we? So here's the deal. Ten million. I'll take your assets off your hands. The whole kit and caboodle. It'll save us both a lot of heartache. Ten mil. That's my final offer. A good offer. An offer, believe me, you'd be out of your mind to pass up."

"What about you buy my stock?"

"No, no, no, no. Not about to saddle myself with a union contract. Just the assets, thank you. Debt free, of course. Look, Skip, I can buy you out or I can compete. I figure it'll cost me a little less in the long run to buy. But either way. You choose. You wanna play fox and hounds, it's okay by me. I've always enjoyed a good chase. You got until midnight Thursday. After that, you're on your own. I will make no more offers, that's a promise. After that, you can go rot in hell for all I care."

Thursday? That meant the buyout vote and the deadline for pledges would have to be moved up a day. Takus knew this, of course. That was the point.

"Well, this is interesting, Nick. What say you give us until next Monday, and we'll think about it?"

"Actually, Skip, I didn't call to negotiate. I called to make an offer. Take it or leave it."

"I need the extra time, Nick."

"Of course you do, but I ain't gonna give it to ya. I run a business here. I ain't got time to sit around with my thumb up my ass. And where does it say I've got to help you out? We're supposed to be competing. Isn't that what the free enterprise system is all about?"

"So I'm told."

"And anyway, this is a pretty good deal, you ask me, a win-win situation. You've just gotta take a close look at it."

Skip was trapped. His situation was absolutely, totally hopeless. But one thing he wouldn't agree to. "If you want a deal, Nick, you've got to push the deadline back twenty-four hours. Friday midnight."

"My proposal stands."

Skip glared at Mel, who had been listening with his usual placid demeanor. "I'll tell you what, Nick. You don't give me the extra time, I'll go to the papers. I don't give a shit what happens. You'll be crucified in Jackson, and you won't get the company, either. After that, the board would never vote to sell it to you. Not only that, but after a stunt like that, the employees will give me the shirts off their backs. You want to compete? We'll compete. So I want midnight Friday. Either that or it's no deal."

For once, Takus didn't immediately come back at Skip. Across the room, Mel frowned and nodded and settled himself more comfortably. Skip took the gestures to mean that he approved of the ultimatum. Push the deadline back, give the employees one last shot, why not? Force Takus to agree to that much at least. But Skip didn't want Takus to agree. Skip wanted to go to the papers and blow this whole damn thing sky-high. For a brief moment, he even fantasized that Takus might be crazy enough to call his bluff.

It was not to be.

"Well," the Modern Meat CEO said at last, "I guess you got yourself a deal. Friday it is. Friday, midnight. But this is just between you and me and your board, okay? If you go out and start blabbing to the papers and making me out to be a steaming cow patty, the deal's off. Explain *that* to your stockholders."

"I'm just trying to stay alive, Nick."

"I know what you're trying to do."

Skip hung up and stared at the phone. "Fuckhead." Then at Mel. "Are you satisfied?"

"What do you think?" Mel asked.

The two of them continued to regard one another across the gulf that had opened between them.

~

Skip polled the board, a pure formality. Takus's offer would be accepted contingent upon the union vote on Friday. And one more thing. Whatever the vote, Skip could forget about continuing without the extra money to upgrade the plant. He had to find that by Friday midnight, too. Or else the assets went to Takus.

# CHAPTER 78

～

Homer slammed his desk, stood up, and walked a couple of paces away before he twisted around, and glared back at Peterson. "You said you wouldn't do this!"

Peterson shook his head, tight little movements, his mouth screwed into a narrow frown. "Not my decision."

"Who then?" Homer demanded.

Peterson regarded him with an expression that might have been resignation or disgust, with a tight smile that contained some of the old Peterson scorn at questions he considered dumb.

"Then why the hell am I dealing with you? Shit, Skip, you said you wouldn't do this!"

"That's right. Didn't say it wouldn't happen."

Homer turned his back on Peterson and took another step away, then changed his mind and returned and sat down at his desk again. "Who should I talk to? Two lousy days from the vote! Who's in charge, Skip? If it isn't you, who?"

Peterson just shook his head. There was no one else to talk to.

It was all too perfect. Homer had been warned. He'd been warned over and over. But he just had to take the chance. He had to believe somehow it would come out different this time. The company wouldn't screw him. Just this one damn time!

"You laid a trap? You son of a bitch."

"It's no trap, Homer. At least, none of my doing."

"Who then?"

Homer kept asking who, but Skip merely shook his head. Homer's sense of betrayal grew. John Michael had been right. It had been pointless to try to save the company.

"You don't seem very damn upset," he accused Peterson, who sat with his arms crossed and his legs crossed, folded into himself.

"A couple hours ago, I was rippin', just like you are now. But I'd known all along that something like this might happen. And if it did, it'd be at the last minute. You did, too."

"Like hell."

"We both knew it, Homer."

"Maybe you did."

Impatiently, Peterson looked away. "Well…no matter. It's done." His gaze, cooler now, returned to Homer. "Remember the day you came up to my office and demanded control out in the plant? Remember that? I hated the idea, I thought it stunk. But you were right. The pill was bitter, but I had to swallow it. And so I did, okay, I did. Out on the floor, you'll be in charge. That was your bottom line." He paused. "That was yours, and this is mine. I've got to have the upgrade money."

"I don't believe you. You've known all along. You've been bullshitting us."

Peterson shook his head. "I pushed the thing as far as I could, Homer. But I'm not the only board member."

"It's over then."

"Is it?"

Homer leaned toward him. "Yeah."

Peterson raised his eyebrows and frowned and tilted his head to the side in a gesture that said maybe and maybe not.

Homer sat quietly for a few moments, almost feeling nothing, but then his anger surged back.

"Shit, *shit*!"

He lurched up from his chair, banging the palms of his hands with a sharp report against his desktop.

Peterson sat way back in his chair, folded in upon himself, perfectly still except for a remnant of the many times he'd shaken his head in the last two minutes. His message had been delivered. He had, for the moment, nothing more to say.

Homer wandered bleakly around his office, ignoring the other man, touching familiar objects. After a time, he became conscious of his anger, and with consciousness, it began to drain away. But his sense of treachery remained.

"You're right, Skip," he admitted, "I *did* expect something like this, some sort of last-minute shenanigans." That was the nature of last minutes. "But I'll tell you what, it doesn't make any difference. It's still for shit. As a matter of fact, it makes it worse. Know why? Because that's the way things have always worked around here. I thought we were trying to do something different. Obviously, I was wrong."

"We *were* trying to do something different. Still are."

"I don't believe you." Homer looked sharply back at Peterson. "Why should I believe you?"

Peterson barely paused before he said, "I can't think of a single reason."

"Neither can I." Peterson represented the stockholders. In their interest, he would lie through his teeth without a second thought. Homer had been a fool to ever imagine it might be otherwise.

Skip stirred himself. "Look, Homer, everyone knows the vote's this Friday, okay? And everyone knows what that means. Naturally, people act in their own interest. Me, too, I'm no different. But you're wrong if you think I don't want to keep on going. I'm not the same guy I was two months ago. I can't prove it, but it's true. You'll just have to believe it. A leap of faith, okay?

"And I know what this does to our chances. We've made some folks nervous, you and I. Suddenly they think we might actually make the buyout work. So they use their power...and it's considerable."

Homer had gone back to wandering. He cast a sidelong glance. "Have you got another offer?"

Peterson shook his head. "If I could tell you, I would."

"Why, thank you."

Peterson's hands flew outward in frustration, then dropped into his lap. Homer turned away and stood staring into the old-fashioned glass-faced bookcase. The room behind him was mirrored in the glass, ghostly shapes obscuring the Iowa Code and NLRB rulings and other volumes. He was aware how shabby everything must appear to Peterson, who never came down to the union offices—windowless, drab, filled with out-of-date furniture. At the supper hour, everyone had gone home, leaving behind a thick silence.

"It's over," he said as he had earlier.

"Maybe."

"You can't believe the membership's going to come up with the extra money, just because you threaten them like this?" Homer went back over and slumped in his chair. The feeling that the whole business was done lifted none of the burden from him. Instead he felt empty and very, very tired.

"It's not a threat."

"An ultimatum then. Whatever." Pointless to quibble.

"People want this to work, Homer, people are still committed to it. We've got to get to Saturday. If we can get to Saturday, we've still got a chance."

Homer listened to the conviction coming back into Peterson's voice but said nothing himself, merely stretched out in his chair and rested his chin on his chest and closed his eyes. It occurred to him that he should still be angry, that one of his flaws was the inability to hold on to anger once he had it. Even now he couldn't, even after this sucker punch.

"My people," he told Skip without opening his eyes, "are free to do whatever they please."

"That's right. But frankly, Homer, I'm not worried about them, not at the moment at least. The person I'm worried about is you. What I want to know is—are *you* still with me?"

Even to ask such a question at such a time seemed the height of arrogance. Homer didn't respond.

"How many years have you been union head, Homer?" Peterson said after a long pause.

"Nine. Why? What difference does it make?"

"Nine. Long time. I can remember how surprised I was when you were elected." Peterson was speaking conversationally now. "No offense, Homer, but you just didn't seem the type. Too easygoing, too nice a guy. Not that we minded upstairs."

If Peterson was trying to get on his good side, he was picking a damn odd way to do it. At the frank assessment, Homer felt a twinge of pain, for he knew many people, his own son included, felt that way about him.

"I was asked by a number of people to run," he told Peterson.

"Yes, I understand, you were the compromise candidate, and then, of course, compromise became the order of the day, so you stayed on. But don't get me wrong, you did a good job, I'm not saying you didn't. You got all there was to get. Still, you know, I've never quite shaken my original impression…that you were a man who would have been happier doing something else."

Homer's thoughts immediately went to a conversation he and Rose had from time to time about the possibility of his becoming a deacon in the Church, a dream he continued to dream, although he had never felt as unworthy as he did at that moment.

"It might surprise you," Peterson had gone on, "but we're quite similar, you and I. In that way, at least. I've often thought I should have done something else. Of course, there was always my family. And the choices we make are not always our own."

This admission, the personal nature of it, wasn't like Peterson, who had never been one to reveal much about himself.

No matter. It was a piss-poor occasion for personal revelations, too little too late. "I'm sure that right about now we all wish we were doing something else," Homer told him.

Peterson, following a line of reasoning of his own, stretched out in his chair, hands clasped on the top of his head, all at once as relaxed as he had been wound tight as a drum earlier. "You know what it's like being an only child?" he asked. "No, I suppose not."

He stared off into space, as motionless as if he had stopped breathing. Someone who walked into the office at that moment could have taken them for a couple of buddies lounging around and shooting the breeze. When Peterson continued, he had dropped the subject of his childhood as abruptly as he raised it. "It's true, I should have done something else, although if you asked me, I couldn't tell you what. Doesn't make any difference, of course, not now. I followed my nose and here I am." He paused again. "I suppose inheritors often feel entitled. I can't say that I did. Or do. Anyway, here I am. Here *we* are. Two guys out of place. Unsuited to the roles we find ourselves playing. But I'll tell you what, Homer, if it wasn't us, it wouldn't be anybody. We're the only reasons this buyout has ever had a ghost of a chance."

Homer wasn't taken in by this invitation to think well of himself. "We should never have tried."

"Perhaps not. But it's too late now."

It surely was, Homer thought. Too late now. He could just imagine how John Michael was going to react to this latest twist in the plot. Boy, oh, boy.

Peterson sat still stretched out and quiet and strangely at ease, very different than the Skip Peterson Homer had always known, the constant movement gone, the slightly distracted air and bursts of intense concentration gone. Something *had* happened. Perhaps he simply realized that the buyout was doomed and was content to play out the string. Perhaps. That might be true. Yet something else radiated from him as well, as it might from a man who after a lifetime of dissatisfactions had at long last come to terms with himself.

He said, "It's a lonely feeling, isn't it, out here in no-man's-land, trying to put this thing together while the people behind us, our own people, do their damnedest to shoot the thing down. I tell you, Homer, what we're doing, why, it just scares the bejesus out of 'em. They're gonna screw us any way they can." He sat up and stretched, like a man rising from a nap. "Be nice if we could ignore them. Course, we can't." Having stretched, he now eyed Homer. "So...it'll happen or it won't. Wha'd'ya think, Hom, is this still worth doing? I say it is."

Homer stared at a bare patch of wall on the far side of the room. He supposed that, despite everything, he really did believe the man. It had always been his fate to believe people, whatever the consequences.

When he spoke, he said, "My eldest son is a sophomore at Reinert. He's nineteen. An A student, always been an A student. A little old-fashioned, I suppose, being your typical union-raised kid. He takes what he finds in books a little too much to heart, too, but he's basically a good kid. Quite different from me, as you can imagine, although I certainly don't love him any the less for it." He wondered how much he wanted to say here. Everything, he guessed. Too little, too late, but he'd say it anyway. "I surely do love him, Skip. But you see, we've been growing apart, my son and me. He thinks I'm weak because of the concessions the union has made over the years. He thinks I'm weak, weaker, because I've agreed to this buyout scheme of yours, which he sees as futile and hurting union locals elsewhere and so forth. Arguments against it aren't hard to find..."

Homer stopped for a moment, and Skip continued for him.

"And now this."

"And now this."

Homer could see that the revelation interested Peterson. He had his hands on his knees, preparing to rise.

"Perhaps after we've made the buyout work," he suggested, "your son will understand."

Homer shook his head. "That's the thing of it. It makes no difference what happens now. Win or lose, he's not going to change his mind."

"I'm sorry."

"Yeah." Having unburdened himself, Homer found that he didn't feel any better. The pain had merely become more clearly focused. John Michael, he knew, still loved him, but it was a love stripped of respect. It was love as duty, love as alms.

A few minutes earlier Skip had come into the room with the shuttered look of a man bearing bad news. Now he sat alertly on the edge of his chair, renewed, ready to spring back up and get on with the business, lacking only Homer's commitment.

"So what's it to be, Homer, you still with me?"

It was interesting, Homer thought bitterly, how little there was to think about here.

"Oh," he told Skip Peterson, "I guess. Gone this far. Pointless to stop now."

# CHAPTER 79

~

Around the perimeter of the Goetzingers' kitchen, drop cloths were spread. Edna had Teddy painting the walls in order to add a little brightness to the room, despite her guilt over the cost. The furniture had been cramped to the middle. Edna and Fritz and the Noels could have gone into the living room, but even in the clutter, the kitchen seemed more comfortable, if that was the right word. Teddy wasn't painting at the moment, nor in the room, although Edna had no doubt he would be keeping quiet someplace in the house where he could hear what was going on.

Almost as soon as Maggie had come through the door, she'd said, "Did you hear? Of course you heard." Billy Noel tagged along reluctantly after his wife. As she had started painfully to shuck off her winter coat, he hurried to catch up and help. She was already turning toward Fritz. "You've been saying all along this would happen."

There was something unintentionally comical about the Noels, Maggie a bit of a thing and Billy so huge, like a Saint Bernard leaning solicitously over a dachshund.

Maggie refused coffee or soda pop, saying they didn't intend to stay. She wouldn't sit down, but thank you. Almost immediately, the phone rang, and Fritz answered it and talked briefly and said he'd call back.

"It's been this way the last three hours," Edna told the Noels.

"I can believe it," Maggie nodded.

Fritz returned to the little group, frowning and shaking his head.

"Everybody's up in arms, I guess," Maggie said, and Edna heard some hopefulness in her tone.

"Looks like," Fritz told her. Since the calls had started, he had become more thoughtful. With another man, that might have been a good sign.

"We want you to tell us everything you know about it," Maggie said eagerly.

Edna—and Billy, too—watched in silence as she grilled Fritz. He told her what he knew, what rumors he had heard, what he thought. His arguments were all well known to Edna and, she imagined, also to Billy, who had sat down himself after moving an empty chair over close to his wife. She seemed intent upon not using it, however, as if that might remove some of the seriousness from the situation. Billy had taken his own coat off, then his woolen beret, turning up the earflaps, and he sat with the two coats and the hat on his lap.

Maggie Noel, a tiny woman made tinier by her arthritis, never went out of her house without getting dressed up, and not this time, either, crisis or no crisis. She wore petite sizes, but they were always too big on her, like the black slacks and shepherd's plaid top she had on at the moment, the top sprouting like epaulets from her shoulders and collapsing around her sunken chest and arms. She nodded furiously as Fritz spoke and put question after question to him, determined to dig out every last little nugget of information. And Fritz happy to oblige, Fritz who had finally, irrevocably given up on the buyout, if he'd ever really believed in it.

Edna felt deeply for Maggie, who had to work so hard to free her mind from her poor knotted up body. Just to look at her caused Edna sympathetic pains. Edna watched her friend's thoughts moving laboriously between inside and outside, the involuntary facial tics as she made small adjustments trying to ease the chronic pain, the quick birdlike moments of concentration as something that Fritz said particularly caught her attention; back and forth she went. In Edna's interactions with others, few things brought her more pleasure than the sudden vivid smile that would sometimes break free on Maggie's face. Her whole life had been one of learning to accept what she could not change. But she was a sharp little thing, and you had to get past that before you could see the rest.

Suddenly, Billy interrupted angrily. "So that's all? We put all this time in, trying to set the thing up, where we was gonna have a say in things, and you're telling me to forget about it, just like that?"

Edna started back, staring at him in amazement. She'd never heard such a violent rush of words out of Billy Noel, not in her whole life. Maggie clasped one gnarled hand in the other and looked at the floor, stricken. Fritz, brought up short as well, turned away and took a deep breath and pressed down a wrinkle in one of the painter's cloths with the toe of his work boot. "Peterson violated his trust, Billy. Said he wouldn't demand the money."

"He didn't say that! He said things could change."

"He knew they'd change. He knew. He's been leading you—us all—around by the nose."

As harsh as his words were, Fritz spoke carefully, sadly, without looking at Billy, and Edna saw that her husband understood the pain he was causing his friend. Maggie had looked up, silently watching the exchange, now between the two men.

Determined, Fritz pressed on. "If this company can be saved, Billy, why hasn't somebody else come forward with the money to do it?"

"It's a long shot, we all know that. But there are a lot of us—you, too—who've worked there our whole lives practically. Since the time of Skip's grandfather." As Billy spoke, he seemed to gather courage. "We know the plant inside out. If anyone can make her competitive, we can." Nothing in his demeanor when he'd arrived had suggested this determination to continue, and now Edna began to suspect the purpose for this visit, Maggie's purpose.

"You think so, Billy?" Fritz asked skeptically. "You think you can save the company?"

Edna noticed that he didn't say "we." If all Fritz's own dreams hadn't come to so little, perhaps he could have shared in this one with Billy. It should have been his. He worked at the Pack, too. But Fritz had a way of not being part of anything he didn't trust.

"Remember, Fritzy," she now reminded him, "this buyout was your idea in the first place."

"Not anymore, it ain't." He turned immediately back toward Billy. "What about Modern Meat?" he challenged him, still speaking softly. "You ready to compete with them?"

"They can't pay a premium to the farmers forever." Billy was slowly swaying side to side on his chair.

"Maybe, but that ain't all. What happens when they got their own brand names, too? It's gonna happen. And when it does, they'll run ad campaigns like you've never seen before."

"Jack 'n' Jill meats are the best in the industry."

"Even if they are, it makes no difference. This is like politics, Billy. The guy with the most money wins."

They continued arguing, but the steam quickly went out of Billy. Edna stood, Fritz stood, and even poor, arthritic Maggie still refused to sit in the chair Billy had moved for her. The three of them crowded around the poor man, who remained stubborn and disconsolate in the center, swaying side to side, at war with himself. After the flare-up of defiance, his doubts had returned full force, and he said sadly, "It's a tough one."

"Do you really believe people are gonna make the sacrifices necessary here?" Fritz asked him. "This isn't like…like, I don't know, farming. You take farming, Billy. It might be a mighty tough way to make a living, but farming's not just a job, it's a way of life. It's in the blood. Working in a packinghouse isn't in anybody's blood."

"Might be you're right," Billy retorted, regaining some of his determination, "maybe the Pack ain't much, but it's all a lot of us got. I can't fall back on my farming the way you can."

Fritz took his time responding. "Without the job at the Pack, Billy, I'll probably lose the farm."

Billy's head came up. "Is that true?"

"We don't know what's going to happen," Edna interposed quickly. Immediately, she thought about Teddy and wondered exactly where he was lurking. Later, when he judged the emotional intensity had eased enough, he'd show his face, and of course, after the Noels had left, there'd be a storm of questions—"Are we really gonna lose the farm, Ma, are we? Are we?"—which she'd struggle to answer, realizing, as she often did with Teddy, what slippery things words could be.

"We've got this chance, Fritz," Billy said, quickly forgetting about anything else and almost pleading with his friend now. "We'll never have another like it. If we don't take it, we've got nobody to blame but ourselves."

"We won't have anybody to blame but ourselves? Is that what you think? Come on, Billy, we didn't mismanage the Pack. You know that. Don't let Peterson sell you this bill of goods."

"I suppose so," Billy admitted, his intensity deserting him again, an awkward silence settling upon the four of them.

"But somehow, you know…" Billy started and then stopped. Edna watched him continuing to struggle with himself. Billy had never been confrontational in his life. "The way you feel, Fritz," he labored on, "why, that doesn't have anything to do with the logic of the thing, I don't think. Maybe it's Skip Peterson's fault, but I don't know how important that is, come right down to it, when you ain't got a job and you're fifty-seven years old, and you don't know how to do anything some other employer might be interested in. I got this picture of myself out of work, sitting in the living room watching soap operas, doin' nothing worth doin'.'"

Billy hung his head and said no more. Arguments with Fritz weren't fair fights, but Billy had hung on despite the setbacks.

And Fritz, Edna could see, was affected. He didn't know how to deal with a situation like this, one he couldn't reduce to a simple matter of right and wrong. For he was not an unkind man.

Edna spoke to the Noels. "I want to say how much I admire you both. Everything is so very difficult for you, I know, Maggie, but you're always such a trooper, it just fills my heart. And you, Billy, what a difficult thing you're trying to do. Another man would have given up long ago, but not you. I think it's wonderful."

"Nobody said it was gonna be easy," Billy managed, a little sourly, the bruises from his exchange with Fritz still showing. "A man's got to be willing to take a chance. Like they say, nothing changes but what people make it change."

"And you're willing to do that, Billy?" Fritz asked. "It's not just you, you know. It's Maggie, too, and your kids."

"Fritzy!"

"I didn't say it. Billy did. A man's gotta take a chance. Okay, fair enough. All I'm tellin' him is it's not just his own life he's putting at risk here."

"Billy knows that." Edna glared at her husband. "And as for you, Mr. Goetzinger, you've said enough." Fritz looked defiantly back at her, but for once kept his mouth shut. "This is the Noels' decision, not yours."

With that, she turned away and tried to regain her equilibrium by concentrating on the others. "What about you, Maggie?" she asked. "You haven't said anything for a long time. What do you think?"

Maggie was looking at her husband, the look distracted and at the same time full of concern, anxiety, and other emotions as well, too many to read.

"Linda's been after us to move down to Tucson, to be near her and the grandkids. What with my disability and Billy's retirement money and in a few years social security, we could just about manage it. Billy doesn't want to leave, of course. He's lived here all his life. I have, too, but I'd go in a minute."

"So you don't want him to put the money into the buyout, is that what you're saying?"

"It's not up to me. I keep telling Billy, it's his decision to make. I'll go along with whatever he decides, but he's got to do it. I know he wants to put the money in. He thinks this is his big chance to do something with his life. Maybe he's right, I don't know. But he's got to decide. If he can't decide about this, what kind of owner will he make? That's the way I look at it. If he can't make up his own mind, what hope is there that he'll stick up for himself when they get to fighting about something or other once the employees own the company? Isn't that right?"

"I think you're right," Edna agreed.

But Maggie wasn't satisfied with the statement. She had shifted her attention from her husband to Edna. "I'd love it, Edna, if Billy contributed and they made a success of it and he got the pride of it, I surely would."

"I understand."

"As much as I want to move down there to Tucson, I would love for Billy to be able to take real pride in something he accomplished."

With a slight start, Edna realized the intensity of Maggie's need for approval here. She had never been one to ask for help. But this was different. She must have been harboring these desires to go to Tucson, maybe saying little or nothing to Billy and feeling guilty because in her heart of hearts she wanted him to forget about the Pack, and at the same time knowing that here was the one real chance he'd ever have to do something special with his life. And wasn't it true that every man wanted nothing so much as to do something special with his life? What a burden, Edna thought, for Maggie to have to carry.

Maggie's sharpness might appear to some people to be mean-spirited. But she never complained about her arthritis. Edna suspected that it took a lot out of her, not complaining about all that pain, chronic and progressive as it was, the endless struggle waged between her mind and her body. So if she groused about other things, more important things in the eye of the world perhaps, but in fact less important given the reality of her life, then what did it really matter?

"I know that you've never wanted anything but the best for Billy," Edna said to her friend. "Billy's your life. So don't you worry that you're not doing right by him. And anyway, what you said is true. If Billy really wants to be part of the buyout, it *is* his decision. Nobody else—not you or anybody—can make it for him."

Edna was conscious of the way she and Maggie were talking about Billy, as if he wasn't present. Had the two women been alone, they would have talked even more frankly, although it appeared they were having something of a private conversation anyway.

"I want to do it," Billy said. That was all.

Edna glared at Fritz, daring him to put his two cents in, but he just shrugged. He'd said his piece. He'd let it go at that. Edna smiled, satisfied.

# CHAPTER 80

~

At a quarter to five the next morning, Fritz stood in his kitchen making a call. The phone on the other end rang three times, and then an answering machine clicked on, Rachel Brandeis saying she wasn't available and to leave a message.

"Rachel? This is Fritz. You awake?" He paused, waiting for her to pick up. What were the chances she was gone by this time in the morning? Not much, he figured, unless she'd spent the night somewhere else. Did she have a boyfriend?

When she didn't answer, he said, "Want you to meet me. You know where Kleinburg is? The JackPack buying station there. Meet me there. An hour from now, quarter to six. Kleinburg. It's out on highway 52, just shy of thirty miles. The buying station."

He hung up, but remained dissatisfied, so a half minute later, he dialed the number again. Edna was moving around upstairs. He wanted to get out of the house before she came down. He listened to the rings impatiently, tapping a finger against the countertop. This time, Rachel answered.

"I heard you, Fritz," she said at once, her voice filled with sleep and irritation.

"Little early for you, is it?"

"What do you want?"

"You know where Kleinburg is?"

"You just told me. What's this about?"

"Tell you when you get there. Got a story for ya."

"Where's the buying station?"

"You know what *klein* means in German? Tiny. That's Kleinburg, tiny. You can find the town, you can find anything in it. Quarter to six." He hung up.

The buying station, in fact, stood at the eastern edge of the town, practically the first thing you ran into when you were coming in from Jackson. Fritz drove out and waited for her, turning the pickup around so it faced back east and leaving the parking lights on. Despite the cold that began at once to seep into the truck, he turned the engine off, preferring the prairie silence. He could make out farms on the far horizon. The blue-black sky rose above the black landscape. A sliver of dying moon hung high in the eastern sky. He liked the darkness and being alone and thinking that the only people awake were his kind of people. The troublemakers didn't get up this early.

From time to time, headlights appeared in the distance, and he watched them disappear and reappear, approaching across the long depressions and rises. Mostly they turned out to be trucks like his, and he wondered if Brandeis would show. Probably she would, he decided, probably just fixing her face. But he couldn't sit there forever, he had to be to work. Every day he got up and went to work and spent eight hours on the kill floor just like he always had.

He had stopped imagining that the lights appearing on the horizon might be hers when a car rose into view close at hand and startled him by turning into the station and sliding to a stop on the loose gravel, nose to nose with the truck. The driver leaned over to the passenger seat to do something, and then used a shoulder to push open the driver-side door and get out. Rachel.

She approached, looking around, taking everything in, her coat wrapped tightly around her, hugging her notebook against her chest. He rolled down his window. Only when she had stopped, a step away, did her gaze come to rest on him.

"So. I'm here."

"Get in. We'll talk."

She went around and climbed in. Fritz considered starting the engine and turning on the heater, then didn't.

"Do you know why Peterson's demanding the 401(k) money?" he asked without preliminaries.

"The wage givebacks aren't enough."

"Why not?"

She could have played dumb and dragged the thing out but didn't. "Probably there's another offer for the company." As she spoke, she inspected the cab of the truck.

"Who from?"

"I don't know."

"Making any effort to find out?"

She said nothing for a few moments, then, "To hell with you. I do my job."

She was annoyed with him. Good. But her response was a bit stronger than he would have expected. He regarded her as he decided how he could avoid getting into a useless conversation about hurt feelings. "Generally, Rachel, when people get touchy, means I hit a sore spot. You're in a difficult position. If there's another offer, only a few people know about it. You've got less than a day now. Most likely not possible to find out, most likely a waste of time…So let me go at the thing another way—just how hard you trying?"

The dashboard lights barely touched her dark hair and the full curve of her cheek. No doubt, Fritz thought as he waited, intelligent reporters like Rachel assumed as a matter of course that others were trying to manipulate them. They were right, of course, people did try. Succeeded, too. Fritz, for his part, never really understood why a person with anything on the ball would go into such a profession.

"If there *is* an offer," she said finally, "it's probably from Modern Meat."

"There's an offer all right. Otherwise, Peterson would take what he could get and make do."

"Hard information?"

"That's your job."

"Then why did you drag me all the way out here?" No fooling around for Miss Brandeis today.

"Okay," he said, "here's the deal. Since Peterson is forcing the employees to put up this extra money, I'm coming out against the buyout."

"Why didn't you tell me this last night when we talked?"

"Didn't know it then."

"What changed?"

"Doesn't matter. What matters is Peterson violated his trust. He's never been up front with the membership. Never treated them like equals. He demands they empty out their pockets, and what does he give in return? Nothing, that's what.

"Most likely, he's been after the 401(k) money all along. First, he had to get everyone all hyped up on this idea they were gonna be running the company themselves. And terrified they'd lose their jobs. He set things up so it was all or nothing. Then he figured he could get anything he wanted."

To jot down her notes, Rachel took off one glove and held a finger of it clamped between her teeth. The truck was getting colder by the minute. She removed the glove from her mouth as she asked again what evidence he had.

"Seems plain as day to me."

"Does it? Tell me, Fritz, it's true you haven't come out against the buyout before, but everybody knows how you feel. Are you against the wages-for-stock part of the deal, too?"

"What difference does it make? Peterson's demanding the other money, so I'm against the buyout."

"You realize it's way too late to get this into paper today."

"That's right."

"You called me out here to give me a story I can't run until tomorrow?"

"Nope. Wanted to show you something." He waited a couple of beats before continuing. "See that house over there?"

She turned to look. A nearby streetlight shone on the for sale sign, the unkempt yard, the empty porch, the carport with no car. "Doesn't look like much, does it? Kind of place you happened on, you'd pass right on by. Turns out, it's of more interest than you might think." He told her about Modern Meat's option to buy it. "You know about that?" he asked.

"No."

"Didn't expect you would. I've been calling around, to the other buying stations. Guess what. Almost everyplace, it's the same story—Modern Meat's taken out an option on some piece of property right nearby. Something your friend Skip Peterson hasn't seen fit to let you in on, although you can bet he knows about it."

She didn't much like this crack, but that was all right. Part of the reason he'd made her come out there was because she wouldn't want to. Hard to get people's attention if you were nice about things.

"Modern Meat's opening their Maquoketa plant," she said. "They'll need buying stations."

"Why the options, then? Why not just buy?"

"You tell me."

"Probably Nick Takus figures he won't have to exercise them. Probably he's made an offer for the Pack."

"Okay."

"But that's not what's really important."

He gave her a few moments to figure it out for herself.

"What's important," he told her when she said nothing and he got sick of waiting, "is *where* Takus has seen fit to buy the options, cheek-by-jowl up against JackPack operations. No reason to do that, not unless you're a bully. Takus is a bully. He enjoys his little cat-and-mouse game with Peterson. My guess is he really doesn't care one way or the other. He'll buy the Pack or he'll drive it out of business, whichever. This isn't news, of course. As soon as he announced he was building the plant in Maquoketa, people knew what would happen. Somehow, in all the shouting about the employees buying the company, it's been forgotten, that's all."

Rachel had become thoughtful, seeming to dispense with the chip on her shoulder for the moment.

"Perhaps," she said, "but all this is surmise on your part, just like your assumptions about the new offer for the company and about Peterson's motives. Do you have a shred of hard evidence, anything at all, aside from the fact that the options exist?"

"That's where you come in. Let's see how good you are at your job. You tell me what's going on. Tell me I'm right, tell me I'm wrong. Or, more to the point of the thing, you tell the employees. They're the ones deserve to know. Right? Isn't that right?"

"Of course."

"I'll say this much. Takus will build his buying stations if he has to. He'll pay a premium for hogs, if he has to, and he'll keep on paying, as long as it takes."

"Won't the farmers remain loyal to the Pack?"

"Some. But mostly they'll sell to the highest bidder. They work on narrow margins. They can't afford to be picky, a man offers them more for their animals."

"But if JackPack closes later on and they *have* to sell to Modern Meat, then they'll be at Takus's mercy."

"That's the future," Fritz said. "It's like the weather. Farmer knows next summer he might get no rain. What's he supposed to do about it? Same thing when it comes to selling hogs. He worries about today, lets tomorrow take care of itself."

Rachel's demeanor had changed completely now, her combativeness gone, replaced by a withdrawn, considering look.

"The buyout's foolish, Rachel," he told her. "As for Peterson and Takus, it's no contest. Takus is a son of a bitch, but he knows what he'd doing. Peterson's out of his league. No matter what he does, he can't make his operation as efficient as Maquoketa. Plus, he's gonna be paying through the nose for his short-term money. And he's lost a good bit of his market, too, and it'll take him years to get it back, maybe never. Takus knows all this, and he knows how to use it."

Rachel nodded, although not as if in agreement, only as if acknowledging that she heard the words.

"Anything else?" she asked.

"That should be more than enough."

"It's something," she conceded. "I can verify that the options exist. As for the rest…"

"The employees deserve to know," he repeated.

As Rachel climbed out of the cab, she said, "That might be true, but if there is another offer, and I find out, that will kill the employee buyout. People will convince themselves they can keep their jobs without buying the company. They'll be wrong, though. Modern Meat will buy the place and close it down. Is that what you want, Fritz? Any other mayor would be the bearer of hope, even against the odds." She paused only long enough to add, "Someone once told me that you can't make things happen, only destroy what other people are trying to do. And you know what? I believe them." She slammed the door shut, not waiting for a response.

~

As daylight crept along the eastern horizon, Rachel drove back into the city, trying to get warm again…and to decide what she should do. Everyone knew Fritz opposed the idea of people putting their savings into the company, not much of a story there. And he'd had barely a good word to say about the buyout for weeks. Coming out against it now would surprise no one. And yet, saying it for the record—JackPack was doomed, JackPack was going down—that still had some shock value, coming from the mayor. She guessed it might scare off just enough people to tip the scales.

She didn't want to write the story. It'd be run on the day of the vote, the last thing the employees read before they had to make up their minds. Fritz knew that, of course. The *momzer*.

What about the Modern Meat offer, assuming it existed? Should she blow off that story, too? Or just go through the motions? It'd be a terrific feather in her cap, of course, breaking such a piece…She said aloud, "To hell with the consequences," just to hear what the words sounded like.

Traffic on the road was light, but there were signs of activity in the houses she passed, people whose workdays began early, people who led lives so different from her own. Driving through the center of a farmstead, the house on one side and barns on the other, she felt bleak and alienated from the scene.

And then, abruptly, her mind cleared. What difference did it make? If an offer existed, no way she'd find out about it, not in twenty-four hours, not with only a handful of people knowing and none of them willing to talk. She could run every reporter's trick in the world, and it wouldn't make a damn bit of difference.

She thought about this, about giving herself permission to try because failure seemed guaranteed. Pathetic.

The landscape came rushing at her, the tires squealing as she rocketed down into a hollow and around an abrupt corner, barely managing to stay on the road. She slowed and proceeded more cautiously, exhaling the sudden intake of air. Okay, she told herself, okay.

She got to the paper at 6:45, much too early to start calling people. She drank her coffee and read the morning paper, lingering over her own piece on events of the previous day, now ancient history, and continuing to mull over the encounter with Goetzinger. She didn't like the man, it was that simple. He was more self-righteous than her father, if that was possible, which, on second thought, it probably wasn't. She regretted once more the part she seemed destined to play.

But what if Fritz was right and the company had no hope of standing up to the predatory Nick Takus? Finding that she resisted the question, she folded her arms and leaned back in the swivel chair and closed her eyes and let her mind go blank.

She wanted the employee buyout to succeed. That was a fact. She did not *want* to want that; she just did. There would, of course, be many interesting pieces to write about an employee-owned company, but that wasn't really the point, only part of it. She simply wanted the buyout to succeed. Her real loyalties were with the employees. To that extent, she was her father's daughter.

So the desire existed, even possessed a moral force. It existed and must be recognized, must be *repeated* so that it wouldn't slip comfortably into the subconscious. She'd long known that she had to guard against her own desires. She might want the buyout to succeed, but that didn't have anything to do with her job. She always had to remember.

All right then. She would spend some time with Homer Budge and watch his last-minute preparations for tomorrow's vote and quote those who remained among the committed. But she would write a sidebar piece detailing Goetzinger's position, too, and a couple of grafs on the buying stations if the options actually existed. Balance. What else? Well, obviously, she had to make some sort of attempt to find out if Modern Meat had made an offer for the company. That was hard news, more important than Homer's last-gasp preparations or Fritz's self-righteous posturings. The employees did have a right to know, even if the knowledge was like being handed a bottle of sleeping pills.

Probability she'd get nothing, *bubkes*. Made no difference. She had to bust her buns trying.

She went down to the caf to get another cup of coffee, and by the time she'd returned, was ready to begin her calls. Still too early for most of them, but one she could make right away. She unlocked the drawer on the right side of her desk and took out her private address book and flipped through it until she found the phone number she was looking for, one she'd dug up some time ago but had been waiting for just the right occasion to use.

She dialed.

"Yes," an impatient voice said.

"Mr. Takus? My name is Rachel Brandeis. I'm a reporter for the *Jackson Tribune* in Jackson, Iowa."

"How did you get my private number?" Takus demanded.

"I apologize for calling so early, Mr. Takus, but I've been told you're a man who thrives on little sleep."

She waited. Would he hang up on her? Would he stay on the line? He didn't make her wait long.

"I know who you are, Miss Brandeis, and that's right, I don't need much sleep. What do you want?"

"You've said people have a right to compete but nobody has a right to make money. Am I quoting you correctly?"

"What do you want?"

Okay, so he wasn't in a chatty mood. She didn't have much time. "My question is this—has Modern Meat made an offer to buy the Jackson Packing Company?"

This time Takus made her wait. When he did speak, he ignored her question. Instead, now that he knew the purpose of the call, he chose to return to her previous comment. "Let's just say, Miss Brandeis, that some folks have accused me of being a little bit on the hard-nosed side. Well, I am. Nothing wrong with that. I compete to win. And let me also say, for the record, that if the employees out there at the Jackson Pack plunk down enough money to buy the place, it's fine by me. I got my doubts about this employee ownership thing, but as you put it, people have a right to compete. And I'm ready to compete, with Skip Peterson, with his people, with anybody. Let the best man win, that's what I say."

Rachel, in turn, ignored Takus's cant. "Have you made an offer for JackPack's stock, Mr. Takus? Or is it an asset buyout?"

"I don't know where you get your information," he told her, "but there is no offer."

"You haven't offered to buy the company?"

"No, I have not. I understand the Jackson Pack employees are voting on this buyout proposal tomorrow."

"That's correct."

"I wish them the best of luck. Like I say, happy to compete."

She asked him a couple of follow-up questions, but he wouldn't answer them.

Instead he said, "By the way, Miss Brandeis, I've been reading your stories. You write damn well. Tell me if you ever decide to go straight. I've got a place in my PR department with your name on it."

He hung up.

Rachel felt flattered by the praise despite herself. She'd gotten diddly-shit out of him, of course, not even a "no comment," which would at least have been suggestive. She supposed he didn't worry overmuch about any distrust that would result if he were caught in an outright lie.

What next? She looked at her watch: 7:03. The East Coast? Her father would be out of the house by now.

As she was debating whether she wanted to talk to her mother, another name occurred to her, one in Jackson, and she fetched a second number out of her private file. It had been months since she'd contacted Kevin Osborn, not since he told her that the Pack was on the point of bankruptcy, her first big breakthrough. She remembered the tone of his voice at the end of their last conversation. He'd still been mad at the company for quashing the case study he'd spent so much of his precious time on, but he clearly didn't have the temperament of a whistle-blower. Sometimes, you can just tell when someone's about to start backpedaling as fast as he can. She'd been relieved to escape with her information intact and decided that as a source, Osborn was pretty much used up. But, she told herself now, he didn't have to talk to her if he didn't want to. She dialed the number.

"Yes?" A woman's voice this time.

"Is Kevin there?"

"Who's calling?"

Rachel identified herself and listened as the woman shouted into another room, "It's that reporter from the *Trib*!" and then a pause and finally in the distance, barely audible, "I'll take it upstairs."

"Hello, Kevin," she said when he came on.

"Rachel?"

"Yes." They both, as if by tacit agreement, waited until they heard the click of the extension being hung up.

"You want to know if there's an offer for the company," he said at once.

"Yes."

"I can't tell you. I don't know anything about it." He was breathless, clearly irritated at the call.

"You're sure?" It was a stupid question, but she didn't know what else to say, confronted with such a sudden and complete denial.

"Of course I'm sure. All I know about is the first. If there's another one, nobody's talking."

"The first? First what? Offer?"

"You didn't know about that? Shit."

"What first offer, Kevin?"

He hesitated. "All right, but this is it, this is all I'm telling you, and you didn't get it from me, okay?"

"Understood."

"There *was* an offer. From Modern Meat. A few weeks ago."

"For how much?"

"I don't know."

"Why was it rejected? It must have been rejected."

"That's right. I'm not sure why. It was way low, I think. An attempt to steal the company and sell it off for parts. I think that must have been the reason."

"You're sure it was from Modern Meat?"

"Yes. That's what I was told."

"Who told you?"

"I'm not going to say. Look, I don't know anything else. There was some dissention on the board, I understand. I don't know if that's true or not."

"What was Skip's role?"

"I don't know. That's all I know. Okay? I've got to go now."

"Is there anybody else I might talk to about this?"

"No. Nobody that I know. I've gotta go now, okay? Please don't call again. Please."

And he hung up on her.

Gingerly, Rachel put the receiver down, thinking she was certainly having trouble at the moment keeping people on the line. Probably she was going to have a lot of short phone calls that day.

She took a sip of coffee, folded her hands in her lap, and sat musing about this latest bit of intelligence. So, an earlier offer, and from Modern Meat. Interesting. She wondered why it had been rejected. Too low, an insult, Takus putting twenty-four dollars and beads on the table? Or maybe the employee offer was already in play and that's why it was refused? This possibility appealed to her, but she knew it was improbable. Businessmen liked to deal with their own kind. Anyway, if one offer had been made, another became more likely. Not inevitable, but definitely more likely. And it gave her another question to ask people.

She looked at her watch and took another sip of coffee and waited until she could begin calling in earnest.

～

Humming to himself, Karl Nevins stood with his hands clasped behind his back, looking out at the rain.

A minute before, he had finished a conversation with one of his oldest clients and remembered at once something that they had forgotten to cover. He debated whether to call him back, but the matter hadn't been pressing and so, instead, feeling restless, he'd

gotten up and gone over to the window, where he now stood looking out at the rain. He always enjoyed the winter rains in California. Monterey Bay lay invisible in the distance. Thick, ragged
fog drifted up the narrow valleys. From his high perch, the valleys
overlapped, one after another, their ridgelines nearly white with
the mist. Near to hand, his grounds were a vivid green, ripe lemons
hanging like lighted bulbs from the trees he had planted fifteen
years earlier.

The phone rang. Ah, Karl thought, he remembered, too.

He went quickly back to his desk and answered with a bright
"Yes," expecting to hear his old friend's voice on the other end of
the line. Instead, it was a woman's.

"Mr. Nevins?"

"Yes."

"This is Rachel Brandeis. I'm calling from Jackson. You and I
met, do you remember, at the Thanksgiving party at your mother's
home last month."

Damn it. The last person he wanted to talk to.

"Why, Miss Brandeis, yes, I do remember. What a surprise."

"I left a message on your machine earlier," she said.

"So you did. Well, it's nice to hear your voice again. And how
are you?" As they exchanged pleasantries, Karl berated himself.
Never assume anything. Always let the fucking machine answer.
Too late now.

Finally, after he judged they'd had sufficient chitchat, he
asked, "And to what do I owe the pleasure of this call?" As if he
didn't know.

She began with a preamble: the run-up to the Pack vote, a
surprising turn of events, the employees' right to know, and finally
the inevitable question.

"Has a new offer been made for the company?"

"I'm afraid that's not a subject I can discuss."

"A lot of people back here believe there is an offer, Mr. Nevins.
And if there isn't, then I have to say I'm confused."

"Why so?"

"It appears at the moment that the employees will be able to come
up with some of the money to modernize the plant, although probably
not all of it. It also seems likely they'll vote to exchange wages for stock.
If there is no new offer, then I can't understand this sudden demand
that they come up with the balance of the upgrade money."

"Sudden demand, Rachel? Now it's my turn to say I'm confused. What sudden demand?"

He listened as she outlined Skip's scheme—with which, of course, Karl was familiar, had been aware of from the beginning—to take however much extra money the employees gave him and repair what he could and keep on going.

When she finished, he said, "There must be some misunderstanding. There's nothing sudden about this. The stipulation from the beginning has been that the employees must come up with *all* the money for the upgrades, that they'd assume real risk, the same as any entrepreneur would."

It ticked Karl off, Skip trying to pull this shit.

"So you're saying nothing has changed?" she persisted.

"That's right." Cautioning himself that he was, after all, talking to a reporter and not just a former dinner companion, he said, "You realize this is not for attribution. I just want you to understand the situation."

"All right. But suppose there is no offer. Suppose it's still just the employees. And suppose they don't come up with every last penny to repair the plant. Then you're telling me you'd declare bankruptcy? You'd really do that?"

It was perhaps interesting to speculate what might have happened given this scenario. Maybe Skip could have convinced a majority of the stockholders to keep on going. As distasteful as that would have been, it might have happened. Anyway, it was purely hypothetical now, and there was only one answer to Brandeis's question.

"Yes, we would declare bankruptcy, that's right. What choice would we have? We'd have to sell the trademarks and so forth for whatever we could get for them. We have the legal obligation to protect the rights of the shareholders."

"I must say, Mr. Nevins, despite what you're saying, there are an awful lot of people here in Jackson who think something has happened to change the situation."

"I'm not responsible for what people think. I just know what the understanding is and has been from the beginning." It pleased him that she was confused. If he could think of a way to nail Skip's hide to the wall, he'd do it.

Brandeis fell silent briefly and then said, "Perhaps we can come back to this later. In the meantime, I have another question."

"Oh?" Some other matter? Karl was beginning to get into the swing of the conversation. "Okay, shoot," he told her. "It's off the record, though."

"I've learned that several weeks ago Modern Meat did, in fact, make an offer for the company. Would you please tell me why it was turned down?"

"An offer for the company?" Karl said, feigning surprise.

"Yes. I know there was an offer. And I know it was rejected. Was it too low, was that the reason?"

Karl held her on the line, trying to determine what else she knew about the first offer, while he wondered how it might be put to use. Then he saw the way.

"Let me repeat, Rachel, we have to be clear here, this is not for attribution."

"I understand."

"So, all right then…Yes, there was an offer, and it came from Modern Meat, but I don't want to get into details."

"Why did you reject it?"

He paused and took a deep breath. No time to think. Did he really want to do this? He'd better make her draw it out of him at least.

"You're right. It was too low."

"How much was it?"

"I'm not going to get into specifics."

"But it was definitely too low?"

"I don't know what you mean by *definitely*. Some of the board members thought it was too low."

"Some? Did you?"

"No. I would have taken it."

"Skip? Did he think it was too low?"

"Yes."

"And the majority agreed with him? Or at least, those controlling a majority of the stock, they agreed with him?"

"Not necessarily."

"Not necessarily?"

"At first, almost everyone was prepared to accept the offer."

"What happened?"

The moment had arrived. Was this a smart thing to do? He didn't know, but, by God, he was going to do it! "What happened? Skip convinced the board that Takus was trying to steal the company and was sure to come back with a better deal later, that's what happened."

She said nothing. Then she asked if he would please repeat what he had just said. After another silence, she said, "And has there been a second offer?" But he could tell she was no longer so interested in this question and asked it mostly for the sake of form.

"As I told you before, I have nothing to say about that. The point is we would have accepted the offer Nick Takus made six weeks ago if we didn't believe Skip when he told us Takus would sweeten the pot later."

"So you didn't believe the employee buyout would work?" Another question she obviously didn't care much about. He could sense her mind working furiously behind the words.

"Our responsibility as a board is to the current stockholders, Rachel. I'm afraid Skip muddies the waters here, but you need to be very clear about this. The board was ready to accept the offer. The only reason we would consider not doing it was if there was a clear understanding that Skip could come up with the money necessary to upgrade the physical plant. We're not talking about a lick and a promise here. If that meant the employees had to dig into their 401(k) portfolios, so be it. Do you remember our conversation at Thanksgiving dinner? I talked about that."

"But you didn't tell me that you were the board member who had recommended reinvesting the money in the company."

"No, I didn't. It's not considered kosher to talk about board business to outsiders. And I wouldn't be doing it now except for my concern that Skip had been misleading the board."

Brandeis was silent for a time and then said, "You're accusing him of a lot more than that. You're suggesting he's been using the employee buyout as a scheme merely to get more money out of Nick Takus. That would be the worst kind of double-dealing." Now they had arrived at the heart of the matter.

"I don't know what Skip's motivations are. I'm just telling you what happened."

"He's trying to save the company."

"If you say so."

He could feel her resistance.

"Look, Rachel, would Skip act against the interests of the stockholders? I don't know. I can only say that he never has in the past."

"And, of course, the majority of stockholders are family members."

"That's right. And there's been a history of animosity between the family and the union, too, so it does seem strange, this sudden alliance between him and Homer Budge. But all I'm saying is what has happened. It could very well be that Skip has turned his back on the family. I don't know. I leave that for you to figure out, if you can."

Another silence as Brandeis thought. This time Karl didn't wait. "I think I've told you as much as I'm going to."

"This is all off the record, is that correct?" she asked.

Karl realized at once that he had a problem. If he did, indeed, leave Skip's two-faced behavior off the record, what could she do with the information? It would be almost impossible to verify, as it was. The other board members would hew to the code of silence.

"I suppose," he said carefully, "this is the sort of thing…that should come out…I suppose…Tell you what. You can use it, but only if you say it came from, oh, I don't know, how about a source close to the board? Not from a board member, okay? Do you understand? A source familiar with activities on the board, but not actually on the board. Okay. *Do you understand?*"

"Yes." She sounded very unhappy.

"Good."

He hung up, glad after all that he had taken the call, thinking, "That'll fix Skip's wagon."

But if Karl felt pleased, he was angry, too. And bitter because he had been forced to resort to such a sordid ploy. It shouldn't have been necessary. But his last name wasn't Peterson, and he'd never been given a chance. He was twice the businessman that Skip would ever be, but he'd never been given a chance. JackPack could have survived. He could have saved the company, he was sure. But not Skip, not the Petersons. Except for old W.F., the Petersons weren't businessmen. They'd ruined the company.

~

Skip smiled. He spoke softly. He said, "This is bullshit."

A tingling feeling prickled along his arms, his vision filled with black spots. He felt like he was going to lose control of his bowels.

Rachel Brandeis sat determined before him. She said, "The charge is a serious one."

"I don't care," he told her, still not raising his voice, "it's bullshit. You can't believe I'd do that."

"What I believe is irrelevant. Did you tell the board that?"

They looked at each other, momentarily at stalemate. Slowly, the tingling sensation had passed, his vision cleared, his bowels quieted.

"I guess," he told her, "I should have expected this. You don't have to tell me where you got it." Karl. It could have been Mel, Skip supposed. No, he decided at once, it had to be Karl. Mel wouldn't discuss board business, no matter the provocation.

"Okay," he said to Rachel, "we need to talk a little bit off the record here."

"No!" she practically yelled, then more softly, "no, nothing more off the record. I'm sorry, Skip, you're always trying to do that to me, to keep the real story untold. I'm not going to do it anymore."

He clicked his fingernails on the desktop as he regarded her. So much had gone wrong in the last forty-eight hours that this new calamity, after the initial shock, now hardly seemed surprising. He felt almost anesthetized. Clearly, he'd failed with Rachel, utterly failed. No surprise there, either, come right down to it. The company had always had piss-poor press relations. And as for his abortive attempts to seduce her—if that's what they were—no matter, he was no lover. He was trying to save his company, that was all.

"There's no way I can put everything on the record, Rachel, you know that."

"I don't care. Say whatever you've got to say. I'll put it in my story. I don't want to hear anything else."

She sat rigidly forward, the knuckles of her hand white where she clutched her notebook. He'd get nowhere with her.

"All right," he said.

He thought to continue at once but found he didn't have the words and instead slumped back in his chair, bowed his head, and raised his hand over his face, thumb and index finger pressing against the corners of his eyes. "All right." He let his hand drop.

Rachel was silent. It was hard to be sure what she thought about anything. He supposed that was the mark of a good reporter. At that moment, her eyes had lifted to meet his, her expression direct but closed. She was, as always, carefully and stylishly dressed, the armor she wore.

"Let me ask you…" he finally began. "After everything you and I have been through, can you really imagine it was all just a scheme to get more money out of Takus?" He spoke now simply as one human being to another. Whatever the story she felt compelled to write, she couldn't possibly believe he was that cynical and calculating. "You have to know I wouldn't do such a thing."

"How am I supposed to *know*?" she replied. "Because you told me? I'm sorry, that's not enough."

He leaned forward, peering at the shuttered, determined countenance that Rachel presented to him. Had Karl convinced her? Wouldn't she see through Karl in a minute? Or was it her family, her background? Businessmen couldn't be trusted. If she'd been a man…But they'd spent too much time together. And she wasn't a man.

"What does your intuition tell you? That I'm a bad guy? I'm sorry, I just don't buy it."

She shook her head. "It's no good. I simply have to know. Did you do that? Did you tell the board that?"

He was wasting his breath. That's all she wanted to know, what happened. She'd closed the door on everything else.

"Just the facts, huh? Nothing else, just the lousy facts."

"That's right," she answered. "And you're right, facts aren't such great things, okay? You think I don't know that?"

This sharpness, betraying her own unhappiness, gave Skip a moment of hope. Or rather, a moment to wonder if there was any point to hope. He decided no. Rachel might not like want she was doing, but it would change nothing. If she was unhappy about it, good. She deserved to be.

"What do you want to say?" she asked again, obviously anxious to get the interview over with. "I'll print any denial you make."

What *did* he want to say? He could tell her the truth, of course, that he *had* told the board that Takus would make a better offer, that he was prepared to tell the board anything in order to keep going, that all he ever wanted was to keep going and that would only happen if the employees bought the company.

"Do you realize this could kill what little chance we've got left to make this thing work?" he said.

She didn't respond, just waited, pen poised.

He slumped back in his chair, shaking his head over and over. He'd been kidding himself when he imagined that the assurance he'd given the board was just a sop thrown to gain time and there wouldn't be any consequences. There were always consequences. There was always someone who remembered, who waited for the right moment...

So should he tell the truth? Make a clean breast of it? But what good would that do? The truth never lay in the future. It was always somewhere behind you, the weapon others used to beat you down with. No, the truth was of no earthly use to him. Anyway, he was doing this thing all the way up, right? This was no time to chicken out.

"You want a quote, Rachel? Okay, here it is. Yes, there was an offer some time ago from Modern Meat. The board of directors rejected it. But I never told them there would be another offer."

"You didn't say that Nick Takus was trying to steal the company and was bound to come back to the table with a better deal?"

"What did I just tell you?"

"So you made no reference to a further offer?"

"No."

"But the person I talked to claimed that you did."

Skip paused, then said, "I can't imagine why anyone would say that, since it didn't happen."

"He seemed pretty definite."

"Perhaps there's a board member who doesn't want the employee buyout to succeed, have you considered that? I live in Jackson. Lived here all my life. Known these people all my life. If Nick Takus were to buy the Pack, he'd close this plant down. Do you think I could possibly want that? I want to keep going."

She scribbled on her pad, relieved, no doubt, to be doing that rather than talking. The words he spoke and her writing them down, these acts separated them even farther. And his statements, one following another, seemed barely linked to anything at all, spears he hurled helplessly against his enemies or a begging bowl he held out to Rachel. In the brief silences between each renewed attempt, tension grew, Skip's irritation mounting into anger and then finally, in one last paroxysm against the injustice of it all, he yelled, "Don't you understand? Or care? This is a bullshit story. For Christ's sake, Rachel, think about what's happening in the industry...companies being driven out of business...tens of thousands of people out on the street! What is this, just another chapter in this awful story? Or do we have something new here? There are people here willing to take a chance, to put all they've got on the line to accomplish something. Are you so damn callous you're willing to destroy that? Tell me, are you?"

She wouldn't respond, merely continued to write down what he said.

~

It was dark by the time Rachel got back to the paper. She returned the calls that had come in during her absence and waited for more to be returned. Some never would.

When she could wait no longer, she got up and took what she had over to Neil Houselog.

He listened and then removed his glasses and cleaned them, although they didn't appear to be dirty. "So what you're saying is the employee buyout effort might be nothing but a con Peterson's been running to get Modern Meat to up its offer?"

"That's one interpretation."

"It's the interpretation our readers will make."

"Yes."

"But you don't think so."

"I'm not sure," she said. "He might have told the board that just to buy time. That makes more sense to me."

Neil put his glasses back on.

"If he sells to the employees," Rachel continued, "he'll probably get to keep his job a little longer." She didn't know if that was his motivation. Probably it was part of the truth. Anyway, a selfish motivation was always useful in selling an argument.

"I suppose," Neil said. "So what are you telling me here? You've got this story, but we shouldn't run it?"

"I don't like the story."

"I'm sure you don't."

"But..."

"Yeah."

Neil rounded up all the editors that were still in the building and led them and Rachel into the conference room where they ranged themselves around the table and she told them about her day. She told them everything, including the dawn exchange with Goetzinger, for that was important, too. She told them without embellishment, giving only the story line and noticing as she did so that she had to make an effort not to call Peterson "Skip" in front of the editors. Neil asked her to name her sources, and she did.

"So," Neil summarized, "here's what we know. There was an offer six weeks ago from Modern Meat. There's probably a new offer on the table, but nobody's talking. The only question is what Skip said or didn't say when the first offer was made. Karl Nevins claims he promised there would be a new offer. Upon hearing Nevins's accusation, Skip said, what was it again, Rachel?"

Her notebook was opened to the page. "'I guess I should have expected this. You don't have to tell me where you got it.'"

"Perhaps that's open to interpretation," Neil suggested. "All the other board members Rachel managed to reach were careful not to deny or affirm, except Mel Coyle, who said…" He nodded toward Rachel.

"'I wouldn't have any problem if you ran the story.'"

"Whatever that means. We can call it a non-affirmative affirmation, I suppose. So that's what we've got. Anything else, Rachel?"

"Yes. I've been thinking about this a lot. At first, I was tempted to dismiss it. Karl Nevins and Mel Coyle are no friends of Skip Peterson. So what if he told the board there'd be another offer? It's irrelevant. The employees will buy the company or they won't, and it makes no difference what games Peterson is playing on the side. And anyway, when the first offer came in, he was probably so desperate to keep the employee buyout in play that he would have told the board just about anything.

"That's one way to look at it. But what if the buyout doesn't work? Or worse, what if people put their life savings in and then the company fails? Fritz Goetzinger believes it's doomed. And he's not alone. The evidence, as a matter of fact, is persuasive. Perhaps Peterson hasn't been cynically using his employees to get a better offer from Nick Takus. Perhaps he's only been stupidly using them, because it's been inevitable from the start that either Takus would get the company or it would go bankrupt.

"This isn't just about tomorrow. It's about what happens afterwards. And if the company does fail, it's about how blame will be assigned." For Rachel remembered the accusation Homer Budge's son had made. It was etched in her mind. "I blame you all."

"I'm sure," she told the editors, "that Skip Peterson said what he said. And…I believe the employees have a right to know."

Around the table, the editors had been attentive, and when she finished, they remained silent. Rachel sat waiting, thinking that it was true, facts were miserable things. They were like stones picked up at random along a beach. What could they tell you about the sand? She just hated it, but what could she do?

Neil stirred himself. "So the question is," he said quietly, "do we have enough to run the story?"

"Cusp," said Harriet Coleman, the feature editor.

"I don't think it's on the cusp," Dan Furst, the night editor, countered. "We don't have two sources here, just one and a half and a bunch of weaselly no-comments."

Neil fingered his tie clasp as he thought. "I tend to agree. This doesn't feel solid enough to me." He jerked his thumb toward the ceiling, in the direction of the penthouse. "Nevertheless, Rachel's got a point. This might be a helluva load of shit to dump on the employees, but if Skip said it, for whatever reason...Other comments?"

The conversation stumbled inconclusively onward until Neil finally said to Rachel, "Go ahead and write it up at least."

She left, but the rest stayed, and as she worked, she could glance across the room, through the glass walls and see them still deep in debate. After they broke up, the managing editor arrived, and he and Neil went back into the conference room and in a few minutes Rachel was called in to repeat her performance of earlier. Then she returned to her story. The two men talked some more. Finally, they left the room and separated.

*According to a source close to the board, a majority of the members were prepared to accept Modern Meat's original offer, but Peterson argued that a better one was likely to come later and they should wait. Eventually, the board accepted his assurances, and the offer was rejected.* She put Skip's denial immediately after. For whatever good it would do him. Just made him out a liar on top of everything else.

She stopped writing, her elbows on the narrow lip of the desk in front of the keyboard, her face cupped in her hands. Why the hell did the schmuck have to say that? With his cousin as a witness!

Right after she closed the story, she went over and told Neil. He said "all right," nothing else, and she walked slowly back to her desk.

For the next hour, she looked his way time and again, although it was impossible to tell whether or not he was reading the piece. He made several phone calls. A couple of the other editors came over to discuss something with him. Rachel could guess what was going on. She was jumpy. On the one hand, she would have been happy if Neil spiked the story. On the other, she didn't know what she felt.

Finally she could take it no longer and went back over to Neil and stood wordlessly.

He leaned back, eyebrows raised, then held his hand, palm up, toward his computer screen. Her story was on it. She read quickly. Only one thing had been changed, the beginning of the key graf, which now read, *According to sources close to the Jackson Packing Company's board of directors...*

"We run it," he told her.

Afterward, she hung around. She could have gone home but didn't feel like it. Nothing to go home to. No reason to stay, either. She considered going over to the bar where the *Trib* people liked to hang. It would've been nice if she was *stinko*—a perfect night to get *stinko*—but too much work if she had to start from scratch. She discarded the idea of calling her girlfriend Sheila back in New York. Conversations with Sheila drained her even when she didn't feel like hell. She could've called her father, instead. He'd approve of her story. He'd tell her she did just the right thing. Right, shmight.

Anyway, it was too much work. And she didn't want to give him the satisfaction. If she wasn't satisfied, why should he be?

She wished she knew what she wanted. She didn't want to work anymore. She didn't want to think. She didn't know what she wanted. To hell with the newspaper life.

After a time, for no particular reason, just to do something, she punched the read button on her computer and scanned her messages.

Sawyer wanted her upstairs. She stared at the message a long time, then got up and walked in a haze over to the elevator and got in. She leaned against the wall, and as the elevator went up, she went down, sliding down the wall, tush on the floor, arms out, pressing her dress down between her flopped-open legs. The elevator door opened, giving her a worm's-eye view of Sawyer's outer office, empty. In a few seconds, the door closed. She had written the story Sawyer had hired her to write. She had thought a thousand times about going up to the penthouse and telling him to go fuck himself, and she hadn't done it.

She continued sitting there, dry-eyed, in the dead silence. If he found her, she'd tell him, she'd tell him now. She practiced what she'd say, but he never came.

# CHAPTER 81

~

At breakfast, Margaret talked about everyday things. It was her way of telling him that whatever he chose to do would be all right.

For Billy's part, he had little to say. He'd come back from the emergency membership meeting the night before still undecided. A few had already made pledges, but most, like Billy, were waiting until the last minute.

He wanted to talk, but what was there left to say? He and Margaret had made the same arguments so many times, the two of them, going this way and that, always looking for some new angle on the thing that would show them the way...and that never came. Nothing more to do, nothing except make up his mind. He would have been happy at that moment if Margaret had told him what he should decide. He would have done it gladly. But she never would, of course. It was his job.

When she came over, moving with her painful slowness, to give Billy his single cup of coffee, she rested a hand on his forehead, as if checking for fever. The arthritis made it impossible to lay her hand flat, and so all he felt were the rough tips of her fingers and the fleshy knob at the base of her thumb.

He left the house just after six in the morning. In the pitch darkness, he drove toward the plant, joining the lines of cars going to work, headlights cast down on the pavement, nosing along as if it was just another weary workday. Suddenly, the idea of spending the next eight hours in the presence of people arguing, continually arguing, oppressed Billy so powerfully that he found himself driving by the massive dark building and out onto the industrial drive leading toward the river.

He stopped at a diner and bought a paper and sat with a cup of coffee, which he barely touched. "D-Day at the Pack," the huge headline across the top said. After reading a couple of paragraphs, he put it aside. When people nearby started talking about the buyout, he got up and left.

Without a destination and because he had always been a conscientious worker, Billy started back toward the plant, but at the last moment, he turned away again and crossed the river and began to drive up the Great River Road. He drove without thinking. The paper lay on the seat beside him.

The bluffs, pressing close along the river, obscured the eastern sky, so he could not see the colors, and dawn came by imperceptible degrees, the blackness dissolving to gray, the landscape filling with ghosts of trees and buildings and passing cars.

Eventually, he'd have to think about the Pack, but at the moment he just wanted to get as far away as he could. In the lifting darkness, the ice on the river glowed a deep blue. He drove through small river towns. About each he knew two or three bits of lore—a former center of the pearl button trade, a town that had once had a socialist mayor, a power plant where eagles overwintered, a place where rattlesnakes in dry years, like the previous summer, came down out of the bluffs. How familiar and restful he found each of these small facts. In ten years, he could drive that road and have those same thoughts.

As the light came up, the river ice lost its magical hue, turning white and gray, strewn about and piled up in the violence of its freezing.

Billy stopped at a couple of cafes and had coffee and tried to read the stories in the paper, but after a short time put them aside. People making the same old arguments. The stories just made him feel guilty.

He continued driving north. He tried not to think, because thinking didn't seem to help.

At turnouts, he would get out of his car and stare down at the river and sloughs. The sloughs were dotted with ice fishing shacks. Zigzags shot across the ice where it had cracked and refrozen, although in still shallows it remained perfectly smooth, the color of bouillon, and his eye would rest on these islands of repose.

As he drove north, he passed farmers hauling hogs in horse trailers to the buying stations. Later, the massive possum bellies went by, bound southward with their loads of animals. In a few weeks, he thought, maybe they would all be heading toward Modern Meat.

He felt badly because he hadn't gone to work. He felt badly because of everything. Although he tried not to think, his mind continued to burden him. Voices arguing at him. Fritz telling him not to do something he'd regret. Margaret saying that if he decided to put their money into the company it would be okay, that this was Jackson, Iowa, not some other place, that Jackson had always been a family town, where people cared and everything would be okay. She said this even though he knew she wanted to move to Tucson. But Billy's roots were in Jackson, six feet deep in the soil of Jackson, as he liked to say. What was he to do?

The Pack could survive, he just knew it. The possibilities had life within him, a vitality so present to him, but when he tried to talk about it, his words couldn't begin to express what he felt, not even to himself. They were like the melodies you hear clearly inside your head but come out all sour notes when you try to sing.

Billy had sat down to figure out what they might invest, his sadness only deepening at the thought of how little they had managed to save over their lifetime together. The struggle he and Margaret were having was over nothing, a few thousand dollars, hardly worth more than the clothes they were wearing on their backs. Could they begrudge the Pack even that?

At noon, he came to a bridge in La Crosse leading back over to the west side of the river, and after hesitating, he crossed it and began to drive south, toward Jackson.

He stopped next to a field of unharvested corn to eat the dinner Margaret had packed for him. The food reminded him of her and made him feel even worse, if that was possible.

He read the stories in the paper.

The stiffened, almost white leaves of the corn stalks vibrated in the gentle breeze. The yellow ears, with rusty colored corn silk, hung exposed where the shucks had peeled back as they dried. At the far edge of the field, he could make out the heads of several browsing deer.

Billy started driving again, going slowly along, other cars impatiently passing on the straightaways. He felt empty, like a man who had filled up only part of his life with living. He tried to imagine what he could have done differently.

At one point, the road swung into a tributary valley, and he was startled to see a broad hillside on which the forest had been leveled, as if by a great wind. It took him a few moments to realize that the trees weren't down at all, that what he gazed at, visible beneath their leafless branches, were their shadows, thousands of shadows, all thrown in the same direction by the afternoon sun. A pickup behind him honked, and he slowed even more and pulled onto the shoulder to let the fellow pass.

Billy readjusted his vision and managed to recapture, although only briefly, the original impression of a massive windfall. Soon the road had emerged from the valley, the vision left behind, and once again he was driving down the Mississippi, toward the city and the decision that couldn't be put off any longer.

∼

Outside the auditorium where they would vote and make their pledges, he met a fellow he knew pretty well, a fellow like himself.

"Well, Billy, this is it."

"I guess."

"Made up your mind yet?"

"Still thinking on it. What about you?"

The fellow made a vaguely helpless gesture.

"A tough one," Billy said.

"Yeah."

They started walking slowly toward the entrance, along with all the others. Through the door, Billy caught a glimpse of the tables that had been set up where people could sign pledge cards. He imagined himself stopping and signing.

"I'm pretty much in favor of the givebacks," he said. "But the retirement money, I don't know…I guess not."

Just before they went inside, the other fellow said, "Yup, suppose that's pretty much the way I feel, too."

~

# PART VII

~

# CHAPTER 82

~

The ice trapping the dredge reached out to mid-river, to a narrow channel of water still open where a curtain of fog boiled high into the clear winter sky, wiping out any trace of the far shore.

Walter Plowman stood with Chuck Fellows, the two of them peering downstream and waiting. The cameraman Walter brought along had shot his footage of the dredge and of the fog and then escaped back into the comfort of the KJTV van, leaving Walter and Chuck at their frigid sentry post. Nothing else to do until Orville Massey showed himself. Walter scanned the fog front, looking for any sign of Orv's boat, but mostly he listened, hoping to catch the first faint thrums of a diesel engine.

"Been calling around to my ag extension and gravedigger friends," he said after a time. "They tell me frost's down three feet in some places."

Chuck looked meditatively into the mist. "It won't come out of the ground."

"Yup." Another condition for a big flood. When the snow melted in March, it'd have no place to go but into the river.

They lapsed back into silence.

A third small storm had passed. Hardly any snow. Too cold. Chuck reached down and wiped flakes from the railing.

"Two centimeters," Walter said.

"Not even that much."

"No. But at that depth, you've got snow cover, at least according to a definition meteorologists use." Last night's storm had been barely a dusting.

"The city standard is one inch," Chuck said. "That's when we put our equipment out on the streets, unless there's ice and we have to go sooner."

Walter enjoyed such facts as these. What else did he know about minimum snow covers?

"There's some sort of minimum to sustain life forms, too," he remembered, "for voles and shrews and other creatures that live under snow." He once knew it and made a mental note to call Jeff Hawthorn up at the U. and find out. It'd make a nice bit of human interest for one of his casts that week.

They had lapsed back into silence until Chuck observed, "Your friend is taking his sweet time."

"He'll get here," Walter assured him, although it was true, Walter would have been somewhat more comfortable about this prediction if Orv had been a weather system.

Close at hand, the complexity of the ice could be seen, swirls and platelets of white locked in a clear matrix, but at a distance, near the open water, the ice field appeared to be uniformly white and granular and solid. Above the curtain of cold steam rising from the river, the sky remained cloudless. The sun at noon shed a brilliant, pale light. Walter held his face up to it but could feel no warmth.

He wondered what Chuck would do if Orv didn't show. Probably too late to get Frank Duccini now, no matter how much Chuck paid him. Walter was distressed at the thought that he might be responsible for cutting the legs out from under Fellows before he had pumped a single grain of sand.

And there was something else, too, something about the failure of the employee buyout at the packing company. The announcement of the purchase by Modern Meat had been all over the news that weekend. No surprise, really, more like the other shoe falling. Still...El had rushed off for a Monday morning meeting with the city manager.

Walter said to Chuck, "Expect now, what with the Pack and all, you're gonna find people a good deal more interested in the dog track."

Chuck didn't respond. His orange forage cap gave him the look of a hunter, and his face, where he shaved, had been rubbed raw by the wind. Even when he wasn't doing anything, there was something tenacious in his expression. Just the sort of fellow the city might look to in tough times. Walter sure hoped that old Orville Massey came through.

"You pull this off," he said to Chuck, "you're gonna make a name for yourself, I bet—the man who dredged the river in the dead of winter."

Walter meant to flatter his new friend, but all that Chuck said was, "If anybody thinks that's special, he's a fool. Just because something's hard doesn't make it worthwhile."

Stung by the harshness of these words, Walter replied, "But you *are* doing it. And it *is* hard."

"I suppose." Chuck said nothing more for a time, and Walter thought he intended to leave it at that, but he did not. "Have you ever noticed, Walt, how people who've got nothing to live for go on living anyway? I've noticed it. Take everything away, life still goes on."

"Not all the time," Walter pointed out, most unhappy at this turn in the conversation, but feeling that he'd been put in the position of the adversary and so ought to respond.

"No," Chuck agreed, "not all the time."

"What say we try to reach Orv on the radio again?" Walter suggested by way of changing the subject.

"Might as well."

As soon as they were inside the machine room, Walter noted the absence of Sam Turner, the black man who Chuck had set to clean up the place. A section of the workbench had been neatly arranged, the rest still a mare's nest.

Walter wasn't surprised that Turner had disappeared, not given El's reaction a few days earlier when he'd made an offhand reference to having seen Turner down cleaning up the dredge. "Not in the drafting room?" she'd asked, her eyes narrowing and her mouth pinched to about half its normal width. "We'll see about that."

Guess she had. Here was something else to feel guilty about, ratting on Chuck, however unintentionally. Walter had meant to give the man a little boost, but so far he'd done nothing but make matters worse. And suppose Orville Massey never showed?

Up in the control room, he checked the two-way radio to make sure he had the right frequency and then spoke sharply into it as he tried to raise his friend.

"Dredge Lydia calling the Itasca. You there, Orv?" Nothing. He tried again, practically shouting.

Suddenly, the line crackled into life, and he heard Massey's calm, humorous voice.

"Guess you ain't looked out the window recently, Walter."

Walter and Chuck immediately turned their attention back to the river, and sure enough, through the dusty pane of glass they could see that a boat had hove into view, moving along the edge of the fog, the port side of the craft visible, dragging the intense white mist along with it.

"Got ya!" Walter cried into the mike. "Coming down, Orv. Over."

Leaving Chuck to bring up the rear, he rushed back onto the deck, stopping only long enough to wave frantically at the cameraman keeping warm in the van.

Out on the river, the Itasca came abreast of the dredge and then turned to the starboard and disappeared into the mist. When she reappeared moments later, she was coming straight toward them, full bore. At the edge of the ice field, she hesitated, then her bow canted up, rising like a whale breaching until the ice failed beneath her and she settled back down. The cameraman was back, his camera mounted on his shoulder and turned toward the Itasca as she came on, riding up over the shell ice, the ice giving way in patches beneath her bow, buckling up at her sides, the boat rising and falling as one patch after another shattered.

"She don't look like much, I'll grant you," Walter said, guessing what Chuck would be thinking. The Itasca was covered with the jigsaw carpentry so popular during the Victorian era, Orv's homage to the old riverboats. "Steamboat Gothic, they call it. But don't let the wedding cake on the outside fool you. She's got a metal hull and a big diesel under the hood. Orv put the engine in when he salvaged the old tug."

"Salvaged?"

"Back in the fifties, she was moored up near Cedar Rapids, on the Cedar River, and used for parties. Until she sank, that is. Ask Orv to tell you the story. It's pretty interesting. Anyway, he got her for nothing, just the cost of hauling her up off the bottom and towing her away."

Despite this odd history and the jigsaw work, however, Walter wasn't so much concerned about Chuck's reaction to the boat. It was his reaction to Orv that he really worried about.

The Itasca came straight for them, and it looked for a long moment that she was bent on ramming the dredge, but at the last second, Walter heard the surge of the diesel as Orv slammed her into reverse. The square bow rose up on the ice skirting the dredge and stopped, tilted at an angle. Slowly, the ice gave way and the little craft settled back down into the water, tipping back and forth on her own wake.

Orv appeared, dodging around the decorations as he came out onto the foredeck. The Itasca began to drift sternward, and he grabbed a heaving line and threw it toward them, almost falling overboard in the process.

"Watch out there, old-timer!" Walter yelled.

Chuck reach out and snatched the line out of the air, took a brief interested glance at the rope ball, like a bolo, on the end, and then reeled the Itasca in.

"That's a monkey's fist," Orv said as he neared. "Use it to concentrate some weight on the end of the line for throwing."

Orv pushed his captain's hat back on his snow-white hair. His ponytail had gotten more wispy over the years, but it still hung down to the middle of his back. His flushed face and rheumy eyes and slightly vacant smile didn't make for much of an impression, Walter had to admit.

"How was the trip up?" he asked.

"Had a helluva time getting out of the slough. Couldn't see a damn thing in the fog, neither. Not much traffic on the river, though," he chuckled. "Liked that. No dingbats out." Orv spoke without taking his eye off Chuck. "Howdy-do, Mr. Fellows? Walter here tells me you could use a hand."

Walter was conscious that during this exchange, Chuck had been peering intently back at the old man, the two of them taking each other's measure.

The cameraman photographed them shaking hands over the small space of water still separating the two craft.

"Just you on board?" Chuck asked.

"Yup. Figure my great-grandson will help me out when he gets out of school. My buddies will come up, too, but they ain't worth spit when it comes to actually doing some work."

"Tell me, Orville, exactly how old are you?"

"Ninety-two. How old are you?"

"Forty-four."

"Got a way to go to catch up, looks like." This was Orv's way of suggesting he didn't much appreciate Chuck's question, at least the tone of it.

Whether or not he noticed the disapproval, Chuck continued to pursue his own line of thought. "I appreciate your willingness to do this," he told the old man, "but you *do* realize it's gonna be damn tough work."

"I'm too old, that what you're saying?"

"Yes, that's what I'm saying." Chuck turned to Walter. "I come out here one morning and find ice frozen around the dredge and your friend Orville here dead on his boat, how do I explain that? The city saves a few bucks by hiring a ninety-two-year-old guy to do a job that by rights should have gone to somebody half his age."

Chuck had a point, although he didn't impress Walter as the kind of chap who would worry overmuch about someone's age, at least so long as he had a clear understanding with him concerning the nature of the work and the risks involved and so forth. Still, Walter was nervous. If Fellows did decide the old man wasn't up to the task, Walter would feel just awful. "What do you say, Orv?" Walter asked. "Work too tough?"

"Mr. Fellows here is right. Might be he'll come down one morning and find I've checked out. Gonna happen someday. Then again, according to your statistics, I've been dead for twenty years. Figure if I keel over tomorrow, I'm still way ahead of the game."

Chuck looked from Orville to the boat to Walter and back to Orville again.

Orv told him, "Long as I've got fuel and food and booze, and my buddies can find their way up here to play a little euchre, I'm a happy man." Orv loved his euchre. "It's up to you, Mr. Fellows. You're game, I'm game. You got some other way you wanna go, no hard feelings."

Chuck obvious didn't like it, but he was half smiling as he shook his head.

"Well," he said at last, "it's not like I've got a shitload of options here. This whole business has been a clusterfuck from the beginning. But...what the hell, let's do it. Thanks. Thanks for coming."

"Glad to help out a friend." Orv nodded toward Walter.

Fellows concluded the exchange with "I'd appreciate it, however, if you didn't croak on me."

"Not planning on it," Orv told him.

Walter's worry turned in a moment to delight. He clapped his hands. This was going to be nifty. An interesting story. Lots of great shots. And, given what had just happened at the Pack, wonderful timing.

As for Chuck, Walter guessed that he was going to find himself at the center of a good deal of attention. Like it or not.

# Chapter 83

~

Homer Budge drove home by the back way. The meeting down at the Five Flags Opera House had gone about as well as could be expected, he supposed. The state and federal people had finally shown up, now that they had a clear-cut disaster on their hands—the packinghouse to be phased out and two thousand people to lose their jobs. The governor had been there, staff from the office of the congressional rep, locals including the mayor, Skip Peterson, a lot of others. The governor had made his statement for the benefit of the press, and the reporters had left so that people could speak freely. He thought about all the harsh things that had been said, all the angry accusations made. But still for the most part it had gone about as well as could be expected, under the circumstances. He would probably end up in charge of the worker relocation center to be set up. That would be something he could do well.

Homer parked in the driveway and got out, and for a few moments contemplated John Michael's VW Beetle, in its usual place. After the vote, Homer had made the confession to his son that he promised he would. John Michael had been right all along, Homer should never have trusted the company. Now the thirty-year-old car, patched and faded, ostentatiously ignored Homer, awaiting the return of its master with blue-collar pride.

Homer went inside and found Rose and John Michael alone together in the kitchen and realized at once, by the look of them, that something else had happened. Please, God, he thought.

"Will you talk to your son?" Rose said. With a flushed expression, she sat at the kitchen table, opposite John Michael. John Michael, the obvious subject of her ire, hunkered, elbows planted, battened down.

"Perhaps," Homer said wearily, "I can take off my coat first."

Mother and son remained silent while he did so. Homer took

his time, in no rush, although not because he was trying to figure out what had gone wrong this time. He unwrapped his scarf and stuffed it into the sleeve and hung the coat back in the tiny unheated mudroom, all more or less in slow motion, as if he was thinking, although he wasn't.

"Okay," he said when he could delay the moment no longer, "what is it this time?"

Rose turned to their son. "Why don't *you* tell him?"

John Michael stirred himself, shucking off the bunkered look. He regarded Homer smugly and announced, "I'm leaving school."

Even as the words came out of his mouth, they seemed already to have been spoken. For a few moments, Homer felt not much of anything. This was followed by a spasm of irritation. And then he found his anger.

"Is this your idea of revenge?" he asked sharply. When John Michael said nothing, Homer yelled, "Is it?"

"I can do what I want," John Michael answered. He was his own man. His life was his own, to ruin if he chose.

"There's more," Rose informed Homer.

"Wonderful." He looked at John Michael. "Well?"

"I'm goin' down to Maquoketa to get a job at Modern Meat and help Uncle Joe organize the place."

"Ah! So that's it," Homer said. This announcement surprised him, but not much. "You're going to help Joe bring back the good ol' days, is that what you're going to do?"

"He's not going anywhere," Rose protested.

Homer supposed that Rose expected him to stop John Michael. She seemed not to grasp the fundamental change that had occurred between father and son. John Michael's expression dared Homer to try to exert his old authority.

All at once, Homer's anger came to a focus on his son's arrogant confidence that he was right.

He moved close to John Michael and said, "You never tried to understand. You're ignorant. You think you know, but you don't."

"I blame Joe Wheeler." This from Rose. "He put the idea in John Michael's head."

"No, he didn't," John Michael protested hotly.

"I think we can leave Joe out of this," Homer told Rose.

Homer studied his son. He understood that nothing was to be done here. This must be accepted, too, along with everything else. But it pissed him off.

"Do yourself a favor," he told his son, "wait till after you get the job before you quit school."

"He's not to quit school, period!" Rose exclaimed.

Irritated by this one-note refrain, Homer snapped at her, "Give it a rest, Rosie." She didn't understand what was going on there.

Homer turned back to his son and spoke quietly but intensely. "If you want to be a fool, go ahead. Just wait until you've got the job."

John Michael got up, saying, "I'm going to Maquoketa, and you can't stop me."

The last thread of the old relationship between them had been severed. Homer saw it. John Michael saw it. They stared at one another as separate beings.

"I don't believe this!" Rose protested, as determined as ever, but finding herself suddenly in the minority.

"Let him go, Rosie," Homer told her. "Let him do what he has to do."

It made no difference that Homer said this. His son would give him no credit for the words. Homer could not say one blessed thing that John Michael wouldn't add to the indictment against him.

As soon as John Michael was gone, Rose rounded on Homer.

"You can't let him quit college, just like that."

"How am I going to stop him?"

Rose just continued to talk tough, not giving an inch. "And I don't care what you say, Homer, I blame Joe Wheeler. He put John Michael up to this."

Rose wouldn't blame John Michael. Children were to be corrected, adults blamed. And of course, in her eyes, John Michael was still a child, although a rather big and troublesome one.

Homer contemplated his wife. His anger had already begun its inevitable passage over into sadness. And pain.

From the whole sorry business, he could glean only a scrap of solace. It wasn't much, but it was something. "Anyway, Rosie," he explained, "it might not be necessary for you to drag John Michael back to school, that much at least. Stop and think for a moment."

The world worked as it worked, and every once in a while bestowed a gift out of that everyday doggedness.

"The Modern Meat people aren't going to hire John Michael," he continued, "not after they figure out who his father is. Which they will."

Rose looked off into space as she let this sink in, clearly resisting the idea, as if nothing would suffice here but that she accomplish it herself.

"I suppose you're right," she said at last. "I suppose that's something, at least."

"Of course, it'll give John Michael one more reason to be mad at me," Homer added, mostly as a comment to himself.

At that moment, Ruthie came into the kitchen, probably an advance scout for the other small Budges, and asked what all the fuss had been about. Was it really true? Was John Michael leaving school? She began rooting around in the fridge. Rose told her that yes, it was true, her brother intended to quit college and go work for Modern Meat. Ruthie found the Coke she was looking for, popped the tab, and took a swallow. As she left, her only comment on the matter was, "What a dweeb."

Homer pulled a chair over so he and Rose could hold hands.

"It's been quite a couple of months," she said, smiling and forgetting about John Michael for a minute.

"Indeed, it has."

How well Homer remembered the morning when they had all been in the kitchen, the Budges at their breakfast convocation, and the fateful call had come from Skip Peterson. Homer took his part of the responsibility for the jobs that had been lost. Now he had lost his son, too. All must be accepted.

It was Tuesday evening. He'd get up at 2:40 tomorrow morning and go to the Power of Prayer, as he did every week, and say the Rosary. He wasn't such great shakes when it came to saying the Rosary, even more scatterbrained than usual as of late. But he would continue to go, every week, no matter what else happened.

And one day John Michael would return.

# CHAPTER 84

~

Chuck Fellows climbed the long, narrow stairs into the small JackPack waiting room and asked for Bart Rule, the company's soon-to-be ex-VP in charge of corporate engineering. Rule appeared almost immediately. The two men didn't know each other, but when Chuck had called ahead and asked for a meeting and told him why, Rule readily assented. "Can't promise you anything," he said over the phone.

In person, he proved to have the usual corporate sheen. But it quickly became clear he wasn't a bullshitter, and although not a young man anymore, he moved in the fluid manner of an athlete. Chuck decided he liked him. As Rule led the way into the bowels of the complex, Chuck questioned him about the future of the company's physical plant.

"Modern Meat's keeping on a few of our people until they close the place down permanently. As for the rest, you'll have to ask them. Packinghouses are pretty much machines with covers, and this facility isn't as efficient as their others, so I expect they'll try to off-load the equipment for whatever they can get, tear down the rest. The site's what's valuable."

They continued chatting, and Rule told Chuck something about the men working for him as they descended flight after flight, never coming out into any of the working areas of the building, while the muted machine noises reverberated all around, as if this was just another day in the life of the company.

The plant's maintenance people had gathered in the room that they obviously used as a point of deployment. Chuck had seen a million such places: a cage where tools could be secured, runs of ductwork, an odor of machine oil and metal and coffee left on the burner too long, old furniture scrounged from someplace, magazines and manuals and lunch buckets. As they waited for whatever

Chuck had on his mind, the men assumed various poses, from which much might have been read had he been one of those people who liked to tailor his presentation to his audience.

After Rule had introduced him, he nodded and said, "Bart here tells me you guys are good at keeping contraptions running."

"Meatpacking is labor intensive, Chuck," Rule interposed. "It doesn't tolerate downtime. These guys have done an amazing job keeping this place online." He had already said this in private, the repetition obviously meant for the benefit of his own people, taking the opportunity to praise them in their presence.

"Tell him about cogeneration, Bart," a fellow with a huge, black beard said.

"Yeah, that's a good example." As Rule spoke, he moved among his men. "We were thinking of installing cogeneration equipment, Chuck, you know, couple the boiler system with our steam turbines. The cogeneration people were proud as punch that they got 95 percent reliability. Trouble was, we needed 99.5. So much for that idea. Too bad, too. Anyway, that ought to give you an idea of the degree of difficulty. So yeah, you better believe it, these guys are good at keeping contraptions running. They wrote the book." As he finished, Rule settled himself in a chair at the back in a manner that suggested his part of the proceedings had been completed.

"Well," Chuck said, "that's interesting, because I've got a little problem with downtime, too. Although I gotta tell you, if I can get my equipment up and running 95 percent of the time, I'll take it. As for 99.5, probably never happen."

"You talkin' about the dredge?" the guy with the big, black beard said. He was no doubt the unofficial leader in the group, so Chuck focused on him.

"You know about that, then?"

Blackbeard nodded. "Oh, yeah, been hearing all about that. Don't see how you can do it, though. Dredging in winter? Damn screwy idea, you ask me."

"Maybe I can, maybe I can't. Maybe with your help."

"Oh, yeah? What makes you think we might be interested?"

"All I know is you're gonna be looking for work."

"Might be."

"I'd say I was looking for a few good men, except I'm Army, not Marines. The Marines in my experience were pretty much a bunch of candy-asses."

"Watch it there, buddy," one of the others piped up, an older guy, looked to be about Korean War vintage.

"A Marine, huh?"

"And damn proud of it."

"Fine. Every man deserves his delusions."

The guy with the beard laughed. "You got a funny way of getting on our good sides, Chuck."

"Not trying to get on anybody's good side, trying to find some men who've got the know-how and like a good challenge."

Blackbeard laughed again. "Tell me, Chuck, suppose the Pack didn't go belly up? Where were you gonna find a crew then?"

"Good question. Most likely, I'd piece one together. Retired guys from the Corps of Engineers looking to make a few extra bucks. People laid off from private dredge outfits for the winter. That sort of thing." This was an option Chuck didn't relish. He'd waste a lot of time and end up with the Dirty Dozen.

"None of us ever been on a dredge, much less tried to run one," Blackbeard pointed out.

"That's okay," Chuck told him. "I'd hate to think somebody had more experience than I do."

"Is that right?" Blackbeard wasn't impressed with this frank admission of ignorance.

Chuck decided there was no point in trying to sugarcoat the thing in the least little way. So he ticked off all the negatives. He described the current state of the dredge, with particular attention to the antiquated types and makes of machinery on board, then mentioned the long apprenticeship he understood was required to become a half-decent dredgeman. He talked about the fact that nobody, so far as he knew, ever tried to do the work in winter, and discussed what he planned to do about the ice in the river. He stressed the miserable conditions they could expect to encounter.

"Ever seen pictures of arctic icebreakers, ice all over the damn place? That's what the dredge is gonna look like once you start pumping sand."

"Hard to see how we could pass up a great job like this," Blackbeard said when the recitation was complete. The rest laughed.

"I know," Chuck agreed. "An impossible job, completely fucked up, and you get to freeze your ass off, to boot. On the plus side, according to Bart, you've got the technical smarts necessary. And we don't have to move the dredge all over the lot, so we don't need all the dredgeman's usual skills."

"Tell me," Blackbeard said, "just so we got an idea of the whole package here, what's it worth to you, this totally fucked up job?" Chuck understood that these guys had already been talking among themselves about whether the dredge work might be something some of them would be interested in. But they weren't going to contribute their services gratis.

"I'll treat you as independent contractors," he told them. "That way I avoid the city's pay scale. I'm prepared to give you what you're getting here, plus a bonus. Call it combat pay."

Chuck couldn't tell how his proposal was going over. Their faces were dim and shadowed. Daylight never penetrated to that subterranean room. The huge complex seemed to press upon them from all sides, and the artificial light petered out in the recesses. Chuck had never liked such places. If he'd worked there, the promise of a job where you could breathe fresh air, even one as deranged as the dredge work, would have been enough for him. But maybe it didn't quite do it for the Pack's maintenance people. Blackbeard stood with his arms crossed, his face hidden behind the massive growth.

"What about the maintenance positions at the track?" he asked. "Once it's built, who gets them?"

"You do. If you work out, that is." Realizing that he might not be able to deliver on such a promise, Chuck added, "This is a public project, so you can figure there'll be some political bs. Whatever happens, I'll go to the wall for you, I can promise you that much. If you don't get the work, it'll be over my dead body."

Blackbeard nodded slowly, and when Chuck left the plant, he had his crew to operate the dredge.

As he went toward his car, he entered the flow of workers leaving the packinghouse at quitting time, men who would soon be out of work and now streamed around him and toward the large, half-empty parking lot. Their expressions revealed little. In their numbers, in the way they carried their heads, in his own sense of having become suddenly invisible as he matched his pace to theirs were resurrected memories of the Vietnamese peasants among whom he'd walked a quarter century ago.

The emotional surge this image recalled didn't last long, for these visitations from his time in Nam, despite their remnant vividness, had lost the power to possess him. His problem was no longer the past; his problem was the future.

At his 4x4, he turned toward the men who continued to advance from the plant, ignoring him. The blank faces were not something they wore, like masks, but exactly the opposite, faces from which masks of civility had been removed to reveal what lay beneath, illegible to Chuck but more basic than the countenances they presented to the world. Mute. Not possessing wisdom or clarity. They were burdened in a way that none of them would have chosen. Yet Chuck envied them the way he'd once envied the Vietnamese, envied them the harshness of their circumstances, their struggles merely to survive, their intimacy with death. He envied them the reality that comes when choice is stripped away.

And as for Chuck himself, what was he? Nothing but a vulture come to consume the liver of the still-living.

Yet he'd do it. He'd use Blackbeard and his pals to pump sand onto the island so Jack Kelley could build his damn racetrack and people could come in buses from Chicago and Milwaukee and Madison to lose their money betting on dogs chasing a lure around a quarter-mile oval. Amusing themselves to death.

And yet he'd do it.

# Chapter 85

~

The kill floor employees were the first to go, furloughed on the Tuesday after Christmas as the first big winter storm approached the city. The cut line would be laid off the next day—in two days, half the employees gone. Stockyard and by-products, too. The people in processed meat would hang on a little longer, until Modern Meat set up a state-of-the-art operation somewhere else to make lean, hickory-smoked bacon and the other products marketed under the Jack 'n' Jill label. The Jackson plant would then be closed.

~

Billy didn't know what had happened to Fritz. The last day, the day they were to be furloughed, and no Fritz. A funny word for it, Billy thought—*furloughed*—as if next week or the week after, they were returning. Billy had no illusions he'd ever be taken back. There wouldn't be any place to be taken back to.

But whatever they called it, last shift or not, he'd put in a good day's work. He'd leave with his head up.

As usual, Fritz's job had been given to the worst of the floaters, not that it made any difference now. Billy wondered where Fritz was at. He needed every cent he could lay his hands on if he wanted to save his farm.

Some words had passed between the two of them since the vote, but mostly they worked silently at their cutting boards and avoided each other.

The plant was filled with angry talk. Skip Peterson hadn't dared to show his face. There were rumors that he'd had a couple of nasty run-ins with plant employees, but Billy didn't know if that was true or not. Might be. There was a lot of anger. As for Billy, well, he wasn't mad. He figured that Skip had just told the board what they wanted to hear. That's what made sense to him.

He felt worse about what Fritz had done.

The work seemed easier now that it was the last day. Adrenaline or something. There were bursts of chatter, but mostly people were pretty subdued. A few of the younger fellows were talking about trying to catch on down in Maquoketa, but Billy was too old. He supposed he and Margaret would move to Tucson if they could sell their house. Margaret wanted him to look for another job or see about getting training. He might. Not right away.

He felt awfully strange. After all these years, the last day. You get it into your mind that something's never going to end, and then it does, just like that.

He went up to the cafeteria for dinner and afterwards returned to the line, only a couple thousand animals left, hardly any time before it would be over. Soon after Billy had put on his mailed glove and taken up his knife, word spread across the floor that despite everything that had happened, despite what people felt, Peterson had come down to say good-bye.

As Billy and the others waited for him to make his way over to their stations at the far end of the kill line, they argued about how to receive him, whether to shake his hand or ignore him or give him an earful. As usual, the chiselers were talking the toughest. Billy said, "I figure all he ever wanted to do was save the company" and let it go at that.

It took Peterson so long to get there that Billy began to think maybe it was just another rumor. But finally he spotted him in the distance. Usually when Skip toured the floor, he went lickety-split, but this time he was stopping at every station along the way, in no hurry to move on to the next. Nobody seemed to be yelling at him, although some ignored him and even made a show of turning their backs. He offered his hand to anyone who wanted to say good-bye and took no account of the others.

When he finally arrived among the headers, he was treated decent, even by the wiseass chiselers. He seemed not to notice that Fritz wasn't there, but simply shook hands with the floater and gave him a few words of encouragement. Then he came around to Billy's station.

Billy wiped his hand as best he could before he took Skip's.

"Well, my friend," Skip said, "we gave it our best shot."

Billy, suddenly feeling the burden of his own failure to pledge, which still bothered him a lot, said, "I'm sorry, Skip."

"Nothing to be sorry about, not a thing."

Like words long damned up and now rushing forward, Billy blurted, "It could've worked."

Skip moved closer, still gripping Billy's hand, and reached out to take hold of his elbow, as well, and lowered his voice so the words were just between the two of them. "You're right, it could have. We could've done a great thing here. We came that close." As he said this, he gripped Billy fiercely, but then he relaxed. "Too late now. Time to move on."

He released Billy and stepped back.

"You take care of yourself, Billy."

"You, too, Skip. God bless."

As Skip moved away, Billy thought of one last thing he wanted to say. "Thanks for coming down."

Skip stopped and turned back for a moment. "Sure."

Billy felt a little better. Skip had taken the trouble to say good-bye, had acknowledged the effort Billy and the others put in, and Billy was grateful. Maybe they hadn't pulled it off, but like Skip said, they'd come pretty damn close. They'd done what they could. And they'd come damn close. They'd almost made it work.

At the end of the shift, Billy went up to the men's locker room. He didn't know who was going to clean out Fritz's locker. He cleaned out his own and went home.

~

Discarding the idea of going upstairs—he'd only find Nick Takus's transition team rummaging through company files and his own dispirited employees—Skip Peterson cut back across the kill floor to a point where he could await the last of the animals. The end of the Jackson Packing Company. Not long now. After eighty-three years. He waited not for sentimental reasons. He didn't quite know why exactly—some sort of emotional need, he supposed. But not sentiment.

For time out of mind, it seemed, he'd been presiding over the death throes of the company, and nobody until the last few months had ever suggested anything but making the patient more comfort-able—profit-sharing, employee attitude surveys, minor improvement in efficiency. They'd all been waiting for the end. Him, too. He was as culpable as anyone else. More culpable.

He glanced at the vacant wall along which beef carcasses had once moved, when they'd been a full-line processor, and he remembered the day he'd toured the plant with Rachel Brandeis. Had he told her about the kosher slaughter, the rabbis who had come from Cincinnati to perform the proper ritual? He couldn't remember. He should have. The rabbis had done the Islamic slaughter, too, using a taped incantation. He could have told her that, as well.

He turned his attention back to the animals as they exited glistening from the dehairing machinery. That had been another of their at-the-margin improvements, the Dutch equipment—pre-drier, singer, polisher. They'd done everything right, and yet the sum had been less than the parts.

People glanced at him from time to time as he stood there, but no one approached, out of respect, no doubt, understanding that he wanted to be alone. He thought about the future and supposed he'd eventually take Farmland up on their offer of a job, but not just yet. Interesting that they wanted to hire him at all, given all the people unhappy with him at the moment, almost everyone, it seemed, for one reason or another. He smiled. Lots of reasons and all of them wrong. Perhaps that explained why he was standing there. It was necessary to assign the proper blame. Not to others. His cousin Karl was a snake, Rachel trapped in the profession she'd chosen, Mel Coyle an ideologue, but Skip was shut of them all, the only responsibility he intended to assign his own.

The last animal appeared, and he watched as it moved relentlessly along the near wall.

The result might have been the same no matter what he'd done, but that wasn't the point. If he couldn't tell for sure what he'd be doing...hell, in ten minutes, how could he know what would happen next week or month or year? But people thought they knew. They set out to manipulate events to justify themselves. And so the history of the company became more than a set of facts; it became a kind of fate.

The racket in the place had begun to die down. The vacant space behind the last animal increased, and the workers prepared to leave, shutting down equipment, washing the floor. It could have been the end of just another workday. Skip, however, was conscious of how the emptiness along one wall now mirrored the emptiness on the opposite.

One of the blue hats was approaching him. He didn't turn yet to see who it was, only aware of the movement out of the corner of his eye. In a few seconds, however, his life would start up again. He could only hope it would be different from the past, the life now behind him, that had, indeed, been a kind of fate.

He turned to see who was coming to talk to him.

~

When the snow began, Fritz would not let Teddy help any longer and drove him back up to the farm in the pickup, pulling the feed wagons they managed to load so far.

"You better stay up here, too," Edna told him as he was augering the corn into the storage bin. "The storm's coming."

"Gonna finish" was all he said to her.

"Are you all right?"

"I'm okay."

Fritz didn't mind doing the rest by himself. He'd rather do it by himself.

Wiping away strands of hair that kept getting in her eyes, her dress whipping around in the wind, Edna asked, "Are you sure?"

He had told her once; he wasn't going to tell her again.

"Don't blame yourself. You were right, Fritzy." She'd been saying that all week. "Skip Peterson couldn't be trusted. It wasn't your fault what happened."

Fritz got into his truck and pulled the empty feed wagons back down to the field next to the river. The storm had begun to intensify, snow swirling in brief tornadoes. He backed the feed wagons into position, got out, and checked around the picker, making sure everything was okay. Then he climbed up into the cab and started harvesting again. Without Teddy, he'd have to drive all the way over to the edge of the field to unload each time the hopper was full. Made no difference. Storm made no difference. He'd harvest the corn.

The picker began its monotonous transits back and forth across the field, snow rushing down from the bluffs and sweeping along the river. At the headlands, the harvester swung slowly around, aligning on the next set of rows, and then moved forward again, the corn falling before it, the noise of the machine lost in the noise of the storm.

Back and forth it went, bleared by the driving snow, on each pass less visible, until finally only the storm remained.

# ACKNOWLEDGMENTS

~

I wish to express my appreciation to the people of Dubuque, who were unfailingly helpful, in ways small and large, during the research for *The Loss of Certainty*. While the city in my work is modeled partially on Dubuque, no one-to-one relationship exists between the two. Jackson is meant to represent an American place, with its own idiosyncrasies, to be sure, but nevertheless a place we can all recognize as the product of America's history and culture.

Two men served practically as *aides-de-camp*, providing me with continuous help, which far outstripped any appreciation I could possibly offer in return.

Upon arriving in the city, I initially spoke with Gent Wittenberg, the administrative assistant to the city manager, and he undertook the initial arrangements necessary to allow me to begin my project. During the research, he served as my mentor, meeting with me regularly to talk about the ins and outs of local governmental activities as well as providing introductions to others who might be helpful. Without Gent, the work would never have been begun much less finished, and for this generosity, I shall always be in his debt.

Bill Banbury, the construction manager for the dog track that was built in Dubuque during my stay, has during the many years of the writing of the trilogy always been available to answer my interminable questions about construction practices and to muse upon the greater meaning of it all. During this often-tedious process of allowing the narrative to evolve out of my experiences on the job site, his interest and helpfulness has never flagged. I also want to thank Bill Schmelling, the field manager, and the construction workers who built the track for their assistance.

This is perhaps as good a place as any to put in a necessary disclaimer. Many of the scenes in this as well as the later volumes are written from the points of view of people who are technically trained. I have attempted to be as accurate as possible in my portrayal of these professions, but if any errors have managed to slip through, they are my responsibility entirely. Furthermore, the characters themselves are fictitious. Any resemblance to actual people is purely coincidental.

I am grateful to the Dubuque City Council, Mayor Jim Brady and City Manager Ken Gearhart for allowing me access to the various city departments.

For the first volume of the trilogy, I needed specialized information on meatpacking and farming. At FDL Foods Inc. the former Dubuque meatpacker, CEO Bob Wahlert provided me with extraordinary access to company employees and practices, allowing me to accompany him on many of his early-morning rounds of the plant and to interview company employees. Among those I talked to and whose work I observed was Fritz Tekippe, a longtime worker on the kill floor. Without the generous help of Bob and Fritz and others at FDL, it would have been simply impossible for me to write credibly about the meatpacking business.

For the farming chapters, I wish to thank the Martens family, who instructed me on some of the intricacies of raising hogs for breeding purposes, and Chuck McCullough, who invited me out to his home farm and allowed me to spend time riding with him as he picked corn.

Information on the practice of TV weather forecasting was generously provided by meteorologist Tim Heller, and knowledge of river biology and lore by Ed Cawley and Gordie Kilgore. Thank you, gentlemen. The research, I can assure you, was the most enjoyable part of the process.

Many others helped as well, including Pat Brunet, Jim Burke, Karen Chesterman, Ed and Joyce Coleman, Wayne Currier, Mary Davis, Mike Denman, Jerry Enzler, Jim Gonyier, Bob Gooch, Betty Hauptli, Jan Hess, Paul Horsfall, Bart Jones, Ric Jones, Pauline Joyce, Jerry Kaufmann, Mark Kisting, Steve Kraske, Don Lang, Barry Lindahl, Deacon Tim LoBianco, Matt Lorenz, John Mauss, Sandy and Arnie McDowell, Bill Miller, Frank Murray, Pam Myre-Gonyier, Harry Neustadt, John North, Roger Osborn, Randy Peck, Ernie Roarig, Buck Schultz, Jim Schute, Ray Steichen, Don Vogt, Marv Vosberg and Ruth Wittenberg. Thank you, one and all.

I also want to acknowledge the encouragement and assistance

of my many readers over the years of the composition of the volumes, in particular Elisabeth Jones and Laura Baker. And finally, I wish to thank Greg Apraham. He'll know the reason why.

Book Two of the Loss of Certainty series coming soon.

# Questions for Discussion

~

1. The novel is set in the "heart of the country." Does it, therefore, seem to be a quintessential America story or is it "off center" in some way? Why?

2. We live in a world where people do their jobs but those jobs are almost always fragments of some larger whole. Father Mike Daugherty, though, refuses to be limited in this way. He believes that his responsibility is to help people in any way he can, including in this instance by pressuring Jack Kelley into arranging the hiring of a parishioner in trouble, the electrician Tony Vasconcellos. Did Mike go to far? If so, what's the boundary that he shouldn't have crossed? Does this suggest that there is no one who should be concerned with the whole person?

3. Should Rachel Brandeis have quit her job at the newspaper when she found out that she had been hired by the publisher Len Sawyer largely because of his personal animosity toward the Petersons, the owners of the meatpacking company?

4. Rachel was manipulated in various ways by officials of The Jackson Packing Company. How might she have avoided this?

5. Given the outcome of the attempt to sell The Jackson Packing Company to its employees, do you think this suggests that all such buyouts are doomed? If that isn't the point to be drawn from the events of the novel, what is?

6. Since the rank-and-file employees lack the specialized knowledge necessary to run a complex operation like JackPack, why should they own the company?

7. The company was trapped in the fallout from the remorseless search for greater efficiencies in the meatpacking industry. This is true of much of the American economy. Is it our fate to have to sacrifice meaningful work in the quest for increased efficiency?

8. If you had been Skip Peterson, what would you have done differently to make the buyout work? Suppose, on the other hand, that you'd been Homer Budge. What, in his shoes, would you have changed?

9. Looking for more fulfilling work, Chuck Fellows wished to move his family to Yellowknife in the Northwest Territories in Canada; his wife, Diane, who didn't intend to leave Jackson, told him that he could go if he wanted but that she and their children were staying. Was she justified?

10. Assuming Sam Turner would need some OJT to refresh his drafting skills, should he have been given a job in the city's drafting room? And after he was given the job, was Chuck Fellows acting responsibly in using him to clean up the dredge rather than making sure his drafting skills were upgraded? When do the needs of human beings take precedence over strictly utilitarian concerns?

11. "Two thousand jobs and one job. He was not fool enough to think there was no connection. Oh, no. Not half fool enough" (pg. 408). These thoughts ran through Johnny Pond's mind at a city council meeting late in the novel. What jobs was he thinking about, and what was the connection he must have had in mind?

12. Given your answer to the last question and what else has occurred in the first volume of The Loss of Certainty, what might you foresee happening in Volume Two?

13. El Plowman censured the narrative that was to be used in the black history exhibit in order to protect the sensitivities of local people with family members who had engaged in racist behavior in the past. Should she have done that?